CANADIAN

Short Fiction

Second Edition

Edited by W.H. New
University of British Columbia

Prentice Hall Canada Inc., Scarborough, Ontario

Canadian Cataloguing in Publication Data

Canadian short fiction

2nd ed.

ISBN 0–13–526153–8

1. Short stories - Canada. I. New, W.H. (William Herbert), 1938–   .

PS8319.C35 1997   C813'0108   C96–931209–1

PR9197.32.C35 1997

 © 1997, 1986 Prentice-Hall Canada Inc., Scarborough, Ontario
A Viacom Company

Prentice-Hall, Inc., Englewood Cliffs, New Jersey
Prentice-Hall International (UK) Limited, London
Prentice-Hall of Australia, Pty. Limited, Sydney
Prentice-Hall Hispanoamericana, S.A., Mexico City
Prentice-Hall of India Private Limited, New Delhi
Prentice-Hall of Japan, Inc., Tokyo
Simon & Schuster Asia Private Limited, Singapore
Editora Prentice-Hall do Brasil, Ltda., Rio de Janeiro

ISBN 0–13–526153–8

Acquisitions Editor: Rebecca Bersagel
Production Editor: Kelly Dickson
Copy Editor: Nick Gamble
Editorial Assistant: Shoshana Goldberg
Production Coordinator: Deborah Starks
Permissions: Marijke Leupen
Cover Design: Petra Phillips
Page Layout: Gail Ferreira Ng-A-Kien

1 2 3 4 5   01 00 99 98 97

Printed and bound in Canada.

Every reasonable effort has been made to obtain permissions for all articles and data used in this edition. If errors or omissions have occurred, they will be corrected in future editions provided written notification has been received by the publisher.

We welcome readers' comments, which can be sent by e-mail to
    collegeinfo_pubcanada@prenhall.com

Contents

Chronological Index of Stories

Thematic Table of Contents

Nature, Place

Indigenous Myths and Tales, Traill, Moodie, Roberts, Duncan, Levine, Munro, Thomas, Adderson, Moore

Science and Technology

Roberts, Leacock (Juggins), Page, Schroeder (See also: stories about shamans and magicians, circuses, and the shape of the universe: e.g. Morriseau, Beaugrand, Tremblay)

Creation, Transformation, Rebirth

Reid and Bringhurst, Buhkwujjenene, Qupiqrualuk, Weyer, Morriseau, Nowlan, Haliburton (Witch), Page, Harris, Glover, Adderson

Fear, Madness

Haliburton (Witch), Ross, Marshall, Page, Gallant, Laurence, Harris, Blaise, Tremblay, Schroeder

Alienation, Intercultural Connection

Haliburton, Moodie, Wilson, Scott, Sime, Gallant, Wiebe, Carrier, Harris, Johnston, McCormack, Blaise, King, Maracle, Bissoondath, Heighton, Adderson

Fantasy, Desire

Haliburton, Beaugrand, Ross, Gallant, Harris, McCormack, Adderson, Moore

Gender, Sexuality

Traill, Thomson, Duncan, Marshall, M. Ferron, Shields, Thomas, Harris, Atwood, Mistry, Adderson, Moore

Art, Language, Artifice

Thomson, Harrison, Leacock, Sime, Munro, Wiebe, Shields, Thomas, Johnston, Hodgins, Atwood, Schroeder, Glover, Heighton

Comic and Ironic Exaggeration

Beaugrand, Haliburton, Thomson, Leacock, Wilson, Gallant (District), Carrier, Johnston, Hodgins, Mitchell, King, Heighton

Storytelling

Haliburton, Wiebe, Harris, King, Glover, Heighton, Adderson

Acknowledgements

I should like to thank Jane Flick, Eva-Marie Kröller, Carole Gerson, Neil Besner, Bruce Nesbitt, and Donald Simpson, for their helpful advice while I was preparing this book; the various copyright-holders for their courtesy; Shoshana Goldberg, Marta Tomins, and Monica Schwalbe for their editorial guidance; and Joyce Marshall, Hugh Hood, Rudy Wiebe, and Jack Hodgins.

Introduction

Prefatory Notes

Most of all, the stories in this anthology are here to be enjoyed. The variety of entertainments includes mysteries, adventures, comic turns, tales of pathos and transformation, stories of resistance and defeat. A variety of subjects and narrative techniques shows up here as well, as does a range of authorial attitudes and cultural presumptions. The "Canada" in *Canadian Short Fiction* invokes a multiple perspective, not a single one, and a rich range of talented writers. It is this range that the collection tries to represent.

The book is organized so as to provide:

1. a guide to thematic recurrences and preoccupations;
2. a sampling of historical practice; and
3. a representation of different formal strategies of storytelling.

Thematically, some of the stories here concern men's and women's independence. Others tell of children's growth to understanding; the politics of art, desire, and the poetics of place; love, war, and social bureaucracy; connections between different cultures (sometimes but not always happy); death, fear, and madness; language; and even storytelling itself. The stories, moreover, are set in all parts of Canada, in Europe, Japan, Trinidad, India, the U.S.A., and the world of the imagination; and while some of the stories are serious or angry or sad, others are variously comic, ironic, self-conscious, parodic, sentimental, cautionary, and playfully fanciful.

The most direct organizational pattern in the anthology is historical; the stories are arranged chronologically by the birthdate of their author—a simple system (which has led to some striking, if accidental, juxtapositions), but one that is not without problems. Readers will be quick to observe that it distorts the chronology of actual composition. Ethel Wilson's 1945 story was written well after Morley Callaghan's 1928 story, for example, but appears before it. Hence the dates of composition are indicated in the headnotes (and in the alternative table of contents) in order to allow readers to follow a different chronology, or to read the stories in the context of their particular time. (The headnotes also briefly probe thematic and technical issues pertinent to the stories in question, and offer suggestions for further reading.)

Modern short fiction in Canada has grown in multiple ways; it has been affected by practice elsewhere, as well as by other writing in Canada. Its sources are many. The focus in this book is on contemporary writing. To

look back at the development of Canadian short fiction, however, is to discover not a single linear progress but a network of interconnecting traditions. To understand the heritage today—and the range and skill of current
practice in the short story form—is to appreciate the many influences that
have shaped the genre. It is wise to remember, too, that Canadian writing is
written in contexts both literary and political, rhetorical and regional, verbal
and cultural. It is marked by the patterns of folk mythology and (domi-
nantly) by the doctrines of Judaeo-Christian belief; it is marked by a consciousness of space and locale and by the impact of an indigenous, European,
American, Asian, and Caribbean presence in the culture; it is marked by
gender and race, and by the writers' individual awareness of their separate
literary forebears—Poe, Dickens, and Gogol; de Maupassant, Mansfield, and
Joyce; Anderson, O'Connor, Malamud, and Borges; and many more.

This collection looks, then, at the form of the Canadian short story over
time, and looks more at questions of *form, structure,* and *tale type* than at regional or thematic representation. The historical structure also emphasizes
the sources of formal variety rather than laying claim to a single national tradition. To write an outline history of short fiction in Canada is, therefore,
to trace the processes of formal adaptation that allowed the art of fiction
to take root in Canada and that subsequently shaped Canadian practice;
it is also to isolate key moments when fictional practice seems to have
opened up to new techniques.

History

Any survey of short fiction in Canada begins in the 19th century. That is the
century in which Poe and others in the United States, France, and Russia
shaped existing forms of prose into the forms we now think of as the conventional "short story"; it is also the century in which Canadian writing in
general clearly began to take shape. But such a survey has to allude to pre-
ceding fictional forms as well, if only to serve as a reminder that the short story
was not born in some form of spontaneous combustion. For centuries there
have been storytellers—"tellers" being the appropriate word; storytelling
(as among the First Nations) was an oral art, and for many people it still is.
Much of the effectiveness of storytelling depends upon voice and pacing. In
oral cultures, storytelling enacted ritual too, and helped to communicate cultural values from one generation to another. But such communication has
been one of the functions of many of the written forms of story as well. Over
the course of history there have been fables (like those of Aesop and
Lafontaine), moral parables, heroic tales (sometimes recorded in epic and
romantic verse, or in drama), sketches of character, and journals of travel

and personal experience. Many of these forms came to bear on 19th-century Canadian writing.

In French, the form that most directly marked 19th-century Canadian storytelling was the folktale, which in turn has a complex history. Writers such as Philippe Aubert de Gaspé, Pamphile Lemay, and Louvigny de Montigny took the tales that were told among the raftsmen, the voyageurs, and the villagers and transformed them into short narratives; rendered anew, many of these same tales were honed by the end of the century— by Honoré Beaugrand and Louis Fréchette—into anecdotal, moralizing, and often sentimental stories, and published in such journals as *La Patrie* and after 1892 in *La Presse.*

There were many English language folktales, too, and in Nova Scotia there was a substantial tradition of animal fables and ghost stories among the black population. But in general, English-language practice in the 19th century seems to have regarded folktales as either primitive or quaint, the forms of a peripheral culture rather than the signs of cultural sophistication and literary maturity. In English, therefore, the two main influences on short story form were quite different ones: those of the romance adventure and the documentary sketch.

The former was probably the most dominant, in that it gave rise to the kinds of story form for which there was a widespread popular market: stories of domestic romance, exotic court intrigue, Oriental journeying, Noble Savages, wild savages, and manly courage. Even in Canada, journals such as the *Literary Garland* and the *Victoria Magazine* patterned themselves on English models, and sought to appeal to European taste. In the process they somehow also managed to transform Canada itself (as a literary setting and subject) into a region of European fancy. "Wilderness" appealed because it was perceived as the fanciful ground of adventure, and "civilization" was equated with "wilderness-under-control"; "civilization," moreover, was displayed in literature not by a mastery of the vernacular speech but by the use of elevated forms of diction.

But for the documentary writers, wilderness was something else. These writers attempted to observe nature directly and so record exactly what they saw, including the apparent chaos of the natural world. They were first of all explorers, travellers, and settlers (Jacques Cartier, Samuel Hearne, Alexander Henry, John Gyles, David Thompson, Anna Jameson, and many more); they emphasized empirical fact. And later documentary writers also recorded the activities of the political and social scene. They were not without bias and subjectivity, however; out of documentary beginnings grew fiction that was just as "inventive" as the fanciful romances were. But the sketch writers appealed to a growing demand for "reality" in literature, and it was they who had the most lasting impact on English-Canadian prose.

To generalize, 19th-century writers such as Susanna Moodie and Rosanna Leprohon wrote early romances; T.C. Haliburton, Catharine Traill, and others—even Susanna Moodie, in her personal sketches—developed the art of literary documentary. But the border between such groups of writers was neither fixed nor always clear. By the end of the century, new journals had developed (*The Week; The Canadian Magazine*); there was a vigorous exchange of editors and ideas between Canada and the United States; and there was a lively mix of cultural influence and literary activity. Some writers (Gilbert Parker, for example) perpetuated the tradition of romanticizing the land and its people, using dialect to show deviations from an educated social norm—hence making stories of the frontier into romance adventures for stay-at-home minds. Other writers (Sir Charles G.D. Roberts, Ernest Thompson Seton) sought to fashion, in the form of the animal tale, a detailed, observant, "realistic"—if anthropomorphic—portrait of the world of nature and "natural" behaviour. Still others, from Sara Jeannette Duncan and Susan Frances Harrison to E.W. Thomson and Grant Allen, were writing satirical social comedies, puncturing the pretensions of the romance writers and determinedly making use of urban settings. Shortly into the new century, however, Stephen Leacock was to begin writing his scores of satiric sketches—his "Nonsense Novels" and "Further Foolishness," his "Literary Lapses" and "Moonbeams from the Larger Lunacy"—looking back at literary conventions and looking out at current fashions, and pillorying all. Fiction in Canada was about to turn in new directions.

In the period between 1890 and 1940, that is, there were signs of different forms of writing as well as signs of a different kind of realism emerging, affecting the subjects of fiction, its stance, and its modes of address. To make a brief list of examples is to telescope much of the history of the period. There were:

1. the psychologically acute sketches of Duncan Campbell Scott (from *In the Village of Viger* in the 1890s to *The Witching of Elspie* in the 1920s)
2. the feminism of J.G. Sime
3. the poetics of Alain Grandbois
4. the solemn moral dilemmas of Frederick Philip Grove
5. the stylistically experimental and rather less fulsome sketches of Morley Callaghan
6. the rural (and to some degree ethnically alternative) realism of Raymond Knister
7. the ironic chronicles of village life by Jean-Aubert Loranger.

Psychology, Suffragism, Rhetoric, Irony: these were watchwords of a changing society. By the 1930s and 1940s, moreover, "reality" was taking different forms again, expressing itself in such ways as these:

1. working class attacks upon economic and class distinctions, as in the stories of Jack Parr
2. the dour psychological narratives of Sinclair Ross
3. the early political fables of A.M. Klein
4. the agrarian realism of Albert Laberge and Ringuet (Philippe Panneton)
5. the social critiques of Roger Lemelin and Yves Thériault
6. the semiautobiographical memoirs of Gabrielle Roy.

There were those who continued to write tales—Thomas Raddall, for example—but for most writers, "Reality" was lodged in political structure and personal experience, and fiction constituted an attempt to represent it. For its part, politics also came to affect literature directly. During the 1940s the CBC began to have some impact on Canadian culture, as did the Massey Commission Report in the 1950s. At the end of the 1950s, the formation of the Canada Council began to affect the number of writers writing and the number of readers reading Canadian literature. With increased attention—both academic and popular—there came to be an increased market for Canadian books. But such visibility did not so much reveal a homogeneous society as it pointed to a cultural mix, and to a culture undergoing further change.

There was an extraordinary range of literary quality among works being published. But in serious short fiction, by the 1960s, much of the sentimentality of romance had been left behind. Writers such as Henry Kreisel and Norman Levine, Anne Hébert and Mavis Gallant, Ethel Wilson and Joyce Marshall and Mordecai Richler—writers with a shrewd eye for social paradox—helped see to that. In their stories characters addressed such issues as chance and change, sometimes glossing them over, desperate to romanticize their often violent implications. But the authors themselves did nothing of the kind. They looked at life not so much straight on as straight out, insisting that their readers stop avoiding the politics of the life they lived and sometimes only pretended to enjoy. From the 1970s into the 1990s, speculative fictions (largely hypotheses about an uncertain future) were to become more common. The theme of sexuality was to become more overt and the language more explicit. And violence (together with terror and anger) came to seem even more traumatic and debilitating, as it does for the characters of David Adams Richards, or Eric McCormack, or Joyce Marshall, or Clark Blaise. And yet these developments did not mean that reality was without comedy, that humour was impossible, or that documentary record was the limit of formal literary growth. Kreisel and Gallant, Ray Guy and Jack Hodgins, Roch Carrier, Ken Mitchell, and Hugh Hood: these are writers of quite different kinds, yet all capable of writing with insight into society *and with wit*. The two do not exclude each other. Indeed, what came to be characteristic of the writing of these decades was an ability to control the apparent disparities between literary order and social chaos—sometimes for ironic ends, sometimes for reformative ones, and sometimes simply to amuse.

In their control over tone and over the nuances of style, many modern writers thereby managed to communicate a kind of double message, one overt and one oblique, one declared and one implied. They drew the reader into their fiction as a kind of conspirator in creating meaning. Hence fantasy did not disappear along with sentiment; if anything it became a more conscious feature of modern fiction than it had been in the stories of the 1900s, and (for all its apparent irrationality) was rooted in real life. The documentary and the fanciful tale came once again to coalesce. Andreas Schroeder and P.K. Page, for example, wrote inventive tales in a loose sort of science fiction, clear narrative inventions with a bearing on social behaviour, as (in some instances) did writers as diverse as Eric McCormack, Caroline Adderson, and Alice Munro. Other writers—J.M. Yates, Virgil Burnett, David Arnason, Lawrence Garber, Sean Virgo, Yves Menard, Elisabeth Vonarburg, Anne Dandurand, and Ray Smith—wrote domestic tales about extraordinary events and extraordinary tales about ordinary language. The stories of Louise Maheux-Forcier played elegantly with the very forms of words, and "metafiction" attracted Leon Rooke, Douglas Glover, Robert Majzels, and a score of others.

Artifice was paramount, but it was not all. For Hugh Hood, master of form, short fiction still carried a substantial moral message. And in the work of Jacques Ferron, Roch Carrier, Gilles Vigneault, and Michel Tremblay, surreal fantasies carried political overtones—especially during the separatist politics of the 1970s. For them and writers like them, vernacular and imaginative challenges to the conventional structures of language in fiction constituted a way of putting words to their challenge to social conventions as well. They opposed both in their politics and in their writing any notion that the existing division of power between "Quebec" and "Canada" was a normative one.

Other writers took up different causes, but tried also to shake language loose from its conventions in order to serve some particular social purpose. "Received" notions of ethnicity and gender roles, for example, came into dispute from the 1970s on, whether in the work of Margaret Laurence, Mordecai Richler, and Jane Rule or in that of Dayv James-French, George Bowering, and Wayson Choy. Women in particular questioned why social constructions of gender seemed so persistently to limit them. Joyce Marshall, Shirley Faessler, Alice Munro, Audrey Thomas, Madeleine Ferron, Marian Engel, Sky Lee, Evelyn Lau, France Theoret, Claire Dé, Claire Harris, Carol Shields, Lee Maracle, Lisa Moore, Edna Alford, J.B. Joe, Janice Kulyk Keefer: all probed in historical and fabular forms, in linear and broken narratives, the curtailments that have affected contemporary cultures and contemporary women. Questions of ethnicity and ethnic borderlines also attracted direct analysis. Authors such as Basil Johnston, George Kenny, Lee Maracle, Thomas King, and Norval Morriseau testified with wit and passion to the unequal position that Natives occupy in modern Canada. Naim Kattan, Austin Clarke, Bill Schermbrucker, Dionne Brand, Philip Kreiner, Fauzia Rafiq, Ann Copeland, Wayson Choy, David Watmough, Neil Bissoondath, Paul Yee, Rohinton Mistry, Steven Heighton, W.P. Kinsella, Ernst Havemann, Abraham Klein, and Rudy Wiebe wrote of characters who try to cross cultural boundaries, whether in fact or in the language of fiction, and in doing so they exposed a whole range of complex social dilemmas. And Dave Godfrey, Hugh Hood, John Metcalf, Malcolm Lowry, Gwendolyn MacEwen, and many others—Guy Vanderhaeghe, Alistair MacLeod, Alden Nowlan, Keath Fraser, W.D. Valgardson, Sandra Birdsell, Veronica Ross, Bonnie Burnard, Diane Schoemperlen, Matt Cohen, Carol Windley, Greg Hollingshead, Linda Svendsen, Cynthia Flood, Sharon Butala, Daphne Marlatt—have given voice to the personality of tradition and the cultural resonances of individual memory. The importance of thus cataloguing these contemporary names—and it is a far from exhaustive list—is to emphasize the vitality, the range, and the quality of current Canadian writing. Not all these writers could be represented in this collection, for the obvious reason of space. The anthology attempts, therefore, to be selective and to be representative; and to represent a range of formal intentions as well as a range of theme, time, and tone. Thus, this survey now returns to the question of short story form, and to those moments in Canadian literary history when fictional practice seemed to change.

History and Formal Change

It is only a small distortion to chart at least some of these moments by date: 1835: the date when T.C. Haliburton's first "Clockmaker" sketches appeared in Joseph Howe's newspaper, *The Novascotian*. There had been political sketches before Haliburton's (those of Thomas McCulloch most notably, in the *Acadian Recorder* in 1821), but it was Haliburton's character Sam Slick who ratified in Canadian prose the power of vernacular speech. That Sam's speech was "gen-u-ine Yankee" and that Sam himself was to go on to influence American prose more directly than Canadian is an irony of history that could scarcely have been predicted at the time; but in Haliburton's command of the cadences of speech lay a concern for the realities of social organization that was to dominate English-Canadian prose for a long time.

1896: the date of the publication of D.C. Scott's *In the Village of Viger*. Often
misread (even today) as a bucolic account of "quaint" French-
Canadian village life, Scott's book challenged many English-Canadian
presumptions about the character of Quebec and probed the more
complex (and often less attractive) motivations that did indeed shape
people's lives. Moreover, the book was structured as a series of stories that altogether formed a coherent unit. This was a form with antecedents in Turgenev's *A Huntsman's Sketches;* it came, however, to
be a recurrent form for 20th-century Canadian—especially English-
Canadian—writers. [The recurrence has, in fact, affected the choice of
stories for this collection. There are a handful of stories here that
come from book-length units of this kind—"The Witch of Inky Dell"
from Haliburton's *The Old Judge*, "Horses of the Night" from Laurence's
A Bird in the House, "Art" from Sime's *Sister Woman*, "Exercisers" from
Mistry's *Tales from Firozsha Baag*, and "The Cage" from Schroeder's
The Late Man. But for the most part readers must treat the book-length
story sequence as a separate form, one to be met in its full length,
in such works as Scott's *In the Village of Viger* (1896), Leacock's *Sunshine
Sketches of a Little Town* (1912), Emily Carr's *Klee Wyck* (1941), Malcolm
Lowry's *Hear Us O Lord From Heaven Thy Dwelling Place* (1961), George
Elliott's *The Kissing Man* (1962), Hugh Hood's *Around the Mountain*
(1967), Dave Godfrey's *Death Goes Better with Coca-Cola* (1967), Mordecai
Richler's *The Street* (1969); shorter sequences by Morley Callaghan
and Raymond Knister; or interrupted-sequence novels like Alden
Nowlan's *Various Persons Named Kevin O'Brien* (1973) and Alice Munro's
Lives of Girls and Women (1972).]

1914: the date of a meeting between Marius Barbeau and the anthropologist Franz Boas at the annual meeting of the American Folklore
Society in New York. Boas's query—were there any old stories in
Canada that corresponded to fairytales elsewhere?—led Barbeau into
his lifelong career as a collector of and commentator upon Canadian
folktales and legends. To some degree Louis Fréchette and Honoré
Beaugrand had preceded him, transforming some folktales into sentimental *contes* in the 1890s. Yet legends such as "Rose Latulipe"
(Aubert de Gaspé's classic tale about a charming devil-stranger-
dancer who seduces a young woman of the village), "Le loup-garou"
(about a man transformed into a werewolf), and "La chasse-galerie"
(about a ride in the devil's canoe) had taken many different forms
in the popular culture by this time. Barbeau preserved the forms of
difference, and (like the important folklorists to follow him: Luc
Lacourcière—who directly influenced the Acadian writer Antonine

Maillet—and Edith Fowke) encouraged a serious interest in the character and function of folk culture, and in its connections with other forms of fiction. When folktales appeared in brief French-language short story form in the 19th century, they gave voice to a cultural fascination with the fantastic and supernatural that persists in Quebec and Acadian New Brunswick even to the present day. Though they have altered somewhat in function and formal character, there are still fantastic *contes* being written; they have become, during the 20th century, more surreal and less fanciful, transforming what was once a form of droll anecdote into a beguiling political fable. Notable current practitioners of the art of the *conte* include Jacques Ferron, Yves Thériault, Madeleine Ferron, Michel Tremblay, Félix Leclerc, and Claudette Charbonneau-Tissot.

1928: the date of the publication of Raymond Knister's anthology *Canadian Short Stories*. While it was praised at the time by B.K. Sandwell, then editor of *Saturday Night,* for bringing together what he considered the great Canadian prose stylists (i.e., the wilderness and romance writers of the turn of the century: Roberts, Thomson, and Gilbert Parker), it is more important in retrospect for having also collected the urbane new writers of the 1920s: Morley Callaghan in particular, Thomas Murtha, and (for his introduction) Knister himself. What the new writers were doing was diminishing their reliance on plot, and emphasizing instead their interest in society and character. Instead of using omniscient narrators to tell about what was happening, in an elegant and formal "received standard" style, the new writers were embodying their meaning in the shapes and cadences of the prose itself, adapting the cadences (in a method that has come to be called "free indirect discourse") to the characters in question, in the moments of their crafted lives in which each story discloses them. Generally, too, the new characters were ordinary people, their command of language often less full than the range of their emotional experience and desperate aspirations. One of the effects of such prose was to reaffirm the connection between crafted fiction and lived life. Another, however, was to assert the preeminence of the artifice, the writer's technique—which was to lead over the course of the next four decades towards the "postmodernist" techniques of many of the writers of the last decades of the century.

1954: the date of the establishment, by Robert Weaver, of the CBC radio programme *Anthology.* Weaver joined the CBC in 1948, and was responsible for arranging for short stories to be read on the air, on such

programmes as *Canadian Short Stories*. The programmes *Anthology* and
CBC Wednesday Night continued to extend this encouragement to writers. Weaver commissioned stories, and helped develop subsequent
CBC prize story competitions; and in print form he also produced
seven anthologies and helped found the influential literary quarterly *Tamarack Review*. Radio programmes (featuring the voices of the
stories of Roger Lemelin, W.O. Mitchell, and many others) confirmed
the literary potential of Canadian speech idiom, hence they retrieved
local speech from the dustbin of "dialect" and so altered formal practice. But above all Weaver initiated opportunities for writers, encouraging an audience for them, and so helping to encourage the art.
Clearly these are not the only moments of change. One could name the
publication dates of other books—those of Jacques Ferron or Alice Munro,
Hugh Hood or Rohinton Mistry—or influential anthologies (e.g., those of
Michael Ondaatje or John Metcalf or Desmond Pacey) as events that reshaped the way it was possible to think about short fiction in Canada. Or
provide dates for the formation of influential writers' groups, such as the
Montreal Story Tellers. Or one could name small presses or particular journals—the *Literary Garland, Liberté, ellipse, Prism, Descant, Malahat Review,* or the
Canadian Fiction Magazine—that have sought to extend the market for serious
short fiction. Or mention the character and quality of journals from elsewhere—*transition, The New Yorker, Atlantic Monthly*—that have published
Canadian writing and affected Canadian literary taste and judgment.

The point here, however, is to stress the changing shape of short fiction
in Canada, both as a way of acknowledging historical differences and as a
way of coming to terms with the issue of short story form.

Form

There is a conventional vocabulary with which most readers of short fiction
are familiar: *plot* (the sequential events in a narrative), *theme* (the subject,
whether overt or implied), *tone* (the narrative attitude), *character* (the actors, personae, whether human or not, animate or not), *setting* (the place
and time of narrative action), *point of view* (the angle of vision the storyteller brings to the story: "first person," perhaps confessional; "third person,"
perhaps limited in knowledge; "omniscient," whether a character actually
in the story or the implied author; or some combination of these), and various descriptions of the language the story is using: *diction, motif, metaphor,
style, irony, metonymy, image*. These terms come into play when people write
about the effects and the workings of fiction.

But there is another vocabulary of form which is also necessary to this anthology, a vocabulary to which the comments on historical change have
already alluded and which requires further codification here. There are,

that is, several strategies of storytelling that have come to be known by different names, strategies which the stories in this collection derive from or exemplify. Among them are these:

1. ANECDOTE: a short, simple, plotless, one-episode narrative.
2. BEAST FABLE: a short FABLE or TALE in which the characters are animals.
3. CHARACTER: a 17th-century prose form that lists the characteristic qualities of a personality type (as distinct from the particular traits of an individual).
4. CONTE: a French story form, often using elements of folktale or fable and telling of fantastic events, roughly comparable to TALE but generally briefer.
5. EXEMPLUM: a narrative "example"—whether short or long—which mediaeval preachers used in their sermons to make a moral point.
6. FABLE: a brief story told to illustrate a moral lesson, with the moral frequently appended to the story as a tag epilogue.
7. JOURNAL: the record of a day's events, as in a logbook or a diary, or a record of an expedition and its observations and discoveries; documentary in form, it can be highly subjective in fact.
8. LEGEND: a special form of FOLKTALE, handed from one generation to another, in which a heroic figure or historical event is made to characterize some feature of national behaviour; or a FOLKTALE form which is declared to be a record of historical truth, even if fantastic.
9. METAFICTION: a work of fiction which takes itself, or the making of fiction in general, as its own subject.
10. MYTH: a story, or group of stories, that explains natural cycles, human behaviour, and the beliefs of a particular culture in terms that usually involve supernatural beings.
11. NOUVELLE: a highly structured French story form, generally longer than the CONTE, in which the focus is on the complexity of character.
12. PARABLE: a story, usually allegorical in nature, which teaches by implication some point about moral behaviour.
13. RÉCIT: a very short French form, often historical or autobiographical in the way it is cast, which generally offers just a glimpse of a single moment of experience.
14. SKETCH: a brief prose form, minimizing (or even eliminating) plot, and emphasizing observable (hence ostensibly documentary) detail, which contrives to convey an objective record of a scene, event, or person, or to convey the impression of being at such a scene or event.
15. TALE: a romantic narrative which depends on emotion, broadly-painted characters, a plotline stressing action, and often an exotic or fanciful setting—functioning sometimes as an escapist entertainment and sometimes as an exploration of dream psychology.

16. TALL TALE: a comic story in which a straightforward narrator totally exaggerates a set of events or the accomplishments of a larger-than-life character.

17. TRANSFORMATION TALE: a tale in which human beings are turned into objects or non-human creatures—told sometimes for the sake of a moral lesson, sometimes to amuse, and sometimes to induce a sense of macabre horror.

As Canadian writers began during the 19th century to experiment with short fiction, they tried out all of these forms, often bringing together several different ones into a single book-length miscellany—as, for example, T.C. Haliburton did with *The Old Judge* in 1849. It would be wrong, therefore, to claim a single source for Canadian short fiction, whether in anecdote and tale, or history and moral exempla, or fable and folktale, or journal and sketch. It would also be wrong to ignore any of them. All these forms came into play, and all of them together helped influence the directions that Canadian prose writing was subsequently to take.

Reading the Anthology

Approximately the first third of this anthology, therefore, assembles examples not just of some of the most important early Canadian writers but also of some of the most influential *forms of story* in Canada, all of which bear on the shape of modern writing. Such forms include *myth and legend* (there are examples of creation, initiation, explanation, and transformation stories of heroes, tricksters, animals, and gods, from Inuit, Micmac, Ojibway, Thompson, Haida, Blackfoot, and Bella Coola sources). There are examples of folktale (Beaugrand's anecdotal, tall-tale version of "La Chasse-Galerie"), *sketch* (Traill and Duncan), *dialect anecdote* (with a moral) and *romantic transformation tale* (Haliburton), ironic and satiric *tales* of manners (Harrison, Thomson), an *animal tale* (Roberts), a narrative version of the *documentary journal* (Scott), and a *parody* of the dialect romance (Leacock). Subsequent stories show, among other things, modern developments from and adaptations of these early forms. For example, Sime and Levine have adapted the techniques of the sketch; Bissoondath and Heighton have demonstrated the contemporary politics of dialect; Wilson, Callaghan, Hood, Schroeder, and Tremblay have retrieved the effects of fable and parable; J. Ferron, M. Ferron, and Vigneault have reshaped the *conte;* Ross has reorganized the plotted tale; Knister, Thomas, Blaise, Shields, Richards, Copeland, Gallant, Metcalf, and Hodgins have all modified the shapes of history and autobiography, and adapted vernacular rhythm to particular effect. Relatedly, Page and McCormack make use of the journal form, linking reality with fantasy; Wiebe and Adderson challenge the exactness of documentary; Munro's linked stories probe the ways in which point of view alters historical "truth"; Glover's metafiction questions storytelling itself. The Maritimer MacLeod writers an initiation story; the Ojibway writer Johnston writes a contemporary trickster anecdote; Mitchell in Saskatchewan writes a colloquial tall tale; Carrier in Quebec writes an ironic small tall tale. Atwood alludes to fairytale, Moore to the rituals of domesticity and romance, King to other fictions, Mistry to Parsi custom and belief, and Harris to the Caribbean folktale of La Diablesse.

The anthology is not circular, of course. Like many another Canadian book, it is cumulative. The items in it can be read in any order. But as the order changes, so does the context for reading the next story, which in turn alters its effect, and in turn and in turn...—making readers part-creators of the stories that they read. That's part of the enjoyment they provide, and to help make it possible is one of the functions of an anthology like this one, which emphasizes the flexibility of the forms of short fiction—in the plural— and the pleasures of reading them for enjoyment and discovery.

For Further Reading

WALTER ALLEN, *The Short Story in English* (Oxford: Clarendon, 1981).

JEANNE DEMERS and LISE GAUVIN, "Le conte écrit, une forme savante," *Etudes françaises* 12.1–2 (avril 1976): 3–24.

———, "Contes—et nouvelles—du Québec," *Stanford French Review* 4 (Spring-Fall 1980): 223–41.

SUZANNE FERGUSON, "Defining the Short Story: Impressionism and Form," *Modern Fiction Studies* 28 (Spring 1982): 13–24; rpt. in Charles May, 218–30.

MICHELLE GADPAILLE, *The Canadian Short Story* (Toronto: Oxford, 1988).

CLARE HANSON, *Short Stories & Short Fictions 1880–1980* (London: Macmillan, 1985).

KARL KROEBER, *Retelling/Rereading: The Fate of Storytelling in Modern Times* (New Brunswick, NJ: Rutgers UP, 1992).

SUSAN LOHAFER, *Coming to Terms with the Short Story* (Baton Rouge & London: Louisiana State UP, 1983).

——— and JO ELLYN CLAREY, eds., *Short Story Theory at a Crossroads* (Baton Rouge & London: Louisiana State UP, 1989).

GERALD LYNCH, "The One and the Many: English-Canadian Short Story Cycles," *Canadian Literature* 130 (Autumn 1991): 91–104.

CHARLES E. MAY, ed., *The New Short Story Theories* (Athens: Ohio UP, 1994).

JOHN METCALF and J.R. (TIM) STRUTHERS, eds., *How Stories Mean* (Erin, Ont.: Porcupine's Quill, 1993).

W.H. NEW, *Dreams of Speech and Violence: The Art of the Short Story in Canada and New Zealand* (Toronto: U Toronto P, 1987).

DESMOND PACEY, "Introduction" to *A Book of Canadian Stories,* rev. ed. (Toronto: Ryerson, 1980) xi–xxxviii.

MARY LOUISE PRATT, "The Short Story: the Long and the Short of It," *Poetics* 10 (June 1981): 45–51; rpt. in Charles May, 91–113.

IAN REID, *The Short Story* (London: Methuen, 1977).

SIMONE VAUTHIER, ed., "La nouvelle canadien anglophone," *Ranam* 16 (1983).

————, *Reverberations: Explorations in the Canadian Short Story* (Concord, Ont.: Anansi, 1993).

AGNÈS WHITFIELD and JACQUES COTNAM, eds., *La nouvelle: écriture(s) et lecture(s)* (Montréal: Editions du XYZ/GREF, 1993).

PART 1

Myths

Indigenous Myths and Tales

The myths collected in this initial section come from a range of indigenous sources, both Indian and Inuit, and represent variations in story form and purpose as well as differences in culture. They also derive both from early collections and from recent retellings of such stories, and hence offer opportunities less for exact anthropological analysis than for contrasts among literary styles. Most important to remember (as the Ojibway shaman/artist Norval Morriseau has observed) is that the telling of myth and tale in First Nations societies was a way not of representing cultural belief but of actively transferring it from speaker to listener. There was—and remains—cultural power in a command of the spoken word. Hence while some stories were told as entertainments (occasionally earthily), even these had their cultural point. Mythological stories communicated ethical models from one generation to another; within these cultures they also explained natural events, spiritual beliefs, origins, and uncertainties.

The myths, then, follow several patterns. "The Raven and the First Men" is a Haida creation story, as retold in 1984 by Bill Reid (the distinguished Haida carver and storyteller, b. 1920, author of *Out of the Silence*, 1971, and *Indian Art of the Northwest Coast*, 1975) and Robert Bringhurst (the American-born poet and student of oral literature, b. 1946, author of *The Beauty of the Weapons*, 1982, and *Ocean Paper Stone*, 1984); the story appeared in *The Raven Steals the Light* (1984). The story of Nanaboozhoo is another creation story, complete with a flood motif, as told in 1878 by the Ojibway chief Buhkwujjenene (c. 1815–1900) to a party of assembled Englishmen; it first appeared in print in the *Algoma Missionary News and Shingwauk Journal* (1 March 1879).

The story of Lumaaq is a Central Eskimo survival tale, as translated from the syllabic text of Aisa Qupiqrualuk and published in *Eskimo Stories* in 1969; "The Myth of Sedna" is a different kind of survival tale, from Cumberland Sound, as recorded by Edward Weyer in *The Eskimos* (1932), and based on the tale that the anthropologist Franz Boas (1858–1942) collected about 1883 and published in the *Bulletin of the American Museum of Natural History* in 1900. It tells of transformation and of haunting. A story of the divinity of the harvest of the sea, it is an inferential explanation tale, indicating among other things why a fishing expedition might fail, and why the mysterious "underwater woman" must be propitiated. It is a tale about diurnal and seasonal cycles, and (through the figure of the dog) also about death.

There are other explanation tales here, too, one of them the complex story by Norval Morriseau (b. 1931 in Fort William); "The Indian that Became a Thunderbird," his ancestral tale about knowledge and the consequences of moral choice, and about the origins of certain marriage customs, appeared in his *Legends of My People the Great Ojibway* (1965). Another explanation tale is of the simplest beast-fable sort ("why the rabbit has a patch on its back")—as familiar to readers of "Br'er Rabbit" and Kipling's "Just So Stories" as to readers of myth—it appears at the heart of the Blackfoot story "The Race," which the American ethnologist George Bird Grinnell (1849–1938) collected in *Blackfoot Lodge Tales* in 1892. More obviously, however, "The Race" is a trickster narrative, one in which Coyote (a name to which Indian speakers gave three syllables) is both hero and villain, and therefore a remarkably human prototype. Coyote figures in "Coyote and the Salmon" as well, a myth of the Thompson (a Salishan) people, retold by Ella Elizabeth Clark in *Indian Legends of Canada* (1960). In the Coyote stories (as in some stories of Rabbit and Nanaboozhoo) the trickster is the bringer of fire and other good things; he is the agency through which the spirits (generally reluctantly) release some of their powers to humankind. As often, however, the trickster proves to be the origin of various pests and plagues as well—to use classical parallels, he is at once Prometheus and Pandora—hence the trickster stories frequently have a double edge to them.

The Bella Coola tale "The Sun Tests His Son-in-Law" is from Stith Thompson's *Tales of the North American Indians* (1929), based on another story gathered by Franz Boas. It is a tale of transformation and initiation, and it provides a particular paradigm of heroic action. And the Micmac legend "The Invisible Boy" is a didactic parable, retold here by the New Brunswick poet and short story writer Alden Nowlan (1933–83), editor of the *Hartland Observer,* and author of *Miracle at Indian River* (1968), and *Nine Micmac Legends* (1983).

There are a number of familiar personages in indigenous myth who are not represented here, for reasons of space: Glooskap, D'Sonoqua, Copper Woman, the monstrous Wendigo. But the characters in the stories collected here are among some of the most recurrent in mythological narrative—mysterious women like Sedna, good and evil brothers like those in Morriseau's story, creator figures like Raven and Old Man, tricksters like Coyote. (Sometimes the roles blur, as they do with Raven and Nanaboozhoo.) And there are a host of minor figures, stylistic touches, and particular twists of narrative that distinguish the stories and give each its flavour. Moreover, the shapes and motifs of these narratives recur through much story writing, not just in the writing of myths; and in Canada there are many modern writers—such as Emily Carr in *Klee Wyck,* for example —who have made the particular figures of myth their own.

For Further Reading

WILLIAM BRIGHT, ed., *Coyote Stories* (Chicago: IJAL Native American Text Series, monograph no. 1, 1978).

EDWARD S. CURTIS, *The North American Indian,* 20 vols. (Cambridge: Harvard UP, 1907–30; Johnson Reprint 1970).

OLIVE PATRICIA DICKASON, *Canada's First Nations: A History of the Founding Peoples from Earliest Times to the Present* (Toronto: McClelland & Stewart, 1992).

———, *The Myth of the Savage* (Edmonton: U Alberta P, 1984).

SAM D. GILL and IRENE F. SULLIVAN, *Dictionary of Native American Mythology* (New York: Oxford, 1992).

DIAMOND JENNESS, *The Indians of Canada* (Ottawa: National Museum of Canada Bulletin 65, Anthropological Series 15, 1932).

LEE MARACLE, "Native Myths: Trickster Alive and Crowing" in *Language in Her Eye: Views on Writing and Gender by Canadian Women,* ed. Libby Scheier, Sarah Sheard, and Eleanor Wachtel (Toronto: Coach House, 1990) 182–87.

R. BRUCE MORRISON and C. RODERICK WILSON, eds., *Native Peoples: The Canadian Experience* (Toronto: McClelland & Stewart, 1986).

ZEBEDEE NUNGAK and EUGENE ARIMA, "A Review of Central Eskimo Mythology" in *Eskimo Stories from Povungnituk, Quebec* (Ottawa: National Museum of Canada Bulletin 235, Anthropological Series 90, 1969) 111–37.

PENNY PETRONE, *Native Literature in Canada from the Oral Tradition to the Present* (Toronto: Oxford, 1990).

———, ed., *First People, First Voices* (Toronto: U Toronto P, 1983).

ROBIN RIDINGTON, *Little Bit Know Something: Stories in a language of anthropology* (Iowa City: U Iowa P, 1990).

———, *Trail to Heaven: Knowledge and Narrative in a Northern Native Community* (Vancouver: Douglas & McIntyre, 1988).

STITH THOMPSON, *Tales of the North American Indians* (1929; rpt. Bloomington: Indiana UP, 1966).

The Raven
and the First Men

Bill Reid and Robert Bringhurst

The great flood which had covered the earth for so long had at last receded, and even the thin strip of sand now called Rose Spit, stretching north from Naikun village, lay dry. The Raven had flown there to gorge himself on the delicacies left by the receding water, so for once he wasn't hungry. But his other appetites—lust, curiosity and the unquenchable itch to meddle and provoke things, to play tricks on the world and its creatures—these remained unsatisfied.

He had recently stolen the light from the old man who kept it hidden in a box in his house in the middle of the darkness, and had scattered it throughout the sky. The new light spattered the night with stars and waxed and waned in the shape of the moon. And it dazzled the day with a single bright shining which lit up the long beach that curved from the split beneath the Raven's feet westward as far as Tao Hill. Pretty as it was, it looked lifeless and so to the Raven quite boring. He gave a great sigh, crossed his wings behind his back and walked along the sand, his shiny head cocked, his sharp eyes and ears alert for any unusual sight or sound. Then taking to the air, he called petulantly out to the empty sky. To his delight, he heard an answering cry—or to describe it more closely, a muffled squeak.

At first he saw nothing, but as he scanned the beach again, a white flash caught his eye, and when he landed he found at his feet, half buried in the sand, a gigantic clamshell. When he looked more closely still, he saw that the shell was full of little creatures cowering in terror of his enormous shadow.

Well, here was something to break the monotony of his day. But nothing was going to happen as long as the tiny things stayed in the shell, and they certainly weren't coming out in their present terrified state. So the Raven leaned his great head close to the shell, and with the smooth trickster's tongue that had got him into and out of so many misadventures during his troubled and troublesome existence, he coaxed and cajoled and coerced the little creatures to come out and play in his wonderful, shiny new world. As you know, the Raven speaks in two voices, one harsh and strident, and the other, which he used

From *The Raven Steals the Light* (Vancouver: Douglas and McIntyre Ltd., 1984). Reprinted by permission of the publisher.

now, a seductive bell-like croon which seems to come from the depth of the sea, or out of the cave where the winds are born. It is an irresistible sound, one of the loveliest sounds in the world. So it wasn't long before one and then another of the little shell-dwellers timidly emerged. Some of them immediately scurried back when they saw the immensity of the sea and the sky, and the overwhelming blackness of the Raven. But eventually curiosity overcame caution and all of them had crept or scrambled out. Very strange creatures they were: two-legged like the Raven, but there the resemblance ended. They had no glossy feathers, no thrusting beak. Their skin was pale, and they were naked except for the long black hair on their round, flat-featured heads. Instead of strong wings, they had thin stick-like appendages that waved and fluttered constantly. They were the original Haidas, the first humans.

For a long time the Raven amused himself with his new playthings, watching them as they explored their much-expanded world. Sometimes they helped one another in their new discoveries. Just as often, they squabbled over some novelty they found on the beach. And the Raven taught them some clever tricks, at which they proved remarkably adept. But the Raven's attention span was brief, and he grew tired of his small companions. For one thing, they were all males. He had looked all up and down the beach for female creatures, hoping to make the game more interesting, but females were nowhere to be found. He was about to shove the now tired, demanding and quite annoying little creatures back into their shell and forget about them when suddenly—as happens so often with the Raven—he had an idea.

He picked up the men, and in spite of their struggles and cries of fright he put them on his broad back, where they hid themselves among his feathers. Then the Raven spread his wings and flew to North Island. The tide was low, and the rocks, as he had expected, were covered with those large but soft-lipped molluscs known as red chitons. The Raven shook himself gently, and the men slid down his back to the sand. Then he flew to the rock and with his strong beak pried a chiton from its surface.

Now, if any of you have ever examined the underside of a chiton, you may begin to understand what the Raven had in his libidinous, devious mind. He threw back his head and flung the chiton at the nearest of the men. His aim was as unerring as only a great magician's can be, and the chiton found its mark in the delicate groin of the startled, shellborn creature. There the chiton attached itself firmly. Then as sudden as spray hitting the rocks from a breaking wave, a shower of chitons broke over the wide-eyed humans, as each of the open-mouthed shellfish flew inexorably to its target.

Nothing quite like this had ever happened to the men. They had never dreamed of such a thing during their long stay in the clamshell. They were astounded, embarrassed, confused by a rush of new emotions and sensations. They shuffled and squirmed, uncertain whether it was pleasure or pain they were experiencing. They threw themselves down on the beach, where a great storm seemed to break over them, followed just as suddenly by a profound calm. One by one the chitons dropped off. The men staggered to their feet and headed slowly down the beach, followed by the raucous laughter of the Raven, echoing all the way to the great island to the north which we now call Prince of Wales.

That first troop of male humans soon disappeared behind the nearest headland, passing out of the games of the Raven and the story of humankind. Whether they found their way back to their shell or lived out their lives elsewhere, or perished in the strange environment in which they found themselves, nobody remembers, and perhaps nobody cares. They had played their roles and gone their way.

Meanwhile the chitons had made their way back to the rock, where they attached themselves as before. But they too had been changed. As high tide followed low and the great storms of winter gave way to the softer rains and warm sun of spring, the chitons grew and grew, many times larger than their kind had ever been before. Their jointed shells seemed about to fly apart from the enormous pressure within them. And one day a huge wave swept over the rock, tore them from their footholds and carried them back to the beach. As the water receded and the warm sun dried the sand, a great stirring began among the chitons. From each emerged a brown-skinned, black-haired human. This time there were both males and females among them, and the Raven could begin his greatest game: one that still goes on.

They were no timid shell-dwellers these, but children of the wild coast, born between the sea and land, challenging the strength of the stormy North Pacific and wresting from it a rich livelihood. Their descendants built on its beaches the strong, beautiful homes of the Haidas and embellished them with the powerful heraldic carvings that told of the legendary beginnings of great families, all the heroes and heroines and the gallant beasts and monsters who shaped their world and their destinies. For many generations they grew and flourished, built and created, fought and destroyed, living according to the changing seasons and the unchanging rituals of their rich and complex lives.

It's nearly over now. Most of the villages are abandoned, and those which have not entirely vanished lie in ruins. The people who remain are changed. The sea has lost much of its richness, and great areas of the land itself lie in waste. Perhaps it's time the Raven started looking for another clamshell.

Nanaboozhoo
Creates the World

Buhkwujjenene

Nanaboozhoo...had a son. He loved his son. He told his son never to go near the
water lest evil should come to him. The son disobeyed his father, he went out
in a canoe and was never seen or heard of more. Nanaboozhoo then vowed
vengeance against the gods of the water who had destroyed his son. There
were two of these gods and one day they lay sleeping on the shore. Nanaboozhoo
was looking everywhere for them, determined to kill them. A loon offered to
show him where they were sleeping. He followed the loon till he found them,
and then he made short work of them with his tomahawk and his war-club. But
lo and behold no sooner were the gods dead than the waters of the great lake
rose up in vengeance; they pursued Nanaboozhoo up on to the dry land, and he
had to run for his life. He sought the highest mountain and climbed to the top
of the highest pine tree. Still the waters pursued him. They rose higher and
higher. What could he do! He broke off a few of the topmost branches, and
made a raft upon which he got and saved himself. He saved also a number of
the animals that were kicking and struggling in the water all around him. At
length he bethought himself of making a new world. How should he do it?
Could he but procure a little of the old world he might manage it. He selected
the beaver from among the animals, and sent it to dive after some earth. When
it came up it was dead. He sent the otter, but it died also. At length he tried the
muskrat. The muskrat dived. When it came up it was dead. But in its claws
was clenched a little earth. Nanaboozhoo carefully took this earth, rubbed it
in his fingers till it was dry, then placed it in the palm of his hand, and blew it
gently over the surface of the water. A new world was thus formed, and
Nanaboozhoo and all the animals landed. Nanaboozhoo sent out a wolf to see
how big the world was. He was gone a month. Again he sent him out and he
was gone a year. Then he sent out a very young wolf. This young wolf died of
old age before it could get back. So Nanaboozhoo said the world was big
enough, and might stop growing.

From *First People, First Voices* (Toronto: University of Toronto Press, 1983). First published in
1879.

Lumaaq

Aisa Qupiqrualuk
Translated by Eugene Arima

These people—a woman with a son who is blind and also a daughter—these are
being come upon by a bear. When the bear peeks through where the window
used to be (the heavy ice pane having melted and fallen in), the mother of the
blind boy is telling him to shoot it with a bow and arrow. Though blind, he is
strong enough; so he shoots. And his mother is lying already, saying, since
they had a dog called Uuka, "You shot Uuka." She lies, but the blind boy hears
the animal hit by his shooting and says, "It sounds as if I shot some beast."
His mother still replies, "No, no. You shot Uuka." Since the bear dies afar off,
his mother and sister will leave him behind because they want the food all to
themselves. When it is almost spring, they leave the blind boy behind in the old
snowhouse. His sister will save him by stealing.

Thus the boy is left in the old abandoned snowhouse. Having shot the bear,
he is being forsaken by his mother because he is blind. But he is fed by his
sister. Loving her blind brother, she used to bring him some of her food inside her parka. She was feeding her brother with stolen food without getting
found out by her mother. He was now in an old snowhouse without a roof (the
spring warmth having melted and collapsed the dome). "My brother, good dog
meat," she always said. Wanting to regain his sight, he will have his eyes
opened since he wants them opened.

Blind, abandoned by his mother and left behind in the old snowhouse, he
is continually seeking to be given sight. So, since he is in an old snowhouse
without a roof, he calls to the loon, and the loon comes. The loon wants to lead
him to the water, and the boy is led there. When they arrive, the loon says,
"Dive down. When you are dying, suffocating and dying, I will bring you up
to the surface." And so he dives underwater. When he moves because he is
choking from lack of breath, he is brought up. Then the loon says, "What do you
see?" The boy says, "I see light." The loon speaks again, "But indeed! Move

Reproduced by permission of the National Museums of Canada, from Zebedee Nungak
and Eugene Arima, *Eskimo Stories from Povungnituk, Quebec,* National Museums of Canada
Bulletin No. 235, Anthropological Series No. 90 (Ottawa, 1969), pp. 49, 51.

only when you are suffocating and dying," and he makes him dive for a second time. The boy moves again because he is choking, and when he is brought up, the loon asks again, "What do you see?" The boy answers, "I see land, but not very clearly." The loon says again, "But indeed! Move only when you are dying of suffocation," and he makes him dive a third time. Because he is dying of suffocation, the boy moves once more, and when he is brought up, the loon asks again, "What do you see?" The boy says, "Far away there on the side of that hill I see a lemming going into its hole." Thus the boy is made to see by the loon and is now back to normal.

Then, since he had regained his sight, he was providing for his mother and sister with game, with tomcods and sculpins. As he was doing so, there were some white whales in close beside the land, and he wanted to harpoon them. To brace against the line, he says to his mother, "When I harpoon, we will brace against the line together. You will be behind me, so tie the line around your waist when I harpoon." And then when he harpoons, just as he is about to pull back against the line, he lets go of it without pulling at all. Hence his mother, because she is tied around the middle, starts running towards the water and plunges under. As she goes under, she says, *"Lumaa, lumaa, lumaa, lumaa, lumaa,"* and also, "If only I could squeeze the water out of my skin on top of that hill, *lumaa.*" These sounds were repeated over and over again as she surfaced with the white whales. Here are the words the boy spoke when his mother plunged underwater: "My mother's hood has become a fish's tail, *iya iyaa.*" So he said as his mother dove down.

The Sedna Myth

as collected by
Edward M. Weyer

A girl named Avilayoq married a dog, who had transformed himself from a speckled stone. She had many offspring, who were Eskimos, white men, and various fantastic creatures. These children were so noisy that the family moved to an island so as not to annoy the girl's father. Every day Avilayoq sent her

From *The Eskimos: Their Environment and Folkways* (New Haven: Yale University Press, 1932). Reprinted by permission of the publisher.

dog-husband to her father for food, which he would put in a pair of boots tied around the dog's neck. One day while her husband was thus absent a man came to the island and induced the girl to go away with him. She lived for some days in the village of her new husband, who turned out to be a petrel instead of a man. Meanwhile, her father set out alone to find her, and succeeding, started back with her hidden in some skins in a boat. Her second husband pursued in his kayak. Upon overtaking them he asked the young woman to show her hand, as he was very anxious to see at least a part of her body. But she did not move. Then he asked her to show her mitten; but still she did not respond. With that he began to cry and so fell far behind. The father proceeded, with his daughter concealed, through calm water. After a time they saw a strange object overhauling them. Sometimes it looked like a man in a kayak, sometimes like a petrel. It flew up and down, then skimmed over the water. Finally, it came up to their boat and circled around it several times, then disappeared again. Suddenly ripples appeared, the waters began to rise, and in a short time a gale was raging. The boat was quite a distance from shore. The old man, fearing that they might be drowned, and dreading his son-in-law's revenge, *threw his daughter overboard. She held on to the gunwales; but her father took his hatchet and chopped off the first joints of her fingers. When they fell into the water they were transformed into whales, the nails becoming the whalebone. Still she clung to the boat. Again he swung his hatchet and he chopped off the last joints of her fingers, which became seals. Now she clung to the boat with only the stumps of her hands; and her father finally wielded his steering oar and knocked out her left eye. Whereupon she fell backward into the sea,* and he paddled ashore. Then he filled with stones the boots in which the first husband, the dog, had been accustomed to carry meat to his family. The dog started to swim across, but when he was halfway the heavy stones dragged him down and he was drowned. The father also became a victim of the sea. *The woman became Sedna, who lives in the lower world,* in her house built of stone and whale ribs. She has but one eye, and she cannot walk, but slides along, one leg bent under, the other stretched out. Her father dwells with her in her house, and the dog lives at the door.

This myth is recorded, with slight variations, from the east coast of Melville Peninsula. The Island where the girl lived with her dog-husband, according to this version, was Qiqertârjuk, close to Iglulik at the eastern end of Fury and Hecla Strait. Her finger tips became seals, the second joints bearded seals, and the third joints walruses; and the girl is called Takánâluk arnâluk, "the woman down there."

The Indian that Became
a Thunderbird

Norval Morriseau

Once in ancient times there lived seven North American Indian brothers. According to this legend these seven brothers had never seen a woman before. How each was born without both parents this legend does not mention. One day the youngest of the seven whose name was Wahbi Ahmik, White Beaver, went hunting in the great forest. There he met Nimkey Banasik, Thunderbird Woman. White Beaver was not afraid for he was glad to see such a beautiful woman. The young warrior took his lady fair to his wigwam where they lived together as man and wife and were very happy. All his brothers liked her except Ahsin, Stone, the oldest brother, who hated her but tried not to show his feelings. One day White Beaver went hunting and was very happy thinking of all the blessings he was given. It was on this day that Ahsin's hate became too much for him to bear.

When White Beaver returned from the hunt he discovered bloodstains around the campfire and near his wigwam. He then rushed into his tent and, not seeing his woman Nimkey Banasik anywhere, his anger grew against his brother Stone because now White Beaver knew that it must have been Stone who hated his wife so much that he killed her.

White Beaver rushed to the tent of Ahsin and said, "I know you hated her, but what wrong did she do to you? It must indeed have been a great wrong. Tell me, Ahsin, what have you done, for I see her blood on the ground leading into the forest?"

Ahsin was not afraid of his brother's anger and replied, "You brought this woman Nimkey Banasik to your wigwam and to my presence when I hate the sight of a woman. I hated her the first time I saw her. We were all happy together before she came, so I planned to get rid of her for good. When you left this morning I saw Nimkey Banasik by the fireside preparing moose meat and cooking for you. I got my sharpest arrow and placed it in my bow. The arrow found its mark in the hip of this woman I hated. After I shot the arrow she jumped up and half ran into the forest, and loud noises of thunder were heard up in the heavens. I was afraid of the thunder and I was afraid to follow her to make sure I had killed her."

From *Legends of My People the Great Ojibway,* ed. Selwyn Dewdney (Toronto: McGraw-Hill Ryerson, 1965). Reprinted by permission of the publisher.

Wahbi Ahmik asked Stone, Ahsin, "Where were my other brothers at the time this took place and why did they not stop you from doing what you did?" Stone answered, "I sent them away. As you see, none have returned yet."

"Now my brother Stone," replied White Beaver, "I am indeed mad enough to kill you, even if you are my blood brother. You are a very foolish man and very evil. Even though I am mad at you, still in a way I am sorry for you. My brother Stone, tell me, did it ever come to your mind what or who Nimkey Banasik was? Could you not think what her name meant—Great Thunderbird Woman? I had meant to tell you but I did not do so right away because I knew you did not like her. This woman could have been the one to boost future generations, if her blood and ours had been mixed together by means of a child. For this woman was a thunderbird in human form. Nimkey Banasik had six sisters. With them we could have founded a great civilization. Now it is too late. And from this day forward Indians to come, from generation to generation, will know that it was you who stopped that progress. But there will be Indians coming from the east whose women our brothers will marry. As for me, I am leaving, never to return until I find this woman, for I shall follow her. I have a feeling that she is still alive, for she had a lot of power."

Then White Beaver followed the trail that led into the forest, over valleys and mountains and far into the great forest, until he reached a huge mountain whose top reached over the very clouds and beyond. He started to climb until the earth could not be seen any more, for now he had reached the very top. There on a blanket of clouds stood a great majestic wigwam that shot forth thunder and lightning bolts. From the wigwam was heard the laughter of many women. All at once it stopped, for his presence was felt. As the wigwam flap opened, there stood Nimkey Banasik looking beautiful as ever, with no sign of blood or of the arrow. She said, "Why did you follow me?"

"I came because you are my life."

Then the woman said, "Come forward. We will give you power to walk on the clouds. Come inside, I want you to meet my parents."

Inside the wigwam were seated two old thunderbirds in human form. Each looked full of power and wisdom. In their eyes he saw light flashing off and on. The Indian was very hungry. The old man said, "What shall we give this Indian? I know he will not eat as we do, for we are of a different nature and we cannot keep him in heaven too long."

So the Indian was asked by the thunderbird sister what he would eat. The Indian said, "I eat moose and deer."

"We will try to obtain some for you."

A big roar of thunder was heard. From the human form the thunderbirds changed into their natural state and flew away. About half an hour later they brought back a big horned snake with two heads and three tails. It was offered to Wahbi Ahmik to eat, but he was unable to do so. Even looking at it made him sick. But each morning he grew more hungry. Again he was asked if he would like something to eat. Two more trips were made but proved unsuccessful. The second time he was offered a snake sturgeon, the third a great big cat demigod. He refused all, as White Beaver could not eat in the same manner as the thunderbirds.

Finally the old woman said to her older daughter, "I am aged in wisdom. I have great knowledge. I know you like this human who is an Indian. As you see, even if he were to be one of us he could not eat as we do. Take him to your great medicine thunderbird uncle, known as Southern Medicine Thunderbird, who lives in the south. Among the thunderbirds there I am sure he will have medicine for this Indian."

White Beaver was laid in a big blanket of cloud that reminded him of a rabbit-skin blanket and he was taken in that manner to the far south. This blanket also covered him, so that he should not look. Before leaving there was a great flash and White Beaver heard thunder and then felt the cloud moving. After some time everything stopped and he was told to get up. As he looked around a big medicine lodge was seen in the middle of a great cloud. Below, on the second layer of clouds, were seen many lodges and wigwams of thunderbirds of many different kinds, who all had human forms. As they entered the medicine lodge Nimkey Banasik spoke to her uncle and said, "My mother, your sister, sent us to try to give medicine to this Indian so that he may eat as we do and if possible become one of us."

For a while the medicine thunderbird stood in silence, then said, "All right, let it be known to this Indian that if he will take the medicine I shall give he will never return to earth but will become a thunderbird, to live up in the heavens for ever." Then the medicine thunderbird took out two small medicine eggs coloured light blue, mixed them together in a small pot and advised Ahmik to drink the first drink.

When White Beaver took it he felt that some power had entered him, and as he looked at his feet he noticed they were those of a thunderbird. At the next drink, the whole amount, he changed into a thunderbird. His human form, the wigwams, the medicine lodge, all had disappeared. Everyone was now a thunderbird. So, being hungry, he flew onward to the home of the female thunderbirds and feasted on the very things he could not eat some short time ago.

But the Indians that lived below remembered this Indian who became a thunderbird. Ahsin's disgrace was known, and the women of the people who came from the east married some of the brothers, and so on from generation to generation until this modern era. This legend is respected among my people. Ojibway belief states that this thunderbird is still heard up in the great heavens and I myself have heard it twice in my lifetime.

The following legend was told to me. Once an Ojibway baby dreamed that a giant bird, a big eagle, grabbed him and flew with him toward a huge, high mountain that had a flat surface. The big eagle left the baby there. Later it would return to devour the child. The child started to cry in his dream and a great thunderbird came out of the skies to help him, and it grabbed the baby with forked lightning and took him from the ground and left him on a great plain, or desert. There the thunderbird spoke to the baby and said, "I will help you only once. So take care, for this will repeat itself in real life." From there the baby travelled home and by the time he reached his own place where he was born he was old. Then the baby woke up.

As he grew into a boy and into a man this dream planted upon his mind a great solid mark of fear. He was always on the look-out for that big eagle. One day this dream came true, as told in a legend of a huge bird that flew a man to a warm country, perhaps the American southeast, or Florida.

One clear, early winter day this Indian was on the ice spearing fish through a hole. As he bent down to look into the hole a wind was heard up above. Looking up he saw a big bird, called Keebonesee, like a huge eagle with enormous claws and a great wing-spread. The Indian could not run any place as the huge bird was about to grab him. With his spear in his hand he was taken up into the air, so far up that the earth was a blur. Finally after flying up in a circle the bird started going straight.

The Indian travelled for some time. Then he noticed the air became hotter. Then he saw mountains and upon the rocks was a huge nest built of big pieces of wood, where the Indian noticed the bones of different animals. The bird made a circle and tried to kill the Indian by hurling him three times against the walls of the huge rocks. His spear prevented this in some way. Finally the bird was either tired or gave up hope of killing him and dropped the Indian into the nest.

As he landed he saw a cave. There he lived for some time. Each day the huge bird would bring back some animal and the Indian ate what was left over. The rocks, or cliff, were very steep and there was no way to go down. The Indian lived each day in hope that one day he would escape. To jump would mean death. Clouds and mist were always there. The mountains were very high and the earth, or tree line, was seen down below in the great far distance.

It cannot be said how long this Indian stayed up there in that lonely cave. One day he noticed the bird brought its mate and began to add more wood and build the huge nest bigger. One morning after this the Indian saw two huge eggs, and again one morning there were newly hatched birds. Hope was in his mind. Now there was a way to escape.

He planned to wait until the young birds grew a little bigger, then he would kill one, take its wings and tie them stretched against his own arms and jump. In this manner he thought that the weight of his body would fall more slowly than if he jumped without them. He succeeded. It took time to jump from one place to another until he set foot on solid ground. Looking up, the Indian saw the two birds flying around making a great noise, perhaps because of his presence or because of the loss of their offspring. Anyway, the Indian headed for the bush, although it was strange to him.

Finally through a medicine dream he started on his journey back home to Ontario. Through many plains and wooded areas and after many hardships he finally reached the place he had left so many moons ago when he was young. By that time he was old and no one was left who knew him. That is all.

The Race

as collected by
George Bird Grinnell

Once Old Man was travelling around, when he heard some very queer singing. He had never heard anything like this before, and looked all around to see who it was. At last he saw it was the cottontail rabbits, singing and making medicine. They had built a fire, and got a lot of hot ashes, and they would lie down in these ashes and sing while one covered them up. They would stay there only a short time though, for the ashes were very hot.

"Little Brothers," said Old Man, "that is very wonderful, how you lie in those hot ashes and coals without burning. I wish you would teach me how to do it."

"Come on, Old Man," said the rabbits, "we will show you how to do it. You must sing our song, and only stay in the ashes a short time." So Old Man began to sing, and he lay down, and they covered him with coals and ashes, and they did not burn him at all.

"That is very nice," he said. "You have powerful medicine. Now I want to know it all, so you lie down and let me cover you up."

So the rabbits all lay down in the ashes, and Old Man covered them up, and then he put the whole fire over them. One old rabbit got out, and Old Man was about to put her back when she said, "Pity me, my children are about to be born."

"All right," replied Old Man. "I will let you go, so there will be some more rabbits; but I will roast these nicely and have a feast." And he put more wood on the fire. When the rabbits were cooked, he cut some red willow brush and laid them on it to cool. The grease soaked into these branches, so even today if you hold red willow over a fire, you will see the grease on the bark. You can see, too, that ever since, the rabbits have a burnt place on their backs, where the one that got away was singed.

Old Man sat down, and was waiting for the rabbits to cool a little, when a coyote came along, limping very badly. "Pity me, Old Man," he said, "you have lots of cooked rabbits; give me one of them."

"Go away," exclaimed Old Man. "If you are too lazy to catch your food, I will not help you."

"My leg is broken," said the coyote. "I can't catch anything, and I am starving. Just give me half a rabbit."

From *Blackfoot Lodge Tales* (Lincoln, Nebraska: University of Nebraska Press, 1962). [1895] Reprinted by permission of the publisher.

"I don't care if you die," replied Old Man. "I worked hard to cook all these rabbits, and I will not give any away. But I will tell you what we will do. We will run a race to that butte, way out there, and if you beat me you can have a rabbit."

"All right," said the coyote. So they started. Old Man ran very fast, and the coyote limped along behind, but close to him, until they got near to the butte. Then the coyote turned round and ran back very fast, for he was not lame at all. It took Old Man a long time to go back, and just before he got to the fire, the coyote swallowed the last rabbit, and trotted off over the prairie.

Coyote and the Salmon

Ella Elizabeth Clark

One time Coyote was crossing a creek which flows into the Thompson River. He fell from the log into the swiftly flowing water and was swept downstream into the river. In danger of being drowned, he turned himself into a small board. As a board, he was carried down the stream to where the Thompson flows into the Fraser River, and from there to the unknown region below.

He floated with the current until he was stopped by a fish-dam, near the mouth of the Fraser. The fish-dam was owned by two old women. When they came to their dam the next morning, they saw the piece of wood.

"That is a nice piece of wood," one of the women said. "It will make a nice dish. I will take it home."

When they had made it into a dish, they placed salmon in it and ate from it. But the fish disappeared so quickly that they could not get enough for a fair meal. One piece of salmon after another they put in the dish, but always it disappeared quickly. At last one of the women became angry and threw the dish into the fire. At once they heard the sound of a baby crying. The sound was coming from the fire.

"Pull it out quickly!" one of the women said. "It is a child! I should like to have a child, to bring up as my own."

So they pulled the child out of the fire, a little boy. He grew up very rapidly. They found him difficult to rear, for he was headstrong and disobedient.

From *Indian Legends of Canada* (Toronto: McClelland and Stewart, 1960). Reprinted by permission of The Canadian Publishers McClelland and Stewart Ltd.

Sometimes they took him with them on their wanderings, and sometimes they left him at home.

In their house these women kept four wooden boxes, each of them fitted with a lid.

"Do not take the lids off these boxes," they warned the boy. "Remember that they must never be taken off. Never."

The boy looked as if he understood.

Salmon, the chief food of the women, was a new food to Coyote. There was no salmon in his country, and the Coyote people knew nothing about it. Below the women's dam the river was full of fish, but of course there were none above it. Coyote made up his mind to break the dam and let the salmon go up the rivers to his people.

One day when the women were away, Coyote broke the dam and then went to the house and opened the four wooden boxes.

From one box, smoke came out; from another, wasps; from the third, salmon-flies; from the fourth, beetles.

Then Coyote, running along the bank of the river, was followed by the salmon. The smoke, the wasps, the flies, and the beetles followed the salmon. The people along the upper river saw the great smoke and wondered what it was. Coyote led some of the salmon up the Thompson River to his people, but most of them went on up the Fraser.

That is why smoke-wasps, salmon-flies, blow-flies, and meat-beetles follow the salmon up the streams, even to this day. They become numerous almost as soon as the salmon begin to run. Until Coyote brought the salmon, these insects were not known to the people of the Fraser River country.

After Coyote had taken salmon up these rivers, he went over to the Columbia and led salmon up that river and up the streams that flow into it. After taking the fish to the headwaters of the Okanagan River, he returned and began to lead them up the Similkameen River. Before he had gone far, he saw some girls bathing near the opposite bank.

He called to them, "Do you want any backbone of the humpback salmon?"

"No," they answered. "But we'd like to have part of a mountain sheep."

"I shall not let their people have any salmon," Coyote said to himself.

So he piled up rocks in the river and made a waterfall.

"Now the salmon can never go any farther up this river," Coyote said to himself.

At the same time he caused great numbers of mountain sheep to appear in the Similkameen country. That is why mountain sheep are still plentiful in that country and why the people have to travel to the Thompson, Okanagan, or Columbia rivers to get their supply of salmon.

All along the rivers, Coyote showed the people how to make equipment for catching salmon, and he taught them how to cook it and how to dry it for winter use.

Then he went to another country. There the people did not know how to hunt. They used clubs and stones for killing animals, and because deer run fast and jump far, the hunters had difficulty in killing anything. So Coyote showed the men how to make bows and arrows and how to use them. He taught the women how to cut up meat, how to cure it, how to dress the skins and make them into clothing.

He did many other wonderful things. He changed mosquitoes from large, fierce creatures that killed people into the tiny insects they are today. He turned grass into shells, to be used for ornaments on buckskin clothes. He turned twigs into berry bushes heavy with fruit. He threw fish skins into the river and they became salmon. Because of Coyote, his people had many kinds of food, and life became much easier than it had been when the world was very young.

Some people say that Coyote was the ancestor of all the Indian tribes that lived between the Cascade Mountains and the Rocky Mountains. Others say that he was not their ancestor, but their chief. All these tribes are known as "Coyote people."

The Sun Tests His Son-in-Law

as collected by
Franz Boas

In a place on Bella Coola River, there used to be a salmon-weir. A chief and his wife lived at this place. One day the wife was cutting salmon on the bank of the river. When she opened the last salmon, she found a small boy in it. She took him out and washed him in the river. She placed him nearby, entered the house, and said to the people, "Come and see what I have found in my salmon!" She had a child in her house, which was still in the cradle. The little boy whom she had found was half as long as her fore-arm. She carried him into the house, and the people advised her to take good care of him. She nursed him with her own baby. When the people were talking in the house, the baby looked around as though he understood what they were saying. On the following day the people were surprised to see how much he had grown, and in a few days he was as tall as any ordinary child. Her own baby also grew up with marvelous rapidity. She gave each of them one breast. After a few days they were able to walk and to talk.

From Stith Thompson, ed., *Tales of the North American Indians* (Bloomington: Indiana University Press, 1966). [1929]

...

[When they mature, the boys go on adventures.]

The two young men were passing by the houses, and looked into the doorways. There was a house in the centre of this town; there they saw a beautiful girl sitting in the middle of the house. Her hair was red, and reached down to the floor. She was very white. Her eyes were large, and as clear as rock crystal. The boy fell in love with the girl. They went on, but his thoughts were with her. The Salmon boy said, "I am going to enter this house. You must watch closely what I do, and imitate me. The Door of this house tries to bite everyone who enters." The Door opened, and the Salmon jumped into the house. Then the Door snapped, but missed him. When it opened again, the boy jumped into the house. They found a number of people inside, who invited them to sit down. They spread food before them, but the boy did not like their food. It had a very strong smell, and looked rather curious. It consisted of algae that grow on logs that lie in the river.

When the boy did not touch it, one of the men said to him, "Maybe you want to eat those two children. Take them down to the river and throw them into the water, but do not look." The two children arose, and he took them down to the river. Then he threw them into the water without looking at them. At the place where he had thrown them down, he found a male and a female Salmon. He took them up to the house and roasted them. The people told him to preserve the intestines and the bones carefully. After he had eaten, one of the men told him to carry the intestines and the bones to the same place where he had thrown the children into the water. He carried them in his hands, and threw them into the river without looking. When he entered the house, he heard the children following him. The girl was covering one of her eyes with her hands. The boy was limping, because he had lost one of his bones. Then the people looked at the place where the boy had been sitting, and they found the eye, and a bone from the head of the male salmon. They ordered the boy to throw these into the water. He took the children and the eye and the bone, and threw them into the river. Then the children were hale and well.

After a while the youth said to his Salmon brother, "I wish to go to the other house where I saw the beautiful girl." They went there, and he said to his Salmon brother, "Let us enter. I should like to see her face well." They went in. Then the man arose, and spread a caribou blanket for them to sit on, and the people gave them food. Then he whispered to his brother, "Tell the girl I want to marry her." The Salmon boy told the girl, who smiled, and said, "He must not marry me. Whoever marries me must die. I like him, and I do not wish to kill him; but if he wishes to die, let him marry me."

...

The woman was the Salmon-berry Bird. After one day she gave birth to a boy, and on the following day she gave birth to a girl. She was the daughter of the Spring Salmon.

After a while the girl's father said, "Let us launch our canoe, and let us carry the young man back to his own people." He sent a messenger to call all the people of the village; and they all made themselves ready, and early the next morning they started in their canoes. The young man went in the canoe of the Spring Salmon, which was the fastest. The canoe of the Sock-eye Salmon came next. The people in the canoe of the Calico Salmon were laughing all the time. They went up the river; and a short distance below the village of the young man's father they landed, and made fast their canoes. Then they sent two messengers up the river to see if the people had finished their salmon-weir. Soon they returned with information that the weir had been finished. Then they sent the young man and his wife, and they gave them a great many presents for the young man's father.

The watchman who was stationed at the salmon-weir saw two beautiful salmon entering the trap. They were actually the canoes of the salmon; but they looked to him like two salmon. Then the watchman put the traps down over the weir, and he saw a great many fish entering them. He raised the trap when it was full, and took the fish out. The young man thought, "I wish he would treat me and my wife carefully"; and his wish came true. The man broke the heads of the other salmon, but he saved the young man and his wife. Then he carried the fish up to the house, and hung them over a pole.

During the night the young man and his wife resumed their human shape. The youth entered his father's house. His head was covered with eagle-down. He said to his father, "I am the fish whom you caught yesterday. Do you remember the time when you lost me? I have lived in the country of the Salmon. The Salmon accompanied me here. They are staying a little farther down the river. It pleases the Salmon to see the people eating fish." And, turning to his mother, he continued, "You must be careful when cutting Salmon. Never break any of their bones, but preserve them, and throw them into the water." The two children of the young man had also entered into the salmon-trap. He put some leaves on the ground, placed red and white cedar-bark over them, and covered them with eagle-down, and he told his mother to place the Salmon upon these.

As soon as he had given these instructions, the Salmon began to come up the river. They crossed the weir and entered the traps. They went up the river as far as Stuick, and the people dried the Salmon according to his instructions. They threw the bones into the water, and the Salmon returned to life, and went back to their own country, leaving their meat behind. The Cohoes Salmon had the slowest canoe, and therefore he was the last to reach the villages. He gave many presents to the Indians. He gave them many-colored leaves, and thus caused the leaves of the trees to change color in the autumn.

Now all the Salmon had returned. The Salmon-berry Bird and her children had returned with them. Then the young man made up his mind to build a small hut, from which he intended to catch eagles. He used a long pole, to which a noose was attached. The eagles were baited by means of Salmon. He spread a mat in his little house, and when he had caught an eagle he pulled out its down. He accumulated a vast amount of down. Then he went back to his house and asked his younger brother to accompany him. When they came to the hut which he had used for catching eagles, he gave the boy a small staff. Then he said to him, "Do not be sorry when I leave you. I am going to visit the Sun. I am not going to stay away a long time. I stayed long in the country of the

Salmon, but I shall not stay long in heaven. I am going to lie down on this mat. Cover me with this down, and then begin to beat time with your staff. You will see a large feather flying upward, then stop." The boy obeyed, and everything happened as he had said. The boy saw the feather flying in wide circles. When it reached a great height, it began to soar in large circles, and finally disappeared in the sky. Then the boy cried, and went back to his mother.

The young man who had ascended to heaven found there a large house. It was the House of Myths. There he resumed his human shape, and peeped in at the door. Inside he saw a number of people who were turning their faces toward the wall. They were sitting on a low platform in the rear of the house. In the right-hand corner of the house he saw a large fire, and women sitting around it. He leaned forward and looked into the house. An old woman discovered him, and beckoned him to come to her. He stepped up to her, and she warned him by signs not to go to the rear of the house. She said, "Be careful! The men in the rear of the house intend to harm you." She opened a small box, and gave him the bladder of a mountain-goat, which contained the cold wind. She told him to open the bladder if they should attempt to harm him. She said that if he opened it, no fire could burn him. She told him that the men were going to place him near the fire, in order to burn him; that one of them would wipe his face, then fire would come forth from the floor, scorching everything. The old woman told him everything that the people were going to do. Now the man in the rear of the house turned around. He was the Sun himself. He was going to try the strength of the visitor. When he saw the young man, he said to the old woman, "Did anybody come to visit you? Let the young man come up to me. I wish him to sit down near me." The young man stepped up to the Sun, and as soon as he had sat down, the Sun wiped his face and looked at the young man (he had turned his face while he was wiping it). Then the young man felt very hot. He tied his blanket tightly round his body, and opened the bladder which the woman had given him. Then the cold wind that blows down the mountains in the winter was liberated, and he felt cool and comfortable. The Sun had not been able to do him any harm. The old man did not say anything, but looked at his visitor.

After a while he said, "I wish to show you a little underground house that stands behind this house." They both rose and went outside. The small house had no door. Access was had to it by an opening in the centre of the roof, through which a ladder led down to the floor. Not a breath of air entered this house. It was made of stone. When they had entered, the Sun made a small fire in the middle of the house; then he climbed up the ladder and closed the door, leaving his visitor inside. The Sun pulled up the ladder, in order to make escape impossible. Then the house began to grow very hot. When the boy felt that he could not stand the heat any longer, he opened the bladder, and the cold wind came out; snow began to fall on the fire, which was extinguished; icicles began to form on the roof, and it was cool and comfortable inside. After a while the Sun said to his four daughters, "Go to the little underground house that stands behind our house, and sweep it," meaning that they were to remove the remains of the young man whom he believed to be burned. They obeyed at once, each being eager to be the first to enter. When they opened the house, they were much surprised to find icicles hanging down from the roof.

When they were climbing down the ladder, the youth arose and scratched them. The youngest girl was the last to step down. The girls cried when the youth touched them, and ran away. The Sun heard their screams, and asked the reason. He was much surprised and annoyed to hear that the young man was still alive. Then he devised another way of killing his visitor. He told his daughters to call him into his house. They went, and the young man re-entered the House of Myths. In the evening he lay down to sleep. Then the Sun said to his daughters. "Early tomorrow morning climb the mountain behind our house. I shall tell the boy to follow you." The girls started while the visitor was still asleep. The girls climbed up to a small meadow which was near a precipice. They had taken the form of mountain-goats. When the Sun saw his daughters on the meadow, he called to his visitor, saying, "See those mountain-goats!" The young man arose when he saw the mountain-goats. He wished to kill them. The Sun advised him to walk up the right-hand side of the mountain, saying that the left-hand side was dangerous. The young man carried his bow and arrow. The Sun said, "Do not use your own arrows! Mine are much better." Then they exchanged arrows, the Sun giving him four arrows of his own. The points of these arrows were made of coal.

Now the young man began to climb the mountain. When he came up to the goats, he took one of the arrows, aimed it, and shot. It struck the animal, but fell down without killing it. The same happened with the other arrows. When he had spent all his arrows, they rushed up to him from the four sides, intending to kill him. His only way of escape was in the direction of the precipice. They rushed up to him, and pushed him down the steep mountain. He fell headlong, but when he was halfway down he transformed himself into a ball of bird's down. He alighted gently on a place covered with many stones. There he resumed the shape of a man, arose, and ran into the house of the Sun to get his own arrows. He took them, climbed the mountain again, and found the mountain-goats on the same meadow. He shot them and killed them, and threw them down the precipice; then he returned. He found the goats at the foot of the precipice, and cut off their feet. He took them home. He found the Sun sitting in front of the house. He offered him the feet, saying, "Count them, and see how many I have killed." The Sun counted them and now he knew that all his children were dead. Then he cried, "You killed my children!" Then the youth took the bodies of the goats, fitted the feet on, and threw the bodies into a little river that was running past the place where they had fallen down. Thus they were restored to life. He had learned this art in the country of the Salmon. Then he said to the girls, "Now run to see your father! He is wailing for you." They gave him a new name, saying, "He has restored us to life." The boy followed them. Then the Sun said, when he entered. "You shall marry my two eldest daughters."

On the next morning the people arose. Then the Sun said to them, "What shall I do to my son-in-law?" He called him, and said, "Let us raise the trap of my salmon-weir." They went up to the river in the Sun's canoe. The water of the river was boiling. The youth was in the bow of the canoe, while the Sun was steering. He caused the canoe to rock, intending to throw the young man into the water. The water formed a small cascade, running down over the weir. He told the young man to walk over the top of the weir in order to reach the trap. He did so, walking over the top beam of the weir. When he reached the baskets, the beam fell over, and he himself fell into the water. The Sun saw him rise twice in the whirlpool just below the weir. When he did not see him rise again, he turned his canoe, and thought, "Now the boy has certainly gone to Nuskyakek." The Sun returned to his house, and said to his daughters, "I lost my son-in-law in the river. I was not able to find him." Then his daughters were very sad.

When the boy disappeared in the water, he was carried to Nuskyakek; and he resumed the shape of a salmon while in the water, and as soon as he landed he resumed human shape and returned to his wife. The Sun saw him coming, and was much surprised. In the evening they went to sleep. On the following morning the Sun thought, "How can I kill my son-in-law?" After a while he said to him, "Arise! We will go and split wood for fuel." He took his tools. They launched their canoe, and went down the river to the sea. When they reached there, it was perfectly calm. There were many snags embedded in the mud in the mouth of the river, some of which were only half submerged. They selected one of these snags a long distance from the shore, and began to split it. Then the Sun intentionally dropped his hammer into the water, and thought at the same time, "Do not fall straight down, but fall sideways, so that he will have much difficulty in finding you." Then he sat down in his canoe, and said, "Oh! I lost my old hammer. I had it at the time when the Sun was created." He looked down into the water, and did not say a word. After a while he said to the young man, "Do you know how to dive? Can you get my hammer? The water is not very deep here." The young man did not reply. Then the Sun continued, "I will not go back without my hammer." Then the boy said, "I know how to dive. If you so wish, I will try to get it." The Sun promised to give him supernatural power if he was able to bring the hammer back. The youth jumped into the water, and then the Sun ordered the sea to rise, and he called the cold wind to make the water freeze. It grew so cold that a sheet of ice a fathom thick was formed at once on top of the sea. "Now," he thought, "I certainly have killed you!" He left his canoe frozen up in the ice, and went home. He said to his daughters, "I have lost my son-in-law. He drifted away when the cold winds began to blow down the mountains. I have also lost my little hammer." But when he mentioned his hammer, his daughters knew at once what had happened. The young man found the hammer, and after he had obtained it he was going to return to the canoe, but he struck his head against the ice, and was unable to get out. He tried everywhere to find a crack. Finally he found a very narrow one. He transformed himself into a fish, and came out of the crack. He jumped about on the ice in the form of a fish, and finally resumed his own shape.

He went back to the Sun's house, carrying the hammer. The Sun was sitting in front of the fire, his knees drawn up, and his legs apart. His eyes were closed, and he was warming himself. The young man took his hammer and

threw it right against his stomach, saying, "Now take better care of your treasures." The young man scolded the Sun, saying, "Now stop trying to kill me. If
you try again, I shall kill you. Do you think I am an ordinary man? You cannot
conquer me." The Sun did not reply.

In the evening he said to his son-in-law, "I hear a bird singing, which I
should like very much to have." The young man asked, "What bird is it?" The
Sun replied, "I do not know it. Watch it early tomorrow morning." The young
man resolved to catch the bird. Very early in the morning he arose, then he
heard the bird singing outside. He knew at once that it was the ptarmigan. He
left the house, and thought, "I wish you would come down!" Then the bird
came down, and when it was quite near by he shot it. He hit one of its wings,
intending to catch it alive. He waited for the Sun to arise. The bird understood
what the young man said, who thus spoke: "The chief here wishes to see you.
Do not be afraid, I am not going to kill you. The chief has often tried to kill
me, but he has been unable to do so. You do not need to be afraid." The young
man continued, "When it is dark I shall tell the Sun to ask you to sit near him,
and when he is asleep I want you to peck out his eyes." When the Sun arose,
the youth went into the house carrying the bird, saying, "I have caught the
bird; now I hope you will treat it kindly. It will awaken us when it is time to
arise. When you lie down, let it sit down near you, then it will call you in the
morning."

In the evening the Sun asked the bird to sit down next to his face. When
he was asleep, the bird pecked out his eyes without his knowing it. Early in the
morning he heard the bird singing. He was going to open his eyes, but he was
not able to do so. Then he called his son-in-law, saying, "The bird has blinded
me." The young man jumped up and went to his father-in-law, and said, "Why
did you wish for the bird? Do you think it is good? It is a bad bird. It has
pecked out your eyes." He took the bird and carried it outside, and thanked it
for having done as it was bidden. Then the bird flew away.

When it was time for the Sun to start on his daily course, he said, "I am
afraid I might fall, because I cannot see my way." For four days he stayed in his
house. He did not eat, he was very sad. Then his son-in-law made up his mind
to cure him. He did not do so before, because he wanted to punish him for his
badness. He took some water, and said to his father-in-law, "I will try to restore
your eyesight." He threw the water upon his eyes, and at once his eyes were
healed and well. He said, "Now you can see what power I have. The water
with which I have washed my face has the power to heal diseases. While I
was in the country of the Salmon, I bathed in the water in which the old Salmon
bathed, in order to regain youth, therefore the water in which I wash makes
everything young and well." From this time on, the Sun did not try to do any
harm to the young man.

Finally he wished to return to his father's village. He left the house, and
jumped down through the hole in heaven. His wife saw him being transformed
into a ball of eagle-down, which floated down gently. Then her father told her
to climb as quickly as she could down his eyelashes. She did so, and reached
the ground at the same time as her husband. He met his younger brother, who
did not recognize him. He had been in heaven for one year.

The Invisible Boy

Alden Nowlan

In the days of the people who are gone, there lived a boy who was invisible, like the wind.

Even his parents could not see him. When he was a baby his mother could find him only by groping in the direction where she heard him crying.

When blankets were wrapped around the baby, they, too, became invisible. When his mother dressed him, the clothing disappeared. As he grew up it was discovered that a bow or spear vanished the moment he took it in his hand.

While still a child, he became a great warrior, for he could walk in broad daylight through the camp of the enemy without being seen. And, being invisible to beasts as well as to men, he became the greatest hunter his village had ever known: stealing upon the wiliest game and driving home his spear so unexpectedly the beast never knew whether it was man or lightning that struck it down.

One day a daughter was born to the parents of the invisible boy and to everyone's astonishment it was discovered that she was the only person in the world who possessed the power to see him. After their parents died, the brother and sister lived together in a large wigwam beside a beautiful lake.

Now, there were many unmarried girls in that country and any one of them would have been happy to have the invisible boy take her as his wife. After all, they reasoned, one who possessed such mysterious power must be favoured by the gods: his wife was certain to bear sons who would do great deeds that would be recorded in the songs of the people. And the family of so mighty a warrior and hunter need never fear hunger, cold or the raids of the enemy.

Of course, they had no way of knowing whether he was handsome or ugly. But since they could not see him they were free to make pictures of him in their minds; and if a girl cannot see her husband's face, well, she can never tire of it, for if the face she has painted in her mind begins to bore her she has only to blink her eyes and it will be replaced by another.

But, alas, his sister insisted that his bride be able to see him. In fact, she promised that the first girl who proved that she could see him would become his wife. So every evening when he came home from the hunt girls would be waiting with his sister outside his wigwam.

"Ah! Here he comes now!" his sister would say. "Do you not see him? He is walking toward us, along the shore of the lake."

From *Nine Micmac Legends* (Hansport, N.S.: Lancelot Press, 1983). Reprinted by permission of the publisher.

A few of the girls—a very few—would admit that they saw nothing. But most would look in the direction toward which the sister was pointing and exclaim: "Yes, yes, I see him! He is the handsomest of all the hunters and, as always when he returns from the hunt, his back is laden with meat."

At this, his sister would pretend to rejoice. She would embrace one of the girls who had spoken and address her as "sister."

"At last!" she would cry, "there is someone besides myself who can see him! How happy he will be! But tell me how he is dressed—I cannot remember what he wore when he left this morning and he is not yet close enough for me to make out his garments."

So cunning was the sister that the girls invariably fell into her trap. They would tell her that his costume was like that of other young men of their village, except that it was richer or more beautiful. Or they would tell her that he wore the skins of animals no other man had ever slain. One might say he wore a jacket made from beaver pelts, another that he was clad in the skin of a white bear and wore the horns of a dragon upon his head. It did not matter. Either way, the sister would know that they were lying and would laugh at them and send them away.

Now, there lived in that village an old man, a widower who had three daughters, the youngest of whom was puny and often sick. The two older girls considered the youngest a great nuisance and shamefully mistreated her: kicking and cuffing her about and burning her hands and face intentionally. When the father came in from the hunt and inquired about the bruises and burns on the girl's body, the older sisters would claim that she had run into a tree or fallen into the fire. "The gods have deprived the little one of her senses," they told him. "Or perhaps she is possessed of an evil spirit. She hurts herself in spite of everything we do to protect her." And they stared in mock pity at the girl, who cowered in the farthest corner of the wigwam, not daring to deny the truth of their words. The people called the girl Oochigeaskw which is translated: She Who Is Covered With Scars.

Both of the older girls had gone to wait for the invisible boy and both had fallen into his sister's trap and been sent home in disgrace.

"Did you see him?" asked Oochigeaskw timidly when they arrived home.

"Certainly, we saw him," they snarled. "But he was so ugly that we fled for fear that we would be made sick by the sight of his face. Why, he was almost as ugly as you!"

Then, as a pleasant way of passing a few idle moments, they each of them cut a stout birch switch and gave their youngest sister a sound thrashing; after which they amused themselves by cutting off her hair and throwing great handfulls of it into the fire. Soon they were enjoying themselves so much that they almost forgot their frustration at having been outwitted by the sister of the invisible boy.

But a fantastic thought had been planted in the mind of little Oochigeaskw. She had decided that she also would find out whether or not she possessed the power to see the invisible boy.

She dared not reveal her plan to her father; it would only have confirmed his belief that the gods had made her mad. But the next day she went to the wigwam where the boy lived with his sister.

She had clothed herself in a dress of birchbark and wore her father's moccasins because they were all she had to wear.

The people laughed at her as she walked through the village. How much harder they would have laughed if they had known her destination!

The girl might have lost her courage and turned back if the boy's sister had not come to meet her.

"Ah, little one," she said, "I perceive you are come to see if you are destined to be my brother's bride. Perchance, you may see him. But would you wish him to see *you*—disfigured with burns and scars and clad like one deprived of her wits?"

Oochigeaskw hung her head and would have slunk away, but the boy's sister took her by the arm and led her into the wigwam.

There she stripped her of her birchbark dress and ungainly moccasins and bathed her and massaged her body with oils so that all the scars and burns disappeared. Then she clothed her in a dress made from the skins of strange and beautiful beasts that the boy had killed; and she reached for a comb with which to comb her hair—

"Do not mock me," Oochigeaskw pleaded, "for you can see that my sisters have cut off my hair."

"Hush," replied the sister of the invisible boy. And, lo, under the touch of her comb the little one's hair grew long and beautiful.

"Now, let us go outside and watch for my brother for it is time for the men to return from the hunt."

The little one did as she was told and the two girls went outside and waited for the invisible boy.

Hardly an instant had passed when Oochigeaskw cried: "I see him! He is coming!"

"And how is he clad?" asked his sister.

"In fabric made from a rainbow," Oochigeaskw answered.

"And of what are his moccasins made?"

"His moccasins are made from strips cut from the summer sky."

"And what does he wear upon his head?"

"A cap made from pieces of the sun and pieces of the moon put together."

"And what does he carry in his hand?"

"He carries a thunderbolt in his hand."

By this time the boy was standing before them.

"Ah, my sister, I see I am discovered," he smiled. And laid down the thunderbolt and reached out and took Oochigeaskw's hand in his.

So she who had been known as She Who Is Covered With Scars became the bride of the invisible boy.

And what happened to the bride's sisters?

Well, there are those who claim they beat one another to death. But it is generally maintained that the sister of the invisible boy turned one into a mosquito and the other into a blackfly. But if such a transformation occurred you must not think it was done for revenge. In their new bodies the sisters went on doing exactly what they had done in their old bodies. And, in any case, who among us is bold enough to argue that the race of flies is unhappier than the race of men?

PART 2

Stories, Sketches and Tales

Thomas Chandler Haliburton

(1796–1865)

BORN IN WINDSOR, NOVA SCOTIA, to a Loyalist family, T.C. Haliburton was educated locally, became a lawyer in 1820, a representative in the provincial assembly between 1820 and 1829, a judge in 1829, and a judge of the Supreme Court of Nova Scotia in 1841. A Tory, he nonetheless performed something of the role of a political gadfly: he vocally opposed the notion of "responsible government," but he advocated a number of "radical" economic and social changes, and he wrote many of his literary sketches and historical works in order to express these views and to champion such causes as the building of a railroad. Dissatisfied with local developments, he moved to England in 1856, and from 1859 till near his death he held a House of Commons seat in London. Both the progressive and the conservative elements of his social politics are apparent in his writings: he admired Yankee ingenuity, but disliked American braggadocio; he espoused political action, and attacked the naiveté and self-satisfaction of local provinciality; he adhered to tradition, yet he adapted the forms of local speech to celebrate his society's individual character. As the internal anecdotes of "The Clockmaker" show, he also made his characters share in many of the social prejudices of the time—as, for example, those that involve gender stereotypes and political biases—but Haliburton may also have been playing some literary jokes here. (His modern editor, George Parker, notes some possible allusions to Laurence Sterne's novel *Tristram Shandy,* and also identifies the real-life American politicians (of the 1810s, 1820s, and 1830s) who are specifically referred to in the text: Governer Cass of Michigan, and Governor Lincoln and General Green of Maine.)

Haliburton published 21 sketches (together called "Recollections of Nova Scotia") in Joseph Howe's paper *The Nova Scotian* in 1835–36; these were modified and brought together as *The Clockmaker* in 1836, reprinted many times (the text varying irregularly with each printer), and sequels detailing further conversations between Sam Slick and the Squire followed in 1838 and 1840. The character of Sam Slick won an immediate following, and Sam appeared in some of Haliburton's other books as well: in *The Attaché* (1843–44) as a member of the American legation in London, and in *Wise Saws and Modern Instances* (1853) as the President's fisheries agent in Nova Scotia. Sam directly influenced subsequent American anecdotal humour (Ward, Twain), and he even (some say) was a model for "Uncle Sam." Haliburton himself later went on to anthologize two volumes of American humour. In his own sketches, however—in satiric dialect and dialogue—his aim was didactic and political; he used the nature of incident and the force of speech to draw a clear moral lesson. Maxims abound in the text of "The Clockmaker," for example, which also draws to a conclusion by declaring directly the lesson to be learned. In his later work he was generally angrier and more openly the essayist in his fiction than he was to begin with. But in *The Old Judge* (1849), he brought together a variety of conventional narrative forms, among them the sentimental tale and the parable; "The Witch of Inky Dell" is from this collection. It is a transformation tale—using all the techniques of romantic exaggeration but asking to be heard as truth. It can be read for its simple adventure, for its historical annotation, or for its psychological implications. (Making "Watt the Tiger" a Loyalist veteran of the Revolutionary War, who fought under the reputedly cruel Lt.-Col. Banastre Tarleton, gives the character both a specific historical role and sufficient motivation for exorcising his previous behaviour in fantasy and narrative.) The story amply demonstrates Haliburton's command of oral narrative and his inventiveness with vernacular diction.

For Further Reading

WALTER S. AVIS, "A Note on the Speech of Sam Slick" in *The Sam Slick Anthology,* ed. R.E. Watters (Toronto: Clarke Irwin, 1969) xix-xxix.

R.A. DAVIES, ed., *The Letters of Thomas Chandler Haliburton* (Toronto: U Toronto P, 1988).

———, *On Thomas Chandler Haliburton: Selected Criticism* (Ottawa: Tecumseh, 1979).

TOM MIDDLEBRO', "Imitatio Inanitatis: Literary Madness and the Canadian Short Story," *Canadian Literature* 107 (Winter 1985): 189–93.

KATHERINE MORRISON, "In Haliburton's Nova Scotia," *Canadian Literature* 101 (Summer 1984): 1–8.

BRUCE NESBITT, ed., *Thomas Chandler Haliburton: Recollections of Nova Scotia* (Ottawa: Tecumseh, 1984), "Introduction" 1–8.

RUTH PANOFSKY, "The Publication of Thomas Chandler Haliburton's *The Clockmaker,* 1st Series," *Canadian Literature* 138–139 (Fall/Winter 1993): 5–20.

GEORGE L. PARKER, "Editor's Introduction" to Thomas Chandler Haliburton, *The Clockmaker, Series One, Two, and Three* (Ottawa: Carleton UP, 1995) xvii-ci.

M.G. PARKS, "Introduction" to Thomas Chandler Haliburton, *The Old Judge* (rpt. Ottawa: Tecumseh, 1978) i-xvii.

The Clockmaker

I had heard of Yankee clock pedlars, tin pedlars, and bible pedlars, especially of him who sold Polyglot Bibles (*all in English*) to the amount of sixteen thousand pounds. The house of every substantial farmer had three substantial ornaments, a wooden clock, a tin reflector, and a Polyglot Bible. How is it that an American can sell his wares, at whatever price he pleases, where a Blue Nose would fail to make a sale at all? I will enquire of the Clockmaker the secret of his success. What a pity it is, Mr. *Slick,* (for such was his name,) what a pity it is, said I, that you, who are so successful in teaching these people the value of *clocks,* could not also teach them the value of *time.* I guess, said he, they have got that ring to grow on their horns yet, which every four year old has in our country. We reckon hours and minutes to be dollars and cents. They do nothing in these parts, but eat, drink, smoke, sleep, ride about, lounge at taverns, make speeches at temperance meetings, and talk about *"House of Assembly."* If a man don't hoe his corn, and he don't get a crop, he says it is all owing to the Bank; and if he runs into debt and is sued, why says the lawyers are a curse to the country. They are a most idle set of folks, I tell you. But how is it, said I, that you manage to sell such an immense number of clocks, (which certainly cannot be called necessary articles,) among a people with whom there seems to be so great a scarcity of money.

Mr. Slick paused, as if considering the propriety of answering the question, and looking me in the face, said, in a confidential tone, Why, I don't care if I do tell you, for the market is glutted, and I shall quit this circuit. It is done by a knowledge of *soft sawder* and *human natur.* But here is Deacon Flint's, said he, I have but one clock left, and I guess I will sell it to him. At the gate of a most comfortable looking farm house stood Deacon Flint, a respectable old man, who had understood the value of time better than most of his neighbors, if one might judge from the appearance of every thing about him. After the usual salutation, an invitation to "alight" was accepted by Mr. Slick, who said, he wished to take leave of Mrs. Flint before he left Colchester. We had hardly entered the house, before the Clockmaker pointed to the view from the window, and, addressing himself to me, said, if I was to tell them in Connecticut, there was such a farm as this away down east here in Nova Scotia, they would'nt believe me—why there aint such a location in all New England. The Deacon has a hundred acres of dyke—seventy, said the Deacon, only seventy. Well, seventy; but then there is your fine deep bottom, why I could run a ramrod into it—Interval, we call it, said the Deacon, who, though evidently pleased at this eulogium, seemed to wish the experiment of the ramrod to be tried in the right

From *The Clockmaker*, 1st Series (Halifax, 1836).

place—well interval if you please, (though Professor Eleazer Cumstick, in his work on Ohio, calls them bottoms,) is just as good as dyke. Then there is that water privilege, worth 3 or $4,000, twice as good as what Governor Cass paid $15,000 for, I wonder, Deacon, you don't put up a carding mill on it: the same works would carry a turning lathe, a shingle machine, a circular saw, grind bark, and ————. Too old, said the Deacon, too old for all those speculations— old, repeated the Clockmaker, not you; why you are worth half a dozen of the young men we see, now-a-days, you are young enough to have—here he said something in a lower tone of voice, which I did not distinctly hear; but whatever it was, the Deacon was pleased, he smiled and said he did not think of such things now. But your beasts, dear me, your beasts must be put in and have a feed; saying which, he went out to order them to be taken to the stable. As the old gentleman closed the door after him, Mr. Slick drew near to me, and said in an under tone, that is what I call "*soft sawder.*" An Englishman would pass that man as a sheep passes a hog in a pasture, without looking at him; or, said he, looking rather archly, if he was mounted on a pretty smart horse, I guess he'd trot away, *if he could.* Now I find—here his lecture on "*soft sawder*" was cut short by the entrance of Mrs. Flint. Jist come to say good bye, Mrs. Flint. What, have you sold all your clocks? yes, and very low, too, for money is scarce, and I wished to close the concern; no, I am wrong in saying all, for I have just one left. Neighbor Steel's wife asked to have the refusal of it, but I guess I won't sell it; I had but two of them, this one and the feller of it, that I sold Governor Lincoln. General Green, the Secretary of State for Maine, said he'd give me 50 dollars for this here one—it has composition wheels and patent axles, it is a beautiful article—a real first chop—no mistake, genuine superfine, but I guess I'll take it back; and beside, Squire Hawk might think kinder harder, that I did not give him the offer. Dear me, said Mrs. Flint, I should like to see it, where is it? It is in a chest of mine over the way, at Tom Tape's store, I guess he can ship it on to Eastport. That's a good man, said Mrs. Flint, jist let's look at it. Mr. Slick, willing to oblige, yielded to these entreaties, and soon produced the clock—a gawdy, highly varnished, trumpery looking affair. He placed it on the chimney-piece, where its beauties were pointed out and duly appreciated by Mrs. Flint, whose admiration was about ending in a proposal, when Mr. Flint returned from giving his directions about the care of the horses. The Deacon praised the clock, he too thought it a handsome one; but the Deacon was a prudent man, he had a watch, he was sorry, but he had no occasion for a clock. I guess you're in the wrong furrow this time, Deacon, it ant for sale, said Mr. Slick; and if it was, I reckon neighbor Steel's wife would have it, for she gives me no peace about it. Mrs. Flint said, that Mr. Steel had enough to do, poor man, to pay his interest, without buying clocks for his wife. It's no concern of mine, said Mr. Slick, as long as he pays me, what he has to do, but I guess I don't want to sell it, and beside it comes too high; that clock can't be made at Rhode Island under 40 dollars. Why it ant possible, said the Clockmaker, in apparent surprise, looking at his watch, why as I'm alive it is 4 o'clock, and if I hav'nt been two hours here—how on airth shall I reach River Philip to-night? I'll tell you what, Mrs. Flint, I'll leave the clock in your care till I return on my way to the States—I'll set it a going and put it to the right time. As soon as this operation was performed, he delivered the key to the deacon with a sort of serio-comic injunction to wind up the clock every Saturday night, which Mrs. Flint said she would take care should be done, and promised to remind her husband of it, in case he should chance to forget it.

That, said the Clockmaker as soon as we were mounted, that I call '*human natur!*' Now that clock is sold for 40 dollars—it cost me just 6 dollars and 50 cents. Mrs. Flint will never let Mrs. Steel have the refusal—nor will the deacon learn until I call for the clock, that having once indulged in the use of a superfluity, how difficult it is to give it up. We can do without any article of luxury we have never had, but when once obtained, it is not '*in human natur*' to surrender it voluntarily. Of fifteen thousand sold by myself and partners in this Province, twelve thousand were left in this manner, and only ten clocks were ever returned—when we called for them they invariably bought them. We trust to '*soft sawder*' to get them into the house, and to '*human natur*' that they never come out of it.

The Witch of Inky Dell

Among the various classes of comers and goers that have at different times visited this country (continued the Judge) witches and apparitions have now nearly ceased to honour or alarm us with their company. Forty years ago they were very numerous, and every village and settlement had its ghost or its sorceress. Many well-authenticated tales are told of their sayings and doings, and of their marvellous power; for when was a story deficient of proof, where people are crafty or credulous? As a sample, I will tell you one that was related to me by a person who had been for some time suffering under the malignant influence of the Witch of Inky Dell, in Cumberland, Nova Scotia.

Shortly after the termination of the American Rebellion, a number of the inhabitants of the old colonies emigrated to this province, the majority of whom were Loyalists, who, relinquishing their homes and possessions, followed the flag of their king into this cold and inhospitable country, while not a few belonged to the opposite side, which they had either disgraced or deserted. Every county of Nova Scotia received great numbers of these "refugees," as they were called, and, among others, Cumberland had a large proportion. Driven from their homes and ordinary occupations, it was a long time before they settled

From *The Old Judge* (London: Colburn, 1849). Reprinted, ed. M.G. Parks (Ottawa: Tecumseh Press, 1978).

themselves in the country of their adoption, and many preserved, during the remainder of their lives, the habits of idleness engendered by war and exile.
Taverns were then places of much greater resort than at the present day, when
they are almost exclusively given up to travellers, and the voice of contention
or merriment scarcely ever ceased within them, either by day or night.

The battles of the recent war were fought over again with renewed zeal,
and it must be admitted that these Loyalists were a most distinguished body of
men, inasmuch as it appeared that every individual was confident that the result of the contest would have been far different if the British Government had
followed his advice. These faithful and wise councillors daily met, deliber-
ated, and decided upon the fate of the nation, but, alas! they had no means to
execute their designs, and the world unfortunately went on as usual without
them.

Among this little loyal band was one Walter Tygart, or Watt the Tiger, as he
was more generally called from the ferocity of his temper. He had held a commission in the celebrated corps of cavalry known as Tarlton's Legion, and was
a strong, well-made, active, daring man; he had distinguished himself during
the war as well by his valour as his cruelty, for it was a favourite maxim of his
that "the Devil was the first rebel," and that therefore to spare a traitor was a devilish and not a Christian act, and was accordingly noted for never having taken
a prisoner, or given quarter to a foe. He was a noisy, rollicking, dissipated fellow, full of anecdote, with some humour, and a strong but dangerous propen-
sity to practical joking. My first recollections of Cumberland are connected
with the "Loyalist Club" and Watt the Tiger, the revolutionary anecdotes they
severally related, or, as the evening advanced, all told together, myself being the
only listener amid the clamorous party.

I remember an absurd anecdote he told of one of their brother members,
who was absent that evening. It is impossible to give you an idea of his manner, though his language may serve to show you the style of man he was. The
story referred to Captain Lybolt, a retired officer of German extraction, who
had recently been appointed a magistrate. He was a vain, pompous, and ignorant man, not very scrupulous in his conduct, and resolved to make his new office as lucrative as possible by means of fines, of which, at that time, no account
was ever exacted or rendered.

"I say, boys, old stick-in-the-mud is made a magistrate; he is, upon my soul!
fact, I assure you, boys. The crittur has begun to fine already, and where the
fine goes the king's fingers will never follow, even if they were as long as a
commissary's. It would have made you die a-laughing if you had seen his first
trial today, as I did, it would, upon my soul, boys! fact, I assure you—I hope I
may die if it wouldn't! A chap crossing his orchard yesterday picked a few of his
apples, and ate them, which, in all Christian countries, is only a sociable, neigh-
bourly act; but old cat-a-nine-tails, dod drot him! called it foraging on the enemy,
marauding, plundering, and what not, and issued a warrant against him for
stealing. 'What is the use of being a justish,' he said, 'if you can't do justish to
yourself!' He did, upon my soul! fact, I assure you! true as thunder, boys!

"To make the court look respectable, and scare the poor devil, with his law and learning, out of his money, he piled up great heaps of books on his table, business and earnest-like, took his seat on one side of it, and made Corporal Cotton, his orderly, sit down on the other, and act as clerk, and then ordered the constable to bring in the prisoner. 'Got for damme, what do you mean, sir?' said he, a-bristling up and a-bridling like a whiskered Lucifer, 'what do you mean by stealing my apples?'—'Who! me?' 'Yes, you?'—'Stealing!' 'Yes, stealing, sir!'—'Do you call that stealing?' 'Stealing! to be sure it is.'

"'Cotton,' said Lybolt, a-whispering to his orderly, 'bring in more book: he don't respect the law, nor the king's appointment, nor the justish. More book, sir;' and Cotton brought in several arms-full of 'more book,' and piled them up on the table. 'Now,' said the Captain, swelling out like a tarnation big bull-frog chock full of wind, 'what do you say for yourself?'—'I didn't think it any great matter,' replied poor pumpkin-headed red-nose, 'to eat a few apples— what a touss you make about nothing!'—'Put that down, Cotton,' said the captain; 'he confesses he stole them, and calls thieving a touss guten himmel. I shall teach him better for all time that shall be passed, that shall be present, or shall come;' and he snorted like as if he seed an indgin, he did, upon my soul, boys!—fact, I assure you, fellows! dod drot me if he didn't! 'Constable, remove the prisoner till the court deliberates on the punishment. Serious offence, this, Captain Tygart,' he said to me, winking and blinking like an owl in the sun, 'a very serious offence, pillaging when on march through the territory of a friendly power. It is death by martial-law;' and he ordered in the prisoner: 'I pronounce you guilty, sir,' said he, 'and now I sentence you—you shall be hanged—you shall be whipped—or you shall pay five pounds, and you shall have your choice which.' The poor crittur, who had no pluck in him, or he would have cap-sized him and his clerk, and buried both of them under their books, paid the five pounds, showed a leg, and made himself scarce. 'Fary good offish, Captain Tygart,' he said with a knowing wink, as he pocketed the fine—'fary good off-ish! fines are more better nor apples—as apples are more better nor nothing. It shall be worth more nor two hundreds in one year'—true as rates, he did, upon my soul, fellows! I hope I may die if he didn't! fact, I assure you, boys!'"

Soon after that, I missed Watt the Tiger from his "accustomed haunts," and understood he was partially deranged. His conduct became suddenly so strange, and he persisted so obstinately in refusing to give any reason for his behaviour, that somebody attributed his melancholy to a disturbed conscience, and remorse for past misdeeds, while not a few believed that he had been visited or claimed by the Devil. It appeared that one night, when returning from the club, his horse arrived at his house before him greatly terrified, followed some time afterwards by his master, whose clothes were torn and soiled, and his countenance and manner much disturbed. Soon after, the same thing occurred again, and he was heard to mutter that he had been ridden hard; that the bit had hurt his mouth, and that his tongue was frost-bitten from exposure to the weather. On another occasion, he complained of having no oats, of being shut in a stable without a halter, and kicked on the leg by a black mare. But, on his last nocturnal excursion, something still more extraordinary happened, for he came home dreadfully fatigued and exhausted, barefooted and bareheaded, having exchanged his own clothes for a red flannel petticoat, that scarcely reached to his knees, and a woman's short dimity bed-gown.

From that time, he never ventured out at night, and by day always carried a small Bible in one pocket, and the Prayer-book in the other, though he was never known to look into either of them. He became reserved, solitary, and moody, and was often found talking or muttering to himself about leaving the country, taking his treasures with him (though, poor fellow! his only possessions were his farm, his cattle, and a pension of fifty pounds a year), and crossing over the seas, and placing his jewels, bars of gold, and chests of money, in the Bank of England, and spending the remainder of his days in the sporting world, far away from all pirates, devils, witches, bridles, side-saddles, and black mares. In fact, his conduct and conversation were so incomprehensible, that he was left to pursue his own meditations unmolested and unquestioned. As soon as he ceased to be a wonder, he ceased to be talked of, and, though not forgotten, his name was seldom mentioned; when, all at once, he awakened, as it were, from this dream of existence, and reappeared among his friends of "the Loyalist Club" at the Cornwallis Arms with all his former uproarious mirth and boisterous behaviour.

It was in the early part of June, 1790, that he rejoined his companions. The day was rendered memorable by one of the most terrific thunderstorms ever known in this country. For several hours, the roar of thunder and incessant flashes of lightning nearly deprived us of the power of vision or hearing, when the whole forest in the neighbourhood of Inky Dell, which lay to the eastward of the village, was suddenly wrapt in flames, that illuminated the heavens with their strong lurid light. It was a fearful spectacle, and great apprehensions were entertained for the safety of the straggling and detached settlements in that vicinity, the inhabitants of which appeared thus suddenly to be deprived both of succour and escape. That portion of the wilderness seemed peculiarly calculated to extend the conflagration, for it consisted chiefly of "soft wood," as the resinous evergreens of America are usually denominated.

The valley was a deep and gloomy hollow, between two high hills, and was clothed with a growth of exceedingly tall, thin, spiral fir-trees, known among lumberers as scantling or ranging timber, which grew so close together as to admit of no underwood or shrubs. It was a forest of spars. For thirty feet, at least, from the ground they exhibited no limbs, after which a few thin branches protruded, loaded with long, pendent streamers of grey moss, resembling straggling locks of hoary hair, while their tops were lost in a thick umbrageous covering, that was impervious to the rays of the sun. It was, consequently, a dark and gloomy wood. The very birds seemed to avoid it, and the hardy little squirrel disdained to feed upon the cones that grew in its dank and stagnant atmosphere. The bat and the owl alone resorted to it, and startled the traveller by their numbers and nocturnal vigilance. Through the centre of it flowed a thick, turbid, and lazy stream, which, from having beds of coal, became perfectly black, and thus imparted to the valley the name of "Inky Dell." The water, besides being discoloured, was as strong as brine, from the numerous salt-springs that flowed into it. The margin of the brook was covered, for some distance, with dead trees and sickly and consumptive dwarf hemlocks, that had perished or languished in the unwholesome moisture with which the subsoil was saturated.

Tall, coarse, slimy, aquatic grass, partaking of the colour of the floods, afforded a shelter for toads and reptiles, that lay concealed in its tangled roots, as if ashamed of their domicile.

The dell was intersected by a gorge which, though not descending as low as the level of the water, furnished a convenient opening for a road, which crossed it at this place. On the western side of the valley and brook stood a small log-house, in a field containing about an acre of land, immediately behind which rose a conical hill, whose base was covered with such timber as I have described. Beyond that was a growth of stunted birches; and at its top, which was uncovered, was a fountain of pure water. It was, probably, the value of this spring that led to the selection of the site for the house. Below the road, the receding hills afforded a small strip of interval, which had once been cleared and sown down with grass seeds, and, though much overgrown, admitted a little light into the landscape. On one side of the house was the prostrate covering of a building, which had evidently been a cow or horse-shed, but which, gradually decaying where it touched the damp earth, had sunk by degrees, until the roof lay by itself without support on the ground.

This wretched and lonely place was the abode of a poor woman, one Nelly Edwards. At the period I have before alluded to, of the emigration from the old colonies, now comprising the United States, she arrived with her husband at Cumberland, and, shortly afterwards, settled at Inky Dell. Who or what they were no one ever knew. They held but little intercourse with their neighbours, were known to live upon very bad terms with each other, and were supposed to have belonged to the rebel party, from whom they, no doubt, had good reason to escape, as soon as law and order were re-established. Edwards had evidently lived much in the backwoods in the early part of his life, for he was a devoted sportsman and hunter. He was averse from industrious habits, and supported himself by trapping and fishing in preference to tilling the soil. They were both in bad repute, and were shunned and avoided by the inhabitants as much as they could have desired themselves.

After a few years of this solitary life, Edwards suddenly disappeared. Whether he had perished in the woods in a conflict with some wild animal; by accident or by illness; or had left the province and his wife in disgust, was not known, nor, indeed, were many inquiries or conjectures ever made. No one felt interested in his fate, and his absence was considered rather as a relief than otherwise by those that travelled the road by that lonely and ill-omened place.

Mrs Edwards was a short, erect, active little woman, that appeared much younger than she really was. Her breeding and extraction, it is said, were lower than those of her husband, who was a man of good address and some education. After his death, or desertion, some advances were made by the neighbours to offer their sympathies or assistance, but her temper was so bad, and her language so coarse and violent, that people became afraid of her, and as some of her imprecations had accidentally come to pass, she began to acquire the not very enviable or desirable appellation of Hag, or Witch. The character of the place well accorded with such a supposition, and the moment it was conceived and circulated, imagination supplied many proofs and corroborations that had previously escaped observation. It was remarked that as soon as a shower of rain had ceased in summer, and the wind had shifted to the west, the spring on the top of the mountain emitted for some time a tall, thin column of vapour, whence it was called the Witch's Fountain, a name it is known by to this day, and probably will always retain. It was also noticed that the fowls about her door were of a different breed from any in the country, being quite black, and that her cat was of the same malignant colour. Her knowledge of herbs and simples, by which she worked many cures among her ignorant neighbours, was also turned against her, and unkindly attributed not to skill but to sorcery, and the very natural inference was drawn that she who could understand the virtues of plants must also know their poisons, and could with equal ease extract the one or the other.

Wearied and annoyed by these surmises and reproaches, she at last availed herself of the superstition of the people to obtain a control over them, and render them obedient to her wishes. She, therefore, foretold fortunes by the assistance of a pack of cards, and the mysterious fountain, that emitted steam without the aid of fire, disclosed where stolen goods might be found, by means of a skilful cross-examination of the applicant or the confession of the thief, and sold cabalistic charms that had the power of warding off misfortunes. The numerous instances in which her prophecies either fulfilled themselves or were accidentally accomplished, are really astonishing, and is it no wonder that the whole country was filled with awe and admiration of the power of "the Witch of Inky Dell;" many a fair one listened in breathless expectation to the sentence that Nelly Edwards was passing on her future life, and returned to rejoice or murmur over the unalterable decree.

There were those, however, who, though willing to believe in her power, were reluctant to intrust her with the secret of their hearts, and, therefore, confined their inquiries to the single point, whether that which they wished, or that which they dreaded, would come to pass. As this evasion implied a doubt, if not of her power, at least of her secrecy, she imposed severe terms on her compliance. The applicant was desired to come to her by moonlight, and compelled to ascend the mount by its dark and winding path, in company with her and no other attendant, and then, filling a cup, marvellously and curiously carved, with the pure water from the fountain, to turn quickly round three times, terminating the evolution with her face to the east, and then to wish and drink. At the full of the moon, the wisher of wishes was requested to repeat the same ceremony; and then the enchantress, after consulting the appearance of the sky and the language of the cards, encouraged or extinguished the hopes of her suppliant.

All, however, were not so credulous, or so obedient; and, among others, Watt the Tiger, who not only threatened her with the penalties of the law and personal chastisement, but claimed Inky Dell as a part of his property, to which it adjoined, and in the grant of which it was included. Many and furious were the wordy contests between these two violent people, who defied and denounced each other; and hag and witch, and the dragon, on the one hand, and marauder, murderer, and the villain on the other, were the mildest terms in their copious vocabulary of abuse.

The locality of the fire was easily distinguished from the windows of the inn. The day on which it occurred was a club day, and several of the members had arrived previous to the storm, and discussed the probable extent and origin of the conflagration. Some attributed it to the natural and probable cause—the lightning; others to the Witch, but most of them to the Devil, who had no doubt claimed the fulfilment of the compact into which he had entered with her, and had come to enforce it, for no doubt was entertained by any one present that the sudden, violent, and extensive fire must have consumed the house and all within it. The lightning was succeeded by a tremendous shower of rain, such as is seldom seen anywhere but in tropical climates, which gradually yielded to a sudden shift of the wind to the westward, that cleared off the clouds, and left everything as smiling and as tranquil as ever. The rain had the effect of arresting and partially extinguishing the fire, which sent forth long, heavy, and black masses of smouldering smoke, that rose gloomily into the sky, and slowly passed away towards the east, until they were lost in the distance.

An arrival from the scene of the fire confirmed our apprehensions: the deep pine and fir forest in Inky Dell was all destroyed, and Mrs Edwards consumed, together with her effects, in her house. Various were the remarks made on this dreadful calamity by the company present. Some commiserated the poor woman's misfortunes and untimely end, and felt as men ought to do under such a dreadful dispensation of Providence. Others thought the country was well rid of such a dangerous inhabitant, and not a few believed it to be the work of her own wicked incantations.

"I never did believe in witchcraft," said one, "and if I had been so weak, this event would have cured me. What's the use of it, if she couldn't foretell the fire in time to get out of the way of it?"

"You don't believe?" said another. "Well, that's good, now! didn't you go to her, when your horse was shot, for advice? and didn't she tell you it was Felix Coon that did it? and didn't you get him convicted?"

"Well, I did; but it was only to please my wife, Miss Lincoln, for I knew it before I went. But women have such infernal curiosity, they will always ax a question as long as there is anybody that will answer it."

"Well, I don't know," said a third; "she is dead now, and it's easy to kick a dead lion, any ass can do that, but I believe she was a powerful woman, and knowed more than a Christian ought to know. She told Patience Fulton, old Caleb's daughter, she was wrong named, for she wouldn't wait patiently, but make a runaway match; and, sure enough, my son Ted helped her one morning next week out of her bed-room window afore her father was up, and they were married by Squire Tommy Watson afore breakfast. Will any one tell me, after that, she wasn't a gifted old lady? Nobody ever prospered that quarrelled with her. There is our old friend Captain Tygart now, he has never been no good since she put the curse and the evil eye on him; he ain't no longer himself, and goes wandering about like one possessed. It's cheap talking about not being afraid of man or devil; once, I don't think the Captain ever was; but hang me if I like to hear people talk so rashly. How comes it he carries the Bible in one pocket, and the Prayer-book in the other, if he ain't timersome of the old witch of Inky Dell? explain that to me, will you? Well, I declare," he continued, slowly and in an alarmed tone, "well, I declare, talk of the Devil, and he is sure to appear! As I'm a living sinner, here is Watt the Tiger, a-galloping down the road like mad, looking as wild and as wide awake as a Cherokee Indgin. I know him of old—he's not safe when he's up in the stirrups that way. He is a wilful man when his blood is up. What's to pay now, I wonder."

He had hardly uttered the words when the Captain pulled up short at the door, dismounted, threw the reins over a post, and burst into the room, saying, "Hullo, boys! are you here? the old devil's dead!—clean gone! burnt up to a cinder! crisp as pie-crust, and twice as tough! she is, upon my soul! I hope I may die if she ain't—fact, I assure you, fellows! not a word of a lie in it—as true as steel. I am a free man now—see if I ain't, boys!" and he took up a chair, broke the legs of it off by a heavy blow on the floor, and then, seizing one of the bars, beat a tattoo violently against the door for the landlord. "How are you, old fellow?" he said, as the door opened. "Hullo! who the devil are you? Where is Mogan?"

"Dead, sir!"

"Dead! the devil he is! I didn't know that. Ah, I suppose she rode him to death, too! Bring me some wine, some of your best, too. I am going to stand a treat tonight, and do you mind, see that it is good—none of your black strap and mother of vinegar, but the best port and madeira. Come, right about! quick march! Poor Mogan! ah! well he was always an everlasting coward—died of fright, I suppose, at seeing that old hag of Inky Dell. Thank fortune, she is gone now, quitted her post, deserted and blown up the magazine. Ah, here is the wine! come, boys! Stop a minute, though; and he rose, and taking the hearth-brush, inserted the handle of it in the neck of one of the decanters that had no stopper in it; then, summoning the maître d'hotel, whom he called old cork-screw, by beating again at the door with a leg of the broken chair. "Is that a fit stopper, sir, for a gentleman? You haven't the honour of knowing me, sir— so I will take the liberty of introducing myself. I am Captain Tygart, sir, at your service, late of Tarlton's legion, a man that gives no quarter and takes no nonsense. If you think you won't know me again, you may stare a while longer; or, if you don't hear me, I'll open your ears for you;" but the terrified man made good his escape.

"Well, boys," he continued, "I am glad to find myself among you again, dot drot me, if I ain't! for it looks like old times. We must make a night of it; so come, fill your glasses, fellows! Here's to poor old Mogan's memory—he was rode to death, I do suppose, poor devil! a hard death that, too, particularly if he was touched in the wind, as I am. That cussed rebel bullet at the Cowpans that went through my lungs spoiled my bellows for me, for I have the heaves now, if I run hard. I should have died, too, if there had been any give in or back out in me; and, as it was, she nearly fixed my flint for me. She is done for herself, though, now, that's a fact, for I've seen her with my own eyes—I went to where the house stood, and felt for her with a long pole among the ashes, so as to be certain of it, and, while poking about, I stirred up something that looked like old Edwards's powder-horn, and off it went like thunder, and scattered her bones all abroad like a bomb-shell. It knocked me over, too, it did upon my soul! but I am not easily scared by gunpowder. Here is a pleasant journey to her, and a happy meeting with her old ally and master, General Scratch, himself! Bars of gold, my boys, diamonds as big as plums; gold and silver saints as big as babies, candlesticks as tall as cornstocks, and graven images from the Spanish main—Joes, half Joes, doubloons, Louis d'ors, guineas, and every sort of coin! They are all mine, fellows! she showed me the place—I know now the spot, the very spot, where the pirates buried them. I'll have them up now, blame my buttons, if I don't! Fill your glasses, boys: here is to the memory of my friends, the pirates! I thought there was luck in store for me—I always had a kind of idea Captain Tygart's services wouldn't go unrewarded. Hurra, boys! here is better luck still."

After the wine was exhausted, materials for making punch were ordered, and the Captain proceeded to brew the intoxicating beverage.

"Two sweet and four sour, two weak and four strong, boys," he said, "with a touch of rael Hyson to flavour it—that's the liquor to warm the heart—hot when you sleep under the table, and cold when you bivouack under a bush in the field. It's the soldier's friend, the ladies' joy, and the world's delight. It's what Tarlton used to call the young man's best companion."

An enormous bowl was filled with it, and placed at the head of the table with a large silver ladle in it, having a golden guinea set in its centre, and a shaft of twisted whalebone to prevent the direct communication of heat to the hand. With this the tumblers were supplied or replenished.

"Come, Tygart," said Major Taylor (the president of the club), "tell us the story of the witch and the pirate's treasure."[1]

"Well, boys," he replied, "I'll tell you; but first fill your glasses. Come, Sandford, if ever you mean to be a judge, you must drink your way to the bench—wine loosens the tongue, sharpens the wit, steadies the nerves, and unlocks the imagination. Here's your health, youngster, and hoping you may have a wig before your head's bald, and a silk gown before you are an old woman! Well, boys, it ain't a very pleasant story to recollect—dod drot me if it is! nor a very credible one for a man of honour to tell, but it's true for all that, it is upon my soul! I hope I may die if it ain't!—fact, I assure you—not a word of a lie in it—I'm booked if it ain't and as you want to hear it, I will tell it to you.

---

[1]Strange as this story may seem, it is nevertheless substantially true, the names and one or two minor circumstances only being changed. The unfortunate man who laboured under this extraordinary hallucination (either from *delirium tremens* acting on a mind pre-occupied with hatred or fear of the Witch of Inky Dell, or from mania of some other kind) not only full believed himself in the reality of the transformation he described, but was so anxious to impress others with a due sense of his veracity, that he reduced the narrative to writing in the form of an affidavit, and attested it before a magistrate. It is well known in Cumberland, where the scene is laid. (TCH)

"Well, you all recollect the last night but two that I spent here. I went home early that evening, certainly not later than two o'clock, sober as a judge (though they ain't always the soberest neither). As I neared Inky Dell, who should I see but Nelly Edwards a-standing in the middle of the road, with her arms akimbo and her chin cocked up in the air, looking as impudent as the Devil. 'How do you do, Captain Tygart?' said she, a-dropping a most gallows polite curtsey at the same time. 'None the better of seeing you,' says I, 'at this time of night.' 'Thank you, sir,' said she; 'and, as you are in such a good humour tonight, I have a small favour to ask of you. Lend me your horse, if you please?' 'I'd see you damned first, you old hag!' said I, 'and then I wouldn't.' 'Don't be rash, Captain,' said she, 'don't be rash. Let me help you off.' 'Stand out of the way!' said I, 'or I'll ride over you!' and I plunged both spurs into the horse, and I did try to knock her down, that's a fact, but old Tarlton reared straight up an eend, and snorted and leaped forward so short and sudden, I fell on the broad of my back in the middle of the road, and off he went as hard as his legs could carry him.

"The way she laughed, and jabbered, and yelled, was enough to wake the dead a'most, and she sat by the wayside and mocked me. 'Who'd a thought the brave Captain Tygart would be afraid of a woman?' she said; 'an old woman, too? I hope you're not hurt. Come to me, and I'll help you up. Why didn't you hold on to the bridle? They tell me you were a trooper, a bold dragoon, a man that was half horse, half devil—but you are a lubberly fellow, at best, a lout, a clown, a mere booby;' and she advanced towards me, and said, 'Get up, sir, this minute.' 'That I will,' said I; 'and if I don't make food for crows of you, you old hag, then say my name is not Watt Tygart—that's all!' and up I got.

"But, boys—you'll hardly believe it—hang me, if I didn't get up on all fours a tall, bony, black horse, and she put a bridle in my mouth, and jumped on my back, and turned my head the other way, and cut and lashed me with a long riding-whip, as savage as a meat axe. When we got on the marsh, we were joined by three other old women on black horses: I won't mention their names, but this I will say, no man on earth would have expected to see such respectable old ladies playing such pranks in such devilish company. Well, away we scampered, over creeks, ditches, honey-pots, bogs, holes, and duckponds, at an awful pace, the old witches laughing, and swearing, and cursing awfully, and a-plying their whips incessantly. I thought I should have died for want of wind, on account of the wound in my lungs; but, at last, we reached Fort Lawrence, and the old women dismounted, and put us into the chaplain's stable, and left us until it was near day-dawn, when back they came in great haste, jabbering and muttering in some unknown tongue, took us into the yard, jumped into their seats, and off like lightning the way they came. At the place where we all met we all separated again, and old Nell hurried me on, punishing me every step with whip and spur most cruelly. At last, she drew up at my gate and got off, and, taking the bridle out of my mouth, and giving me a cut across the hind quarters, said, 'Jump, sir!' and I jumped and cleared it, and fell down from exhaustion the other side, and when I got up, I rose in my own shape and dress—dod drot me, if I didn't! and went to my own house, and turned into bed, ashamed, mortified, fatigued, and worried to death. I dare say you won't believe it, boys—but it's a fact, I assure you—I hope I may die if it ain't—it is upon my soul! true as training. My sides ached for a week, and were very tender where I was spurred, and my mouth and tongue were very sore from the rusty old bit, and my heart it was nearly broke to be saddled and made a beast of, by that old she dragon, in such a shameful manner.

"The next time I was here, I walked home, with a good stout stick in my hand, so as to be secured against a fall, and to defend myself against her if I could, and I positively made up my mind, if I caught hold of the old screech owl, to beat her to death. Well, just as I was returning, I met her again at the self-same spot. 'Good evening, Captain,' she said; 'so you are walking tonight?'—'What the devil is that to you?' I replied. 'Nothing,' she said; 'I only wanted to borrow your horse, but you will do yourself, I suppose, instead, though I must say you are about the slowest and clumsiest beast I ever rode.' 'Mother Edwards,' said I, 'none of your cussed nonsense now. Stand off, I beseech you; for if you dare to come within reach of me, I'll murder you—I will, upon my soul! and if I have no power over you at night, seeing that you're leagued with the Devil or some of his imps, I'll kill you by day, as sure as there is a Heaven above us!'— 'Don't talk of Heaven, you villain!' she said, most provoking cool; 'you have neither lot nor part in it. But come, give me your hand, and promise to behave like a man, a neighbour, and a Christian, and relinquish your claim to Inky Dell, and I will forgive you.'—'Avaunt, Satan!' said I, 'and get behind me.' With that she uttered a fearful yell, and flew round as quick as a wink and jumped on my back, and clung to me like a tiger, and my arms were turned into legs, and myself into a black horse again, in little less than half no time, and whack went the whip, and dig went the spur; and off we dashed as before, like a streak of lightning; and the same old women, mounted in the same way, joined us again, and away we scampered over that everlasting long old Tantramar marsh to the fort. As I arrived last I was turned into the stable loose, without being put into a stall, and got dreadfully kicked in the breast and legs, by a wicked devil of a black mare, that laid me up for months; and I was rode home, and leaped over the gate as before, and, when I got my own shape, and looked round for that wretched old miscreant, she was clean gone out of sight. It was a dreadful ride that, boys, you may depend; and my tongue, being kept out by the bits, got frostbitten, so it was actually too big for my mouth, and I had to keep snow on it all winter to cure it. It feels so cold now even at the thought of it, that I must have some more punch to warm. Come, fellows, fill your glasses! Sandford, you young rogue, stand up to your collar like a man, and do your part—no heel taps, my fine fellows: it ain't fair.

"Well, boys, to make a long story short, the next time I was here, and that was the last time I ever darkened these doors, was in June, just three years ago this month. I loaded a pair of pistols that hitch, and put them into my pocket, and was determined to have a crack at her, and, if that didn't do, to stay at home always at night, when evil spirits are abroad on the face of the earth. Well, she met me again, as usual, at the same spot. The very sight of her put me into a cold sweat—dod drot me, if it didn't!—'You are late tonight, Captain,' said she, with a sort of mock softness of voice and sweetness of manner.—'Better late than never,' said I; and I up and fired right into her face. 'I thought you was a good shot, Captain,' she said, coolly, 'but your hand is out; it's some time now since you killed women and children, and, besides, it's dark. Fire again, for you have another pistol there—be cool now: take good aim, for a murderer's arm is always unsteady.' 'Take that, you old hag,' said I, 'for your impudence!' and I fired again right into her, and threw the pistol at her with all my might. 'Missed it again, my bold dragoon,' she said, laughing ready to kill herself. 'Come, we must be off, my pretty charger, for our time is short'—then she waved her hand, and in a moment I was wrapped in horse-hide the third time, and off we flew, as before, only faster, for she was in a desperate hurry, and thrashed me all the way, and called me a brute, a cart-horse, a broken-winded beast, and anything she could lay her tongue to.

"Well, we went through the same manoeuvre as on the other two visits to the fort, but I was so out of breath on my return, that before I reached my gate, I stumbled and fell, and, when I got up, there I was in my own shape, and there was old Nelly with the bridle in her hand. 'Mrs. Edwards,' said I, 'I have a favour to ask of you.' 'What is it?' says she; 'anything I can do for you in the world I will do with pleasure.' 'Kill me on the spot,' says I, 'but don't treat me like a beast.' 'Kill you, Watty, dear!' she said; 'I wouldn't hurt a hair of your head for anything under heaven. You are a brave man, and I honour you— a handsome man, and I love you, dear. Kill you! no, never.' 'Then, give me my clothes, madam, and let me go to my house.' 'Your clothes!' says she; 'dear me! I dropped them near the haystack on Deacon Fulton's marsh. Come, I'll show you where they are;' and she seized my hand and walked back; but, heavens and earth ! her walk was so everlastingly fast, the utmost I could possibly do by running as hard as I could lay leg to the ground was to keep up with her, it was actually worse than the horse-gallop. When we came to creeks, and sloughs, and miry places, she walked over them dry-footed, and I nearly sank up to my middle, when she would drag me out by the arm, till she nearly dragged that out, too.

"At last, we came to the Deacon's Honeypot, where so many colts were smothered, and, as I had no shoes on, the bones of the critters hurt my feet dreadfully. When I got out of that, I looked about the nastiest thing in all creation, covered over with red slime that way, and she laughed like anything. 'Come,' said she, 'take a swim now across this creek, and wash yourself; for on the other side is the haystack and your clothes.' There was the stump of an old willow-tree there, and I turned my back on her and sat down, and rested my elbows on my knees, and buried my head in my hands, devoured internally by sorrow and rage, and externally by black flies, musquitoes, and ants, that had built a den in the dead log. My heart bled, and my back bled, and my feet bled, and I felt about the meanest of all living sinners. 'Captain Tygart,' said she, 'you are a brave man; I respect your courage and endurance;' but I made her no answer, 'There is no back out in you.' I said nothing, but I thought to myself, 'Oh, my stars! I wish to goodness I could back out of the old Witch's clutches!' 'And you are a handsome man,' she continued, 'the handsomest man in these

parts. I really admire and love you.' That word love made my very blood cur-
dle with disgust; it made me sick at the stomach—dod drot me, if it didn't!
'Will you marry me, Watty?' she asked. 'I'll see you d——d first,' I said, 'and then
I wouldn't!' 'Don't be rash, Watty,' she said, coaxingly, and a-brushing the flies
off my back with some bulrushes; 'don't be rash, dear. I will be a fond and
good wife to you, and I am not so old as you think. I am a young woman. Press
your hand firmly on your eyes, and tell me what you see.' Well, what I saw
absolutely took away all my voice, it astonished me so, and I didn't speak.
'What do you see?' she said, again. 'I see a beautiful girl,' said I, 'one of the
most beautiful creatures I ever beheld.' 'Well, that's me, Watty, dear; turn round,
and look at me—that's a love;' and I turned round, and sure enough there was
old Nell put back in years to twenty-four or twenty-five years of age, as handsome and blooming as I suppose she might have been at that time of life. Still
I knew it was all witchcraft, and I shuddered all over, and turned back again,
and put my hands to my face. 'Will you marry me now, Watty, dear?' she said.
'I will give up sorcery, and remain a young and loving bride.' 'Kill me,' said I,
'if you like—drown me in this Honeypot among Deacon Fulton's colts—do
what you like with me—but I never will ally myself to the Powers of Darkness.
So no, there, now. Marry! no, never! I'll be darned to darnation, if I do!' 'Don't
be rash, dear,' she said again; 'you don't know what you are refusing. I have un-
told gold.' 'I don't care if you have your weight of it twice over.' 'Yes, but I
have fifty times that amount. I know where the pirates' treasures are concealed—say but the word, and they are yours. Press your hands on your eyes
again, and I will show them to you. What do you see now?' 'I see a large bay,'
said I, 'filled with islands;' and my heart jumped to my mouth the moment I beheld it, for I knew it the first glimpse I got of it. It was La Haive Bay, where we
were at anchor three days in a calm, on our way to Halifax; but I didn't let on
that I know'd it. 'Look again: do you see a light I have put on one of those islands, to mark it for you?' 'I do,' says I. 'Well, what else do you see?' Before I
answered her, I counted the islands right and left of it, and took the bearings
from the river, and the distance from the Cape all in my mind, so as to be sure
to know it again, and I do know it, boys—I do, upon my soul! I hope I may die,
if I don't—fact, I assure you, boys—true as Gospel! 'Well, what do you see?' said
she. 'I see a cave,' said I, 'and chests of gold bars in it, and others filled with images, crucifixes, censers, and long candlesticks of the same metal.' 'They are
prizes from the Spanish main, dear,' said she. 'What else do you see? for that ain't
half that's there.' 'Why, boxes of gold, coins of all sorts, and great heaps of
money piled up; and trunks of jewels of every size and variety.' 'Consent, and
I will give you all that and another hoard on the mainland more rich than that,'
says she, 'Watty, and we will leave this country and go where we ain't known,
and live rich and happy all the days of our life.'

"Well, I won't say I warn't tempted, because that would be a lie which never
yet disgraced Captain Tygart's lips. A little loose talk I plead guilty to, for soldiers are not parsons, and preaching by general orders is the duty of a chaplain,
but a lie!—I scorn it as I do a nigger. I was tempted—that's a fact. It made my
mouth water so it actually choked me a'most, and made me drivel like an idiot;

but then I thought what's the use of all that wealth, after all, if ill got. The pirates had to hide it, and leave it, and it didn't save them from getting hanged; and if I get it by witchcraft, perhaps it wouldn't make me happy neither. It would be better to take it hereafter by right of discovery. 'What do you say, Watty dear, now? Will you marry me?' 'No,' says I; 'never!' 'Then take that,' said she, 'you good-for-nothing, stupid, heartless wretch!' fetching me a blow on the side of the head, that knocked me down insensible on the ground.

"When I awoke, it was broad full day, the sun was up a considerable piece, and actually blistered me all over where the insects had bit me. I was lame, stiff, sore, and faint; and how in the world I was to get home I couldn't tell for the soul of me. I couldn't get back the way I came, for that was impossible, on account of the miry ground; and to head all the creeks, and go round all the Honeypots, and leap all the ditches, seemed past my strength; but it was neck or nothing, and I tried it, and at last got off the marsh, and reached Ned Dykins' place, and, seeing the stable-door open, I thought Ned might be there a-feeding of his cattle, and I went in to beg him to lend me some clothes to make myself decent, and to give me something to eat, for I was e'en a'most beat out. The first person I saw, when I entered, was Mrs Dykins a-milking of her cows, and, as soon as she got sight of me, she screamed, upset her bucket, and off like a shot out of the other door, and I after her, calling on her, for Heaven's sake, to stop and speak to me; but, the more I called, the more she screamed; and away she flew to the house, and set the dogs on me, and barred the door. The cussed critters made at me so wicked, I was obliged to draw a stake from the fence, and stretch two of them out before I could get away.

"Then off I goes to Jerusha Chubbs. Well, Chubbs was away to the militia-training, and all the men folk with him; and, when I came to the door, his daughter was stooping down at the wood-pile, a picking up chips in her apron; and when she saw a naked man coming up, she dropt the chips, and off like a shot too, yelling like all possessed; and old Mother Chubbs, the she devil, got down the duck gun, and swore she would shoot me, if I attempted to come in, and I knew she would be as good as her word, too, for she pinked more nor one of the rebels that came plundering about her father's house in the war.

"It seemed to me as if all the world had turned agin me, and I had a great mind to lie right down, and cuss all creation and die; and I believe I should, if it hadn't been that the thoughts of the pirates' treasures kind of cheered me a little. While I was standing doubting what to do, I spied a clothes-line hanging in the yard, with ever so many things on it, so I went there, to see if I could find anything to put on, but, as ill luck would have it, they was all women's garments. And there I was in another fix: at last I got desperate, pulled off a red flannel petticoat of the old woman's, and jumped into it, and then got a short bedgown, and squeezed into that, after a few rips, and splits, and tears, in stretching it; and off I went home, where I scared even my own servants out of their wits.

"I took to my bed, and kept it ever so long, for shame and vexation; and at last I came to a resolution never to go out at night, when the Powers of Darkness were let loose; and by day to carry the Bible in one pocket, and the Prayer-book in the other, for protection, seeing pistols were no good; and there I have been a prisoner ever since, till this day, when the Devil flew away with the Witch of Inky Dell. Now, that's a fact, boys, I assure you—it is, upon my soul! I hope I may die if it ain't!

"You may talk, boys, about civilized warfare, such as pitched battles, and sieges, and ambushes, and skirmishes, and cavalry charges, and hand to hand work, but what is it, after all, fellows?—for I've been in them all—why, just good schooling for a soldier, and nothing more. And you may talk about Indian warfare (where a man wants all his wits about him, I can tell you), and boast of tommyhawking, and scalping, and pistolling, and all that. And pretty hard work it is, too, to have bullets flying about you everywhere, and you not see your enemy; but what is it, after all, but duelling at a hundred yards, with the butt of a tree to cover you? It's cowardly work! The weapon for a man, boys, is a bayonet, and then it's a hurrah, a charge, and a squeak, and it's all over.

"If the British Government had taken my advice, that cussed rebellion would have been ended in six weeks. Says I to Sir Harry Clinton, 'Sir Harry,' says I, 'hang every d——d rebel taken in arms, and the game's ours in no time.' Says he, 'I'm afraid the rebels will hang their prisoners in return.'—'Serve them right,' says I; 'd——n them! I hope they will. Let them die fighting like men, and they will escape hanging like dogs.' 'It will exasperate the colonists,' says he. 'It exasperates them much more, your Excellency,' says I, 'to see you pardon them villains that way. Sir Harry,' said I, 'mark my words, *conciliation is the father, and clemency the mother, of rebellion, and a d——d pretty child it is, too; having all the ignorance and meanness of one parent, and the hypocrisy and cowardice of the other.'*

"But that is neither here nor there, fellows. As I was a-saying, talk of civilized warfare, or Indian warfare, or any warfare you please; but the Lord preserve me from Spiritual warfare! Fact, I assure you, boys—it is, upon my soul! I hope I may die if it ain't—true as fate! Fill your glasses, boys, then let's have another brew, and then hurrah for a song—the Major's song:

> The rebel flag waved high in air,
> Above the ragged crew,
> When Tarlton, &c."

As Captain Tygart had promised, they certainly made a night of it—such a night, indeed, as I never saw before, and hope never to witness again.

Poor Watt, the Tiger, is long since dead. He lost his life in a vain attempt to raise the pirates' treasure, that the Witch of Inky Dell disclosed to him in La Haive Island. It was a very remarkable adventure; and, some other evening, I will relate to you how he came to his end, in endeavouring to——undermine and blow up the Devil.

Catharine Parr Traill

(1802–1899)

BORN IN KENT, Catharine Strickland grew up in Suffolk with her four sisters and two brothers, most of whom later became writers at some point in their careers. Her sister Agnes Strickland made a reputation as a biographer and children's writer; and her sister Susanna Moodie, known at the time for her romances, is best remembered now as the author of the set of pioneer sketches called *Roughing It in the Bush* (1853). Catharine, Susanna, and their brother Samuel Strickland all in due course emigrated to Canada, variously suffering the deprivations that frontier isolation worked on people whose notions of civilization depended on books, education, social community, and received taste. Catharine's literary career began—before her marriage to Thomas Traill and her emigration to the Peterborough area in 1832, to take up a military land grant—with a collection of moralistic and didactic sketches, *The Tell Tale* (1818), and a series of books aimed at children, including *The Young Emigrant* (1826). Michael Peterman describes this work as a "conduct book, advocating an adventurer's spirit, British resoluteness, and a Crusoe-like acceptance of untoward fate, all in the context of domestic solidarity." In fact Catharine apparently adapted to frontier Canada better than Mr. Traill did, and domestic solidarity depended substantially on the income that derived from her writing. Several practical, commonsense books characterize her later literary work, e.g. *The Backwoods of Canada* (1836) and *The Female Emigrant's Guide, and Hints on Canadian Housekeeping* (1854). Something of a naturalist, Catharine also wrote *Canadian Wild Flowers* (1868), which was illustrated by Susanna's daughter Agnes Fitzgibbon, and numerous articles and sketches concerning bush life. These she wrote for such journals as the *Literary Garland* in Montreal and *Chambers's Edinburgh Journal*. Her sketch of "Female Trials in the Bush" first appeared in *The Anglo-American Magazine* in April 1853.

For Further Reading

CARL BALLSTADT, "Catharine Parr Traill (1802–1899)" in *Canadian Writers and Their Works*, Fiction Series, I, ed. Robert Lecker et al. (Toronto: ECW, 1983) 149–93.

CAROLE GERSON and KATHY MEZEI, eds., *The Prose of Life: Sketches from Victorian Canada* (Toronto: ECW, 1981), "Introduction" 1–15.

CLARA THOMAS, "The Strickland Sisters" in *The Clear Spirit*, ed. Mary Quayle Innis (Toronto: U Toronto P, 1966) 42–73.

Female Trials in the Bush

It has been remarked how much more prone to discontent, the wives of the emigrants are than their husbands; and it generally is the fact, but why is it so? A little reflection will show the cause. It is generally allowed that woman is by nature and habit more strongly attached to home and all those domestic ties and associations that form her sources of happiness, than man. She is accustomed to limit her enjoyments within a narrow circle; she scarcely receives the same pleasures that man does from travelling and exchange of place; her little world is *home,* it is or should be her sphere of action, her centre of enjoyment, the severing her at once forever from it makes it dearer in her eyes, and causes her the severest pangs. #1

It is long before she forms a home of comfort to herself like that she has left behind her, in a country that is rough, hard and strange; and though a sense of duty will, and does, operate upon the few to arm them with patience to bear, and power to act, the larger proportion of emigrant wives sink into a state of hopeless apathy, or pining discontent, at least for a season, till time, that softener of all human woes, has smoothed, in some measure, the roughness of the colonists' path, and the spirit of conformity begins to dispose faithful wives to the endeavour to create a new home of comfort, within the forest solitudes.

There is another excuse for the unhappy despondency too frequently noticed among the families of the higher class of emigrants; and as according to an old saying, "prevention is better than cure," I shall not hesitate to plead the cause of my sex, and point out the origin of the domestic misery to which I allude.

There is nothing more common than for a young settler of the better class, when he has been a year or two in the colony, and made some little progress in clearing land and building, to go to England for a wife. He is not quite satisfied with the paucity of accomplishments and intellectual acquirements among the daughters of the Canadians, he is ambitious of bringing out a young lady, fit to be the companion of a man of sense and taste, and thoughtlessly induces some young person of delicate and refined habits to unite her fate to his. Misled by his sanguine description of his forest home and his hopes of future independence, she listens with infinite satisfaction to his account of a large number of acres, which may be valuable or nearly worthless, according to the local advantages they possess; of this, she of course knows nothing, excepting from the impressions she receives from her lover.

He may in a general way tell her that as a bush settler's wife, she must expect to put up with some privations at first, and the absence of a few of those elegant refinements of life which she has been accustomed to enjoy; but these evils are often represented as temporary, for he has rarely the candour to tell her the truth, the whole truth and nothing but the truth.

From *The Anglo-American Magazine* (April 1853).

＃2

Deceived by her lover and deceiving herself into the fond belief that her love for him will smooth every difficulty, she marries, and is launched upon a life for which she is totally unfitted by habits, education and inclination, without due warning of the actual trials she is destined to encounter.

There is not only cruelty but even want of worldly wisdom in these marriages. The wife finds she has been deceived, and becomes fretful, listless and discontented; and the husband, when too late, discovers that he has transplanted a tender exotic, to perish beneath the withering influence of an ungenial atmosphere, without benefitting by its sweetness or beauty. I need hardly dwell on the domestic evils arising from this state of things, but I would hold such marriages up as a warning to both parties.

Some will say, but are these things so? and is the change really so striking between a life in England and one in the colonies? I speak that which I have seen, and testify that which I do know. Even under the fairest and most favorable circumstances, the difference must necessarily be great between a rich fertile country, full of resources, and one where all has to be created or supplied at the expense of time and money. But I speak more especially of those, who, living in the less cultivated and populous portions of the colony, are of course exposed to greater privations and disadvantages, as settlers in the bush must be.

In towns and populous districts these hardships are less remarkable.

I remember among many instances that have fallen under my notice, one somewhat remarkable for the energetic trials of female fortitude that were called forth by a train of circumstances, most adverse and unexpected.

A young man residing in our neighbourhood, of sanguine disposition and slender property, had contrived by means of credit and a little money to start a large concern, a saw mill, a store, tavern, and other buildings, which were to form the germ of a large village. Full of hopes of the most extravagant kind, if he deceived others, I believe he also deceived himself into the vain belief that all his various castles, were destined to make his individual fortune, and confer a lasting benefit on the country where they were situated. Under this delusion, and finding moreover that it was absolutely necessary to raise resources for carrying on his schemes, he went home, and was not long in forming an acquaintance with an accomplished young lady of some fortune. She was an orphan, and charmed with the novelty of the life he described, she consented to marry him and become the queen of the village of which he gave her so glowing a picture. Perhaps at that period he was not fully aware of the fact, that the property of the young lady was under the control of trustees, and that the interest only was at her command, and fortunate it was for her that the guardians were inflexible in their principles, and resisted every solicitation to resign any part of the capital.

The young bride, accustomed to the domestic beauties and comforts of the mother country, beheld with dismay the long tract of gloomy pine wood through which she journeyed to her forest home, and the still more unseemly fields, blackened by charred pine and cedar stumps, in the midst of which rose the village, whose new and half finished buildings failed to excite any feeling in the breast but bitter disappointment and aversion; and she wept and sighed for all that was fair and beautiful in her own beloved country, rendered now ten times more lovely by the contrast with all she beheld around her; yet though she was miserable and discontented, she clung with passionate love to her husband and, with womanly fondness, made every sort of excuse for him—even to herself, and always to others. It was this love which, as it increased, upheld her as the sad reality of ruin arrived. Misfortune, as an armed man, came fast upon the devoted pair—every fair and flattering prospect vanished. Unable to provide for the satisfaction of his importunate creditors as he had expected to do from his wife's property, they would no longer be put off and he became a perfect prisoner in his own house. The land, buildings, all, faded as it were from his grasp; even the yearly income arising from her money, had been forestalled, and all her costly clothing went by degrees, all her pretty ornaments and little household business were disposed of piece-meal, to supply their daily wants. All, all were gone, and with fresh trials, fresh privations, came unwonted courage and energy to do and to bear. She was now a mother, and the trials of maternity were added to her other arduous duties. She often lamented her want of knowledge and ability in the management of her infant, for she had been totally unaccustomed to the trouble of young children. To add to her sorrows, sickness seized her husband, he who had been used to a life of activity and bustle, scarcely caring to rest within doors, unless at meal-times was sunk under the effects of confinement, chagrin and altered diet, and a long obstinate intermittent ensued.

Though to some persons it might appear a trifling evil, there was nothing in all her sad reverse of condition that seemed so much to annoy my poor friend as the discolouring of her beautiful hands; she would often sigh as she looked down on them and say, "I used to be so vain of them, and never thought to employ them in menial offices, such as necessity has driven us to."

Poor thing! she had not been trained to such servile tasks as I have seen her occupied in, and I pitied her the more because I saw her bearing up so bravely under such overwhelming trials; she who had come out to our woods, not two years before, a bride, a proud fastidious woman, unable and unwilling to take part in the best household labour, who would sit on the side of her bed while a servant drew the silk stocking and satin slippers on her tiny white feet, and dressed her from head to foot—who despised the least fare that could be set before her by any of her neighbors—who must despatch a messenger almost daily to the distant town for fresh meat and biscuits—and new white bread, was now compelled to clothe herself and her babe, to eat the coarsest fare, black tea unsweetened and only softened with milk, instead of rich cream which she walked twice or thrice a week to fetch from my house or that of my sister-in-law, bearing her stone pitcher in one hand, with the additional weight of her baby on her arm. So strange a thing is woman's love, that she, whom I had been wont to consider decidedly selfish, now showed a generous and heroic devotion towards the man whose thoughtlessness had reduced her to that state of poverty and privation that seemed to make her regardless of poverty. What personal sacrifices did she not make, what fatigues undergo? I have met her coming from a small field where oats had been sown, with a sheaf on her back, which she had cut with her own fair hands to feed an old ox—the only remnant of stock that escaped the creditors, and which was destined to supply the household with beef the ensuing fall. Yet she was quite cheerful and almost laughed at her unusual occupation. There was a poor Irish girl who staid with her to the last and never forsook her in her adverse fortune, but she had been kind and considerate to her when many mistresses would have turned her out of their house, and now she staid with her and helped her in her time of need.

One day I came to visit her, fearing from her unusual absence, that something was amiss with the child or herself. I found her lying on a rude sort of sofa, which she had very ingeniously made, by nailing some boards together, and covered with chintz, after having stuffed it with hay,—for she was full of contrivances; "they amused her, and kept her from thinking of her troubles," she said. She looked very pale, her fair hair being neglected, and there was an air of great languor and fatigue visible in her frame. But when I expressed my apprehension that she, too, had fallen a prey to ague or fever, she eagerly replied,— "Oh, no, I am only dreadfully tired. Do you know, I was wandering in the woods a great part of the night!"

"On what errand?" I inquired, in some surprise,—on which she related her adventures, in these words:—

"I had reason to suppose that English letters of some consequence had arrived by post, and as I had no one to send for them, to whom I dared trust them, I made up my mind, yesterday morning, to walk down for them myself. I left my little boy to the care of Jane and his father, for, carrying him a distance of so many miles, and through such roads, was quite beyond my strength. Well, I got my letters and a few necessary articles that I wanted, at the store; but what with my long walk, and the delay one always meets with in town, it was nearly sunset before I began to turn my steps homeward. I then found, to my great distress, that I had lost my faithful 'Nelson' [a great Newfoundland dog that accompanied her wherever she went]. I lingered a good while in the hope that my brave dog would find me out, but concluding, at last, that he had been shut up in one of the stores, I hurried on, afraid of the moon setting before I should be out of the dark wood. I thought, too, of my boy, and wondered if his father would waken and attend to him if he cried or wanted feeding. My mind was full of busy and anxious thoughts, as I pursued my solitary way through these lonely woods, where everything was so death-like in its solemn silence, that I could hear my own footsteps, or the fall of a withered leaf, as it parted from the little boughs above my head and dropped on the path before me. I was so deeply absorbed with my own perplexing thoughts that I did not at first notice that I had reached where two paths branched off in nearly parallel directions, so that I was greatly puzzled which of the two was my road. When I had walked a few yards down one, my mind misgave me that I was wrong, and I retraced my steps without being at all satisfied that the other was the right one. At last I decided upon the wrong, as it afterwards turned out, and I now hurried on, hoping to make up, by renewed speed, for the time I had lost by my indecision. The increasing gloom of the road thickly shaded with hemlocks and cedars, now convinced me I was drawing near swampy ground, which I did not remember to have traversed in my morning walk. My heart thrilled with terror, for I heard the long-drawn yell of wolves, as I imagined in the distance. My first impulse was to turn and flee for my life, but my strength suddenly failed, and

I was compelled to sit down upon a pine log by the side of the path to recover myself. 'Alas! alas!' said I, half-aloud, 'alone, lost in these lonely woods, perhaps to perish miserably, to be torn by wild beasts, or starved with hunger and cold, as many have been in this savage country! Oh my God! forsake me not, but look upon the poor wanderer with the eyes of mercy!' Such was my prayer when I heard the rapid gallop of some animal fast approaching—the sudden crashing of dry boughs, as the creature forced his way through them, convinced me it was too near for escape to be possible. All I could do was to start to my feet, and I stood straining my eyes in the direction of the sound, while my heart beat so audibly that I seemed to hear nothing else. You may judge of the heartfelt relief I experienced when I beheld my dear old dog, my faithful Nelson, rush bounding to my side, almost as breathless as his poor terror-stricken mistress.

"You know that I don't often indulge in tears, even when overwhelmed with trouble, but this time I actually cried for joy, and lifted up my heart in fervent thankfulness to Him who had guided my dumb protector through the tangled bush to my side that night. 'Come, Nelson,' I said, aloud, 'you have made a man of me. Richard is himself again, dear fellow, I shall fear neither wolf nor bear while you are with me.' I then fastened my bundle about his neck for my arm ached with carrying it, and on we trudged. At first I thought it would be best to retrace my steps, but I fancied I saw light like a clearing breaking through the trees, and conjectured that this bye-road led in all likelihood to some of the bush farms or lumberer's shanties. I resolved to pursue my way straight onwards; nor was I mistaken, for some minutes after brought me to the edge of a newly burnt fallow, and I heard the baying of dogs, which no doubt were the same sounds, I, in my fright, had taken for wolves.

"The moon was now nearly set, and I judged it must be between one and two o'clock. I peeped into the curtainless window of the shanty, the glimmering light from a few burning brands and the red embers of the huge back-log in the wide clay-built chimney showed the inmates were all asleep, and as the barking and growling of the dogs, who, frightened by Nelson's great size, had retreated to a respectful distance, had failed to rouse them, I took bush-leave, opened the door, and stepped in without further ceremony. On a rude bed of cedar sticks slept two females, the elder of whom was not undressed but lay sleeping on the outside of the coverlet, and it was with great difficulty that I managed to rouse her to a consciousness of my presence and my request for a guide to the mills. 'Och! och! och! my dear crayter' she said, raising herself at last upon her brawny arm and eyeing me from under her black and tangled locks with a cunning and curious look, 'what should a young thing like yourself be doing up and abroad at sich a time of night as this?'

'Good mother,' I said, 'I have lost my way in the bush, and want a lad or some one to show me the way to the mills.'

'Sure,' said the old woman, 'this is not a time to be asking the boys to leave their beds, but sit down there, and I will speak with the master.' She then pushed a rude seat in front of the fire, and roused up the logs with a huge handspike, which she wielded with strength of arm that proved she was no stranger to the work of closing in logheaps, and even chopping, and then proceeded to wake her partner, who, with three or four big boys, occupied another bed at the farthest end of the shanty.

After some parleying with the man it was agreed that at day-break one of the elder boys should be sent to guide me home, but not sooner. 'There Mistress' said the man, 'you may just lie down on my old woman's bed, the girl has the ague, but she is as quiet as a lamb, and will not disturb you.' I preferred sitting on my rude seat before the now blazing fire, to sharing the girl's couch, and as to a refreshment of fried pork and potatoes which my hostess offered to get ready for me, I had no appetite for it, and was glad when my host of the shanty and his partner retired to bed, and left me to my own cogitations and mute companionship of Nelson. One feeling was uppermost in my mind—gratitude to God for my present shelter, rude as it was; the novelty of my situation almost amused me, and then graver thoughts came over me as I cast my eyes curiously around upon smoke-stained walls and unbarked rafters from whence moss and grey lichens waved in a sort of fancied drapery above my head. I thought of my former life of pride and luxury. What a singular contrast did it present to my situation at that moment. The red flashing glare of the now fiercely burning logs illumined every corner of the shanty, and showed the faces of the sleepers in their humble beds. There lay close beside me on her rude pallet, the poor sick girl, whose pale visage and labouring breath excited my commiseration, for what comfort could she have, either mental or bodily, I asked myself. The chinking in many parts, had been displaced, and the spaces stuffed with rags, straw, moss, wool and a mass of heterogeneous matter, that would have plainly told from what part of the world the inmates had come, if their strong South of Ireland brogue had not declared it past all disputing. Few and scanty were the articles of furniture and convenience. Two or three unplaned pinewood shelves, on which were arranged some tinware and a little coarse delf, a block of wood sawn from the butt end of a large timber tree, and a rude ricketty table, with a pork and flour barrel, some implements of husbandry, among which gleamed brightly the Irish spade, an instrument peculiar to the Irish laborers' cabin, and a gun which was supported against the log walls by two carved wooden hooks, or rests, such was the interior of the shanty. I amused myself with making a sort of mental inventory of its internal economy, till by degrees weariness overcame me, and leaning my back against the frame of the poor sick girl's bed, I fell sound asleep, and might have slept on till broad day, had not my slumbers been suddenly broken by the rolling of one of the big logs on the hearth, and looking over, I almost started at the sight of the small, sinister-looking eyes of my host, which were bent upon me with so penetrating a glance, that I shrank from before them. In good truth more stout-hearted persons might have been justified in the indulgence of a cowardly feeling, if they had been placed in a similar situation, so utterly helpless and alone; but my courage quickly returned. I thought it wisest not to show distrust, and addressed the uncouth-looking personage before me with a cheerful air, laughing at his having caught me napping. Yet I remember the time, when I was a youthful romance reader, I should have fancied myself into a heroine, and my old Irishman into a brigand; but in my intercourse with the lower class of Irish emigrants, I have learnt that there is little cause for fear in reality. Their wild passions are often roused to a fearful degree of violence by insult, either against their religion or their nation, to acts of vengence; but such a thing as murdering or robbing a helpless, unoffending stranger, seeking the hospitable shelter of their roofs, I never yet heard of, nor do I believe them capable of an act of covetousness or cruelty so unprovoked. While I thought on these things my confidence returned, so that I would not have hesitated to take the man for my guide through the lone woods I had to pass, trusting to this impression of the Irish character, which, with many defects, has many virtues, while that of hospitality is certainly one of the most prominent.

"The first streak of daylight saw the old woman stirring, to prepare their morning meal of pork and potatoes, of which I was glad to partake.

"One by one came stealing sleepily from their nests four ragged urchins, whose garments I verily believe were never removed for weeks, either by day or night. They all had the same peculiar smoke-dried complexion, a sort of dusky greyish tint, grey eyes, with thick black lashes, and broad black eyebrows, with a squareness of head and a length of chin which I have not unfrequently noticed as a characteristic feature in the less comely inhabitants of the Irish cabins. The boys stole looks of wonder and curiosity at me, but no one spoke or ventured to ask a question; however, they bestowed great marks of attention on Nelson, and many were the bits of meat and potatoes with which they strove to seduce him from my feet.

"When our meal was ended, I gave the old woman a small piece of silver, and, accompanied by Master Michael, the biggest boy, I left the shanty, and was glad enough to seek my own home, and find all as well as when I had left them, though some anxiety had been felt for my unusual absence."

Such were the midnight adventures of my poor friend. It was only one of many trials that she afterwards underwent before she once more regained her native land. She used often to say to me, "I think, if you ever write another book on the backwoods, some of my adventures might furnish you with matter for its pages."

I would not have it inferred from these pages that, because some young men have erred in bringing out wives, unsuited by their former state of life, to endure the hardships of a bush-settling life, there are no exceptions. I would warn all who go home for British wives, to act openly, and use no deception, and to choose wisely such as are by habits and constitution able to struggle with the trials that may await them. It is not many who have the mental courage that was displayed by her whose adventures I have just narrated.

Susanna Moodie

(1803–1885)

SUSANNA (STRICKLAND) MOODIE WAS BORN IN SUFFOLK, ENGLAND, into a family that became widely known for its literary endeavours. Her sisters Agnes and Elizabeth Strickland, who remained in England, were popular biographers; her brother Samuel and her sister Catharine Parr Traill, who (like Susanna) emigrated to Canada, wrote commentaries on colonial society, natural history, and other subjects. Susanna emigrated somewhat unwillingly in 1832, just over a year after her marriage to Lt. J.W. Dunbar Moodie (he left the army with half pay and a grant of land in Upper Canada). Mostly she wrote conventional romances—yet in subsequent years she has become more recognized for her two books of pioneer sketches: *Roughing It in the Bush* (1852, rev. 1871) and *Life in the Clearings versus the Bush* (1853). "A Visit to Grosse Isle," in its more genteel, revised form, appeared in the earlier of these volumes; the lively first version of the sketch, collected here, appeared under the general title "Scenes in Canada" in the first issue of *The Victoria Magazine* (a journal that Mrs. Moodie edited with her husband, designing it in the "hope of inducing a taste for polite literature among the working classes") in September 1847.

Susanna Moodie's view of life was deeply affected by her Methodist commitment to faith and good works, her patriotic commitment to English social order, and her literary commitment to "elevated" language and verbal propriety. In her writing, she was much influenced by Mary Russell Mitford's collection of Suffolk sketches, *Our Village* (1824). But in recording local scenes, local speech, local characters, and bush life, Susanna Moodie also grew to appreciate that neither the values she emigrated with, nor the prejudices and fears, were fixed. "A Visit to Grosse Isle" (the quarantine station in the St. Lawrence River) gives some indication of her state of mind on arriving in Canada. In 1852 she was warning unprepared would-be settlers not to emigrate at all. (Her own tribulations, in due course, became the subject of a play by Robertson Davies and a book of poems by Margaret Atwood.) By 1871, however—in an essay called "Canada: A Contrast," which prefaced the reprint of her 1852 sketches—she was writing that "the rough has become smooth, the crooked has been made straight, the forests have been converted to fruitful fields." Some of these changes will have taken place in the environment around her, some in her own capacity to see and appreciate the land where she made her home.

For Further Reading

CARL BALLSTADT, "Susanna Moodie and the English Sketch," *Canadian Literature,* 51 (Winter 1972): 32–38.

————, "Editor's Introduction" to Susanna Moodie, *Roughing It in the Bush or Life in Canada* (Ottawa: Carleton, 1988) xvii-lx.

SUSANNA MOODIE, *Letters of a Lifetime,* ed. Carl Ballstadt, Elizabeth Hopkins, and Michael Peterman (Toronto: U Toronto P, 1985).

————, *Letters of Love and Duty: The Correspondence of John and Susanna Moodie,* ed. Carl Ballstadt, Elizabeth Hopkins, and Michael Peterman (Toronto: U Toronto P, 1993).

MICHAEL PETERMAN, "Susanna Moodie (1803–1885)," in *Canadian Writers and Their Works,* ed. Robert Lecker, Jack David, and Ellen Quigley (Toronto: ECW, 1983), I: 63–104.

JOHN THURSTON, ed., *Voyages: Short Narratives of Susanna Moodie* (Ottawa: U Ottawa P, 1991), "Introduction" vii-xxix.

A Visit to Grosse Isle

Alas! that man's stern spirit ere should mar
A scene so pure, so exquisite as this.

The dreadful Cholera was depopulating Quebec and Montreal, when our ship cast anchor off Grosse Isle, on the 30th of August, 1832; and we were boarded a few minutes after by the health officers. One of these gentlemen, a little, shrivelled up Frenchman, from his solemn aspect, and spectral, attenuated figure, would have made no bad representation of him who sat upon the pale horse. He was the only grave Frenchman I ever saw, and I naturally enough regarded him as a phenomenon. His companion, a fine looking, fair-haired, florid young Scotchman, though a little consequential in his manners, looked like one who in his own person could combat and vanquish all the diseases to which flesh is heir. Such was the contrast between these doctors, that they would have formed very good emblems—one of vigorous health, the other of hopeless decay.

Our Captain, whom I shall call old Boreas, a rude, blunt old sailor, possessing as much politeness as might be expected from a bear, received his sprucely dressed visitors upon deck, with very little courtesy, and followed them down into the cabin with various uncouth mutterings, which sounded very like short growls. The officials were no sooner seated, than glancing round the cabin, they commenced the following dialogue:

'Captain, where are you from?'

Now, the Captain had a peculiar lingo of his own, from which he invariably expunged all the connecting links. Small words, like 'and,' 'the,' and 'but,' he contrived to dispense with altogether, as my readers will perceive by his laconic reply— 'Scotland—sailed from Port o' Leith—bound for Quebec—Montreal—general cargo, seventy-two steerage, four cabin passengers—crew, eight men—brig ninety-two tons burden.' Here he produced his credentials and handed them to the gentlemen. The Scotchman just glanced his eye over the papers, and laid them on the table. 'Had you a good passage out?' 'Tedious—baffling winds—heavy fogs—detention for three weeks on banks—foul weather making the gulf—people short of water—ship nearly out of provisions—steerage passengers starving.'

'Any sickness or deaths on board?'

'None.'

'Any births?' lisped the little Frenchman.

The Captain screwed up his mouth, scratched his head, and after a moment's

---

From *The Victoria Magazine* (September, 1847).

reflection, replied, 'Why, yes; now I think on't, gentlemen, we had one female on board who produced three at once.'

'Indeed! that's uncommon,' said the Scotch doctor. 'Are the children alive and well—are they males or females? I should like much to see them.' He started up, and knocked his head, for he was very tall, against the ceiling. 'Confound your low cribs; I have nearly knocked out my brains.'

'A hard task, that,' looked the Captain. He did not say it, but I knew by his sarcastic grin, what was uppermost in his thoughts. 'The young ones are all males—very fine, thriving creatures. Step upon deck, Sam Frazer, (turning to his steward,) and bring them down, for the Doctors to see.'

I looked hard at old Boreas, wondering all the while, what he was at. Sam appeared to comprehend him in a moment, for he vanished with a knowing wink to his superior; and quickly returned, bearing in his arms three fat, chuckle-headed bull-terrier pups, whom I had christened Neptune, Triton, and Bowswain. The sagacious slut followed close at his heels, as if she dreaded some sinister design upon the part of Sam towards her young, and looked ready to give and take offence on the slightest provocation.

'Well, gentlemen, here are the young 'uns.—They do credit to the nursing of the brindled slut,' cried the old tar, chuckling and rubbing his hands together.

'Sacre! do you tink us dogs, to try and pass your tam puppies on us for babies?' screamed the enraged little Frenchman.

"Hout, man! don't be angry," said the Scotchman, stifling a laugh, 'you see 'tis only a joke.'

'Joke! tam his joke—me no understand such joke,' retorted his angry comrade, bestowing a hearty kick on one of the unoffending pups, who was frisking about his feet. The pup yelped—the slut barked and leaped furiously at the offender, and was only kept from biting him, by Sam, who could scarcely hold her back, for laughing. The Captain was uproarious in his mirth, and the Frenchman alone maintained a serious countenance.

The dogs were at length dismissed, and peace restored. After some further questioning, a bible was required for the Captain to take his oath; but mine was mislaid, and there was none at hand. 'Confound it!' muttered the old sailor, tossing over the papers in his desk, 'I don't think there's one in the ship. Oh yes, here it is at last. That scoundrel, Sam, always stows all my traps out of the way;' and taking up Voltaire's History of Charles XII, from the table, he handed it, with as grave a face as he could assume, to the Frenchman.

The official received it with the dignity of one who has authority. The Captain kissed the book with an air of mock sanctity, and the gentlemen returned to the deck. Here they requested old Boreas to give them a few feet of oak, to mend their sailing boat, which had sustained some damage in going on board a vessel, the day before. This the Captain could not do, which circumstance put them into a very bad humor; and in no very gentle tones they ordered him instantly to prepare the boats to put his passengers on shore.

'I'll be sunk, if I do!' returned the bluff old sailor. 'Stiff wind—short sea—great danger in making land—the boats heavily laden will be swamped. Not a soul shall leave the vessel tonight!'

'You must comply with our orders.'

'I won't; that's poz. I know my duty—you stick to yours. If the wind falls off, I'll go off with them myself; but not a life shall be risked to please you!'

The officers left the vessel in high disdain; and we could but applaud the Captain's firmness when we saw eleven people drowned from another vessel, in attempting to obey the same orders.

The next day all was confusion and bustle on board our vessel. I watched boat after boat depart for the shore, full of people and goods, and envied them the glorious privilege of once more treading their native earth. How ardently we anticipate pleasure, which in the end proves positive pain; such was my case, when indulged in the gratification I so eagerly desired. As cabin passengers, we were not involved in the general order of purification; but were obliged to send all the clothes and bedding we had used during the voyage, on shore with our servant, to be washed.

The ship was soon emptied of all her live cargo. My husband alone remained to bear me company, and he intended to reconnoitre the Island, the first time the boats returned to the vessel. We paced the deck nearly all day—the baby, and the slut and her family, our sole companions; and more than this, we were doomed to undergo a strict fast. All our provisions were consumed; some of the steerage passengers had been out of food for days, and were half-starved. The Captain was to bring a supply of soft bread, from the store-ship, which came daily from Quebec with supplies for the people on the Island. How we reckoned upon once more tasting bread and fresh butter;—the very thought of the treat in store for us, served to sharpen my appetite, and make the long fast more irksome. I could now fully realize Mrs. Bowdich's feelings in her longing so for English bread and butter, after her three years' travels through the burning African deserts, with her talented and devoted husband.

'When we arrived at the hotel at Plymouth,' said she, 'and were asked what refreshments we chose—Tea and home-made bread and butter—brown bread, if you please, and plenty of it.—I never enjoyed any luxury like it; I was positively ashamed of asking the waiter to re-fill the plate. After the execrable African messes, and the hard ship-buscuit, only imagine the luxury of a good slice of English bread and butter!'

I laughed heartily at the lively energy with which that charming and lovely woman related this little incident in her eventful history; but just at that moment I fully realized it all.

As the sun rose above the horizon, all these matter-of-fact circumstances were gradually forgotten, and merged in the surpassing beauty of the scene, which rose majestically before us. The previous day had been dark and stormy, and a heavy fog had concealed the mountain chain which forms the stupendous back-ground to this sublime scenery, entirely from our view. As the clouds rolled away from the hoary peaks of their grey, bald brows, and cast a denser shadow upon the vast forest belt that girdled them round, and they loomed out like mighty giants, Titans of the earth, in all their wild and awful grandeur, a thrill of wonder and delight pervaded my mind; the spectacle floated dimly on my sight, for my eyes were blinded with tears;—blinded with the excess of beauty. I turned to the right and the left; I looked up and down the glorious river;—never had I beheld so many striking objects in one landscape—nature had lavished all her noblest features in producing that enchanting scene. The rocky Isle in front, with its neat farm houses at the eastern point, and its high bluff, crowded with the telegraph towards the west;—the middle space, occupied by sheds for the cholera patients and its shores dotted over with motley groups washing their clothes, added not a little to the picturesque effect of the whole land-scene.—Then the river, covered with boats, darting to and fro, and conveying passengers from twenty-five vessels, of various size and tonnage, which rode at anchor, with their flags flying, gave an air of life and interest to the whole.

Turning to the south side of the river, we were not less struck with its low, fertile shores, white houses, and neat churches, whose lofty spires and tin roofs glittered like silver, as they caught the first rays of the sun. As far as the eye could reach, this line of buildings extended along the shore, its back-ground formed by the dense purple hue of the interminable forest. It was a scene unlike any we had ever beheld; and to which Britain contains no parallel; and this recalls to my memory a remark made by an old Scotch dragoon, who was one of our passengers, when he rose in the morning and saw the Parish of St. Thomas for the first time: 'Weil, it beats a'. It looks jist for a' the warld like claes hung out to drie. Can they white clouts be a' houses?'

There really was some truth in this strange simile; and for many minutes I could scarcely convince myself of the fact that the white patches, scattered so thickly over the opposite bank, were the dwellings of a busy, lively population.

'What sublime views of the north side of the river those inhabitants of St. Thomas must enjoy,' thought I; 'but perhaps familiarity with the scene has made them indifferent to its beauty.'

Eastward, the view down the St. Lawrence towards the Gulf, is the finest of all; perhaps unsurpassed by any in the world. Your eye follows the long range of mountains until their blue summits are blended and lost in the blue of the sky. Some of these, partially cleared, are sprinkled with neat cottages, and the green slopes which spread around them are covered with flocks and herds. The surface of the splendid river is diversified with islands of every size and shape; some in wood, others partially cleared, and adorned with orchards and white farm houses. As the morning sun streamed upon the most prominent of these, leaving the others in deep shadow, the effect was wonderfully grand and imposing. In more remote regions, where the forest has never yet echoed to the woodman's axe, or received the impress of civilization, the first approach to the shores inspires a solemn awe, which almost becomes painful in its intensity.

> Land of vast hills and mighty streams,
> The lofty sun that o'er thee beams
> On fairer clime sheds not his ray,
> When basking in the noon of day
> Thy waters dance in silver light,
> And o'er them, frowning dark as night,
> Thy shadowy forests, soaring high,
> Stretch far beyond the aching eye,
> And blend in distance with the sky.

And silence, awful silence, broods
Profoundly o'er these solitudes;
Naught but the lapsing of the floods
Awakes the stillness of the woods—
A sense of desolation reigns
O'er those unpeopled forest plains,
Where sounds of life ne'er wake a tone
Of cheerful praise round nature's throne—
Man finds himself with God—alone.

From such meditations we were aroused by the return of the boat, and the Captain, who brought a note for M——, from the Captain who commanded the station, inviting us to spend the afternoon in his tent, and proposing to show us all that was worthy of notice on the Island. 'This is very kind,' said M——; 'Captain —— claims a former acquaintance with me; but to tell you the truth, S——, I have not the least recollection of him.—Do you wish to go?'

'Oh by all means,' cried I joyfully,—'whosoever he may be I shall owe him a debt of gratitude, for giving me an opportunity of seeing this lovely Island. It looks a perfect Paradise.'

The Captain smiled to himself, as he assisted in placing the baby and me in the boat. 'Don't be too sanguine, Mrs. M——.' But the very idea of going on shore—of putting my foot upon the New World for the first time, after nine weeks of sea and rough weather, had transported me into the seventh heaven. I was in no humor to have listened to reason, had an angel delivered the lecture.

It was four o'clock when we landed on the rocks, and the heat of an intensely warm day had rendered them so hot that I could scarcely stand upon them. How the people without shoes bore it, I cannot imagine. Never shall I forget the extraordinary spectacle that met our view the moment we passed the low range of bushes which formed a screen in front of this strange scene.

A crowd of some four thousand Irish emigrants had been landed during the present and former day; and all, men, women and children, who were not confined by sickness to the sheds, (which greatly resembled penns for cattle,) were busily employed in washing clothes;—the men and boys in the water, and the women trampling their bedding in tubs, or in holes of the rocks, which the retiring tide had left half full of water. Those who had not the good luck to possess either tubs or iron pots, or even a good hole in the rocks, were running impatiently to and fro—swearing at, and scolding, in no measured terms, the poor soldiers, who stood by to keep them in order; wondering no doubt at their want of success, and the wilful and perverse nature of the women critters.

'For God's sake! woman, let me go!' cried the sergeant—a tall, handsome young fellow—vainly endeavoring to extricate his coat tails from the grasp of a hard-featured, sun-burnt, middle-aged harpy, who clung to him with the most provoking pertinacity.

'Give me a kettle—I can't wash without a kettle!'

'My good woman, I don't keep a hardware store—I have no kettles to lend or sell.'

'A wash-tub, then—do you hear? A wash-tub—I must and will ha' a tub!'

'Wash in the holes of the rocks, like the rest;' cried the soldier, losing all patience, and hurling her off. 'Confound the hag! she has torn the facings from my coat.'

The savage shook them in his face with a grin, and I thought him very lucky to escape with so little damage from her grasp; for I shrunk from the red-fisted virago with a feeling almost approaching to fear, as she pushed past me in the crowd.

I had heard and read much of savages; and have since seen somewhat of un-civilized life among the Indians, whilst dwelling in the bush; but the Indian is one of Nature's gentlemen; he never does nor says a rude or vulgar thing;—but the vicious, uneducated barbarians, who form the surplus of over-populated Christian countries, are far behind them in delicacy of feeling and natural cour-tesy. The people who covered the island appeared perfectly destitute of shame, or a sense of common decency. We turned from the revolting scene in disgust, but were unable to leave the spot until the captain had satisfied a noisy group of his own people, who were demanding from him a supply of stores. Fortunately, M—— discovered a woodland path that led to the back of the is-land, where, sheltered by some hazel bushes from the intense heat of the sun, we sat down, by the cool, gushing river, out of sight, but not out of hearing, of the noisy, riotous crowd which we had left. Could we have shut out the profane sounds which came to us on every breeze, how deeply should we have en-joyed the tranquil beauty of that retired and lovely spot. The rocky banks of the island were adorned with beautiful ever-greens, which sprang up sponta-neously from every crevice. I remarked many of our most highly esteemed or-namental shrubs among these wildings of nature. The filagree, with its dark, glossy narrow leaves; the privet, with its modest white blossoms and purple berries; the Lignum Vitæ, with its strong resinous odor; the Burnet Rose, and a great variety of elegant unknowns. Here, the indenturation of the shores of the island and main land, receding from each other, formed a small cove, over-hung with lofty trees; and the dense shadows cast upon the waters by the mountains, which towered to the height of some thousand feet above us, gave them an ebon hue. The sunbeams, dancing through the thick quivering foliage, fell in stars of gold, or long lines of dazzling brightness upon the deep, still, black waters, producing the most novel, and at the same time, the most beau-tiful effect in the world. It was a scene over which the spirit of peace might brood in silent adoration; and how was it marred by the discordant yells of the filthy beings who were performing their necessary but unpoetical ablu-tions on that enchanting spot, sullying the purity of the air and waters by their contaminating influence.

We were now joined by the sergeant, who very kindly brought us his cap full of ripe plums and hazel nuts, the natural growth of the Island, and a note from his superior, who found he had made a mistake in his supposed knowledge of M——, and politely apologising for not being allowed by the health offi-cers, to receive any emigrant beyond the bounds appointed for the performance of Quarantine.

'I don't envy you the task of keeping these wild savages in order,' said M——.

'You may well say that, Sir. But our night scenes far exceed any thing which could strike you during the day. Why, lord, sir, you would think they were incarnate devils;—singing, drinking, dancing, shouting, and cutting antics which would surprise the leader of a circus. And then, sir, they are such thieves that they rob one another of the little which they possess. The healthy actually run the risk of taking the cholera, by robbing the sick. If you have not hired one or two stout honest fellows among your passengers to guard your clothes while they are drying, you will never see half of them again. They are a sad set. We could perhaps manage the men; but the women— the women, sir, are the devil!'

We could not help laughing heartily at this graphic description, though we both felt a little disappointed in not getting a sight of the uninfected and cultivated portions of the island, which, viewed at a distance, appeared beautiful. There was, however, no help for it, and we were obliged to remain until sundown in our retired nook. We were hungry and tired, with our long fast;—the musquitos swarmed in myriads round us, tormenting the poor baby, who, not at all pleased with her first visit to the new world, filled the air with her cries.

The captain at last came to tell us that the boat was ready. Oh welcome sound—and forcing our way once more through the squabbling crowd, we gained the landing place. Here we met a boat just landing a fresh cargo of these lively savages. One fellow, of gigantic proportions, whose long great coat reaching below the calves of his bare red legs, partly concealed the want of other garments, leaped upon the rocks, flourishing aloft a shillelah, and bounding and capering about, like one of the wild goats from his native mountains—'Whurrah! my boys!' he cried, 'we are now in 'Meriky, the land o' liberty! Shure we'll all be jintilmin here!'

'What a set of wild devils!' said the captain. 'He belongs to the light pocket and cool breeches set; I could almost envy the fellow his devil-may-care spirits. Well, Mrs. ——, I hope you have had enough of Grosse Isle. But could you have witnessed the scenes which I did this morning—'

Here he was interrupted by a stout Scotch woman, the wife of the old dragoon, suddenly grasping his arm as he stepped into the boat, and looking up into his face in what she meant to be a very fascinating manner—'Captain, dinna forget.'

'Forget what?' Here she whispered something in his ear. 'Oh, the bottle of brandy!' he responded, aloud. 'I should have thought, Mrs. M'Kenzie, you had had enough of that same on yon island?'

'Aye, sic a place for dasent folk,' returned the drunken body, shaking her head—'One needs a drap o' comfort, captain, to keep up one's heart, at a'.'

The captain set up one of his boisterous laughs as he pushed the boat from the shore. 'Hollo! there, Sam Frazer! steer in—we've forgotten the stores.'

'I hope not, captain,' said I—'I am starving since day-break!'

'Bless my soul! I forgot you. Well, well, I've made a good catholic of you, at any rate!'

'The bread, the butter, the onions, and the beef,' said Sam, particularizing each article, 'are here, sir.'

'Pull away, then—all right. Mrs. ——, we'll have a glorious supper; and mind you don't dream of Grosse Isle!'

Honoré Beaugrand
(1848–1906)

BORN IN LANORAIE, QUEBEC, Honoré Beaugrand attended the Montreal Military School, and at the age of 17 fought for the Emperor Maximilian in the Mexican War (1865–67). After two years in France, he moved to the U.S.A. and followed a newspaper career in Massachusetts, Missouri, then came back to Canada. In 1879 he founded *La Patrie,* a reform paper in Montreal. He became mayor of Montreal in 1885, and shortly afterwards he left to travel abroad, and write. He wrote a number of travel essays, and one novel—a pro-American political work called *Jeanne-la-Fileuse* (1878)—and by the 1890s he was deeply involved in retelling and commenting on French-Canadian folklore. His *La chasse-galerie: légendes canadiennes* was published in both English and French in 1900. The title tale was first published in *La Patrie* in French; in English it appeared in 1892, in *Century Magazine* in New York. Repeatedly, the folk versions of "La chasse-galerie" on which this story is based are told as though they were reports of true-life experience. "Often" (reports say) the voyageurs and the workers in the lumber camps accepted Beelzebub's help so that they might fly to visit their sweethearts.

In his preface to the English version (which was strikingly illustrated by Henri Julien), Beaugrand wrote: "It is hardly necessary to apologize for having used in the narrative expressions typical of the ruder life and character whose language and superstitions it is the intention of the writer to portray."

For Further Reading

RICHARD M. DORSON, "Canadiens" in *Bloodstoppers and Bearwalkers* (Cambridge: Harvard UP, 1959) 69–102.

EDITH FOWKE, *Folktales of French Canada* (Toronto: NC Press, 1981).

LUC LACOURCIERE, *Oral Tradition: New England and French Canada* (Québec: Laval, 1972).

FRANÇOIS RICARD, "Préface" to Honoré Beaugrand, *La chasse-galerie: légendes canadiennes* (Montréal: Fides, 1973) 7–16.

La Chasse-Galerie

I

"Well, then, since you seem to desire it so very much, I will tell you a roarin' story that ought to be a lesson to all of you. If there is among the crowd any renegade who intends to run *la chasse-galerie* or the *loup-garou*, he had better skip and go outside to see whether the owls are screeching in the storm, in converse with Old Nick himself, because I intend to begin my story by making a big sign of the cross. That will be a regular set-back to *le diable*, who always tries, at this time, to snatch a poor shantyman's soul by promising him all kinds of nonsense. I have had enough of that in my young days to understand his tricks."

Not a man moved. On the contrary, all gathered closer round the fireplace, where the cook had dragged the provision-chest, and upon which he had taken his seat on a camp-stool, preparatory to relating his experience under the wiles of the *mauvais esprit*.

It was on New Year's eve of the year 1858, in the depth of the forest, in the Ross timber camp, at the head of the Gatineau River. The winter had fairly set in, and the snow outside had already piled up to the roof of the shanty. The boss, according to custom, had ordered the distribution of the contents of a small barrel of Jamaica rum among the men, and the cook had terminated early his preparations of a succulent *ragoût* of pig's feet and of a large tin full of *glissantes* for the New Year's dinner. A big kettle, half full of molasses, was already simmering on the fire, as there was to be a candy-pull to finish the evening's entertainment.

Every man had filled his pipe with good strong Canadian tobacco, and a thick cloud of smoke darkened the interior of the shanty. A few pine-branches thrown at intervals on the fire produced a reddish glare that illuminated the rude faces of the men with curious effects of *clair-obscur*.

Joe, the cook, was a homely little man who laughed at his own physical defects, and who did not take offense when his comrades chaffed him on the subject, and called him *le bossu*, the hunchback. He had worked in the shanties for the last forty years and his experience was only equaled by the facility with which he could relate his adventures when he had taken a glass of *bonne vieille Jamaique*.

"I was telling you," said Joe, "that I was a *pendard* in my youth, but it is long since I mended my ways, and now I never joke about religious matters. I go to confession regularly every year, and what I am about to relate took place years and years ago, when I feared *ni Dieu, ni diable*. It was on a night like this, a New Year's eve, thirty-four or thirty-five years ago. Gathered round the fireplace with all the *camarades*, we made merry; and if it is true, as we say in French, that

From *La chasse-galerie: légendes canadiennes* (Montréal: Pelletier, 1900).

'small rivulets make large rivers,' it is just as true that small drinks empty large barrels. And in those days, people drank more than today, and evenings of this kind generally ended in a boxing-match, outside, in the snow. The *rhum* was no better than it is tonight, but it was *bougrement bon*, I can assure you. I will be frank with you and tell you that about eleven o'clock my head began to feel dizzy, and I lay down on my buffalo-robe to take a nap, while waiting for the midnight jump that we always take over the head of a pork-barrel, from the old year into the new one. We will repeat the same thing tonight before we go to visit the neighboring camps to wish them the compliments of the season.

II

"I had slept for quite a while, when I was rudely awakened by a second boss, Baptiste Durand, who said to me: Joe, it is past midnight, and you are late for the barrel-jump. The *camarades* have gone to the other camps, and I am going to Lavaltrie to see my sweetheart. Will you come with me?"

"'To Lavaltrie,' said I, 'are you crazy? We are three hundred miles away from there, and you could not travel the distance in two months, through the forest, when there are no roads beaten in the snow. And what about our work the day after tomorrow?'

"'*Imbicile!* don't you understand me? We will travel in our bark canoe, and tomorrow morning at six o'clock we will be back here for breakfast.'

"I understood. Baptiste Durand proposed that I should join him and run *la chasse-galerie;* risk the salvation of my soul for the fun of going to give a New Year's kiss to my *blonde* at Lavaltrie. That was a little too much for me. It was true that I was a *mauvais sujet,* that I did not practise *la religion,* and that I took a drink too much now and then; but between that and the fact of selling my soul to *le diable* there was a big difference, and I said: 'No, siree! *Pas un tonnerre!*'

"'Oh, you are a regular old woman,' answered Baptiste tauntingly. 'There is no danger whatever. We can go to Lavaltrie and back in six hours. Don't you know that with *la chasse-galerie* we can travel 150 miles an hour, when one can handle the paddles as well as we all do. All there is to it is that we must not pronounce *le nom du bon Dieu* during the voyage, and that we must be careful not to touch the crosses on the steeples when we travel. That's easy enough, and, to be all right, all a man has to do is to look where he goes, think about what he says, and not touch a drop of liquor on the way. I have made the trip five times, and *le diable* has not got me yet. Come, *mon vieux,* stiffen up your courage, and in two hours we will be at Lavaltrie. Think of Liza Guimbette, and the pleasure you will have in kissing her "a happy New Year." There are already seven of us to make the trip, but we must be two, four, six, or eight, to make up the crew of the canoe.'

"'Yes, that's all right, but you must make an engagement with *le diable,* and he is not the kind of a *bourgeois* that I want to make any bargain with.'

"A simple formality if we are careful where we go and not to drink. A man is not a child, *pardieu!* Come on! The *camarades* are waiting outside, and the canoe is already in the clearing. Come, come!'

"And I was led outside of the shanty, where I saw the six men who were awaiting us, paddle in hand. The large canoe was lying on a snowbank, and before I had time to think twice about it, I was seated in the bow, awaiting the signal to go. I must say that my mind was somewhat confused, but Baptiste Durand, who was a hard customer,—for, it was said, he had not been to confession for seven years,—gave me no time for reflection. He was standing in the stern, and exclaimed in a ringing voice:

"'Are you ready?'

"'Ready.'

"'Repeat after me.'

"'And we repeated together:

"'*Satan!* king of the infernal regions, we promise to sell you our souls, if within the following six hours we pronounce *le nom du bon Dieu,* your master and ours, or if we touch a cross on the voyage. On that condition you will transport us through the air, wherever we may want to go, and bring us back sound and safe to the shanty. *Acabris, Acabras, Acabram! Fais-nous voyager par-dessus les montagnes!'*

III

"The last words were hardly pronounced, when we felt the canoe rising in the air to a height of five or six hundred feet. I felt as light as a feather, and at Baptiste's command, we commenced paddling like sorcerers that we were. At the first stroke of the paddle, the canoe shot out like an arrow, and off we went under the protecting wing of *le diable* himself. It fairly took my breath away, and I could hear the bow of the canoe whizzing through the crisp air of the night.

"We went faster than the wind, and during the first fifteen minutes we sailed over the forest, without perceiving anything else than the dark heads of the great pines. It was a beautiful night, and a full moon lighted up the sky like the midday sun. It was terribly cold though, and our mustaches were fairly frozen, while our bodies were all in a perspiration. We were paddling like demons at work in the lower regions. We soon perceived a bright, glistening belt of clear ice, that shone like a mirror. That was the Gatineau River; and then the lights in the farm-houses, which were mostly lit up on New Year's eve. We began passing the tin-covered steeples as quickly as telegraph-poles fly past in a railway-train, and the spires shone in the air like the bayonets of the soldiers drilling on the Champ de Mars, in Montreal. On we went like *tous les diables,* passing over forests, rivers, towns, villages, and leaving behind us a trail of sparks. It was Baptiste Durand, the *possédé,* who steered the canoe because he knew the route, and we soon came to the Ottawa River, which we followed down to the *Lac des Deux Montagnes!*

"'Look out there!' said Baptiste; 'we will just skim over Montreal and frighten some of the fellows who may be out at this hour of the night. Joe, clear your whistle and get ready to sing your best canoe-song, "*Canot d'écorce,*" my boy.'

"The excitement of the trip had braced me up, and I was ready for anything. Already we could see the lights of the great city, and with an adroit stroke of his paddle, Baptiste brought us down on a level with the summit of the towers of Notre-Dame. I cleared my throat and sang '*Canot d'écorce,*' while my *camarades* joined heartily in the chorus.

"'Mon père n'avait fille que moi,
Canot d'écorce qui va voler,
Et dessus la mer il m'envoie:
Canot d'écorce qui vole, qui vole,
Canot d'écorce qui va voler!'

Et dessus la mer il m'envoie,
Canot d'écorce qui va voler,
Le marinier qui me menait:
Canot d'écorce qui vole, qui vole,
Canot d'écorce qui va voler!

Le marinier qui me menait,
Canot d'écorce qui va voler,
Me dit ma belle embrassez-moi:
Canot d'écorce qui vole, qui vole,
Canot d'écorce qui va voler!

Me dit ma belle embrassez-moi,
Canot d'écorce qui va voler,
Non, non, monsieur, je ne saurais:
Canot d'écorce qui vole, qui vole,
Canot d'écorce qui va voler!

Non, non, monsieur, je ne saurais,
Canot d'écorce qui va voler,
Car si mon papa le savait:
Canot d'écorce qui vole, qui vole,
Canot d'écorce qui va voler!

Car si mon papa le savait,
Canot d'écorce qui va voler,
Ah! c'est bien sur qu'il me battrait:
Canot d'écorce qui vole, qui vole,
Canot d'écorce qui va voler!

IV

"Although it was well on toward two o'clock in the morning, we saw some groups of men who stopped in the middle of the street to watch us go by, but we went so fast that in a twinkle we had passed Montreal and its suburbs. We were nearing the end of our voyage, and we commenced counting the steeples, Longue-Pointe, Pointe-aux-Trembles, Repentigny, St. Sulpice, and at last we saw the two shining spires of Lavaltrie that gleamed among the dark-green pines of the domain.

"'Look out over there' shouted Baptiste. 'We will land on the edge of the wood, in the field of my godfather, Jean-Jean-Gabriel. From there we will proceed on foot to go and surprise our acquaintances in some *fricot* or dance in the neighborhood.'

"We did as directed, and five minutes later our canoe lay in a snowbank, at the edge of the wood of Jean-Jean-Gabriel. We started in Indian file to go to the village. It was no small job, because the snow reached to our waists and there was no trace of any kind of a road. Baptiste, who was the most daring of the crowd, went and knocked at the door of his godfather's house, where we could see a light, but there was no one there except a servant, who told us that the old folks had gone to a *snaque* at old man Robillard's place, and that the young people of the village—boys and girls—were across the St. Lawrence at Batissette Augé's, at the *Petite Misère*, below Contrecoeur, where there was a New Year's hop.

"'Let us go to the dance at Batissette Augé's,' said Baptiste; 'we are sure to find our sweethearts over there.'

"'Let us go to Batissette Augé's!'

"'And we returned to our canoe, while cautioning one another against the great danger that there was in pronouncing certain words, in touching anything in the shape of a cross, and especially in drinking liquor of any kind. We had only four hours before us, and we must return to the shanty before six o'clock in the morning, if we wanted to escape from the clutches of Old Nick, with whom we had made such a desperate bargain. And we all knew that he was not the kind of a customer to let us off, in the event of any delay on our part.

"'Acabris, Acabras, Acabram! Fais-nous voyager par-dessus les montagnes!' shouted Baptiste once more.

"And off we went again, paddling through the air, like renegades that we were, every one of us. We crossed the river in less time than it requires to tell it, and we descended in a snowbank close to Batissette Augé's house, where we could hear the laughter of the dancers, and see their shadows through the bright windows.

"We dragged our canoe on the riverside, to hide it among the hummocks produced by the ice-shove.

"'Now,' said Baptiste, in a last warning, 'no nonsense! Do you hear? Dance as much as you can, but not a single glass of rum or whisky. And at the first sign, follow me out without attracting attention. We can't be too careful!'

"And we went and knocked at the door.

V

"Old Batissette came and opened the door himself, and we were received with opened arms by the guests, who knew us all.

"'Where do you come from?'

"'I thought you were in the *chantiers*, up the Gatineau?'

"'What makes you come so late?'

"'Come and take a smile.'

"Baptiste came to the rescue by saying: 'First and foremost, let us take our coats off, and give us a chance to dance. That's what we came here for, and if you still feel curious in the morning, I will answer all your questions.'

"For my part, I had already spied Liza Guimbette, who was chatting away with little Boisjoli, of Lanoraie. I made my *reverence* in due style, and at once asked for the favor of the next dance, which was a four-handed reel. She accepted with a smile that made me forget that I had risked the salvation of my soul to have the pleasure of pressing her soft white hand in mine and of cutting pigeonwings as her partner. During two hours the dancing went on without stopping, and, if I do say so myself, we shanty fellows cut a shine in the dance that made the hayseeds tired before morning. I was so busy with my partner that at first I did not notice that Baptiste was visiting the *buffet* rather often with some of the other boys, and once I caught him lifting his elbow in rather a suspicious manner. But I had no idea that the fellow would get tipsy, after all the lecturing he had given us on the road. When four o'clock struck, all the members of our crew began to edge out of the house without attracting attention, but I had to drag Baptiste before he would consent to go. At last we were all out, with just two hours before us to reach the camp, and three hundred miles to ride in our canoe, under the protection of Beelzebub. We had left the dance like wild Indians without saying good-bye to anybody, not even to Liza Guimbette, whom I had invited for the next *cotillon*. I always thought that she bore me a grudge for that, because when I reached home the next summer she was Madame Boisjoli.

"We found our canoe all right in the hummocks, but I need hardly tell you that we were all put out when we found that Baptiste Durand had been drinking. He was to steer the boat, and we had no time to lose in humoring the fancies of a drunken man. The moon was not quite so bright as when we started from the camp, and it was not without misgivings that I took my place in the bow of the canoe, well decided to keep a sharp lookout ahead for accidents. Before starting I said to Baptiste:

"'Look out, Baptiste, old fellow! Steer straight for the mountain of Montreal, as soon as you can get a glimpse of it.'

"'I know my business,' answered Baptiste sharply, 'and you had better mind yours.'

"What could I do? And before I had time for further reflections:

"'*Acabris, Acabras, Acabram! Fais-nous voyager par-dessus les montagnes!*'

VI

"And up we went again like lightning, steering southwest, if the wild way in which Baptiste managed our boat could be called steering. We passed over the steeple of the church of Contrecoeur, coming pretty close to it, but instead of going west Baptiste made us take a sheer toward the Richelieu River. A few minutes later we were skimming over Beloeil Mountain, and we came within ten feet of striking the big cross that the bishop of Quebec planted there, during a temperance picnic held a few years before by the clergy of his diocese.

"'To the right, Baptiste! steer to the right, or else you will send us all to *le diable* if you keep on going that way.'

"And Baptiste did instinctively turn to the right, and we steered straight for the mountain of Montreal, which we could perceive in the distance by the dim lights of the city. I must say that I was becoming frightened, because if Baptiste kept on steering as he had done, we would never reach the Gatineau alive, and *le diable* was probably smacking his lips, as I supposed, at the bare idea of making a New Year's mess of us. And I can tell you that the disaster was not long in coming. While we were passing over the city, Baptiste Durand uttered a yell, and, flourishing his paddle over his head, gave it a twist that sent us plunging into a snowdrift, in a clearing on the mountain-side. Luckily the snow was soft, and none of us were hurt, nor was the canoe injured in anyway. But Baptiste got out and declared most emphatically that he was going down-town to have *un verre*. We tried to reason with him, but our efforts proved useless, as is generally the case with *les ivrognes*. He would go down if *le diable* himself were to catch hold of him on the way. I held a moment's consultation with *mes camarades*, and before Baptiste knew what we were about, we had him down in the snow, where we bound him hand and foot so as to render him incapable of interfering with our movements. We placed him in the bottom of the canoe, and gagged him so as to prevent him from speaking any words that might give us up to perdition.

"And *'Acabris! Acabras! Acabram!'* up we went again, this time steering straight for the Gatineau. I had taken Baptiste's place in the stern. We had only a little over an hour to reach camp, and we all paddled away for dear life and eternal salvation. We followed the Ottawa River as far as the Pointe-Gatineau, and then steered due north by the polar star for our shanty. We were fairly flying in the air, and everything was going well when that rascal of a Baptiste managed to slip the ropes we had bound him with and to pull off his gag. We had been so busy paddling that, the first thing we knew, he was standing in the canoe, paddle in hand, and was swearing like a pagan. I felt that our end had come if he pronounced a certain sacred word, and it was out of the question to appease him in his frenzy. We had only a few miles to go to reach camp, and we were floating over the pine forest. The position was really terrible. Baptiste was using his paddle like a shilalah and making a *moulinet* that threatened every moment to crush in some one's head. I was so excited that by a false movement of my own paddle I let the canoe come down on a level with the pines, and it was upset as it struck the head of a big tree. We all fell out and began dropping down from branch to branch like partridges shot from the tamarack-tops. I don't know how long I was coming down, because I fainted before we reached the snow beneath, but my last recollection was like the dream of a man who feels himself dropping down a well without ever reaching bottom.

VII

"About eight o'clock the next morning, I awoke in my bunk, in the cabin, whither some of our *camarades* had conveyed us after having found us to our necks in a neighboring snow-bank, at the foot of a monster pine-tree. Happily, no one was seriously hurt, although we were all more or less bruised and scratched, some having secured even black eyes in our way down from the tree-top. We were all thankful that nothing worse had befallen us, and when the *camarades* said that they had found us sleeping away in the snow the effects of the previous night's frolic, not one of us had anything to say to the contrary. We all felt satisfied that our *escapade* with Old Nick remained unknown in the camp, and we preferred leaving our chums under the impression that we had taken *un verre* too many, to telling them of the bargain we had made to satisfy a passing fancy. So far as Baptiste Durand was concerned, there is no doubt that he had forgotten the latter part of his voyage, but he never alluded to the fact, and we followed his example. It was not till many years afterward that I related the story of our *aventures,* just as they happened on that memorable New Year's eve.

"All I can say, my friends, is that it is not so amusing as some people might
think, to travel in mid-air, in the dead of winter, under the guidance of
Beelzebub, running *la chasse-galerie,* and especially if you have *un
ivrogne* to steer your bark canoe. Take my advice, and don't listen
to any one who would try to rope you in for such a trip. Wait
until summer before you go to see your sweethearts, for
it is better to run all the rapids of the Ottawa and the
St. Lawrence on a raft, than to travel in partner-
ship with *le diable* himself." And Joe, the
cook, dipped a ladleful of boiling molasses from the big kettle on the fire,
and declared that everything
was now ready for the
candy-
pull.

Edward William Thomson

(1849–1924)

E.W. THOMSON GREW UP ON THE FAMILY FARM IN YORK TOWNSHIP (now part of Toronto) before embarking on his itinerant career. He fought briefly with the Union forces in the American Civil War in 1864, and in 1866 against the Fenians. He studied civil engineering and became a surveyor, then a political journalist for the Toronto *Globe* between 1878 and 1891. Subsequently he took on the position of Revising Editor for the Boston weekly *Youth's Companion* (an experience he drew on for the writing of "Miss Minnely's Management"), and later still he returned to the Canadian paper.

He contributed stories to a number of journals. One of his most famous narratives—"The Privilege of the Limits"—appeared in *Harper's Weekly* in 1891, and "Miss Minnely's Management" was run in Sir Andrew Macphail's Montreal quarterly *The University Magazine* in 1910. The author of some poetry and several juveniles, Thomson was most famous in his day for the bucolic dialect wisdom of his title character in *Old Man Savarin and Other Stories* (1895), a work he revised in 1917 (removing two stories and adding three more recent ones, including "Miss Minnely's Management") as *Old Man Savarin Stories: Tales of Canada and Canadians*. The effect of the revision was to shift something of the book's emphasis: away from portraits of a world of rural canniness to a general picture of a world slightly jaundiced by its awareness of social manipulations. The irony of "Miss Minnely's Management" is part of this general tendency. It's a story about survival in many ways; it's also a story that focusses on language—on the way language changes and is changed, on the way it is manipulated to sell art and morality, and on the power it yet possesses to resist containment.

For Further Reading

LORRAINE MCMULLEN, "Tales of Canada and Canadians," *Journal of Canadian Fiction* 11 (Summer 1973): 191–94.

LINDA SHESHKO, "Introduction" to E.W. Thomson, *Old Man Savarin Stories* (Toronto: U Toronto P, 1974) vii-xxxvi.

Miss Minnely's Management

I

George Renwick substituted "limb" for "leg," "intoxicated" for "drunk," and "undergarment" for "shirt," in "The Converted Ringmaster," a short-story-of-commerce, which he was editing for "The Family Blessing." When he should have eliminated all indecorum it would go to Miss Minnely, who would "elevate the emotional interest." She was sole owner of "The Blessing," active director of each of its multifarious departments. Few starry names rivalled hers in the galaxy of American character-builders.

Unaware of limitations to her versatility, Miss Minnely might have dictated all the literary contents of the magazine, but for her acute perception that other gifted pens should be enlisted. Hence many minor celebrities worshipped her liberal cheques, whilst her more extravagant ones induced British titled personages to assuage the yearning of the American Plain People for some contact with rank.

Renwick wrought his changes sardonically, applying to each line a set of touchstones—"Will it please Mothers?" "Lady schoolteachers?" "Ministers of the Gospel?" "Miss Minnely's Taste?" He had not entirely converted The Ringmaster when his door was gently opened by the Chief Guide to the Family Blessing Building.

Mr. Durley had grown grey under solemn sense of responsibility for impressions which visitors might receive. With him now appeared an unusually numerous party of the usual mothers, spinsters, aged good men, and anxious children who keep watch and ward over "The Blessing's" pages, in devotion to Miss Minnely's standing editorial request that "subscribers will faithfully assist the Editors with advice, encouragement, or reproof." The Mature, with true American gentleness, let the Young assemble nearest the open door. All necks craned toward Renwick. Because Mr. Durley's discourse to so extensive a party was unusually loud. Renwick heard, for the first time, what the Chief Guide was accustomed to murmur at his threshold: "De-ar friends, the gentleman we now have the satisfaction of beholding engaged in a sitting posture at his editorial duties is Mr. George Hamilton Renwick, an American in every—."

"He *looks* like he might be English," observed a matron.

Mr. Durley took a steady look at Renwick: "He *is* some red complected, Lady, but I guess it's only he is used to out of doors." He resumed his customary drone:—"Mr. Renwick, besides he is American in every fibre of his being, is a first rate general purpose editor, and also a noted authority on yachting, boating, canoeing, rowing, swimming, and every kind of water amusements of a kind calculated to build up character in subscribers. Mr. George Hamilton

---

From *Old Man Savarin Stories: Tales of Canada and Canadians* (Toronto: Gundy, 1917).

Renwick's engagement by 'The Family Blessing' exclusively is a recent instance of many evidences that Miss Minnely, the Sole Proprietress, spares no expense in securing talented men of genius who are likewise authorities on every kind of specialty interesting, instructive, and improving to first-class respectable American families. Ladies and gentlemen, and de-ar children, girls, and youths, we will now pass on to Room Number Sixteen, and behold Mr. Caliphas C. Cummins, the celebrated author and authority on Oriental and Scriptural countries. Mr. Cummins is specially noted as the author of 'Bijah's Bicycle in Babylonia,' 'A Girl Genius at Galilee,' and many first-class serials published exclusively in 'The Family Blessing.' He may—"

Mr. Durley softly closed Renwick's door.

The Improving Editor, now secluded, stared wrathfully for some moments. Then he laughed, seized paper, and wrote in capitals:

"When the editor in this compartment is to be exhibited, please notify him by knocking on this door before opening it. He will then rise from his sitting posture, come forward for inspection, and turn slowly round three times, if a mother, a school teacher, or a minister of the Gospel be among the visiting subscribers."

Renwick strode to his door. While pinning the placard on its outside he overheard the concluding remarks of Mr. Durley on Mr. Cummins, whose room was next in the long corridor: "Likewise talented editor of the Etiquette Department and the Puzzle Department. Mr. Cummins, Sir, seven lady teachers from the State of Maine are now honouring us in this party."

Renwick stood charmed to listen. He heard the noted author clack forward to shake hands all round, meantime explaining in thin, high, affable volubility: "My de-ar friends, you have the good fortune to behold me in the very act of composing my new serial of ten Chapters, for 'The Blessing' exclusively, entitled 'Jehu and Jerusha in Jerusalem,' being the experiences of a strenuous New England brother and sister in the Holy Land, where our Lord innogerated the Christian religion, now, sad to say, under Mohammetan subjection. In this tale I am incorporating largely truthful incidents of my own and blessed wife's last visit to the Holy Places where—"

Renwick slammed his door. He flung his pen in a transport of derision. Rebounding from his desk, it flew through an open window, perhaps to fall on some visitor to "The Blessing's" lawn. He hastened to look down. Nobody was on gravel path or bench within possible reach of the missile. Renwick, relieved, mused anew on the singularities of the scene.

The vast "Blessing" Building stands amid a city block devoted largely to shaven turf, flower beds, grassed mounds, and gravel paths. It is approached from the street by a broad walk which bifurcates at thirty yards from the "Richardson" entrance, to surround a turfed truncated cone, from which rises a gigantic, severely draped, female figure. It is that bronze of Beneficence which, in the words of the famous New England sculptress, Miss Angela C. Amory Pue, "closely features Miss Martha Minnely in her grand early womanhood." In the extensive arms of the Beneficence a bronze volume so slants that spectators may read on its back, in gilt letters, "THE FAMILY BLESSING." Prettily pranked out in dwarf marginal plants on the turfy cone these words are pyramided:

"LOVE. HEAVEN. BENEFICENCE. THE LATEST FASHIONS. MY COUNTRY, 'TIS OF THEE."

Not far from the statue slopes a great grassed mound which displays still more conspicuously in "everlastings," "THE FAMILY BLESSING. CIRCULATION 1915, 1,976,709. MONTHLY. COME UNTO ME ALL YE WEARY AND HEAVILY LADEN. TWO DOLLARS A YEAR."

The scheme ever puzzled Renwick. Had some demure humour thus addressed advertisements as if to the eternal stars? Or did they proceed from a pure simplicity of commercial taste? From this perennial problem he was diverted by sharp rapping at his door. Durley again? But the visitor was Mr. Joram B. Buntstir, veteran among the numerous editors of "The Blessing," yet capable of jocularities. He appeared perturbed.

"Renwick, you are rather fresh here, and I feel so friendly to you that I'd hate to see you get into trouble unwarned. Surely you can't wish Miss Minnely to see *that*."

"What? Oh, the placard! That's for Durley. He must stop exhibiting me."

"Mr. Durley won't understand. Anyway, he couldn't stop without instructions from Miss Minnely. He will take the placard to her for orders. You do not wish to hurt Miss Minnely's feelings, I am sure." Mr. Buntstir closed the door behind him.

"Bah—Miss Minnely's feelings can't be so tender as all that!"

"No, eh? Do you know her so thoroughly?"

"I don't know her at all. I've been here three months without once seeing Miss Minnely. Is she real? Half the time I doubt her existence."

"You get instructions from her regularly."

"I get typewritten notes, usually voluminous, signed 'M. Minnely,' twice a week. But the Business Manager, or Miss Heartly, may dictate them, for all I know."

"Pshaw! Miss Minnely presides in seclusion. Her private office has a street entrance. She seldom visits the Departments in office hours. Few of her staff know her by sight. She saves time by avoiding personal interviews. But she keeps posted on everybody's work. I hope you may not have to regret learning how very real Miss Minnely can be. She took me in hand, once, eight years ago. I have been careful to incur no more discipline since—kind as she was. If she sees your placard—"

"Well, what?"

"Well, she can be very impressive. I fear your offer to turn round before visitors may bring you trouble."

"I am looking for trouble. I'm sick and tired of this life of intellectual shame."

"Then quit!" snapped Buntstir, pierced. "Be consistent. Get out. Sell your sneers at a great established publication to some pamphlet periodical started by college boys for the regeneration of Literature. Don't jeer what you live by. That is where intellectual shame should come in."

"You are right. A man should not gibe his job. I must quit. The 'Blessing' is all right for convinced devotees of the mawkish. But if a man thinks sardonically of his daily work, that damns the soul."

"It may be an effect of the soul trying to save itself," said Buntstir, mollified. "Anyway, Renwick, remember your trouble with 'The Reflex.' Avoid the name of a confirmed quitter. Stay here till you can change to your profit. Squealing won't do us any good. A little grain of literary conscience ought not to make you *talk* sour. It's cynical to satirize our bread and butter—imprudent, too."

"That's right. I'll swear off, or clear out. Lord, how I wish I could. My brain must rot if I don't. 'The Blessing's' 'emotional'! Oh, Buntstir, the stream of drivel! And to live by concocting it for trustful subscribers. Talk of the sin of paregoricking babies!"

"Babies take paregoric because they like it. Pshaw, Renwick, you're absurdly sensitive. Writing-men must live, somehow—usually by wishy-washiness. Unpleasant work is the common lot of mankind. Where's *your* title to exemption? Really, you're lucky. Miss Minnely perceives zest in your improvements of copy. She says you are naturally gifted with 'The Blessing's' taste."

"For Heaven's sake, Buntstir!"

"She did—Miss Heartly told me so. And yet—if she sees that placard—no one can ever guess what she may do in discipline. You can't wish to be bounced, dear boy, with your family to provide for. Come, you've blown off steam. Take the placard off your door."

"All right. I will. But Miss Minnely can't bounce me without a year's notice. That's how I engaged."

"A year's notice to quit a life of intellectual shame!"

"Well, it is one thing to jump out of the window, and another to be bounced. I wouldn't stand that."

Buntstir laughed. "I fancy I see you, you sensitive Cuss, holding on, or jumping off or doing anything contra to Miss Minnely's intention." He went to the door. "Hello, where's the placard?" he cried, opening it.

"Gone!" Renwick sprang up.

"Gone, sure. No matter how. It is already in Miss Minnely's hands. Well, I told you to take it down twenty minutes ago."

"Wait, Buntstir. What is best to be done?"

"Hang on for developments—and get to work."

Buntstir vanished as one hastens to avoid infection.

II

Renwick resumed his editing of "The Converted Ringmaster" with resolve to think on nothing else. But, between his eyes and the manuscript, came the woeful aspect of two widows, his mother and his sister, as they had looked six months earlier, when he threw up his political editorship of "The Daily Reflex" in disgust at its General Manager's sudden reversal of policy. His sister's baby toddled into the vision. He had scarcely endured to watch the child's uncertain steps during the weeks while he wondered how to buy its next month's modified milk. To "The Reflex" he could not return, because he had publicly burned his boats, with the desperate valour of virtue conscious that it may weaken if strained by need for family food.

Out of that dangerous hole he had been lifted by the Sole Proprietress of "The Family Blessing." She praised his "public stand for principle" in a note marked "strictly confidential," which tendered him a "position." He had secretly laughed at the cautious, amiable offer, even while her laudation gratified his self-importance. Could work on "The Blessing" seem otherwise than ridiculous for one accustomed to chide presidents, monarchs, bosses, bankers, railway magnates? But it was well paid, and seemed only too easy. The young man did not foresee for himself that benumbing of faculty which ever punishes the writer who sells his facility to tasks below his ambition. At worst "The Blessing" seemed harmless. Nor could his better nature deny a certain esteem to that periodical which affectionate multitudes proclaimed to be justly named.

Renwick, viewing himself once more as a recreant breadwinner, cursed his impetuous humour. But again he took heart from remembrance of his engagement by the year, little suspecting his impotency to hold on where snubs must be the portion of the unwanted. Twelve months to turn round in! But after? What if an editor, already reputed impractical by "The Reflex" party, should be refused employment everywhere, after forsaking "The Blessing" office, in which "positions" were notoriously sought or coveted by hundreds of "literary" aspirants to "soft snaps"? So his veering imagination whirled round that inferno into which wage earners descend after hazarding their livelihood.

From this disquiet he sprang when his door was emphatically knocked. It opened. Mr. Durley reappeared with a throng closely resembling the last, except for one notable wide lady in street costume of Quakerish gray. Her countenance seemed to Renwick vaguely familiar. The fabric and cut of her plain garb betokened nothing of wealth to the masculine eye, but were regarded with a degree of awe by the other ladies present. She appeared utterly American, yet unworldly, in the sense of seeming neither citified, suburbanish, nor rural. The experienced placidity of her countenance reminded Renwick of a familiar composite photograph of many matrons chosen from among "The Blessing's" subscribers.

"Her peculiarity is that of the perfect type," he pondered while listening to Durley's repetition of his previous remarks.

At their close, he briskly said: "Mr. Renwick, Sir, Miss Minnely wishes you to know that your kind offer is approved. We are now favoured with the presence of four mothers, six lady teachers, and a minister of the Gospel."

Renwick flushed. His placard approved! It promised that he would come forward, and turn round thrice for inspection. Durley had received instructions to take him at his word! Suddenly the dilemma touched his facile humour. Explanation before so many was impossible. Gravely he approached the visitors, held out the skirts of his sack coat, turned slowly thrice, and bowed low at the close.

The large lady nodded with some reserve. Other spectators clearly regarded the solemnity as part of "The Blessing's" routine. Mr. Durley resumed his professional drone:—"We will now pass on to Room Number Sixteen, and behold Mr. Caliphas C. Cummins in—" Renwick's door closed.

Then the large lady, ignoring the attractions of Mr. Cummins, went to the waiting elevator, and said "down."

Renwick, again at his desk, tried vainly to remember of what or whom the placid lady had reminded him. A suspicion that she might be Miss Minnely fled before recollection of her street costume. Still—she *might* be. If so—had his solemnly derisive posturing offended her? She had given no sign. How could he explain his placard to her? Could he not truly allege objections to delay of his work by Durley's frequent interruptions? He was whirling with conjecture and indecision when four measured ticks from a lead pencil came on his outer door.

There stood Miss Heartly, Acting Manager of the Paper Patterns Department. Her light blue eyes beamed the confidence of one born trustful, and confirmed in the disposition by thirty-five years of popularity at home, in church, in office. In stiff white collar, lilac tie, trig grey gown, and faint, fading bloom of countenance, she well represented a notable latter day American type, the Priestess of Business, one born and bred as if to endow office existence with some almost domestic touch of Puritan nicety. That no man might sanely hope to disengage Miss Heartly from devotion to "The Family Blessing" was as if revealed by her unswerving directness of gaze in speech.

"I have called, Mr. Renwick, by instruction of the Sole Proprietress. Miss Minnely wishes me, first, to thank you for this."

It was the placard!

Renwick stared, unable to credit the sincerity in her face and tone. She *must* be making game of him while she spoke in measured links, as if conscientiously repeating bits each separately memorized:

"Mr. Renwick—Miss Minnely desires you to know that she has been rarely more gratified—than by this evidence—that your self-identification with 'The Blessing'—is cordial and complete. But—Miss Minnely is inclined to hope—that your thoughtful and kind proposal—of turning round for inspection—may be—modified—or improved. For instance—if you would carefully prepare—of course for revision by her own taste—a short and eloquent welcoming discourse—to visitors—that could be elevated to an attraction—for subscribers—of that she is almost, though not yet quite, fully assured. Miss Minnely presumes, Mr. Renwick, that you have had the pleasure of—hearing Mr. Cummins welcome visitors. Of course, Mr. Renwick, Miss Minnely would not have *asked* you—but—as you have volunteered—in your cordial willingness—*that* affords her an opportunity—for the suggestion. But, Mr. Renwick, if you do not *like* the idea—then Miss Minnely would not wish—to pursue the suggestion further." A child glad to have repeated its lesson correctly could not have looked more ingenuous.

In her fair countenance, open as a daybook, Renwick could detect no guile. Her tone and figure suggested curiously some flatness, as of the Paper Patterns of her Department. But through this mild deputy Miss Minnely must, he conceived, be deriding him. With what subtlety the messenger had been chosen! It seemed at once necessary and impossible to explain his placard to one so guiltless of humour.

"I hoped it might be understood that I did not intend that placard to be taken literally, Miss Heartly."

"Not literally!" she seemed bewildered.

"To be pointed at as 'a first class general purpose editor' is rather too much, don't you think?"

"I know, Mr. Renwick," she spoke sympathetically. "It sort of got onto your humility, I presume. But Miss Minnely thinks you *are* first class, or she would never have instructed Mr. Durley to *say* first class. That is cordial to you, and good business—to impress the visitors, I mean."

"Miss Minnely is very appreciative and kind. But the point is that I did not engage to be exhibited to flocks of gobemouches."

Miss Heartly pondered the term. "Please, Mr. Renwick, what are gobemouches?"

"I should have said The Plain People."

"Perhaps there have been rude ones—not subscribers," she said anxiously.

"No, all have acted as if reared on 'The Blessing.' "

She sighed in relief—then exclaimed in consternation:—"Can Mr. Durley have been—*rude?*" She hesitated to pronounce the dire word.

"Not at all, Miss Heartly. I do not blame Mr. Durley for exhibiting us as gorillas."

"But how *wrong.*" There was dismay in her tone. "Miss Minnely has warned him against the least bit of deception."

"Oh, please, Miss Heartly—I was speaking figuratively."

Her fair brow slightly wrinkled, her fingers went nervously to her anxious lips, she looked perplexed;—"Figuratively! If you would kindly explain, Mr. Renwick. I am not very literary."

"Do the ladies of the Paper Patterns Department *like* to be exhibited?" he ventured.

"Well, I could not exactly be warranted to say 'like'—Scripture has such warnings against the sinfulness of vanity. But we are, of course, cordially pleased to see visitors—it is so good for the Subscription Department."

"I see. And it is not hard on you individually. There you are, a great roomful of beautiful, dutiful, cordial young ladies. You keep one another in countenance. But what if you were shown each in a separate cage?"

Her face brightened. "Oh, now I understand, Mr. Renwick! You mean it would be nicer for the Editors, too, to be seen all together."

Renwick sighed hopelessly. She spoke on decisively: "That may be a valuable suggestion, Mr. Renwick." On her pad she began pencilling shorthand. "Of course I will credit you with it. Perhaps you do not know that Miss Minnely always pays well for valuable suggestions." She wrote intently, murmuring: "But is it practicable? Let me think. Why, surely practicable! But Miss Minnely will decide. All partitions on the Editorial Flat could be removed! Make it cool as Prize Package or Financial Department!" She looked up from her paper, glowing with enterprise, and pointed her pencil straight at Renwick. "And so impressive!" She swept the pencil in a broad half circle, seeing her picture. "Thirty Editors visible at one comprehensive glance! All so literary, and busy, and intelligent, and cordial! Fine! I take the liberty, temporarily, of calling that a first-class suggestion, Mr. Renwick. It may be worth hundreds to you, if Miss Minnely values it. It may be forcibly felt in the Subscription List—if Miss Minnely approves. It may help to hold many subscribers who try to get away after the first year. I feel almost sure Miss Minnely *will* approve. I am so glad. I thought something important was going to come when Miss Minnely considered your placard so carefully."

"But some of the other Editors may not wish to be exhibited with the whole collection," said Renwick gravely. "For instance, consider Mr. Cummins' literary rank. Would it gratify him to be shown as a mere unit among Editors of lesser distinction?"

"You are most fore-thoughtful on every point, Mr. Renwick. That is so *fine*. But Mr. Cummins is also most devoted. I feel sure he would cordially yield, if Miss Minnely approved. I presume you will wish me to tell her that you are grateful for her kind message?"

"Cordially grateful seems more fitting, Miss Heartly—and I am—especially for her choice of a deputy."

"Thank you, Mr. Renwick. I will tell her that, too. And may I say that you will be pleased to adopt her suggestion that you discourse a little to visitors, pending possible changes in this Flat, instead of just coming forward and turning around. Literary men are so clever—and—ready." He fleetingly suspected her of derision.

"Please say that I will reflect on Miss Minnely's suggestion with an anxious wish to emulate, so far as my fallen nature will permit, Miss Heartly's beautiful devotion to 'The Blessing's' interests."

"Oh, thank you again, so much, Mr. Renwick." And the fair Priestess of Business bowed graciously in goodbye.

III

Renwick sat dazed. From his earliest acquaintance with "The Family Blessing" he had thought of its famous Editress and Sole Proprietress as one "working a graft" on the Plain People by consummate sense of the commercial value of cordial cant. Now he had to conceive of her as perfectly ingenuous. Had she really taken his placard as one written in good faith? He remembered its sentences clearly:

"When the editor in this compartment is to be exhibited, please notify him by knocking on this door before opening it. He will then rise from his sitting posture, come forward for inspection, and turn slowly around three times if a school teacher, a mother, or a minister of the Gospel be among the visiting subscribers."

Miss Minnely took that for sincere! Renwick began to regard "The Blessing" as an emanation of a soul so simple as to be incapable of recognizing the diabolic element, derision. He was conceiving a tenderness for the honesty which could read his placard as one of sincerity. How blessed must be hearts innocent of mockery! Why should he not gratify them by discoursing to visiting subscribers? The idea tickled his fancy. At least he might amuse himself by writing what would edify Durley's parties if delivered with gravity. He might make material of some of Miss Minnely's voluminous letters of instruction to himself. From his pigeon-hole he drew that file, inspected it rapidly, laughed, and culled as he wrote.

Twenty minutes later he was chuckling over the effusion, after having once read its solemnities aloud to himself.

"Hang me if I don't try it on Durley's next party?" he was telling himself, when pencil tickings, like small woodpecker tappings, came again on his outer door. "Miss Heartly back! I will treat her to it!" and he opened the door, discourse in hand.

There stood the wide, wise-eyed placid, gray-clad lady!

"I am Miss Minnely, Mr. Renwick. Very pleased to introduce myself to a gentleman whose suggestion has pleased me deeply." Her wooly voice was as if steeped in a syrup of cordial powers. Suddenly he knew she had reminded him of Miss Pue's gigantic bronze Beneficence.

"Thank you, Miss Minnely. I feel truly honoured." Renwick, with some concealed trepidation, bowed her to his revolving chair.

"Mr. Renwick." She disposed her amplitude comfortably; then streamed on genially and authoritatively. "You may be gratified to learn that I was pleased—on the whole—by your cordial demeanour while—er—revolving—not long ago—on the occasion of Mr. Durley's last visiting party. Only—you will permit me to say this in all kindness—I did not regard the—display of—er—form—as precisely *adapted*. Otherwise your appearance, tone, and manner were eminently suitable—indeed such as mark you strongly, Mr. Renwick, as conforming—almost—to my highest ideal for the conduct of Editors of 'The Blessing.' Consequently I deputed Miss Heartly—with a suggestion. She has informed me of your cordial willingness, Mr. Renwick—hence I am here to thank you again—and instruct. Your short discourse to visitors will—let me explain—not only edify, but have the effect of, as it were, obviating any necessity for the—er—revolving—and the display of—er—form. Now, you are doubtless aware that I invariably edit, so to speak, every single thing done on behalf of our precious 'Family Blessing.' For due performance of that paramount duty I must give account hereafter. My peculiar gift is Taste—you will understand that I mention this fact with no more personal vanity than if I mentioned that I have a voice, hands, teeth, or any other endowment from my Creator—*our* Creator, in fact. Taste—true sense of what our subscribers like on their *higher* plane. My great gift must be entitled to direct what we *say* to visitors, just as it directs what 'The Blessing' publishes on its story pages, its editorial columns, its advertisements, letter heads, everything of every kind done in 'The Blessing's' name. I am thorough. And so, Mr. Renwick, I desire to hear your discourse beforehand. What? You have already prepared it? Excellent! Promptitude—there are few greater business virtues! We will immediately use your draft as a basis for further consultation."

So imposing was her amiable demeanour that Renwick had no wish but to comply. He glanced over what he had written, feeling now sure that its mock gravity would seem nowise sardonic to Miss Minnely.

"In preparing these few words," he remarked, "I have borrowed liberally from your notes of instruction to me, Miss Minnely."

"Very judicious. Pray give me the pleasure."

He tendered the draft.

"But no, please *deliver* it." She put away the paper. "Suppose me to be a party of our de-ar visiting subscribers. I will stand here, you there. Now do not hesitate to be audible, Mr. Renwick." She beamed as a Brobdignagian child at a new game.

Renwick, quick to all humours, took position, and began with unction: "Dear friends, dear visitors—"

She interrupted amiably:—"De-ar friends, de-ar visitors. Make two syllables of the de-ar. The lingering is cordial in effect. I have observed that carefully—de-ar softens hearts. Dwell on the word—dee-ar—thus you will cause a sense of affectionate regard to cling to visitors' memories of 'The Blessing's' editorial staff. You understand, Mr. Renwick?"

He began again: "De-ar friends, de-ar visitors, de-ar mothers, de-ar teachers," but again she gently expostulated, holding up a flat hand to stop his voice.

"Please, Mr. Renwick—no, I think not—it might seem invidious to discriminate by specifying some before others. All alike are our de-ar friends and visitors."

"De-ar friends, de-ar visitors," Renwick corrected his paper, "I cannot hope to express adequately to you my feelings of delight in being introduced to your notice as a first class general purpose editor, and eminent authority on—"

She graciously interposed:—"It might be well to pencil *this* in, Mr. Renwick, 'introduced to you by our de-ar colleague, Mr. Durley, the most experienced of our guides to the "Family Blessing" Building, as general purpose editor, etc.' That would impress, as hinting at our corps of guides, besides uplifting the rank of our valued colleague, Mr. Durley, and by consequence 'The Blessing,' through the respectful mention made of one of our more humble employees. Elevate the lowly, and you elevate all the superior classes—that is a sound American maxim. In business it is by such fine attention to detail that hearts and therefore subscribers are won. But, Mr. Renwick, *nothing* could be better than your 'I cannot hope to express adequately my feelings of delight,' etc.—that signifies cordial emotion—it is very good business, indeed."

Sincerity was unclouded in her gaze. He pencilled in her amendment, and read on:—"and eminent authority on water amusements of a character to build up character in first-class respectable American families."

"Very good—I drilled Mr. Durley in that," she put in complacently.

"Dear friends," he resumed.

"De-ar," she reminded him.

"De-ar friends, you may naturally desire to be informed of the nature of the duties of a general purpose editor, therefore—"

"Let me suggest again, Mr. Renwick. Better say 'Dear friends, closely associated with "The Family Blessing," as all must feel who share the privilege of maintaining it, you will naturally desire to be informed,' etc. Don't you agree, Mr. Renwick? It is well to neglect no opportunity for deepening the sense of our de-ar subscribers that the 'Blessing' is a privilege to their households. I do everything possible to make our beloved ones feel that they *own* 'The Blessing,' as in the highest sense they do. They like that. It is remunerative, also."

Renwick jotted in the improvement, and read on: "A general purpose editor of 'The Blessing' is simply one charged with promoting the general purpose of 'The Blessing.' To explain what that is I cannot do better than employ the words of the Sole Proprietress, Miss Minnely herself, and—."

The lady suggested, "*I cannot do so well as to employ the words of*—it is always effective to speak most respectfully of the absent Proprietress—that touches their imagination favourably. It is good business."

"I appreciate it, Miss Minnely. And now I venture to adapt, *verbatim*, parts of your notes to me."

"It was forethoughtful to preserve them, Mr. Renwick. I am cordially pleased."

He read on more oratorically:—"De-ar friends, 'The Blessing' has a Mission, and to fulfil that Mission it must, first of all, entertain its subscribers on their *higher plane*. This cannot be done by stimulating in them any latent taste for coarse and inelegant laughter, but by furnishing entertainingly the wholesome food from which mental pabulum is absorbed and mental growth accomplished."

"Excellent! My very own words."

"The varieties of this entertaining pabulum must be *conscientiously* prepared, and administered in small quantities so that each can be assimilated unconsciously by Youth and Age without mental mastication. Mind is *not* Character, and—"

"How true. Character-building publications must *never* be addressed to mere *Mind*."

"The uplifting of the Mind, or Intellect," Renwick read on, "is not the general purpose of 'The Family Blessing.' It is by the Literature of the Heart that Character is uplifted. Therefore a general purpose editor of 'The Blessing' must ever seek to maintain and to present the *truly cordial*. That is what most widely attracts and pleases all these sections of the great American people who are uncorrupted by worldly and literary associations which tend to canker the Soul with cynicism."

"I remember my glow of heart in writing those inspiring, blessed, and inspired words!" she exclaimed. "Moreover, they are true. Now, I think that is about enough, Mr. Renwick. Visitors should never be too long detained by a single attraction. Let me advise you to memorize the discourse carefully. It is cordial. It is impressive. It is informative of 'The Blessing's' ideal. It utters my own thoughts in my own language. It is admirably adapted to hold former subscribers, and to confirm new. All is well." She pondered silently a few moments. "Now, Mr. Renwick, I would be strictly just. The fact that an editor, and one of those not long gathered to our happy company, has suggested and devoted himself to this novel attraction, will have noblest effect in rousing our colleagues of every Department to emulative exertion. Once more, I thank you cordially. But the Sole Proprietress of the remunerative 'Blessing' holds her place in trust for all colleagues, and she is not disposed to retire with mere thanks to one who has identified himself so effectually with her and its ideals. Mr. Renwick, your honorarium—your weekly pay envelope," again she paused reflectively, "it will hereafter rank you with our very valued colleague, Mr. Caliphas C. Cummins himself! No—no-no, Mr. Renwick—do not thank me—

thank your happy inspiration—thank your cordial devotion—thank your *Taste*—thank your natural, innate identification, in high ideals, with me and 'The Family Blessing.' As for me—it is for me to thank you—and I do so, again, cordially, cordially, cordially!" She beamed, the broad embodiment of Beneficence, in going out of the room.

Renwick long stared, as one dazed, at the story of "The Converted Ringmaster." It related in minute detail the sudden reformation of that sinful official. The account of his rapid change seemed no longer improbable nor mawkish. Any revolution in any mind might occur, since his own had been so swiftly hypnotized into sympathy with Miss Minnely and her emanation "The Blessing." How generous she was! Grateful mist was in his eyes, emotion for the safety of the widows and the orphan whose bread he must win.

Yet the derisive demon which sat always close to his too sophisticated heart was already gibing him afresh:—"You stand engaged," it sneered, "as assistant ringmaster to Durley's exhibition of yourself!"

New perception of Miss Minnely and Miss Heartly rose in his mind. Could mortal women be really as simple as those two ladies had seemed? Might it not be they had managed him with an irony as profound as the ingenuousness they had appeared to evince?

Susan Frances Harrison

(1859-1935)

BORN IN TORONTO, Susan Frances Riley was educated there and in Montreal. In 1879 she married a musician and moved to Ottawa, then back to Toronto. An authority on French-Canadian folksong, she was also known as a musician in her own right. She edited the Toronto journal *The Week* for several months; and, using the pen-names "Gilbert King" and "Seranus," she contributed regularly to Canadian, British, and American magazines. She wrote a number of books of poetry and two romantic novels, of which *The Forest of Bourg-Marie* (1898), a dramatic rendering of the breakup of French Canadian society, was the most noted. Her story collection *Crowded Out and Other Sketches* (1886), from which "The Gilded Hammock" is taken, is a miscellany of mannered comedies and didactic sketches. The title story tacitly rebels against the colonial-mindedness of British publishers who (the story declares) refused to acknowledge anything but stereotypical versions of a wilderness Canada; Britain, argues Harrison, was therefore closed to realistic Canadian writers. But America was open. "The Gilded Hammock," which reflects the close editorial and literary connections that existed between Canada and New England in the latter decades of the 19th century, asserts something of the urban realities of the place and the time. Nonetheless, Harrison's irony exposes various kinds of social shallowness in the process, and her urbanity reveals one of several alternatives to the image of the Canadian wilds that was perpetrated by conventional romantic tales.

For Further Reading

ELAINE SHOWALTER, *A Literature of Their Own* (Princeton: Princeton UP, 1977).

The Gilded Hammock

Who does not know the beautiful Miss De Grammont? Isabel De Grammont, who lives by herself and is sole mistress of the brown-stone mansion in Fifth Avenue, the old family estate on the Hudson, the villa at Cannes, the first floor of a magnificently decayed palace at Naples, who has been everywhere, seen everything and—cared for nobody?

She reclines now in her latest craze—a hammock made of pure gold wire, fine and strong and dazzling as the late October sun shines upon it stretched from corner to corner of her regally-furnished drawing-room. Two gilded tripods securely fastened to the floor hold the ends of the hammock in which she lies. The rage for yellow holds her as it holds everyone who loves beauty and light and sunshine. Cushions of yellow damask support her head, and a yellow tiger-skin is under her feet. The windows are entirely hidden with thick amber draperies, and her own attire is a clinging gown of some soft silk of a deep creamy tint that as she sways to and fro in the hammock is slightly lifted, displaying a petticoat of darker tint, and Russian slippers of bronzed kid. Amber, large clear and priceless, gleams in its soft waxy glow in her hair, on her neck, round her waist, where it clasps a belt of thick gold cloth and makes a chain for a fan of yellow feathers.

Because you see, although it is autumn, it is very warm all through Miss De Grammont's mansion, as she insists on fires, huge bonfires, you may call them, of wood and peat in every room and on every hearth. Out of the fires grew the desire for the hammock.

"Why," says Miss De Grammont, with a faint yawn, "why must I only lie in a hammock in the Summer, and then, where nobody can see me? I will have a hammock made for the winter, to lie in and watch my fires by."

And so she did, for money is law and beauty creates duty, and one day, when the fashionable stream, the professional cliques and the artistic hangers-on called upon her "from three to six," they were confronted by the vision of an exquisitely beautiful woman dressed in faint yellow with great bunches of primroses in brass bowls from Morocco on a table by her side, who received them in a "gilded hammock," with her feet on a tiger-skin, and her chestnut hair catching a brighter tinge from the flames of her roaring fire, and the sunlight as it came in through the amber medium of the silken-draped windows.

The tea was Russian, like the slippers, and the butler who presented it was a mysterious foreigner who spoke five languages. The guests all wondered, as people always did at De Grammont. Nobody knew quite what she had done with herself since she had been left an orphan at the age of nineteen. She suddenly shot up into a woman, beautiful, with that patrician and clear-cut loveliness with yet a touch of the *bohémienne* about it which only *les belles Américaines* know. Then she took unto herself a maid, two dogs, and three Saratoga trunks

From *Crowded Out and Other Sketches* (Ottawa: *Evening Journal,* 1886).

and went over to Europe wandering about everywhere. At Cannes, she met and subjugated the heir to the crown; of this friendship the tiger-skin remained as a *souvenir.* The heir to the crown was not generous. Next came various members of embassies, all proud, all poor, and all frantically in love. She laid all manner of traps for her lovers and discovered in nearly every case that these men were after her money. A certain Russian Grand Duke, from whom had come some superb amber ornaments—he being a man of more wealth than the others—never forgave her the insult she offered him. He sent her these ornaments from the same shop in Paris that he ordered—at the same time—a diamond star for a well-known ballet dancer, and the two purchases were charged to his account. Through some stupidity, the star came to her. She ordered her horses and drove the same day to the jeweler, who was most humble and anxious to retrieve his error. He showed her the amber. She examined it carefully. "It is genuine, and very fine," she said gravely. "I have lived in Russia and I know. I am very fond of amber. I will buy this myself from you, and you may inform His Highness of the fact."

The delighted shop-keeper did not ask her very much more than its genuine value and next day all Paris knew of the transaction and flocked to the Opera to see her in the ornaments which had cost the Russian Duke his friendship for the bearer. But though eccentric, impulsive and domineering, no whisper had ever attached itself to her name. On her return to her native New York, was she not welcomed, fêted, honored, besieged with invitations everywhere? People felt she was different from the girl who went away. *She* had been undecided, emotional, a trifle vain, self-conscious, guilty of moods—no small offence in society; this glorious creature was a queen, a goddess, always calm, always serene, always a trifle bored, always superbly the same. Her house she re-furnished altogether. The three Saratoga trunks were now represented by nine or ten English ones, dress baskets, large packing cases, and one mysterious long box which when opened contained several panels of old Florentine carved wood-work which interested all New York immensely. Pictures and tapestries, armor and screens, and a gate of mediaeval wrought iron were all among her art treasures. The foreign butler was her *chargé d'affaires,* and managed everything most wisely and even economically. He engaged a few servants in New York, her maid, housekeeper and the two housemaids she had brought out with her. Her house was the perfect abode of the most faultless aestheticism. It was perfection in every detail and in the *ensemble* which greeted the eye, the ear, every sense, and all mental endowments, from the vestibule in marble and rugs to the inner boudoir and sanctum of the mistress of the house, hung with pale rose and straw-color in mingled folds of stamped Indian silks, priceless in color and quality. Two Persian cats adorned the lounge and one of her great dogs—a superb mastiff—occupied the rug before the door night and day, almost without rest.

Such were the general surroundings of Isabel De Grammont. Art and letters, music and general culture were inseparable from the daily life of such a woman as well as immediate beautiful presences, so that into this faultless house came everything new that the world offered in books, magazines, songs and new editions. Thanks to European travel, there was no language she could not read, no modern work she had not studied. Also came to her receptions the literary lions of New York. Aspiring journalists, retiring editors, playwrights and composers, a few actors and crowds of would-be poets flocked to the exquisite drawing-rooms hung with yellow, wherein the owner of so much magnificence lounged in her golden hammock. Sonnets were written of her descriptive of orioles flying in the golden west, and newspaper paragraphs indited weekly in her praise referred to her as the "Semiramus of a new and adoring society world." Baskets of flowers, tubs of flowers, barrels of flowers were sent weekly to her address, and she was solicited—on charitable, fashionable, religious, communistic, orthodox and socialistic grounds as lady patroness of this or member of that and subscriber to the other. In short, she was a success, and as nothing succeeds like success, we may take it that as the months rolled on, and the great house still maintained its superb hospitality and Miss De Grammont still appeared in her sumptuous carriage either smothered in furs or laces according to the seasons, she still maintained in like manner her position in society and her right to the homage and admiration of all classes.

But this was not the case. Even a worm will turn and public opinion is very often a little vermicular, let us say. And it happened, that public opinion in the case of Miss De Grammont, began to turn, to raise itself up in fact and look a little about it and beyond it as we have all seen worms do—both in cheeses and out of them—when the fact that she lay most of the time in a gilded hammock swung in front of her drawing-room fire was announced from the pulpits of society journals. It may have been that her friends were devoid of imagination, that they were cold, prudish, satirical, unpoetical, unaesthetic, anything we like to call them, that will explain their action in the matter, for they clearly, one and all, disliked the notion of the hammock. One spoke of it disparagingly to another, who took it up and abused it to a third, who described it to a friend who "wrote for the papers." This gifted gentleman who lodged with a lady of the same temper and edited a fashion journal, concocted with her help a description of the thing which soon found its way into his paper and was then copied into hers. The public grew uneasy. It would swallow any story it was told about the Heir apparent, for instance and a Russian Grand Duke—is it not the sublime prerogative of American women to dally with such small game as those gentlemen—but it kicked against the probability of such an actual fact as the hammock already described which seemed too ridiculous a whim to possess any real existence. However, the tongues of the fashionable callers, the professional cliques and the artistic hangers-on coincided in the affair to that extent that soon the existence of the gilded hammock was established and from that time Miss De Grammont's popularity was on the wane. Dowagers looked askance and matrons posed in a patronizing manner, the flippant correspondents of society journals and the compilers of sonnets in which that very hammock had been eulogized and metaphored to distraction now waited upon her, if at all in an entirely different manner. Strange how all classes began to recall the many peculiar or unaccountable things she had done, the extraordinary costumes she had worn, the fact that she lived alone, and the other fact that she made so few friends. From aspersions cast on her house, her equipage, her dresses, there came to be made strictures on her private character, her love affairs, her friends and career in Europe, her *ménage* at present in New York and the members thereof. Finally public opinion finding that all this made very little impression outwardly, upon the regal disdain of Miss De Grammont in her carriage or in her Opera-stall, however she might writhe and chafe when safely ensconced within that rose and straw-colored boudoir, made up its mind that the secret of the whole three volume novel, the key to the entire mystery lay with the—butler.

That black-moustached functionary, they whispered, had his mistress in his power. He had been a courier, and she had fallen in love with him abroad. Or he had been a well-known conjurer and coerced her through means little less than infernal to run away with him. He was a mesmerist, so they said, and could send her into trances at will. Then he had been the famous Man Milliner of Vienna, whose disappearance one fine day with the entire trousseau of an Austrian Grand Duchess had been a nine days' wonder. These dresses she wore, strange mixtures never seen on earth before of violet and blue, pink and pea green, rose and lemon, were the identical ones prepared for the Grand Duchess. Finally, he was an Italian Prince rescued from a novel of "Ouida's," whom she had found living in exile, having to suffer punishment for some fiendish crime perpetrated in the days of his youth.

When the stories had reached this point, Miss De Grammont, to whom they were conveyed through papers, notes from "confidential friends," her maid and others, wrote a letter one day directed to the

> Rev. Luke Fielding,
> Pastor Congregational Church,
> Phippsville, Vermont.

A week or ten days after, Miss De Grammont, seated—not in the gilded hammock though it still swung gracefully before the glowing fire—but in the cushions which graced her window looking on the front of the house, saw a gentleman arrive in a cab. She rose hastily and opened the door of the room herself for her visitor. This was the Rev. Luke Fielding, a gentleman of the severest Puritanical cut and a true New Englander to boot. With his hat in his hand he advanced with an expression on his face of the deepest amazement and dismay which increased momentarily as he saw not only the gorgeous coloring and appointments of the room but the fair figure of its occupant. To be sure, she had with infinite difficulty selected the plainest dress she could find in her wardrobe to receive him in, a gown of dark green velvet made very simply and high to the throat. But alas! there was no disguising the priceless lace at her wrists, or the gems that glittered on her firm white hands.

"My dear cousin!" said the lady, giving him both her hands.

"My dear cousin Isabel," returned the minister, laying his hat down on a plush-covered chair on which it looked curiously out of place, and taking her hands in his.

"My dear cousin Isabel, after so many years!"

"It is only eight years, cousin," returned the lady.

"True," replied the minister gravely. "Yet to one like myself that seems a long time. You sent for me, cousin." His gaze wandered round the room and then fastened once more upon Miss De Grammont.

"Yes," she said faintly. "I could not tell you all in my letter. I wanted—I want still—somebody's help."

"And it is very natural you should apply for mine, cousin. I will do anything I can. I have"—the minister grew sensibly more severe, more grave—"I have this day, on the train, seen a paper—a new kind of paper to me, I confess,—a *Society Journal* it calls itself, in which a name is mentioned. Is your—trouble—connected with that?"

Miss De Grammont blushed deeply. "Yes. That is my name. I would not have troubled you—but I must ask your advice, for you are the only one of the family, of my mother's family—" Her voice broke.

"Yes, cousin, you are right."

The minister rose and stood up before her, a stern though not unsympathetic figure in his stiff black coat and iron gray hair. "I know what you are going to ask me to do. You will ask me to see these people, these editors, reviewers, whatever they are, to talk to them, to impress upon them what you are and who you are, and who your mother was, and what is the end of the base man who imagines lies and the end of all the workers of iniquity. You will ask me to tell them that it is all false, all abominable intrigue and treachery and I shall demand in your name and in my own as your only near relative and a minister of the Gospel, an apology. It is but jealousy, cousin. Forgive me, but you are too beautiful and too young to live alone in such a house, in such a manner. You must marry. Or else you must give up such a life. It maketh enemies within your gates and behold! there shall be no man to say a good thing of thee!"

The minister had lifted up his voice as if he had been in the pulpit and for one instant laid his hand on his cousin's hair. Then he went back to his seat.

Miss De Grammont was profoundly moved. Great tears coursed down her cheeks and until they had stopped she could not trust herself to speak.

"The paper!" she said dismally. "You have seen a paper, you say, with—my—my name in it! There is nothing new in that. I have been in the papers for months past. I am never out of them. And this one says—"

The minister drew it out of his pocket.

"That with you, in this house lives, in the character of a butler, an exiled Italian Prince who committed grave personal and political offences many years ago and was sent to prison. That you are married to him. My dear cousin, it is monstrous!"

Miss De Grammont took out her handkerchief already wet through with her tears and pressed it to her eyes.

"It is not monstrous," she said, "but it is most extraordinary. He *is* an Italian Prince, and I *am* married to him."

To use a hackneyed phrase, the room swam around Mr. Fielding for an instant. When he recovered he could only sit and gaze at the beautiful woman before him. The details of village life in Vermont had not educated him up to exigencies of this sort. A fearful chasm seemed to have opened under his feet, and he began to comprehend dimly that there were other lives than his own and that of his estimable but commonplace wife being daily lived out in this world.

"Yes," said Miss De Grammont, a little more bravely now that the worst shock was over. "That is quite true. And the extraordinary part of it is that they can only have guessed at it; evolved it, as it were from the depths of their inner consciousness, they can't possibly have discovered it. It isn't known anywhere, save perhaps to one or two in Italy."

"In Italy," murmured the Rev. Mr. Fielding. "You met him in Italy? And why keep it secret? My dear cousin, you have made a great mistake. And all this sad and singular story is true?"

"Very nearly true. All but the offences. *They* never happened."

"Your husband is not a political character then?"

"Oh! not in the least. He knows nothing of politics. My José! He couldn't hurt anything, moreover!"

"José is a Spanish name, surely,' said Mr. Fielding.

"His mother was a Castilian, fair and proud as only a Castilian can be. She named him José. But he has other names, three, all Italian—Antonio—"

"I see," said the minister dryly. "I am sorry that I cannot give you all the sympathy in this matter that you may desire, but you have entered on a course of action which is perplexing at least, to say no more. I feel, my dear cousin, that as a—married woman—your confidences are—ill placed and I must ask you to withdraw them. You must settle this matter with your—ahem—husband." Mr. Fielding took up his hat and in another moment would have been gone forever, but that turning at the door he saw such intense supplication in his cousin's eyes that his orthodox heart melted.

"Forgive me cousin," he said coming back. "There may be still a way out of it. Will you tell me all?" Miss De Grammont then related her different heart episodes abroad, entanglements, half-engagements, desperate flirtations and all the rest of it to this sober, black-coated gentleman. Such a revelation poured forth in truly feminine style nearly drove him away the second time, but true to his word, he remained nevertheless, sitting bolt upright in a padded chair only meant for lounging. Finally, she told him of her snares to catch lovers and how one day she was caught herself by the dark-browed, eloquent Prince Corunna. She fell in love herself for the first time in her life, and he with her, so he declared. But he was miserably poor and with the pride of a Castilian would not woo her because of her money. She hated it, yet she could not live without it.

The Minister smiled pityingly.

However she made him marry her, and then proposed as a test, in which he joyfully acquiesced, that he should make himself of use to her, be in fact, her major-domo, steward, butler, amanuensis, anything and everything.

"It is most unprecedented," sighed the minister. "That a man with Castilian blood in his veins—"

Miss De Grammont interrupted him. "He was happier so, dear cousin. But I—I grew most unhappy. And since I have been here, I have been very unhappy still. We are both in a false position and now—thanks to that unlucky hammock—our secret has become common property."

"The hammock!" said Mr. Fielding. "What has that got to do with it? It is a pretty idea."

"So I think," said Miss De Grammont, delighted beyond measure. Then she told him about the paragraphs, large and small, the confidential friends, the small beginnings that had led insensibly up to the culminating point—that of scandal.

"I am being dropped gradually," she said.

"Of course you are," said the minister. "Of course you are. Soon you will be—forgive me—a dead letter. There is only one thing to be done and that I can do at once. A letter must be written to this paper, stating calmly in as few words as possible that this paragraph is true, that you *are* married to Prince—ah—Corunna, that he *is* a political offender and for that reason the marriage *was* kept secret, but that now of course as informers must already have given the secret away, you are obliged to endorse it yourself."

"But José is not a political offender! Never did anything wrong in his life!"

"Of course not," said the minister. "Some of us others, even clergymen, are not so fortunate. Now that must be included, else there is no good reason for having kept your marriage secret. Other explanations will not be taken. Besides this will entitle you to sympathy at once. Will you write the letter and I can leave it at the office for you? There is time for me to do that before my train starts."

Miss De Grammont wrote her letter as dictated by her cousin. He put it in his pocket and rose to go.

"Will you not stay and see my husband?" she said timidly.

"Thank you, no," returned Mr. Fielding. "I haven't met many foreigners. I don't think, perhaps, we should get on. Down in Phippsville—well, my circle is so different from yours, Isabel. It is the fashion I hear to live abroad now, and desert America—at least to depreciate it, and not to care about its opinion—but that hasn't spread yet to our little village. It seems as if it might have been better for instance, had you stayed in Europe. You see, having married an Italian, all this trouble would have been avoided—I mean—it could have gone on over there—but now—well, riches are a snare, my dear cousin, as you have by this time found. Good-bye, dear cousin, and God be with you."

When a letter addressed to the editor of the *Society Journal* appeared the next day signed Isabel Corunna (*née* De Grammont) with its paralysing statement in a few concise words, New York was startled to its foundation. Public opinion which for a week had been at the culminating point of distrust, malevolence and resentment, turned the corner in a moment and for the moment believed implicitly in the faith of the lady it had abandoned. The greatest sympathy was shown Madame La Princesse Corunna, or Princess Corunna, or Miss De Grammont that *was*, or whatever her friends chose to call her. The butler disappeared for ever and the Prince came in. It was a transformation scene equal to Beauty and the Beast. Dark-browed and eloquent as ever, the Prince was a social success whenever he chose to be, but as time went on, he and his wife became more and more absorbed in each other and the world saw little of either of them. For a time he posed as a political offender which gave his wife no end of amusement. They were so far reinstated into public favor that the hammock—source of mingled joy and woe—was again considered as a thing of beauty and a thing to be imitated. There are a dozen such hammocks now in New York City.

But there are still a few ill-natured people, dowagers, matrons, an old love or two, and a handful of shrivelled spinsters who declare that the Prince is no Prince at all, but a Pastrycook.

Sir Charles G.D. Roberts

(1860–1943)

BORN IN DOUGLAS, N.B., and educated at the University of New Brunswick, Charles G.D. Roberts went on to become a translator, a writer of boys' books, a novelist, editor, leading poet of the "Confederation Group" (with Archibald Lampman, Bliss Carman, Wilfred Campbell, and D.C. Scott), and an innovative story writer who developed the art of the contemporary animal tale. His first book of poems, *Orion* (1880), served as a stimulus to later 19th-century poets in Canada, combining a sense of tradition with an effort to record exact descriptive detail. Roberts became editor of *The Week* in 1883, but left shortly after for the United States, adopting the life of the professional writer from 1897 on, not returning to Canada until 1925.

Credited with transforming the animal tale from a traditional beast fable into a contemporary scientific and psychological record, Roberts influenced such writers as Rudyard Kipling and Ernest Thompson Seton, who in turn influenced Sir Robert Baden-Powell—out of whose version of wilderness emerged the Boy Scout Movement. Roberts published his first animal story in *Harper's Magazine* in 1892, and in his "Introductory" remarks to his collection *Kindred of the Wild* (1902), he specified that an animal story was "a psychological romance constructed on a framework of natural science." The emphasis must be on "romance" as much as on "science"; anthropomorphic in presumption, the stories convey an illusion of documentary objectivity, but Roberts was actually interpreting "natural" behaviour and the "reality" of the wilderness quite subjectively. Attacked by some (by Theodore Roosevelt, for example) as fakery, the wilderness stories won a wide popular audience. Some seventeen of Roberts' animal story collections appeared between 1904 and 1936, among them *Red Fox* (1905), *The Haunters of the Silences* (1907), *The Feet of the Furtive* (1912), and *Hoof and Claw* (1914). "When Twilight Falls on the Stump Lots" appeared in *Kindred of the Wild*. Roberts' stories set the tone for much of Canadian writing of the earlier 20th century: discovering natural morality in the wilderness, the nature writers made a version of wilderness into the typifying image of Canadian culture at large. In Roberts' stories, "scientific nature" was a challenge to the vapid settings of 19th-century romance; other writers of the time, however, saw it as yet another form of artifice, which was in turn open to satiric and realistic challenge.

For Further Reading

LAUREL BOONE, ed., *The Collected Letters of Charles G.D. Roberts* (Fredericton: Goose Lane, 1989).

JOHN BURROUGHS, "Real and Sham Natural History," *Atlantic Monthly* 91 (March 1903): 298–304.

JOSEPH GOLD, "The Precious Speck of Life," *Canadian Literature* 26 (Autumn 1965): 22–32.

R.H. MACDONALD, "The Revolt Against Instinct," *Canadian Literature* 84 (Spring 1980): 18–29.

T.D. MACLULICH, "The Animal Story and the 'Nature Faker' Controversy," *Essays on Canadian Writing* 33 (Fall 1986): 112–24.

W.H. MAGEE, "The Animal Story," *Dalhousie Review* 44 (1964–65): 156–64.

MICHEL POIRIER, "The Animal Story in Canadian Literature," *Queen's Quarterly* 34 (1927): 398–419.

JAMES POLK, *Wilderness Writers* (Toronto: Clarke Irwin, 1972).

When Twilight Falls
on the Stump Lots

The wet, chill first of the spring, its blackness made tender by the lilac wash of the afterglow, lay upon the high, open stretches of the stump lots. The winter-whitened stumps, the sparse patches of juniper and bay just budding, the rough-mossed hillocks, the harsh boulders here and there up-thrusting from the soil, the swampy hollows wherein a coarse grass began to show green, all seemed anointed, as it were, to an ecstasy of peace by the chrism of that paradisal colour. Against the lucid immensity of the April sky the thin tops of five or six soaring ram-pikes aspired like violet flames. Along the skirts of the stump lots a fir wood reared a ragged-crested wall of black against the red amber of the horizon.

Late that afternoon, beside a juniper thicket not far from the centre of the stump lots, a young black and white cow had given birth to her first calf. The little animal had been licked assiduously by the mother's caressing tongue till its colour began to show of a rich dark red. Now it had struggled to its feet, and, with its disproportionately long, thick legs braced wide apart, was beginning to nurse. Its blunt wet muzzle and thick lips tugged eagerly, but somewhat blunderingly as yet, at the unaccustomed teats; and its tail lifted, twitching with delight, as the first warm streams of mother milk went down its throat. It was a pathetically awkward, unlovely little figure, not yet advanced to that youngling winsomeness which is the heritage, to some degree and at some period, of the infancy of all the kindreds that breathe upon the earth. But to the young mother's eyes it was the most beautiful of things. With her head twisted far around, she nosed and licked its heaving flanks as it nursed; and between deep, ecstatic breathings she uttered in her throat low murmurs, unspeakably tender, of encouragement and caress. The delicate but pervading flood of sunset colour had the effect of blending the ruddy-hued calf into the tones of the landscape; but the cow's insistent blotches of black and white stood out sharply, refusing to harmonise. The drench of violet light was of no avail to soften their staring contrasts. They made her vividly conspicuous across the whole breadth of the stump lots, to eyes that watched her from the forest coverts.

The eyes that watched her—long, fixedly, hungrily—were small and red. They belonged to a lank she-bear, whose gaunt flanks and rusty coat proclaimed a season of famine in the wilderness. She could not see the calf, which was hidden by a hillock and some juniper scrub; but its presence was very legibly conveyed to her by the mother's solicitous watchfulness. After a mo-

From *The Kindred of the Wild* (Boston: Page, 1902). Reprinted by permission of The Canadian Publishers McClelland and Stewart Ltd.

tionless scrutiny from behind the screen of fir branches, the lean bear stole noiselessly forth from the shadows into the great wash of violet light. Step by step, and very slowly, with the patience that endures because confident of its object, she crept toward that oasis of mothering joy in the vast emptiness of the stump lots. Now crouching, now crawling, turning to this side and to that, taking advantage of every hollow, every thicket, every hillock, every aggressive stump, her craft succeeded in eluding even the wild and menacing watchfulness of the young mother's eyes.

The spring had been a trying one for the lank she-bear. Her den, in a dry tract of hemlock wood some furlongs back from the stump lots, was a snug little cave under the uprooted base of a lone pine, which had somehow grown up among the alien hemlocks only to draw down upon itself at last, by its superior height, the fury of a passing hurricane. The winter had contributed but scanty snowfall to cover the bear in her sleep; and the March thaws, unseasonably early and ardent, had called her forth to activity weeks too soon. Then frosts had come with belated severity, sealing away the budding tubers, which are the bear's chief dependence for spring diet; and worst of all, a long stretch of intervale meadow by the neighbouring river, which had once been rich in ground-nuts, had been ploughed up the previous spring and subjected to the producing of oats and corn. When she was feeling the pinch of meagre rations, and when the fat which a liberal autumn of blueberries had laid up about her ribs was getting as shrunken as the last snow in the thickets, she gave birth to two hairless and hungry little cubs. They were very blind, and ridiculously small to be born of so big a mother; and having so much growth to make during the next few months, their appetites were immeasurable. They tumbled, and squealed, and tugged at their mother's teats, and grew astonishingly, and made huge haste to cover their bodies with fur of a soft and silken black; and all this vitality of theirs made a strenuous demand upon their mother's milk. There were no more bee-trees left in the neighbourhood. The long wanderings which she was forced to take in her search for roots and tubers were in themselves a drain upon her nursing powers. At last, reluctant though she was to attract the hostile notice of the settlement, she found herself forced to hunt on the borders of the sheep pastures. Before all else in life was it important to her that these two tumbling little ones in the den should not go hungry. Their eyes were open now—small and dark and whimsical, their ears quaintly large and inquiring for their roguish little faces. Had she not been driven by the unkind season to so much hunting and foraging, she would have passed near all her time rapturously in the den under the pine root, fondling those two soft miracles of her world.

With the killing of three lambs—at widely scattered points, so as to mislead retaliation—things grew a little easier for the harassed bear; and presently she grew bolder in tampering with the creatures under man's protection. With one swift, secret blow of her mighty paw she struck down a young ewe which had strayed within reach of her hiding-place. Dragging her prey deep into the woods, she fared well upon it for some days, and was happy with her growing cubs. It was just when she had begun to feel the fasting which came upon the exhaustion of this store that, in a hungry hour, she sighted the conspicuous markings of the black and white cow.

It is altogether unusual for the black bear of the eastern woods to attack any quarry so large as a cow, unless under the spur of fierce hunger or fierce rage. The she-bear was powerful beyond her fellows. She had the strongest possible incentive to bold hunting, and she had lately grown confident beyond her wont. Nevertheless, when she began her careful stalking of this big game which she coveted, she had no definite intention of forcing a battle with the cow. She had observed that cows, accustomed to the protection of man, would at times leave their calves asleep and stray off some distance in their pasturing. She had even seen calves left all by themselves in a field, from morning till night, and had wondered at such negligence in their mothers. Now she had a confident idea that sooner or later the calf would lie down to sleep, and the young mother roam a little wide in search of the scant young grass. Very softly, very self-effacingly, she crept nearer step by step, following up the wind, till at last, undiscovered, she was crouching behind a thick patch of juniper, on the slope of a little hollow not ten paces distant from the cow and the calf.

By this time the tender violet light was fading to a grayness over hillock and hollow; and with the deepening of the twilight the faint breeze, which had been breathing from the northward, shifted suddenly and came in slow, warm pulsations out of the south. At the same time the calf, having nursed sufficiently, and feeling his baby legs tired of the weight they had not yet learned to carry, laid himself down. On this the cow shifted her position. She turned half round, and lifted her head high. As she did so a scent of peril was borne in upon her fine nostrils. She recognised it instantly. With a snort of anger she sniffed again; then stamped a challenge with her fore hoofs, and levelled the lance-points of her horns toward the menace. The next moment her eyes, made keen by the fear of love, detected the black outline of the bear's head through the coarse screen of the juniper. Without a second's hesitation, she flung up her tail, gave a short bellow, and charged.

The moment she saw herself detected, the bear rose upon her hindquarters; nevertheless she was in a measure surprised by the sudden blind fury of the attack. Nimbly she swerved to avoid it, aiming at the same time a stroke with her mighty forearm, which, if it had found its mark, would have smashed her adversary's neck. But as she struck out, in the act of shifting her position, a depression of the ground threw her off her balance. The next instant one sharp horn caught her slantingly in the flank, ripping its way upward and inward, while the mad impact threw her upon her back.

Grappling, she had her assailant's head and shoulders in a trap, and her gigantic claws cut through the flesh and sinew like knives; but at the desperate disadvantage of her position she could inflict no disabling blow. The cow, on the other hand, though mutilated and streaming with blood, kept pounding with her whole massive weight, and with short tremendous shocks crushing the breath from her foe's ribs.

Presently, wrenching herself free, the cow drew off for another battering charge; and as she did so the bear hurled herself violently down the slope, and gained her feet behind a dense thicket of bay shrub. The cow, with one eye blinded and the other obscured by blood, glared around for her in vain, then, in a panic of mother terror, plunged back to her calf.

Snatching at the respite, the bear crouched down, craving that invisibility which is the most faithful shield of the furtive kindred. Painfully, and leaving a drenched red trail behind her, she crept off from the disastrous neighbourhood. Soon the deepening twilight sheltered her. But she could not make haste; and she knew that death was close upon her.

Once within the woods, she struggled straight toward the den that held her young. She hungered to die licking them. But destiny is as implacable as iron to the wilderness people, and even this was denied her. Just a half score of paces from the lair in the pine root, her hour descended upon her. There was a sudden redder and fuller gush upon the trail; the last light of longing faded out of her eyes; and she lay down upon her side.

The merry little cubs within the den were beginning to expect her, and getting restless. As the night wore on, and no mother came, they ceased to be merry. By morning they were shivering with hunger and desolate fear. But the doom of the ancient wood was less harsh than its wont, and spared them some days of starving anguish; for about noon a pair of foxes discovered the dead mother, astutely estimated the situation, and then, with the boldness of good appetite, made their way into the unguarded den.

As for the red calf, its fortune was ordinary. Its mother, for all her wounds, was able to nurse and cherish it through the night; and with morning came a searcher from the farm and took it, with the bleeding mother, safely back to the settlement. There it was tended and fattened, and within a few weeks found its way to the cool marble slabs of a city market.

Sara Jeannette Duncan

(1861–1922)

BORN OF CELTIC STOCK AND RAISED IN BRANTFORD, Sara Jeannette Duncan attended Toronto Normal School but soon abandoned teaching to take up journalism. The new career provided certain unconventional opportunities for travel, and as early as 1884 she was in New Orleans, working as a freelance contributor (as, later, she was an editorial writer and reviewer) for the Washington *Post*. Through the 1880s, using the pseudonym "Garth Grafton," she was also a columnist for the *Globe, The Week,* and the *Montreal Star*. A trip around the world in 1888—her sketches of her travels appeared in fictional form as *A Social Departure* (1890)—led to her meeting Everard Cotes, a museum official in Calcutta, who went on to become a newspaper editor. She married him in 1890 and spent the rest of her life in India and England.

An acquaintance of such writers as W.D. Howells, Henry James, and E.M. Forster, she was not untouched by the character of their writing. A highly articulate observer of words and mores, she wrote ironic comedies of manners and politics, describing—in such novels as *Cousin Cinderella* (1908) and *An American Girl in London* (1891)—the differing role (and language) of women in Canada, Britain, and the U.S.A. Another novel, *The Imperialist* (1904), is a politically adept account of the Imperial Federation Movement and of late 19th century shifts in Ontario political attitudes. *The Pool in the Desert* (1903) is a collection of short stories. "A Visit to a Carmelite Convent," which appeared first on 10 November 1887 in *The Week,* is characteristic of much of her journalism; paying close attention to detail, she managed to sketch evocative pictures of persons and places, which approach (though stop short of) the character of fiction; by carefully controlling the irony of her sketches, she managed to reach past the ostensible objectivity of the sketch form, and to reveal in what she observed a set of social implications that might not otherwise be so readily apparent.

For Further Reading

MISAO DEAN, *A Different Point of View: Sara Jeannette Duncan* (Montreal: McGill-Queen's UP, 1990).

CAROLE GERSON and KATHY MEZEI, Introduction to *The Prose of Life: Sketches from Victorian Canada* (Toronto: ECW, 1981) 1–15.

THOMAS E. TAUSKY, ed., *Sara Jeannette Duncan: Selected Journalism* (Ottawa: Tecumseh, 1978).

A Visit to a Carmelite Convent

Let us walk awhile first. We shall find plenty along these narrow streets to repay us for exercise we are unaccustomed to in flat Ontario—pedestrianism at an angle of forty-five degrees. The first thing one looks for on arriving in Montreal is lodgings and a laundress; the next an alpenstock. By the time the first two are satisfactorily got we don't want the alpenstock. We are accustomed to the hills, and like them.

Dozens of loveable, habitable-looking, fine, old stone houses! That one especially, there on the corner of Bleury and another street that we must not mention, because we can easily see from the outside of it that the inhabitants do not love publicity. Is not that very good to look at with its suggestion of strength and endurance and comfort, and all the sentiment that gathers about a home! In architecture unpretentiously square, not at all grand in size but big enough to suggest comfortable capacity. Wide, hospitable eaves and old-fashioned projecting porch, tiny panes in the windows that make the people behind them feel as if they were indoors. Hard to keep clean? I suppose so; but few things that are worth having are got very easily. You think your broad sheets of plateglass an improvement perhaps? Well, I don't. I like best the many broken pictures that the narrow panes make. Plate-glass is for invalids. If healthy people want all out-of-doors they can put on their hats and go out and get it. And of course there are trees about our old house, and places where flowers bloomed, I suppose, in June, and a barn that is as solidly built as the house itself. There is this advantage about the Quebec climate: it compels people to build houses that future generations may comfortably live in, and put their money into strength and solidity instead of ornamentally hideous exterior kickshaws, which lose even their tawdry worth in ten or fifteen years.

Judging from appearances the human boy is not the reviled member of society in Montreal that he is elsewhere. He is, in fact, conspicuously "wanted." Every other shop window bears the placard *"garçon demandé"*—which limited advertisement the boys disdain to notice apparently, for it remains there week after week. It appears to the sojourner that the Montreal *garçon* declines almost all his legitimate occupations. He does not cry the papers to any extent; he is no bootblack, nor crossing-sweeper, he! Nor does he drive grocers' carts nor run errands nearly so much as with us, which is perhaps owing to the fact that his father is content to do it. Altogether, unless the factories swallow him up, the small boy of Montreal may be believed to lead a life of enervating and luxurious leisure.

Next to the oft-quoted *Fameuse*—which by the way is neither more nor less than our own more modestly christened "snow-apple"—the fruit of the land ap-

From *The Week* (10 November, 1887).

pears to be the oyster. One does not require much capital to start in the bi-valve business in Montreal. A pile of shells on either side of the door, to attest public appreciation and a flourishing trade; inside, half a barrel of stock, a broken knife and castor that has seen better days, and perhaps a wooden chair on which the proprietor sits and smokes his native tobacco at ten cents a pound and ponders, doubtless upon the advantages of unrestricted trade. The shells are the only indication the intelligent public requires, but some osten-tatious firms scrawl the additional legend, "*huitres,*" in chalk above the door. This is the humble beginning of the business; it ends somewhere in the mag-nificence of the Windsor, and all the way up one is struck with the diversity of its forms. Oysters not only at the fruiterer's and the fishmonger's, but in the market, at the grocer's, the confectioner's, the little woman's who sells odds and ends of buttons, lace, and the evening papers; oysters by the glass, quart, gallon, peck, small measure, basket, and barrel. I have not yet seen them in the millinery shops by the yard, but am willing to believe that they are sold covertly even there.

But we are a long way down St. Catharine Street, and our car is coming. Where are we going? To Hochelaga I think, to see the convent there. Our guide, who is a lively little French-Canadian lady, and luckily for us speaks English, says it is "the la-argest in Kennada—that convent;" and surely with the October sun shining on its pillared front, and the last yellow largesse of autumn scat-tered about its solid base, and the broad blue St. Lawrence flowing grandly past, it is the most beautiful in "Kennada." We are admitted to the reception room, which is really quite a large *salon,* adorned with oil paintings of His Holiness the Pope, the sister who founded the Order very humbly at Longueuil across the river there, and the usual religious subjects. This lady in the black habit and the plain white hood, which, with the veil, is the dress of the sisters of Jesus and Mary, who presents each cheek to be kissed by our French friend, and bows pleasantly to the rest of us, is the Mother Superior of the whole Order. The responsibility of her charge may be imagined when we hear that it has missions in Florida, California, British Columbia. She looks like an or-ganiser and directress this nun, with her keen, intellectual face, ready speech, and nervous, energetic manner. She has been for eighteen years at the head of a mission in California, and it is a little odd to note the traces of Americanism in her voice and ways. One looks for national traits in secular flocks, but expects, somehow, nuns to be feminogeneous, if I may coin a word. The Superioress chats with us for a while, and hands us over to a smiling little English nun, who shows us the school-rooms, where one hundred and sixty-five young ladies, all the way from five to eighteen are receiving the usual convent instruction, and the chapel, a perfect copy of that of St. Marie Maguere of Rome, and very beau-tiful with carvings, and white statues of Saints, and dusky corners where sin-gle candles are burning.

"I will show you our Saint," says the little nun, as she leads the way to the place near the altar, where lies a wax figure, representing a beautiful young girl dead with a gash in her throat. "St. Aurelia," says the little nun in a whis-per, "and the hair"—which is very long, shining, and curly—"was given by our sister St. Aurelia when she entered."

"Was it—was she—was the saint made here?" I enquire, in misery of uncertainty as to the proper pronoun.

"The head and hands and feet were sent from Paris," she responds, "but we made the body here and put it together, and all the embroidery of the dress was done here."

The embroidery is of gold on a robe of white satin, and a marvel of handiwork.

"Perhaps," says the little nun, "I can show you our other most precious relics." And she goes to see. Alas! she cannot show them to us—perhaps because we are heretics, and who knows what a heretic will do or say.

Just across the road from the Convent of Jesus and Mary stands a grim building with a very high thick stone wall. I have never seen so impassable a wall around a prison as this which confines inmates who have imposed a life sentence on themselves. The building is the worldly face of the cloistered cells of the Carmelites, and the wall is built about their garden. And this is the only Carmelite convent in America. In Spain, in France, in Italy there are others, but not on *this* continent. The Order has existed here since 1875 only. The money to establish it was given by a Madame Frémont of Quebec, and the French Carmelite *fondatrice* who came from Paris is dead now. So are all her sisters except three. The severity of their lives in our rigorous climate killed them. There are fifteen now cloistered here, but twelve are French-Canadian. You know, of course, what it means to take the vows of a Carmelite. It means the most literal renouncement of the world possible to a human being. The face of the Carmelite nun is never seen after her entrance except by her immediate relatives, and then only for half an hour once a month, through heavy gratings. Her hand is never touched save by her sisters. From behind the little door that is barred upon her on the day of parting with our pleasant world she never comes again. Her cell is of the barest; she sleeps on a mattress with one coverlet. Her diet is of the poorest, and meat never enters it. Her habit is of coarse brown cloth, with a veil of a similar colour and kind, and she wears sandals on her feet. Her occupation is prayer and penance, and the making of church decorations. She is a "favourite soul."

We ring, and the sound reverberates within, hollow and chill. A nun dressed like those of the convent opposite opens the door, and, after a whispered conference with our French friend, admits us. The hall we stand in is narrow, cold, and ill-ventilated, and we shiver as we pass along to a small, bare room with an opening in the wall about four feet square. From the iron bars which guard it project spikes half a foot long. On the other side of the opening is another barred network, and behind that hangs a black veil. The room is in semi-darkness, but we can read above the spikes and bars the words—

> *Au Carmel comme au jugement,*
> *Dieu seul et moi.*

They strike through the stillness upon one's consciousness like a text of half-comprehended truth. *Dieu seul et moi!* There is a ring of awful solemnity about that. This is where the Carmelite comes to get her pitiful sight of someone she loved in the days before she became a "favourite soul"; and these are the bars through which that loved one strains aching eyes for the tortured glimpse of the recluse. Through double bars—and then the tears! "Mark well and consider, all you who pass this way," runs a printed text upon the wall; "is there any sorrow like my sorrow?"

Yes, we may have speech with one of the nuns, the sister who let us in comes to tell us. This is by grace of the French lady, who is high in favour in her church. But not here. So we are conducted to another little room, where a circular shelf revolves in the wall for the admission of necessaries to the hospital. Behind this stands the nun. Madame addresses her. We cannot. We have a kind of fear as to what we might say, our conversation being in the world. We shrink from the possible profanation of the strange stillness that surrounds the life behind these thrice-mortared gray walls. But Madame does not shrink. She addresses the shelf with a sort of reverential gaiety, if there is such a thing, and enquires for the health of "*ma soeur.*" And in tremulous tones the nun responds that she is very well—oh, very well, indeed, and is Madame well? How her voice shakes as they talk in French, Madame turning occasionally to tell us that the Superioress is very ill; that if we desire the prayers of the nun we may have them; that the garden has not been very successful this year! It is a great license, this of conversing with strangers behind a heavy partition, and she must be very, very mindful not to forget for an instant that these are not "favourite souls." And she can speak in English? Yes, but can we?

"Are you happy, *ma soeur?*" I falter.

"I am most happy," comes the answer in a quiet cadence.

"And when you die, *ma soeur,* where are you buried?" I query.

"In the vault below," she responded, and I fancy I do detect a trace of hopefulness in the way she says this.

Do they sell the things they make? Oh yes, and if we wish to buy, some will be put on the shelf. And presently a box of wax flowers is pushed slowly around—pansies and camelias and roses, white and red, exquisitely wrought. How much? For the roses five or six cents apiece; for the pansies three. And, after getting change for the price of our souvenirs, she is distressed that we will not take the two or three coppers that are due us.

It is late in the afternoon when we go again through the narrow hall to the door, yet we must have a look at the chapel on the other side. So through another long passage we follow our guide, and into the rather empty, dreary, and bare edifice, where a candle or two burn dimly, and we can just make out the figures of a few bead-telling worshippers. As we stand silent a sound—a song(?)—a dirge sweeps through the gloom from somewhere behind the altar and beyond the knowable. It sinks and swells in its inexpressible mournfulness, as waves might beat on a desolate shore. It is the call—the cry—the chant of the Carmelite nuns.

Duncan Campbell Scott

(1862–1947)

BORN INTO A METHODIST MINISTER'S FAMILY IN OTTAWA, D.C. Scott attended school at Smiths Falls, Ontario, and in Stanstead, Quebec. In 1879, he entered the Indian Branch of the federal civil service, rose to become Deputy Superintendent of Indian Affairs in 1923, and retired in 1932. A 1905 trip to James Bay as Commissioner for the area resulted in an insightful journal of his observations; and many of his best poems and some of his stories drew on Indian themes, shifting Canadian literary representations of Indian culture away from noble savage stereotypes. Committed to tradition and to a doctrine that equated art with a quest for beauty, he was nonetheless articulate about the inevitable, necessary changes taking place in poetic form, especially during World War I. His presidential address to the Royal Society in 1922, called "Poetry and Progress," meditates on what these tensions between belief and literary method meant to him. His first collection of poetry appeared in 1893, and several others followed over the next five decades. Scott was also a biographer and novelist; he wrote sketches for the "At the Mermaid Inn" column of the *Globe* during 1892–93; and his letters to the critic E.K. Brown reveal the aesthetic aspirations of his later years.

His first collection of stories, a unified work called *In the Village of Viger* (1896), mistakenly won him a reputation as a bucolic regionalist, the elegist of a dying French Canadian culture. But he was more properly read as a psychological realist, subtly modifying the conventional forms of storytelling in order to make them tell a different-from-conventional story. His French Canada was not idyllic, for all its embrace of folktale and myth; Scott recognized the forms for what they are: not quaint or unsophisticated fictions but sophisticated patterns of reality. In his second collection, *The Witching of Elspie* (1923), appeared a variety of stories ranging in form from the title folktale to "Labrie's Wife," a consciously crafted fictional documentary journal, which reveals the blindness of the first-person narrator/journalist to what he sees and what he writes, and his blundering stupidity about what he does. Scott's last volume, *The Circle of Affection* (1947), was a miscellaneous gathering of previously uncollected poems and prose.

For Further Reading

ALLAN DOUGLAS BRODIE, "Canadian Short-Story Writers," *Canadian Magazine* 4.4 (February 1895): 334–44.

STAN DRAGLAND, *Floating Voice: Duncan Campbell Scott and the Literature of Treaty 9* (Concord, Ont.: Anansi, 1994).

KLAY DYER, "Passing Time and Present Absence: Looking to the Future in *In the Village of Viger,*" *Canadian Literature* 141 (Summer 1994): 86–106.

CAROLE GERSON, "The Piper's Forgotten Tune," *Journal of Canadian Fiction* 16 (1976): 138–43.

Labrie's Wife

[BEING AN EXCERPT FROM THE MANUSCRIPT JOURNAL OF
ARCHIBALD MUIR, CLERK OF THE HONOURABLE THE HUD-
SON'S BAY COMPANY, AT NEPIGON HOUSE IN THE YEAR OF
OUR LORD 1815.]

May Twenty-second, 1815

Today something happened which is bound to be of consequence in this outlandish place, and that I will set down here and make of record. Alec, who is getting more gumption now, although as unsteady in all his performances as he was ever, returned from his trip to the Flat Rock, and arrived safe with his two canoes and Ogemah-ga-bow, little Needic and his two sons. It appears they had, by reason of the rough weather, to lay by at Dry Beaver Islands and had like to have starved if the wind had not gone down, for these fools of Indians will never learn not to devour half their rations in the first day out from the Post. They came in looking like wasps, their belts girt so tightly about their middles.

I could tell the moment I clapped eyes upon Alec that he had some bee in his bonnet, for he can no more control his countenance than an otter can help fishing. His face was all of a jump, and he spoke as if he had no spittal under his tongue. I have a plan to let the youngster speak when he is ready, and by this means I have the enjoyment of witnessing him cast about to get me to question him and assist him out with his story. When we were having a bit of dinner he fairly simmered, but he did not boil until I lit my pipe. Then he could stand my coolness no longer.

"We're to have an opposition!" he blurted out. I did not want to show any astonishment, but I nearly dropped my pipe, such a matter never having been thought of in the Nepigon before. "You see," he went on, "I determined when I was at that part of the lake to go over to Keg Island and see if the cache was all right, and on St. Paul's Island, when we went ashore to roast some fish, we found two canoes loaded, and a Frenchman and three Indians."

"He asked me if I was with the English, and I lied to him straight enough, and said No! I was trading alone. Then he wanted to know where our Post was, and I said it was beyond the large island to the west. He said his name was Labrie, and that he was for the North West Company, and was sent in opposition to the English on the lake. So I decided to camp where I was, and not to go to Keg Island, but to come on here. I told him to keep due west, and not to land until he struck the big island, which was Cariboo Island, and not for any reason to camp on a little flat island half way there, which was full of snakes."

The youngster was mighty proud of himself at outwitting the Frenchman, but,

From *The Witching of Elspie* (Toronto: McClelland and Stewart, 1923). Reprinted by permission of The Canadian Publishers McClelland and Stewart Ltd.

to take down his pride a bit, I provoked him by saying, "Well, poor Donald used to call you a clavering idiot, but if he had lived to this day he'd have had to invent a new kind of word for you. If your Labrie is anything of a trader he watched you away in the morning, and he will treat us in good Hudson's Bay Company rum when we first meet, having visited your little flat island full of snakes." Off went Alec trying to bite his beard, aping Donald's manner, poor lad; but he has yet a beard no longer than a pinfeather.

May Twenty-third, 1815

I was up before sun this day, as I had a restless night, thinking what I should do now we were to have opposition on the lake, a thing new to me who have scant experience. I determined to be smooth with them and observe them closely, and spoil them if I might with a fair face, and in all events to fight them with what weapons they may choose. I had wakened from a light doze with the sudden thought that I should possess myself of the point of land below the Post where I have always said the buildings should have been placed, which commands and oversees our present position. If it were seized by these pirates of Frenchmen, what then would become of our trade? They would eat it like a bear eats honey-comb. Alec could not see that, and provoked me with much grumbling that it was a useless work and a weary waste of muscle. It is curious how blockheaded he is about all matters connected with trade: he has some acuteness belike but of what sort God alone knows. In the end I was mightily satisfied to see a stout staff with the ensign flying, and a small boat-landing, with one of the boats moored. We had the work done before mid-day, and for the rest of the time I had pleasure in looking down at the point which had an inhabited and secure look, under the Hudson's Bay Company's flag. If the Frenchmen have any idea of the shore about here there will be some *sacréing* when they find the point taken up, for northwards there is no place for a foothold, and only in a cove, half a mile to the south, can they find level land enough for building upon. So when our Indians come down, and they should be here in a matter of four weeks, they are bound to reach the Post first, and I can keep my eye upon the rascals, who would, if they could, trade with the newcomers and forget old kindnesses and obligations.

May Twenty-fourth, 1815

Ogemah-ga-bow came up to say that one of Needic's boys had died last night, having over-eaten himself after his fast on the Dry Beaver Islands. Rain to-day.

May Twenty-sixth, 1815

Sun-down yesterday on my bench before the door, whereby Needic had made a smudge to keep off the flies, which are now very bad, when I saw a canoe that was none of ours land at the point, and a man step out onto the new boat landing. He looked all about him as if he was making an inventory of the place, and then he came slowly up the hill. He was a stout-shouldered, low-set fellow, with a black beard and small, bad eyes. Said I to myself as I saw him approach, "There is something mainly dishonest in your make-up, my man, and whatever one may have to do to keep trade from you it won't be very savoury in the doing if your methods are to be used."

"My name's Labrie," he said, running his hand through his hair.

I got upon my legs and said politely, "I heard of your being in the Lake from my man. Will you be seated?"

He said "No" and looked over his shoulder at the Point.

"You have the Point under your flag," he remarked.

"Aye," I said, as dry as I could.

"The work has marks of newness."

"You are right, it was only finished yesterday."

The blood came into his face in an ugly way.

"Well, there can be no great objection to my trading a little."

"Not there," said I bluntly. "Under my company's flag what we take we claim and keep."

He breathed rather heavily, but held his tongue, and was going to walk away.

"Hold on," said I, "strangers are not treated so here, you must have a dram."

I called Alec, who brought the rum and the glasses. We drank healths courteously, that were ready to cut one another's throats.

"Did you ever taste better than that?" said I.

"I have as good," said he, "though it is the best I can match it."

"Match it!" said I in a tone of surprise, winking at Alec, who flew as red as a bubble jock. We parted then but just as he was getting away he said over his shoulder, "Your man there has a damned queer idea of direction."

May Twenty-seventh, 1815

Sent Needic and his live boy and Ogemah-ga-bow's brother to Poplar Lodge, to have news of the hunters. The Osnaburgh packs from the north should now be two weeks out, unless the ice is later this year than last. To-morrow I will put Alec and Ogemah-ga-bow to work clearing out the storehouse and setting things to rights. I am much exercised in mind over my responsibilities. It was bad enough last year, but now I have the whole management, and this opposition to contend with upon the back of it. I begin to be worn with it, what with loss of sleep at night, and thinking about nought else in the day. No sign of Labrie or any of his party.

May Thirtieth, 1815

This morning Labrie came up to borrow an adze, which I lent to him without any question. He seemed to want to be civil enough. When I asked him, however, if Madame Labrie had arrived, he seemed quite put about and mumbled something in his beard, which sounded nearly like "What affair is that of yours?" I paid no attention to him, not wishing to quarrel yet awhile, and without any further parley off he went with the adze, which I am fortunate if I ever see again.

Heat intense to-day, bringing on a great storm of thunder and much rain. Had a great debate with Alec, when we were indoors, as to when the Osnaburgh packs will be in. I calculate in three weeks, as the water is like to be high, they will take the route through Mud Lakes to Negodina, as I wrote Godfrey. The old route to Wabinosh would take them much longer and, what with broken water and two desperate, long carries, there is a great risk of loss by that way. Alec thinks they will be down sooner. There is no doubt they have had a fine winter and if the pack can be safely landed it will be a great matter, and no doubt I shall hear good of it from the partners.

May Thirty-first, 1815

This morning when I was cleaning my pistols I heard a clear sound of laughter. Now laughter is an uncommon thing in this country, visiting us very infrequently. To be sure the Indians laugh, but that to me always has an unmeaning sound, and sometimes a bestial. Moreover, this laughter was different in kind, and one must have listened to it however absorbed he might have been. It was high-pitched and very clear and had something merry and withal innocent about it. It was contagious also and the mere sound of it made my very muscles twitch. There was no one visible, but after I had gazed awhile I saw Alec come up the steps from the warehouse. Not to appear interested before the lad I went back to my work. After a little he came in. I noticed his face was flushed and his manner excited. I paid no attention to him until he had knocked a dish off the table. It broke into three pieces. I was angry with him, good crockery not being by any means very plentiful in this country.

"Good God, man!" I cried. "If you're in such a state that you cannot avoid breaking the dishes, will you lie upon your bed for a while." He glared at me terribly, but had not a word to say. Then I kept quiet for as much as a quarter of an hour, and I could see it was fretting him; he fidgeted about greatly. Then he got up and went to the door.

"It seems to me you take mighty small interest in things."

I said never a word.

"Are you deaf this morning?"

I made no sound. He made no move for a minute, then he said, just as he was going out of the door, in an exasperated way, "That was Labrie's wife."

I could have laughed to myself, but when I had thought upon it for a time I began to perceive something bitter in his tone, and I reflected that of late I had treated him much as poor Donald used unthinkingly to treat me, and that he must be occupying my old position of complaint, and my heart was softened a bit, and I resolved to be more kind to him in future, who is in much a good boy and canny in a sort about many things.

June First, 1815

I saw Labrie's wife for the first time this morning. An uncommon looking wench, with black hair and eyes and a mouthful of white teeth. I discussed her thoroughly with Alec, who sticks up for it that she is a handsome one. So she is, after her manner, though that I do not acknowledge to Alec. She looked me all over as if I were for sale, and when I coolly turned my back on her, that she might have a good look at that, she went off in a mighty huff.

Alec reports that there are two other women in Labrie's party, rather old and haggish. I have not clapped eyes upon them, not having visited the Cove. Although she went off in a huff, the young wench is a merry one, and it amuses her to hear Alec so aboundingly polite to her with his "Madame Labrie." "Madame Labrie" this and "Madame Labrie" that, whereupon she giggles or breaks out into wild laughter.

June Third, 1815

Needic back from Poplar Lodge, where everything is all right. Had an amusing conversation with the lad Alec anent Labrie's wife. The huzzy comes about the house constantly, even when we are not here.

"Now what is she after?" said I.

"You have no understanding of women," he replied. "Of course she will come back when you treat her in that way."

"Now in what way?" said I. "Never do I look at her or pass the time of day with her."

"That is it," he retorts. "You are fairly insulting her, and she comes back."

"Do you try and be sweet to her and mayhap she would stay away."

"It is different with me," he says, biting his whiskers (?) and shrugging up his shoulders, just as the wench does herself. He has taken on a sort of mincing, balancing, half-Frenchified accent, and shrugs his shoulders.

"Are you afrait she would fall into the love weez you, Alec?" I remarked, trying hard to imitate the accent.

"It is not me she will be in love with."

"No, who then? Needic?"

"Needic!" he cried, going off with a great French shrug.

June Fourth, 1815

No word from Godfrey about the packs. I am getting a trifle anxious. Alec says there are more guns than yardsticks in Labrie's quarters, and makes out they are on for a fight. Labrie's wife came up at noon and made us an omelette with gull's eggs and fresh onion-tops. She is a clever wench and sat looking at me as I devoured it. I talked a bit to her. After she left, Alec sat frowning.

"You were very free with her."

"I merely spoke to her, but then she made a good omelette."

"You said too much to her. You nearly told her we expected the packs at Negodina by the Mud Lake route this year instead of Wabinosh."

"Well, and if I did?"

"It is all she wanted to know."

"Well, you seem to be always ready to stand up for the spy, if she be one," said I, turning the French accent upon him. This made him wroth, as it always does.

"You never seem to understand that a woman's not like a man. The best of them you have to watch, and more particularly when one of them is in love with you."

"That does not apply here," I said, "unless you have her assurances yourself."

"I would not make love to a married woman," he said hotly.

"That's why you guard yourself so carefully, is it? You are mighty pious. It is a pity you are not like me. Now for me, Mr. Labrie's wife has no attraction whatever, commandments or no commandments."

This set him off again.

"Be careful you, Archibald Muir, that is what I have to say to you."

We could hear the lady herself laughing down at the landing, and it sounded so innocent that I could not refrain from smiling at the boy.

June Fifth, 1815

We had a scene last night with Labrie's wife, for which Alec has to be thanked, and in which I think he had a small revenge for my baiting of him. I will set down the occurrence here although it be against myself, and our national instrument. She had been hardly before the house, and it was in the dusk of the evening, when she asked me to play upon the pipes.

"Will you play upon the bag-pipes, Mr. Muir?" she said in a very civil voice. "I have never heard the bag-pipes."

Now I am always at pains to oblige a lady, if it be possible, so I went in and got the pipes, hearing Alec urge me also, so I had two willing to be pleased.

Well, scarcely had I begun to get the skin filled with wind when Labrie's wife began to laugh. Now I am willing to admit that the foreword to a performance on the pipes may be dispiriting, but I charge that what follows after when the instrument is well controlled, and when the melody pours forth in full cry, would serve to obliterate a greatly more dispiriting prelude. But in this case I did not get beyond that stage, for Labrie's wife laughed with so little judgment that I was put about. I saw something in Alec's face which led me to think that the whole matter was preconceived by him, and with that I laid down my pipes on the bench beside me. Not another note would I play. I am not much versed in women's ways, and what Labrie's wife did puzzled me. But of that I shall give Alec's explanation. At first she kept on laughing, and then she stopped suddenly and came forward looking sober enough, but with the wrinkles of the laughter not yet gone out of her face. There she stood about four feet from me with a bit of her dress in her hand, as I have seen school girls stand abashed having been found at fault.

"You are angry because I laughed?" she said.

I did not answer.

"Are you angry with me because I could not help laughing?"

I did not answer.

Then she came close to me and made as if to put her hands upon my shoulders, and when I looked straight upon her eyes she dropped her hands, made a sound in her throat, and turned and went away.

Then young Alec began to strut about like a bantam cock.

"I have to thank you for that performance," I said.

"Why would you prevent a woman from laughing?" says he, in a rage. "Don't you know enough of women to let them laugh and let them talk?"

"I can lay no claim to such a knowledge as yourself," said I, in a mighty sneering voice. "In truth I know naught about them."

"You have proved that this night," retorted Alec.

"Expound that, you young oracle," said I.

"Expound? You have sent her away with a sore heart, and she was minded to be playful with you, and that cuts sore on a heart such as hers. Don't you see it, man?" he cried, sort of dashing his hands down.

"I see nothing of the sort. She was angry simply because I wouldn't speak back to her."

"You might have spoken to her or not spoken, and she would never have minded if you hadn't looked at her in the way you did."

I saw it was no use my trying to fathom the young donkey, so I would speak no more to him.

June Sixth, 1815

Labrie's wife was up last night but I would not go out to see her, being tired of the body and her endless chatter. Alec and she talked for an hour; the boy would be contented to go on vapouring forever, I believe. I pretended to be busy with my papers, and in the end she went away. She came to the window just before she went, and I heard her fingers on the sash, but I did not look up, and I heard her low gurgling laugh as she ran away from Alec, who would go down to the landing with her.

He is as polite to her and as formal as if he were living by a code of court etiquette. I twitted him with that.

"Well," he says, mighty stiff, and pulling a solemn face, "she is a woman, and she is another man's wife."

"The last is her great virtue," said I, with a tone of sarcasm, at which he looked scornful and exceeding pious.

June Seventh, 1815

Good news yesterday. Toma came in with a message from Godfrey. The Osnaburgh packs are safe at Cache Point on the Mud Lake route. The water is high and they have not had a mishap. In three days they should reach Negodina at the end of the lake. It is, as I have always said, a route more clean and handy than the Wabinosh route, and it will be adopted now from this out.

June Eighth, 1815

Woke up with a mighty sore head this morning and had words with Alec. It is inconceivable how domineering that lad has become.

"You were drinking with Madame Labrie last night," he said.

"And my lord is jealous," I replied, sneering at him.

"Ye have made a fool of yourself. What did you tell her?"

"Nothing that I rightly remember. Since when were you ordained my catechist?"

"Now I have told you many times," he said in a parsoning way, "that you did not understand the nature of women, and that you would let slip something that Labrie wanted to know. Now you have done so, I believe, between a glass too much of whiskey and a pretty woman."

"Do you call yon a pretty woman?" I said, mocking his accent.

"I pity you!" he said, with great contempt.

He went away swinging his shoulders, much more the master than the man.

To set down the truth, although it be against myself, Labrie's wife came up in the evening of yesterday. I was more decent with the bitch having had the good news, and I treated her to some whiskey, and drank with her. Alec was off watching Toma, as he thought Labrie might try to get hold of him. I do not just remember when she went away. God forgive me, I do not rightly remember anything about it.

Hardly had Alec dismissed himself when he came back very greatly excited, but in anger this time.

"They have gone," said he.

"Who?" said I, not thinking for a moment.

"Who! My God! Who? Why, Labrie."

"Well, what of that?" I said. "It is a good riddance of a vile lot of thieves out of God's country."

"That is all you see to it?" he said.

"Well, what more?" I replied.

"I seem to see that last night you told Madame Labrie the packs were coming by the Mud Lake route to Negodina, and that they have gone to stop them. I have my doubt they will not barter with them. I seem to see that they will capture the furs and that by no very gentle means."

"You have said it before," I cried out, wroth with him and with myself. "So yon slut is what I have always supposed her to be."

A dark look came into his face. "Choose your words!" he cried, taking a step towards me.

"I'll neither pick nor choose my words," I said. "What do you call her then that would take our hospitality and then do us wrong?"

"Madaline would do no such thing," he cried, strutting about in a way that looked comical to me. I laughed at him.

"Madaline! Madaline! We shall see what Madaline will have done when we lose our furs. Why, man, you said out of your own mouth that she had done it."

"You lie," he cried, but it was here not impudence, so I paid no attention to him.

After some parley and conversation, I sent him with three canoes and all the able men, except Needic, to Negodina to see what had fallen out. He is to send me back a letter, as soon as he can, with the word. I am here now quite alone, and in mind very much put about. I have been striving to recall what passed between Labrie's wife and myself, but without any clear recollection. Ah, those women! I well remember my father used to say, "At the bottom of every trouble, there you will find a woman," and my mother used to retort, "And likewise at the bottom of every happiness." Whereupon he would kiss her.

June Tenth, 1815

Last night—waiting for word from Alec. This morning I went down to Labrie's camp with Needic. They had left two tents and some rubbish, and a little green box marked "M. L." Turning the lot over I found two empty kegs marked "H. B. Co.," once full of rum, which they had stolen from the cache on Keg Island. So we heaped all together and set fire to it. It burned merrily, and they are at least by that much the poorer.

June Eleventh, 1815

I am in great spirits today. Last night I was wakened by Needic, who had his boy with him. Everything had reached Negodina safely, and there was no sign anywhere of Labrie's party. They will push on at once.

June Twelfth, 1815

This morning Labrie came back. Needic came up and told me, so about noon I took my pistols and went down with him to the cove. They had one tent up and the women were making the fire. The men went off and none of them would speak to us. I stood smiling in a taunting way, and just as I was about to leave, Labrie's wife came over to me. I perceived she had her arm wound in a cloth.

"Well, Madame Labrie, how did you hurt your arm?"

"Why do you call me Madame Labrie?"

"One must call you something. My boy Alec calls you Madaline."

Her face grew a darker red.

"You have been away for a while?"

"Yes," she said, "we were at Wabinosh, and I see you burned my box when I was gone.

"Were you ever in love?" she asked suddenly.

"Never," said I, "praise be to God."

"When you are I pray heaven you may be tortured in it."

"I am thankful for your good wishes."

"The other night you told me your packs were coming by Negodina. You understand? It was Labrie who shot me through the arm. He wanted to kill me for taking them to Wabinosh, but the others would not let him."

"The low rascal," I said, "to shoot a woman."

"And *you* have nothing to say about *me?*" She looked at me curiously, and put an odd emphasis on the *you* and the *me.*

"It is fortunate you made a mistake."

"A mistake!" said she. "Your boy Alec is twice the man that you are."

The huzzy said that with a fluff of pride.

"Good-bye," said I from my canoe.

"Is that all, Archibald Muir, is that all?"

"Good-bye," said I, "and I hope your husband won't shoot at you again."

I looked back when we had gone a bit, and she still stood there. She did not make any sign towards me, though I waved to her in courtesy. Then she covered up her face in her hands.

No word of Godfrey and Alec. I sent Needic to Labrie's wife with two gold guineas for the box I had burned, probably the only gold she ever clapped her eyes on, as it is unknown in this trade almost.

June Thirteenth, 1815

The packs came in yesterday evening. Godfrey and the men all well. I mixed a keg of spirits for them and they made a hideous night of it. Too busy to write much now, but can do nothing more to-night. Looking back in the store ledgers I can see no such winter's catch. Great good luck. Labrie's party still hanging around. Alec went down as soon as he got back, and stayed longer than he ought, so I berated him soundly. To-night at supper he said;

"Labrie shot her through the arm because she had taken them to Wabinosh and had misled them."

I paid no attention to him. By and by he said:

"You will be glad to know that she says you told her nothing about the packs."

"Did she?" said I, puzzled, as she had told me the contrary.

"I don't believe her," he added.

"You're complimentary to the ladies," I remarked.

"Here is something she asked me to give you."

It was the money I had sent her for that box of hers I burnt.

June Fourteenth, 1815

Busy all day between the storehouse and the fur press. Half the Indians are drunk yet. Alec says Labrie and his party have gone. May the devil's luck go with them. I thought Alec looked a trifle white in the face, and as if he was impatient to make me talk, but I had no time to be spending with him.

June Fifteenth, 1815

A wonderfully warm day, and the flies very bad, enough to madden one. Have pressed all the packs and now everything is in order for a move. What a grand night for the partners it will be when they see our canoes full of the finest come to land at Fort William. It should be of profit to me, and I expect to come back here or go somewhere a factor, if I comprehend the rules properly. About an hour ago I had just finished writing the last words when Alec's shadow came over the window. He seemed to stand there over long, and I was just on the point of crying out to him when he moved off. In a moment he came in to me. I did not look up from my writing when he flung a scrap of paper down before me.

"There!" he said, in an odd voice. "I found it under the sash. It fell face down, so, as I saw printing on the back, I thought it was but a scrap torn off a fur bill."

"Read it," said he.

I turned it over and observed that there were some words in writing on the other side. I made them out to be: "Why do you call me Labrie's wife? She is my aunt. Do you think I would marry an ugly fellow like Labrie. They brought me up here to help their plans. We shall see. If you want to know my name it's Madaline Lesage. I learned to write from the Sister St. Theresa at Wikwemikong. Is it not pretty? M. L."

Then I recalled how she had come to the window, one night not very long ago, when I opine she had left the paper there.

"Well?" I said coolly, "and what is it now that you have to say about Madaline Lesage?"

His face had a tortured look upon it. He tried to speak. "She was—she was the bravest, the dearest"—he stopped there and hung down his head. "Oh, my God, you cannot understand. You can never understand!"

He moved away and stood by the door. I thought upon what he had said. No, I did not understand. Then I tried once more to go on with my page. But I was detained by a sound which is as uncommon as that of laughter in these outlandish parts. The sound of sobbing. Just for a moment it brought back to me the sound of my sister's voice as she sobbed for her lover when they brought him back dead and dripping out of the sea. I had a vision of it as if it were snapped upon my eye in a flash of lightning, she leaning her forehead upon her wrists against the wall. I looked up at Alec and there he was leaning at the door-post, his shoulders all moving with his sobs. I understood in a flash. I pray God to forgive me for the sin of blindness, and for always being so dead to others in my own affairs. I went towards him knowing that I could not give him any comfort. So he went out from the house and walked alone through the gloaming. I perceived that a change had come over him. I had always considered him a bit of a boy to be ordered about, but there was a man walking away from me, resolute in his steps, big in his bulk, and weighed down as if he was carrying a load, bearing it as if he were proud of it, with energy and trust in himself.

Stephen Leacock

(1869–1944)

BORN IN SWANMOOR, HANTS., ENGLAND, Stephen Butler Leacock moved to Canada when his parents emigrated to the Lake Simcoe area in 1876; "I decided to accompany them," he wrote in an autobiographical sketch, with characteristic understatement. His father later left the family, leaving Leacock's mother to bring up eleven children. Leacock himself, educated at Upper Canada College and the University of Toronto, subsequently went on to study political economy under Thorstein Veblen at the University of Chicago, receiving his doctorate in 1903 and moving to Montreal, where he became a professor of economics and political science at McGill. While he published a number of works in economic and social history—including a highly successful political science text—he rapidly became known as a comic lecturer and writer, winning a huge international readership.

His sketches appeared in *Grip, Saturday Night,* and elsewhere, before he collected them into his more than thirty books. Among these are *Literary Lapses* (1910), *Nonsense Novels* (1911), *Arcadian Adventures with the Idle Rich* (1914), and—a work based loosely on his Orillia background—*Sunshine Sketches of a Little Town* (1912). Influenced by Dickens and Twain, Leacock nonetheless shaped his own characteristic humorous style; delighting in puns and incremental, farcical repetitions, he manipulated oral anecdotes towards absurd climax and crashingly deliberate anticlimaxes. And he wrote several illuminating essays on the social basis of humour. Apparently gentle, much of his writing has a sharp sting to it. When he parodied romance conventions, as in "Hannah of the Highlands" (from *Saturday Night,* 1910, collected in *Nonsense Novels*) or when he told extended pseudological, pseudoscientific anecdotes, as in "The Retroactive Existence of Mr. Juggins" (from *Behind the Beyond,* 1913), he was exposing what he saw as the absurdities of human behaviour and not just exaggerating human foible. But the bitter edge that surfaces in some of his writing is less evident here; for all their explicit violence and implicit criticism, these stories—especially if heard aloud—ultimately dissolve into amiable nonsense.

For Further Reading

CARL BERGER, "The Other Mr. Leacock," *Canadian Literature* 55 (Winter 1973): 23–40.

ALAN BOWKER, ed., *The Social Criticism of Stephen Leacock* (Toronto: U Toronto P, 1973), "Introduction" ix-xlviii.

D.A. CAMERON, *Faces of Leacock* (Toronto: Ryerson, 1967).

ROBERTSON DAVIES, *Stephen Leacock* (Toronto: McClelland & Stewart, 1970).

Hannah of the Highlands: or The Laird of Loch Aucherlocherty

Sair maun ye greet, but hoot awa!
There's muckle yet, love isna' a'—
Nae more ye'll see, howe'er ye whine
The bonnie breeks of Auld Lang Syne!

The simple words rang out fresh and sweet upon the morning air.

It was Hannah of the Highlands. She was gathering lobsters in the burn that ran through the Glen.

The scene about her was typically Highland. Wild hills rose on both sides of the burn to a height of seventy-five feet, covered with a dense Highland forest that stretched a hundred yards in either direction. At the foot of the burn a beautiful Scotch loch lay in the hollow of the hills. Beyond it again, through the gap of the hills, was the sea. Through the Glen, and close beside the burn where Hannah stood, wound the road that rose again to follow the cliffs along the shore.

The tourists in the Highlands will find no more beautiful spot than the Glen of Aucherlocherty.

Nor is there any spot which can more justly claim to be historic ground.

It was here in the Glen that Bonnie Prince Charlie had lain and hidden after the defeat of Culloden. Almost in the same spot the great boulder still stands behind which the Bruce had lain hidden after Bannockburn; while behind a number of lesser stones the Covenanters had concealed themselves during the height of the Stuart persecution.

Through the Glen Montrose had passed on his fateful ride to Killiecrankie; while at the lower end of it the rock was still pointed out behind which William Wallace had paused to change his breeches while flying from the wrath of Rob Roy.

Grim memories such as these gave character to the spot.

Indeed, most of the great events of Scotch history had taken place in the Glen, while the little loch had been the scene of some of the most stirring naval combats in the history of the Grampian Hills.

But there was little in the scene which lay so peaceful on this April morning to recall the sanguinary history of the Glen. Its sides at present were covered with a thick growth of gorse, elderberry, egg-plants, and ghillie flower, while the woods about it were loud with the voice of the throstle, the linnet, the magpie, the jackdaw, and other song-birds of the Highlands.

It was a gloriously beautiful Scotch morning. The rain fell softly and quietly,

From *Nonsense Novels* (Toronto: John Lane, 1911). Reprinted by permission of The Canadian Publishers McClelland and Stewart Ltd.

bringing dampness and moisture, and almost a sense of wetness to the soft moss underfoot. Grey mists flew hither and thither, carrying with them an invigorating rawness that had almost a feeling of dampness.

It is the memory of such a morning that draws a tear from the eye of Scotchmen after years of exile. The Scotch heart, reader, can be moved to its depths by the sight of a raindrop or the sound of a wet rag.

And meantime Hannah, the beautiful Highland girl, was singing. The fresh young voice rose high above the rain. Even the birds seemed to pause to listen, and as they listened to the simple words of the Gaelic folk song, fell off the bough with a thud on the grass.

The Highland girl made a beautiful picture as she stood.

Her bare feet were in the burn, the rippling water of which laved her ankles. The lobsters played about her feet, or clung affectionately to her toes, as if loath to leave the water and be gathered in the folds of her blue apron.

It was a scene to charm the heart of a Burne-Jones, or an Alma Tadema, or of anybody fond of lobsters.

The girl's golden hair flowed widely behind her, gathered in a single braid with a piece of stovepipe wire.

'Will you sell me one of your lobsters?'

Hannah looked up. There, standing in the burn a few yards above her, was the vision of a young man.

The beautiful Highland girl gazed at him fascinated.

He seemed a higher order of being.

He carried a fishing-rod and basket in his hand. He was dressed in a salmon-fishing costume of an English gentleman. Salmon-fishing boots reached to his thighs, while above them he wore a fishing-jacket fastened loosely with a fishing-belt about his waist. He wore a small fishing-cap on his head.

There were no fish in his basket.

He drew near to the Highland girl.

Hannah knew as she looked at him that it must be Ian McWhinus, the new laird.

At sight she loved him.

'Ye're sair welcome,' she said, as she handed to the young man the finest of her lobsters.

He put it in his basket.

Then he felt in the pocket of his jacket and brought out a sixpenny piece.

'You must let me pay for it,' he said.

Hannah took the sixpence and held it a moment, flushing with true Highland pride.

'I'll no be selling the fush for money,' she said.

Something in the girl's speech went straight to the young man's heart. He handed her half a crown. Whistling lightly, he strode off up the side of the burn. Hannah stood gazing after him spellbound. She was aroused from her reverie by an angry voice calling her name.

'Hannah, Hannah,' cried the voice, 'come away ben; are ye daft, lass, that ye stand there keeking at a McWhinus?'

Then Hannah realized what she had done.

She had spoken with a McWhinus, a thing that no McShamus had done for a hundred and fifty years. For nearly two centuries the McShamuses and the McWhinuses, albeit both dwellers in the Glen, had been torn asunder by one of those painful divisions by which the life of the Scotch people is broken into fragments.

It had arisen out of a point of spiritual belief.

It had been six generations agone at a Highland banquet, in the days when the unrestrained temper of the time gave way to wild orgies, during which the theological discussions raged with unrestrained fury. Shamus McShamus, an embittered Calvinist, half crazed perhaps with liquor, had maintained that damnation could be achieved only by faith. Whimper McWhinus had held that damnation could be achieved also by good works. Inflamed with drink, McShamus had struck McWhinus across the temple with an oatcake and killed him. McShamus had been brought to trial. Although defended by some of the most skilled lawyers of Aucherlocherty, he had been acquitted. On the very night of his acquittal, Whangus McWhinus, the son of the murdered man, had lain in wait for Shamus McShamus, in the hollow of the Glen road where it rises to the cliff, and had shot him through the bagpipes. Since then the feud had raged with unquenched bitterness for a century and a half.

With each generation the difference between the two families became more acute. They differed on every possible point. They wore different tartans, sat under different ministers, drank different brands of whisky, and upheld different doctrines in regard to eternal punishment.

To add to the feud the McWhinuses had grown rich, while the McShamuses had become poor.

At least once in every generation a McWhinus or a McShamus had been shot, and always at the turn of the Glen road where it rose to the edge of the cliff. Finally, two generations gone, the McWhinuses had been raised to sudden wealth by the discovery of a coal mine on their land. To show their contempt for the McShamuses they had left the Glen to live in America. The McShamuses, to show their contempt for the McWhinuses, had remained in the Glen. The feud was kept alive in their memory.

And now the descendant of the McWhinuses had come back, and bought out the property of the Laird of Aucherlocherty beside the Glen. Ian McWhinus knew nothing of the feud. Reared in another atmosphere, the traditions of Scotland had no meaning for him. He had entirely degenerated. To him the tartan had become only a piece of coloured cloth. He wore a kilt as a masquerade costume for a Hallowe'en dance, and when it rained he put on a raincoat. He was no longer Scotch. More than that, he had married a beautiful American wife, a talcum-powder blonde with a dough face and the exquisite rotundity of the packing-house district of the Middle-West. Ian McWhinus was her slave. For her sake he had bought the lobster from Hannah. For her sake, too, he had scrutinized closely the beautiful Highland girl, for his wife was anxious to bring back a Scotch housemaid with her to Chicago.

And meantime Hannah, with the rapture of a new love in her heart, followed her father, Oyster McOyster McShamus, to the cottage. Oyster McOyster, even in advancing age, was a fine specimen of Scotch manhood. Ninety-seven years of age, he was approaching the time when many of his countrymen begin to show the ravages of time. But he bore himself straight as a lath, while his tall stature and his native Highland costume accentuated the fine outline of his form. This costume consisted of a black velvet beetle-shell jacket, which extended from the shoulder halfway down the back, and was continued in a short kilt of the tartan of the McShamuses, which extended from the waist halfway to the thigh. The costume reappeared again after an interval in the form of rolled golf stockings, which extended halfway up to the knee, while on his feet a pair of half-shoes were buckled halfway up with a Highland clasp. On his head halfway between the ear and the upper superficies of the skull he wore half a Scotch cap, from which a tall rhinoceros feather extended halfway into the air.

A pair of bagpipes were beneath his arm, from which, as he walked, he blew those deep and plaintive sounds which have done much to imprint upon the characters of those who hear them a melancholy and resigned despair.

At the door of the cottage he turned and faced his daughter.

"What said Ian McWhinus to you i' the burnside?" he said fiercely.

"'Twas nae muckle,' said Hannah, and she added, for the truth was ever more to her than her father's wrath, 'he gi'ed me a saxpence for a fush.'

'Siller!' shrieked the Highlander. 'Siller from a McWhinus!'

Hannah handed him the sixpence. Oyster McOyster dashed it fiercely on the ground, then picking it up he dashed it with full force against the wall of the cottage. Then, seizing it again he dashed it angrily into the pocket of his kilt.

They entered the cottage.

Hannah had never seen her father's face so dour as it looked that night.

Their home seemed changed.

Hannah and her mother and father sat down that night in silence to their simple meal of oatmeal porridge and Scotch whisky. In the evening the mother sat to her spinning. Busily she plied her work, for it was a task of love. Her eldest born, Jamie, was away at college at Edinburgh, preparing for the ministry. His graduation day was approaching, and Jamie's mother was spinning him a pair of breeches against the day. The breeches were to be a surprise. Already they were shaping that way. Oyster McShamus sat reading the Old Testament in silence, while Hannah looked into the peat fire and thought of the beautiful young Laird. Only once the Highlander spoke.

'The McWhinus is back,' he said, and his glance turned towards the old flint-lock musket on the wall. That night Hannah dreamed of the feud, of the Glen and the burn, of love, of lobsters, and of the Laird of Loch Aucherlocherty. And when she rose in the morning there was a wistful look in her eyes, and there came no song from her throat.

The days passed.

Each day the beautiful Highland girl saw the young Laird, though her father knew it not.

In the mornings she would see him as he came fishing to the burn. At times he wore his fishing-suit, at other times he had on a knickerbocker suit of shepherd's plaid with a domino pattern *négligé* shirt. For his sake the beautiful

Highland girl made herself more beautiful still. Each morning she would twine a Scotch thistle in her hair, and pin a spray of burdock at her heart.

And at times he spoke to her. How Hannah treasured his words. Once, catching sight of her father in the distance, he had asked her who was the old sardine in the petticoats, and the girl had answered gladly that it was her father for, as a fisherman's daughter, she was proud to have her father mistaken for a sardine.

At another time he had asked her if she was handy about the work of the house. How Hannah's heart had beat at the question. She made up her mind to spin him a pair of breeches like the ones now finishing for her brother Jamie.

And every evening as the sun set Hannah would watch in secret from the window of the cottage waiting for the young Laird to come past in his motor car, down the Glen road to the sea. Always he would slacken the car at the sharp turn at the top of the cliff. For six generations no McWhinus had passed that spot after nightfall with his life. But Ian McWhinus knew nothing of the feud.

At times Oyster McOyster would see him pass, and standing at the roadside would call down Gaelic curses on his head.

Once, when her father was from home, Hannah had stood on the roadside, and Ian had stopped the machine and had taken her with him in the car for a ride. Hannah, her heart beating with delight, had listened to him as he explained how the car was worked. Had her father known that she had sat thus beside a McWhinus, he would have slain her where she sat.

The tragedy of Hannah's love ran swiftly to its close.

Each day she met the young Laird at the burn.

Each day she gave him the finest of her lobsters. She wore a new thistle every day.

And every night, in secret as her mother slept, she span a new concentric section of his breeches.

And the young Laird, when he went home, said to the talcum blonde, that the Highland fisher-girl was not half such a damn fool as she seemed.

Then came the fateful afternoon.

He stood beside her at the burn.

'Hannah,' he said, as he bent towards her, 'I want to take you to America.'

Hannah had fallen fainting in his arms.

Ian propped her against a tree, and went home.

An hour later, when Hannah entered her home, her father was standing behind the fireplace. He was staring fixedly into the fire, with the flint-lock musket in his hands. There was the old dour look of the feud upon his face, and there were muttered curses on his lips. His wife Ellen clung to his arm and vainly sought to quiet him.

'Curse him,' he muttered, 'I'll e'en kill him the night as he passes in his deil machine.'

Then Hannah knew that Oyster McShamus had seen her with Ian beside the burn. She turned and fled from the house. Straight up the road she ran towards the manor house of Aucherlocherty to warn Ian. To save him from her father's wrath, that was her one thought. Night gathered about the Highland girl as she ran. The rain clouds and the gathering storm hung low with fitful lightning overhead. She still ran on. About her was the rolling of the thunder and the angry roaring of the swollen burn. Then the storm broke upon the darkness with all the fury of the Highland gale. The sky was rent with the fierce play of the elements. Yet on Hannah ran. Again and again the lightning hit her, but she ran on still. She fell over the stones, tripped and stumbled in the ruts, butted into the hedges, cannoned off against the stone walls. But she never stopped. She went quicker and quicker. The storm was awful. Lightning, fire, flame, and thunder were all about her. Trees were falling, hurdles were flying, birds were being struck by lightning. Dogs, sheep, and even cattle were hurled through the air.

She reached the manor house, and stood a moment at the door. The storm had lulled, the rain ceased, and for a brief moment there was quiet. The light was streaming from the windows of the house. Hannah paused. Suddenly her heart misgave her. Her quick ear had caught the sound of a woman's voice within. She approached the window and looked in. Then, as if rooted to the spot, the Highland girl gazed and listened at the pane.

Ian lay upon a sofa. The *négligé* dressing-gown that he wore enhanced the pallid beauty of his face. Beside him sat the talcum-powder blonde. She was feeding him with chocolates. Hannah understood. Ian had trifled with her love. He had bought her lobsters to win her heart, only to cast it aside.

Hannah turned from the window. She plucked the thistle from her throat and flung it on the ground. Then, as she turned her eye, she caught sight of the motor standing in the shed.

'The deil machine!' she muttered, while the wild light of Highland frenzy gathered in her eye; then, as she rushed to it and tore the tarpaulin from off it, 'Ye'll no be wanting of a mark the night, Oyster McShamus,' she cried.

A moment later, the motor, with Hannah at the wheel, was thundering down the road to the Glen. The power was on to the full, and the demented girl clung tight to the steering-gear as the machine rocked and thundered down the descent. The storm was raging again, and the thunder mingled with the roar of the machine as it coursed madly towards the sea. The great eye of the motor blazed in front. The lurid light of it flashed a second on the trees and the burn as it passed, and flashed blinding on the eyes of Oyster as he stood erect on the cliff-side below, musket in hand, and faced the blazing apparition that charged upon him with the old Highland blood surging in his veins.

It was all over in a moment—a blinding flash of lightning, the report of a musket, a great peal of thunder, and the motor bearing the devoted girl hurled headlong over the cliff.

They found her there in the morning. She lay on her side motionless, half buried in the sand, upturned towards the blue Highland sky, serene now after the passing of the storm. Quiet and still she lay. The sea birds seemed to pause in their flight to look down on her. The little group of Scotch people that had gathered stood and gazed at her with reverential awe. They made no attempt to put her together. It would have been useless. Her gasoline tubes were twisted and bent, her tank burst, her sprockets broken from their sides, and her steering-gear an utter wreck. The motor would never run again.

After a time they roused themselves from their grief and looked about for Hannah. They found her. She lay among the sand and seaweed, her fair hair soaked in gasoline. Then they looked about for Oyster McShamus. Him, too, they found, lying half buried in the grass and soaked in whiskey. Then they looked about for Ellen. They found her lying across the door of the cottage half buried in Jamie's breeches.

Then they gathered them up. Life was not extinct. They chafed their hands. They rubbed their feet. They put hot bricks upon their stomachs. They poured hot whisky down their throats. That brought them to.

Of course.

It always does.

They all lived.

But the feud was done for. That was the end of it. Hannah had put it to the bad.

The Retroactive Existence of Mr. Juggins

I first met Juggins, really to notice him, years and years ago as a boy out camping. Somebody was trying to nail up a board on a tree for a shelf and Juggins interfered to help him.

"Stop a minute," he said, "you need to saw the end of that board off before you put it up." Then Juggins looked round for a saw, and when he got it he had hardly made more than a stroke or two with it before he stopped. "This saw," he said, "needs to be filed up a bit." So he went and hunted up a file to sharpen the saw, but found that before he could use the file he needed to put a proper handle on it, and to make a handle he went to look for a sapling in the bush, but to cut the sapling he found that he needed to sharpen up the axe. To do this, of course, he had to fix the grindstone so as to make it run properly. This involved making wooden legs for the grindstone. To do this decently Juggins decided to make a carpenter's bench. This was quite impossible without a better set of tools. Juggins went to the village to get tools, and, of course, he never came back.

He was re-discovered, weeks later, in the city, getting prices on wholesale tool machinery.

After that first episode I got to know Juggins very well. For some time we were students at college together. But Juggins somehow never got far with his

From *Behind the Beyond* (Toronto: John Lane, 1913). Reprinted by permission of The Canadian Publishers McClelland and Stewart Ltd.

studies. He always began with great enthusiasm and then something happened. For a time he studied French with tremendous eagerness. But he soon found that for a real knowledge of French you need first to get a thorough grasp of Old French and Provençal. It proved impossible to do anything with these without an absolutely complete command of Latin. This Juggins discovered could only be obtained, in any thorough way, through Sanskrit, which of course lies at the base of it. So Juggins devoted himself to Sanskrit until he realised that for a proper understanding of Sanskrit one needs to study the ancient Iranian, the root-language underneath. This language however is lost.

So Juggins had to begin over again. He did, it is true, make some progress in natural science. He studied physics and rushed rapidly backwards from forces to molecules, and from molecules to atoms, and from atoms to electrons, and then his whole studies exploded backward into the infinities of space, still searching a first cause.

Juggins, of course, never took a degree, so he made no practical use of his education. But it didn't matter. He was very well off and was able to go straight into business with a capital of about a hundred thousand dollars. He put it at first into a gas plant, but found that he lost money at that because of the high price of the coal needed to make gas. So he sold out for ninety thousand dollars and went into coal mining. This was unsuccessful because of the awful cost of mining machinery. So Juggins sold his shares in the mine for eighty thousand dollars and went in for manufacturing mining machinery. At this he would have undoubtedly made money but for the enormous cost of gas needed as motive-power for the plant. Juggins sold out of the manufacture for seventy thousand, and after that he went whirling in a circle, like skating backwards, through the different branches of allied industry.

He lost a certain amount of money each year, especially in good years when trade was brisk. In dull times when everything was unsaleable he did fairly well.

Juggins's domestic life was very quiet.

Of course he never married. He did, it is true, fall in love several times; but each time it ended without result. I remember well his first love story, for I was very intimate with him at the time. He had fallen in love with the girl in question utterly and immediately. It was literally love at first sight. There was no doubt of his intentions. As soon as he had met her he was quite frank about it. "I intend," he said, "to ask her to be my wife."

"When?" I asked; "right away?"

"No," he said, "I want first to fit myself to be worthy of her."

So he went into moral training to fit himself. He taught in a Sunday-school for six weeks, till he realised that a man has no business in Divine work of that sort without first preparing himself by serious study of the history of Palestine. And he felt that a man was a cad to force his society on a girl while he is still only half acquainted with the history of the Israelites. So Juggins stayed away. It was nearly two years before he was fit to propose. By the time he was fit, the girl had already married a brainless thing in patent leather boots who didn't even know who Moses was.

Of course Juggins fell in love again. People always do. And at any rate by this time he was in a state of moral fitness that made it imperative.

So he fell in love—deeply in love this time—with a charming girl, commonly known as the eldest Miss Thorneycroft. She was only called eldest because she had five younger sisters; and she was very poor and awfully clever and trimmed all her own hats. Any man, if he's worth the name, falls in love with that sort of thing at first sight. So, of course, Juggins would have proposed to her; only when he went to the house he met her next sister, who, of course, was younger still, and, I suppose, poorer, for she made not only her own hats but her own blouses. So Juggins fell in love with her. But one night when he went to call, the door was by the sister younger still, who not only made her own blouses and trimmed her own hats, but even made her own tailor-made suits. After that Juggins backed up from sister to sister till he went through the whole family, and in the end got none of them.

Perhaps it was just as well that Juggins never married. It would have made things very difficult because, of course, he got poorer all the time. You see, after he sold out his last share in his last business he bought with it a diminishing life annuity, so planned that he always got rather less next year than this year, and still less the year after. Thus, if he lived long enough, he would starve to death.

Meantime he has become a quaint-looking elderly man, with coats a little too short and trousers a little above his boots—like a boy. His face too is like that of a boy, with wrinkles.

And his talk now has grown to be always reminiscent. He is perpetually telling long stories of amusing times that he has had with different people that he names.

He says, for example—

"I remember a rather queer thing that happened to me in a train one day—"

And if you say "when was that, Juggins?" he looks at you in a vague way as if calculating and says, "In 1875, or 1876, I think, as near as I recall it."

I notice, too, that his reminiscences are going further and further back. He used to base his stories on his recollections as a young man, now they are further back.

The other day he told me a story about himself and two people that he called the Harper brothers, Ned and Joe. Ned, he said, was a tremendously powerful fellow.

I asked how old Ned was and Juggins said that he was three. He added that there was another brother not so old, but a very clever fellow about—here Juggins paused and calculated—eighteen months.

So then I realised where Juggins' retroactive existence is carrying him to. He has passed back through childhood into infancy, and presently, just as his annuity runs to a point and vanishes, he will back up clear through the Curtain of Existence and die, or be born, I don't know which to call it.

Meantime he remains to me as one of the most illuminating allegories I have met.

Jessie Georgina Sime

(1868–1958)

AVAILABLE INFORMATION CONCERNING J.G. SIME indicates that she was the daughter of writers and related both to the English novelist Mrs. Oliphant and to Sir Daniel Wilson, a principal of the University of Toronto. Born in Scotland, she grew up in London, was educated at home and at Queen's College, London, then studied music in Berlin for three years. After a short career as a singer, she helped her father as a reader for Macmillan's in London. She then began to write short stories, and between trips to France and Italy, reviewed for the *Athenaeum,* contributed a weekly column to the *Pall Mall Gazette,* and became a reader for Nelson and Co. in Edinburgh, sometimes using the pen name "Jacob Salviris." She moved to Canada in 1907, took up residence in Montreal, and began to publish a number of novels, essays, and biographical works, including *Rainbow Lights* (a transatlantic study of women). *The Mistress of All Work* (a 1916 pocket manual describing how the modern business woman can cope with practical problems of domestic life), *Canada Chaps* (1917), *Our Little Life* (1921, about immigrant life in Quebec), and *In a Canadian Shack* (1937, a series of sketches of life and character in rural "mountain" Quebec). One of her stories about Irish Catholic Montreal appeared in May Lamberton Becker's American anthology *Golden Tales of Canada* (1938). Among at least seven other books are two novels Sime wrote with her friend Frank Nicholson, *A Tale of Two Worlds* (1953) and *Inez and Her Angel* (1954). She was active in the Canadian Women's Press Club, the P.E.N. Clubs, and the Authors' Association. She returned to the U.K. after World War II.

But it is for her 1919 story collection *Sister Woman* that she now warrants closer attention. Cast as a frame tale, *Sister Woman* begins when a man asks his woman friend what it is that women are after, and why they won't just say what it is. The woman replies that she has to explain by means of stories, and the rest of the book unfolds as a demonstration by example. Skilled in the art of representing Scots and English dialect, Sime had her character tell of divorce, of cruelty in marriage, of single parenthood, of economic and social disparities, of alcoholism, motherhood, and stillbirth, and of a variety of problems involving immigrant attitudes. "Art" is one of the sketch-stories—or perhaps moral exempla—from this collection.

For Further Reading

SANDRA CAMPBELL, "'Gently Scan': Theme and Technique in J.G. Sime's *Sister Woman*," *Canadian Literature* 133 (Summer 1992): 40–52.

W.H. NEW, "Jessie Georgina Sime" in *Canadian Writers, 1890–1920, Dictionary of Literary Biography* 92 (Detroit: Gale, 1990) 356–61.

K. JANE WATT, "Introduction" to J.G. Sime, *Our Little Life: A Novel of Today* (rpt. Ottawa: Tecumseh, 1994) vii-xl.

Art

There is nothing so wearisome in all the wearisome possibilities of this world as to be talked to about Art. I dislike to be talked to about anything beginning with a capital letter—Love, Art, Vice—anything of that sort. The more people talk about such things the less do they do them; and unless you do a thing what can you possibly have to say that is worth listening to about it? I haven't known many criminals—to give them their technical name—but I'll be bound that if I did know them they wouldn't talk to me about Vice. They might spin me a yarn about housebreaking, perhaps, and very diverting it would be, but they wouldn't call it by the name of Vice. They would call it—whatever the slang for burglary may be. As to lovers—none that I have known ever talked of Love—while artists are generally too busy to be talking much at all. Art, indeed, may be described as a thing to be done and not talked about. I dare say the War will help it on its way—so far, at least, as not talking about it is concerned. But why, as Mr. Granville Barker says, worry with it at all? If it is there you can't miss it, and if it isn't there no talking about it will produce it. Let it take its chance with love—which is much in the same box.

This was not the point of view of Charlie Ralston when he came out to Canada—five or six years ago, before the War. How well I remember his advent among us—Charlie, pleasant-voiced, intensely and passionately interested in all sorts of things that didn't seem to the Canadians to matter, unpractical, artified to a degree, and with a way of saying: "Quite a charming person!" or "What a delicious little bit!" that set the Dominion's teeth on edge and made it writhe. Canada didn't like him. Oh, not at all; it didn't.

I am sorry to say he talked about Art. I hate to say or even to hint anything about my countrymen and countrywomen—of whom I am and want to be so proud; but when they come to Canada a demon seems to enter into them, and too often not one demon but seven demons; and nothing seems able to cast them out again. I mean the demons. Long ago in Paris, before we were at all popular there, it used to be pointed out to me that all Englishwomen had rabbit mouths, with teeth sticking out in front where no teeth should be. This I indignantly denied. But when the Parisians of those far-off days took me walking on the boulevards, lo! all the English we met *had* rabbit mouths with teeth sticking out in front. I can't explain it—so it was. And reluctantly I had to admit the fact. In Canada it isn't teeth that stick out of the English; it is opinions. Canadians (before the War, also when we were not so popular as we are today) used to point out to me the angularity and the Himalayan superiority of the English once they crossed the ocean. This, in the face of anecdote and even of proof, I indignantly denied. But when the Canadians took me walking on their wharves, lo! all the English, as they disembarked, *had* opinions sticking

From *Sister Woman* (London: Grant Richards Ltd., 1919).

out all over them where no opinions should be—chiefly opinions inimical to Canada and the Canadians. And these opinions they—the English—did not desist from mentioning until they reached the wharves to go away again. They were Pauline in their power of mentioning things in season and out of season. And the Canadians didn't—and don't now—like it at all.

Charlie Ralston was no exception to the rule. Once more I do not attempt any explanation. I merely mention. He went on talking about Art and why it wasn't in Canada and why it should be and what was the way to bring it there instanter, until the Canadians, if they weren't the most long-suffering people on earth, would have tarred and feathered him and sent him home with the freight unpaid. Being, as they are, *the* long-suffering people *par excellence,* they listened. They had lots of opportunity. When they asked Charlie to dinner he talked about Art. What Futurist music is and isn't. What is the reason of the Canadian being unable to understand it. Why he—and still more she—probably never will. And the pity of it. He talked. He did talk. Oh my, he talked a lot!

Once I remember sitting next to him at lunch. First he told me silly, would-be-funny stories of his landlady—"such a charming person!" And then he told me all the "little bits" he had been "jotting down." And then he told me things I couldn't understand—and wouldn't let me talk to anyone else. All in the name of Art. (What is it?) After lunch was over it was worse. He drew—yes, he did—from his pocket a slim book full of—imagine what! Aphorisms. Yes, aphorisms, as I'm a woman. And he read them. He read them all, and as they were pretty Futurist he had to act the meaning in a sort of drawing-room lecture. We sat round. Yes, we did. We sat there listening with a cerebral indigestion growing on the lot of us—don't tell me, after that, Canadians aren't a long-suffering race. He read them every one...he exhibited them internally, as doctors say.

R̶

La Rochefoucauld m̨ i

Aq.   Fill the bottle.

To be taken as directed after food.

That was the prescription.

Another time it was a play he read, one that "a manager" said was excellent. The first Act, said the manager, was something fine. Ditto the second. He didn't happen to be in want of plays just then, otherwise he would have——— Charlie read it to us. Well, we won't say anything more about it. It was a play. *Requiescat in pace,* and please not *resurgat!*

So Charlie Ralston was a bore, as will be seen. A bore of the first water. And yet Canada put up with him. He talked at it, he openly corrected it, he criticised its way of dress, its ways of speech, its ways of life—and Canada went on asking him to dinner. Canadians are a funny folk. Instead of turning on the English when they come and grow their rabbit teeth across the ocean, Canadians bear with them. The English criticise, find fault, put the Canadians in the corner; Canadians grumble, they don't like the drubbing—but they bear it. Whether the War will——— But that's not what I have to say. It's Charlie.

After a bit Charlie took up with a Canadian girl. She was pretty, not un-kindly, practical, with hands on her and no ideas to speak of. Good ground to clear and plough. I don't know what *she* saw in Charlie, unless it was his vio-let eyes, which should have been a girl's. Anyway, they were together as often as they could be—and people looked at them and said to one another: "Is there anything *in* it? Freda Wanham's gone on *him!*" She was. I met them on their way to somewhere once. She was fresh in her white frock, walking beside him as if he was the King. Why can a woman never hide her feelings if she loves a man—not from another woman anyway? Do men read men like that? There was in Freda's face that morning the look you can't mistake, that look of some-thing that's not far from adoration—her eyes were brimming, her cheeks were flushed, her body swayed towards his. And her little happy laugh rang out, that happy little laugh—not humorous at all—a woman has when she is walk-ing with the man she loves. Freda was very sweet that morning. She didn't even see me as I passed them—her eyes were seeking his.

Charlie didn't see me either. He was settled down with Charlie Ralston. He liked the pretty girl beside him, but his thoughts and aspirations were firmly on himself. He looked nice, good-looking, well-set-up. His tie was suitable. Under his arm, poor boy, was a Shelley or some such thing—I fancy he meant to read to her when their secluded spot was reached. Well, she could look at him as he was reading. I daresay she was happy.

That came to nothing. Freda's brother said that Charlie was "the Goddamnedest fool...!" That was his calm opinion—and the family more or less agreed. I don't know whether that influenced Freda or whether Charlie stuck to Shelley and didn't "handle" poetry as a matrimonial theme, but, anyway, Freda married someone else—a practical man who talked of Mergers, not of Art. I daresay Freda's safer with him than she would have been with Charlie. Marriages are ticklish things at any time, and international marriages are—well, they are dif-ficult. England and Canada are separated by more than water. They are relations, and relations, we all know, are apt to differ. I think Charlie and Freda, on the whole, are best apart. "Will the love that you're so rich in light a fire in the kitchen?" I'm sure that Charlie when he came to Canada couldn't have lit a fire with all the love he had at his command. Since then the War has taught him things.

What made me think of him tonight was that I read a letter from him. It was to Mrs. Wanham, Freda's mother. Charlie wrote to tell her that her son, Lieutenant Wanham—the very one who said that Charlie was the Goddamnedest fool!—had died in France. And Charlie Ralston used no apho-risms in writing. He told quite simply all he could. He put down every little fact he thought might lighten grief. He thought of everything, all the details; he wrote as if he were beside the mother, talking, consoling, watching the changes on her face and comforting her with every tiny thing she wished to know. Charlie writing that way! It was a revelation of him. And then I re-membered how one day Charlie had come to see me, and how suddenly, un-expectedly, as happens sometimes when you talk alone with someone, affectation had dropped away from him. He had talked simply, told me of "home," talked of his mother, told me foolish little tender jokes about her—"the old lady!" that was what he called her. We had talked all afternoon that day and never mentioned Art. There was no improvement—we discussed nothing. We just sat and talked of England, of the spring there—the starry primroses—the English birds—their song—the perfume of the English flowers. Perhaps that *was* Art—I never thought of it till now.

Anyway, when Charlie went away that day I thought: "What a pity!" Here was a nice boy growing rabbit teeth just out of cussedness—and partly out of shyness too, perhaps. Why do English people come out to Canada and antagonise the whole Dominion? Why? Why can't they be the natural, kindly people that we mostly are at home—and let Art take its chance? As I said before, after the War, perhaps, things will be different. We shall be *doing* then, please God, not talking quite so much. There's lots to do....

As I finished reading Charlie's letter I stopped to think what I should say— it's hard to think of things at times like that—and as I paused I glanced at Freda. Freda's a married woman now, as I have said. She has another love, a little one that *is* Art, but can't talk about it. She's happy. But as I glanced at her I saw her eyes fixed on the letter in my hand...and in her eyes was something— something that was there the day I met them on the hill. She's quite happy. But women, when they've cared for someone, keep a feeling—they don't forget. They can't. I fancy if you said to Freda: "Who is your favourite poet?" she would answer: "Shelley." The present Mr. Freda never heard of Percy Bysshe and doesn't want to.

When I began I thought there was a story, but it seems there isn't. The thing I really had to say was—what a pity English people do themselves injustice when they come out here! How often have I blushed for English men and women in the past ten years! How often! When I've heard them puffing, blowing, boasting—or, on the other tack, freezing, extinguishing, well, I've suffered. They come out here and set us right on every possible point...it's hard to bear—it really is. I can't help hoping that the day will come when they'll be less superior, and when I can feel truly proud of all the opinions that stick out of them. English like that there are at home. Why can't they stay like that when they come out to Canada?

Charlie is learning, anyway—that letter shows it. I hope he has the best of luck and comes back here after the War to show us what an Englishman can be! I use Canadian phraseology and the present tense just to encourage him in—Art!

Ethel Wilson

(1888–1980)

ETHEL DAVIS BRYANT WAS BORN IN PORT ELIZABETH, SOUTH AFRICA, the daughter of a Methodist missionary. On the death of her mother in 1890, she was sent to relatives in England, and when her father died eight years later, she went to live with her grandmother in Vancouver. The details of growing up in this environment she later loosely fictionalized in her affectionate novel about idiosyncrasy and change, *The Innocent Traveller* (1949). A teacher in Vancouver from 1907 to 1920, she married in 1921, and later in life turned to writing. The first of her stories appeared in the *New Statesman and Nation* in the late 1930s, though none was collected until *Mrs. Golightly and Other Stories* (1961). Among her novels are *Hetty Dorval* (1947) and *Swamp Angel* (1954), and two novellas were combined as *The Equations of Love* (1952). Through all her fiction run two apparently contradictory strains of humour and violence. But Wilson argues that civilization is paper thin, a mere veneer over irrationality, uncertainty, and barbarism. Civilized individuals are susceptible to violence, and civilized societies (even societies with rich traditions of art) are open to barbaric distortions of behaviour. "We Have to Sit Opposite" (first published in *Chatelaine* in 1945) is an allegorical, political fable about such vulnerability experienced about the time of World War II. The modal change in the story is also instructive. Beginning in witty repartee, the story shifts to cold fear as the tourists come to realize how— just by responding—they have opened themselves up to engagement and complicity.

For Further Reading

BLANCHE GELFANT, "The Hidden Mines in Ethel Wilson's Landscape," *Canadian Literature* 93 (Summer 1982): 4–23.

LORRAINE MCMULLEN, ed., *The Ethel Wilson Symposium 1981* (Ottawa: U Ottawa P, 1982).

DAVID STOUCK, ed., *Ethel Wilson: Stories, Essays and Letters* (Vancouver: U British Columbia P, 1987).

ETHEL WILSON, "A Cat Among the Falcons," *Canadian Literature* 2 (Autumn 1959): 10–19.

"Women and War" issue, *Canadian Literature* 151 (Winter 1996).

We Have to Sit Opposite

Even in the confusion of entering the carriage at Salzburg, Mrs. Montrose and her cousin Mrs. Forrester noticed the man with the blue tooth. He occupied a corner beside the window. His wife sat next to him. Next to her sat their daughter of perhaps seventeen. People poured into the train. A look passed between Mrs. Montrose and Mrs. Forrester. The look said, "These people seem to have filled up the carriage pretty well, but we'd better take these seats while we can as the train is so full. At least we can have seats together." The porter, in his porter's tyrannical way, piled their suitcases onto the empty rack above the heads of the man with the blue tooth, and his wife, and his daughter, and departed. The opposite rack was full of baskets, bags and miscellaneous parcels. The train started. Here they were. Mrs. Montrose and Mrs. Forrester smiled at each other as they settled down below the rack which was filled with miscellaneous articles. Clinging vines that they were, they felt adventurous and successful. They had travelled alone from Vienna to Salzburg, leaving in Vienna their doctor husbands to continue attending the clinics of Dr. Bauer and Dr. Hirsch. And now, after a week in Salzburg, they were happily on their way to rejoin their husbands, who had flown to Munich.

Both Mrs. Montrose and Mrs. Forrester were tall, slight and fair. They were dressed with dark elegance. They knew that their small hats were smart, suitable and becoming, and they rejoiced in the simplicity and distinction of their new costumes. The selection of these and other costumes, and of these and other hats in Vienna had, they regretted, taken from the study of art, music and history a great deal of valuable time. Mrs. Montrose and Mrs. Forrester were sincerely fond of art, music and history and longed almost passionately to spend their days in the Albertina Gallery and the Kunsthistorische Museum. But the modest shops and shop windows of the craftsmen of Vienna had rather diverted the two young women from the study of art and history, and it was easy to lay the blame for this on the museums and art galleries which, in truth, closed their doors at very odd times. After each day's enchanting pursuits and disappointments, Mrs. Montrose and Mrs. Forrester hastened in a fatigued state to the café where they had arranged to meet their husbands who by this time had finished their daily sessions with Dr. Bauer and Dr. Hirsch.

This was perhaps the best part of the day, to sit together happily in the sunshine, toying with the good Viennese coffee or a glass of wine, gazing and being gazed upon, and giving up their senses to the music that flowed under the chestnut trees. (Ah Vienna, they thought, Vienna, Vienna.)

From *Mrs. Golightly and Other Stories* (Toronto: Macmillan, 1961). First published in *Chatelaine* in 1945. Reprinted by permission of The University of British Columbia Library.

No, perhaps the evenings had been the best time when after their frugal pension dinner they hastened out to hear opera or symphony or wild atavistic gypsy music. All was past now. They had been very happy. They were fortunate. Were they too fortunate?

Mrs. Montrose and Mrs. Forrester were in benevolent good spirits as they looked round the railway carriage and prepared to take their seats and settle down for the journey to Munich to meet their husbands. In their window corner, opposite the man with the blue tooth, was a large hamper. "*Do* you mind?" asked Mrs. Montrose, smiling sweetly at the man, his wife, and his daughter. She prepared to lift the hamper on which the charming view from the carriage window was of course wasted, intending to move it along the seat, and take its place. The man, his wife, and his daughter had never taken their eyes off Mrs. Montrose and Mrs. Forrester since they had entered the carriage.

"*If* you please," said the man loudly and slowly in German English, "*if* you please, that place belongs to my wife or to my daughter. For the moment they sit beside me, but I keep that place for my wife or my daughter. That seat is therefore reserved. It is our seat. You may of course use the two remaining seats."

"I'm sorry," said Mrs. Montrose, feeling snubbed, and she and Mrs. Forrester sat down side by side on the two remaining seats opposite the German family. Beside them the hamper looked out of the window at the charming view. Their gaiety and self-esteem evaporated. The train rocked along.

The three continued to stare at the two young women. Suddenly the mother leaned toward her daughter. She put up her hand to her mouth and whispered behind her hand, her eyes remaining fixed on Mrs. Montrose. The daughter nodded. She also stared at Mrs. Montrose. Mrs. Montrose flushed. The mother sat upright again, still looking at Mrs. Montrose, who felt very uncomfortable, and very much annoyed at blushing.

The man ceased staring at the two young women. He looked up at the rack above him, which contained their suitcases.

"Those are your suitcases," he asked, or rather announced.

"Yes," said Mrs. Montrose and Mrs. Forrester without smiles.

"They are large," said the man in a didactic manner, "they are too large. They are too large to be put on racks. A little motion, a very little motion, and they might fall. If they fall they will injure myself, my wife, or my daughter. It is better," he continued instructively, "that if they fall, they should fall upon your heads, not upon our heads. That is logical. They are not my suitcases. They are your suitcases. You admit it. Please to move your suitcases to the opposite rack, where, if they fall, they will fall upon your own heads." And he continued to sit there motionless. So did his wife. So did his daughter.

Mrs. Montrose and Mrs. Forrester looked at the suitcases in dismay. "Oh," said Mrs. Forrester, "they are so heavy to move. If you feel like that, please won't you sit on this side of the carriage, and we will move across, under our own suitcases, though I can assure you they will not fall. Or perhaps you would help us?"

"We prefer this side of the carriage," said the man with the blue tooth. "We have sat here because we prefer this side of the carriage. It is logical that you should move your suitcases. It is not logical that my wife, my daughter and I should give up our seats in this carriage, or remove your suitcases."

Mrs. Montrose and Mrs. Forrester looked at each other with rage in their hearts. All their self-satisfaction was gone. They got up and tugged and tugged as the train rocked along. They leaned resentfully across the erectly sitting man, and his wife and his daughter. They experienced with exasperation the realization that they had better make the best of it. The train, they knew, was crowded. They had to remain in this carriage with this disagreeable family. With much pulling and straining they hauled down the heavy suitcases. Violently they removed the parcels of the German family and lifted their own suitcases onto the rack above their heads, disposing them clumsily on the rack. Panting a little (they disliked panting), they settled down again side by side with high colour and loosened wisps of hair. They controlled their features so as to appear serene and unaware of the existence of anyone else in the railway carriage, but their hearts were full of black hate.

The family exchanged whispered remarks, and then resumed their scrutiny of the two young women, whose elegance had by this time a sort of tipsy quality. The girl leaned toward her mother. She whispered behind her hand to her mother, who nodded. Both of them stared at Mrs. Forrester. Then they laughed.

"Heavens!" thought the affronted Mrs. Forrester, "this is outrageous! Why can't Alice and I whisper behind our hands to each other about these people and make them feel simply awful! But they wouldn't feel awful. Well, we can't, just because we've been properly brought up, and it would be too childish. And perhaps they don't even know they're rude. They're just being natural." She breathed hard in frustration, and composed herself again.

Suddenly the man with the blue tooth spoke. "Are you English?" he said loudly.

"Yes—well—no," said Mrs. Forrester.

"No—well—yes," said Mrs. Montrose, simultaneously.

A derisive look came over the man's face. "You must know what you are," he said, "either you are English or you are not English. Are you, or are you not?"

"No," said Mrs. Montrose and Mrs. Forrester, speaking primly. Their chins were high, their eyes flashed, and they were ready for discreet battle.

"Then are you Americans?" said the man in the same bullying manner.

"No," said Mrs. Montrose and Mrs. Forrester.

"You can't deceive *me*, you know," said the man with the blue tooth, "I know well the English language. You *say* you are not English. You *say* you are not American. What, then, may I ask, are you? You must be something."

"We are Canadians," said Mrs. Forrester, furious at this catechism.

"*Canadians,*" said the man.

"Yes, Canadians," said Mrs. Montrose.

"This," murmured Mrs. Forrester to Mrs. Montrose, "is more than I can bear!"

"What did you say?" said the man, leaning forward quickly, his hands on his knees.

"I spoke to my friend," said Mrs. Forrester coldly, "I spoke about my bear."

"Yes," said Mrs. Montrose, "she spoke about her bear."

"Your bear? Have you a bear? But you cannot have a bear!" said the man with some surprise.

"In Canada I have a bear. I have two bears," said Mrs. Forrester conceitedly.

"That is true," said Mrs. Montrose nodding, "she has two bears. I myself have five bears. My father has seven bears. That is nothing. It is the custom."

"What do you do with your bears?" asked the man.

"We eat them," said Mrs. Forrester.

"Yes," said Mrs. Montrose, "we eat them. It is the custom."

The man turned and spoke briefly to his wife and daughter, whose eyes opened wider than ever.

Mrs. Montrose and Mrs. Forrester felt pleased. This was better.

The man with the blue tooth became really interested. "Are you married?" he asked Mrs. Forrester.

"Yes," she replied. (We'll see what he'll say next, then we'll see what we can do.)

"And you?" he enquired of Mrs. Montrose. Mrs. Montrose seemed uncertain. "Well, yes, in a way, I suppose," she said.

The man with the blue tooth scrutinized Mrs. Montrose for a moment. "*Then,*" he said, as though he had at last found her out, "if you are married, where is your husband?"

Mrs. Montrose took out her pocket handkerchief. She buried her face in her hands, covering her eyes with her handkerchief. She shook. Evidently she sobbed.

"Now you see what you've done!" said Mrs. Forrester. "You shouldn't ask questions like that. Just look at what you've done."

The three gazed fascinated on Mrs. Montrose. "Is he dead or what is he?" asked the man of Mrs. Forrester, making the words almost quietly with his mouth.

"Sh!!" said Mrs. Forrester very loudly indeed. The three jumped a little. So did Mrs. Montrose.

There was silence while Mrs. Montrose wiped her eyes. She looked over the heads opposite. The wife leaned toward her husband and addressed him timidly behind her hand. He nodded, and spoke to Mrs. Forrester.

"Well," he said, "at least you admit that *you* have a husband. If you have a husband then, where is he?"

"Oh, I don't know," said Mrs. Forrester lightly.

"No, she doesn't know," said Mrs. Montrose.

The three on the opposite seat went into a conference. Mrs. Montrose and Mrs. Forrester did not dare to look at each other. They were enjoying themselves. Their self-esteem had returned. They had impressed. Unfavourably, it is true. But still they had impressed.

The man with the blue tooth pulled himself together. He reasserted himself. Across his waistcoat hung a watch chain. He took his watch out of his pocket and looked at the time. Then to the surprise of Mrs. Montrose and Mrs.

Forrester he took another watch out of the pocket at the other end of the chain. "You see," he said proudly, "I have two watches."

Mrs. Montrose and Mrs. Forrester were surprised, but they had themselves well in hand.

Mrs. Montrose looked at the watches disparagingly. "My husband has six watches," she said.

"Yes, that is true," nodded Mrs. Forrester, "her husband *has* got six watches, but my husband, like you, unfortunately, has only two watches."

The man put his watches back. Decidedly the battle was going in favour of the two young women. How horrid of us, he was so pleased with his watches, thought Mrs. Montrose. Isn't it true that horridness just breeds horridness. We're getting horrider every minute. She regarded the man, his wife and his daughter with distaste but with pity.

"You *say*," said the man, who always spoke as though their statements were open to doubt, which of course they were, "that you come from Canada. Do you come from Winnipeg? I know about Winnipeg."

"No," said Mrs. Montrose, and she spoke this time quite truthfully, "I come from Vancouver." Mrs. Forrester remained silent.

"And you, where do you come from?" persisted the man in a hectoring tone, addressing Mrs. Forrester. Mrs. Forrester remained silent, she had almost decided to answer no more questions.

"Oh, do not tell, please do not tell," begged Mrs. Montrose in an anguished way.

"No," said Mrs. Forrester importantly, "I shall not tell. Rest assured. I shall not tell."

"Why will she not tell?" demanded the man. He was tortured by curiosity. So was his wife. So was his daughter.

"Sh!!" said Mrs. Montrose very loudly.

The man seemed ill at ease. By this time nothing existed in the world for him, or for his wife, or for his daughter but these two Canadian women who ate bears.

"How is it," asked the man, "that you no longer buy my trousers?"

"I beg your pardon?" faltered Mrs. Montrose. For a moment she lost ground.

"I said," replied the man, "why is it that you no longer buy my trousers?"

The ladies did not answer. They could not think of a good answer to that one.

"I," said the man, "am a manufacturer of trousers. I make the most beautiful trousers in Germany. Indeed in the world." (You do not so, thought Mrs. Forrester, picturing her husband's good London legs.) "For three years I receive orders from Winnipeg for my trousers. And now, since two years, yes, since 1929, I receive no more orders for my trousers. Why is that?" he asked, like a belligerent.

"Shall we tell him?" asked Mrs. Forrester, looking at Mrs. Montrose. Neither of them knew why he had received no more orders for his trousers, but they did not wish to say so. "Shall we tell him?" asked Mrs. Forrester.

"You tell him," said Mrs. Montrose.

"No, *you* tell him," said Mrs. Forrester.

"I do not like to tell him," said Mrs. Montrose, "I'd rather you told him."

The man with the blue tooth looked from one to the other.

"Very well. I shall tell him," said Mrs. Forrester. "The fact is," she said, looking downward, "that in Canada men no longer wear trousers."

"What are you saying? That is not true, never can that be true!" said the man in some confusion.

"Yes," said Mrs. Montrose, corroborating sombrely. "Yes, indeed it is true. When they go abroad they wear trousers, but in Canada, no. It is a new custom."

"It is the climate," said Mrs. Forrester.

"Yes, that is the reason, it is the climate," agreed Mrs. Montrose.

"But in Canada," argued the man with the blue tooth, "your climate is cold. Everyone knows your climate is cold."

"In the Arctic regions, yes, it is really intensely cold, we all find it so. But not in Winnipeg. Winnipeg is very salubrious." (That's a good one, thought Mrs. Montrose.)

The man turned and spoke rapidly to his wife. She also turned, and looked askance at her daughter. The expressions of the man, his wife, and his daughter were a blend of pleasure and shock. The two liars were delighted.

At last the man could not help asking, "But they *must* wear something! It is not logical."

"Oh, it's logical, all right!" said Mrs. Forrester.

"But what *do* they wear?" persisted the man.

"I never looked to see," said Mrs. Montrose. "*I* did, I looked," said Mrs. Forrester.

"Well?" asked the man.

"Oh, they just wear kilts," said Mrs. Forrester.

"Kilts? What are kilts? I do not know kilts," said the man.

"I would rather not tell you," said Mrs. Forrester primly.

"Oh," said the man.

Mrs. Montrose took out her vanity case, and inspected herself, powder puff in hand.

"I do not allow my wife and daughter to paint their faces so," said the man with the blue tooth.

"No?" said Mrs. Montrose.

"It is not good that women should paint their faces so. Good women do not do that. It is a pity."

(Oh, Alice, thought Mrs. Forrester in a fury, he shall not dare!) "It is a pity," she hissed, "that in your country there are no good dentists!"

"Be careful, be careful," whispered Mrs. Montrose.

"What do you mean?" demanded the man with the blue tooth.

(She will go too far, I know she will, thought Mrs. Montrose, alarmed, putting out her hand.)

"In our country," said the rash Mrs. Forrester, "anyone needing attention is taken straight to the State Dentist by the Police. This is done for aesthetic reasons. It is logical."

"I am going to sleep," said Mrs. Montrose very loudly, and she shut her eyes tight.

"So am I," said Mrs. Forrester, in a great hurry, and she shut her eyes too. This had been hard work but good fun for Mrs. Montrose and Mrs. Forrester. They felt, though, that they had gone a little bit too far. It might be as well if they slept, or pretended to sleep, until they reached Munich. They felt that outside their closed eyes was something frightening. The voice of the man with the blue tooth was saying, "I wish to tell you, I wish to tell you..." but Mrs. Montrose was in a deep sleep, and so was Mrs. Forrester. They sat with their eyes tightly closed, beside the hamper which still occupied the seat with the view by the darkening window. Mrs. Montrose had the inside corner, and so by reason of nestling down in the corner, and by reason of having an even and sensible temperament, she really and truly fell asleep at last.

Not so Mrs. Forrester. Her eyes were tightly closed, but her mind was greatly disturbed. Why had they permitted themselves to be baited? She pondered on the collective mentality that occupied the seat near to them (knees almost touching), and its results which now filled the atmosphere of the carriage so unpleasantly. She had met this mentality before, but had not been closely confined with it, as now. What of a world in which this mentality might ever become dominant? Then one would be confined with it without appeal or relief. The thought was shocking. She felt unreasonably agitated. She felt rather a fool, too, with her eyes shut tightly. But, if she opened them, she would have to look somewhere, presumably at the family, so it seemed safer to keep them closed. The train sped on. After what seemed to her a very long time, she peeped. The wife and daughter were busy. The husband sat back, hands on knees, chin raised, expectant, eyes closed. His wife respectfully undid his tie, his collar, and his top shirt button. By this time the daughter had opened the hamper, and had taken from it a bottle and a clean napkin. These she handed to her mother. The wife moistened the napkin from the bottle and proceeded to wash her husband, his face, his ears, round the back of his neck, and inside his shirt collar, with great care. "Like a cat," thought Mrs. Forrester, who had forgotten to shut her eyes.

The man with the blue tooth lowered his raised chin and caught her. "You see," he said loudly, "you see, wives should look properly after their husbands, instead of travelling alone and..." But Mrs. Forrester was fast asleep again. The whole absurd encounter had begun to hold an element of terror. They had been tempted into folly. She knew—as she screwed up her closed eyes—that they were implicated in fear and folly.

The two young women took care to sleep until the train reached Munich. Then they both woke up.

Many people slept until they reached Munich. Then they all began to wake up.

Raymond Knister

(1899–1932)

BORN IN RUSCOMB, ESSEX COUNTY, ONTARIO, Raymond Knister grew up on his father's farm, and later attended Victoria College (Toronto) and Iowa State
University. In 1923 he moved to Iowa to edit *The Midland,* and he published in
that journal as well as in *This Quarter,* the *Toronto Star Weekly,* and *Saturday Night.*
By 1928 he was back in Canada, editing for Macmillan the first major anthology of Canadian short stories. The author of two novels, some poems, a set of
delightful "Corncob Corners" sketches, and many short stories, he was (like
other writers of his generation: Callaghan, Thomas Murtha, Dorothy Livesay)
interested in the plight of working people and in the ways that ordinary words
could be invested with literary power. Still at the beginning of his career,
Knister drowned in 1932, in a swimming accident.

A collection of his stories—including "The First Day of Spring" and other
works which had been left in manuscript—appeared as *The First Day of Spring and
Other Prose,* edited by Peter Stevens in 1976. The title story of this volume tells
at one level of a simple initiation (a boy's realization of horrors in life that he
has not dreamed of, a realization made palpable in the image of the colt, and an
understanding made clear in his treatment of the colt); but it is also a story of
the restrained voices of two generations, separate and interweaving. The voices
embody a whole range of desires—to connect, to communicate, to change, to part,
to stay—and they tell of the way that authority and choice pass from one generation to another. The story concerns the many faces of change. Its craft lies in
the careful pacing.

For Further Reading

IMOGEN GIVENS, "Raymond Knister—Man or Myth?" *Essays on Canadian
  Writing* 16 (Fall/Winter 1979–80): 5–19.

MICHAEL GNAROWSKI, "Introduction" to *Selected Stories of Raymond Knister*
  (Ottawa: U Ottawa P, 1972) 11–16.

RAYMOND KNISTER, "Dissecting the T.B.M.," *Saturday Night* (6 Sept. 1930): 5.

PETER STEVENS, ed., *The First Day of Spring and Other Prose* (Toronto: U Toronto
  P, 1976), "Introduction" xi-xxx.

The First Day of Spring

It had been a mild winter, and yet when March came, and days in which wheels threw the snow like mud in stretches of road where snow still lay, the world was changed.

This change was more than seeming. Who misses the first day of spring? Snow may linger on the ground and return, but the new smell is there, more potent perhaps than it is ever to be in lush days of blossoms. The blue of the sky softens, the air lifts, and it is as though the lightness of a life above the earth were being made ready, an entering spirit to pervade the uncoloured and frost-clogged flesh of the world; or perhaps it is as though this flesh had suddenly sighed in its sleep, an exhalation intoxicating to men and beasts. It is as though sunlight on their bare boughs has at last awakened the trees, and the wind through them is now more than a gesture remembered only by the grass.

Perhaps it was the effect of spring on a boy which made me forgetful. Musing in the darkness of the cow-stable after such a day, I allowed Bess, one of the cows, to sip up all the water in a second pail, when her stall mate, Rose, had had only one. I started and pulled the pail away. There was still a very little in the bottom, and this I offered to Rose. She did not want the water, or doubted its existence in the bottom of the pail, so I decided not to get her another. The ground was soft and deep to the narrow hooves of cows, so they were not turned out to find their way to the well at the foot of the hill.

In the other end of the building, where the horses were kept, I could hear my father backing the 'driver' out of her stall, and I knew that he was going to town. As I walked across the barnyard, the straw and loose dirt gave way under my feet with sudden crunches, where the old ice had melted, honey-combed by a few afternoons of warm sun. I ran ahead to open the gate, and Cherry was led through. A long-haired bay mare with trim legs, she held her head high, and trod sedately in the slippery mud of the lane.

This made me smile, for I thought of the chase she had led the colts that morning from 'the other farm' a mile away. After the early chores we had walked to the back of this farm, and captured the more or less unneeded horses which had been wintered there. They had pawed the snow for long grass, and with occasional loads of corn-fodder had kept fat on their ribs. Only in times of storm were they brought into the barn.

They crowded about us, snorting trumpets of fog in the thin spring sunshine—turning, shying, shattering films of ice on the puddles. Father got the halter on Kate, a 'general purpose' mare weighing about fifteen hundred pounds,

From *The First Day of Spring: Stories and Other Prose,* ed. Peter Stevens (Toronto: University of Toronto Press, 1976). Reprinted by permission of University of Toronto Press.

who, as the senior member of the party, could be expected to lead it safely to the barn. Then he hoisted me on her back, first twisting the halter shank into her mouth; for since the sudden breath of spring had caused the excursion we had set forth without bridles. He came along behind on foot to see that the others did not linger or stray.

But he needn't have worried about that. The whole herd of horses and colts jumped across the weedy ditch and set up a gallop, strung along the lane, splashing impartially through mud, blue puddles, and dark drifts of snow. The air was like a cool bright tide, and the fresh sound of hens cackling on a neighbouring farm seemed to cry us forward. Old Kate was not to be outdone, in spite of my pulling. I saw that she meant to take me home without stopping at the barn on this place; so I jumped from her back, out far enough to have a purchase on her halter. I got her stopped, tearing the grass at the roadside with my boots. But the colts galloped gaily right on past the gate, never hearing my calls and Kate's rib-shaking whinny—straight to the home place, led in a businesslike trot by this same old driver, Cherry.

She was very mild now, Cherry, as though she meditated on the dusk of the evening and the vicissitude of her fortune. My father pulled the long-unused buggy from the shed, and cautioned me: 'Watch her, she'll be feeling those two feeds of clover hay and oats.' But as we pulled the shafts over her and fastened the traces, she helped by easing back slightly, appearing meanwhile to give heed to a lonely-sounding 'plunk-plash' where another rig was passing along the muddy road. I looked up at her large tilted eyes and high-held head averted while Father went to the house for his overcoat, and told her, with a boy's faith:

'Sure, you'd stand, wouldn't you, Cherry. Not run away.'

Like a dog the driver made a gesture of glancing at me, but retained her statuesque pose, and grinding a stray stem of hay in her mouth, still considered the sound from the road, beyond the hedge.

'Well; now we've forgotten the buggy-cushion,' my father said, interrupting my day-dream, and went into the drive-shed for it. 'Now's no time for automobiles. Wasn't so bad, a mild winter like this, but from now on, until the frost is all out—' He picked up the lines and stepped into the buggy.

Preferring the automobile to the buggy, I pretended to be annoyed.

'Yes, I suppose when the horses are working hard and other people are getting their cars out, we'll begin to use a horse and rig.'

But I really didn't care, and my words seemed to thin away into the chill tranquil evening. I put my hands into my pockets; for—significant of spring—I had mislaid my mitts that afternoon...everything was satisfying. This day had been brisk and active, banishing in a stroke the long winter in which the world had seemed so far away and the chores so inevitable and tame. Now we seemed remotely interesting and strange to one another, the quiet horse, my father, and myself.

'I saw Fred Keith and that Merrill girl trying to get through the mud yesterday with their car, and that was a good example of how foolish it is.'

'Muriel?' I asked, in surprise. 'I didn't know either of them was back.'

'And what do you think—You knew he was pretty well gone on her before they moved down east. He must have been, or he wouldn't have up and sold his store and all and moved down there near them. True, he had a good offer, but then, he didn't need to go just *there*. You know, he got the girl in trouble.' He spoke as man to man, as though I was old enough, now, for that. I was seventeen.

'Not Muriel?' I was convinced that he was mistaken. 'I hardly knew they were going together, even, till they had gone.'

'Got her in the family way. Going together! I guess! He was too wise. I knew all along where things were heading. I used to see him hanging around there all kinds of hours. Why, one time last spring, quite late, May maybe,—I was passing along to the other place about four or five in the morning to sow cloverseed, and there was his glass coup' at the road, all the windows covered with fog, and I thought there was nobody in it, but just as I got by I heard a giggle, and you hate to look back—just getting home. Poor girl, I guess if she'd known how it would turn out—'

Father buttoned his overcoat. He sat erect in the buggy, joggling the whip, while Cherry bent an ear alternately to him and to the road. It seemed that his words were a long time reaching me. Then I wanted to be indignant, and could not, in the face of his calm acceptance. He did not gossip until there was something to talk about.

'Why—why, she was just the same age as me. We were in the same class at school.'

'The foolish age. It's all the worse—when some fellow gets them going wrong, I mean. All the more foolish. What I was going to say, I saw them yesterday, stuck in the mud in his coup'. It seemed the thing had caught fire—'

'Caught fire, how?'

But I was scarcely listening, for everything seemed irrelevant beside this strange, half-expected news of Muriel, which yet struck me like a blow. It seemed only a few weeks since I had used to tease her at school, and she had been so pretty that I had wondered secretly if some day I might not be bold enough to try to keep company with her myself. Her auburn hair, and narrow blue eyes, saucy nose, returned to me as I had seen her in the lamplight when she had recited at an entertainment a year ago.

It seemed that I was just getting to know her when the family moved away; and oddly she seemed to me younger then than in the years before. She had been always like a complete, demurely perfect creature in her way, not liable to the imperfections of growth, stages in which most girls are gawky or giggling. I had looked at her as from a distance, and I still remember her somehow as one recalls an early love-affair with a woman older than himself.

'Why, it simply caught fire. They had coal oil in the radiator... It does seem one trouble just attracts others to it.'

'But how—'

'How did they get it out? Well, I guess it burnt itself out, like. I suppose the oil burnt off the engine, never got to the gasoline or anything. I was surprised to see them a hundred miles from where they belonged. He had a piece of fence-rail and was trying to pry the mud out of the wheels. Had his hat off and his good clothes plastered. I yelled at him. "Hello, Fred, what's the matter with your plug-hat car?" He seemed glad to see me and tell his story. But he didn't feel much like joking, I can tell you. He wanted to get on, as though he was in a hurry, all excited. I seen Muriel in the coup' and started to ask her how the family was. She kind of ducked down, almost, and didn't want to talk to me. He says, all excited, "Congratulate us, congratulate us, we're married!"

I twisted the heel of my rubber boot in the ground.

'Yes, married. But it's too late. I wouldn't be surprised if they were in jail by this time. By George! I bet they were trying to get to Detroit and the other side. They were in a hurry, all right. They couldn't have been very pleased to see me, though I did stop and get them out of the hole. No, nor they didn't seem to be very pleased with each other. You wouldn't have known them for the same pair, so...down-in-the-mouth. But that's how it goes.'

I did not have a word to say, or I had more than I could say. It was growing dusk, but a strange new robin called sharply somewhere in the thick jumbled limbs of a crab-apple tree in the garden. A couple of pigeons alighted on the barn ridge, one facing each way, watchfully; we had had a pigeon pie or two lately. Some air over the buildings, a new strange echo of our voices, yet one so old I wondered how I could have forgotten it, filled my heart with a mixture of feelings.

A girl's voice came from across the fields, a few words of singing, a voice with something wild and strong in it.

'Hear her? That's the other one. Pretty much alike, for cousins. Remember how they used to call to each other from one house to the other? Could hear them as plain, when the air was like this! On a Monday morning, when they'd both be putting out washings, they'd try singing a duet, and laugh back and forth.... Nothing can stop her singing when she gets out.'

But the girl's voice had stopped.

'Well, Cherry,' Father addressed the horse. 'It seems like old times, sitting behind your ornery old hide. Horses are going to want a lot of time to get used to the work. They'll be mighty soft. Got to break in those colts one of these days too, can't get at it too soon. Is there anything you want me to get in town?'

'How about—what you said—he—they might be arrested?'

'Oh. Oh, the way of that, I suppose you should know such things. They was out after her, the police, so I heard when I got to town yesterday. And me just seeing them—When the time came, you see, she had a child.'

'Couldn't he marry her?'

'Course, yes, but then, they hadn't, so... They might have had a fall-out before that time. Well, what she done, by all accounts, her father went out one morning, and he was stirring the swill-barrel and singing, like you know he used to. The girl got that honest. Quite early it was. He carried a couple of pailsful to the trough at the pigpen, and he wondered, they didn't squeal like they usually did when he began to feed them. But of course, a lot of fat hogs like that, he couldn't see anything amongst them, until they got lined up at the trough.'

'But what about Muriel?' I asked, and my voice seemed shrill. I had overcome a sense of shame in mentioning her name, a relic of shyness before the girl herself, perhaps.

'Well, she—Muriel I guess had—she'd left just a few minutes before. She, well, what she done—The baby may have been dead before she—She must have gone straight to Fred, and they lit out.'

But almost as soon as he had begun to speak I had turned to walk away. I couldn't bear what loomed over the image of that girl in my mind. Why, she must have gone through things that were incredible...I turned to face my father.

'Well, of course, you read of these things, but you never think they're going to happen to people you know. But that's how it is when young people start to go wrong. Might have happened right here when they lived here.' He chirped, and tightened the lines.

The old mare swung at once into her long road-stride. 'Don't bother any more with the chores. I'll fix them when I get home.' Father called from the lane, looking back.

From across the fields the light hidden voice came reaching again, and then it stopped, as though for an answer. The air was chill, and with the darkness winter seemed to be returning.

After a few minutes I moved away toward the barn. In the gloom of the stable I stroked the warm nose of a colt. 'You're going to be broken in,' I whispered. He was strangely quiet.

Morley Callaghan

(1903–1990)

BORN IN TORONTO, Morley Callaghan attended St. Michael's College and (though he never practised law) Osgoode Hall Law School. He became a cub reporter for the *Toronto Star* in the 1920s, when Ernest Hemingway worked there, and he early began to publish stories, encouraged by Hemingway and noticed by other luminaries of the period such as Scott Fitzgerald. The main influence on his writing, however, was that of the American author Sherwood Anderson, whose *Winesburg, Ohio* explored the "grotesques" of a precise locale, and whose technique surrendered plot to the effects of cadence and simple diction. Style, for Callaghan, had to convey both region (for him, Toronto) and the moral dilemmas that ordinary people recurrently faced and attempted to resolve, often unsuccessfully. Callaghan published in the most prestigious literary journals of the 1920s and 1930s, and on a trip to Paris in 1929 met many of the famous literary exiles then resident there: Hemingway, Joyce, Fitzgerald, and the Canadian John Glassco. Glassco's journal *Memoirs of Montparnasse* (1970) and Callaghan's *That Summer in Paris* (1963) contrastingly record the time. Callaghan himself returned directly to Canada, and followed a successful career as playwright, as author of juveniles, novels, and short stories, as journalist, and as a CBC radio and television personality. Among his novels are *Such Is My Beloved* (1931), *The Loved and the Lost* (1951), and *A Time for Judas* (1983). Collections of his stories were published in 1929 and 1936; an omnibus collection, *Morley Callaghan's Stories,* first appeared in 1959; and *The Lost and Found Stories of Morley Callaghan* appeared in 1985.

First published, respectively, in *The Exile* (1928) and *Atlantic Monthly* (1932), "Ancient Lineage" and "A Sick Call" were collected in their unrevised form in *A Native Argosy* (1929) and *Now That April's Here and Other Stories* (1936). The texts here are from *Morley Callaghan's Stories.* They demonstrate some of the moral and stylistic dimensions of Callaghan's early short fiction. Apparently without ornament, the opening paragraphs of "Ancient Lineage," for example, convey by their rhythm, by their semantic presumptions, and by the metonymy of the setting itself some hint of the turns that the subsequent story will take. Equally revelatory, "A Sick Call" is more of a parable, drawing on Biblical antecedents (for contrast more than parallel) in order to explore the moral limitations of the human universe, and the relative choices that people make even in the name of an absolute good.

For Further Reading

GARY BOIRE, *Morley Callaghan: literary anarchist* (Toronto: ECW, 1994).

MORLEY CALLAGHAN, "An Ocean Away," *Times Literary Supplement* (4 June 1964): 493.

BRANDON CONRON, *Morley Callaghan* (New York: Twayne, 1966).

VICTOR HOAR, *Morley Callaghan* (Toronto: Copp Clark, 1969).

E. W. PITCHER, "Family Secrets in Callaghan's 'Ancient Lineage,' " *Canadian Notes & Queries* 49 (1995): 18–20.

DAVID STAINES, ed., *The Callaghan Symposium* (Ottawa: U Ottawa P, 1981).

ROBERT WEAVER, "A Talk with Morley Callaghan," *Tamarack Review* 7 (Spring 1958): 3–29.

Ancient Lineage

The young man from the Historical Club with a green magazine under his arm got off the train at Clintonville. It was getting dark but the station lights were not lit. He hurried along the platform and jumped down on the sloping cinder path to the sidewalk.

Trees were on the lawns alongside the walk, branches drooping low, leaves scraping occasionally against the young man's straw hat. He saw a cluster of lights, bluish-white in the dusk across a river, many lights for a small town. He crossed the lift-lock bridge and turned on to the main street. A hotel was at the corner.

At the desk a bald-headed man in a blue shirt, the sleeves rolled up, looked critically at the young man while he registered. "All right, Mr. Flaherty," he said, inspecting the signature carefully.

"Do you know many people around here?" Mr. Flaherty asked.

"Just about everybody."

"The Rowers?"

"The old lady?"

"Yeah, an old lady."

"Sure, Mrs. Anna Rower. Around the corner to the left, then turn to the right on the first street, the house opposite the Presbyterian church on the hill."

"An old family," suggested the young man.

"An old-timer all right." The hotel man made it clear by a twitching of his lips that he was a part of the new town, canal, water power, and factories.

Mr. Flaherty sauntered out and turned to the left. It was dark and the street had the silence of small towns in the evening. Turning a corner he heard girls giggling in a doorway. He looked at the church on the hill, the steeple dark against the sky. He had forgotten whether the man had said beside the church or across the road, but could not make up his mind to ask the fellow who was watering the wide church lawn. No lights in the shuttered windows of the rough-cast house beside the church. He came down the hill and had to yell three times at the man because the water swished strongly against the grass.

"All right, thanks. Right across the road," Mr. Flaherty repeated.

Tall trees screened the square brick house. Looking along the hall to a lighted room, Mr. Flaherty saw an old lady standing at a sideboard. "She's in all right," he thought, rapping on the screen door. A large woman of about forty, dressed in blue skirt and blue waist, came down the stairs. She did not open the screen door.

"Could I speak to Mrs. Anna Rower?"

From *Morley Callaghan's Stories* (Toronto: Macmillan, 1967). First published in *The Exile,* 1928. Reprinted by permission of Macmillan Canada.

"I'm Miss Hilda Rower."

"I'm from the University Historical Club."

"What did you want to see Mother for?"

Mr. Flaherty did not like talking through the screen door. "I wanted to talk to her," he said firmly.

"Well, maybe you'd better come in."

He stood in the hall while the large woman lit the gas in the front room. The gas flared up, popped, showing fat hips and heavy lines on her face. Mr. Flaherty, disappointed, watched her swaying down the hall to get her mother. He carefully inspected the front room, the framed photographs of dead Conservative politicians, the group of military men hanging over the old-fashioned piano, the faded greenish wallpaper and the settee in the corner.

An old woman with a knot of white hair and good eyes came into the room, walking erectly. "This is the young man who wanted to see you, Mother," Miss Hilda Rower said. They all sat down. Mr. Flaherty explained he wanted to get some information concerning the Rower genealogical tree for the next meeting of his society. The Rowers, he knew, were a pioneer family in the district, and descended from William the Conqueror, he had heard.

The old lady laughed thinly, swaying from side to side. "It's true enough, but I don't know who told you. My father was Daniel Rower, who came to Ontario from Cornwall in 1830."

Miss Hilda Rower interrupted. "Wait, Mother, you may not want to tell about it." Brusque and businesslike, she turned to the young man. "You want to see the family tree, I suppose."

"Oh, yes."

"My father was a military settler here," the old lady said.

"I don't know but what we might be able to give you some notes," Miss Hilda spoke generously.

"Thanks awfully, if you will."

"Of course you're prepared to pay something if you're going to print it," she added, smugly adjusting her big body in the chair.

Mr. Flaherty got red in the face; of course he understood, but to tell the truth he had merely wanted to chat with Mrs. Rower. Now he knew definitely he did not like the heavy nose and unsentimental assertiveness of the lower lip of this big woman with the wide shoulders. He couldn't stop looking at her thick ankles. Rocking back and forth in the chair she was primly conscious of lineal superiority; a proud unmarried woman, surely she could handle a young man, half-closing her eyes, a young man from the University indeed. "I don't want to talk to her about the University," he thought.

Old Mrs. Rower went into the next room and returned with a framed genealogical tree of the house of Rower. She handed it graciously to Mr. Flaherty, who read, "The descent of the family of Rower, from William the Conqueror, from Malcom 1st, and from the Capets, Kings of France." It bore the *imprimatur* of the College of Arms, 1838.

"It's wonderful to think you have this," Mr. Flaherty said, smiling at Miss Hilda, who watched him suspiciously.

"A brother of mine had it all looked up," old Mrs. Rower said.

"You don't want to write about that," Miss Hilda said, crossing her ankles. The ankles looked much thicker crossed. "You just want to have a talk with Mother."

"That's it," Mr. Flaherty smiled agreeably.

"We may write it up ourselves some day." Her heavy chin dipped down and rose again.

"Sure, why not?"

"But there's no harm in you talking to Mother if you want to, I guess."

"You could write a good story about that tree," Mr. Flaherty said, feeling his way.

"We may do it some day but it'll take time," she smiled complacently at her mother, who mildly agreed.

Mr. Flaherty talked pleasantly to this woman, who was so determined he would not learn anything about the family tree without paying for it. He tried talking about the city, then tactfully asked old Mrs. Rower what she remembered of the Clintonville of seventy years ago. The old lady talked willingly, excited a little. She went into the next room to get a book of clippings. "My father, Captain Rower, got a grant of land from the Crown and cleared it," she said, talking over her shoulder. "A little way up the Trent River. Clintonville was a small military settlement then..."

"Oh, Mother, he doesn't want to know all about that," Miss Hilda said impatiently.

"It's very interesting indeed."

The old woman said nervously, "My dear, what difference does it make? You wrote it all up for the evening at the church."

"So I did too," she hesitated, thinking the young man ought to see how well it was written. "I have an extra copy." She looked at him thoughtfully. He smiled. She got up and went upstairs.

The young man talked very rapidly to the old lady and took many notes.

Miss Rower returned. "Would you like to see it?" She handed Mr. Flaherty a small gray booklet. Looking quickly through it, he saw it contained valuable information about the district.

"The writing is simply splendid. You must have done a lot of work on it."

"I worked hard on it," she said, pleased and more willing to talk.

"Is this an extra copy?"

"Yes, it's an extra copy."

"I suppose I might keep it," he said diffidently.

She looked at him steadily. "Well...I'll have to charge you twenty-five cents."

"Sure, sure, of course, that's fine." He blushed.

"Just what it costs to get them out," the old lady explained apologetically.

"Can you change a dollar?" He fumbled in his pocket, pulling the dollar out slowly.

They could not change it but Miss Rower would be pleased to go down to the corner grocery store. Mr. Flaherty protested. No trouble, he would go. She insisted on asking the next-door neighbour to change it. She went across the room, the dollar in hand.

Mr. Flaherty chatted with the nice old lady and carefully examined the family tree, and wrote quickly in a small book till the screen door banged, the curtains parted, and Miss Hilda Rower came into the room. He wanted to smirk, watching her walking heavily, so conscious of her ancient lineage, a virginal mincing sway to her large hips, seventy-five cents' change held loosely in drooping fingers.

"Thank you," he said, pocketing the change, pretending his work was over. Sitting back in the chair he praised the way Miss Rower had written the history of the neighbourhood and suggested she might write a splendid story of the family tree, if she had the material, of course.

"I've got the material, all right," she said, trying to get comfortable again. How would Mr. Flaherty arrange it and where should she try to sell it? The old lady was dozing in the rocking-chair. Miss Rower began to talk rather nervously about her material. She talked of the last title in the family and the Sir Richard who had been at the court of Queen Elizabeth.

Mr. Flaherty chimed in gaily, "I suppose you know the O'Flahertys were kings in Ireland, eh?"

She said vaguely, "I daresay, I daresay," conscious only of an interruption to the flow of her thoughts. She went on talking with hurried eagerness, all the fine talk about her ancestors bringing her peculiar satisfaction. A soft light came into her eyes and her lips were moist.

Mr. Flaherty started to rub his cheek, and looked at her big legs, and felt restive, and then embarrassed, watching her closely, her firm lower lip hanging loosely. She was talking slowly, lazily, relaxing in her chair, a warm fluid oozing through her veins, exhausting but satisfying her.

He was uncomfortable. She was liking it too much. He did not know what to do. There was something immodest about it. She was close to forty, her big body relaxed in the chair. He looked at his watch and suggested he would be going. She stretched her legs graciously, pouting, inviting him to stay a while longer, but he was standing up, tucking his magazine under his arm. The old lady was still dozing. "I'm so comfortable," Miss Rower said, "I hate to move."

The mother woke up and shook hands with Mr. Flaherty. Miss Rower got up to say good-bye charmingly.

Half-way down the path Mr. Flaherty turned. She was standing in the doorway, partly shadowed by the tall trees, bright moonlight filtering through leaves touching soft lines on her face and dark hair.

He went down the hill to the hotel unconsciously walking with a careless easy stride, wondering at the change that had come over the heavy, strong woman. He thought of taking a walk along the river in the moonlight, the river on which old Captain Rower had drilled troops on the ice in the winter of 1837 to fight the rebels. Then he thought of having a western sandwich in the café across the road from the hotel. That big woman in her own way had been hot stuff.

In the hotel he asked to be called early so he could get the first train to the city. For a long time he lay awake in the fresh, cool bed, the figure of the woman whose ancient lineage had taken the place of a lover in her life, drifting into his thoughts and becoming important while he watched on the wall the pale moonlight that had softened the lines of her face, and wondered if it was still shining on her bed, and on her throat, and on her contented, lazily relaxed body.

A Sick Call

Sometimes Father Macdowell mumbled out loud and took a deep wheezy breath as he walked up and down the room and read his office. He was a huge old priest, white-headed except for a shiny baby-pink bald spot on the top of his head, and he was a bit deaf in one ear. His florid face had many fine red interlacing vein lines. For hours he had been hearing confessions and he was tired, for he always had to hear more confessions than any other priest at the cathedral; young girls who were in trouble, and wild but at times repentant young men, always wanted to tell their confessions to Father Macdowell, because nothing seemed to shock or excite him, or make him really angry, and he was even tender with those who thought they were most guilty.

While he was mumbling and reading and trying to keep his glasses on his nose, the house girl knocked on the door and said, "There's a young lady here to see, father. I think it's about a sick call."

"Did she ask for me especially?" he said in a deep but slightly cracked voice.

"Indeed she did, father. She wanted Father Macdowell and nobody else."

So he went out to the waiting-room, where a girl about thirty years of age, with fine brown eyes, fine cheek bones, and rather square shoulders, was sitting daubing her eyes with a handkerchief. She was wearing a dark coat with a gray wolf collar. "Good evening, father," she said. "My sister is sick. I wanted you to come and see her. We think she's dying."

"Be easy, child; what's the matter with her? Speak louder, I can hardly hear you."

"My sister's had pneumonia. The doctor's coming back to see her in an hour. I wanted you to anoint her, father."

"I see, I see. But she's not lost yet. I'll not give her extreme unction now. That may not be necessary. I'll go with you and hear her confession."

"Father, I ought to let you know, maybe. Her husband won't want to let you see her. He's not a Catholic, and my sister hasn't been to church in a long time."

"Oh, don't mind that. He'll let me see her," Father Macdowell said, and he left the room to put on his hat and coat.

When he returned, the girl explained that her name was Jane Stanhope, and her sister lived only a few blocks away. "We'll walk and you tell me about

From *Morley Callaghan's Stories* (Toronto: Macmillan, 1967). First published in *Atlantic Monthly,* 1932. Reprinted by permission of Macmillan Canada.

your sister," he said. He put his black hat square on the top of his head, and pieces of white hair stuck out awkwardly at the sides. They went to the avenue together.

The night was mild and clear. Miss Stanhope began to walk slowly, because Father Macdowell's rolling gait didn't get him along the street very quickly. He walked as if his feet hurt him, though he wore a pair of large, soft, specially constructed shapeless shoes. "Now, my child, you go ahead and tell me about your sister," he said, breathing with difficulty, yet giving the impression that nothing could have happened to the sister which would make him feel indignant.

There wasn't much to say, Miss Stanhope replied. Her sister had married John Williams two years ago, and he was a good, hard-working fellow, only he was very bigoted and hated all church people. "My family wouldn't have anything to do with Elsa after she married him, though I kept going to see her," she said. She was talking in a loud voice to Father Macdowell so that he could hear her.

"Is she happy with her husband?"

"She's been very happy, father. I must say that."

"Where is he now?"

"He was sitting beside her bed. I ran out because I thought he was going to cry. He said if I brought a priest near the place he'd break the priest's head."

"My goodness. Never mind, though. Does your sister want to see me?"

"She asked me to go and get a priest, but she doesn't want John to know she did it."

Turning into a side street, they stopped at the first apartment house, and the old priest followed Miss Stanhope up the stairs. His breath came with great difficulty. "Oh dear, I'm not getting any younger, not one day younger. It's a caution how a man's legs go back on him," he said. As Miss Stanhope rapped on the door, she looked pleadingly at the old priest, trying to ask him not to be offended at anything that might happen, but he was smiling and looking huge in the narrow hallway. He wiped his head with his handkerchief.

The door was opened by a young man in a white shirt with no collar, with a head of thick, black, wavy hair. At first he looked dazed, then his eyes got bright with excitement when he saw the priest, as though he were glad to see someone he could destroy with pent-up energy. "What do you mean, Jane?" he said. "I told you not to bring a priest around here. My wife doesn't want to see a priest."

"What's that you're saying, young man?"

"No one wants you here."

"Speak up. Don't be afraid. I'm a bit hard of hearing," Father Macdowell smiled rosily. John Williams was confused by the unexpected deafness in the priest, but he stood there, blocking the door with sullen resolution as if waiting for the priest to try to launch a curse at him.

"Speak to him, father," Miss Stanhope said, but the priest didn't seem to hear her; he was still smiling as he pushed past the young man, saying, "I'll go in and sit down, if you don't mind, son. I'm here on God's errand, but I don't mind saying I'm all out of breath from climbing those stairs."

John was dreadfully uneasy to see he had been brushed aside, and he followed the priest into the apartment and said loudly, "I don't want you here."

Father Macdowell said, "Eh, eh?" Then he smiled sadly. "Don't be angry with me, son," he said. "I'm too old to try and be fierce and threatening." Looking around, he said, "Where's your wife?" and he started to walk along the hall, looking for the bedroom.

John followed him and took hold of his arm. "There's no sense in your wasting your time talking to my wife, do you hear?" he said angrily.

Miss Stanhope called out suddenly, "Don't be rude, John."

"It's he that's being rude. You mind your business," John said.

"For the love of God let me sit down a moment with her, anyway. I'm tired," the priest said.

"What do you want to say to her? Say it to me, why don't you?"

Then they both heard someone moan softly in the adjoining room, as if the sick woman had heard them. Father Macdowell, forgetting that the young man had hold of his arm, said, "I'll go in and see her for a moment, if you don't mind," and he began to open the door.

"You're not going to be alone with her, that's all," John said, following him into the bedroom.

Lying on the bed was a white-faced, fair girl, whose skin was so delicate that her cheek bones stood out sharply. She was feverish, but her eyes rolled toward the door, and she watched them coming in. Father Macdowell took off his coat, and as he mumbled to himself he looked around the room, at the mauve-silk bed light and the light wallpaper with the tiny birds in flight. It looked like a little girl's room. "Good evening, father," Mrs. Williams whispered. She looked scared. She didn't glance at her husband. The notion of dying had made her afraid. She loved her husband and wanted to die loving him, but she was afraid, and she looked up at the priest.

"You're going to get well, child," Father Macdowell said, smiling and patting her hand gently.

John, who was standing stiffly by the door, suddenly moved around the big priest, and he bent down over the bed and took his wife's hand and began to caress her forehead.

"Now, if you don't mind, my son, I'll hear your wife's confession," the priest said.

"No, you won't," John said abruptly. "Her people didn't want her, and they left us together, and they're not going to separate us now. She's satisfied with me." He kept looking down at her face as if he could not bear to turn away.

Father Macdowell nodded his head up and down and sighed. "Poor boy," he said. "God bless you." Then he looked at Mrs. Williams, who had closed her eyes, and he saw a faint tear on her cheek. "Be sensible, my boy," he said, "You'll have to let me hear your wife's confession. Leave us alone a while."

"I'm going to stay right here," John said, and he sat down on the end of the bed. He was working himself up and staring savagely at the priest. All of a sudden he noticed the tears on his wife's cheeks, and he muttered as though bewildered, "What's the matter, Elsa? What's the matter, darling? Are we bothering you? Just open your eyes and we'll go out of the room and leave you alone till the doctor comes." Then he turned and said to the priest, "I'm not going to leave you here with her, can't you see that? Why don't you go?"

"I could revile you, my son. I could threaten you; but I ask you, for the peace of your wife's soul, leave us alone." Father Macdowell spoke with patient tenderness. He looked very big and solid and immovable as he stood by the bed. "I liked your face as soon as I saw you," he said to John. "You're a good fellow."

John still held his wife's wrist, but he rubbed one hand through his thick hair and said angrily, "You don't get the point, sir. My wife and I were always left alone, and we merely want to be left alone now. Nothing is going to separate us. She's been content with me. I'm sorry, sir; you'll have to speak to her with me here, or you'll have to go."

"No; you'll have to go for a while," the priest said patiently.

Then Mrs. Williams moved her head on the pillow and said jerkily, "Pray for me, father."

So the old priest knelt down by the bed, and with a sweet unruffled expression on his florid face he began to pray. At times his breath came with a whistling noise as though a rumbling were inside him, and at other times he sighed and was full of sorrow. He was praying that young Mrs. Williams might get better, and while he prayed he knew that her husband was more afraid of losing her to the Church than losing her to death.

All the time Father Macdowell was on his knees, with his heavy prayer book in his two hands, John kept staring at him. John couldn't understand the old priest's patience and tolerance. He wanted to quarrel with him, but he kept on watching the light from overhead shining on the one baby-pink bald spot on the smooth, white head, and at last he burst out, "You don't understand, sir! We've been very happy together. Neither you nor her people came near her when she was in good health, so why should you bother her now? I don't want anything to separate us now; neither does she. She came with me. You see you'd be separating us, don't you?" He was trying to talk like a reasonable man who had no prejudices.

Father Macdowell got up clumsily. His knees hurt him, for the floor was hard. He said to Mrs. Williams in quite a loud voice, "Did you really intend to give up everything for this young fellow?" and he bent down close to her so he could hear.

"Yes, father," she whispered.

"In Heaven's name, child, you couldn't have known what you were doing."

"We loved each other, father. We've been very happy."

"All right. Supposing you were. What now? What about all eternity, child?"

"Oh, father, I'm very sick and I'm afraid." She looked up to try to show him how scared she was, and how much she wanted him to give her peace.

He sighed and seemed distressed, and at last he said to John, "Were you married in the church?"

"No, we weren't. Look here, we're talking pretty loud and it upsets her."

"Ah, it's a crime that I'm hard of hearing, I know. Never mind, I'll go." Picking up his coat, he put it over his arm; then he sighed as if he were very tired, and he said, "I wonder if you'd just fetch me a glass of water. I'd thank you for it."

John hesitated, glancing at the tired old priest, who looked so pink and white and almost cherubic in his utter lack of guile.

"What's the matter?" Father Macdowell said.

John was ashamed of himself of appearing so sullen, so he said hastily, "Nothing's the matter. Just a moment. I won't be a moment." He hurried out of the room.

The old priest looked down at the floor and shook his head; and then, sighing and feeling uneasy, he bent over Mrs. Williams, with his good ear down to her, and he said, "I'll just ask you a few questions in a hurry, my child. You answer them quickly and I'll give you absolution." He made the sign of the cross over her and asked if she repented for having strayed from the Church, and if she had often been angry, and whether she had always been faithful, and if she had ever lied or stolen—all so casually and quickly as if it hadn't occurred to him that such a young woman could have serious sins. In the same breath he muttered, "Say a good act of contrition to yourself and that will be all, my dear." He had hardly taken a minute.

When John returned to the room with the glass of water in his hand, he saw the old priest making the sign of the cross. Father Macdowell went on praying without even looking up at John. When he had finished, he turned and said, "Oh, there you are. Thanks for the water. I needed it. Well, my boy, I'm sorry if I worried you."

John hardly said anything. He looked at his wife, who had closed her eyes, and he sat down on the end of the bed. He was too disappointed to speak.

Father Macdowell, who was expecting trouble, said, "Don't be harsh, lad."

"I'm not harsh," he said mildly, looking up at the priest. "But you weren't quite fair. And it's as though she turned away from me at the last moment. I didn't think she needed you."

"God bless you, bless the both of you. She'll get better," Father Macdowell said. But he felt ill at ease as he put on his coat, and he couldn't look directly at John.

Going along the hall, he spoke to Miss Stanhope, who wanted to apologize for her brother-in-law's attitude. "I'm sorry if it was unpleasant for you, father," she said.

"It wasn't unpleasant," he said. "I was glad to meet John. He's a fine fellow. It's a great pity he isn't a Catholic. I don't know as I played fair with him."

As he went down the stairs, puffing and sighing, he pondered the question of whether he had played fair with the young man. But by the time he reached the street he was rejoicing amiably to think he had so successfully ministered to one who had strayed from the faith and had called out to him at the last moment. Walking along with the rolling motion as if his feet hurt him, he muttered, "Of course they were happy as they were ... in a worldly way. I wonder if I did come between them?"

He shuffled along, feeling very tired, but he couldn't help thinking, "What beauty there was to his staunch love for her!" Then he added quickly "But it was just a pagan beauty, of course."

As he began to wonder about the nature of this beauty, for some reason he felt inexpressibly sad.

Sinclair Ross

(1908–1996)

JAMES SINCLAIR ROSS was born in Shellbrook, Saskatchewan, near Prince Albert. Except for four years in the army, he worked for the Union Bank of Canada (later absorbed by the Royal Bank) in Saskatchewan, Winnipeg, and Montreal, until he retired in 1966. He moved then to Greece and Spain, and in 1980 to Vancouver. His four novels and two collections of short stories, most characteristically, are psychological analyses of suppressed desires. In his best-known work, *As For Me and My House* (1941), a failed minister's barren wife tries to come to terms with envy, bitterness, hypocrisy, adultery, thwarted creativity, and the pressures of the 1930s prairie drought. In *Sawbones Memorial* (1974), a medical doctor's personal history—recorded through flashbacks, at the time of his retirement—can provide moments of equanimity only after his repressed memories have been made plain. Of Ross's story collections, the most important is *The Lamp at Noon and Other Stories* (1968); *The Race and Other Stories* (1982) brings together a miscellany of early and late works, but *The Lamp at Noon* is a coherent picture of Depression life on the prairies. Impoverishment (both emotional and economic), mental depression, suspicion, psychological strain: these constitute the implicit subjects, the empirical truth, behind stories like "The Lamp at Noon" (1938) and "The Painted Door" (1942). On the surface the stories tell also of tensions in families, tension between generations, and the tensions of isolation.

At one level a simple, realistic, plotted narrative, "One's a Heifer"—which first appeared in 1944 in Ralph Gustafson's anthology *Canadian Accent*—is also a story about various kinds of bias. It asks what we really know and what we just think we know when we act the way we do—or when we interpret behaviour, whether in fiction or in life. It also acknowledges that the forms of repression and sublimation are sometimes conscious choices, deliberate attempts to live out symbolically what sometimes cannot be lived or accepted in fact.

For Further Reading

MARILYN CHAPMAN, "Another Case of Ross's Mysterious Barn," *Canadian Literature* 103 (Winter 1984): 184–86.

KEATH FRASER, "Futility at the Pump," *Queen's Quarterly* 77 (Spring 1970): 72–80.

LORRAINE MCMULLEN, *Sinclair Ross* (Boston: Twayne, 1979).

F.H. WHITMAN, "The Case of Ross's Mysterious Barn," *Canadian Literature* 94 (Autumn 1982): 168–69.

One's a Heifer

My uncle was laid up that winter with sciatica, so when the blizzard stopped
and still two of the yearlings hadn't come home with the other cattle, Aunt
Ellen said I'd better saddle Tim and start out looking for them.

"Then maybe I'll not be back tonight," I told her firmly. "Likely they've
drifted as far as the sandhills. There's no use coming home without them."

I was thirteen, and had never been away like that all night before, but, busy
with the breakfast, Aunt Ellen said yes, that sounded sensible enough, and
while I ate, hunted up a dollar in silver for my meals.

"Most people wouldn't take it from a lad, but they're strangers up towards
the hills. Bring it out independent-like, but don't insist too much. They're more
likely to grudge you a feed of oats for Tim."

After breakfast I had to undress again, and put on two suits of underwear
and two pairs of thick, home-knitted stockings. It was a clear, bitter morning.
After the storm the drifts lay clean and unbroken to the horizon. Distant farm-
buildings stood out distinct against the prairie as if the thin sharp atmosphere
were a magnifying glass. As I started off Aunt Ellen peered cautiously out of
the door a moment through a cloud of steam, and waved a red and white check-
ered dish-towel. I didn't wave back, but conscious of her uneasiness rode erect,
as jaunty as the sheepskin and two suits of underwear would permit.

We took the road straight south about three miles. The calves, I reasoned,
would have by this time found their way home if the blizzard hadn't carried
them at least that far. Then we started catercornering across fields, riding over to
straw-stacks where we could see cattle sheltering, calling at farmhouses to ask
had they seen any strays. "Yearlings," I said each time politely. "Red with white
spots and faces. The same almost except that one's a heifer and the other isn't."

Nobody had seen them. There was a crust on the snow not quite hard enough
to carry Tim, and despite the cold his flanks and shoulders soon were steaming.
He walked with his head down, and sometimes, taking my sympathy for
granted, drew up a minute for breath.

My spirits, too, began to flag. The deadly cold and the flat white silent miles
of prairie asserted themselves like a disapproving presence. The cattle round the
straw-stacks stared when we rode up as if we were intruders. The fields stared,
and the sky stared. People shivered in their doorways, and said they'd seen
no strays.

At about one o'clock we stopped at a farmhouse for dinner. It was a single
oat sheaf half thistles for Tim, and fried eggs and bread and tea for me. Crops
had been poor that year, they apologized, and though they shook their heads

From *The Lamp at Noon and Other Stories* (Toronto: McClelland and Stewart, 1968). Reprinted
by permission of The Canadian Publishers McClelland and Stewart Ltd.

when I brought out my money I saw the woman's eyes light greedily a second, as if her instincts of hospitality were struggling hard against some urgent need. We too, I said, had had poor crops lately. That was why it was so important that I find the calves.

We rested an hour, then went on again. "Yearlings," I kept on describing them. "Red with white spots and faces. The same except that one's a heifer and the other isn't."

Still no one had seen them, still it was cold, still Tim protested what a fool I was.

The country began to roll a little. A few miles ahead I could see the first low line of sandhills. "They'll be there for sure," I said aloud, more to encourage myself than Tim. "Keeping straight to the road it won't take a quarter as long to get home again."

But home now seemed a long way off. A thin white sheet of cloud spread across the sky, and though there had been no warmth in the sun the fields looked colder and bleaker without the glitter on the snow. Straw-stacks were fewer here, as if the land were poor, and every house we stopped at seemed more dilapidated than the one before.

A nagging wind rose as the afternoon wore on. Dogs yelped and bayed at us, and sometimes from the hills, like the signal of our approach, there was a thin, wavering howl of a coyote. I began to dread the miles home again almost as much as those still ahead. There were so many cattle straggling across the fields, so many yearlings just like ours. I saw them for sure a dozen times, and as often choked my disappointment down and clicked Tim on again.

And then at last I really saw them. It was nearly dusk, and along with fifteen or twenty other cattle they were making their way towards some buildings that lay huddled at the foot of the sandhills. They passed in single file less than fifty yards away, but when I pricked Tim forward to turn them back he floundered in a snowed-in water-cut. By the time we were out they were a little distance ahead, and on account of the drifts it was impossible to put on a spurt of speed and pass them. All we could do was take our place at the end of the file, and proceed at their pace towards the buildings.

It was about half a mile. As we drew near I debated with Tim whether we should ask to spend the night or start off right away for home. We were hungry and tired, but it was a poor, shiftless-looking place. The yard was littered with old wagons and machinery; the house was scarcely distinguishable from the stables. Darkness was beginning to close in, but there was no light in the windows.

Then as we crossed the yard we heard a shout, "Stay where you are," and a man came running towards us from the stable. He was tall and ungainly, and, instead of the short sheepskin that most farmers wear, had on a long black overcoat nearly to his feet. He seized Tim's bridle when he reached us, and glared for a minute as if he were going to pull me out of the saddle. "I told you to stay out," he said in a harsh, excited voice. "You heard me, didn't you? What do you want coming round here anyway?"

I steeled myself and said, "Our two calves."

The muscles on his face were drawn together threateningly, but close to him like this and looking straight into his eyes I felt that for all their fierce look there was something about them wavering and uneasy. "The two red ones with the white faces," I continued. "They've just gone into the shed over there with yours. If you'll give me a hand getting them out again I'll start for home now right away."

He peered at me a minute, let go the bridle, then clutched it again. "They're all mine," he countered. "I was over by the gate. I watched them coming in."

His voice was harsh and thick. The strange wavering look in his eyes steadied itself for a minute to a dare. I forced myself to meet it and insisted, "I saw them back a piece in the field. They're ours all right. Let me go over a minute and I'll show you."

With a crafty tilt of his head he leered, "You didn't see any calves. And now, if you know what's good for you, you'll be on your way."

"You're trying to steal them," I flared rashly. "I'll go home and get my uncle and the police after you—then you'll see whether they're our calves or not."

My threat seemed to impress him a little. With a shifty glance in the direction of the stable he said, "All right, come along and look them over. Then maybe you'll be satisfied." But all the way across the yard he kept his hand on Tim's bridle, and at the shed made me wait a few minutes while he went inside.

The cattle shed was a lean-to on the horse stable. It was plain enough: he was hiding the calves before letting me inside to look around. While waiting for him, however, I had time to reflect that he was a lot bigger and stronger than I was, and that it might be prudent just to keep my eyes open, and not give him too much insolence.

He reappeared carrying a smoky lantern. "All right," he said pleasantly enough, "come in and look around. Will your horse stand, or do you want to tie him?"

We put Tim in an empty stall in the horse stable, then went through a narrow doorway with a bar across it to the cattle shed. Just as I expected, our calves weren't there. There were two red ones with white markings that he tried to make me believe were the ones I had seen, but positive I hadn't been mistaken, I shook my head and glanced at the doorway we had just come through. It was narrow, but not too narrow. He read my expression and said, "You think they're in there. Come on, then, and look around."

The horse stable consisted of two rows of open stalls with a passage down the centre like an aisle. At the far end were two box-stalls, one with a sick colt in it, the other closed. They were both boarded up to the ceiling, so that you could see inside them only through the doors. Again he read my expression, and with a nod towards the closed one said, "It's just a kind of harness room now. Up till a year ago I kept a stallion."

But he spoke furtively, and seemed anxious to get me away from that end of the stable. His smoky lantern threw great swaying shadows over us; and the deep clefts and triangles of shadow on his face sent a little chill through me, and made me think what a dark and evil face it was.

I was afraid, but not too afraid. "If it's just a harness room," I said reck-
lessly, "why not let me see inside? Then I'll be satisfied and believe you."

He wheeled at my question, and sidled over swiftly to the stall. He stood in
front of the door, crouched down a little, the lantern in front of him like a
shield. There was a sudden stillness through the stable as we faced each other.
Behind the light from his lantern the darkness hovered vast and sinister. It
seemed to hold its breath, to watch and listen. I felt a clutch of fear now at my
throat, but I didn't move. My eyes were fixed on him so intently that he seemed
to lose substance, to loom up close a moment, then recede. At last he disappeared completely, and there was only the lantern like a hard hypnotic eye.

It held me. It held me rooted, against my will. I wanted to run from the stable, but I wanted even more to see inside the stall. Wanting to see and yet
afraid of seeing. So afraid that it was a relief when at last he gave a shame-
faced laugh and said, "There's a hole in the floor—that's why I keep the door
closed. If you didn't know, you might step into it—twist your foot. That's what
happened to one of my horses a while ago."

I nodded as if I believed him, and went back tractably to Tim. But regaining
control of myself as I tried the saddle girths, beginning to feel that my fear had
been unwarranted, I looked up and said, "It's ten miles home, and we've been
riding hard all day. If we could stay a while—have something to eat, and then
get started—"

The wavering light came into his eyes again. He held the lantern up to see me
better, such a long, intent scrutiny that it seemed he must discover my designs.
But he gave a nod finally, as if reassured, brought oats and hay for Tim, and
suggested, companionably, "After supper we can have a game of checkers."

Then, as if I were a grown-up, he put out his hand and said, "My name is
Arthur Vickers."

Inside the house, rid of his hat and coat, he looked less forbidding. He had a
white nervous face, thin lips, a large straight nose, and deep uneasy eyes. When
the lamp was lit I fancied I could still see the wavering expression in them,
and decided it was what you called a guilty look.

"You won't think much of it," he said apologetically, following my glance
around the room. "I ought to be getting things cleaned up again. Come over
to the stove. Supper won't take long."

It was a large, low-ceilinged room that for the first moment or two struck me
more like a shed or granary than a house. The table in the centre was littered
with tools and harness. On a rusty cook-stove were two big steaming pots of
bran. Next to the stove stood a grindstone, then a white iron bed covered with
coats and horse blankets. At the end opposite the bed, weasel and coyote skins
were drying. There were guns and traps on the wall, a horse collar, a pair of rubber boots. The floor was bare and grimy. Ashes were littered around the stove.
In a corner squatted a live owl with a broken wing.

He walked back and forth a few times looking helplessly at the disorder,
then cleared off the table and lifted the pots of bran to the back of the stove. "I've
been mending harness," he explained. "You get careless, living alone like this.
It takes a woman anyway."

My presence, apparently, was making him take stock of the room. He picked up a broom and swept for a minute, made an ineffective attempt to straighten the blankets on the bed, brought another lamp out of a cupboard and lit it. There was an ungainly haste to all his movements. He started unbuckling my sheepskin for me, then turned away suddenly to take off his own coat. "Now we'll have supper," he said with an effort at self-possession. "Coffee and beans is all I can give you—maybe a little molasses."

I replied diplomatically that that sounded pretty good. It didn't seem right, accepting hospitality this way from a man trying to steal your calves, but theft, I reflected, surely justified deceit. I held my hands out to the warmth and asked if I could help.

There was a kettle of plain navy beans already cooked. He dipped out enough for our supper into a frying pan, and on top laid rashers of fat salt pork. While I watched that they didn't burn he rinsed off a few dishes. Then he set out sugar and canned milk, butter, molasses, and dark heavy biscuits that he had baked himself the day before. He kept glancing at me so apologetically all the while that I leaned over and sniffed the beans, and said at home I ate a lot of them.

"It takes a woman," he repeated as we sat down to the table. "I don't often have anyone here to eat with me. If I'd known, I'd have cleaned things up a little."

I was too intent on my plateful of beans to answer. All through the meal he sat watching me, but made no further attempts at conversation. Hungry as I was, I noticed that the wavering, uneasy look was still in his eyes. A guilty look, I told myself again, and wondered what I was going to do to get the calves away. I finished my coffee and he continued:

"It's worse even than this in the summer. No time for meals—and the heat and flies. Last summer I had a girl cooking for a few weeks, but it didn't last. Just a cow she was—just a big stupid cow—and she wanted to stay on. There's a family of them back in the hills. I had to send her home."

I wondered should I suggest starting now, or ask to spend the night. Maybe when he's asleep, I thought, I can slip out of the house and get away with the calves. He went on, "You don't know how bad it is sometimes. Weeks on end and no one to talk to. You're not yourself—you're not sure what you're going to say or do."

I remembered hearing my uncle talk about a man who had gone crazy living alone. And this fellow Vickers had queer eyes all right. And there was the live owl over in the corner, and the grindstone standing right beside the bed. "Maybe I'd better go now," I decided aloud. "Tim'll be rested, and it's ten miles home."

But he said no, it was colder now, with the wind getting stronger, and seemed so kindly and concerned that I half forgot my fears. "Likely he's just starting to go crazy," I told myself, "and it's only by staying that I'll have a chance to get the calves away."

When the table was cleared and the dishes washed he said he would go out and bed down the stable for the night. I picked up my sheepskin to go with him, but he told me sharply to stay inside. Just for a minute he looked crafty and forbidding as when I first rode up on Tim, and to allay his suspicions I nodded compliantly and put my sheepskin down again. It was better like that anyway, I decided. In a few minutes I could follow him, and perhaps, taking advantage of the shadows and his smoky lantern, make my way to the box-stall unobserved.

But when I reached the stable he had closed the door after him and hooked it from the inside. I walked round a while, tried to slip in by way of the cattle shed, and then had to go back to the house. I went with a vague feeling of relief again. There was still time, I told myself, and it would be safer anyway when he was sleeping.

So that it would be easier to keep from falling asleep myself I planned to suggest coffee again just before we went to bed. I knew that the guest didn't ordinarily suggest such things, but it was not time to remember manners when there was someone trying to steal your calves.

When he came in from the stable we played checkers. I was no match for him, but to encourage me he repeatedly let me win. "It's a long time now since I've had a chance to play," he kept on saying, trying to convince me that his shortsighted moves weren't intentional. "Sometimes I used to ask her to play, but I had to tell her every move to make. If she didn't win she'd upset the board and go off and sulk."

"My aunt is a little like that too," I said. "She cheats sometimes when we're playing cribbage—and, when I catch her, says her eyes aren't good."

"Women talk too much ever to make good checker players. It takes concentration. This one, though, couldn't even talk like anybody else."

After my long day in the cold I was starting to yawn already. He noticed it, and spoke in a rapid, earnest voice, as if afraid I might lose interest soon and want to go to bed. It was important for me too to stay awake, so I crowned a king and said, "Why don't you get someone, then, to stay with you?"

"Too many of them want to do that." His face darkened a little, almost as if warning me. "Too many of the kind you'll never get rid of again. She did, last summer when she was here. I had to put her out."

There was silence for a minute, his eyes flashing, and wanting to placate him I suggested, "She liked you, maybe."

He laughed a moment, harshly. "She liked me all right. Just two weeks ago she came back—walked over with an old suitcase and said she was going to stay. It was cold at home, and she had to work too hard, and she didn't mind even if I couldn't pay her wages."

I was getting sleepier. To keep awake I sat on the edge of the chair where it was uncomfortable and said, "Hadn't you asked her to come?"

His eyes narrowed. "I'd had trouble enough getting rid of her the first time. There were six of them at home, and she said her father thought it time that someone married her."

"Then she must be a funny one," I said. "Everybody knows that the man's supposed to ask the girl."

My remark seemed to please him. "I told you didn't I?" he said, straightening a little, jumping two of my men. "She was so stupid that at checkers she'd forget whether she was black or red."

We stopped playing now. I glanced at the owl in the corner and the ashes littered on the floor, and thought that keeping her would maybe have been a good idea after all. He read it in my face and said, "I used to think that too sometimes. I used to look at her and think nobody knew now anyway and that she'd maybe do. You need a woman on a farm all right. And night after night she'd be sitting there where you are—right there where you are, looking at me, not even trying to play—"

The fire was low, and we could hear the wind. "But then I'd go up in the hills, away from her for a while, and start thinking back the way things used to be, and it wasn't right even for the sake of your meals ready and your house kept clean. When she came back I tried to tell her that, but all the family are the same, and I realized it wasn't any use. There's nothing you can do when you're up against that sort of thing. The mother talks just like a child of ten. When she sees you coming she runs and hides. There are six of them, and it's come out in every one."

It was getting cold, but I couldn't bring myself to go over to the stove. There was the same stillness now as when he was standing at the box-stall door. And I felt the same illogical fear, the same powerlessness to move. It was the way his voice had sunk, the glassy, cold look in his eyes. The rest of his face disappeared; all I could see were his eyes. And they filled me with a vague and overpowering dread. My own voice a whisper, I asked, "And when you wouldn't marry her—what happened then?"

He remained motionless a moment, as if answering silently; then with an unexpected laugh like a breaking dish said, "Why, nothing happened. I just told her she couldn't stay. I went to town for a few days—and when I came back she was gone."

"Has she been back to bother you since?" I asked.

He made a little silo of checkers. "No—she took her suitcase with her."

To remind him that the fire was going down I went over to the stove and stood warming myself. He raked the coals with the lifter and put in poplar, two split pieces for a base and a thick round log on top. I yawned again. He said maybe I'd like to go to bed now, and I shivered and asked him could I have a drink of coffee first. While it boiled he stood stirring the two big pots of bran. The trouble with coffee, I realized, was that it would keep him from getting sleepy too.

I undressed finally and got into bed, but he blew out only one of the lamps, and sat on playing checkers with himself. I dozed a while, then sat up with a start, afraid it was morning already and that I'd lost my chance to get the calves away. He came over and looked at me a minute, then gently pushed my shoulders back on the pillow. "Why don't you come to bed too?" I asked, and he said, "Later I will—I don't feel sleepy yet."

It was like that all night. I kept dozing on and off, wakening in a fright each time to find him still there sitting at his checker board. He would raise his head sharply when I stirred, then tiptoe over to the bed and stand close to me listening till satisfied again I was asleep. The owl kept wakening too. It was down in the corner still where the lamplight scarcely reached, and I could see its eyes go on and off like yellow bulbs. The wind whistled drearily around the house. The blankets smelled like an old granary. He suspected what I was planning to do, evidently, and was staying awake to make sure I didn't get outside.

Each time I dozed I dreamed I was on Tim again. The calves were in sight, but far ahead of us, and with the drifts so deep we couldn't overtake them. Then instead of Tim it was the grindstone I was straddling, and that was the reason, not the drifts, that we weren't making better progress.

I wondered what would happen to the calves if I didn't get away with them. My uncle had sciatica, and it would be at least a day before I could be home and back again with some of the neighbours. By then Vickers might have butchered the calves, or driven them up to a hiding place in the hills where we'd never find them. There was the possibility, too, that Aunt Ellen and the neighbours wouldn't believe me. I dozed and woke—dozed and woke—always he was sitting at the checker board. I could hear the dry tinny ticking of an alarm clock, but from where I was lying couldn't see it. He seemed to be listening to it too. The wind would sometimes creak the house, and then he would give a start and sit rigid a moment with his eyes fixed on the window. It was always the window, as if there was nothing he was afraid of that could reach him by the door.

Most of the time he played checkers with himself, moving his lips, muttering words I couldn't hear, but once I woke to find him staring fixedly across the table as if he had a partner sitting there. His hands were clenched in front of him, there was a sharp, metallic glitter in his eyes. I lay transfixed, unbreathing. His eyes as I watched seemed to dilate, to brighten, to harden like a bird's. For a long time he sat contracted, motionless, as if gathering himself to strike, then furtively he slid his hand an inch or two along the table towards some checkers that were piled beside the board. It was as if he were reaching for a weapon, as if his invisible partner were an enemy. He clutched the checkers, slipped slowly from his chair and straightened. His movements were sure, stealthy, silent like a cat's. His face had taken on a desperate, contorted look. As he raised his hand the tension was unbearable.

It was a long time—a long time watching him the way you watch a finger tightening slowly in the trigger of a gun—and then suddenly wrenching himself to action he hurled the checkers with such vicious fury that they struck the wall and clattered back across the room.

And everything was quiet again. I started a little, mumbled to myself as if half-awakened, lay quite still. But he seemed to have forgotten me, and after standing limp and dazed a minute got down on his knees and started looking for the checkers. When he had them all, he put more wood in the stove, then returned quietly to the table and sat down. We were alone again; everything was exactly as before. I relaxed gradually, telling myself that he'd just been seeing things.

The next time I woke he was sitting with his head sunk forward on the table. It looked as if he had fallen asleep at last, and huddling alert among the bed-clothes I decided to watch a minute to make sure, then dress and try to slip out to the stable.

While I watched, I planned exactly every movement I was going to make. Rehearsing it in my mind as carefully as if I were actually doing it, I climbed out of bed, put on my clothes, tiptoed stealthily to the door and slipped outside. By this time, though, I was getting drowsy, and relaxing among the blankets I decided that for safety's sake I should rehearse it still again. I rehearsed it four times altogether, and the fourth time dreamed that I hurried on successfully to the stable.

I fumbled with the door a while, then went inside and felt my way through the darkness to the box-stall. There was a bright light suddenly and the owl was sitting over the door with his yellow eyes like a pair of lanterns. The calves, he told me, were in the other stall with the sick colt. I looked and they were there all right, but Tim came up and said it might be better not to start for home till morning. He reminded me that I hadn't paid for his feed or my own supper yet, and that if I slipped off this way it would mean that I was stealing, too. I agreed, realizing now that it wasn't the calves I was looking for after all, and that I still had to see inside the stall that was guarded by the owl. "Wait here," Tim said, "I'll tell you if he flies away," and without further questioning I lay down in the straw and went to sleep again.... When I woke coffee and beans were on the stove already, and though the lamp was still lit I could tell by the window that it was nearly morning.

We were silent during breakfast. Two or three times I caught him watching me, and it seemed his eyes were shiftier than before. After his sleepless night he looked tired and haggard. He left the table while I was still eating and fed raw rabbit to the owl, then came back and drank another cup of coffee. He had been friendly and communicative the night before, but now, just as when he first came running out of the stable in his long black coat, his expression was sullen and resentful. I began to feel that he was in a hurry to be rid of me.

I took my time, however, racking my brains to outwit him still and get the calves away. It looked pretty hopeless now, his eyes on me so suspiciously, my imagination at low ebb. Even if I did get inside the box-stall to see the calves—was he going to stand back then and let me start off home with them? Might it not more likely frighten him, make him do something desperate, so that I couldn't reach my uncle or the police? There was the owl over in the corner, the grindstone by the bed. And with such a queer fellow you could never tell. You could never tell, and you had to think about your own skin too. So I said politely, "Thank you, Mr. Vickers, for letting me stay all night," and remembering what Tim had told me took out my dollar's worth of silver.

He gave a short dry laugh and wouldn't take it. "Maybe you'll come back," he said, "and next time stay longer. We'll go shooting up in the hills if you like—and I'll make a trip to town for things so that we can have better meals. You need company sometimes for a change. There's been no one here now quite a while."

His face softened again as he spoke. There was an expression in his eyes as if he wished that I could stay on now. It puzzled me. I wanted to be indignant, and it was impossible. He held my sheepskin for me while I put it on, and tied the scarf around the collar with a solicitude and determination equal to Aunt Ellen's. And then he gave his short dry laugh again, and hoped I'd find my calves all right.

He had been out to the stable before I was awake, and Tim was ready for me, fed and saddled. But I delayed a few minutes, pretending to be interested in his horses and the sick colt. It would be worth something after all, I realized, to get just a glimpse of the calves. Aunt Ellen was going to be skeptical enough of my story as it was. It could only confirm her doubts to hear me say I hadn't seen the calves in the box-stall, and was just pretty sure that they were there.

So I went from stall to stall, stroking the horses and making comparisons with the ones we had at home. The door, I noticed, he had left wide open, ready for me to lead out Tim. He was walking up and down the aisle, telling me which horses were quiet, which to be careful of. I came to a nervous chestnut mare, and realized she was my only chance.

She crushed her hips against the side of the stall as I slipped up to her manger, almost pinning me, then gave her head a toss and pulled back hard on the halter shank. The shank, I noticed, was tied with an easy slip-knot that the right twist and a sharp tug would undo in half a second. And the door was wide open, ready for me to lead out Tim—and standing as she was with her body across the stall diagonally, I was for the moment screened from sight.

It happened quickly. There wasn't time to think of consequences. I just pulled the knot, in the same instant struck the mare across the nose. With a snort she threw herself backwards, almost trampling Vickers, then flung up her head to keep from tripping on the shank and plunged outside.

It worked as I hoped it would. "Quick," Vickers yelled to me, "the gate's open—try and head her off"—but instead I just waited till he himself was gone, then leaped to the box-stall.

The door was fastened with two tight-fitting slide-bolts, one so high that I could scarcely reach it standing on my toes. It wouldn't yield. There was a piece of broken whiffle-tree beside the other box-stall door. I snatched it up and started hammering on the pin. Still it wouldn't yield. The head of the pin was small and round, and the whiffle-tree kept glancing off. I was too terrified to pause a moment and take careful aim.

Terrified of the stall though, not of Vickers. Terrified of the stall, yet compelled by a frantic need to get inside. For the moment I had forgotten Vickers, forgotten even the danger of his catching me. I worked blindly, helplessly, as if I were confined and smothering. For a moment I yielded to panic, dropped the piece of whiffle-tree and started kicking at the door. Then, collected again, I forced back the lower bolt, and picking up the whiffle-tree tried to pry the door out a little at the bottom. But I had wasted too much time. Just as I dropped to my knees to peer through the opening Vickers seized me. I struggled to my feet and fought a moment, but it was such a hard, strangling clutch at my throat that I felt myself go limp and blind. In desperation then I kicked him, and with a blow like a reflex he sent me staggering to the floor.

But it wasn't the blow that frightened me. It was the fierce, wild light in his eyes.

Stunned as I was, I looked up and saw him watching me, and, sick with terror, made a bolt for Tim. I untied him with hands that moved incredibly, galvanized for escape. I knew now for sure that Vickers was crazy. He followed me outside, and, just as I mounted, seized Tim again by the bridle. For a second or two it made me crazy too. Gathering up the free ends of the rein I lashed him hard across the face. He let go of the bridle, and, frightened and excited too now, Tim made a dash across the yard and out of the gate. Deep as the snow was, I kept him galloping for half a mile, pommelling him with my fists, kicking my heels against his sides. Then of his own accord he drew up short for breath, and I looked around to see whether Vickers was following. He wasn't—there was only snow and the hills, his buildings a lonely little smudge against the whiteness—and the relief was like a stick pulled out that's been holding up tomato vines or peas. I slumped across the saddle weakly, and till Tim started on again lay there whimpering like a baby.

We were home by noon. We didn't have to cross fields or stop at houses now, and there had been teams on the road packing down the snow so that Tim could trot part of the way and even canter. I put him in the stable without taking time to tie or unbridled him, and ran to the house to tell Aunt Ellen. But I was still frightened, cold and a little hysterical, and it was a while before she could understand how everything had happened. She was silent a minute, indulgent, then helping me off with my sheepskin said kindly, "You'd better forget about it now, and come over and get warm. The calves came home themselves yesterday. Just about an hour after you set out."

I looked up at her. "But the stall, then—just because I wanted to look inside he knocked me down—and if it wasn't the calves in there—"

She didn't answer. She was busy building up the fire and looking at the stew.

Joyce Marshall

(b. 1913)

BORN IN MONTREAL AND EDUCATED AT MCGILL, Toronto freelance writer Joyce Marshall has had many of her works broadcast over the CBC. Widely applauded for her translations of some of the fiction of Gabrielle Roy and other writers, she is also noted for her own short stories and two novels, *Presently Tomorrow* (1946) and *Lovers and Strangers* (1957). Seven of her powerful stories—written over three decades, from the 1950s to the 1970s—were collected in *A Private Place* (1975), and several more stories have appeared since.

Uncertainty constitutes a recurrent theme in them. Sometimes it is a direct threat, and sometimes it works indirectly, as when the fear of being uncertain becomes a debilitating obsession for a character. The stories—like "The Enemy," which was broadcast on CBC *Anthology* before being collected in 1975—then ask how people might guard themselves against attack and against disintegration. The answers are not always comforting. People do have some systems of social support around them—and if they can draw on an inner strength of will, then that, too, is a valuable ally—but their real-life choices of how to act are seldom clearcut. For example, women in Marshall's stories are repeatedly put in a position where they can choose to engage actively with society or to withdraw defensively from it. Neither choice is intrinsically "right" (though Marshall's bias is clearly towards "engagement" and "activity"). Both choices, moreover, are somehow "dangerous"; and against the dangers there are few adequate defences. When the dangers are irrational, there are no defences at all, for that's what "irrationality" implies: the inability to plan for it, to fit it into a reasonable, logical order. The result—as in "The Enemy"—can be stark terror. And the terror is all the more horrific because of the quiet, conversational, profoundly ordinary manner in which the story discusses the blunt and ugly fact of violation.

For Further Reading

TIMOTHY FINDLEY, "Afterword" to Joyce Marshall, *Any Time at All and Other Stories* (Toronto: McClelland & Stewart, 1993) 212–19.

W.H. NEW, "Joyce Marshall" in *Canadian Writers, 1920–1959,* second series, *Dictionary of Literary Biography* 88 (Detroit: Gale, 1989) 197–204.

PATRICIA MEYER SPACKS, *The Female Imagination* (New York: Knopf, 1975).

The Enemy

"Unless it's happened to you," she always begins, "you couldn't understand, you couldn't possibly." Having repeated it all so many times—many more times than is useful to herself or of possible concern to anyone else—she uses not only the same phrases and words but the same stresses, her voice rising on its own, clinging to certain pitches, slipping back. She often wishes she might find different words for the events because then, she feels, she might no longer describe them, would not need to. For it is need that keeps her at it. She knows that. Need to discover something, something she has missed, perhaps even wanted and still wants to miss. So she goes on explaining that it wasn't as if anyone hated her. Nobody ever has. Her life, though certainly not blameless, has not harmed others.

Everyone agrees, as everyone always agrees now with Miranda. But they like her less, she knows, than in the days when she used to explain nothing, was even a little mysterious. Mysteriously married seven or eight years ago to a painter many years older. Divorced without pain. Mother of a small child, a girl of about six. Mysteriously well-off, with child-support arriving more or less regularly from Spain or Portugal and something much larger known vaguely as "money from my father." (No-one even knew she had a mother living in Winnipeg, till the mother turned up "to help" after the disaster. Or that Winnipeg was Miranda's home town. Or, for that matter, that Miranda was just a name she'd given herself.) She tried for a while to get them to call her Mary but no-one could get into the way of it. She had too definitely become Miranda, one of those thin prettyish young women with long legs and a tiny rump and a gift for dressing herself up or down so that in Miranda's case her various outfits and adornments are always more memorable than the shape and colour of her eyes or the precise shade of greeny-yellow of her rain of hair. She still lives much as before in the bottom flat of the high, orphaned half-house she owns just off Church Street—rather sloppily with that wasteful sort of sloppiness only the well-to-do can manage. Buying things, breaking them, giving them away. She still takes in strays though the strays now get nervous very quickly and wander off. But her older friends, who are all more or less in her debt and have only recently become aware of it, are patient and try to listen at least. Thinking, she knows: My God, all this fuss about a lot of old junk. Yes, Miranda's mind echoes: junk—*my* junk. And buys or makes another lamp. Strings popcorn into necklaces. Or sees some starved young man selling *Guerilla* on Yonge Street and takes him home to dinner. For she must do as she's always done, be what she was in the days when she didn't have to wonder what that was.

No-one points out that she doesn't tell the story as it happened but breaks right into the climax as if she's forgotten how slowly and intermittently it

---

From *A Private Place* (Ottawa: Oberon Press, 1975). Reprinted by permission of the author.

began. (There was cleverness in this, she came to realize but no longer seems to remember.) She sees herself now as trudging through the slush of that February day, groceries in one arm, the small blonde child at her side, happy and innocent, very much herself, opening the door into her big cluttered living room and then, abruptly, ruin at her feet. Actually she didn't even notice, till it crunched, that the shade from the centre fixture lay in shards on the rug. Her mind, as she swept up the bits, was busy with Chet, her unpaying tenant on the second floor, whom she'd met in the hall and impulsively, because his little airedale face looked so pinched and unhappy, invited to dinner. She did not even think to mention it when he came or during their quite ordinary evening.

Chet did some of his "magic" tricks and, after dinner, put the child to bed. Maidy, a sixteen-year-old runaway from Timmins Miranda had found sleeping in the laundromat and installed on the top floor, came down to borrow ten dollars for grass. Miranda gave it to her because, as she explained later to Chet, who thought Maidy was exploiting her, it was better than having the girl go back on the street. Maidy was straightening out, Miranda had taught her to dip candles and every now and then she took a batch over to Kensington to sell, but you couldn't expect too much too quickly. Chet sniffed. He would have remained a perfectly conventional youth, Miranda thought with pity, if he hadn't chosen to evade the draft, come to Toronto just when it was hardest to find jobs and grow that untidy beard. Miranda was trying to help him get enough points to become a landed immigrant but what could the poor kid do except—why, of course, wave hankies and pull cards from ears to the delight of children. Immediately she called half a dozen people and persuaded two of them to hire him to perform at children's parties they hadn't known they were going to have. Chet cheered, first slightly, then considerably, and after discussing his future for a while, they went to bed. He now accepted this culmination to their evenings as calmly as she did. We like it and we're good, she'd had to tell him with some pains; her being older had alarmed him, made him search for motives. She suspected sometimes that he saw it as his way of thanking her—for the free quarters and the frequent free meals—and, because this pleased him, she allowed it. Though she was not at that time analytical of herself or others, she knew she disliked obligation and saw anything that could release it as a good thing.

She was busy during the next few days rounding up other party dates for Chet but found time to shop for a new lampshade—real flowers pressed between two sheets of frosted glass. A week later it was broken, lying in fragments on the rug. The pieces, it occurred to her as she swept them up, looked dirty as if someone had ... She ran to the windows. The one in the kitchen was unhooked. It often was. She stood for a moment looking out at the backs of apartments old and new, the few scattered houses like her own, one of them seemingly crowned by a crane that as she watched it slowly shifted. But only when she was buying the third shade—fringed and silken and unbreakable—did she wholly admit what she now accepted: Someone had done those things. She formed the habit of checking hooks and fastenings before she went out, glancing about quickly when she came in.

Nothing happened for several weeks and then one evening Steve came home with her after the opening of his new show. She hadn't been sure he would. He was unreliable on these occasions, his shyness pushed to its limits talking to reviewers and possible buyers, which he did well and gaily but with deep shame. His paintings would sell as always; he would be glad, she knew, if just for once they didn't. But he was glib in his work and, sadly, knew it. Other more innovative painters, his friends, didn't even envy him his success. He knew that too.

The child was spending the night with Maidy because Miranda hadn't been able to get a sitter. Maidy liked to be given a responsibility now and then, not too many responsibilities or too often. So Miranda played the stereo rather loud and they had several more drinks and, when Steve tried to pull off her dress, she helped him and lay half-naked across his lap while he quizzed her—about her marriage, about the various men who wandered in and out of her life. Was she, in fact, just what she seemed—a nice warm communal earth-mother or—?

"A mixed-up rich kid out for kicks?" she suggested.

"No, no, that wasn't what I—Hey—why are you watching me?"

"Am I?" She was, of course. He was using her as he often did to work out something for himself. He might turn brutal if she wasn't careful and with Steve brutality, even verbal brutality, which was all he ever permitted himself, led always to humiliation. Steve went fairly far back in her life for he was a friend of Rodney, to whom she'd been married.

"Ah, why do you put up with me?" he asked.

"Why not?" she said and got up to lead the way to the other room.

"No sensible person would," he said. "I've got a jeezly great paunch. And I'm too boiled to be any use to you."

He fell across her as she eased under the covers of her low bed. So she took it cold across her narrow rump—garbage, a nasty little pile of it, identified, when she wrenched him off and switched on the light, as tomato peel, tea-leaves, something vaguely sour and soupy.

Steve helped her check windows after she'd washed, shaking, in the bathroom. There was that kitchen window unfastened again. Had she remembered to lock it?

"Mightn't it have been the kid?" Steve suggested.

"No—I never drink tea—this isn't my—Steve, don't tell anyone. Promise."

"Why in hell not?"

She couldn't say. So he promised and, suddenly sober, helped her rinse the sheets, made coffee, sat with her a while and left. But after the next time, about a week later, it was she who told, told everyone, talked and talked.

For it was a pair of the child's socks, cut up small and placed in the refrigerator, all coated with something that might have been excrement or mud; she had plucked them out with tongs and flung them away before she could tell. She knew now that someone hated her, someone who knew her, knew where things were kept. A few days later it was definitely excrement, wrapped in leaves, tucked in among her underwear. Someone who had leisure, wasn't afraid, knew her habits. And then a smear that might be vomit trodden into the living-room rug.

"Tell the police," people said. "Move. This is a maniac. Some day you'll come in and surprise him and he'll kill you."

She wouldn't tell the police. It mustn't be some outsider who discovered the culprit. *She* must do it, though she wasn't sure why. Everyone professed to be sold on the theory of the maniac behaving randomly. She pretended to accept this too, had safety catches put on the windows and a bolt on the back door. She thought of having the lock of her apartment changed—she had given away so many keys—but a new lock was just as vulnerable as the old to wax impression or wire. (Everyone had a different theory of how thieves or vandals got in.) She so loathed this new need for bolting and barricading that from time to time she deliberately left the back door unlocked when she went over to Church Street to shop. (The smear on the living-room rug appeared after one such lapse. But the next incident—a rough phallus drawn with some sort of filth on the bathroom mirror—occurred when the place was tightly sealed.)

She began to explain herself. She'd never felt the need to, believing that others accepted her on her own terms. She now discovered that she didn't know what those were. She seemed to have lived a completely unexamined life. But if unexamined, it was surely also inoffensive. I've always given as much as I've got, she insisted. I have never taken a man from anyone else. I have never clung. If I've been promiscuous, and I know that is a word some people might want to use about me, I have not been mean or niggardly. I have never used sex as a weapon. To defend herself, she began to name the men she'd gone to bed with. Having no practice in confiding, she didn't know how to stop once started, even when uneasiness on the faces of people who'd wanted to know more about her showed that they hadn't wanted to know this much. She defended the upbringing she was giving the child, unable to forget what might have been a rather blatant message in the little socks. She had never tried to thrust her own standards on the child. Never would. And you just had to look at her—

Everyone agreed that the child looked and behaved like a happy, solid little person. No-one argued with anything she said about herself. No-one showed any indication of the hatred someone felt. She was not convinced, went on explaining and watching for signs. She entertained a lot. (Everyone thought she feared being alone.) She called people she had not seen for years who might feel resentment towards her—men she had left behind or who had left her.

She tried to lay traps, would tell a number of people she was going to a play or a concert, duly leave, then come back after half an hour.

Once she found Maidy at the door.

"I thought I heard something," the girl said.

They stared at one another, fat little shaggy Maidy blinking up from behind her hair.

"When," Miranda asked her, "are you going to do something about paying your way around here? You people seem to think that just because I have money, I'm your own built-in pushover. Well, we were poor when I was a kid. Do you know that? My mother worked as a nurse on the four-to-midnight shift. I never saw her. And do you know why? My father was killed in that war you know nothing about. He had money from his family and he left it in trust for me when I was 21—his unborn child he called me in his will because that's what I was then. I guess my mother was hurt. She wouldn't even spend the interest—"

"Gee, I'm sorry," Maidy said. "But look—if gratitude's what you want, why don't you choose someone who's got something to be grateful with?"

"All I want," said Miranda, "is for you to stop thinking you invented everything, invented suffering, invented injustice—"

She slammed the door in the girl's face but next day was ashamed, apologized to Maidy and asked her to sit with the child. And she said nothing at all a week later when Chet came in to say he hoped she'd understand, there was something sick going on, he'd better move, because if it blew up into a real hassle before he got his landed immigrant's status...

He kept one or two of the performing dates she'd made for him, then disappeared; she heard he'd hitch-hiked out to the west coast.

"Have you thought," Steve asked, "that he might have been the one who did it?"

Miranda didn't answer. For she had indeed thought this. Or even that it might have been Steve himself. There could have been time that evening for him to sneak into the bedroom while she was in the kitchen or the can. Having nursed that garbage in his pocket all through the opening of his show? Could he be that sick? Could anyone? What did she really know of him, when you came to it, except that he was a great paunchy man who drank too much, was limited and knew it? What did she know of any of the people she summed up in easy phrases and considered her friends? And while there was no-one she could imagine doing those things, there was no-one she could not imagine doing them.

After the scrawl on the bathroom mirror, nothing happened. Throughout the wind and wet of March her belongings were unmolested. But she still locked or negligently failed to lock, carefully inspected everything when she came in. Her enemy had made these changes in her way of living, watched now, she supposed, and was pleased to have shaken her so.

Then one April afternoon she fell into conversation at the laundromat with a young man who had an idea for a film and even a small amount of backing. She invited him to dinner and, after the child was in bed, they talked for a while and then made love. And as they lay afterwards, discussing how he might best apply for subsidy—she knew a number of people who might be useful—she suddenly saw herself acting just as she always did, as if she'd never been attacked, and found herself telling him about all the ugly little acts.

"Yeah, people are hung up in all sorts of ways," he said and soon afterwards decided to get up and dress and leave.

He tried to see her again but the child got chicken pox and needed nursing and then Miranda came down with it herself and was very ill. Maidy brought odd little meals of cereal and brown rice and took the child out. Steve and others sat in turn by Miranda's bed. When she felt strong enough she arranged to rent a cottage in Muskoka for six weeks. She sat in the sun and swam and taught the child to do the dog paddle and play a couple of simple card-games. The days dripped past like honey and it seemed to her that she was almost as empty as the child. When her ex-husband's monthly cheque was forwarded to her, she sat down to write her usual report of their daughter's well-being, found herself telling him instead that he ought not to have married her, so much younger, he had so clearly disliked marriage, she hadn't cared all that much for it herself, had been glad when he suggested packing it up but even so it hadn't been fair, next time he should pick someone a little more—She stopped, shocked by a resentment she hadn't known she felt, this was the enemy's doing, he didn't want to leave her with anything. She tore up the letter and in a few days wrote the sort of formal account she usually sent. The child began to answer the usual appellation of "child" with "My name's Anne," so there was more of her perhaps than there was of her mother who long ago, for some reason or lack of reason, had adopted a name that wasn't her own. And she couldn't imagine how she was to return to Toronto and that apartment, have friends and men and go on living.

The only two things of real value—the television and the stereo—had been spared. Everything else was smashed, splintered, ribboned, rent—every garment of her own and the child's, all the dishes, the curtains, the ornaments and the lamps. Even the mattresses had been ripped open with a knife, the pictures slashed. The chairs and tables must have been wrenched apart with great strength. And there was a trail of filth through the room.

Sobbing on her knees at the phone, clutching the child, Miranda dialed several numbers till she found Steve at home. Steve proved immediately practical, arrived only minutes after the police, whom he had notified, and answered the first questions very sensibly. But even he couldn't explain why Miranda hadn't reported the earlier incidents or why, with so much reason for anxiety, she hadn't asked the police to keep an eye on the flat. (Or for that matter the caretaker, who, summoned, knew and had heard nothing. He was only in the building an hour or so a day.) Neighbours? The middle flat had stood empty since Chet left. Maidy was rooted out of her attic, large-eyed. She hadn't heard anything either.

When Miranda felt sufficiently composed, she began to speak in a rapid voice. "Why should I tell all sorts of people I have enemies? Who would want to admit that? Would you?"

The policeman, who was young and painfully clean-shaven and held his chin so firmly up-tilted that his expression, whether of concern or contempt, couldn't be seen, ignored this and went on talking to Steve. Fingerprint men and photographers were summoned, came and went. Reporters arrived with more photographers. Miranda talked, told them she was going to buy a savage dog, she was alone with her child and in grave danger. She and Anne were pushed in and out of various groups, some of which included, as well as Maidy and Steve, mysterious persons she'd never seen before. Miranda talked until suddenly she was alone with Steve, who was sitting on the floor with the child asleep on his lap while she told him she couldn't go out to eat, she had to guard her stereo. Late in the evening came a sharp ring and knock and in walked her mother, summoned from Winnipeg—when?—by Steve, who seemed to have known—how?—her name and where she lived. And then, Miranda talking still, they were all in a taxi going to a hotel. When she awakened next morning rather late, it was with the sense, almost the weight, of eyes on her face. But her mother, in a chair near the window, was reading a newspaper spread across her knees.

"Ah there," she said, as Miranda propped herself on an elbow, and began to fill in space with her light firm voice, eyes down still towards the paper (this woman with the pansy-crumpled face, glasses and little mouth who'd edged Miranda's childhood, nursed her when ill, worked for her clothes and her music and skating lessons, organized the mechanics of her life but left her thoughts loose to go where they chose and now was afraid—or unwilling—to look at her in disarray). That nice little thing from upstairs, she said—what a curious name, was it short for Maiden?—had come to take Anne for the day; they were off to the island. And that charming Steve was busy with the caretaker at this very moment sweeping up the place. So, she concluded, she'd order up breakfast and then they'd go out, buy one or two—

"No," Miranda said. "I'm not going back to that apartment. Mother, let me come home to Winnipeg with you."

"I haven't room for you," said her mother. She probably has a man, Miranda thought, she's really quite attractive. And she felt sad trying to edge her mind into her mother's life, all strange to her.

"I can't live alone, I don't know how to," she said. "I live like a slut. I neglect the—Anne."

"I doubt that," said her mother. "She doesn't look neglected. Child—" Oh call me by my name, Miranda thought, I haven't heard it for so long, I want to. "Why are you so sure it's someone you know?" And when Miranda didn't answer, "It's natural," her mother said. "A form of egotism. Wanting to deserve things—it's so much less demeaning than being a victim. But we all have to come to it at times. So be as sensible as I think you are and get up."

Miranda did and three days later went back with Anne and some borrowed furniture to the apartment. Her mother remained in the city for another week, then returned to Winnipeg and her own life. Miranda did buy a dog, a boxer said to be fierce, but walking him was a chore and neighbours who had missed the sounds of destruction were not so deaf to the howling of the dog when left alone at night. So she found him a home in the suburbs. She had discovered, anyway, that she was not afraid. The enemy would not return. He did not need to, having done his worst. He had thrust her all the way to the dark side and though there might not have been anything very bad there, there was nothing very good either.

In September another young woman's apartment was wrecked, a block away. On his third attempt the vandal was caught. Photographs showed him small and hollow-cheeked, a classic nonentity. He lived in one of the older buildings in the neighbourhood and had few acquaintances. He spoke a good deal about a mission. The girls, he insisted, were nothing, he did not know or choose them, they were chosen. He did not come to trial, which Miranda re-gretted. Not that she wanted to have to testify against him; she was too fright-ened of what she might say, would surely think. But she would have liked to see for once and close at hand the face of what is the real enemy, whether within or without. She might have known something then—not why she was marked out since that seems to have been sheer savage randomness but why, chosen, she was so open, her life so ready to come apart. She knows her two fel-low victims by sight now, thinks of asking them but never does; they do not look damaged.

And where are the other threats? She knows there will be others, that they only wait. Perhaps that is why she goes on talking about it, living one day and one day. And almost trusting.

P.K. Page

(b. 1916)

PATRICIA KATHLEEN PAGE WAS BORN IN SWANAGE, ENGLAND, and came to Alberta in 1919, where she grew up. Taking on a variety of jobs—in commerce, in radio, and as a research assistant—she became a scriptwriter for the National Film Board in 1946, and in 1950 she married W.A. Irwin, then Film Board Commissioner, who later became Canadian High Commissioner and Ambassador to Australia, Brazil, and Mexico. Already a published poet by this time—Page had been active in the journal *Preview* in the 1940s, and under the name "Judith Cape" had published a novel called *The Sun and the Moon* in 1944 (it was reprinted in *The Sun and the Moon and Other Fictions* in 1973)—she benefitted greatly from the years she spent abroad. In Brazil, for example (she records in her published journal), she learned to draw; and as P.K. Irwin, she developed another career as a fine-line pen-and-ink artist. Australia shaped some of her finest poems (e.g., "Cook's Mountains") and sharpened her talent for effective metaphor. From her early poems (which recurrently explored psychological types), she moved towards more oracular utterances, and explorations of the psychological and artistic implications of bicameral brain research.

"Unless the Eye Catch Fire..." (which first appeared in *Malahat Review* in 1979) became the prose centre to a book of poetry called *Evening Dance of the Grey Flies* (1981). A journal in form, it reflects not only on the idea that the universe might end in fire, but also on the poetic dimensions of fiction itself.

For Further Reading

MARGARET ATWOOD, "Canadian Monsters: Some Aspects of the Supernatural in Canadian Fiction" in *Second Words* (Toronto: House of Anansi, 1982) 238–44.

ANDREA PARADIS, ed., *Out of This World: Canadian Science Fiction & Fantasy Literature* (Ottawa: Quarry/National Library of Canada, 1995).

Unless the Eye
Catch Fire...

Unless the eye catch fire
The God will not be seen...

—THEODORE ROSZAK,
Where the Wasteland Ends

Wednesday, September 17.
The day began normally enough. The quails, cockaded as antique foot soldiers, arrived while I was having breakfast. The males black-faced, white-necklaced, cinnamon-crowned, with short, sharp, dark plumes. Square bibs, Payne's grey; belly and sides with a pattern of small stitches. Reassuring, the flock of them. They tell me the macadamization of the world is not complete.

A sudden alarm, and as if they had one brain among them, they were gone in a rush—a sideways ascending Niagara—shutting out the light, obscuring the sky and exposing a rectangle of lawn, unexpectedly emerald. How bright the berries on the cotoneaster. Random leaves on the cherry twirled like gold spinners. The garden was high-keyed, vivid, locked in aspic.

Without warning, and as if I were looking down the tube of a kaleidoscope, the merest shake occurred—moiréed the garden—rectified itself. Or, more precisely, as if a range-finder through which I had been sighting, found of itself a more accurate focus. Sharpened, in fact, to an excoriating exactness.

And then the colours changed. Shifted to a higher octave—a *bright spectrum*. Each colour with its own *light*, its own *shape*. The leaves of the trees, the berries, the grasses—as if shedding successive films—disclosed layer after layer of hidden perfections. And upon these rapidly changing surfaces the 'range-finder'—to really play hob with metaphor!—sharpened its small invisible blades.

I don't know how to describe the intensity and speed of focus of this gratuitous zoom lens through which I stared, or the swift and dizzying adjustments within me. I became a 'sleeping top,' perfectly centred, perfectly—sighted. The colours vibrated beyond the visible range of the spectrum. Yet I saw them. With some matching eye. Whole galaxies of them, blazing and glowing, flowing in rivulets, gushing in fountains—volatile, mercurial, and making lackluster and off-key the colours of the rainbow.

I had no time or inclination to wonder, intellectualize. My mind seemed astonishingly clear and quite still. Like a crystal. A burning glass.

And then the range-finder sharpened once again. To alter space.

From *Evening Dance of the Grey Flies* (Toronto: Oxford University Press, 1981). Reprinted by permission of the author.

The lawn, the bushes, the trees—still super-brilliant—were no longer *there*. *There*, in fact, had ceased to exist. They were now, of all places in the world, *here*. Right in the centre of my being. Occupying an immense inner space. Part of me. Mine. Except the whole idea of ownership was beside the point. As true to say I was theirs as they mine. I and they were here; they and I, there. (*There*, *here*...odd...but for an irrelevant, inconsequential 't' which comes and goes, the words are the same.)

As suddenly as the world had altered, it returned to normal. I looked at my watch. A ridiculous mechanical habit. As I had no idea when the experience began it was impossible to know how long it had lasted. What had seemed eternity couldn't have been more than a minute or so. My coffee was still steaming in its mug.

The garden, through the window, was as it had always been. Yet not as it had always been. Less. Like listening to mono after hearing stereo. But with a far greater loss of dimension. A grievous loss.

I rubbed my eyes. Wondered, not without alarm, if this was the onset of some disease of the retina—glaucoma or some cellular change in the eye itself—superlatively packaged, fatally sweet as the marzipan cherry I ate as a child and *knew* was poison.

If it *is* a disease, the symptoms will recur. It will happen again.

Tuesday, September 23.
It *has* happened again.

Tonight, taking Dexter for his late walk, I looked up at the crocheted tangle of boughs against the sky. Dark silhouettes against the lesser dark, but beating now with an extraordinary black brilliance. The golden glints in obsidian or the lurking embers in black opals are the nearest I can come to describing them. But it's a false description, emphasizing as it does, the wrong end of the scale. This was a *dark spectrum*. As if the starry heavens were translated into densities of black—black Mars, black Saturn, black Jupiter; or a master jeweller had crossed his jewels with jet and set them to burn and wink in the branches and twigs of oaks whose leaves shone luminous—a leafy Milky Way—fired by black chlorophyll.

Dexter stopped as dead as I. Transfixed. His thick honey-coloured coat and amber eyes glowing with their own intense brightness, suggested yet another spectrum. A *spectrum of light*. He was a constellated dog, shining, supra-real, against the foothills and mountain ranges of midnight.

I am reminded now, as I write, of a collection of lepidoptera in Brazil—one entire wall covered with butterflies, creatures of daylight—enormous or tiny— blue, orange, black. Strong-coloured. And on the opposite wall their anti-selves—pale night flyers spanning such a range of silver and white and lightest snuff-colour that once one entered their spectral scale there was no end to the subtleties and delicate nuances. But I didn't think like this then. All thought, all comparisons were prevented by the startling infinities of darkness and light.

Then, as before, the additional shake occurred and the two spectrums moved swiftly from without to within. As if two equal and complementary circles centred inside me—or I in them. How explain that I not only *saw* but actually *was* the two spectrums? (I underline a simple, but in this case, exactly appropriate anagram.)

Then the range-finder lost its focus and the world, once again, was back to normal. Dexter, a pale, blurred blob, bounded about within the field of my peripheral vision, going on with his doggy interests just as if a moment before he had not been frozen in his tracks, a dog entranced.

I am no longer concerned about my eyesight. Wonder only if we are both mad, Dexter and I? Angelically mad, sharing hallucinations of epiphany. *Folie à deux?*

Friday, October 3.
It's hard to account for my secrecy, for I *have* been secretive. As if the cat had my tongue. It's not that I don't long to talk about the colours but I can't risk the wrong response—(as Gaby once said of a companion after a faultless performance of *Giselle:* 'If she had criticised the least detail of it, I'd have hit her!').

Once or twice I've gone so far as to say, 'I had the most extraordinary experience the other day...' hoping to find some look or phrase, some answering, 'So did I.' None has been forthcoming.

I can't forget the beauty. Can't get it out of my head. Startling, unearthly, indescribable. Infuriatingly indescribable. A glimpse of—somewhere else. Somewhere alive, miraculous, newly-made yet timeless. And more important still—significant, luminous, with a meaning of which I was part. Except that I—the I who is writing this—did not exist; was flooded out, dissolved in that immensity where subject and object are one.

I have to make a deliberate effort now not to live my life in terms of it; not to sit, immobilized, awaiting the shake that heralds a new world. Awaiting the transfiguration.

Luckily the necessities of life keep me busy. But upstream of my actions, behind a kind of plate glass, some part of me waits, listens, maintains a total attention.

Tuesday, October 7.
Things are moving very fast.

Some nights ago my eye was caught by a news item. 'Trucker Blames Colours,' went the headline. Reading on: 'R. T. Ballantyne, driver for Island Trucks, failed to stop on a red light at the intersection of Fernhill and Spender. Questioned by traffic police, Ballantyne replied: "I didn't see it, that's all. There was this shake, then all these colours suddenly in the trees. Real bright ones I'd never seen before. I guess they must have blinded me." A breathalizer test proved negative.' Full stop.

I had an overpowering desire to talk to R. T. Ballantyne. Even looked him up in the telephone book. Not listed. I debated reaching him through Island Trucks in the morning.

Hoping for some mention of the story, I switched on the local radio station, caught the announcer mid-sentence:

'...to come to the studio and talk to us. So far no one has been able to describe just what the "new" colours are, but perhaps Ruby Howard can. Ruby, you say you actually *saw* "new" colours?'

What might have been a flat, rather ordinary female voice was sharpened by wonder. 'I was out in the garden, putting it to bed, you might say, getting it ready for winter. The hydrangeas are dried out—you know the way they go. Soft beiges and greys. And I was thinking maybe I should cut them back, when there was this—shake, like—and there they were shining. Pink. And blue. But not like they are in life. Different. Brighter. With little lights, like...'

The announcer's voice cut in, 'You say "not like they are in life". D'you think this wasn't life? I mean, do you think maybe you were dreaming?'

'Oh, no,' answered my good Mrs. Howard, positive, clear, totally unrattled. 'Oh, no, I wasn't *dreaming*. Not *dreaming*—... Why—*this* is more like dreaming.' She was quiet a moment and then, in a matter-of-fact voice, 'I can't expect you to believe it,' she said. 'Why should you? I wouldn't believe it myself if I hadn't seen it.' Her voice expressed a kind of compassion as if she was really sorry for the announcer.

I picked up the telephone book for the second time, looked up the number of the station. I had decided to tell Mrs. Howard what I had seen. I dialled, got a busy signal, depressed the bar and waited, cradle in hand. I dialled again. And again.

Later.

J. just phoned. Curious how she and I play the same game over and over.

J: Were you watching Channel 8?

Me: No, I...

J: An interview. With a lunatic. One who sees colours and flashing lights.

Me: Tell me about it.

J: He was a logger—a high-rigger—not that that has anything to do with it. He's retired now and lives in an apartment and has a window-box with geraniums. This morning the flowers were like neon, he said, flashing and shining...*Hon*estly!

Me: Perhaps he saw something you can't...

J: (*Amused*) I might have known you'd take his side. Seriously, what *could* he have seen?

Me: Flashing and shining—as he said.

J: But they couldn't. Not geraniums. And you know it as well as I do. *Hon*estly, Babe... (She is the only person left who calls me the name my mother called me.) Why are you always so perverse?

I felt faithless. I put down the receiver, as if I had not borne witness to my God.

October 22.

Floods of letters to the papers. Endless interviews on radio and TV. Pros, cons, inevitable spoofs.

One develops an eye for authenticity. It's as easy to spot as sunlight. However they may vary in detail, true accounts of the colours have an unmistakable common factor—a common factor as difficult to convey as sweetness to those who know only salt. True accounts are inarticulate, diffuse, unlikely—impossible.

It's recently crossed my mind that there may be some relationship between having seen the colours and their actual manifestation—something as improbable as *the more one sees them the more they are able to be seen*. Perhaps they are always there in some normally invisible part of the electro-magnetic spectrum and only become visible to certain people at certain times. A combination of circumstances or some subtle refinement in the organ of sight. And then—from quantity to quality perhaps, like water to ice—a whole community changes, is able to see, catches fire.

For example, it was seven days between the first time I saw the colours and the second. During that time there were no reports to the media. But once the reports began, the time between lessened appreciably *for me*. Not proof, of course, but worth noting. And I can't help wondering why some people see the colours and others don't. Do some of us have extra vision? Are some so conditioned that they're virtually blind to what's there before their very noses? Is it a question of more, or less?

Reports come in from farther and farther afield; from all walks of life. I think now there is no portion of the inhabited globe without 'shake freaks' and no acceptable reason for the sightings. Often, only one member of a family will testify to the heightened vision. In my own small circle, I am the only witness—or so I think. I feel curiously hypocritical as I listen to my friends denouncing the 'shakers'. Drugs, they say. Irrational—possibly dangerous. Although no sinister incidents have occurred yet—just some mild shake-baiting here and there—one is uneasily reminded of Salem.

Scientists pronounce us hallucinated or mistaken, pointing out that so far there is no hard evidence, no objective proof. That means, I suppose, no photographs, no spectroscopic measurement—if such is possible. Interestingly, seismographs show very minor earthquake tremors—showers of them, like shooting stars in August. Pundits claim 'shake fever'—as it has come to be called—is a variant on flying saucer fever and that it will subside in its own time. Beneficent physiologists suggest we are suffering (why is it *always* suffering, never enjoying?) a distorted form of *ocular spectrum* or after-image. (An after-image of what?) Psychologists disagree among themselves. All in all, it is not surprising that some of us prefer to keep our experiences to ourselves.

January 9.
Something new has occurred. Something impossible. Disturbing. So disturbing, in fact, that according to rumour it is already being taken with the utmost seriousness at the highest levels. TV, press and radio—with good reason—talk of little else.

What seemingly began as a mild winter has assumed sinister overtones. Farmers in southern Alberta are claiming the earth is unnaturally hot to the touch. Golfers at Harrison complain that the soles of their feet burn. Here on the coast, we notice it less. Benign winters are our specialty.

Already we don't lack for explanations as to why the earth could not be hotter than usual, nor why it is naturally 'unnaturally' hot. Vague notes of re-assurance creep into the speeches of public men. They may be unable to ex-plain the issue, but they can no longer ignore it.

To confuse matters further, reports on temperatures seem curiously incon-sistent. What information we get comes mainly from self-appointed 'earth touchers'. And now that the least thing can fire an argument, their conflicting readings lead often enough to inflammatory debate.

For myself, I can detect no change at all in my own garden.

Thursday...?
There is no longer any doubt. The temperature of the earth's surface *is* in-creasing.

It is unnerving, horrible, to go out and feel the ground like some great beast, warm, beneath one's feet. As if another presence—vast, invisible—attends one. Dexter, too, is perplexed. He barks at the earth with the same indignation and, I suppose, fear, with which he barks at the first rumblings of earth-quake.

Air temperatures, curiously, don't increase proportionately—or so we're told. It doesn't make sense, but at the moment nothing makes sense. Countless explanations have been offered. Elaborate explanations. None adequate. The fact that the air temperature remains temperate despite the higher ground heat must, I think, be helping to keep panic down. Even so, these are times of great tension.

Hard to understand these two unexplained—unrelated?—phenomena: the first capable of dividing families; the second menacing us all. We are like an-imals trapped in a burning building.

Later.
J. just phoned. Terrified. Why don't I move in with her, she urges. After all she has the space and we have known each other forty years. (Hard to believe when I don't feel even forty!) She can't bear it—the loneliness.

Poor J. Always so protected, insulated by her money. And her charm. What one didn't provide, the other did...diversion, services, attention.

What do I think is responsible for the heat, she asks. But it turns out she means who. Her personal theory is that the 'shake-freaks' are causing it—in-voluntarily, perhaps, but the two are surely linked.

'How could they possibly cause it?' I enquire. 'By what reach of the imagi-nation...?'

'Search *me*!' she protests. 'How on earth should *I* know?' And the sound of the dated slang makes me really laugh.

But suddenly she is close to tears. 'How can you *laugh*?' she calls. 'This is nightmare. Nightmare!'

Dear J. I wish I could help but the only comfort I could offer would terrify her still more.

September.

Summer calmed us down. If the earth was hot, well, summers *are* hot. And we were simply having an abnormally hot one.

Now that it is fall—the season of cool nights, light frosts—and the earth like a feverish child remains worryingly hot, won't cool down, apprehension mounts.

At last we are given official readings. For months the authorities have assured us with irrefutable logic that the temperature of the earth could not be increasing. Now, without any apparent period of indecision or confusion, they are warning us with equal conviction and accurate statistical documentation that it has, in fact, increased. Something anyone with a pocket-handkerchief of lawn has known for some time.

Weather stations, science faculties, astronomical observatories all over the world, are measuring and reporting. Intricate computerized tables are quoted. Special departments of government have been set up. We speak now of a new Triassic Age—the Neo-Triassic—and of the accelerated melting of the ice caps. But we are elaborately assured that this could not, repeat not, occur in our lifetime.

Interpreters and analysts flourish. The media are filled with theories and explanations. The increased temperature has been attributed to impersonal agencies such as bacteria from outer space; a thinning of the earth's atmosphere; a build-up of carbon-dioxide in the air; some axial irregularity; a change in the earth's core (geologists are reported to have begun test borings). No theory is too far-fetched to have its supporters. And because man likes a scapegoat, blame has been laid upon NASA, atomic physicists, politicians, the occupants of flying saucers and finally upon mankind at large—improvident, greedy mankind—whose polluted, strike-ridden world is endangered now by the fabled flames of hell.

We are also informed that Nostradamus, the Bible, and Jeane Dixon have all foreseen our plight. A new paperback, *Let Edgar Casey Tell You Why* sold out in a matter of days. Attendance at churches has doubled. Cults proliferate. Yet even in this atmosphere, we, the 'shake freaks', are considered lunatic fringe. Odd-men out. In certain quarters I believe we are seriously held responsible for the escalating heat, so J. is not alone. There have now been one or two nasty incidents. It is not surprising that even the most vocal among us have grown less willing to talk. I am glad to have kept silent. As a woman living alone, the less I draw attention to myself the better.

Our lives are greatly altered by this overhanging sense of doom. It is already hard to buy certain commodities. Dairy products are in very short supply. On the other hand, the market is flooded with citrus fruits. We are threatened with severe shortages for the future. The authorities are resisting rationing but it will have to come if only to prevent artificial shortages resulting from hoarding.

Luckily the colours are an almost daily event. I see them now, as it were, with my entire being. It is as if all my cells respond to their brilliance and become light too. At such times I feel I might shine in the dark.

No idea of the date.

It is evening and I am tired but I am so far behind in my notes I want to get something down. Events have moved too fast for me.

Gardens, parks, every tillable inch of soil have been appropriated for food crops. As an able, if aging body, with an acre of land and some knowledge of gardening, I have been made responsible for soy-beans—small trifoliate plants rich with the promise of protein. Neat rows of them cover what were once my vegetable garden, flower beds, lawn.

Young men from the Department of Agriculture came last month, bulldozed, cultivated, planted. Efficient, noisy desecrators of my twenty years of landscaping. Dexter barked at them from the moment they appeared and I admit I would have shared his indignation had the water shortage not already created its own desolation.

As a government gardener I'm a member of a new privileged class. I have watering and driving permits and coupons for gasoline and boots—an indication of what is to come. So far there has been no clothes rationing.

Daily instructions—when to water and how much, details of mulching, spraying—reach me from the government radio station to which I tune first thing in the morning. It also provides temperature readings, weather forecasts and the latest news releases on emergency measures, curfews, rationing, insulation. From the way things are going I think it will soon be our only station. I doubt that newspapers will be able to print much longer. In any event, I have already given them up. At first it was interesting to see how quickly drugs, pollution, education, Women's Lib., all became by-gone issues; and, initially, I was fascinated to see how we rationalized. Then I became bored. Then disheartened. Now I am too busy.

Evening.

A call came from J. Will I come for Christmas?

Christmas! Extraordinary thought. Like a word from another language learned in my youth, now forgotten.

'I've still got some Heidseck. We can get tight.'

The word takes me back to my teens. 'Like old times...'

'Yes.' She is eager. I hate to let her down. 'J., I can't. How could I get to you?'

'In your *car*, silly. *You* still have gas. You're the only one of us who has.' Do I detect a slight hint of accusation, as if I had acquired it illegally?

'But J., it's only for emergencies.'

'My God, Babe, d'you think *this* isn't an emergency?'

'J., dear...'

'*Please,* Babe,' she pleads. 'I'm so afraid. Of the looters. The eeriness. You must be afraid too. *Please!*'

I should have said, yes, that of course I was afraid. It's only natural to be afraid. Or, unable to say that, I should have made the soothing noises a mother makes to her child. Instead, 'There's no reason to be afraid, J.,' I said. It must have sounded insufferably pompous.

'No reason!' She was exasperated with me. 'I'd have thought there was every reason.'

She will phone again. In the night perhaps when she can't sleep. Poor J. She feels so alone. She *is* alone. And so idle. I don't suppose it's occurred to her yet that telephones will soon go. That a whole way of life is vanishing completely.

It's different for me. I have the soy-beans which keep me busy all the daylight hours. And Dexter. And above all I have the colours and with them the knowledge that there are others, other people, whose sensibilities I share. We are invisibly, inviolably related to one another as the components of a molecule. I say 'we'. Perhaps I should speak only for myself, yet I feel as sure of these others as if they had spoken. Like the quails, we share one brain—no, I think it is one heart—between us. How do I know this? How *do* I know? I know by knowing. We are less alarmed by the increasing heat than those who have not seen the colours. I can't explain why. But seeing the colours seems to change one—just as certain diagnostic procedures cure the complaint they are attempting to diagnose.

In all honesty I admit to having had moments when this sense of community was not enough, when I have had a great longing for my own kind—for so have I come to think of these others—in the way one has a great longing for someone one loves. Their presence in the world is not enough. One must see them. Touch them. Speak with them.

But lately that longing has lessened. All longing, in fact. And fear. Even my once great dread that I might cease to see the colours has vanished. It is as if through seeing them I have learned to see them. Have learned to be ready to see—passive; not striving to see—active. It keeps me very wide awake. Transparent even. Still.

The colours come daily now. Dizzying. Transforming. Life-giving. My sometimes back-breaking toil in the garden is lightened, made full of wonder, by the incredible colours shooting in the manner of children's sparklers from the plants themselves and from my own work-worn hands. I hadn't realized that I too am part of this vibrating luminescence.

Later.

I have no idea how long it is since I abandoned these notes. Without seasons to measure its passing, without normal activities—preparations for festivals, occasional outings—time feels longer, shorter or—more curious still—simultaneous, undifferentiated. Future and past fused in the present. Linearity broken.

I had intended to write regularly, but the soy-beans keep me busy pretty well all day and by evening I'm usually ready for bed. I'm sorry however to have missed recording the day-by-day changes. They were more or less minor at first. But once the heat began its deadly escalation, the world as we have known it—'our world'—had you been able to put it alongside 'this world'—would have seemed almost entirely different.

No one, I think, could have foreseen the speed with which everything has broken down. For instance, the elaborate plans made to maintain transportation became useless in a manner of months. Private traffic was first curtailed, then forbidden. If a man from another planet had looked in on us, he would have been astonished to see us trapped who were apparently free.

The big changes only really began after the first panic evacuations from the cities. Insulated by concrete, sewer pipes and underground parkades, high density areas responded slowly to the increasing temperatures. But once the heat penetrated their insulations, Gehennas were created overnight and whole populations fled in hysterical exodus, jamming highways in their futile attempts to escape.

Prior to this the government had not publicly acknowledged a crisis situation. They had taken certain precautions, brought in temporary measures to ease shortages and dealt with new developments on an *ad hoc* basis. Endeavoured to play it cool. Or so it seemed. Now they levelled with us. It was obvious that they must have been planning for months, only awaiting the right psychological moment to take everything over. That moment had clearly come. What we had previously thought of as a free world ended. We could no longer eat, drink, move without permits or coupons. This was full-scale emergency.

Yet nothing proceeds logically. Plans are made only to be re-made to accommodate new and totally unexpected developments. The heat, unpatterned as disseminated sclerosis, attacks first here, then there. Areas of high temperature suddenly and inexplicably cool off—or vice versa. Agronomists are doing everything possible to keep crops coming—taking advantage of hot-house conditions to force two crops where one had grown before—frantically playing a kind of agricultural roulette, gambling on the length of time a specific region might continue to grow temperate-zone produce.

Mails have long since stopped. And newspapers. And telephones. As a member of a new privileged class, I have been equipped with a two-way radio and a permit to drive on government business. Schools have of course closed. An attempt was made for a time to provide lessons over TV. Thankfully the looting and rioting seem over. Those desperate gangs of angry citizens who for some time made life additionally difficult, have now disappeared. We seem at last to understand that we are all in this together.

Life is very simple without electricity. I get up with the light and go to bed as darkness falls. My food supply is still substantial and because of the soy-bean crop I am all right for water. Dexter has adapted well to his new life. He is outdoors less than he used to be and has switched to a mainly vegetable diet without too much difficulty.

Evening.

This morning a new order over the radio. All of us with special driving privileges were asked to report to our zone garage to have our tires treated with heat resistant plastic.

I had not been into town for months. I felt rather as one does on returning home from hospital—that the world is unexpectedly large, with voluminous airy spaces. This was exaggerated perhaps by the fact that our whole zone had been given over to soy-beans. Everywhere the same rows of green plants—small pods already formed—march across gardens and boulevards. I was glad to see the climate prove so favourable. But there was little else to make me rejoice as I drove through ominously deserted streets, paint blistering and peeling on fences and houses, while overhead a haze of dust, now always with us, created a green sun.

The prolonged heat has made bleak the little park opposite the garage. A rocky little park, once all mosses and rhododendrons, it is bare now, and brown. I was seeing the day as everyone saw it. Untransmuted.

As I stepped out of my car to speak to the attendant I cursed that I had not brought my insulators. The burning tarmac made me shift rapidly from foot to foot. Anyone from another planet would have wondered at this extraordinary quirk of earthlings. But my feet were forgotten as my eyes alighted a second time on the park across the way. I had never before seen so dazzling and variegated a display of colours. How could there be such prismed brilliance in the range of greys and browns? It was as if the perceiving organ—wherever it is—sensitized by earlier experience, was now correctly tuned for this further perception.

The process was as before: the merest shake and the whole park was 'rainbow, rainbow, rainbow'. A further shake brought the park from *there* to *here*. Interior. But this time the interior space had increased. Doubled. By a kind of instant knowledge that rid me of all doubt, I knew that the garage attendant was seeing it too. *We saw the colours.*

Then, with that slight shift of focus, as if a gelatinous film had moved briefly across my sight, everything slipped back.

I really looked at the attendant for the first time. He was a skinny young man standing up naked inside a pair of loose striped overalls cut off at the knee, *sidney* embroidered in red over his left breast pocket. He was blond, small-boned, with nothing about him to stick in the memory except his clear eyes which at that moment bore an expression of total comprehension.

'You...' we began together and laughed.

'Have you seen them before?' I asked. But it was rather as one would say 'how do you do'—not so much a question as a salutation.

We looked at each other for a long time, as if committing each other to memory.

'Do you know anyone else?' I said.

'One or two. Three, actually. Do you?'

I shook my head. 'You are the first. Is it...is it...always like that?'

'You mean...?' he gestured towards his heart.

I nodded.

'Yes,' he said, 'Yes, it is.'

There didn't seem anything more to talk about. Your right hand hasn't much to say to your left, or one eye to the other. There was comfort in the experience, if comfort is the word, which it isn't. More as if an old faculty had been extended. Or a new one activated.

Sidney put my car on the hoist and sprayed its tires.

Some time later.

I have not seen Sidney again. Two weeks ago when I went back he was not there and as of yesterday, cars have become obsolete. Not that we will use that word publicly. The official word is *suspended.*

Strange to be idle after months of hard labor. A lull only before the boys from the Department of Agriculture come back to prepare the land again. I am pleased that the soy-beans are harvested, that I was able to nurse them along to maturity despite the scorching sun, the intermittent plagues and the problems with water. Often the pressure was too low to turn the sprinklers and I would stand, hour after hour, hose in hand, trying to get the most use from the tiny trickle spilling from the nozzle.

Sometimes my heart turns over as I look through the kitchen window and see the plants shrivelled and grotesque, the baked earth scored by a web of fine cracks like the glaze on a plate subjected to too high an oven. Then it comes to me in a flash that of course, the beans are gone, the harvest is over.

The world is uncannily quiet. I don't think anyone had any idea of how much noise even distant traffic made until we were without it. It is rare indeed for vehicles other than Government mini-cars to be seen on the streets. And there are fewer and fewer pedestrians. Those who do venture out, move on their thick insulators with the slow gait of rocking-horses. Surreal and alien, they heighten rather than lessen one's sense of isolation. For one *is* isolated. We have grown used to the sight of helicopters like large dragon-flies hovering overhead—addressing us through their P.A. systems, dropping supplies—welcome but impersonal.

Dexter is my only physical contact. He is delighted to have me inside again. The heat is too great for him in the garden and as, officially, he no longer exists, we only go out under cover of dark.

The order to destroy pets, when it came, indicated more clearly than anything that had gone before, that the Government had abandoned hope. In an animal-loving culture, only direct necessity could validate such an order. It fell upon us like a heavy pall.

When the Government truck stopped by for Dexter, I reported him dead. Now that the welfare of so many depends upon our cooperation with authority, law breaking is a serious offence. But I am not uneasy about breaking this law. As long as he remains healthy and happy, Dexter and I will share our dwindling provisions.

No need to be an ecologist or dependent on non-existent media to know all life is dying and the very atmosphere of our planet is changing radically. Already no birds sing in the hideous hot dawns as the sun, rising through a haze of dust, sheds its curious bronze-green light on a brown world. The trees that once gave us shade stand leafless now in an infernal winter. Yet, as if in the masts and riggings of ships, St. Elmo's fire flickers and shines in their high branches, and bioplasmic pyrotechnics light the dying soy-beans. I am reminded of how the ghostly form of a limb remains attached to the body from which it has been amputated. And I can't help thinking of all the people who don't see the colours, the practical earth-touchers with only their blunt senses to inform them. I wonder about J. and if, since we last talked, she has perhaps been able to see the colours too. But I think not. After so many years of friendship, surely I would be able to sense her, had she broken through.

Evening...?
The heat has increased greatly in the last few weeks—in a quantum leap. This has resulted immediately in two things: a steady rising of the sea level throughout the world—with panic reactions and mild flooding in coastal areas; and, at last, a noticeably higher air temperature. It is causing great physical discomfort.

It was against this probability that the authorities provided us with insulator spray. Like giant cans of pressurized shaving cream. I have shut all rooms but the kitchen and by concentrating my insulating zeal on this one small area, we have managed to keep fairly cool. The word is relative, of course. The radio has stopped giving temperature readings and I have no thermometer. I have filled all cracks and crannies with the foaming plastic, even applied a layer to the exterior wall. There are no baths, of course, and no cold drinks. On the other hand I've abandoned clothes and given Dexter a shave and a haircut. Myself as well. We are a fine pair. Hairless and naked.

When the world state of emergency was declared we didn't need to be told that science had given up. The official line had been that the process would reverse itself as inexplicably as it had begun. The official policy—to hold out as long as possible. With this in mind, task forces worked day and night on survival strategy. On the municipal level, which is all I really knew about, everything that could be centralized was. Telephone exchanges, hydro plants, radio stations became centres around which vital activities took place. Research teams investigated the effects of heat on water mains, sewer pipes, electrical wiring; work crews were employed to prevent, protect or even destroy incipient causes of fire, flood and asphyxiation.

For some time now the city has been zoned. In each zone a large building has been selected, stocked with food, medical supplies and insulating materials. We have been provided with zone maps and an instruction sheet telling us to stay where we are until ordered to move to what is euphemistically called our 'home'. When ordered, we are to load our cars with whatever we still have of provisions and medicines and drive off *at once*. Helicopters have already dropped kits with enough gasoline for the trip and a small packet, somewhat surprisingly labelled 'emergency rations' which contains one cyanide capsule—grim reminder that all may not go as the planners plan. We have been asked to mark our maps, in advance, with the shortest route from our house to our 'home', so that in a crisis we will know what we are doing. These instructions are repeated *ad nauseam* over the radio, along with hearty assurances that everything is under control and that there is no cause for alarm. The Government station is now all that remains of our multi-media. When it is not broadcasting instructions, its mainly pre-recorded tapes sound inanely complacement and repetitive. Evacuation Day, as we have been told again and again, will be announced by whistle blast. Anyone who runs out of food before that or who is in need of medical aid is to use the special gas ration and go 'home' at once.

As a long-time preserver of fruits and vegetables, I hope to hold out until E. Day. When that time comes it will be a sign that broadcasts are no longer possible, that contact can no longer be maintained between the various areas of the community, that the process will not reverse itself in time and that, in fact, our world is well on the way to becoming—oh, wonder of the modern kitchen—a self-cleaning oven.

Spring, Summer, Winter, Fall.
What season is it after all?
I sense the hours by some inner clock. I have applied so many layers of insulating spray that almost no heat comes through from outside. But we have to have air and the small window I have left exposed acts like a furnace. Yet through it I see the dazzling colours; sense my fellow-men.

Noon.
The sun is hidden directly overhead. The world is topaz. I see it through the minute eye of my window. I, the perceiving organ that peers through the house's only aperture. We are one, the house and I—parts of some vibrating sensitive organism in which Dexter plays his differentiated but integral role. The light enters us, dissolves us. We are the golden motes in the jewel.

Midnight.
The sun is directly below. Beneath the burning soles of my arching feet it shines, a globe on fire. Its rays penetrate the earth. Upward beaming, they support and sustain us. We are held aloft, a perfectly balanced ball in the jet of a golden fountain. Light, dancing, infinitely upheld.

Who knows how much later.
I have just 'buried' Dexter.

This morning I realized this hot little cell was no longer a possible place for a dog.

I had saved one can of dog food against this day. As I opened it Dexter's eyes swivelled in the direction of so unexpected and delicious a smell. He struggled to his feet, joyous, animated. The old Dexter. I was almost persuaded to delay, to wait and see if the heat subsided. What if tomorrow we awakened to rain? But something in me, stronger than this wavering self, carried on with its purpose.

He sat up, begging, expectant.

I slipped the meat out of the can.

'You're going to have a really good dinner,' I said, but as my voice was unsteady, I stopped.

I scooped a generous portion of the meat into his dish and placed it on the floor. He was excited, and as always when excited about food, he was curiously ceremonial, unhurried—approaching his dish and backing away from it, only to approach it again at a slightly different angle. As if the exact position was of the greatest importance. It was one of his most amusing and endearing characteristics. I let him eat his meal in his own leisurely and appreciative manner and then, as I have done so many times before, I fed him his final *bon bouche* by hand. The cyanide pill, provided by a beneficent government for me, went down in a gulp.

I hadn't expected it to be so sudden. Life and death so close. His small frame convulsed violently, then collapsed. Simultaneously, as if synchronized, the familiar 'shake' occurred in my vision. Dexter glowed brightly, whitely, like phosphorus. In that dazzling, light-filled moment he was no longer a small dead dog lying there. I could have thought him a lion, my sense of scale had so altered. His beautiful body blinded me with its fires.

With the second 'shake' his consciousness must have entered mine for I felt a surge in my heart as if his loyalty and love had flooded it. And like a kind of ground bass, I was aware of scents and sounds I had not known before. Then a great peace filled me—an immense space, light and sweet—and I realized that this was death. Dexter's death.

But how describe what is beyond description?

As the fires emanating from his slight frame died down, glowed weakly, residually, I put on my insulators and carried his body into the now fever-hot garden. I laid him on what had been at one time an azalea bed. I was unable to dig a grave in the baked earth or to cover him with leaves. But there are no predators now to pick the flesh from his bones. Only the heat which will, in time, dessicate it.

I returned to the house, opening the door as little as possible to prevent the barbs and briars of burning air from entering with me. I sealed the door from inside with foam sealer.

The smell of the canned dog food permeated the kitchen. It rang in my nostrils. Olfactory chimes, lingering, delicious. I was intensely aware of Dexter. Dexter immanent. I contained him as simply as a dish contains water. But the simile is not exact. For I missed his physical presence. One relies on the physical more than I had known. My hands sought palpable contact. The flesh forgets slowly.

Idly, abstractedly, I turned on the radio. I seldom do now as the batteries are low and they are my last. Also, there is little incentive. Broadcasts are intermittent and I've heard the old tapes over and over.

But the government station was on the air. I tuned with extreme care and placed my ear close to the speaker. A voice, faint, broken by static, sounded like that of the Prime Minister.

'...all human beings can do, your government has done for you.' (Surely not a political speech *now*?) 'But we have failed. Failed to hold back the heat. Failed to protect ourselves against it; to protect you against it. It is with profound grief that I send this farewell message to you all.' I realized that this, too, had been pre-recorded, reserved for the final broadcast. 'Even now, let us not give up hope...'

And then, blasting through the speech, monstrously loud in the stone-silent world, the screech of the whistle summoning us 'home'. I could no longer hear the P.M.'s words.

I began automatically, obediently, to collect my few remaining foodstuffs, reaching for a can of raspberries, the last of the crop to have grown in my garden when the dawns were dewy and cool and noon sun fell upon us like golden pollen. My hand stopped in mid-air.

I would not go 'home'.

The whistle shrilled for a very long time. A curious great steam-driven cry—man's last. Weird that our final utterance should be this anguished inhuman wail.

The end.

Now that it is virtually too late, I regret not having kept a daily record. Now that the part of me that writes has become nearly absorbed. I feel obliged to do the best I can.

I am down to the last of my food and water. Have lived on little for some days—weeks, perhaps. How can one measure passing time? Eternal time grows like a tree, its roots in my heart. If I lie on my back I see winds moving in its high branches and a chorus of birds is singing in its leaves. The song is sweeter than any music I have ever heard.

My kitchen is as strange as I am myself. Its walls bulge with many layers of spray. It is without geometry. Like the inside of an eccentric styrofoam coconut. Yet, with some inner eye, I see its intricate mathematical structure. It is as ordered and no more random than an atom.

My face is unrecognizable in the mirror. Wisps of short damp hair. Enormous eyes. I swim in their irises. Could I drown in the pits of their pupils?

Through my tiny window when I raise the blind, a dead world shines. Sometimes dust storms fill the air with myriad particles burning bright and white as the lion body of Dexter. Sometimes great clouds swirl, like those from which saints receive revelations.

The colours are almost constant now. There are times when, light-headed, I dance a dizzying dance, feel part of that whirling incandescent matter—what I might once have called inorganic matter!

On still days the blameless air, bright as a glistening wing, hangs over us, hangs its extraordinary beneficence over us.

We are together now, united, indissoluble. Bonded.

Because there is no expectation, there is no frustration.

Because there is nothing we can have, there is nothing we can want.

We are hungry of course. Have cramps and weakness. But they are as if in *another body. Our* body is inviolate. Inviolable.

We share one heart.

We are one with the starry heavens and our bodies are stars.

Inner and outer are the same. A continuum. The water in the locks is level. We move to a higher water. A high sea.

A ship could pass through.

Jacques Ferron

(1921–1985)

IN MANY WAYS THE PREMIER STORYTELLER OF HIS GENERATION IN QUEBEC, Jacques Ferron was born in Louiseville, and educated at Laval, where he graduated in medicine. He went on into general practice in the Gaspé, in working-class Montreal, and then in Longeuil. An articulate socialist by political persuasion, he was a playwright, a novelist and storyteller, constantly puncturing the pretensions of French-Canadian elitism and attacking English-Canadian intrusions into Quebec life. Highly visible in politics, he played a particularly important role as a negotiator in helping to resolve the October Crisis in 1970. On the federal scene, he was perhaps most recognized as the founder of the satirical Rhinoceros Party.

He wrote numerous articles on medicine, history, and politics; and his novels include *La charette* (1968) and *Le Saint-Elias* (1972), both of which teach a moral lesson by demonstrating parallels between modern cultural experiences and some extraordinary events in the past. His stories, deeply marked by the folk forms of Gaspé storytelling, include *Contes du pays incertain* (1962)—a collection telling of the decay of both rural and urban local culture—and *Contes inédits* (1968). *Tales from the Uncertain Country* (1972) is a selection of his *contes* as translated by Betty Bednarski. "Martine, continued" appeared in *Contes anglais et autres* (1964) and in Larry Shouldice's English translation in 1974. A kind of absurdist drama in form, the story speaks of a variety of choices in life and art that resist "happy endings." The fairytale chronicle, alluded to throughout, is thus problematically tilted askew.

For Further Reading

BETTY BEDNARSKI, "Introduction" to *Selected Tales of Jacques Ferron* (Toronto: House of Anansi, 1984) 11–16.

J.-P. BOUCHER, *Les Contes de Jacques Ferron* (Montréal: l'Aurore, 1974).

BARBARA GODARD, "The Oral Tradition and Contemporary Fiction," *Essays on Canadian Writing*, 7–8 (Fall 1977): 46–62.

PIERRE L'HENAULT, *Jacques Ferron, cartographe de l'imaginaire* (Montréal: Presses de l'université de Montréal, 1980).

DONALD SMITH, "Jacques Ferron ou la géographie d'un pays incertain," *Journal of Canadian Fiction* 25–26 (1979): 175–85.

MARY ZIROFF, *A Study Guide to Jacques Ferron's Tales from the Uncertain Country* (Toronto: House of Anansi, 1977).

Martine, continued

Translated by Larry Shouldice

Until a short time ago, the city was not very well cemented together; the countryside kept invading it.

MARTINE

My father used to be an exuberant man whose generous wife presented him with a child every year and never gave it a second thought. She remained rosy-cheeked and beautiful, as comely as the house, which was clean and bright under the willows. We owned several acres of land around the house, enough to feed a cow and her calf, and some pigs. I was brought up with these animals, which is why I kept healthy. The city, however, having encircled our domain, kept gnawing away at it insidiously. My father let one piece of land go, then another, and then a third, so that in the end there wasn't enough hay for the cow. She went dry, and what can you do with a cow that doesn't give milk except eat her? Which we did.

The next spring we had no calf. My father ended up selling the little island of countryside on Mount Royal Street which, without the cow and her calf, had lost its meaning. Finally, it was the pigs' turn. When the last one had been eaten, the neighbours moved closer. They glued their houses to ours. We were caught up in the whole thing. And my mother started to suffer from shortness of breath.

The countryside, which had slipped in through the cracks to the very heart of the city, with cows, pigs, chickens, vegetables and trees, retreated little by little, taking back its animals, the clean air, and the joy. The houses, welded to each other, still kept their role as dwellings, but also served now as walls. The cracks were repaired. No more escape, no more space: now the city was well cemented together.

THE WINO

I didn't used to be a wino. I was something more honourable: a vagabond. Not the kind who frightens women and is given a penny to keep away bad luck, but the kind of vagabond known throughout the province, who is welcomed with joy and even asked to stay, for he brings wisdom and dreams in his pack. As long as the mild season lasted, I would keep to the roads. At night I

Jacques Ferron, "Martine, continued," in Philip Stratford, ed., *Stories from Québec* (Toronto: Van Nostrand Reinhold Canada, 1974). Translated byLarry Shouldice. Jacques Ferron, *Contes, édition intégrale: Contes du pays incertain – Contes anglais – Contes inédits* (Montréal: Hurtubise HMH, 1968, second edition revised 1985). Translated by Larry Shouldice. Originally published in *Contes anglais* (Montréal: Editions Hurtubise, 1964).

would stop in some house where I would spend the evening conjuring up before the eyes of my hosts a world that had no reality, but through which you could still perceive the one that had been swallowed up by the shadows. The next day, on the road again, I would feel that I hadn't come in vain and that I had left behind more order than before: a brighter day, the farms more clearly set out, faces more human. No, I wasn't a tramp. I didn't beg for anything, and what I received couldn't be compared to what I had given. I was a bum, but I was also kind of a great lord wandering the world to give it a bit more substance, to give it a little style.

THE WIDOWER
I was young when a passer-by, unknown in the village, looked behind my ears and predicted to my father that I would never be happily wed. My father remembered this when the time came for me to marry. He chose me the gentlest and humblest of girls. Never was there a more tender wife in the whole world. But she died, and I loved her. The passer-by hadn't been wrong.

THE WINO
In winter I'd come back to town and find my buddies again; then they were vagabonds, now they're winos. We would exchange wisdom and dreams, waiting for the end of the flood. For winter is a flood. Each house becomes an ark in which the memory of springtime lives on; that's how the springtime returns again. We would watch for it, and as soon as the air was quivering with an aimless desire, as soon as its shining sign appeared, we would quickly say good-bye to one another. Each would take up his pack of wisdom and dreams and discreetly leave town. The winding roads were good for roving, and walking was still possible. A horse doesn't go much faster than a man and the difference isn't worth the trouble of an extra animal. We moved along at a lively pace. Sometimes, in one season, we could visit the whole province.

Then the horses disappeared, replaced by machines. The roads became straighter and harder. It was no longer possible to walk. How can you expect a man to compete with those speed machines that tear through space on ribbons of smoking asphalt? Walking didn't get you anywhere any more; you were just as far ahead to stay put. So we stopped roving. Without our tales the country became confused again.

We don't leave the city now, and we've swapped our packs for the bottle; we've traded wisdom and dreams for poison. Wisdom and dreams don't belong in the city, but the bottle gives us a taste of the great escape.

MARTINE
When we had eaten the cow, the calf, and the pigs, my father took to drink, and misfortune struck our household. His wife became an awful thing, a withered mass of sallow flesh, who still found strength enough to wield a broom. You can guess the rest of my story. Oh my, yes, she really used to lay into me! Still, I can't forget my childhood and happiness for me is a cow chewing her cud near Mount Royal Street, or a cup of warm milk with a bit of froth on it, just enough to leave a white moustache under your nose.

The countryside used to come into the city, while the tramps with packs on their backs were leaving it. Between the country and the city there was an exchange of wisdom and health. But now this trading has stopped. The city has kept its goods and the country hers, so each has lost everything, both wisdom and health. The one doesn't come without the other. Exchanges are sometimes necessary. A fable will help you to understand.

THE WINO

Once there was a man who was a widower. He had large ears and a daughter, and this daughter was courted by a boy who was the son of another widower, and this widower had ears as large, as red, and as shameful as those of the first. Which is not surprising, since outlandish ears seem to favour widowerhood. Friendship consoled the two men in their fate, and this gentle bond not only promoted their children's friendship but also made their work more effective.

Mutual help is necessary on continents, and all the more so on a deserted island. The two widowers had landed on such an island one morning, each with a child on his back, after a shipwreck from which they were the only survivors. They had not landed together. The widower with the daughter built his house in the north of the island, while the widower with the son built his in the south. Then, having met each other while out exploring and struck up a friendship, they decided to farm in the middle of the island so that they could work together. Theirs was an equal friendship; one didn't have to walk any farther to work than the other.

The children, however, were keeping house, one in the north and one in the south, and it was by chance that they came to know each other. Down on the shore the boy picked up a little compass that had been left there after his father's shipwreck, and it led him straight to the girl. Love itself couldn't have guided him better, for which we can be thankful; otherwise he might have drowned. There are attractions that lead towards life as well as towards death and love is one of these. This time, thanks to the compass and the positions of the two houses, love was well directed. While the fathers were labouring in the middle of the island, the children, in the house to the north, were practising to become lovers. A beard sprouted on the boy; a sigh stirred the girl. Their passion increased as the days went by. The girl sighed so well and so often that her bosom remained swelled from a sigh that she couldn't let out. These burgeoning breasts and the budding beard called forth other amorous weapons.

The young lovers at last were on the point of confrontation when, most inopportunely, the widowers with the big ears, catching wind of something, stopped working harmoniously in the middle of the island, took off their masks of friendship and showed each other faces of hostility. Their children's skirmishing was none of their business; why were these two old fools interfering? Widowers have strange ways and these two, because their children were falling in love, set out to kill one another. Then they thought it would be safer to go back home, one to the house in the south, and the other to the house in the north, in which the latter found the son of his new enemy. He booted him out the door with vigorous kicks to the backside. Jack and Jill were separated. It was the end of their romance; the blossom did not bear fruit. The lovers were kept confined by the widowers, each of whom cleared a garden around his own house. The middle of the island became wild and overgrown with underbrush. The lovers' hearts, likewise.

After two years of this regime, the son of the widower in the south was a vague, nervous, sickly creature, no longer a boy. The daughter of the widower in the north was a vague, nervous, sickly creature, no longer a girl. And the widowers' ears stuck out in anguish. One night they heard footsteps. The next morning, in the undergrowth in the middle of the island, they found the two children. They had come back together again to die.

The fable doesn't tell us anything more. What became of the widowers? Were they changed into donkeys? It's quite probable but the fable doesn't say. It has nothing more to say than to make us understand that among human beings certain exchanges are necessary.

Exchanges are necessary between lovers, between the mind and the body, between the city and the country. But a thousand rows of walls enclose the city, and the imprisoned lovers only meet again in death. The wedding procession gets lost in the underbrush and is replaced by a funeral procession. No one can cry out. Substitutions are made without anyone protesting them, and in an anguished silence the undertakers are always ready to take advantage of dissension. Exchanges are necessary between two shores, but the bridges have been burned. Above the common waters the willow branches are no longer intertwined from bank to bank. The arch between the two walls has fallen, and hands reach out to the sky without joining. Exchanges are necessary among men, but men group together in isolation. They would like to get along but are unable to speak to one another. They arrange to meet and then slam the door in each other's face. Everyone, in an inner prison, is his own jailer. And there are some in vaults who see their own agony through the eyes of an undertaker. A lonely man is his own prey. Solitude is the sign of our times. There are no more exchanges, there is no more society. A grotesque discordance reigns supreme, and in the thin air the wing of oblivion brushes the world.

THE WINO
I don't feel its approach anymore. For a long time now I've been hearing the whistle of its wings. Haven't you noticed it?

MARTINE
A shadowy and bloody wing it is, herding the flocks before it. Men come to me, absurd and pitiful. At least rats, when they panic, throw themselves in droves into the sea. But men keep up appearances; they stay in line, hats in hand, in spite of their anguish. And they come to me for God-knows-what deliverance, as if I could open the world to them. Their lovemaking seems to be a last escape. They press against me and tumble me, but it's all in vain. A bit of a tumble can generate a lot of emotion, but it can't alter fate.

SALVARSAN
If oblivion threatens the world, men, for their part, are spreading madness. We live in a strange age.

The world evolves, but the forms in which we apprehend it barely change. Apprehending the world changelessly, we think nothing. It follows that mind without nourishment breeds a creeping uneasiness.

SALVARSAN

My breath came shorter. *I'm getting old,* I thought. And my temperament changed. I felt a greater pity for my patients; their recovery brought me a quicker joy. When I received my fees, I compared myself to the girl who, having given herself willingly, found it painful to hold out her hand. Poverty, along with the humiliation of an inferior situation, is the cause of a lot of sickness and many premature deaths. Attending one of these deaths, I had the feeling that I was participating in a human sacrifice. More clearly every day I could see behind the social system a blood-thirsty idol, greedy for children, young men and young women. I called him Baal. I could have found other names for him. My sense of perspective had changed and medicine began to seem rather futile.

THE WIDOWER

My wife accidentally swallowed a germ that stayed in her chest, and it was impossible to get rid of it. And yet she took all the drugs. As the doctor said, science is not yet perfect. The day will come, however, when there will be an effective drug for every germ. Men will keep on dying, but it will be from natural causes. A natural death is the flower of old age.

SALVARSAN

Once upon a time there was a man whose son was condemned to death. I don't know why. This man, crazed by his sorrow, imagined that he would save his son by killing the hangman. And it was a second hangman who executed both the son and the father.

THE WINO

Another time there was a young prince who lived in the most beautiful castle in the world. His father was the king of the land. When he was twenty years old he fell into a sort of lethargy. He had no desires. The finest foods nauseated him. The king summoned his doctors, but their knowledge was useless. As a last resort wise men were sent for. Yet they were as foolish as the doctors, except for one of them who said to the king, "Sire, in the city there is an old lady who is dying of hunger. By saving her you will save your son." The old woman was given food, and the young prince again found the will to live. The next day, however, he fell back into his lethargy. The king summoned the wise man again. "There is," said the wise man, "a baby who is crying from thirst. His mother has no more milk, and his father is not rich enough to buy cow's milk for him." The baby was given milk to drink, and the young prince again found the will to live. But the next day he fell back into his lethargy. "There is," said the wise man, "a young girl who has been badly done by and who..." The king interrupted, shouting that there would be no end to it. "No," replied the wise man, "for there is no end to human misery." And the king, who loved his palace and his banquets, let his son, the young prince, die.

No one mends old clothes with new cloth, for the new patch pulls away part of the clothing and the tear becomes worse. Neither is new wine stored in old casks....

MARTINE
To keep the old casks they have sacrificed the new wine. The blood of our children flows in the mud.

Madeleine Ferron

(b. 1922)

A NATIVE OF LOUISEVILLE, QUEBEC, Madeleine Ferron went to school in Lachine, and attended the University of Montreal, where she studied ethnography. She now lives in the Beauce region of Quebec, and draws on local folk fables in her own work. She has written plays for Chicoutimi and Montreal radio, and several *contes* and *nouvelles* for the periodicals *Chatelaine* and *L'Information médicale et paramédicale*. Her works of fiction include *La fin des loups-garous* (1966); and, appearing in that same year, a collection of her *contes* (including "Be Fruitful and Multiply") entitled *Coeur de sucre*. The story was translated in 1974 by Sheila Watson (herself the author of a collection of myth-based short fiction, *Four Stories,* 1979). Ferron's feminist fable, which seems placid on the surface, is in reality a cry of rage—against a life that servitude has emptied of meaning (for men and women alike), and against the mechanical rituals of social custom that are mistaken for the measure of normal behavior. The title "Be Fruitful and Multiply" is thus resonant with irony, and the customary implications of its allusion are overturned.

For Further Reading

MAURICE LEMIRE, ed., *Dictionnaire des oeuvres littéraires du Québec,* IV: 1960–1969 (Montréal: Fides, 1984) 184–85.

Be Fruitful and Multiply

Translated by Sheila Watson

About eight o'clock they woke with a start. Amazed and confused, she shrank from the unexpectedness of her waking. She wasn't dreaming. It was true. She had been married the day before and was waking up with her husband in a bed in the neighbour's house. He was pushing back his hair and swearing as he painfully lifted his head. He had gone to bed dead drunk. "You cannot refuse," they said. "After all, you are the bridegroom."

Half way through the evening he was drunk already and a shock of brown hair had fallen forward over his face without his making any effort at all to throw it back with a shake of his head as he usually did. Shifting from leg to leg, her senses blunted with sleep, she watched, heavy-eyed, the progress of the festivity, diverted from time to time by the almost wild pleasure he was taking in his own wedding feast.

Since it was her wedding too, she resolutely stayed awake, all the while envying her cousin who slept peacefully, her head against the corner of the wall. They were the same age—thirteen-and-a-half. At that age sleep could be pardoned, she had heard them say again and again. Of course, but not on the night of one's wedding.

It was long after midnight when at last he signalled her to follow him. They went through the garden so that no one could see them or play mean tricks on them. She helped him to jump over the fence, to cross the ditch, and to climb the stairs. He fell across the bed and began to snore at once, his hands clenched like a child's. He was eighteen. She slept, curled round on an empty corner of the mattress.

They got up quickly as soon as they woke, ashamed to have stayed in bed so long. He ran to hitch up a buggy which he drove around in front of his in-laws' house. His wife's trunk was loaded on and he helped her up. He was formal, embarrassed; she, almost joyful. Then he turned the horse at a trot towards the property that had been prepared for them. He was to be the second neighbour down the road. She waved happily again and again and her mother, who was crying, kept watching, until they had rounded the corner, the blond braid that swung like a pendulum over the back of the buggy seat.

All day they worked eagerly getting settled. In the evening they went to bed early. He embraced her eagerly. Face to face with a heat that flamed and entangled her in its curious movement, she was frightened.

Madeleine Ferron, "Be Fruitful and Multiply," in Philip Stratford, ed., *Stories from Québec* (Toronto: Van Nostrand Reinhold Canada, 1974). Translated by Sheila Watson. Originally published in *Coeur de sucre* (Montréal: Editions HMH, 1966).

"What are you doing?" she asked.

He answered quietly, "You are the sheep and I am the ram."

"Oh," she said. It was simple when one had a reference point.

On the first mornings of their life together, after he had left for the fields, she ran quickly to her mother's.

"Are you managing?" her mother always asked.

"Yes," the child replied smiling.

"Your husband, is he good to you?"

"Oh yes," she said. "He says I am a pretty sheep."

Sheep...sheep. The mother, fascinated, watched her daughter attentively but did not dare to question her further.

"Go back to your husband now," she said. "Busy yourself about the house and get his meal ready."

Since the girl hesitated uncertainly as if she did not understand, her mother sprinkled sugar on a slice of bread spread with cream, gave it to her and pushed her gently toward the door. The child went down the road eating her bread and the mother, reassured, leaned sadly against the wall of the house watching the thick swaying braid until the girl turned the corner of the road.

Little by little the young wife spaced her visits. In autumn when the cold rain began to fall, she came only on Sundays. She had found her own rhythm. Was she too eager, too ambitious? Perhaps she was simply inattentive. Her tempo was too swift. She always hurried now. She wove more bed covers than her chest could hold, cultivated more vegetables than they could eat, raised more calves than they knew how to sell.

And the children came quickly—almost faster than nature permits. She was never seen without a child in her arms, one in her belly, and another at her heels. She raised them well, mechanically, without counting them; accepted them as the seasons are accepted; watched them leave; not with fatalism or resignation but steadfast and untroubled, face to face with the ineluctable cycle that makes the apple fall when it is ripe.

The simple mechanism she had set in motion did not falter. She was the cog wheel that had no right to oversee the whole machine. Everything went well. Only the rhythm was too fast. She outstripped the seasons. The begetting of her children pressed unreasonably on that of her grandchildren and the order was broken. Her daughters and her sons already had many children when she was still bearing others—giving her grandsons uncles who were younger than they were and for whom they could have no respect.

She had twenty-two children. It was extravagant. Fortunately, as one child was carried in the front door, beribboned and wailing, one went out the rear door alone, its knapsack on its back. Nevertheless, it was extravagant. She never realized it.

When her husband was buried and her youngest son married, she caught her breath, decided finally on slippers and a rocking chair. The mechanism could not adjust to a new rhythm. It broke down. She found herself disoriented, incapable of directing the stranger she had become, whom she did not know, who turned round and round with outstretched arms, more and more agitated.

"And if I should visit my family?" she asked her neighbour one day. She had children settled in the four corners of the province, some even exiled to the United States. She would go to take the census or, rather, she would go like a bishop to make the rounds of the diocese.

She had been seen leaving one morning, walking slowly. She had climbed into the bus, a small black cardboard suitcase in her hand. She had smiled at her neighbours but her eyes were still haggard.

She went first to the States. She was introduced to the wife of her grandson who spoke no French and to all the others whom she looked at searchingly.

"That one," she said, "is she my child or my child's child?"

The generations had become confused. She no longer knew.

She went back to Sept-Isles. One day, when she was rocking on the veranda with one of her sons, he pointed out a big dark-haired young man who was coming down the street.

"Look, mother," her son said, "He is my youngest." He was eighteen and a shock of hair fell forward over his face. She began to cry.

"It is he," she said, "It is my husband."

The next day she was taken to the home of one of her daughters, whom she called by her sister's name. Her daughter took care of her for several days and then took her to the house of the other daughter who, after much kindness, took her to the home of one of the oldest of the grandsons. She asked no questions. She cried.

Finally, one of her boys, chaplain in a home for the aged, came to get her. She followed him obediently. When he presented her to the assembled community, she turned to him and said quietly, "Tell me, are all these your brothers?"

Mavis Gallant

(b. 1922)

BORN MAVIS DE TRAFFORD YOUNG, IN MONTREAL, Mavis Gallant attended school in that city and in the eastern U.S.A. Fluently bilingual, and a highly articulate observer and chronicler of social mores and the politics of cultural history, she worked for several years in the 1940s for the National Film Board and as a reporter, reviewer, and caption-writer for the *Montreal Standard*. In 1950 she left for Europe, and except for the year 1983–84, which she spent as writer-in-residence at the University of Toronto, she has lived in Europe ever since, most recently in Paris. The author of a play (*What Is To Be Done?*, first performed at Toronto's Tarragon Theatre in 1982), numerous essays, novels, and story collections, and many uncollected stories, she commands a sizeable readership. Most of her stories have appeared in the *New Yorker*, as has some of her recent political journalism. She also wrote the informative introduction to *The Affair of Gabrielle Russier* (1971) and for some years has been engaged in researching a book on the Dreyfus Case.

Her collections include *My Heart Is Broken* (1964; called *An Unmarried Man's Summer* in its British edition), *The Pegnitz Junction* (1973), *Home Truths* (1981), and *In Transit* (1988). Some of the stories in the early collections, and the "Linnet Muir" stories of *Home Truths*, adopt Canadian settings, and variously probe the limits of Canadian political and personal naiveté. And the naiveté that disrupts the lives of whole cultures constitutes a recurrent feature of the stories in *The Pegnitz Junction*, to which "The Latehomecomer" thematically and formally relates. Both "The Latehomecomer" (*New Yorker*, 1974) and "From the Fifteenth District" (*New Yorker*, 1978) appeared in *From the Fifteenth District* (1979). "From the Fifteenth District"—while it, too, reveals paradoxical disparities between people's experience and their versions of reality—demonstrates yet another feature of Gallant's stylistic skill: her coruscating wit. Both stories show her sensitivity to the lives of individuals, and her sympathy particularly for those whose lives are caught out of phase with the social system that frames them. Relationship is a key issue in Gallant's writing—specific relations between people, in families, in cultures—but the nature of relationship itself as well. She asks what is meant by such discriminatory terms as "likeness," "difference," "contrast," or by temporal and spatial terms like "here" and "before." The verbal textures of her elegant prose amply record these issues, and by drawing readers into the style itself draw them also into a more vivid appreciation of the comedy, agony, and private pathos of daily life.

For Further Reading

NEIL BESNER, *The Light of Imagination: Mavis Gallant's Fiction* (Vancouver: U British Columbia P, 1988).

GEOFF HANCOCK, ed., Mavis Gallant issue, *Canadian Fiction Magazine* 28 (1978).

JANICE KULYK KEEFER, *Reading Mavis Gallant* (Toronto: Oxford, 1989).

LAWRENCE MATHEWS, "Ghosts and Saints: Notes on Mavis Gallant's *From the Fifteenth District*," *Essays on Canadian Writing* 42 (Winter 1990): 154–72.

GRAZIA MERLER, *Mavis Gallant: Narrative Patterns and Devices* (Ottawa: Tecumseh, 1978).

DANIELLE SCHAUB, "Structural Patterns of Alienation and Disjunction in Mavis Gallant's Firmly Structured Stories," *Canadian Literature* 136 (Spring 1993): 45–57.

The Latehomecomer

When I came back to Berlin out of captivity in the spring of 1950, I discovered I had a stepfather. My mother had never mentioned him. I had been writing from Brittany to "Grete Bestermann," but the "Toeppler" engraved on a brass plate next to the bellpull at her new address turned out to be her name, too. As she slipped the key in the lock, she said quietly, "Listen, Thomas. I'm Frau Toeppler now. I married a kind man with a pension. This is his key, his name, and his apartment. He wants to make you welcome." From the moment she met me at the railway station that day, she must have been wondering how to break it.

I put my hand over the name, leaving a perfect palm print. I said, "I suppose there are no razor blades and no civilian shirts in Berlin. But some ass is already engraving nameplates."

Martin Toeppler was an old man who had been a tram conductor. He was lame in one arm as the result of a working accident and carried that shoulder higher than the other. His eyes had the milky look of the elderly, lighter round the rim than at the center of the iris, and he had an old woman's habit of sighing, "Ah, yes, yes." The sigh seemed to be his way of pleading, "It can't be helped." He must have been forty-nine, at the most, but aged was what he seemed to me, and more than aged—useless, lost. His mouth hung open much of the time, as though he had trouble breathing through his nose, but it was only because he was a chronic talker, always ready to bite down on a word. He came from Franconia, near the Czech border, close to where my grandparents had once lived.

"Grete and I can understand each other's dialects," he said—but we were not a dialect-speaking family. My brother and I had been made to say "bread" and "friend" and "tree" correctly. I turned my eyes to my mother, but she looked away.

Martin's one dream was to return to Franconia; it was almost the first thing he said to me. He had inherited two furnished apartments in a town close to an American military base. One of the two had been empty for years. The occupants had moved away, no one knew where—perhaps to Sweden. After their departure, which had taken place at five o'clock on a winter morning in 1943, the front door had been sealed with a government stamp depicting a swastika and an eagle. The vanished tenants must have died, perhaps in Sweden, and now no local person would live in the place, because a whole family of ghosts rattled about, opening and shutting drawers, banging on pipes, moving chairs and ladders. The ghosts were looking for a hoard of gold that had been left behind, Martin thought. The second apartment had been rented to a family who had dis-

From *From The Fifteenth District* (Toronto: Macmillan, 1979). Reprinted by permission of Georges Borchardt, Inc. Copyright © 1979 by Mavis Gallant.

appeared during the confused migrations of the end of the war and were probably dead, too; at least they were dead officially, which was all that mattered.
Martin intended to modernize the two flats, raise them up to American standards—he meant by this putting venetian blinds at the windows and gas-
heated water tanks in the bathrooms—and let them to a good class of American
officer, too foreign to care about a small-town story, too educated to be afraid of
ghosts. But he would have to move quickly; otherwise his inheritance, his sole
postwar capital, his only means of getting started again, might be snatched
away from him for the sake of shiftless and illiterate refugees from the Soviet
zone, or bombed-out families still huddled in barracks, or for latehomecomers.
This last was a new category of persons, all one word. It was out of his mouth
before he remembered that I was one, too. He stopped talking, and then he
sighed and said, "Ah, yes, yes."

   He could not keep still for long: he drew out his wallet and showed me a picture of himself on horseback. He may have wanted to substitute this country
image for any idea I had of him on the deck of a tram. He held the snapshot at
arm's length and squinted at it. "That was Martin Toeppler once," he said. "It
will be Martin Toeppler again." His youth, and a new right shoulder and arm,
and the hot, leafy summers everyone his age said had existed before the war
were waiting for him in Franconia. He sounded like a born winner instead of
a physically broken tram conductor on the losing side. He put the picture away
in a cracked celluloid case, pocketed his wallet, and called to my mother, "The
boy will want a bath."

   My mother, who had been preparing a bath for minutes now, had been receiving orders all her life. As a girl she had worked like a slave in her mother's
village guesthouse, and after my father died she became a servant again, this
time in Berlin, to my powerful Uncle Gerhard and his fat wife. My brother
and I spent our winters with her, all three sleeping in one bed sometimes, in
a cold attic room, sharing bread and apples smuggled from Uncle Gerhard's
larder. In the summer we were sent to help our grandmother. We washed the
chairs and tables, cleaned the toilets of vomit, and carried glasses stinking
with beer back to the kitchen. We were still so small we had to stand on stools
to reach the taps.

   "It was lucky you had two sons," Uncle Gerhard said to my mother once.
"There will never be a shortage of strong backs in the family."

   "No one will exploit my children," she is supposed to have replied, though
how she expected to prevent it only God knows, for we had no roof of our
own and no money and we ate such food as we were given. Our uniforms
saved us. Once we had joined the Hitler Jugend, even Uncle Gerhard never
dared ask, "Where are you going?" or "Where have you been?" My brother
was quicker than I. By the time he was twelve he knew he had been trapped;
I was sixteen and a prisoner before I understood. But from our mother's point
of view we were free, delivered; we would not repeat her life. That was all
she wanted.

   In captivity I had longed for her and for the lost paradise of our poverty,
where she had belonged entirely to my brother and to me and we had slept

with her, one on each side. I had written letters to her full of remorse for past neglect and containing promises of future goodness: I would work hard and look after her forever. These letters, sent to blond, young, soft-voiced Grete Bestermann, had been read by Grete Toeppler, whose greying hair was pinned up in a sort of oval balloon, and who was anxious and thin, as afraid of things to come as she was of the past. I had not recognized her at the station, and when she said timidly, "Excuse me? Thomas?" I thought she was her own mother. I did not know then, or for another few minutes, that my grandmother had died or that my rich Uncle Gerhard, now officially de-Nazified by a court of law, was camped in two rooms carved out of a ruin, raising rabbits for a living and hoping that no one would notice him. She had last seen me when I was fifteen. We had been moving toward each other since early this morning, but I was exhausted and taciturn, and we were both shy, and we had not rushed into each other's arms, because we had each been afraid of embracing a stranger. I had one horrible memory of her, but it may have been only a dream. I was small, but I could speak and walk. I came into a room where she was nursing a baby. Two other women were with her. When they saw me they started to laugh, and one said to her, "Give some to Thomas." My mother leaned over and put her breast in my mouth. The taste was disgustingly sweet, and because of the two women I felt humiliated: I spat and backed off and began to cry. She said something to the women and they laughed harder than ever. It must have been a dream, for who could the baby have been? My brother was eleven months older than I.

She was cautious as an animal with me now, partly because of my reaction to the nameplate. She must have feared there was more to come. She had been raised to respect men, never to interrupt their conversation, to see that their plates were filled before hers—even, as a girl, to stand when they were sitting down. I was twenty-one, I had been twenty-one for three days, I had crossed over to the camp of the bullies and strangers. All the while Martin was talking and boasting and showing me himself on horseback, she crept in and out of the parlor, fetching wood and the briquettes they kept by the tile stove, carrying them down the passage to build a fire for me in the bathroom. She looked at me sidelong sometimes and smiled with her hand before her mouth—a new habit of hers—but she kept silent until it was time to say that the bath was ready.

My mother spread a towel for me to stand on and showed me a chair where, she said, Martin always sat to dry his feet. There was a shelf with a mirror and comb but no washbasin. I supposed that he shaved and they cleaned their teeth in the kitchen. My mother said the soap was of poor quality and would not lather, but she asked me, again from behind the screen of her hand, not to leave it underwater where it might melt and be wasted. A stone underwater might have melted as easily. "There is a hook for your clothes," she said, though of course I had seen it. She hesitated still, but when I began to unbutton my shirt she slipped out.

The bath, into which a family could have fitted, was as rough as lava rock. The water was boiling hot. I sat with my knees drawn up as if I were in the tin tub I had been lent sometimes in France. The starfish scar of a grenade wound was livid on one knee, and that leg was misshapen, as though it had been pressed the wrong way while the bones were soft. Long underwear I took to be my stepfather's hung over a line. I sat looking at it, and at a stiff thin towel hanging next to it, and at the water condensing on the cement walls, until the skin of my hands and feet became as ridged and soft as corduroy.

There is a term for people caught on a street crossing after the light has changed: "pedestrian-traffic residue." I had been in a prisoner-of-war camp at Rennes when an order arrived to repatriate everyone who was under eighteen. For some reason, my name was never called. Five years after that, when I was in Saint-Malo, where I had been assigned to a druggist and his wife as a "free worker"—which did not mean free but simply not in a camp—the police sent for me and asked what I was doing in France with a large "PG," for "*prisonnier de guerre*," on my back. Was I a deserter from the Foreign Legion? A spy? Nearly every other prisoner in France had been released at least ten months before, but the file concerning me had been lost or mislaid in Rennes, and I could not leave until it was found—I had no existence. By that time the French were sick of me, because they were sick of the war and its reminders, and the scheme of using the prisoners the Americans had taken to rebuild the roads and bridges of France had not worked out. The idea had never been followed by a plan, and so some of the prisoners became farm help, some became domestic servants, some went into the Foreign Legion because the food was better, some sat and did nothing for three or four years, because no one could discover anything for them to do. The police hinted to me that if I were to run away no one would mind. It would have cleared up the matter of the missing file. But I was afraid of putting myself in the wrong, in which case they might have an excuse to keep me forever. Besides, how far could I have run with a large "PG" painted on my jacket and trousers? Here, where it would not be necessary to wear a label, because "latehomecomer" was written all over me, I sensed that I was an embarrassment, too; my appearance, my survival, my bleeding gums and loose teeth, my chronic dysentery and anemia, my craving for sweets, my reticence with strangers, the cast-off rags I had worn on arrival, all said "war" when everyone wanted peace, "captivity" when the word was "freedom," and "dry bread" when everyone was thinking "jam and butter." I guessed that now, after five years of peace, most of the population must have elbowed onto the right step of the right staircase and that there was not much room left for pedestrian-traffic residue.

My mother came in to clean the tub after I was partly dressed. She used fine ash from the stove and a cloth so full of holes it had to be rolled into a ball. She said, "I called out to you but you didn't hear. I thought you had fallen asleep and drowned."

I was hard of hearing because of the anti-aircraft duty to which I'd been posted in Berlin while I was still in high school. After the boys were sent to the front, girls took our places. It was those girls, still in their adolescence, who defended the grown men in uniform, down in the bunkers. I wondered if they had been deafened, too, and if we were a generation who would never hear anything under a shout. My mother knelt by the tub, and I sat on Martin's chair, like Martin, pulling on clean socks she had brought me. In a low voice, which I heard perfectly, she said that I had known Martin in my childhood. I said I had not. She said then that my father had known him. I stood up and waited until she rose from her knees, and I looked down at her face. I was afraid of touching her, in case we should both cry. She muttered that her family must surely have known him, for the Toepplers had a burial plot not far from the graveyard where my grandmother lay buried, and some thirty miles from where my father's father had a bakery once. She was looking for any kind of a link.

"I wanted you and Chris to have a place to stay when you came back," she said, but I believed she had not expected to see either of us again and that she had been afraid of being homeless and alone. My brother had vanished in Czechoslovakia with the Schörner army. All of that army had been given up for dead. My Uncle Gerhard, her only close relative, could not have helped her even if it had occurred to him; it had taken him four years to become officially and legally de-Nazified, and now, "as white as a white lilac," according to my mother, he had no opinions about anything and lived only for his rabbits.

"It is nice to have a companion at my age," my mother said. "Someone to talk to." Did the old need more than conversation? My mother must have been about forty-two then. I had heard the old men in prison camp comparing their wives and saying that no hen was ever too tough for boiling.

"Did you marry him before or after he had this apartment?"

"After." But she had hesitated, as if wondering what I wanted to hear.

The apartment was on the second floor of a large dark block—all that was left of a workers' housing project of the nineteen-twenties. Martin had once lived somewhere between the bathroom window and the street. Looking out, I could easily replace the back walls of the vanished houses, and the small balconies festooned with brooms and mops, and the moist oily courtyard. Winter twilight must have been the prevailing climate here until an air raid let the seasons in. Cinders and gravel had been raked evenly over the crushed masonry now; the broad concourse between the surviving house—ours—and the road beyond it that was edged with ruins looked solid and flat.

But no, it was all shaky and loose, my mother said. Someone ought to cause a cement walk to be laid down; the women were always twisting their ankles, and when it rained you walked in black mud, and there was a smell of burning. She had not lost her belief in an invisible but well-intentioned "someone." She then said, in a hushed and whispery voice, that Martin's first wife, Elke, was down there under the rubble and cinders. It had been impossible to get all the bodies out, and one day a bulldozer covered them over for all time. Martin had inherited those two apartments in a town in Franconia from Elke. The Toepplers were probably just as poor as the Bestermanns, but Martin had made a good marriage.

"She had a dog, too," said my mother. "When Martin married her she had a white spitz. She gave it a bath in the bathtub every Sunday." I thought of Martin Toeppler crossing this new wide treacherous front court and saying, "Elke's grave. Ah, yes, yes." I said it, and my mother suddenly laughed loudly and dropped her hand, and I saw that some of her front teeth were missing.

"The house looks like an old tooth when you see it from the street," she said, as though deliberately calling attention to the very misfortune she wanted to hide. She knew nothing about the people who had lived in this apartment, except that they had left in a hurry, forgetting to pack a large store of black-market food, some pretty ornaments in a china cabinet, and five bottles of wine. "They left without paying the rent," she said, which didn't sound like her.

It turned out to be a joke of Martin Toeppler's. He repeated it when I came back to the parlor wearing a shirt that I supposed must be his, and with my hair dark and wet and combed flat. He pointed to a bright rectangle on the brown wallpaper. "That is where they took Adolf's picture down," he said. "When they left in a hurry without paying the rent."

My father had been stabbed to death one night when he was caught tearing an election poster off the schoolhouse wall. He left my mother with no money, two children under the age of five, and a political reputation. After that she swam with the current. I had worn a uniform of one kind or another most of my life until now. I remembered wearing civilian clothes once, when I was fourteen, for my confirmation. I had felt disguised, and wondered what to do with my hands; from the age of seven I had stuck my thumbs in a leather belt. I had impressions, not memories, of my father. Pictures were frozen things; they told me nothing. But I knew that when my hair was wet I looked something like him. A quick flash would come back out of a mirror, like a secret message, and I would think, There, that is how he was. I sat with Martin at the table, where my mother had spread a lace cloth (the vanished tenants') and over which the April sun through lace curtains laid still another design. I placed my hands flat under lace shadows and wondered if they were like my father's, too.

She had put out everything she could find to eat and drink—a few sweet biscuits, cheese cut almost as thin as paper, dark bread, small whole tomatoes, radishes, slices of salami arranged in a floral design on a dish to make them seem more. We had a bottle of fizzy wine that Martin called champagne. It had a brown tint, like watered iodine, and a taste of molasses. Through this murk bubbles climbed. We raised our glasses without saying what we drank to, other than my return. Perhaps Martin drank to his destiny in Franconia with the two apartments. I had a plan, but it was my own secret. By a common accord, there was no mutual past. Then my mother spoke from behind the cupped hand and said she would like us to drink to her missing elder son. She looked at Martin as she said this, in case the survival of Chris might be a burden, too.

Toward the end of that afternoon, a neighbor came in with a bottle of brandy— a stout man with three locks of slick grey hair across his skull. All the fat men of comic stories and of literature were to be Willy Wehler to me, in the future. But he could not have been all that plump in Berlin in 1950; his chin probably showed the beginnings of softness, and his hair must have been dark still, and there must have been plenty of it. I can see the start of his baldness, the two deep peninsulas of polished skin running from the corners of his forehead to just above his ears. Willy Wehler was another Franconian. He and Martin began speaking in dialect almost at once. Willy was at a remove, however—he mispronounced words as though to be funny, and he would grin and look at me. This was to say that he knew better, and he knew that I knew. Martin and Willy hated Berlin. They sounded as if they had been dragged to Berlin against their will, like displaced persons. In their eyes the deepest failure of a certain political authority was that it had enticed peace-loving persons with false promises of work, homes, pensions, lives afloat like little boats at anchor; now these innocent provincials saw they had been tricked, and they were going back where they had started from. It was as simple to them as that—the equivalent of an insurance company's no longer meeting its obligations. Willy even described the life he would lead now in a quiet town, where, in sight of a cobbled square with a fountain and an equestrian statue, he planned to open a perfume-and-cosmetics shop; people wanted beauty now. He would live above the shop—he was not too proud for that—and every morning he would look down on his blue store awnings, over window boxes stuffed with frilled petunias. My stepfather heard this with tears in his eyes, but perhaps he was thinking of his two apartments and of Elke and the spitz. Willy's future seemed so real, so close at hand, that it was almost as though he had dropped in to say goodbye. He sat with his daughter on his knees, a baby not yet three. This little girl, whose name was Gisela, became a part of my life from that afternoon, and so did fat Willy, though none of us knew it then. The secret to which I had drunk my silent toast was a girl in France, who would be a middle-aged woman, beyond my imagining now, if she had lived. She died by jumping or accidentally falling out of a fifth-floor window in Paris. Her parents had locked her in a room when they found out she was corresponding with me.

This was still an afternoon in April in Berlin, the first of my freedom. It was one day after old Adolf's birthday, but that was not mentioned, not even in dialect or in the form of a Berlin joke. I don't think they were avoiding it; they had simply forgotten. They would always be astonished when other people turned out to have more specific memories of time and events.

This was the afternoon about which I would always say to myself, "I should have known," and even "I knew"—knew that I would marry the baby whose movements were already so willful and quick that her father complained, "We can't take her anywhere," and sat holding both her small hands in his; otherwise she would have clutched at every glass within reach. Her winged brows reminded me of the girl I wanted to see again. Gisela's eyes were amber in color, and luminous, with the whites so pure they seemed blue. The girl in France had eyes that resembled dark petals, opaque and velvety, and slightly tilted. She had black hair from a Corsican grandmother, and long fine lashes. Gisela's lashes were stubby and thick. I found that I was staring at the child's small ears and her small perfect teeth, thinking all the while of the other girl, whose smile had been spoiled by the malnutrition and the poor dentistry of the Occupation. I should have realized then, as I looked at Willy and his daughter, that some people never go without milk and eggs and apples, whatever the landscape, and that the sparse feast on our table had more to do with my mother's long habit of poverty—a kind of fatalistic incompetence that came from never having had enough money—than with a real shortage of food. Willy had on a white nylon shirt, which was a luxury then. Later, Martin would say to me, "That Willy! Out of a black uniform and into the black market before you could say 'democracy,' " but I never knew whether it was a common Berlin joke or something Martin had made up or the truth about Willy.

Gisela, who was either slow to speak for her age or only lazy, looked at me and said, "Man"—all she had to declare. Her hair was so silky and fine that it reflected the day as a curve of mauve light. She was all light and sheen, and she was the first person—I can even say the first *thing*—I had ever seen that was un-flawed, without shadow. She was as whole and as innocent as a drop of water, and she was without guilt.

Her hands, released when her father drank from his wineglass, patted the tablecloth, seized a radish, tried to stuff it in his mouth.

My mother sat with her chair pushed back a few respectful inches. "Do you like children, Thomas?" she said. She knew nothing about me now except that I was not a child.

The French girl was sixteen when she came to Brittany on a holiday with her father and mother. The next winter she sent me books so that I would not drop too far behind in my schooling, and the second summer she came to my room. The door to the room was in a bend of the staircase, halfway between the phar-macy on the ground floor and the flat where my employers lived. They were sup-posed to keep me locked in this room when I wasn't working, but the second summer they forgot or could not be bothered, and in any case I had made a key with a piece of wire by then. It was the first room I'd had to myself. I whitewashed the walls and boxed in the store of potatoes they kept on the floor in a corner. Bunches of wild plants and herbs the druggist used in pre-scriptions hung from hooks in the ceiling. One whole wall was taken up with shelves of drying leaves and roots—walnut leaves for treating anemia, camomile for fainting spells, thyme and rosemary for muscular cramps, and nettles and mint, sage and dandelions. The fragrance in the room and the view of the port from the window could have given me almost enough happiness for a lifetime, except that I was too young to find any happiness in that.

How she escaped from her parents the first afternoon I never knew, but she was a brave, careless girl and had already escaped from them often. They must have known what could happen when they locked that wild spirit into a place where the only way out was a window. Perhaps they were trying to see how far they could go with a margin of safety. She left a message for them: "To teach you a lesson." She must have thought she would be there and not there, lost to them and yet able to see the result. There was no message for me, except that it is a terrible thing to be alone; but I had already learned it. She must have knelt on the windowsill. The autumn rain must have caught her lashes and hair. She was already alien on the windowsill, beyond recognition.

I had made my room as neat for her as though I were expecting a military in-spection. I wondered if she knew how serious it would be for both of us if we were caught. She glanced at the view, but only to see if anyone could look in on us, and she laughed, starting to take off her pullover, arms crossed; then stopped and said, "What is it—are you made of ice?" How could she know that I was retarded? I had known nothing except imagination and solitude, and the preying of old soldiers; and I was too old for one and repelled by the other. I thought she was about to commit the sacrifice of her person—her physical self and her immortal soul. I had heard the old men talking about women as if women were dirt, but needed for "that." One man said he would cut off an ear for "that." Another said he would swim the Atlantic. I thought she would lie in

some way convenient to me and that she would feel nothing but a kind of sorrow, which would have made it a pure gift. But there was nothing to ask; it
was not a gift. It was her decision and not a gift but an adventure. She hadn't
come here to look at the harbor, she told me, when I hesitated. I may even
have said, "No," and it might have been then that she smiled at me over crossed
arms, pulling off her sweater, and said, "Are you made of ice?" For all her jaun-
tiness, she thought she was deciding her life, though she continued to use the
word "adventure." I think it was the only other word she knew for "love." But
all we were settling was her death, and my life was decided in Berlin when
Willy Wehler came in with a bottle of brandy and Gisela, who refused to say
more than "Man." I can still see the lace curtains, the mark on the wallpaper, the
china ornaments left by the people who had gone in such a hurry—the chimney sweep with his matchstick broom, the girl with bobbed orange hair sitting
on a crescent moon, the dog with the ruff around his neck—and when I remember this I say to myself, "I must have known."

We finished two bottles of Martin's champagne, and then my mother jumped
to her feet to remove the glasses and bring others so that we could taste Willy
Wehler's brandy.

"The dirty Belgian is still hanging around," he said to Martin, gently rocking the child, who now had her thumb in her mouth.

"What does he want?" said my stepfather. He repeated the question; he was
slow and he thought that other people, unless they reacted at once and with a
show of feeling, could not hear him.

"He was in the Waffen-S.S.—he says. He complains that the girls here won't
go out with him, though only five or six years ago they were like flies."

"They are afraid of him," came my mother's timid voice. "He stands in the
court and stares..."

"I don't like men who look at pure young girls," said Willy Wehler. "He
said to me, 'Help me; you owe me help.' He says he fought for us and nobody
thanked him."

"He did? No wonder we lost," said Martin. I had already seen that the survivors of the war were divided into those who said they had always known how
it would all turn out and those who said they had been indifferent. There are
also those who like wars and those who do not. Martin had never been committed to winning or to losing or to anything—that explained his jokes. He
had gained two apartments and one requisitioned flat in Berlin. He had lost a
wife, but he often said to me later that people were better off out of this world.

"In Belgium he was in jail," said Willy. "He says he fought for us and then
he was in jail and now we won't help him and the girls won't speak to him."

"Why is he here?" my stepfather suddenly shouted. "Who let him in? All
this is his own affair, not ours." He rocked in his chair in a peculiar way, perhaps only imitating the gentle motion Willy made to keep Gisela asleep and
quiet. "Nobody owes him anything," cried my stepfather, striking the table
so that the little girl started and shuddered. My mother touched his arm and
made a sort of humming sound, with her lips pressed together, that I took to
be a signal between them, for he at once switched to another topic. It was a
theme of conversation I was to hear about for many years after that afternoon.

It was what the old men had to say when they were not boasting about women or their own past, and it was this: What should the Schörner army have done in Czechoslovakia to avoid capture by the Russians, and why did General Eisenhower (the villain of the story) refuse to help?

Eisenhower was my stepfather's left hand, General Schörner was his right, and the Russians were a plate of radishes. I turned very slightly to look at my mother. She had the sad cast of feature women have when their eyes are fixed nowhere. Her hand still lay lightly on Martin Toeppler's sleeve. I supposed then that he really was her husband and that they slept in the same bed. I had seen one or two closed doors in the passage on my way to the bath. Of my first prison camp, where everyone had been under eighteen or over forty, I remembered the smell of the old men—how they stopped being clean when there were no women to make them wash—and I remembered their long boasting. And yet, that April afternoon, as the sunlight of my first hours of freedom moved over the table and up along the brown wall, I did my boasting, too. I told about a prisoner I had captured. It seemed to be the thing I had to say to two men I had never seen before.

"He landed in a field just outside my grandmother's village," I told them. "I was fourteen. Three of us saw him—three boys. We had French rifles captured in the 1870 war. He'd had time to fold his parachute and he was sitting on it. I knew only one thing in English; it was 'Hands up.' "

My stepfather's mouth was open, as it had been when I first walked into the flat that day. My mother stood just out of sight.

"We advanced, pointing our 1870 rifles," I went on, droning, just like the old prisoners of war. "We all now said, 'Hands up.' The prisoner just—" I made the gesture the American had made, of chasing a fly away, and I realized I was drunk. "He didn't stand up. He had put everything he had on the ground—a revolver, a wad of German money, a handkerchief with a map of Germany, and some smaller things we couldn't identify at once. He had on civilian shoes with thick soles. He very slowly undid his watch and handed it over, but we had no ruling about that, so we said no. He put the watch on the ground next to the revolver and the map. Then he slowly got up and strolled into the village, with his hands in his pockets. He was chewing gum. I saw he had kept his cigarettes, but I didn't know the rule about that, either. We kept our guns trained on him. The schoolmaster ran out of my grandmother's guesthouse—everyone ran to stare. He was excited and kept saying in English, 'How do you do? How do you do?' but then an officer came running, too, and he was screaming, 'Why are you interfering? You may ask only one thing: Is he English or American.' The teacher was glad to show off his English, and he asked, 'Are you English or American?' and the American seemed to move his tongue all round his mouth before he answered. He was the first foreigner any of us had ever seen, and they took him away from us. We never saw him again."

That seemed all there was to it, but Martin's mouth was still open. I tried to remember more. "There was hell because we had left the gun and the other things on the ground. By the time they got out to the field, someone had stolen the parachute—probably for the cloth. We were in trouble over that, and we never got credit for having taken a prisoner. I went back to the field alone later on. I wanted to cry, for some reason—because it was over. He was from an adventure story to me. The whole war was a Karl May adventure, when I was fourteen and running around in school holidays with a gun. I found some small things in the field that had been overlooked—pills for keeping awake, pills in transparent envelopes. I had never seen that before. One envelope was called 'motion sickness.' It was a crime to keep anything, but I kept it anyway. I still had it when the Americans captured me, and they took it away. I had kept it because it was from another world. I would look at it and wonder. I kept it because of *The Last of the Mohicans,* because, because."

This was the longest story I had ever told in my life. I added, "My grandmother is dead now." My stepfather had finally shut his mouth. He looked at my mother as if to say that she had brought him a rival in the only domain that mattered—the right to talk everyone's ear off. My mother edged close to Willy Wehler and urged him to eat bread and cheese. She was still in the habit of wondering what the other person thought and how important he might be and how safe it was to speak. But Willy had not heard more than a sentence or two. That was plain from the way the expression on his face came slowly awake. He opened his eyes wide, as if to get sleep out of them, and—evidently imagining I had been talking about my life in France—said, "What were you paid as a prisoner?"

I had often wondered what the first question would be once I was home. Now I had it.

"Ha!" said my stepfather, giving the impression that he expected me to be caught out in a monstrous lie.

"One franc forty centimes a month for working here and there on a farm," I said. "But when I became a free worker with a druggist the official pay was three thousands francs a month, and that was what he gave me." I paused. "And of course I was fed and housed and had no laundry bills."

"Did you have bedsheets?" said my mother.

"With the druggist's family, always. I had one sheet folded in half. It was just right for a small cot."

"Was it the same sheet as the kind the family had?" she said, in the hesitant way that was part of her person now.

"They didn't buy sheets especially for me," I said. "I was treated fairly by the druggist, but not by the administration."

"Ah ha," said the two older men, almost together.

"The administration refused to pay my fare home," I said, looking down into my glass the way I had seen the men in prison camp stare at a fixed point when they were recounting a grievance.

"A prisoner of war has the right to be repatriated at administration expense. The administration would not pay my fare because I had stayed too long in France—but that was their mistake. I bought a ticket as far as Paris on the pay I had saved. The druggist sold me some old shoes and trousers and a jacket of his. My own things were in rags. In Paris I went to the Y.M.C.A. The Y.M.C.A. was supposed to be in charge of prisoners' rights. The man wouldn't listen to me. If I had been left behind, then I was not a prisoner, he said; I was a tourist. It was his duty to help me. Instead of that, he informed the police." For the first time my voice took on the coloration of resentment. I knew that this complaint about a niggling matter of train fare made my whole adventure seem small, but I had become an old soldier. I remembered the police commissioner, with his thin lips and dirty nails, who said, "You should have been repatriated years ago, when you were sixteen."

"It was a mistake," I told him.

"Your papers are full of strange mistakes," he said, bending over them. "There, one capital error. An omission, a grave omission. What is your mother's maiden name?"

"Wickler," I said.

I watched him writing "W-i-e-c-k-l-a-i-r," slowly, with the tip of his tongue sticking out of the corner of his mouth as he wrote. "You have been here for something like five years with an incomplete dossier. And what about this? Who crossed it out?"

"I did. My father was not a pastry cook."

"You could be fined or even jailed for this," he said.

"My father was not a pastry cook," I said. "He had tuberculosis. He was not allowed to handle food."

Willy Wehler did not say what he thought of my story. Perhaps not having any opinion about injustice, even the least important, had become a habit of his, like my mother's of speaking through her fingers. He was on the right step of that staircase I've spoken of. Even the name he had given his daughter was a sign of his sensitivity to the times. Nobody wanted to hear the pagan, Old Germanic names anymore—Sigrun and Brunhilde and Sieglinde. Willy had felt the change. He would have called any daughter something neutral and pretty—Gisela, Marianne, Elisabeth—any time after the battle of Stalingrad. All Willy ever had to do was sniff the air.

He pushed back his chair (in later years he would be able to push a table away with his stomach) and got to his feet. He had to tip his head to look up into my eyes. He said he wanted to give me advice that would be useful to me as a latehomecomer. His advice was to forget. "Forget everything," he said. "Forget, forget. That was what I said to my good neighbor Herr Silber when I bought his wife's topaz brooch and earrings before he emigrated to Palestine. I said, 'Dear Herr Silber, look forward, never back, and forget, forget, forget.' "

The child in Willy's arms was in the deepest of sleeps. Martin Toeppler followed his friend to the door, they whispered together; then the door closed behind both men.

"They have gone to have a glass of something at Herr Wehler's," said my mother. I saw now that she was crying quietly. She dried her eyes on her apron and began clearing the table of the homecoming feast. "Willy Wehler has been kind to us," she said. "Don't repeat that thing."

"About forgetting?"

"No, about the topaz brooch. It was a crime to buy anything from Jews."

"It doesn't matter now."

She lowered the tray she held and looked pensively out at the wrecked houses across the street. "If only people knew beforehand what was allowed," she said.

"My father is probably a hero now," I said.

"Oh, Thomas, don't travel too fast. We haven't seen the last of the changes. Yes, a hero. But too late for me. I've suffered too much."

"What does Martin think that he died of?"

"A working accident. He can understand that."

"You could have said consumption. He did have it." She shook her head. Probably she had not wanted Martin to imagine he could ever be saddled with two sickly stepsons. "Where do you and Martin sleep?"

"In the room next to the bathroom. Didn't you see it? You'll be comfortable here in the parlor. The couch pulls out. You can stay as long as you like. This is your home. A home for you and Chris." She said this so stubbornly that I knew some argument must have taken place between her and Martin.

I intended this room to be my home. There was no question about it in my mind. I had not yet finished high school; I had been taken out for anti-aircraft duty, then sent to the front. The role of adolescents in uniform had been to try to prevent the civilian population from surrendering. We were expected to die in the ruins together. When the women ran pillowcases up flagpoles, we shinnied up to drag them down. We were prepared to hold the line with our 1870 rifles until we saw the American tanks. There had not been tanks in our Karl May adventure stories, and the Americans, finally, were not out of *The Last of the Mohicans*. I told my mother that I had to go back to high school and then I would apply for a scholarship and take a degree in French. I would become a schoolmaster. French was all I had from my captivity; I might as well use it. I would earn money doing translations.

That cheered her up. She would not have to ask the ex-tram conductor too many favors. "Translations" and "scholarship" were an exalted form of language, to her. As a schoolmaster, I would have the most respectable job in the family, now that Uncle Gerhard was raising rabbits. "As long as it doesn't cost *him* too much," she said, as if she had to say it and yet was hoping I wouldn't hear.

It was not strictly true that all I had got out of my captivity was the ability to speak French. I had also learned to cook, iron, make beds, wait on table, wash floors, polish furniture, plant a vegetable garden, paint shutters. I wanted to help my mother in the kitchen now, but that shocked her. "Rest," she said, but I did not know what "rest" meant. "I've never seen a man drying a glass," she said, in apology. I wanted to tell her that while the roads and bridges of France were still waiting for someone to rebuild them I had been taught how to make a tomato salad by the druggist's wife; but I could not guess what the word "France" conveyed to her imagination. I began walking about the apartment. I looked in on a store cupboard, a water closet smelling of carbolic, the bathroom again, then a room containing a high bed, a brown wardrobe, and a table covered with newspapers bearing half a dozen of the flowerless spiky dull green plants my mother had always tended with so much devotion. I shut the door as if on a dark past, and I said to myself, "I am free. This is the beginning of life. It is also the start of the good half of a rotten century. Everything ugly and corrupt and vicious is behind us." My thoughts were not exactly in those words, but something like them. I said to myself, "This apartment has a musty smell, an old and dirty smell that sinks into clothes. After a time I shall probably smell like the dark parlor. The smell must be in the cushions, in the bed that pulls out, in the lace curtains. It is a smell that creeps into night-clothes. The blankets will be permeated." I thought, I shall get used to the smell, and the smell of burning in the stone outside. The view of ruins will be my view. Every day on my way home from school I shall walk over Elke. I shall get used to the wood staircase, the bellpull, the polished nameplate, the white enamel fuses in the hall—my mother had said, "When you want light in the parlor you give the center fuse in the lower row a half turn." I looked at a framed drawing of cartoon people with puffy hair. A strong wind had blown their umbrella inside out. They would be part of my view, like the ruins. I took in the ancient gas bracket in the kitchen and the stone sink. My mother, washing glasses without soap, smiled at me, forgetting to hide her teeth. I reëxamined the tiled stove in the parlor, the wood and the black briquettes that would be next to my head at night, and the glass-fronted cabinet full of the china ornaments God had selected to survive the Berlin air raids. These would be removed to make way for my books. For Martin Toeppler need not imagine he could count on my pride, or that I would prefer to starve rather than take his charity, or that I was too arrogant to sleep on his dusty sofa. I would wear out his soap, borrow his shirts, spread his butter on my bread. I would hang on Martin like an octopus. He had a dependent now—a ravenous, egocentric, late-homecoming high-school adolescent of twenty-one. The old men owed this much to me—the old men in my prison camp who would have sold mother and father for an extra ounce of soup, who had already sold their children for it; the old men who had fouled my idea of women; the old men in the bunkers who had let the girls defend them in Berlin; the old men who had dared to survive.

The bed that pulled out was sure to be all lumps. I had slept on worse. Would it be wide enough for Chris, too?

People in the habit of asking themselves silent useless questions look for an-swers in mirrors. My hair was blond again now that it had dried. I looked less like my idea of my father. I tried to see the reflection of the man who had gone out in the middle of the night and who never came back. You don't go out alone to tear down election posters in a village where nobody thinks as you do—not unless you *want* to be stabbed in the back. So the family had said.

"You were well out of it," I said to the shadow that floated on the glass panel of the china cabinet, though it would not be my father's again unless I could catch it unaware.

I said to myself, "It is quieter than France. They keep their radios low."

In captivity I had never suffered a pain except for the cramps of hunger the first years, which had been replaced by a scratching, morbid anxiety, and the pain of homesickness, which takes you in the stomach and the throat. Now I felt the first of the real pains that were to follow me like little dogs for the rest of my life, perhaps; the first compressed my knee, the second tangled the nerves at the back of my neck. I discovered that my eyes were sensitive and that it hurt to blink.

This was the hour when, in Brittany, I would begin peeling the potatoes

for dinner. I had seen food my mother had never heard of—oysters, and arti-
chokes. My mother had never seen a harbour or a sea.

My American prisoner had left his immediate life spread on an alien meadow—
his parachute, his revolver, his German money. He had strolled into captivity
with his hands in his pockets.

"I know what you are thinking," said my mother, who was standing behind me. "I know that you are judging me. If you could guess what my life
has been—the whole story, not only the last few years—you wouldn't be hard
on me."

I turned too slowly to meet her eyes. It was not what I had been thinking.
I had forgotten about her, in that sense.

"No, no, nothing like that," I said. I still did not touch her. What I had been
moving along to in my mind was: Why am I in this place? Who sent me here?
Is it a form of justice or injustice? How long does it last?

"Now we can wait together for Chris," she said. She seemed young and
happy all at once. "Look, Thomas. A new moon. Bow to it three times. Wait—
you must have something silver in your hand." I saw that she was hurrying
to finish with this piece of nonsense before Martin came back. She rummaged
in the china cabinet and brought out a silver napkin ring—left behind by the
vanished tenants, probably. The name on it was "Meta"—no one we knew.
"Bow to the moon and hold it and make your wish," she said. "Quickly."

"You first."

She wished, I am sure, for my brother. As for me, I wished that I was a few
hours younger, in the corridor of a packed train, clutching the top of the open
window, my heart hammering as I strained to find the one beloved face.

From the Fifteenth District

Although an epidemic of haunting, widely reported, spread through the
Fifteenth District of our city last summer, only three acceptable complaints
were lodged with the police.

Major Emery Travella, 31st Infantry, 1914–18, Order of the Leopard, Military
Beech Leaf, Cross of St. Lambert First Class, killed while defusing a bomb in a
civilian area 9 June, 1941, Medal of Danzig (posthumous), claims he is haunted
by the entire congregation of St. Michael and All Angels on Bartholomew Street.
Every year on the Sunday falling nearest the anniversary of his death, Major

From *From The Fifteenth District* (Toronto: Macmillan, 1979). Reprinted by permission of
Georges Borchardt, Inc. Copyright © 1979 by Mavis Gallant.

Travella attends Holy Communion service at St. Michael's, the church from which he was buried. He stands at the back, close to the doors, waiting until all the communicants have returned to their places, before he approaches the altar rail. His intention is to avoid a mixed queue of dead and living, the thought of which is disgusting to him. The congregation sits, hushed and expectant, straining to hear the Major's footsteps (he drags one foot a little). After receiving the Host, the Major leaves at once, without waiting for the Blessing. For the past several years, the Major has noticed that the congregation doubles in size as 9 June approaches. Some of these strangers bring cameras and tape recorders with them; others burn incense under the pews and wave amulets and trinkets in what they imagine to be his direction, muttering pagan gibberish all the while. References he is sure must be meant for him are worked into the sermons: "And he that was dead sat up, and began to speak" (Luke 7:15), or "So Job died, being old and full of days" (Job 42:17). The Major points out that he never speaks and never opens his mouth except to receive Holy Communion. He lived about sixteen thousand and sixty days, many of which he does not remember. On 23 September, 1914, as a young private, he was crucified to a cart wheel for five hours for having failed to salute an equally young lieutenant. One ankle was left permanently impaired.

The Major wishes the congregation to leave him in peace. The opacity of the living, their heaviness and dullness, the moisture of their skin, and the dustiness of their hair are repellent to a man of feeling. It was always his habit to avoid civilian crowds. He lived for six years on the fourth floor in Block E, Stoneflower Gardens, without saying a word to his neighbors or even attempting to learn their names. An affidavit can easily be obtained from the former porter at the Gardens, now residing at the Institute for Victims of Senile Trauma, Fifteenth District.

•••

Mrs. Ibrahim, aged thirty-seven, mother of twelve children, complains about being haunted by Dr. L. Chalmeton of Regius Hospital, Seventh District, and by Miss Alicia Fohrenbach, social investigator from the Welfare Bureau, Fifteenth District. These two haunt Mrs. Ibrahim without respite, presenting for her ratification and approval conflicting and unpleasant versions of her own death.

According to Dr. Chalmeton's account, soon after Mrs. Ibrahim was discharged as incurable from Regius Hospital he paid his patient a professional call. He arrived at a quarter past four on the first Tuesday of April, expecting to find the social investigator, with whom he had a firm appointment. Mrs. Ibrahim was discovered alone, in a windowless room, the walls of which were coated with whitish fungus a quarter of an inch thick, which rose to a height of about forty inches from the floor. Dr. Chalmeton inquired, "Where is the social investigator?" Mrs. Ibrahim pointed to her throat, reminding him that she could not reply. Several dark-eyed children peeped into the room and ran away. "How many are yours?" the Doctor asked. Mrs. Ibrahim indicated six twice with her fingers. "Where do they sleep?" said the Doctor. Mrs. Ibrahim indicated the floor. Dr. Chalmeton said, "What does your husband do for a living?" Mrs.

Ibrahim pointed to a workbench on which the Doctor saw several pieces of finely wrought jewelry; he thought it a waste that skilled work had been lavished on what seemed to be plastics and base metals. Dr. Chalmeton made the patient as comfortable as he could, explaining that he could not administer drugs for the relief of pain until the social investigator had signed a receipt for them. Miss Fohrenbach arrived at five o'clock. It had taken her forty minutes to find a suitable parking space: the street appeared to be poor, but everyone living on it owned one or two cars. Dr. Chalmeton, who was angry at having been kept waiting, declared he would not be responsible for the safety of his patient in a room filled with mold. Miss Fohrenbach retorted that the District could not resettle a family of fourteen persons who were foreign-born when there was a long list of native citizens waiting for accommodation. Mrs. Ibrahim had in any case relinquished her right to a domicile in the Fifteenth District the day she lost consciousness in the road and allowed an ambulance to transport her to a hospital in the Seventh. It was up to the hospital to look after her now. Dr. Chalmeton pointed out that housing of patients is not the business of hospitals. It was well known that the foreign poor preferred to crowd together in the Fifteenth, where they could sing and dance in the streets and attend one another's weddings. Miss Fohrenbach declared that Mrs. Ibrahim could easily have moved her bed into the kitchen, which was somewhat warmer and which boasted a window. When Mrs. Ibrahim died, the children would be placed in foster homes, eliminating the need for a larger apartment. Dr. Chalmeton remembers Miss Fohrenbach's then crying, "Oh, why do all these people come here, where nobody wants them?" While he was trying to think of an answer, Mrs. Ibrahim died.

In her testimony, Miss Fohrenbach recalls that she had to beg and plead with Dr. Chalmeton to visit Mrs. Ibrahim, who had been discharged from Regius Hospital without medicines or prescriptions or advice or instructions. Miss Fohrenbach had returned several times that April day to see if the Doctor had arrived. The first thing Dr. Chalmeton said on entering the room was "There is no way of helping these people. Even the simplest rules of hygiene are too complicated for them to follow. Wherever they settle, they spread disease and vermin. They have been responsible for outbreaks of aphthous stomatitis, hereditary hypoxia, coccidioidomycosis, gonorrheal arthritis, and scleroderma. Their eating habits are filthy. They never wash their hands. The virus that attacks them breeds in dirt. We took in the patient against all rules, after the ambulance drivers left her lying in the courtyard and drove off without asking for a receipt. Regius Hospital was built and endowed for ailing Greek scholars. Now it is crammed with unteachable persons who cannot read or write." His cheeks and forehead were flushed, his speech incoherent and blurred. According to the social investigator, he was the epitome of the broken-down, irresponsible old rascals the Seventh District employs in its public services. Wondering at the effect this ranting of his might have on the patient, Miss Fohrenbach glanced at Mrs. Ibrahim and noticed she had died.

Mrs. Ibrahim's version of her death has the social investigator arriving first, bringing Mrs. Ibrahim a present of a wine-colored dressing gown made of soft, quilted silk. Miss Fohrenbach explained that the gown was part of a donation of garments to the needy. Large plastic bags, decorated with a moss rose, the emblem of the Fifteenth District, and bearing the words "Clean Clothes for the Foreign-Born," had been distributed by volunteer workers in the more prosperous streets of the District. A few citizens kept the bags as souvenirs, but most had turned them in to the Welfare Bureau filled with attractive clothing, washed, ironed, and mended, and with missing buttons replaced. Mrs. Ibrahim sat up and put on the dressing gown, and the social investigator helped her button it. Then Miss Fohrenbach changed the bed linen and pulled the bed away from the wall. She sat down and took Mrs. Ibrahim's hand in hers and spoke about a new, sunny flat containing five warm rooms which would soon be available. Miss Fohrenbach said that arrangements had been made to send the twelve Ibrahim children to the mountains for special winter classes. They would be taught history and languages and would learn to ski.

The Doctor arrived soon after. He stopped and spoke to Mr. Ibrahim, who was sitting at his workbench making an emerald patch box. The Doctor said to him, "If you give me your social-security papers, I can attend to the medical insurance. It will save you a great deal of trouble." Mr. Ibrahim answered, "What is social security?" The Doctor examined the patch box and asked Mr. Ibrahim what he earned. Mr. Ibrahim told him, and the Doctor said, "But that is less than the minimum wage." Mr. Ibrahim said, "What is a minimum wage?" The Doctor turned to Miss Fohrenbach, saying, "We really must try and help them." Mrs. Ibrahim died. Mr. Ibrahim, when he understood that nothing could be done, lay face down on the floor, weeping loudly. Then he remembered the rules of hospitality and got up and gave each of the guests a present—for Miss Fohrenbach a belt made of Syriac coins, a copy of which is in the Cairo Museum, and for the Doctor a bracelet of precious metal engraved with pomegranates, about sixteen pomegranates in all, that has lifesaving properties.

Mrs. Ibrahim asks that her account of the afternoon be registered with the police as the true version and that copies be sent to the Doctor and the social investigator, with a courteous request for peace and silence.

•••

Mrs. Carlotte Essling, née Holmquist, complains of being haunted by her husband, Professor Augustus Essling, the philosopher and historian. When they were married, the former Miss Holmquist was seventeen. Professor Essling, a widower, had four small children. He explained to Miss Holmquist why he wanted to marry again. He said, "I must have one person, preferably female, on whom I can depend absolutely, who will never betray me even in her thoughts. A disloyal thought revealed, a betrayal even in fantasy, would be enough to destroy me. Knowing that I may rely upon some one person will leave me free to continue my work without anxiety or distraction." The work was the Professor's lifelong examination of the philosopher Nicolas de Malebranche, for whom he had named his eldest child. "If I cannot have the unfailing loyalty I have described, I would as soon not marry at all," the Professor added. He had just begun work on *Malebranche and Materialism.*

Mrs. Essling recalls that at seventeen this seemed entirely within her possibilities, and she replied something like "Yes, I see," or "I quite understand," or "You needn't mention it again."

Mrs. Essling brought up her husband's four children and had two more of her own, and died after thirty-six years of marriage at the age of fifty-three. Her husband haunts her with proof of her goodness. He tells people that Mrs. Essling was born an angel, lived like an angel, and is an angel in eternity. Mrs. Essling would like relief from this charge. "Angel" is a loose way of speaking. She is astonished that the Professor cannot be more precise. Angels are created, not born. Nowhere in any written testimony will you find a scrap of proof that angels are "good." Some are merely messengers; others have a paramilitary function. All are stupid.

After her death, Mrs. Essling remained in the Fifteenth District. She says she can go nowhere without being accosted by the Professor, who, having completed the last phase of his work *Malebranche and Mysticism,* roams the streets, looking in shopwindows, eating lunch twice, in two different restaurants, telling his life story to waiters and bus drivers. When he sees Mrs. Essling, he calls out, "There you are!" and "What have you been sent to tell me?" and "Is there a message?" In July, catching sight of her at the open-air fruit market on Dulac Street, the Professor jumped off a bus, upsetting barrows of plums and apricots, waving an umbrella as he ran. Mrs. Essling had to take refuge in the cold-storage room of the central market, where, years ago, after she had ordered twenty pounds of raspberries and currants for making jelly, she was invited by the wholesale fruit dealer, Mr. Lobrano, aged twenty-nine, to spend a holiday with him in a charming southern city whose Mediterranean Baroque churches he described with much delicacy of feeling. Mrs. Essling was too startled to reply. Mistaking her silence, Mr. Lobrano then mentioned a northern city containing a Gothic cathedral. Mrs. Essling said that such a holiday was impossible. Mr. Lobrano asked for one good reason. Mrs. Essling was at that moment four months pregnant with her second child. Three stepchildren waited for her out in the street. A fourth stepchild was at home looking after the baby. Professor Essling, working on his *Malebranche and Money,* was at home, too, expecting his lunch. Mrs. Essling realized she could not give Mr. Lobrano one good reason. She left the cold-storage room without another word and did not return to it in her lifetime.

Mrs. Essling would like to be relieved of the Professor's gratitude. Having lived an exemplary life is one thing; to have it thrown up at one is another. She would like the police to send for Professor Essling and tell him so. She suggests that the police find some method of keeping him off the streets. The police ought to threaten him; frighten him; put the fear of the Devil into him. Philosophy has made him afraid of dying. Remind him about how he avoided writing his *Malebranche and Mortality.* He is an old man. It should be easy.

Norman Levine

(b. 1923)

NORMAN LEVINE GREW UP IN OTTAWA, the setting (and subject) of "In Lower Town." Like all of Levine's work, this story has an autobiographical basis. His war novel *The Angled Road* (1952) grew from his experience in the RCAF; his polemical travel book *Canada Made Me* (1958) exposed the complacencies he found in his native culture; and the stories of *One-way Ticket* (1961), *I don't want to know anyone too well* (1972), and *Thin Ice* (1979) characteristically take autobiographical form as well, sketching details of marriage, family, and daily experience. By careful selection and arrangement, however, Levine manages to transform simple, mundane events into resonant moments of insight into contemporary behaviour. His often anthologized story "We all begin in a little magazine" comments on the nature of modern artistry. Many other stories describe more directly the details of life in England. After World War II, Levine attended McGill, then moved to St. Ives, Cornwall, till he returned to Canada in 1980. He now lives in Toronto.

"In Lower Town" was first published in *Encounter* in 1973; it was broadcast over the CBC, first appeared in book form in *Selected Stories* (1975), and was published as a separate book, by Commoner's Publishing, in 1977, together with photographs of Ottawa's Lower Town by Johanne McDuff. It appears again in his 1982 collection, *Champagne Barn*. The documentary quality of the story lends itself to photographic illustration, but it is also important to recognize the subjectivity of the sketch form in Levine's hands. The narrative stance is at once removed and critical, and involved and bemused. Levine makes the *apparent* memoir, the *apparent* interview, the *apparent* record of conversation and observation into an impressionistic account of the nature of change and the impact of change on the lives of women and men.

For Further Reading

"Interview with Norman Levine," *Quill & Quire* 51.3 (March 1985): 49–50.

IRA BRUCE NADEL, "*Canada Made Me* and Canadian Autobiography," *Canadian Literature* 101 (Summer 1984): 69–81.

FREDERICK SWEET, "Norman Levine" in Jeffrey M. Heath, ed., *Profiles in Canadian Literature* 4 (Toronto & Charlottetown: Dundurn, 1982) 29–36.

In Lower Town

When I was a kid we lived in Lower Town, Ottawa. The first house was on Guigues Street. It was a brick house on a corner. On one side was King Edward Avenue with its boulevard of tall elms, their roots above the ground. And on the other, our neighbour, Nadolny. Mr. Nadolny, a nice-looking man in glasses, had been something different in Europe. Here in Ottawa he was, like my father, a fruit pedlar. The rest of Guigues Street was French Canadian.

It was a large three-storey house and to help things out my mother took in boarders. All of them were recent immigrants from Europe.

There was Isaac and his wife Ethel. He looked like a professor with his monocle, and worked in a jewelry store uptown, doing watch repairs. She stayed home as she was pregnant. She looked a bit scatty with her blond fuzzy hair that she had difficulty in combing, and her large pale eyes. She also couldn't speak English. When she started to have labour pains, she called out to me.

"Me hoits. Me hoits."

They soon left Ottawa for California.

And there was Bobeh and Zaydeh Saslove. They were brought over by their sons when they were in their late sixties. He was short and quiet and had a long beard and not much to do except go to the synagogue. In Poland, when he was younger, he was something in wood. Here he would go to the market and buy, in summer, the wood we needed for the winter. I'd see him come back with the horse and wagon and blocks of wood piled high in the back. He made several trips. Then he spent days building the blocks of wood carefully together along the back fence near where the wild cucumbers were growing. He took care and had the wood meshed evenly—like I tried to do on the table with matches. After he had stacked the couple of cords he would ask us to come out and see how it looked. We all said it looked very nice. A couple of days later he would knock it all down flat. And then start to build it up again, very neatly.

Both he and his wife spoke in whispers. And they ate their meals together out of the same bowl.

My father only knew a few words of English and a few words of French. When I was twelve—and we had moved from Guigues to Murray Street where just about everyone was either a fruit or a rag pedlar—I decided to help my father with the peddling. When school finished at the end of June, I left the house early in the morning and walked to the market and helped him load the wagon with

---

"In Lower Town" was first broadcast on CBC's *Anthology,* and first published in *Encounter* (1973). It is also included in Levine's story collection *Champagne Barn* (Toronto: Penguin, 1984). Reprinted by permission of the author.

the fruit and vegetables that he bought from the farmers and the wholesale stores. Then we went out—the white horse pulling the high red wagon, over Rideau, along Nicholas Street, by the jail, over Laurier Bridge and across the Rideau Canal, to the first street with my father's customers—Gloucester.

It was a quiet street with lots of trees and squirrels on the grass lawns and wooden houses with verandahs painted green or brown. In the middle of the block there was a grey stone convent where someone was always practising the piano.

It was a humid day and our shirts were damp when my father asked me to come along to his first customer—to help break me in.

We walked around to the back of the house to the kitchen. He knocked on the screen door. A pretty woman in a black slip appeared. She was in her thirties. She began to ask questions as to the price of the corn, bananas, tomatoes, cucumbers, potatoes—and she started to squeeze the peach I had, as a sample, in my wicker basket.

"*Kvetch, Kvetch.*" My father began to talk in Yiddish. "I bet you know how to squeeze in bed."

I looked at the woman's face trying to pretend I didn't hear what my father was saying.

"How much are the spring onions?" she asked.

"Three bunches for twenty cents," I said.

"Look at the prostitute," my father said in Yiddish. (The word he used was *curveh*, which is much more evocative.) "You can see she's got nothing on underneath."

"How much are the cherries?" the woman asked with a nice smile.

"Twenty-five cents a box," I said, looking at her brown eyes, the dark hair cut short, the even teeth.

I tried to keep a straight face while she gave me her order and my father went on, in Yiddish, about her likely performance in bed.

As we walked back to the wagon to get her order made up, I felt embarrassed and pleased. I had never heard my father say anything like this before. Without turning my head, I glanced at his face. He was grinning like a kid.

That evening—after he had put the horse in the stable and had his supper—he came outside to sit with my mother and sister on the verandah. He was the same self I had known before, in his chair, in the corner, by the hanging Morning Glory, drinking Kik. And looking at the families sitting outside on the other verandahs doing much the same.

I thought it was only my father who behaved differently away from Lower Town until I happened to be in one of the wealthier West End streets a couple of days later. By now I knew the route as well as the horse. And I used to go well ahead of the horse and wagon so I could sit on a verandah, in the shade, and rest a bit while my father served his customers.

I was sitting like this when I saw old man Pleet—our neighbour on one side in Murray Street. He had a broken-down horse pulling a shabby wagon with old mattresses, old bed-springs, bottles and sacks. But instead of calling out "rags, rags for sale," which he did in Lower Town; here he was saying, in a slight sing-song, the evening service of the synagogue. He didn't see me. As the horse and wagon went by I looked at his face. Mr. Pleet was miles and miles away.

Another time, also in a wealthier street, in Rockcliffe, I saw Mr. Slack, another rag pedlar from Murray Street. He too was going through with his horse and wagon, very slowly, on this hot summer's day. Junk piled behind him. And calling out sadly in Yiddish.

"Thieves. Thieves. Nothing but a bunch of thieves live here."

I guess they knew that once away from Lower Town they might as well have been in a foreign country. And they also knew that they could never become part of it.

But I would.

At school I not only played with the other Lower Town kids but also with kids whose parents only spoke English. Had nice jobs in the government. Some of these kids asked me back to their houses. (It was a very democratic place.) Large houses with maids and with trees and bushes and lots of grass. I remember being asked back by a classmate whose father was an aide-de-camp to the Governor General. And when I arrived there was a garden party on the lawn. Another time a doctor's son asked me. And after we had nice things to eat in a large gloomy house we went in their white boat along the Rideau Canal. Another time a blond girl in the class asked me back for her birthday party— it was to a large house off the Driveway. We had to take our shoes off because the floors were new.

I couldn't invite them back to the house in Murray Street. They had made me ashamed of where I lived, of the house that smelled of the stable, and of parents who couldn't speak English.

I used to go to school day-dreaming that I had other parents, pretending I lived somewhere else. And wondering when I could get away from here.

I did get away when I was eighteen and a half. The war was on. I joined up, went overseas. And after the war I went away to university in Montreal. Then moved over to England and thought I had put all this very far behind me.

But what happened?

Now that most of the fruit and rag pedlars are dead and Lower Town has changed—I find I am unable to stay away from it. It's become like a magnet. Whenever I can, I return.

The last time was this summer. I was supposed to go to Montreal and Toronto. But I only spent a short time in those places. I wanted to be in Ottawa. And though I stayed in a hotel with everything modern and neat, I kept on walking through the streets of Lower Town.

On Rideau, I went into Nate's delicatessen. And saw some of the kids I grew up with—children of those men who used to go out with a horse and wagon.

"You've really made it," Moe Slack said, shaking my hand. "Both the *Citizen* and the *Journal* gave you a full page. My wife bought your last book when it came out. I tried to read it but gave up halfway. Why don't you write dirty books? That's what people want to read."

Harvey Reinhardt came in. He was the same size as me but had put on more weight.

"How are you?" I asked after he sat down.

"I'm impotent," he said.

(Except he pronounced it important.)

"Ten years ago I had five dames going at the same time—"

"What do you mean?"

"I had five mistresses," he said. "My mother caught me with one at home. She said if you don't get that woman out of the house, I'll cut my throat right here. Do me a favour, I said, go out on the lawn. You'll spoil the carpet. I was a real bastard," he said with a grin.

We were sitting around a table in the back of Nate's. Moe Slack and I were having smoked-meat sandwiches and coffee and there was a blown-up informal photograph of Trudeau on the wall. We were now about the same age as those fruit and rag pedlars.

Harvey Reinhardt ordered a kipper.

"I like an English breakfast," he said. "The English girls—do they like to screw? What is it?" he asked me.

"It must be the damp climate," I said.

"You think so?"

The kipper came.

"Have you ever gone to these group things?" Harvey Reinhardt said.

"No," I said, eager to hear more.

"Very high-class people," said Harvey. "They only let you come with your wife or your girlfriend. It starts off like a real party. They give you a drink. Then you start dancing. And you go off to a room. I had this beautiful twenty-five year old. And I couldn't do a thing."

"Didn't she know what to do, to help things along?" I asked.

"She knew what to do," Harvey said. "But it was no good. She said she worked at some agricultural place with boars. And when some boars overdid it they were no good after that. I think this has happened to me. Later I saw her go off with some other fellow into a bedroom. I don't think I'll go again. There's no fun in it for me."

"You're a millionaire—I hear," Moe said to Harvey.

Harvey takes out a cigar and winces. "Who knows?" he said.

I left them at Nate's, remembering when they were younger and I was younger, remembering their mothers and fathers, their sisters and brothers. And crossed into Lower Town.

The streets were being altered, the wooden houses demolished and other houses had doors and windows boarded up waiting to be pulled down.

I walked along York, Clarence, Murray, St. Patrick, Rose, McGee—

Here my father's horse got loose from the stable and came out into the street one summer evening. And then the whole street came out to watch the men coax him back.

In this courtyard I saw a wedding where the young red-haired bridegroom broke the glass on the ground under the held canopy. And the white bits of fluff from the dandelions, or the trees, were blown across by the summer wind so that it looked like falling snow.

Here in winter we hired two horses and a long sleigh without sides. About ten boys and ten girls. We rode at night to the sound of bells on the harness. The overhead street-light showed the hard-packed snow. And in the shadows, on either side, the wooden houses moved slowly by. We pushed one another into the snowbanks, then ran to get back onto the sleigh....

I came to the small park at the end of King Edward Avenue, sat on a green bench, and felt strangely timeless. The white Minto bridges across the hardly moving Rideau river, the swans, the blackbird in the tall grass seemed—like the streets—to be frozen like a photograph. And in an extraordinary stillness.

I went to see my mother.

"Where have you been?" she asked.

"I walked along Murray Street and St. Patrick and down to King Edward Park."

"I haven't been back there for over ten years," she said.

"They're knocking the wooden houses down," I said. "And changing the streets. Soon there will be nothing left of the place the way it was."

"You'll see how nice they'll make it," she said. "All those wooden houses— that's past. We need high-rises, motorways. It will be a lot better. You can write about that," she said. "Tell how nice everything is here. Look at that high-rise across the park. At night, when the apartments put on their lights, it looks like a ship.... You won't write any more about fruit-and-rag pedlars?"

"No," I said.

"That's the old life—it's finished."

She fussed over me, giving me things to eat. And as soon as I finished something on a plate she quickly took the plate away and I could hear her washing it up in the kitchen. Her whole flat was spotless, everything in place. After a while, all this neatness was getting me down. Until I went to look in the drawer of a dresser in the living-room for the old photographs. And saw, to my relief, that the neatness, everything in its place, was only on the surface. That in the drawers, in the dresser, things were still jumbled up.

I looked at the faces of people in the Lower Town of not so long ago. There was a photograph of my mother in her early twenties with two friends...my father on the verandah...a family picture in front of the house...a photograph of my sister and me by a large elm on King Edward Avenue when I was five and she was three...a gathering at someone's wedding....

My mother watched me. "When I'm gone," she said, indicating the photographs with her hand and then sweeping her hand downwards. "*In* the garbage! *All* in the garbage. You'll see."

She said it almost defiantly.

On the day I arrived for this visit men in yellow machines were busy knocking down the large convent on Rideau Street. I asked Harvey Reinhardt why they were knocking down a perfectly good convent.

"You can't make a buck out of a convent on Rideau Street," he said.

A few weeks later all that was still standing was part of the chapel. I could see a large painting painted on one wall of the chapel. It showed a young nun in a black-and-sky-blue habit. And coming down from the top left of the picture, down to the upturned eyes of the nun, was a wide ray of sunshine. Several cherubim were in this ray of the sun. They had curly blond hair and wings.

On the day I left Ottawa the chapel had also been knocked down, the rubble cleared. It was all very tidy. Nothing to show that there ever had been a convent there at all.

Margaret Laurence

(1926–1987)

BORN JEAN MARGARET WEMYSS IN NEEPAWA, MANITOBA, Margaret Laurence went on to become the best-known Canadian novelist of her generation, noted for such works as *The Stone Angel* (1964) and *The Diviners* (1974). She grew up in Neepawa—brought up by her aunt, after both her parents died. She attended United College (Winnipeg), and her prairie background resurfaced in her fiction, transformed into the world that as early as 1939 she had named "Manawaka."

Most of her early writings, however, depict African settings. These drew on her observations of Somaliland and Ghana, where she lived with her husband, an engineer, between 1950 and 1957. She wrote a travel book (*The Prophet's Camel Bell,* 1963), a novel (*This Side Jordan,* 1960), stories (collected as *The Tomorrow-Tamer and other stories,* 1963), and translations of Somali folk tales. Living in Africa—learning to appreciate the complexities of an oral culture—led her not only to sharpen her own anti-colonialist feelings but also to re-examine the past, to listen again to the voices of her own society and to chart the "Manawaka" experience.

"Manawaka" became a microcosm of Western Canadian social history, a world in which generational, sexual, and ethnic tensions all epitomized the kinds of social adjustment that during the 20th century transformed a provincial outpost into a place that might be called home. With its graphic account of Depression pressures on thwarted women and displaced men, "Horses of the Night"—first published in *Winter's Tales 9* (1967) and collected as a central story in *A Bird in the House* (1970)—testifies to the kinds of mask that people put on to defend themselves against reality, and to the kinds of reality that they must nevertheless learn to face. Formally, the story is a carefully crafted work of art as well as an historical record. The title allusion (to Marlowe's *Doctor Faustus* and, through it, to Ovid's *Amores*) and the imagery (of rooms and boxes, for example) work out the temptations of permanence, youth, and freedom that the central character has to deal with, as she herself grows up.

In her last years, Margaret Laurence lived in Lakefield, Ontario, where she was active in the anti-nuclear movement, served as Chancellor of Trent University in Peterborough, and wrote the essays in autobiography that were posthumously published as *Dance on the Earth: A Memoir* (1989).

For Further Reading

Tom Middlebro', "Imitatio Inanitatis: Literary Madness and the Canadian Short Story," *Canadian Literature* 107 (Winter 1985): 189–93.

Patricia Morley, *Margaret Laurence: The Long Journey Home* (Montreal: McGill-Queen's UP, 1991).

W.H. New, "No Longer Living There: Margaret Laurence's *A Bird in the House*" in *Dreams of Speech and Violence* (Toronto: U Toronto P, 1987) 187–200.

Clara Thomas, *The Manawaka World of Margaret Laurence* (Toronto: McClelland & Stewart, 1975).

Horses of the Night

I never knew I had distant cousins who lived up north, until Chris came down to Manawaka to go to high school. My mother said he belonged to a large family, relatives of ours, who lived at Shallow Creek, up north. I was six, and Shallow Creek seemed immeasurably far, part of a legendary winter country where no leaves grow and where the breath of seals and polar bears snuffled out steamily and turned to ice.

"Could plain people live there?" I asked my mother, meaning people who were not Eskimos. "Could there be a farm?"

"How do you mean?" she said, puzzled. "I told you. That's where they live. On the farm. Uncle Wilf—that was Chris's father, who died a few years back— he got the place as a homestead, donkey's years ago."

"But how could they grow anything? I thought you said it was up north."

"Mercy," my mother said, laughing, "it's not *that* far north, Vanessa. It's about a hundred miles beyond Galloping Mountain. You be nice to Chris, now, won't you? And don't go asking him a whole lot of questions the minute he steps inside the door."

How little my mother knew of me, I thought. Chris had been fifteen. He could be expected to feel only scorn towards me. I detested the fact that I was so young. I did not think I would be able to say anything at all to him.

"What if I don't like him?"

"What if you don't?" my mother responded sharply. "You're to watch your manners, and no acting up, understand? It's going to be quite difficult enough without that.

"Why does he have to come here, anyway?" I demanded crossly. "Why can't he go to school where he lives?"

"Because there isn't any high school up there," my mother said. "I hope he gets on well here, and isn't too homesick. Three years is a long time. It's very good of your grandfather to let him stay at the Brick House.

She said this last accusingly, as though she suspected I might be thinking differently. But I had not thought of it one way or another. We were all having dinner at the Brick House because of Chris's arrival. It was the end of August, and sweltering. My grandfather's house looked huge and cool from the outside, the high low-sweeping spruce trees shutting out the sun with their dusky out-fanned branches. But inside it wasn't cool at all. The woodstove in the kitchen was going full blast, and the whole place smelled of roasting meat.

Grandmother Connor was wearing a large mauve apron. I thought it was a nicer colour than the dark bottle-green of her dress, but she believed in wearing sombre shades lest the spirit give way to vanity, which in her case was

From *A Bird in the House* (Toronto: McClelland and Stewart, 1970). Reprinted by permission of The Canadian Publishers McClelland and Stewart Ltd.

certainly not much of a risk. The apron came up over her shapeless bosom and obscured part of her cameo brooch, the only jewellery she ever wore, with its portrait of a fiercely bearded man whom I imagined to be either Moses or God.

"Isn't it nearly time for them to be getting here, Beth?" Grandmother Connor asked.

"Train's not due until six," my mother said. "It's barely five-thirty now. Has Father gone to the station already?"

"He went an hour ago," my grandmother said.

"He would," my mother commented.

"Now, now, Beth," my grandmother cautioned and soothed.

At last the front screen door was hurled open and Grandfather Connor strode into the house, followed by a tall lanky boy. Chris was wearing a white shirt, a tie, grey trousers. I thought, unwillingly, that he looked handsome. His face was angular, the bones showing through the brown skin. His grey eyes were slightly slanted, and his hair was the colour of couchgrass at the end of summer when it has been bleached to a light yellow by the sun. I had not planned to like him, not even a little, but somehow I wanted to defend him when I heard what my mother whispered to my grandmother before they went into the front hall.

"Heavens, look at the shirt and trousers—must've been his father's, the poor kid."

I shot out into the hall ahead of my mother, and then stopped and stood there.

"Hi, Vanessa," Chris said.

"How come you knew who I was?" I asked.

"Well, I knew your mother and dad only had one of a family, so I figured you must be her," he replied, grinning.

The way he spoke did not make me feel I had blundered. My mother greeted him warmly but shyly. Not knowing if she were expected to kiss him or to shake hands, she finally did neither. Grandmother Connor, however, had no doubts. She kissed him on both cheeks and then held him at arm's length to have a proper look at him.

"Bless the child," she said.

Coming from anyone else, this remark would have sounded ridiculous, especially as Chris was at least a head taller. My grandmother was the only person I have ever known who could say such things without appearing false.

"I'll show you your room, Chris," my mother offered.

Grandfather Connor, who had been standing in the living room doorway in absolute silence, looking as granite as a statue in the cemetery, now followed Grandmother out to the kitchen.

"Train was forty minutes late," he said weightily.

"What a shame," my grandmother said. "But I thought it wasn't due until six, Timothy."

"Six!" my grandfather cried. "That's the mainline train. The local's due at five-twenty."

This was not correct, as both my grandmother and I knew. But neither of us contradicted him.

"What on earth are you cooking a roast for, on a night like this?" my grandfather went on. "A person could fry an egg on the sidewalk, it's that hot. Potato salad would've gone down well."

Privately I agreed with this opinion, but I could never permit myself to acknowledge agreement with him on anything. I automatically and emotionally sided with Grandmother in all issues, not because she was inevitably right but because I loved her.

"It's not a roast," my grandmother said mildly. "It's mock-duck. The stove's only been going for an hour. I thought the boy would be hungry after the trip."

My mother and Chris had come downstairs and were now in the living room. I could hear them there, talking awkwardly, with pauses.

"Potato salad," my grandfather declaimed, "would've been plenty good enough. He'd have been lucky to get it, if you ask me anything. Wilf's family hasn't got two cents to rub together. It's me that's paying for the boy's keep."

The thought of Chris in the living room, and my mother unable to explain, was too much for me. I sidled over to the kitchen door, intending to close it. But my grandmother stopped me.

"No," she said, with unexpected firmness. "Leave it open, Vanessa."

I could hardly believe it. Surely she couldn't want Chris to hear? She herself was always able to move with equanimity through a hurricane because she believed that a mighty fortress was her God. But the rest of us were not like that, and usually she did her best to protect us. At the time I felt only bewilderment. I think now that she must have realised Chris would have to learn the Brick House sooner or later, and he might as well start right away.

I had to go into the living room. I had to know how Chris would take my grandfather. Would he, as I hoped, be angry and perhaps even speak out? Or would he, meekly, only be embarrassed?

"Wilf wasn't much good, even as a young man," Grandfather Connor was trumpeting. "Nobody but a simpleton would've taken up a homestead in a place like that. Anybody could've told him that land's no use for a thing except hay."

Was he going to remind us again how well he had done in the hardware business? Nobody had ever given him a hand, he used to tell me. I am sure he believed that this was true. Perhaps it even was true.

"If the boy takes after his father, it's a poor lookout for him," my grandfather continued.

I felt the old rage of helplessness. But as for Chris—he gave no sign of feeling anything. He was sitting on the big wing-backed sofa that curled into the bay window like a black and giant seashell. He began to talk to me, quite easily, just as though he had not heard a word my grandfather was saying.

This method proved to be the one Chris always used in any dealings with my grandfather. When the bludgeoning words came, which was often, Chris never seemed, like myself, to be holding back with a terrible strained force for fear of letting go and speaking out and having the known world unimaginably fall to pieces. He would not argue or defend himself, but he did not apologise, either. He simply appeared to be absent, elsewhere. Fortunately there was very little need for response, for when Grandfather Connor pointed out your shortcomings, you were not expected to reply.

But this aspect of Chris was one which I noticed only vaguely at the time. What won me was that he would talk to me and wisecrack as though I were his same age. He was—although I didn't know the phrase then—a respecter of persons.

On the rare evenings when my parents went out, Chris would come over to mind me. These were the best times, for often when he was supposed to be doing his homework, he would make fantastic objects for my amusement, or his own—pipecleaners twisted into the shape of wildly prancing midget men, or an old set of Christmas-tree lights fixed onto a puppet theatre with a red velvet curtain that really pulled. He had skill in making miniature things of all kinds. Once for my birthday he gave me a leather saddle no bigger than a matchbox, which he had sewn himself, complete in every detail, stirrups and horn, with the criss-cross lines that were the brand name of his ranch, he said, explaining it was a reference to his own name.

"Can I go to Shallow Creek sometime?" I asked one evening.

"Sure. Some summer holidays, maybe. I've got a sister about your age. The others are all grown up."

I did not want to hear. His sisters—for Chris was the only boy—did not exist for me, not even as photographs, because I did not want them to exist. I wanted him to belong only here. Shallow Creek existed, though, no longer filled with ice mountains in my mind but as some beckoning country beyond all ordinary considerations.

"Tell me what it's like there, Chris."

"My gosh, Vanessa, I've told you before, about a thousand times."

"You never told me what your house is like."

"Didn't I? Oh well—it's made out of trees grown right there beside the lake."

"Made out of trees? Gee. Really?"

I could see it. The trees were still growing, and the leaves were firmly and greenly on them. The branches had been coaxed into formations of towers and high-up nests where you could look out and see for a hundred miles or more.

"That lake, you know," Chris said. "It's more like an inland sea. It goes on for ever and ever amen, that's how it looks. And you know what? Millions of years ago, before there were any human beings at all, that lake was full of water monsters. All different kinds of dinosaurs. Then they all died off. Nobody knows for sure why. Imagine them—all those huge creatures, with necks like snakes, and some of them had hackles on their heads, like a rooster's comb only very tough, like hard leather. Some guys from Winnipeg came up a few years back, there, and dug up dinosaur bones, and they found footprints in the rocks."

"Footprints in the *rocks?*"

"The rocks were mud, see, when the dinosaurs went trampling through, but after trillions of years the mud turned into stone and there were these mighty footprints with the claws still showing. Amazing, eh?"

I could only nod, fascinated and horrified. Imagine going swimming in those waters. What if one of the creatures had lived on?

"Tell me about the horses," I said.

"Oh, them. Well, we've got these two riding horses. Duchess and Firefly. I raised them, and you should see them. Really sleek, know what I mean? I bet I could make racers out of them."

He missed the horses, I thought with selfish satisfaction, more than he missed his family. I could visualise the pair, one sorrel and one black, swifting through all the meadows of summer.

"When can I go, Chris?"

"Well, we'll have to see. After I get through high school, I won't be at Shallow Creek much."

"Why not?"

"Because," Chris said, "what I am going to be is an engineer, civil engineer. You ever seen a really big bridge, Vanessa? Well, I haven't either, but I've seen pictures. You take the Golden Gate Bridge in San Francisco now. Terrifically high—all those thin ribs of steel, joined together to go across this very wide stretch of water. It doesn't seem possible, but it's there. That's what engineers do. Imagine doing something like that, eh?"

I could not imagine it. It was beyond me.

"Where will you go?" I asked. I did not want to think of his going anywhere.

"Winnipeg, to college," he said with assurance.

The Depression did not get better, as everyone had been saying it would. It got worse, and so did the drought. That part of the prairies where we lived was never dustbowl country. The farms around Manawaka never had a total crop failure, and afterwards, when the drought was over, people used to remark on this fact proudly, as though it had been due to some virtue or special status, like the Children of Israel being afflicted by Jehovah but never in real danger of annihilation. But although Manawaka never knew the worst, what it knew was bad enough. Or so I learned later. At the time I saw none of it. For me, the Depression and drought were external and abstract, malevolent gods whose names I secretly learned although they were concealed from me, and whose evil I sensed only superstitiously, knowing they threatened us but not how or why. What I really saw was only what went on in our family.

"He's done quite well all through, despite everything," my mother said. She sighed, and I knew she was talking about Chris.

"I know," my father said. "We've been over all this before, Beth. But quite good just isn't good enough. Even supposing he managed to get a scholarship, which isn't likely, it's only tuition and books. What about room and board? Who's going to pay for that? Your father?"

"I see I shouldn't have brought up the subject at all," my mother said in an aloof voice.

"I'm sorry," my father said impatiently. "But you know, yourself, he's the only one who might possibly—"

"I can't bring myself to ask Father about it, Ewen. I simply cannot do it."

"There wouldn't be much point in asking," my father said, "when the answer is a foregone conclusion. He feels he's done his share, and actually, you know, Beth, he has, too. Three years, after all. He may not have done it gracefully, but he's done it."

We were sitting in the living room, and it was evening. My father was slouched in the grey armchair that was always his. My mother was slenderly straight-backed in the blue chair in which nobody else ever sat. I was sitting on the footstool, beige needlepoint with mathematical roses, to which I had staked my own claim. This seating arrangement was obscurely satisfactory to me, perhaps because predictable, like the three bears. I was pretending to be colouring into a scribbler on my knee, and from time to time my lethargic purple crayon added a feather to an outlandish swan. To speak would be to invite dismissal. But their words forced questions in my head.

"Chris isn't going away, is he?"

My mother swooped, shocked at her own neglect.

"My heavens—are you still up, Vanessa? What am I thinking of?"

"Where is Chris going?"

"We're not sure yet," my mother evaded, chivvying me up the stairs. "We'll see."

He would not go, I thought. Something would happen, miraculously, to prevent him. He would remain, with his long loping walk and his half-slanted grey eyes and his talk that never excluded me. He would stay right here. And soon, because I desperately wanted to, and because every day mercifully made me older, quite soon I would be able to reply with such a lightning burst of knowingness that it would astound him, when he spoke of the space or was it some black sky that never ended anywhere beyond this earth. Then I would not be innerly belittled for being unable to figure out what he would best like to hear. At that good and imagined time, I would not any longer be limited. I would not any longer be young.

I was nine when Chris left Manawaka. The day before he was due to go, I knocked on the door of his room in the Brick House.

"Come in," Chris said. "I'm packing. Do you know how to fold socks, Vanessa?"

"Sure. Of course."

"Well, get folding on that bunch there, then."

I had come to say goodbye, but I did not want to say it yet. I got to work on the socks. I did not intend to speak about the matter of college, but the knowledge that I must not speak about it made me uneasy. I was afraid I would blurt out a reference to it in my anxiety not to. My mother had said, "He's taken it amazingly well—he doesn't even mention it, so we mustn't either."

"Tomorrow night you'll be in Shallow Creek," I ventured.

"Yeh." He did not look up. He went on stuffing clothes and books into his suitcase.

"I bet you'll be glad to see the horses, eh?" I wanted him to say he didn't care about the horses any more and that he would rather stay here.

"It'll be good to see them again," Chris said. "Mind handing over those socks now, Vanessa? I think I can just squash them in at the side here. Thanks. Hey, look at that, will you? Everything's in. Am I an expert packer or am I an expert packer?"

I sat on his suitcase for him so it would close, and then he tied a piece of rope around it because the lock wouldn't lock.

"Ever thought what it would be like to be a traveller, Vanessa?" he asked.

I thought of Richard Halliburton, taking an elephant over the Alps and swimming illicitly in the Taj Mahal lily pool by moonlight.

"It would be keen," I said, because this was the word Chris used to describe the best possible. "That's what I'm going to do someday."

He did not say, as for a moment I feared he might, that girls could not be travellers.

"Why not?" he said. "Sure you will, if you really want to. I got this theory, see, that anybody can do anything at all, anything, if they really set their minds to it. But you have to have this total concentration. You have to focus on it with your whole mental powers, and not let it slip away by forgetting to hold it in your mind. If you hold it in your mind, like, then it's real, see? You take most people, now. They can't concentrate worth a darn."

"Do you think I can?" I enquired eagerly, believing that this was what he was talking about.

"What?" he said. "Oh—sure. Sure I think you can. Naturally."

Chris did not write after he left Manawaka. About a month later we had a letter from his mother. He was not at Shallow Creek. He had not gone back. He had got off the northbound train at the first stop after Manawaka, cashed in his ticket, and thumbed a lift with a truck to Winnipeg. He had written to his mother from there, but had given no address. She had not heard from him since. My mother read Aunt Tess's letter aloud to my father. She was too upset to care whether I was listening or not.

"I can't think what possessed him, Ewen. He never seemed irresponsible. What if something should happen to him? What if he's broke? What do you think we should do?"

"What can we do? He's nearly eighteen. What he does is his business. Simmer down, Beth, and let's decide what we're going to tell your father."

"Oh Lord," my mother said. "There's that to consider, of course."

I went out without either of them noticing. I walked to the hill at the edge of the town, and down into the valley where the scrub oak and poplar grew almost to the banks of the Wachakwa River. I found the oak where we had gone last autumn, in a gang, to smoke cigarettes made of dried leaves and pieces of newspaper. I climbed to the lowest branch and stayed there for a while.

I was not consciously thinking about Chris. I was not thinking of anything. But when at last I cried, I felt relieved afterwards and could go home again.

Chris departed from my mind, after that, with a quickness that was due to the other things that happened. My Aunt Edna, who was a secretary in Winnipeg, returned to Manawaka to live because the insurance company cut down on staff and she could not find another job. I was intensely excited and jubilant about her return, and could not see why my mother seemed the opposite, even though she was as fond of Aunt Edna as I was. Then my brother Roderick was born, and that same year Grandmother Connor died. The strangeness, the unbelievability, of both these events took up all of me.

When I was eleven, almost two years after Chris had left, he came back without warning. I came home from school and found him sitting in our living room. I could not accept that I had nearly forgotten him until this instant. Now that he was present, and real again, I felt I had betrayed him by not thinking of him more.

He was wearing a navy-blue serge suit. I was old enough now to notice that it was a cheap one and had been worn a considerable time. Otherwise, he looked the same, the same smile, the same knife-boned face with no flesh to speak of, the same unresting eyes.

"How come you're here?" I cried. "Where have you been, Chris?"

"I'm a traveller," he said. "Remember?"

He was a traveller all right. One meaning of the word *traveller* in our part of the world, was a travelling salesman. Chris was selling vacuum cleaners. That evening he brought out his line and showed us. He went through his spiel for our benefit, so we could hear how it sounded.

"Now look, Beth," he said, turning the appliance on and speaking loudly above its moaning roar, "see how it brightens up this old rug of yours? Keen, eh?"

"Wonderful," my mother laughed. "Only we can't afford one."

"Oh well—" Chris said quickly, "I'm not trying to sell one to you. I'm only showing you. Listen, I've only been in this job a month, but I figure this is really a going thing. I mean, it's obvious, isn't it? You take all those old wire carpet-beaters of yours, Beth. You could kill yourself over them and your carpet isn't going to look one-tenth as good as it does with this."

"Look, I don't want to seem—" my father put in, "but, hell, they're not exactly a new invention, and we're not the only ones who can't afford—"

"This is a pretty big outfit, you know?" Chris insisted. "Listen, I don't plan to stay, Ewen. But a guy could work at it for a year or so, and save—right? Lots of guys work their way through university like that."

I needed to say something really penetrating, something that would show him I knew the passionate truth of his conviction.

"I bet—" I said, "I bet you'll sell a thousand, Chris."

Two years ago, this statement would have seemed self-evident, unquestionable. Yet now, when I had spoken, I knew that I did not believe it.

The next time Chris visited Manawaka, he was selling magazines. He had the statistics worked out. If every sixth person in town would get a subscription to *Country Guide,* he could make a hundred dollars in a month. We didn't learn how he got on. He didn't stay in Manawaka a full month. When he turned up again, it was winter. Aunt Edna phoned.

"Nessa? Listen, kiddo, tell your mother she's to come down if it's humanly possible. Chris is here, and Father's having fits."

So in five minutes we were scurrying through the snow, my mother and I, with our overshoes not even properly done up and our feet getting wet. We need not have worried. By the time we reached the Brick House, Grandfather Connor had retired to the basement, where he sat in the rocking chair beside the furnace, making occasional black pronouncements like a subterranean oracle. These loud utterances made my mother and aunt wince, but Chris didn't seem to notice any more than he ever had. He was engrossed in telling us about the mechanism he was holding. It had a cranker handle like an old-fashioned sewing machine.

"You attach the ball of wool here, see? Then you set this little switch here, and adjust this lever, and you're away to the races. Neat, eh?"

It was a knitting machine. Chris showed us the finished products. The men's socks he had made were coarse wool, one pair in grey heather and another in maroon. I was impressed.

"Gee—can I do it, Chris?"

"Sure. Look, you just grab hold of the handle right here."

"Where did you get it?" my mother asked.

"I've rented it. The way I figure it, Beth, I can sell these things at about half the price you'd pay in a store, and they're better quality."

"Who are you going to sell them to?" Aunt Edna enquired.

"You take all these guys who do outside work—they need heavy socks all year round, not just in winter. I think this thing could be quite a gold mine."

"Before I forget," my mother said, "how's your mother and the family keeping?"

"They're okay," Chris said in a restrained voice. "They're not short of hands, if that's what you mean, Beth. My sisters have their husbands there."

Then he grinned, casting away the previous moment, and dug into his suitcase.

"Hey, I haven't shown you—these are for you, Vanessa, and this pair is for Roddie."

My socks were cherry-coloured. The very small ones for my brother were turquoise.

Chris only stayed until after dinner, and then he went away again.

After my father died, the whole order of life was torn. Nothing was known or predictable any longer. For months I lived almost entirely within myself, so when my mother told me one day that Chris couldn't find any work at all because there were no jobs and so he had gone back to Shallow Creek to stay, it made scarcely any impression on me. But that summer, my mother decided I ought to go away for a holiday. She hoped it might take my mind off my father's death. What, if anything, was going to take her mind off his death, she did not say.

"Would you like to go to Shallow Creek for a week or so?" she asked me. "I could write to Chris's mother."

Then I remembered, all in a torrent, the way I had imagined it once, when he used to tell me about it—the house fashioned of living trees, the lake like a sea where monsters had dwelt, the grass that shone like green wavering light while the horses flew in the splendour of their pride.

"Yes," I said. "Write to her."

The railway did not go through Shallow Creek, but Chris met me at Challoner's Crossing. He looked different, not only thinner, but—what was it? Then I saw that it was the fact that his face and neck were tanned red-brown, and he was wearing denims, farm pants, and a blue plaid shirt open at the neck. I liked him like this. Perhaps the change was not so much in him as in myself, now that I was thirteen. He looked masculine in a way I had not been aware of, before.

"C'mon, kid," he said. "The limousine's over here."

It was a wagon and two horses, which was what I had expected, but the nature of each was not what I had expected. The wagon was a long and clumsy one, made of heavy planking, and the horses were both plough horses, thick in the legs, and badly matched as a team. The mare was short and stout, matronly. The gelding was very tall and gaunt, and he limped.

"Allow me to introduce you," Chris said. "Floss—Trooper—this is Vanessa."

He did not mention the other horses, Duchess and Firefly, and neither did I, not all the fortnight I was there. I guess I had known for some years now, without realising it, that the pair had only ever existed in some other dimension.

Shallow Creek wasn't a town. It was merely a name on a map. There was a grade school a few miles away, but that was all. They had to go to Challoner's Crossing for their groceries. We reached the farm, and Chris steered me through the crowd of aimless cows and wolfish dogs in the yard, while I flinched with panic.

It was perfectly true that the house was made out of trees. It was a fair-sized but elderly shack, made out of poplar poles and chinked with mud. There was an upstairs, which was not so usual around here, with three bedrooms, one of which I was to share with Chris's sister, Jeannie, who was slightly younger than I, a pallid-eyed girl who was either too shy to talk or who had nothing to say. I never discovered which, because I was so reticent with her myself, wanting to push her away, not to recognise her, and at the same time experiencing a shocked remorse at my own unacceptable feelings.

Aunt Tess, Chris's mother, was severe in manner and yet wanting to be kind, worrying over it, making tentative overtures which were either ignored or repelled by her older daughters and their monosyllabic husbands. Youngsters swam in and out of the house like shoals of nameless fishes. I could not see how so many people could live here, under the one roof, but then I learned they didn't. The married daughters had their own dwelling places, nearby, but some kind of communal life was maintained. They wrangled endlessly but they never left one another alone, not even for a day.

Chris took no part at all, none. When he spoke, it was usually to the children, and they would often follow him around the yard or to the barn, not pestering but just trailing along in clusters of three or four. He never told them to go away. I liked him for this, but it bothered me, too. I wished he would return his sisters' bickering for once, or tell them to clear out, or even yell at one of the kids. But he never did. He closed himself off from squabbling voices just as he used to do with Grandfather Connor's spearing words.

The house had no screens on the doors or windows, and at meal times the flies were so numerous you could hardly see the food for the iridescent-winged blue-black bodies squirming all over it. Nobody noticed my squeamishness except Chris, and he was the only one from whom I really wanted to conceal it.

"Fan with your hand," he murmured.

"It's okay," I said quickly.

For the first time in all the years we had known each other, we could not look the other in the eye. Around the table, the children stabbed and snivelled, until Chris's oldest sister, driven frantic, shrieked, *Shut up shut up shut up*. Chris began asking me about Manawaka then, as though nothing were going on around him.

They were due to begin haying, and Chris announced that he was going to camp out in the bluff near the hayfields. To save himself the long drive in the wagon each morning, he explained, but I felt this wasn't the real reason.

"Can I go, too?" I begged. I could not bear the thought of living in the house with all the others who were not known to me, and Chris not here.

"Well, I don't know—"

"Please. Please, Chris. I won't be any trouble. I promise."

Finally he agreed. We drove out in the big hayrack, its slatted sides rattling, its old wheels jolting metallically. The road was narrow and dirt, and around it the low bushes grew, wild rose and blueberry and wolf willow with silver leaves. Sometimes we would come to a bluff of pale-leaved poplar trees, and once a red-winged blackbird flew up out of the branches and into the hot dusty blue of the sky.

Then we were there. The hayfields lay beside the lake. It was my first view of the water which had spawned saurian giants so long ago. Chris drove the hayrack through the fields of high coarse grass and on down almost to the lake's edge, where there was no shore but only the green rushes like floating meadows in which the water birds nested. Beyond the undulating reeds the open lake stretched, deep, green-grey, out and out, beyond sight.

No human word could be applied. The lake was not lonely or untamed. These words relate to people, and there was nothing of people here. There was no feeling about the place. It existed in some world in which man was not yet born. I looked at the grey reaches of it and felt threatened. It was like the view of God which I had held since my father's death. Distant, indestructible, totally indifferent.

Chris had jumped down off the hayrack.

"We're not going to camp *here*, are we?" I asked and pleaded.

"No. I just want to let the horses drink. We'll camp up there in the bluff." I looked. "It's still pretty close to the lake, isn't it?"

"Don't worry," Chris said, laughing. "You won't get your feet wet."

"I didn't mean that."

Chris looked at me.

"I know you didn't," he said. "But let's learn to be a little tougher, and not let on, eh? It's necessary."

Chris worked through the hours of sun, while I lay on the half-formed stack of hay and looked up at the sky. The blue air trembled and spun with the heat haze, and the hay on which I was lying held the scents of grass and dust and wild mint.

In the evening, Chris took the horses to the lake again, and then he drove the hayrack to the edge of the bluff and we spread out our blankets underneath it. He made a fire and we had coffee and a tin of stew, and then we went to bed. We did not wash, and we slept in our clothes. It was only when I was curled up uncomfortably with the itching blanket around me that I felt a sense of unfamiliarity at being here, with Chris only three feet away, a self-consciousness I would not have felt even the year before. I do not think he felt this sexual strangeness. If he wanted me not to be a child—and he did—it was not with the wish that I would be a woman. It was something else.

"Are you asleep, Vanessa?" he asked.

"No. I think I'm lying on a tree root."

"Well, shift yourself, then," he said. "Listen, kid, I never said anything before, because I didn't really know what to say, but—you know how I felt about your dad dying, and that, don't you?"

"Yes," I said chokingly. "It's okay. I know."

"I used to talk with Ewen sometimes. He didn't see what I was driving at, mostly, but he'd always listen, you know? You don't find many guys like that."

We were both silent for a while.

"Look," Chris said finally. "Ever noticed how much brighter the stars are when you're completely away from any houses? Even the lamps up at the farm, there, make enough of a glow to keep you from seeing properly like you can out here. What do they make you think about, Vanessa?"

"Well—"

"I guess most people don't give them much thought at all, except maybe to say—*very pretty*—or like that. But the point is, they aren't like that. The stars and planets, in themselves, are just not like that, not *pretty*, for heaven's sake. They're gigantic—some of them burning—imagine those worlds tearing through space and made of pure fire. Or the ones that are absolutely dead—just rock or ice and no warmth in them. There must be some, though, that have living creatures. You wonder what *they* could look like, and what they feel. We won't ever get to know. But somebody will know, some day. I really believe that. Do you ever think about this kind of thing at all?"

He was twenty-one. The distance between us was still too great. For years I had wanted to be older so I might talk with him, but now I felt unready.

"Sometimes," I said, hesitantly, making it sound like *Never.*

"People usually say there must be a God," Chris went on, "because otherwise how did the universe get here? But that's ridiculous. If the stars and planets go on to infinity, they could have existed forever, for no reason at all. Maybe they weren't ever created. Look—what's the alternative? To believe in a God who is brutal. What else could He be? You've only got to look anywhere around you. It would be an insult to Him to believe in a God like that. Most people don't like talking about this kind of thing—it embarrasses them, you know? Or else they're not interested. I don't mind. I can always think about things myself. You don't actually need anyone to talk to. But about God, though—if there's a war, like it looks there will be, would people claim that was planned? What kind of a God would pull a trick like that? And yet, you know, plenty of guys would think it was a godsend, and who's to say they're wrong? It would be a job, and you'd get around and see places."

He paused, as though waiting for me to say something. When I did not, he resumed.

"Ewen told me about the last war, once. He hardly ever talked about it, but this once he told me about seeing the horses into the mud, actually going under, you know? And the way their eyes looked when they realised they weren't going to get out. Ever seen horses' eyes when they're afraid, I mean really berserk with fear, like in a bush-fire? Ewen said a guy tended to concentrate on the horses because he didn't dare think what was happening to the men. Including himself. Do you ever listen to the news at all, Vanessa?"

"I—"

I could only feel how foolish I must sound, still unable to reply as I would have wanted, comprehendingly. I felt I had failed myself utterly. I could not speak even the things I knew. As for the other things, the things I did not know, I resented Chris's facing me with them. I took refuge in pretending to be asleep, and after a while Chris stopped talking.

•••

Chris left Shallow Creek some months after the war began, and joined the Army. After his basic training he was sent to England. We did not hear from him until about a year later, when a letter arrived for me.

"Vanessa—what's wrong?" my mother asked.

"Nothing."

"Don't fib," she said firmly. "What did Chris say in his letter, honey?"

"Oh—not much."

She gave me a curious look and then she went away. She would never have demanded to see the letter. I did not show it to her and she did not ask about it again.

Six months later my mother heard from Aunt Tess. Chris had been sent home from England and discharged from the Army because of a mental breakdown. He was now in the provincial mental hospital and they did not know how long he would have to remain there. He had been violent, before, but now he was not violent. He was, the doctors had told his mother, passive.

Violent. I could not associate the word with Chris, who had been so much the reverse. I could not bear to consider what anguish must have catapulted him into that even greater anguish. But the way he was now seemed almost worse. How might he be? Sitting quite still, wearing the hospital's grey dressing-gown, the animation gone from his face?

My mother cared about him a great deal, but her immediate thought was not for him.

"When I think of you, going up to Shallow Creek that time," she said, "and going out camping with him, and what might have happened—"

I, also, was thinking of what might have happened. But we were not thinking of the same thing. For the first time I recognised, at least a little, the dimensions of his need to talk that night. He must have understood perfectly well how impossible it would be, with a thirteen-year-old. But there was no one else. All his life's choices had grown narrower and narrower. He had been forced to return to the alien lake of home, and when finally he saw a means of getting away, it could only be into a turmoil which appalled him and which he dreaded even more than he knew. I had listened to his words, but I had not really heard them, not until now. It would not have made much difference to what happened, but I wished it were not too late to let him know.

Once when I was on holiday from college, my mother got me to help her clean out the attic. We sifted through boxes full of junk, old clothes, schoolbooks, bric-a-brac that once had been treasures. In one of the boxes I found the miniature saddle that Chris had made for me a long time ago.

"Have you heard anything recently?" I asked, ashamed that I had not asked sooner.

She glanced up at me. "Just the same. It's always the same. They don't think there will be much improvement."

Then she turned away.

"He always used to seem so—hopeful. Even when there was really nothing to be hopeful about. That's what I find so strange. He *seemed* hopeful, didn't you think?"

"Maybe it wasn't hope," I said.

"How do you mean?"

I wasn't certain myself. I was thinking of all the schemes he'd had, the ones that couldn't possibly have worked, the unreal solutions to which he'd clung because there were no others, the brave and useless strokes of fantasy against a depression that was both the world's and his own.

"I don't know," I said. "I just think things were always more difficult for him than he let on, that's all. Remember that letter?"

"Yes."

"Well—what it said was that they could force his body to march and even to kill, but what they didn't know was that he'd fooled them. He didn't live inside it any more."

"Oh Vanessa—" my mother said. "You must have suspected right then."

"Yes, but—"

I could not go on, could not say that the letter seemed only the final heartbreaking extension of that way he'd always had of distancing himself from the absolute unbearability of battle.

I picked up the tiny saddle and turned it over in my hand.

"Look. His brand, the name of his ranch. The Criss-Cross."

"What ranch?" my mother said, bewildered.

"The one where he kept his racing horses. Duchess and Firefly."

Some words came into my head, a single line from a poem I had once heard. I knew it referred to a lover who did not want the morning to come, but to me it had another meaning, a different relevance.

Slowly, slowly, horses of the night—

The night must move like this for him, slowly, all through the days and nights. I could not know whether the land he journeyed through was inhabited by terrors, the old monster-kings of the lake, or whether he had discovered at last a way for himself to make the necessary dream perpetual.

I put the saddle away once more, gently and ruthlessly, back into the cardboard box.

Hugh Hood

(b. 1928)

BORN IN TORONTO to a bilingual family, Hugh Hood grew up in that city, and received his Ph.D. from the University of Toronto in 1955. He now lives in Montreal, teaches English at the University of Montreal, and is a prolific crafts-man in the art of fiction. His several volumes of short stories include *Flying a Red Kite* (1962), *The Fruit Man, the Meat Man & the Manager* (1971), and *None Genuine Without This Signature* (1980), which variously (with consummate wit and with sombre vision) shape in stylized forms his meditations on observed reality, historical repetition, and ethical choice. *Around the Mountain* (1967) is an inte-grated, calendrical cycle of twelve sketches, recording the shifting moods of Montreal life. *The Governor's Bridge Is Closed* is a 1973 collection of essays on fic-tion and society. Like his stories, these and his many other essays are deeply in-fluenced by his Roman Catholicism. Hood has also written books on hockey, several novels, and is currently involved in an ambitious 12-volume novel cycle—called *The New Age*—which follows the life of a character named Matthew Goderich, through whom the reader comes to recognize the details of local Canadian history and the involvement of Canada in the larger paradigms (both civil and moral) of 20th-century world events.

Active (with Clark Blaise, John Metcalf, Ray Smith, and Ray Fraser) in a 1970s group called The Montreal Story Tellers, Hood acknowledges his affini-ties with his colleagues and with writers as diverse as Turgenev, Leacock, and Morley Callaghan, but he insists on his independence from all artistic cate-gories. Each story, for him, is an independent design, drawing its meaning from cadence and patterns of recurrence as much as from any overt "subject." "Going Out as a Ghost," for example, which appeared in *Fiddlehead* in 1974 and was collected in *Dark Glasses* (1976), is a story of contrasts and alternatives: of boys and girls, solstice and equinox, face and mask, past and present, dark and White, confinement and freedom—all of them focussing finally not on the identifiability but on the ambivalence of right and wrong.

For Further Reading

ROBERT FULFORD, "An Interview with Hugh Hood," *Tamarack Review* 66 (June 1975): 65–77.

HUGH HOOD, "Sober Coloring: The Ontology of Super-realism" in *The Narrative Voice*, ed. John Metcalf (Toronto: McGraw-Hill Ryerson, 1972) 95–101.

ROBERT LECKER, *On the Line* (Toronto: ECW, 1982).

J.R. (TIM) STRUTHERS, ed., Hood issue, *Essays in Canadian Writing* 13–14 (Winter-Spring 1978–79).

Going Out as a Ghost

The children were preparing for Halloween, a festival they preferred to Christmas. The sombre mysterious end of October, when it grows colder and nobody yet knows how cold it may become, had always seemed more inviting to them than the steady weather of the solstice. They set great store by their costumes—had in different years presented themselves as Laurel and Hardy, four Marx brothers, knights in armour and hairy serfs, the two ends of a horse. They were a quartet agreeably near in age inclined to form pairs, liking to complement one another: master and slave, fat man and thin.

Their father, a confused man, joked with them about the reach and complication of these conceptions. "Going to go out this year?" he would inquire as they grew older. "What are you going out as?" The boys would argue between themselves, the girls exchange secret smiles, giving nothing away.

"I'll throw a sheet over my head and cut holes in it," their father would say at the very last minute. "I'm going out as a ghost." And the entire family would laugh uproariously, for this struck them as the lowest deep of impoverished fantasy. "Going out as a ghost," they all sang together, laughing, but inwardly troubled by the concept of dressing up as a clown or a cowboy. Such children could—probably did—miss altogether the intense, absorbed September and October during which the dress-up box was emptied, filled, emptied: old organdy and silk from costumes of years past held to the light. They had also a property box filled with daggers, stilettos, swords, false noses, wigs, grotesque false ears. Theatrical make-up was available, nose putty, crêpe hair. A family half sunk in show-business. All this began in late summer with vacation still in progress.

"If you're going into town, bring back my gorilla mask," said the older of the boys to his father on a Wednesday in late August. "I want to compare the fur."

"Where is it in the house? In your closet?"

"It's hanging on the light fixture in our room," said the younger boy. "I hung it there to make it look like a head sticking out of the wall."

"There should be a gorilla's hind-end sticking out of the wall in the next bedroom," said the father. He chatted amusingly with the children, but the image of the gorilla mask stayed with him disagreeably as he drove into the city. One of those rubber, over-the-head, monster disguises which can be found at theatrical costumers, it had been a birthday gift to his son, who had a collection of them: Dracula, Frankenstein's monster, the Wolf-Man, the Gorilla. In a poor light the thing was genuinely horrific and might prove shocking to householders on that dreary night nine weeks in the future. He was troubled by the human cast of the bestial shape. The coarse red of the cheeks, upturned snout, matted dangling hair, the powdery texture of the pliant rubbery skin. The boys

From *Dark Glasses* (Ottawa: Oberon Press, 1976). Reprinted by permission of the author.

played up certain simian characteristics in their movements; they liked to lower their hands around their knees by flexing the knee-joints. They would gibber in simulated ape-language. The younger boy often hung head downward in trees. With the gorilla mask over either head, full disguise was at once effected, a whole transformation of behaviour threatened. "Now I'm going to tear you limb from limb," they would say.

He had further worries, minor repairs impending on his automobile, which gave trouble as he drove along; the radiator leaked, spreading the odour of coolant through the passenger compartment, the smell of ethylene glycol, and some sweetish, doubtless wholly poisonous additive—radiator cleanser or sealer; there might be holes in the hoses. Late in the day he arrived in his city neighbourhood and left the auto with a local service man who at once, before his eyes, dismantled it, rendering it inoperative. "Tomorrow, one o'clock," said the mechanic, a highly trustworthy man.

"Going back to the country in the afternoon."

"You can have it by one. Not before."

He was glad to leave his car sitting on the lot, always felt better about it at such times, as one does about the seriously-ill member of the family who is at last "in good hands." As he walked the short distance to his empty house, it began to rain, then in the next hour settled into a steady downpour. He let himself in, stepped over the pile of mail lying on the floor below the letter slot, into the quiet hall. He had always liked the look of this house in the late afternoon with no electric light on; what light there was entered freely through large windows front and rear, then diffused itself into the corners of dark halls. He mounted to the second floor and standing in the doorway of his sons' bedroom he saw the gorilla mask hanging over the light socket, from which the bulb had been removed. Outside the rain continued to fall; it was now very dark for this time of year. The house was shut tight and stuffy, yet the mask moved and lifted slightly in some faint air current. He stared. He decided to have his evening meal delivered, Chinese, or barbecued chicken, no need to go out again. He might call a friend, see if he wanted to watch a late movie. What else had the kids asked for, was it masking tape?

Later he shuffled through the mail, discarded almost all, phoned for chicken, phoned David, who agreed to drive round at 9.30. Unmarried, self-employed, chronically at loose ends at night, David seemed pleased to be asked. "There are two good films on tonight," he said. "I hope my car starts." He came a little early, barely past nine, surprising his host, who was ensconced before the TV in the basement, picking chicken from the spaces between his teeth, listening to the rain, not making much sense of the program he watched, which was loud. The doorbell rang several times before he grasped that it was not part of the soundtrack, which might well have had bells in it.

He switched on the porch light and peered out at the rain. Might as well be Halloween, he thought, and opened the door for David. "You're early."

"You said any time. You're alone, right? How much do you charge to haunt a house anyway?"

"What makes you say that?"

"I just thought of it. Your house is always a little haunted, you know." This seemed a disobliging comment which he could only ignore; they descended to the TV which they watched with pleasure for over an hour, until the telephone rang. This bell, different in tone from the doorbell, could not be assimilated to the sound of TV, had to be answered at once or attention would stray. He climbed unwillingly to the ground floor and went to the telephone in the studio at the very back of the house, where he fondled the clamorous instrument, gazing through the huge window at shining wetness. He put the receiver to his ear.

"Bet you don't know who this is," said a melodious voice. The line clicked and crackled strangely; the voice echoed, seemed familiar, then wholly unrecognizable. He had heard it, he knew, but how very long ago. "Bet you don't know who this is...this is...is...who?"

"We were in school together," he said firmly, shutting off the unsteady echoes.

The voice cooed, "You're getting close."

He listened harder; he had heard the voice somewhere in the past. There was a *castrato* music to it, high, sexually elastic though certainly male. "It's Philly White."

"Who?"

"Philly White. We went to parish school together, don't you remember the Whites, my brother Bob, my sister Pauline? We made our First Holy Communion together."

"So we did. So we did. Of course I remember. You had smallpox when we were in, the third grade?"

He could remember the effects of the disease vividly, the spoiled face, the depth of indentation of the small round scars, about the size of a flake of confetti. His complexion had been like his name, white, the holes in his face changing colour as embarrassment or exposure moved the boy. He had often been in trouble with the teachers, hadn't been heard from in forty years. The voice was irrefutable testimony, when linked to a past and a name.

"I'm here at the Prevention Centre on Parthenais Street." The voice in the receiver pronounced the name wrong, as an Ontarian would, and translated the name of the institution too literally. *Centre de Prevention* doesn't mean "prevention centre," it means "detention centre," a quasi-jail where persons are held to await trial or, in certain cases, sentencing after conviction. Until now he had never heard of the place or seen it, knew nothing about it, couldn't have identified it from glimpses at a distance. It is a deceptive building. It is the embodiment of a lie. It doesn't look like what it is; suicide is routine inside. Men have spent fifteen months there awaiting trial, the presumed innocent often treated far worse than the proven guilty—because the innocence is purely formal and presumptive. Most inmates are habitual offenders. None of this was familiar to him. "What are they holding you for?" he asked.

"Some trouble about a cheque. Well, actually two cheques. Three. You knew my family, you knew Bob was ordained, you knew...I was married there for a while; then I moved out west. I had a car business in Vancouver and then came back east. Two little girls. We're separated now of course...you're the only one here in the city...I don't want my wife to know yet. I was hoping for a reconciliation. I want to get straightened out and start again."

"What's the charge?" He felt proud of the way he phrased the question; he had no contact with police, courts, criminals, or even people who were being held, detained, prevented. "Have they got anything to go on?"

"Actually..." indecision floated into the quavering voice. "I can't talk any more; they're taking me back. They might let you see me. Could you try to see me?"

"The charge?"

"Matter of two years...I've been sentenced..." He never found out whether the term of the sentence was two years, or whether a longer term might be reduced to two for good conduct. "They're deciding whether to send me to a dry-out clinic. There's a problem of alcoholism. And they're waiting for information from Vancouver."

"What sort of information?" He felt damp; the studio was damp.

"...conviction for fraud...not serious."

"What else?"

"Hotel bills in Dorval. They brought me in from Dorval. I was there a month. I have to go now." It sounded as if the call had been cut off at the main switchboard. He put the receiver into its cradle and took several deep breaths, then called downstairs. In a few moments, David appeared from the depths. "You're missing some good takeoffs," he said.

"Will you do me a favour?"

"Yes."

"My car's in for repair and I have to go out unexpectedly. Would you do me a great kindness and drive me across town? I'm not sure exactly where to go. Do you know where Parthenais is?"

They had to unearth David's street-guide in the glove compartment, then consult its small print as they drove along Sherbrooke in the persistent rain; the windows kept fogging over; it was difficult to see. Parthenais was well out toward the east end, past De Lorimier almost at D'Iberville. They turned south when they came to it, down the steep hill toward De Maisonneuve. In a few minutes a massive dark shape stood up indistinctly before them, an ultra-modern office building fourteen stories high, in glassy black plastic siding, standing on a small plot of land surrounded by chain-link fence topped with multiple strands of shining barbed wire. It reminded him of a shiny polished dark monolith seen in some science-fiction film. Some sort of object of perverse worship. Close up, the building looked like most others built around 1969. They parked across the narrow street and approached the main entrance which opened into a spacious glassed-in hall two stories high, with an elevator bank to the right and a reception desk nearby. One or two guards idled in corners, paying no attention to them. He asked at the desk if he would be able to see Philly White, and the receptionist—perfectly agreeable and forthcoming—laughed jovially.

"Tomorrow, 1.30. Come back then."

"He seemed in pain or frightened. Could he be afraid of something?"

"Tomorrow, 1.30. Come back then."

One of the guards moved indecisively.

Time to get out of here while we still can, he thought. He felt great waves of imaginary fugitive guilt washing over him. Hundreds of movies lodged in his memory now rose up to frighten, to accuse. He thought of the fearful ending of *I Am a Fugitive from a Chain Gang* and hastened away. "What do you do, how do you live?" "I steal."

Driving homeward, David said, "I didn't care much for the atmosphere..."

He had to force himself to return the next afternoon. Just before he left the house, he got a call from a police sergeant in Dorval. "...heard from Philly White this morning—he's not a bad fellow, Philly, he wouldn't hurt anybody. He has no violence on his record."

"Record? What record?"

"Oh a long, long record. Four convictions in B.C. Fraudulent auto sales with forgery. Fraudulent roofing contracts. But no violence, I was glad when he told me he found a friend to help him out. If I come by your house, can I give you his radio? He left it in the cells here and I know he'll miss it. That Parthenais...it isn't like the Dorval Jail. It's no picnic, you bet." He recited a series of calamitous occurrences which had taken place at the detention centre. Group suicides, self-mutilations. "So you see if old Philly has a friend to help, I'll be glad. His family won't do nothing."

"His family aren't here. His mother is dead and they all live in Toronto."

"Did he tell you that? His mother lives in Montréal with one of his sisters and one brother. They don't go to see him. His wife and kids are here too."

"Does his wife know he's awaiting sentence?"

"No, she doesn't know a thing...nobody knows anything about Philly White for sure. Can I drop off his radio?"

"I'm not sure I'm going to be here. I have to go to the country. I have to go pick up my car. I don't believe I can make it; the family's expecting me back. I have to go and..."

"He'll be disappointed. He said you were coming down."

"He seems to say whatever he likes."

"That's right."

"Mail him the radio. I'll be away."

"No. No. I think I'll deliver it by hand."

The car was ready when he went over to get it. "It's ready; it's ready. You said it would be," he said happily; the garageman looked at him in surprise.

"It always is."

"A pleasure...a pleasure."

The building on Parthenais looked more horrible in bright sunshine than in rainy darkness. Huge, slab-sided, far too glassy. Your gaze went right through it and out the other side. He went in, explained his errand to the man on the desk—the same man as the night before; didn't he ever sleep? And ascended to the tenth floor in an ordinary elevator. At the third, fifth and eighth floors it stopped automatically; he peered out without ostentation. Each floor seemed perfectly normal; you could see across the hall and out the windows. Ordinary office space. The view grew progressively more distant and spreadout as the car rose in the shaft. He was prepared for a handsome prospect as he stepped out on ten, and was chilled and repelled by the barred, electrically-locked gate, the approaches beyond it to heavy steel doors. The four top floors of the building form a maximum security jail. There is no exercise yard. There is no sports

program. Prisoners may use one of three small recreation areas for periods of up
to one hour, every second day, if they aren't receiving special discipline.

"...you are not permitted to see him. What gave you the idea you could see
him? Are you a relative?"

"No, he told me on the phone that..."

"I'm sorry, sir. His case is awaiting disposition. Only relatives."

"He told me he had no relatives nearer than Toronto."

"He told you a lie."

"Does his wife come to see him? How long has he been in here? I want to try
to help."

"You aren't an officer of the John Howard Society?"

"No, nothing like that."

"Not a lawyer conferring with a judge about the sentence?"

"No, no."

The walls of this dreadful bullpen—a long counter or booth like that in a government liquor store or customs house—were painted a very pale grey-blue
which did nothing to conceal their metallic chill. He began to look around
wildly.

"What is your name, sir? Why did you come here?"

"This man called me on the telephone last night and told me he was in trouble; he didn't say how serious it was, but I gathered that he felt pretty desperate..."

"...they'll all tell you that."

"Yes, I'm sure they will. I would myself, I think, if I had to stay here. Can't
you tell me anything at all?"

"I've never seen the man."

"How do you know so much about him?"

"I'm simply following general regulations, sir."

"And he has no right to a visitor, like he claimed?"

"Certain relatives, his lawyer of record, officially authorized prison visitors."

"All right, then, a sergeant from Dorval is bringing in his radio. He left it
there. Would you see that he gets it?"

"I don't know anything about that at all."

He left the bullpen and walked quickly through the massive doors. He felt
very glad that they opened for him, that the elevator came, some time after he
pressed the DOWN button. All the way out to the street and into the driver's
seat of his car, he felt as if a hand might descend on his shoulder. There was a
parking ticket under the left windshield wiper. The rubberized gorilla mask
smiled up at him from where he had dropped it on the front seat. He felt intensely happy to see it there, happy that he'd remembered it, that his children
enjoyed having it. He made the best of his way out of town.

The mask alone was not enough, naturally. Four imaginative new costumes
were required. The boys decided to go out as soldiers of the American Civil
War, one in blue uniform, one in grey; design and fitting of these intricate costumes occupied much of September and early October.

"What are you going out as?"

"Soldiers of the War Between the States, as they would have been dressed at Gettysburg." The younger son was a student of Civil War history and a bitter partisan of the North, an admirer of Lincoln and Grant.

"But don't you think Lee was the greatest general of that war?"

"He lost, didn't he?"

Not much to be said to that.

And of course, he reflected, on the essential issue of slavery the North had been in the right. He was certain of that; what could possibly be urged in favour of slavery, of imprisonment, detention, referral to clinic? He felt mixed up, his head crowded with civilized misgiving. He started to get letters addressed to Philly White, in his care. He wouldn't open them and couldn't decide what to do with them. Some were postmarked Vancouver. One looked like an Income Tax refund cheque. A month after the first phone call, there came another. "Yes, it's me. I want to thank you for everything you've done for me. Sergeant Bastien told me how you helped him."

"The man from Dorval with your radio."

"He said how kind you were."

"Were you actually talking to Sergeant Bastien?" It had become important to extract some unambiguous, verifiable statement.

"Not actually talking to him in so many words...exactly."

"How then?"

"Well, he got through to me all right. These veteran police officers have ways of dealing with things that you and I wouldn't think of."

"I didn't do anything for you, White. I have no intention of doing anything for you." He at least could be unambiguous, or hoped he could.

"But you came down to the Prevention Centre to see me, didn't you?"

"I did. Anybody would have done that."

"But you came twice, didn't you?"

"How do you know?"

"I know." There was a noxious appeal to this way of talking. He felt himself being drawn into the position of co-conspirator and even accomplice. He had enough free-floating fear of having done something criminal in his imagination without this.

"Just handle my mail for me," begged White.

"Why can't it go directly to jail?" He felt dreadfully like laughing. He thought, "Go directly to Jail; do not pass GO; do not collect $200"; he remembered the cards in the pile marked "Get out of Jail free."

"Would you like your wife to have to send her letters to such a place?"

"No."

"Do this for me then, for the sake of the old days."

"What old days? Do you know, I can barely remember you. That's 40 years ago. I don't have any responsibility for you."

"We are all responsible for one another," said White.

"Then why did you...never mind."

"I can use your address?"

"I'll forward anything that arrives."

The call was abruptly ended by that strange echoing click suggestive of constant switchboard surveillance. He wondered who was listening, and thought of making misleading and ambiguous remarks the next time White telephoned, just to give the listeners something to think about, realizing at the same moment that such an action would cause them to set up a dossier on him, which would then have the assured and interminable existence of an official file.

A flood of correspondence ensued, much of it from distant provinces, all addressed to his quiet Montréal street, all for Philly White. He would wait for three or four days till he had a dozen or so items, then bundle them together in a single large envelope and forward it to Parthenais Street. Certain letters obviously got through to White, who discussed them in later phone calls. Some were perhaps suppressed by the authorities or censored by them, but on the whole White seemed well abreast of his outside affairs; he had now been at the Centre de Prevention for August, September, most of October—almost thirteen weeks; this was nothing compared to the detention of other unfortunates. The top floors were designed to hold 250 inmates, all in one way or another of special status. Either they could not be brought to trial because the prosecutor's case was incomplete, or the dockets were overburdened, or their lawyers were evading the event for tactical reasons: those in this last category might wait forever without their process coming on. Many died on Parthenais Street without receiving either condemnation or justification. And there were always more than 300 crowded into the cells.

There were many like White whose guilt had been legally established. Convicted, criminals in the eyes of the law, sentenced, as yet undisposed of, they could not be conveniently put away and forgotten in this or that prison because a humane penology wished to "cure" them—in White's case apparently to dry the liquor out of him and begin treatment for alcoholism. A cured alcoholic, he might no longer be a fraud-artist and con-man, but this was doubtful. The alcoholism and the pathological addiction to lying might be elements of deeper ruin, probably were.

Nobody knows what is truly criminal, who are culpable. There are legal definitions, always abstract, inexact. There is observably bad—at least socially unacceptable—behaviour: what is called the "psychopathic personality" where social responsibility is rejected together with the possibility of truthfulness. What oppressed the listener to Philly White's phone calls was that he never, even by accident, said the plain truth.

Disguise abounded; cold came on. Toward the end of the month the boys completed their Civil War costumes and began to parade around the house in them, looking from a short distance wonderfully authentic. The younger lad had constructed one of those flat, forward-slanting Confederate caps with a badge of crossed rifles over the peak, and the letters C.S.A. sewn into it irregularly. The effect was truly persuasive. He had a cardboard musket and a water bottle. He kept saying, "Pickett's charge represented the high-water mark of the Confederacy," and his father never managed to establish what that meant. The other boy had decided to approach the northern infantryman's dress with less historical correctness and more freedom of interpretation. He carried a powder-horn—more appropriate for the Revolutionary War—and wore a shaggy false beard made of stuff chopped from an old Borghana coat of their mother's, which gave him an unexpectedly Russian air.

The girls hovered over alternatives. Then in a late fury of artistic creation they evolved two superb and original designs. For the younger girl, the baby of the family, they made a horse's body from a painted and draped cardboard carton fitted around her waist like an Eskimo's kayak. This was completed by floppy artificial legs hanging from a painted saddle—a caricature of a circus equestrienne. Her sister had then simply to dress herself as a ringmaster: red coat, tall hat, white breeches, riding whip, and the illusion was perfect and striking.

Mixed images of strangely-caparisoned, smallish persons capering around him wound their way into their father's worried judgment. All day on the 31st of the month he lazed around the house among orange and black festoons, expecting some sort of resolution of the affair of White the bunco steerer. The weekend before, all clocks had been put back. It was full dark by six pm. The children departed for their exciting annual night walk, gangs of neighbourhood kids beginning to press the doorbell. The phone rang in the midst of other urgent pealings, as he raised his coffee cup to his lips. Of course it was his old friend on Parthenais Street, with his first concrete demand for money. "If you'll just make the one payment for me, $184.80, we can retain ownership, they won't repossess. It's in the wife's name. I'll tell you where to send your cheque, and thanks for what you're trying to do. I really mean it."

He felt great anger squeezing his throat. "You don't mean it at all," he said, "you're just trying it on. I knew it would get to this point. A hundred and eighty from the poor sucker for openers, eh? It's finished, White, you get me? That's it. Don't call again and don't have any more mail sent here. I thought you needed me, I thought you meant it. All just a big con. You're still at it even though they've locked you up. You've been sentenced. How come they don't put you where you belong?"

"*They're* trying to help me."

"Let them! Whoever *they* are."

"I'm only trying to make contact."

"Good-bye White. Don't call again."

He hoped the listeners got it all; there wouldn't be any more calls. The doorbell rang and he walked through the house, opened the door and confronted a small visitant dressed as a ghost. He handed this person many sugary treats, then shut the door. I did right, he told himself, I did right (wrong), I did right, right (wrong), I did right...

Gilles Vigneault

(b. 1928)

BORN IN NATASHQUAN, QUEBEC, and educated at Laval, Gilles Vigneault taught school for some years before debuting in 1960 as a chansonnier. In this second career he established a culture-wide reputation; songwriter and performer, poet and tale-teller, he came for many people to embody their cultural aspirations. His song "Mon pays"—"mon pays, ce n'est pas un pays, c'est l'hiver"—became a Quebec anthem during the late 1960s, and another song—"Gens du pays"—an unofficial separatist theme song during the 1970s. A collection of his songs, with music, appeared as *Gilles Vigneault* in Paris in 1977.

He has published some sixteen volumes of poetry, and several collections of contes, among them *Contes sur la pointe des pieds* (1960; translated by Paul Allard in 1972), *Contes du coin de l'oeil* (1966), including "Le mur," and *La petite heure* (1979). In its English translation, by Jacqueline de Puthod, "The Wall" appeared in 1974. An enigmatic parable, it can be read for its psychological observations, its political implications, or its moral message.

For Further Reading

MAURICE LEMIRE, ed., *Dictionnaire des oeuvres littéraires du Québec* (Montréal: Fides, 1984) 205–06, 209–11.

DONALD SMITH, *Gilles Vigneault, conteur et poète* (Montréal: Québec/Amérique, 1984).

The Wall

Translated by Jacqueline de Puthod

A former mason, sentenced to twenty years' hard labour, was repairing with surprising care the exterior wall of his prison. He was of course closely guarded, and although the work was compulsory and under scrupulous surveillance, the taste for perfection he exhibited at it was a source of amazement to passersby and even to his two guards. Someone expressed his surprise and the former mason, without lifting his eyes from his work, replied as if he had expected the question all along: "What pleasure would there be in escaping from a prison that was poorly built?"

Then, before the anxious prison guards who had become more watchful than ever, he went on as though talking to himself: "When you've put your own hand to the making of a wall, it tells you more about human freedom than all the philosophers put together."

This saying spread far and wide until it reached the ears of a monk. The monk came to visit the mason. They talked together at length. And the mason, without disturbing a soul, left the prison by the main gate wearing a habit and a rope belt.

The prison director, a subtle man though he didn't show it, recently asked a professional burglar to repair a window sash. The work was so well done that one feels something is bound to happen, despite the formal order issued that day forbidding anyone to speak to a prisoner at work.

Gilles Vigneault, "The Wall," in Philip Stratford, ed., *Stories from Québec* (Toronto: Van Nostrand Reinhold Canada, 1974). Translated by Jacqueline de Puthod Stratford. Originally published in *Contes du coin de l'oeil* (Montréal: Nouvelles Editions de l'Arc, 1966).

Basil Johnston

(b. 1929)

BORN IN PARRY ISLAND, ONTARIO, Basil Johnston graduated from Loyola College in Montreal in 1954 and went on to teach history in the Toronto secondary school system. In 1969 he joined the staff of the Royal Ontario Museum, and in 1972 became a member of the ethnology department. Fluent in Ojibway, he has translated a number of works into that language, and produced an Ojibway language course and beginners' lexicon for the federal Indian Affairs branch. A guest editor of the Indian magazine *Tawow,* he has contributed articles, stories, and poems to a variety of magazines and anthologies, and he has produced several books, for children and for adults, on Ojibway myth and culture. Among these are *Ojibway Heritage* (1976), *Tales Our Elders Told* (1981), and *Ojibway Ceremonies* (1983). *Moose Meat and Wild Rice* (1978) is a collection of seriocomic short stories; "Cowboys and Indians," a wry oral story about a contemporary trickster, is marked by its laconic idiom and its detached amusement at the uninformed bustle of Hollywood manner. It appeared first in *The Ontario Indian* in 1981, was collected in Penny Petrone's anthology *First People First Voices* in 1983, and is based on a story told to Johnston by Benjamin Pease.

For Further Reading

KENT GOODERHAM, ed., *I Am an Indian* (Toronto: Dent, 1969).

BASIL JOHNSTON, "Indians, Métis and Eskimos," in *Read Canadian,* ed. Robert Fulford et al. (Toronto: James Lewis & Samuel, 1972) 168–74.

———, "Is That All There Is?" *Canadian Literature* 128 (Spring 1991): 54–62.

———, "One Generation from Extinction," *Canadian Literature* 124–125 (Spring-Summer 1990): 10–15.

WILLIAM PATTERSON, *The Canadian Indian* (Toronto: Collier-Macmillan, 1971).

Cowboys and Indians

Hollywood grew fast and big. By the 1930s there were many studios employing many actors in the production of many motion pictures. Within the same few years as the studios got bigger, techniques improved; as techniques improved so did the quality of acting; and as acting got better, so did the range and variety of themes enlarge. And of course viewers' tastes became more refined and discriminating, requiring of Hollywood and the studios more authenticity and less artificiality in their productions.

And the studios were willing to oblige.

It was decided by the producer and director of a major studio planning a western picture with either Hoot Gibson, Tom Mix, or Ken Maynard as the principal star, to hire real Indians to take part in the production. With real Indians the advantages were obvious. Besides lending authenticity to the motion picture, Indians represented a substantial saving. Their natural pigmentation would reduce expenses in cosmetics and make-up artistics; their natural horsemanship would save time and expenses usually incurred in training greenhorns to ride; their possession of herds of ponies would save time and outlay in the rental and feeding of horses; and their natural talent for art would obviate the need for anthropologists to act as consultants in authenticating Indian art and design. The only expense to be incurred was the fee of $2.00 per day for movie extras.

Management calculated that 500 Indians along with 500 horses were needed for no more than two days to shoot an attack upon a wagon-train. The producer and the director also decided that there would be substantial savings by establishing the location of the filming near an Indian reservation somewhere in the west.

Inquiries, preliminary and cursory, made of historians and the Bureau of Indian Affairs in Washington indicated that the Crow Indians of Montana, having retained their traditions and still owning large herds of horses, would be best suited for a motion picture of the kind planned by the studio. Besides, the terrain in the area was genuine honest-to-goodness Indian country, excellent for camera work.

Negotiations with the Bureau of Indian Affairs for permission to treat with the Crows for their services as actors and for the provision of horses began at once. Permission was granted by Washington; and the Crows were more than willing to take part.

Crew and cast arrived by train in Billings, Montana. Anxious to get started and to finish shooting the siege of a wagon-train in as short a time as possible, the producer and director sent a limousine to the reservation to fetch the chief.

First published in *The Ontario Indian,* Vol. 4, No. 8 (August, 1981). Reprinted by permission of the author.

Over a meal with the chief and his retinue of councillors and hangers-on, the
producer, portly and bald, beneath a cloud of smoke produced by a fat cigar, informed the chief that it was a great privilege to work with the Crows and that
it was an honour and a distinction for his studio to set precedent in the entire
industry by being the first to use real, live, honest-to-goodness Indians in a
motion picture. For the Crows, it would mean fame and national recognition...and money...$2.00 a day for those taking part; $1.00 per day for those
providing horses, and $1.00 per day for those providing art work and the loan
of teepees.

An interpreter translated for the chief.

The producer smiled and blew a cloud of smoke out of the side of his mouth.
The Crow responded "How! How! How!"

"It shouldn't take long chief, three or four days...no more. A day to get ready
and two or three to film the scene. We don't want to interfere too much in your
affairs, you've probably got a lot to do and...we are working under a pretty
tight schedule."

The interpreter relayed this information to the chief.

"Now chief. We want 500 warriors; 500 horses; bows and arrows and...maybe
fifty or so rifles...feathers, head-dresses, buckskin jackets, and...buckskin leg-
gings...and four or five people who can paint designs on horses and put make-
up on warriors." The producer continued, "The scene itself will be easy. The
warriors will attack the wagon-train at daybreak. It shouldn't take more than
half an hour. Very easy, really don't need any rehearsals. My colleague will
tell you what to do. Probably the easiest two bucks you'll ever make...cash as
soon as the scene's shot. Can you get all this stuff by tomorrow night, chief?"
And the producer flicked ashes from his fat cigar.

The interpreter prattling in Crow to his chief and councilors pounded the
table, slashed the air, shrugged his shoulders to emphasize his message to his
listeners, who looked dumbfounded. Nevertheless they injected a "How! How!"
frequently enough into the discourse to intimate some understanding.

The chief said something.

"How many horses?"

"500, the producer might even settle for 450."

The interpreter addressed his chief who shook his head grunting "How!"

"Ain't got 500 horses," the interpreter said sadly.

"450?"

"Ain't dat many on de reservation."

"300?"

"No, not dat many: not like long time ago."

"Well! How many have you got?" the producer asked, his face pinching into
worried lines and his voice losing its cheer and vitality.

"Maybe 10...20...an' not very good dem."

"Keeee...rice...!" And the producer bit a chunk of cigar, crushing the other
end in the ashtray. "Are there any horses around here?"

"Yeah. Ranchers and farmers got dem."

To his assistant, the producer instructed "Get 500 horses by tomorrow evening. We have to shoot that scene next morning with the Indians charging down the slope."

The interpreter whispered to his chief who shook his head.

"Say, mister," the interpreter addressed the producer, "how about saddles?"

"Saddles?" the word erupted.

"Yeah, saddles."

There was a moment of cosmic silence. "Saddles!" the producer repeated mouthing the word in disbelief. "What do you mean...saddles! You're all going to ride bare-back. This film is going to be authentic...who ever heard of Indians riding on saddles...supposed to be the finest horsemen in the world."

The interpreter stiffened in fright at the thought that he might be one of the warriors to ride bare-back, and he hung his head.

"Don't know how to ride...us. Forgot how...long time ago...Need saddles...might fall off an' git hurt...us."

"This is incredible!...unbelievable!...no horses!...can't ride!..." the producer gasped as he sank into the chair. "Keeeeee-rice."

Hope waning from his brow and voice, the producer tried "You still got bows an' arrows?"

The interpreter slouched even lower "No! Got none of dem t'ings, us."

"Buckskin outfits?"

"No," another shameful shrug.

"Moccasins?"

"Some," a little brighter.

"Head-dresses?"

"Maybe two, three—very old dem."

"Teepees?"

"No more—live in houses us."

"Anyone know Indian designs...you know—war paint for warriors...and horses?"

"Don't t'ink so...everybody forgot."

The producer groaned. "This is astounding...I can't believe it...No horses...can't ride...no teepees...no buckskin...no...no moccasins...no...no head-dresses...and...probably not even loin-cloths..." and he was quivering. "It boggles the mind."

"What do we do?" the director asked.

For several moments the producer assessed the circumstances, and possessing an analytical mind he stated what needed to be done.

"With all our crew and cast here, and with our wagon-train and cannon and horses, we can't very well go back now. We'll have to train these Indians to ride. Now...Adams," the producer's assistant, "I want you to get on the line right away. Get a guy who knows something about Indians, from the Bureau of Indian Affairs. I want you to get maybe a dozen chiefs' outfits; and 500 loincloths, bows an' arrows for everyone, about a dozen head-dresses and moccasins...everything we need to make these Indians...*Indians.* Is that clear? And get those horses by tomorrow night."

"Yes sir!"

"In the meantime, I'll call the studio office for more money. Let's get movin'."
The assistant went out.

"How long we gotta stay in this miserable God-forsaken cow-town?" Ken Maynard inquired.

"Coupla weeks...maybe."

Ken Maynard groaned.

"Now!" directing his cigar at the interpreter and his remarks to the chief, the producer said, "Tell the chief to get 500 young men to learn to ride bare-back, an' to learn fast."

The interpreter apprised his chief of the message. The chief responded.

"He say $2.00 a day!"

"Keeee-rice! Tell him, okay."

Two mornings later, 500 horses borrowed and rented from the local ranchers were delivered to the Indian reservation. 500 Crows began practising the art of horsemanship at once, and in earnest. And while it is true that many Crows shied away from the horses, just as many horses shied away from the Crows, so that there was much anxious circling of horses around Indians and Indians around horses, pulling, and jerking midst the clamour of pleas "Whoa! Whoa! Steady there Nellie! Easy there!" all in Crow, and the horses perhaps because they were unfamiliar with Crow refusing to "whoa." Eventually, horses and Crows overcame their mutual distrust and suspicions and animosities to enable the Indians to mount their beasts.

There were of course some casualties, a few broken legs, sprained ankles, cracked ribs, and bruised behinds suffered by the novices on the first day. But by the third day most of the young men, while not accomplished equestrians, were able to ride passably well; that is, they fell off their mounts less often.

With the arrival of the equipment, bows and arrows, head-dresses, moccasins, loin-cloths, shipped by express from Washington, one day was set aside for the Crow warriors to practise shooting arrows from bows, first from a standing position and then from horseback. There were a few more casualties but nothing serious.

Along with the equipment came twelve make-up artists accompanied by an anthropologist to advise the artists in war-paint designs and to instruct the Crow in war-whooping. Twelve immense pavilions were erected, outside of each billboards bearing symbols and markings representative of warrior war-paint and horse-paint designs. Each Indian having selected the design that best suited his taste and his horse entered a pavilion where he and his steed were painted, emerging at the other end of the massive tent looking very fierce and ready for war.

The movie moguls decided that they would film the siege of the wagon-train at 5 a.m. regardless of the readiness of the Indians. "So what if a few Red-skins fall off their horses...be more realistic."

As planned and according to script ten Crows, dressed in white buckskin heavily beaded and wearing war-bonnets to represent leadership, along with 450 warriors wearing only loin-cloths and armed with bows and arrows were assembled in a shallow depression unseen from the wagon-train. The horses pawed the ground and snorted and whinnied, while the director, producer, assorted assistants, and camera-men waited for the sun to cast its beams upon the wagon-train. When that critical moment occurred, signalled by an assistant with a wave of an arm, the director shouted "Action! Cameras roll!"

450 Indians on 450 horses erupted over the lip of the valley a 'hoopin' an' a hollerin', their savage war-cries splitting the air while 1800 hooves thundered down the slope, shaking the earth. Wagon-train passengers spilled out of covered-wagons, splashed up from blankets, seized rifles, yelling "Injuns! Injuns!" and hurled themselves behind boxes and crates and barrels and began firing. At one end of the valley, Ken Maynard on his white charger waited for his cue; at the other end fifty cavalrymen waited to charge to the rescue, Bang! Bang! Bang! The Crows, a 'hoopin' an' a hollerin' were riding round and round the wagon-train, firing their arrows into the covered wagons and into boxes and crates and barrels. Bang! Bang! Bang! Round and round rode the Crows.

"Cut! Cut! Cut!" everyone was shouting. "Cut! Cut! Cut!" everyone was waving his arms. Cut! Cut! Cut! 450 Crows, yelling whoa! whoa! whoa! brought their steeds to a halt.

The director, also on a horse, was livid with rage. He almost choked "Somebody's gotta die; when you're shot, you fall off your horse and die. Don't you understand?"

The Indians nodded and grunted "How! How!"

The director in disgust rode off leaving the cast and crew to repair 3000 to 4000 punctures and perforations inflicted by arrows on the canvas of the covered wagons. Six members of the cast suffering injuries from stray arrows needed medical attention. The Indians, with the arrows they had recovered, retired to the reservation to mend their weapons.

Just before sun-up next day there was a final admonition. "Get it done right this time!" The warriors responded "How! How!"

At the hand signal, "Action! Cameras roll!" were uttered.

450 Indians on 450 horses boiled over the lip of the valley, a 'hoopin' an' a hollerin', their savage war cries rending the peace, while 1800 hooves pounded down the slope convulsing the ground. Wagon-train patrons scurried out of covered wagons, sprang from blankets, seized their rifles, yelling "Injuns! Injuns!" and dove behind boxes and crates and barrels and began firing. Bang! Bang! Bang!

Seventy-five of the Crows, a 'hoopin' an' a hollerin' fell off their horses. Bang! Bang! Bang! 200 more Crows, a 'hoopin' an' a hollerin' spun off their mounts. Bang! Bang! Bang! The rest pitched off their steeds which fled in all directions.

"Cut! Cut! Cut!" everyone was shouting. 450 Crows suspended their moanin' an' a groanin' an' a rollin' on the ground, even though many had sustained real injuries, to listen to and to watch the director.

There was a torrent of curses, sulphuric glares, which eventually subsided into mutterings, the gist of which was relayed by the interpreter to the chiefs and warriors "that not everyone should have fallen off his horse." To this the chief replied $2.00.

The scene was re-enacted the next day without incident. After the shooting there were hand-shakes all around; and expressions of admiration tendered by Ken Maynard to the Crows for the speed with which they had developed horsemanship, remarking that "it must be in-bred."

Crew and cast were celebrating over wine and whiskey, cheese and crackers, when the film editor summoned the director. "Come here and look at these," he said, thrusting a magnifying glass to his superior. The director held the film strip against the light; he applied the magnifying glass to the stills.

"Sun-glasses! Keeee-rice...sun-glasses...those damned Indians. Keeee-rice...what next..."

When told, the producer kicked a chair after hurling a bottle into a corner: for close to ten minutes he cursed Indians. But it was useless, the scene had to be shot again.

Horses and Indians had to be recalled and reassembled for retakes for which the good chief demanded $2.00 for his people. It took another week before the wagon-train siege was filmed to the satisfaction of the producer and his director. In the interim there were two days of rain, one filming aborted by several Crows wearing watches, an extra filming of a prairie fire ignited by Ken Maynard that miscarried because several Crow warriors, supposedly dead, moved to avoid getting burned during a critical segment of the filming. When the first real epic of "Cowboys and Indians" was finally done, the Crows were jubilant, indebted to their chief for the prosperity and lasting renown that he exacted during difficult times. The producer and director, cast and crew, departed in disquiet over having exceeded their budget.

But whatever doubts the producer and the director might have entertained were more than vindicated by reviews of the film in which the horsemanship of the Crow was acclaimed and the genius of the producer for his vision and for his foresight in using Indians in motion pictures.

Alice Munro

(b. 1931)

ALICE (LAIDLAW) MUNRO WAS BORN IN WINGHAM, ONTARIO. Much of her fiction records—with apparent photographic fidelity—this region of rural Ontario: its space and its restrictions, its oblique speech, many ties, and close connections. Some stories, too, refer to the environment of the West Coast, and to Victoria in particular, a city Munro moved to shortly after her first marriage in 1951. Yet much of Munro's work concerns itself not with documenting the landscape at all but with the processes by which people—women especially—break free of closed worlds. They break free in fantasy, in memory, in delusion, in madness, by choice, by profession, and in art. But as so many of her stories reveal—"The Office," for example, the other stories in *Dance of the Happy Shades* (1968), or the episodes of her novel *Lives of Girls and Women* (1971)—the knowledge that comes from art is at once as pressureful, dangerous, and potentially isolating as experience itself, even though it can only ever approximate the empirical life to which it is related.

It is this sense of paradox and parallel, of apparent objectivity and relative understanding, which constitutes the core of Munro's work. The techniques she uses—oxymoron, irony—emphasize the meaning that derives from apparent contradictions, and delineate the kinds of uncertainty and dislocation with which people find they must live. In collections such as *Something I've Been Meaning to Tell You* (1974) and *Who Do You Think You Are?* (1978), the stories frequently deal with the processes of accommodation. Subsequent volumes, such as *The Moons of Jupiter* (1982), *Friend of My Youth* (1990), and *Open Secrets* (1994), emphasize the resonance of indeterminacy, or inconclusiveness. Stories never conclude with "answers," these volumes reveal; they give rise only to more stories. Admittedly, characters sometimes think they "know" answers—such is the persuasiveness of invention. But ambiguity and uncertainty prove more durable, and they have their own attractions.

The linked stories that make up "Chaddeleys and Flemings"—first published separately (and in slightly different form) in *Chatelaine* in 1978 and *Saturday Night* in 1979—were brought together in *The Moons of Jupiter*. They further illustrate how shifts in perspective alter facts, alter histories, until the processes of memory and the art of selecting and arranging details surface as the effective shapers of accepted "truth."

Alice Munro's work has been widely praised, and she has won numerous awards. She now divides her time between Clinton, Ontario, and Vancouver Island.

For Further Reading

E.D. BLODGETT, "Winging It," *Canadian Literature* 97 (Summer 1983): 98–101.

JAMES CARSCALLEN, *The Other Country: patterns in the writing of Alice Munro* (Toronto: ECW, 1993).

HELIANE CATHERINE DAZIRON, "The Preposterous Oxymoron," *Literary Half-Yearly* 24 (July 1983): 116–24.

AJAY HEBLE, *The Tumble of Reason: Alice Munro's Discourse of Absence* (Toronto: U Toronto P, 1994).

LOUIS K. MACKENDRICK, ed., *Probable Fictions: Alice Munro's Narrative Acts* (Toronto: ECW, 1983).

ALICE MUNRO, "What Is Real?" in *Making It New,* ed. John Metcalf (Toronto: Methuen, 1982) 223–26.

KAREN E. SMYTHE, *Figuring Grief: Gallant, Munro and the Poetics of Elegy* (Montreal: McGill-Queen's UP, 1992).

Chaddeleys and Flemings

1. Connection

Cousin Iris from Philadelphia. She was a nurse. Cousin Isabel from Des Moines. She owned a florist shop. Cousin Flora from Winnipeg, a teacher; Cousin Winifred from Edmonton, a lady accountant. Maiden ladies, they were called. Old maids was too thin a term, it would not cover them. Their bosoms were heavy and intimidating—a single, armored bundle—and their stomachs and behinds full and corseted as those of any married woman. In those days it seemed to be the thing for women's bodies to swell and ripen to a good size twenty, if they were getting anything out of life at all; then, according to class and aspirations, they would either sag and loosen, go wobbly as custard under pale print dresses and damp aprons, or be girded into shapes whose firm curves and proud slopes had nothing to do with sex, everything to do with rights and power.

My mother and her cousins were the second sort of women. They wore corsets that did up the side with dozens of hooks and eyes, stockings that hissed and rasped when they crossed their legs, silk jersey dresses for the afternoon (my mother's being a cousin's hand-me-down), face powder (rachel), dry rouge, eau de cologne, tortoise-shell, or imitation tortoise-shell, combs in their hair. They were not imaginable without such getups, unless bundled to the chin in quilted satin dressing-gowns. For my mother this style was hard to keep up; it required ingenuity, dedication, fierce effort. And who appreciated it? She did.

They all came to stay with us one summer. They came to our house because my mother was the only married one, with a house big enough to accommodate everybody, and because she was too poor to go to see them. We lived in Dalgleish in Huron County in Western Ontario. The population, 2,000, was announced on a sign at the town limits. "Now there's two thousand and four," cried Cousin Iris, heaving herself out of the driver's seat. She drove a 1939 Oldsmobile. She had driven to Winnipeg to collect Flora, and Winifred, who had come down from Edmonton by train. Then they all drove to Toronto and picked up Isabel.

"And the four of us are bound to be more trouble than the whole two thousand put together," said Isabel. "Where was it—Orangeville—we laughed so hard Iris had to stop the car? She was afraid she'd drive into the ditch!"

The steps creaked under their feet.

"Breathe that air! Oh, you can't beat the country air. Is that the pump where you get your drinking water? Wouldn't that be lovely right now? A drink of well water!"

My mother told me to get a glass, but they insisted on drinking out of the tin mug.

From *The Moons of Jupiter* by Alice Munro © Alice Munro 1982. Reprinted by permission of Macmillan Canada.

They told how Iris had gone into a field to answer nature's call and had looked up to find herself surrounded by a ring of interested cows.

"Cows baloney!" said Iris. "They were steers."

"Bulls for all you'd know," said Winifred, letting herself down into a wicker chair. She was the fattest.

"Bulls! I'd know!" said Iris. "I hope their furniture can stand the strain, Winifred. I tell you it was a drag on the rear end of my poor car. Bulls! What a shock, it's a wonder I got my pants up!"

They told about the wild-looking town in Northern Ontario where Iris wouldn't stop the car even to let them buy a Coke. She took one look at the lumberjacks and cried, "We'd all be raped!"

"What is raped?" said my little sister.

"Oh-oh," said Iris. "It means you get your pocketbook stolen."

Pocketbook: an American word. My sister and I didn't know what that meant either but we were not equal to two questions in a row. And I knew that wasn't what rape meant anyway; it meant something dirty.

"Purse. Purse stolen," said my mother in a festive but cautioning tone. Talk in our house was genteel.

Now came the unpacking of presents. Tins of coffee, nuts and date pudding, oysters, olives, ready-made cigarettes for my father. They all smoked, too, except for Flora, the Winnipeg schoolteacher. A sign of worldliness then; in Dalgleish, a sign of possible loose morals. They made it a respectable luxury.

Stockings, scarves emerged as well, a voile blouse for my mother, a pair of stiff white organdy pinafores for me and my sister (the latest thing, maybe, in Des Moines or Philadelphia but a mistake in Dalgleish, where people asked us why we hadn't taken our aprons off). And finally, a five-pound box of chocolates. Long after all the chocolates were eaten, and the cousins had gone, we kept the chocolate-box in the linen-drawer in the dining-room sideboard, waiting for some ceremonial use that never presented itself. It was still full of the empty chocolate cups of dark, fluted paper. In the wintertime I would sometimes go into the cold dining room and sniff at the cups, inhaling their smell of artifice and luxury; I would read again the descriptions on the map provided on the inside of the box-top: hazelnut, creamy nougat, Turkish delight, golden toffee, peppermint cream.

The cousins slept in the downstairs bedroom and on the pulled-out daybed in the front room. If the night was hot they thought nothing of dragging a mattress on to the verandah, or even into the yard. They drew lots for the hammock. Winifred was not allowed to draw. Far into the night you could hear them giggling, shushing each other, crying, "What was that?" We were beyond the street-lights of Dalgleish, and they were amazed at the darkness, the large number of stars.

Once they decided to sing a round.

Row, row, row your boat
Gently down the stream,
Merrily, merrily, merrily, merrily,
Life is but a dream.

They didn't think Dalgleish was real. They drove uptown and reported on the oddity of the shopkeepers; they imitated things they had overheard on the street. Every morning the coffee they had brought filled the house with its unfamiliar, American fragrance, and they sat around asking who had an inspiration for the day. One inspiration was to drive out into the country and pick berries. They got scratched and overheated and at one point Winifred was completely penned in, immobilized, by thorny branches, bellowing for a rescue party; nevertheless they said they had mightily enjoyed themselves. Another inspiration was to take my father's fishing-rods and go down to the river. They came home with a catch of rock bass, a fish we generally threw back. They organized picnics. They dressed up in old clothes, in old straw hats and my father's overalls, and took pictures of each other. They made layer cakes, and marvelous molded salads which were shaped like temples and colored like jewels.

One afternoon they put on a concert. Iris was an opera singer. She took the cloth off the dining-room table to drape herself in, and sent me out to collect hen feathers to put in her hair. She sang "The Indian Love Call," and "Women Are Fickle." Winifred was a bank-robber, with a water-pistol she had bought at the five-and-ten. Everybody had to do something. My sister and I sang, two songs: "Yellow Rose of Texas," and the Doxology. My mother, most amazingly, put on a pair of my father's trousers and stood on her head.

Audience and performers, the cousins were for each other, every waking moment. And sometimes asleep. Flora was the one who talked in her sleep. Since she was also the most ladylike and careful, the others stayed awake to ask her questions, trying to make her say something that would embarrass her. They told her she swore. They said she sat bolt upright and demanded, "Why is there no damned chalk?"

She was the one I liked least because she attempted to sharpen our minds— my sister's and mine—by throwing out mental-arithmetic questions. "If it took seven minutes to walk seven blocks, and five blocks were the same length but the other two blocks were double the length—"

"Oh, go soak your head, Flora!" said Iris, who was the rudest.

If they didn't get any inspiration, or it was too hot to do anything, they sat on the verandah drinking lemonade, fruit punch, ginger ale, iced tea, with maraschino cherries and chunks of ice chipped from the big chunk in the icebox. Sometimes my mother prettied up the glasses by dipping the rims in beaten egg whites, then in sugar. The cousins would say they were prostrated, they were good for nothing; but their complaints had a gratified sound, as if the heat of summer itself had been created to add drama to their lives.

Drama enough already.

In a larger world, things had happened to them. Accidents, proposals, encounters with lunatics and enemies. Iris could have been rich. A millionaire's widow, a crazy old woman with a wig like a haystack, had been wheeled into the hospital one day, clutching a carpetbag. And what was in the carpetbag but jewels, real jewels, emeralds and diamonds and pearls as big as pullet eggs. Nobody but Iris could do a thing with her. It was Iris who persuaded her at last to throw the wig into the garbage (it was crawling with fleas), and let the jewels go into the bank vault. So attached did this old woman become to Iris that she wanted to remake her will, she wanted to leave Iris the jewels and the stocks and the money and the apartment houses. Iris would not allow it. Professional ethics ruled it out.

"You are in a position of trust. A nurse is in a position of trust."

Then she told how she had been proposed to by an actor, dying from a life of dissipation. She allowed him to swig from a Listerine bottle because she didn't see what difference it would make. He was a stage actor, so we wouldn't recognize the name even if she told us, which she wouldn't.

She had seen other big names, too, celebrities, the top society of Philadelphia. Not at their best.

Winifred said that she had seen things too. The real truth, the real horrible truth about some of those big wheels and socialites came out when you got a look at their finances.

We lived at the end of a road running west from Dalgleish over some scrubby land where there were small wooden houses and flocks of chickens and children. The land rose to a decent height where we were and then sloped in wide fields and pastures, decorated with elm trees, down to the curve of the river. Our house was decent too, an old brick house of a fair size, but it was drafty and laid out in an inconvenient way and the trim needed paint. My mother planned to fix it up and change it all around, as soon as we got some money.

My mother did not think much of the town of Dalgleish. She was often harking back, to the town of Fork Mills, in the Ottawa Valley, where she and the cousins had gone to high school, the town their grandfather had come to from England; and to England itself, which of course she had never seen. She praised Fork Mills for its stone houses, its handsome and restrained public buildings (quite different, she said, from Huron County's, where the idea had been to throw up some brick monstrosity and stick a tower on it), for its paved streets, the service in its stores, the better quality of things for sale and the better class of people. The people who thought so highly of themselves in Dalgleish would be laughable to the leading families of Fork Mills. But then, the leading families of Fork Mills would themselves be humbled if they came into contact with certain families of England, to whom my mother was connected.

Connection. That was what it was all about. The cousins were a show in themselves, but they also provided a connection. A connection with the real, and prodigal, and dangerous, world. They knew how to get on in it, they had made it take notice. They could command a classroom, a maternity ward, the public; they knew how to deal with taxi drivers and train conductors.

The other connection they provided, and my mother provided as well, was to England and history. It is a fact that Canadians of Scottish—which in Huron County we called Scotch—and Irish descent will tell you quite freely that their ancestors came out during the potato famine, with only the rags on their backs, or that they were shepherds, agricultural laborers, poor landless people. But anyone whose ancestors came from England will have some story of black sheep or younger sons, financial reverses, lost inheritances, elopements with unsuitable partners. There may be some amount of truth in this; conditions in Scotland and Ireland were such as to force wholesale emigration, while Englishmen may have chosen to leave home for more colorful, personal reasons.

This was the case with the Chaddeley family, my mother's family. Isabel and Iris were not Chaddeleys by name, but their mother had been a Chaddeley; my mother had been a Chaddeley, though she was now a Fleming; Flora and Winifred were Chaddeleys still. All were descended from a grandfather who left England as a young man for reasons they did not quite agree on. My mother believed that he had been a student at Oxford, but had lost all the money his family sent him, and had been ashamed to go home. He lost it by gambling. No, said Isabel, that was just the story; what really happened was that he got a servant girl in trouble and was compelled to marry her, and take her to Canada. The family estates were near Canterbury, said my mother. (Canterbury pilgrims, Canterbury bells.) The others were not sure of that. Flora said that they were in the west of England, and that the name Chaddeley was said to be related to Cholmondeley; there was a Lord Cholmondeley, the Chaddeleys could be a branch of that family. But there was also the possibility, she said, that it was French, it was originally *Champ de laiche,* which means field of sedge. In that case the family had probably come to England with William the Conqueror.

Isabel said she was not an intellectual and the only person she knew from English history was Mary Queen of Scots. She wanted somebody to tell her if William the Conqueror came before Mary Queen of Scots, or after?

"Sedge fields," said my father agreeably. "That wouldn't exactly make them a fortune."

"Well, I wouldn't know sedge from oats," said Iris. "But they were prosperous enough in England, according to Grandpa, they were gentry there."

"Before," said Flora, "and Mary Queen of Scots wasn't even English."

"I knew that from the name," said Isabel. "So ha-ha."'

Every one of them believed, whatever the details, that there had been a great comedown, a dim catastrophe, and that beyond them, behind them, in England, lay lands and houses and ease and honor. How could they think otherwise, remembering their grandfather?

He had worked as a postal clerk, in Fork Mills. His wife, whether she was a seduced servant or not, bore him eight children, then died. As soon as the older children were out to work and contributing money to the household—there was no nonsense about educating them—the father quit work. A fight with the Postmaster was the immediate reason, but he really had no intention of working any longer; he had made up his mind to stay at home, supported by his children. He had the air of gentleman, was widely read, and full of rhetoric and self-esteem. His children did not balk at supporting him; they sank into their commonplace jobs, but pushed their own children—they limited themselves to one or two apiece, mostly daughters—out to Business School, to Normal School, to Nurses Training. My mother and her cousins, who were these children, talked often about their selfish and wilful grandfather, hardly ever about their decent, hard-working parents. What an old snob he was, they said, but how handsome, even as an old man, what a carriage. What ready and appropriate insults he had for people, what scathing judgments he could make. Once, in faraway Toronto, on the main floor of Eaton's as a matter of fact, he was accosted by the harnessmaker's wife from Fork Mills, a harmless, brainless woman who cried, "Well, ain't it nice to meet a friend so far from home?"

"Madam," said Grandfather Chaddeley, "you are no friend of mine."

Wasn't he the limit, they said. *Madam, you are no friend of mine!* The old snob. He paraded around with his head in the air like a prize gander. Another lower-class lady—lower-class according to him—was kind enough to bring him some soup, when he had caught cold. Sitting in his daughter's kitchen, not even his own roof over his head, soaking his feet, an ailing and in fact a dying man, he still had the gall to turn his back, let his daughter do the thanking. He despised the woman, whose grammar was terrible, and who had no teeth.

"But he didn't either! By that time he had no teeth whatever!"

"Pretentious old coot."

"And a leech on his children."

"Just pride and vanity. That's the sum total of him."

But telling these stories, laughing, they were billowing with pride themselves, they were crowing. They were proud of having such a grandfather. They believed that refusing to speak to inferior people was outrageous and mean, that preserving a sense of distinction was ridiculous, particularly when your teeth were gone, but in a way they still admired him. They did. They admired his invective, which was lost on his boss, the plodding Postmaster, and his prideful behavior, which was lost on his neighbors, the democratic citizens of Canada. (Oh what a shame, said the toothless neighbor, the poor old fellow, he don't even reckinize me.) They might even have admired his decision to let others do the work. A gentleman, they called him. They spoke ironically, but the possession of such a grandfather continued to delight them.

I couldn't understand this, at the time or later. I had too much Scottish blood in me, too much of my father. My father would never have admitted there were inferior people, or superior people either. He was scrupulously egalitarian, making it a point not to "snivel," as he said, to anybody, not to kowtow, and not to high-hat anybody either, to behave as if there were no differences. I took the same tack. There were times, later, when I wondered if it was a paralyzing prudence that urged this stand, as much as any finer sentiment, when I wondered if my father and I didn't harbor, in our hearts, intact and unassailable notions of superiority, which my mother and her cousins with their innocent snobbishness could never match.

It was not of much importance to me, years later, to receive a letter from the Chaddeley family, in England. It was from an elderly lady who was working on a family tree. The family did exist, in England, after all, and they did not spurn their overseas branches, they were seeking us out. My great-grandfather was known to them. There was his name on the family tree: Joseph Ellington Chaddeley. The marriage register gave his occupation as butcher's apprentice. He had married Helena Rose Armour, a servant, in 1859. So it was true that he had married a servant. But probably not true about the gaming debts at Oxford. Did gentlemen who were embarrassed at Oxford go and apprentice themselves to butchers?

It occurred to me that if he had stayed with butchering, his children might have gone to high school. He might have been a prosperous man in Fork Mills. The letter-writer did not mention the Cholmondeley connection, or the fields of sedge, or William the Conqueror. It was a decent family we belonged to, of servants and artisans, the occasional tradesman or farmer. At one time I would have been shocked to discover this, and would hardly have believed it. At another, later, time, when I was dedicated to tearing away all false notions, all illusions, I would have been triumphant. By the time the revelation came I did not care, one way or the other. I had almost forgotten about Canterbury and Oxford and Cholmondeley, and that first England I had heard of from my mother, that ancient land of harmony and chivalry, of people on horseback, and good manners (though surely my grandfather's had broken, under the strain of a cruder life), of Simon de Montfort and Lorna Doone and hounds and castles and the New Forest, all fresh and rural, ceremonious, civilized, eternally desirable.

And I had already had my eyes opened to some other things, by the visit of Cousin Iris.

That happened when I was living in Vancouver. I was married to Richard then. I had two small children. On a Saturday evening Richard answered the phone and came to get me.

"Be careful," he said. "It sounds like Dalgleish."

Richard always said the name of my native town as if it were a clot of something unpleasant, which he had to get out of his mouth in a hurry.

I went to the phone and found to my relief that it was nobody from Dalgleish at all. It was Cousin Iris. There was a bit of the Ottawa Valley accent still in her speech, something rural—she would not have suspected that herself and would not have been pleased—and something loud and jolly, which had made Richard think of the voices of Dalgleish. She said that she was in Vancouver, she was retired now and she was taking a trip, and she was dying to see me. I asked her to come to dinner the next day.

"Now, by dinner, you mean the evening meal, don't you?"

"Yes."

"I just wanted to get it straight. Because when we visited at your place, remember, your folks always had dinner at noon. You called the noon meal dinner. I didn't think you still would but I wanted to get it straight."

I told Richard that a cousin of my mother's was coming to dinner. I said she was, or had been, a nurse, and that she lived in Philadelphia.

"She's all right," I said. I meant decently educated, well enough spoken, moderately well-bred. "She's travelled all over. She's really quite interesting. Being a nurse she's met all sorts of people—" I told about the millionaire's widow and the jewels in the carpetbag. And the more I talked, the more Richard discerned of my doubts and my need for reassurance, and the more noncommittal and unreassuring he became. He knew he had an advantage, and we had reached the point in our marriage where no advantage was given up easily.

I longed for the visit to go well. I wanted this for my own sake. My motives were not such as would do me credit. I wanted Cousin Iris to shine forth as a relative nobody need be ashamed of, and I wanted Richard and his money and our house to lift me forever, in Cousin Iris's eyes, out of the category of poor relation. I wanted all this accomplished with a decent subtlety and restraint and the result to be a pleasant recognition of my own value, from both sides.

I used to think that if I could produce one rich and well-behaved and important relative, Richard's attitude to me would change. A judge, a surgeon, would have done very well. I was not sure at all how Iris would serve, as a substitute. I was worried about the way Richard had said *Dalgleish,* and that vestige of the Ottawa Valley—Richard was stern about rural accents, having had so much trouble with mine—and something else in Iris's voice which I could not identify. Was she too eager? Did she assume some proprietary family claim I no longer believed was justified?

Never mind. I started thawing a leg of lamb and made a lemon meringue pie. Lemon meringue pie was what my mother made when the cousins were coming. She polished the dessert forks, she ironed the table napkins. For we owned dessert forks (I wanted to say to Richard); yes, and we had table napkins, even though the toilet was in the basement and there was no running water until after the war. I used to carry hot water to the front bedroom in the morning, so that the cousins could wash. I poured it into a jug like those I now see in antique stores, or on hall tables, full of ornamental grasses.

But surely none of this mattered to me, none of this nonsense about dessert forks? Was I, am I, the sort of person who thinks that to possess such objects is to have a civilized attitude to life? No, not at all; not exactly; yes and no. Background was Richard's word. *Your background.* A drop in his voice, a warning. Or was that what I heard, not what he meant? When he said Dalgleish, even when he wordlessly handed me a letter from home, I felt ashamed, as if there was something growing over me; mold, something nasty and dreary and inescapable. Poverty, to Richard's family, was like bad breath or running sores, an affliction for which the afflicted must bear one part of the blame. But it was not good manners to notice. If ever I said anything about my childhood or my family in their company there would be a slight drawing-back, as at a low-level obscenity. But it is possible that I was a bit strident and self-conscious, like the underbred character in Virginia Woolf who makes a point of not having been taken to the circus. Perhaps that was what embarrassed them. They were tactful with me. Richard could not afford to be so tactful, since he had put himself in a chancy position, marrying me. He wanted me amputated from that past which seemed to him such shabby baggage; he was on the lookout for signs that the amputation was not complete; and of course it wasn't.

My mother's cousins had never visited us again, en masse. Winifred died suddenly one winter, not more than three or four years after that memorable visit. Iris wrote to my mother that the circle was broken now and that she had suspected Winifred was diabetic, but Winifred did not want to find that out because of her love of food. My mother herself was not well. The remaining cousins visited her, but they did so separately, and of course not often, because of distances. Nearly every one of their letters referred to the grand time they had all had, that summer, and near the end of her life my mother said, "Oh, Lord, do you know what I was thinking of? The water-pistol. Remember that concert? Winifred with the water-pistol! Everybody did their stunt. What did I do?"

"You stood on your head."

"Ah yes I did."

•••

Cousin Iris was stouter than ever, and rosy under her powder. She was breathless from her climb up the street. I had not wanted to ask Richard to go to the hotel for her. I would not say I was afraid to ask him; I simply wanted to keep things from starting off on the wrong foot, by making him do what he hadn't offered to do. I had told myself that she would take a cab. But she had come on the bus.

"Richard was busy," I said to her, lying. "It's my fault. I don't drive."

"Never mind," said Iris staunchly. "I'm all out of puff just now but I'll be all right in a minute. It's carrying the lard that does it. Serves me right."

As soon as she said *all out of puff,* and *carrying the lard,* I knew how things were going to go, with Richard. It hadn't even taken that, I knew as soon as I saw her on my doorstep, her hair, which I remembered as gray-brown, now gilt and sprayed into a foamy pile, her sumptuous peacock-blue dress decorated at one shoulder with a sort of fountain of gold spray. Now that I think of it, she looked splendid. I wish I had met her somewhere else. I wish I had appreciated her as she deserved. I wish that everything had gone differently.

"Well, now," she said jubilantly. "Haven't you done all right for yourself!" She looked at me, and the rock garden and the ornamental shrubs and the expanse of windows. Our house was in Capilano Heights on the side of Grouse Mountain. "I'll say. It's a grand place, dear."

I took her in and introduced her to Richard and she said, "Oh-ho, so you're the husband. Well, I won't ask you how's business because I can see it's good."

Richard was a lawyer. The men in his family were either lawyers or stockbrokers. They never referred to what they did at work as any kind of business. They never referred to what they did at work at all. Talking about what you did at work was slightly vulgar; talking about how you did was unforgivably so. If I had not been still so vulnerable to Richard it might have been a pleasure to see him met like this, head on.

I offered drinks at once, hoping to build up a bit of insulation in myself. I had got out a bottle of sherry, thinking that was what you offered older ladies, people who didn't usually drink. But Iris laughed and said, "Why, I'd love a gin and tonic, just like you folks."

"Remember that time we all went to visit you in Dalgleish?" she said. "It was so dry! Your mother was still a small-town girl, she wouldn't have liquor in the house. Though I always thought your father would take a drink, if you got him off. Flora was Temperance, too. But that Winifred was a devil. You know she had a bottle in her suitcase? We'd sneak into the bedroom and take a nip, then gargle with cologne. She called your place the Sahara. Here we are crossing the Sahara. Not that we didn't get enough lemonade and iced tea to float a battleship. Float four battleships, eh?"

Perhaps she had seen something when I opened the door—some surprise, or failure of welcome. Perhaps she was daunted, though at the same time immensely pleased by the house and the furnishings, which were elegant and dull and not all chosen by Richard, either. Whatever the reason, her tone when she spoke of Dalgleish and my parents was condescending. I don't think she wanted to remind me of home, and put me in my place; I think she wanted to establish herself, to let me know that she belonged here, more than there.

"Oh, this is a treat, sitting here and looking at your gorgeous view! Is that Vancouver Island?"

"Point Grey," said Richard unencouragingly.

"Oh, I should have known. We went out there on the bus yesterday. We saw the University. I'm with a tour, dear, did I tell you? Nine old maids and seven widows and three widowers. Not one married couple. But as I say, you never know, the trip's not over yet."

I smiled, and Richard said he had to move the sprinkler.

"We go to Vancouver Island tomorrow, then we're taking the boat to Alaska. Everybody said to me back home, what do you want to go to Alaska for, and I said, because I've never been there, isn't that a good enough reason? No bachelors on the tour, and do you know why? They don't live to be this old! That's a medical fact. You tell your hubby. Tell him he did the right thing. But I'm not going to talk shop. Every time I go on a trip they find out I'm a nurse and they show me their spines and their tonsils and their whatnots. They want me to poke their livers. Free diagnosis. I say enough of that. I'm retired now and I mean to enjoy life. This beats the iced tea a mile, doesn't it? But she used to go to such a lot of trouble. The poor thing. She used to frost the glasses with egg white, remember?"

I tried to get her to talk about my mother's illness, new treatments, her hospital experiences, not only because that was interesting to me, but because I thought it might calm her down and make her sound more intelligent. I knew Richard hadn't gone out at all but was lurking in the kitchen.

But she said, no shop.

"Beaten egg white, then sugar. Oh, dear. You had to drink through straws. But the fun we had there. The john in the basement and all. We did have fun."

Iris's lipstick, her bright teased hair, her iridescent dress and oversized brooch, her voice and conversation, were all part of a policy which was not a bad one: she was in favor of movement, noise, change, flashiness, hilarity, and courage. Fun. She thought other people should be in favor of these things too, and told about her efforts on the tour.

"I'm the person to get the ball rolling. Some people get downhearted on a trip. They get indigestion. They talk about their constipation. I always get their minds off it. You can always joke. You can start a singsong. Every morning I can practically hear them thinking, what crazy thing is that Chaddeley going to come up with today?"

Nothing fazed her, she said. She told about other trips. Ireland. The other women had been afraid to get down and kiss the Blarney Stone, but she said, "I've come this far and I'm going to kiss the damn thing!" and did so, while a blasphemous Irishman hung on to her ankles.

We drank; we ate; the children came in and were praised. Richard came and went. Nothing fazed her; she was right. Nothing deflected her from her stories of herself; the amount of time she could spend not talking was limited. She told about the carpetbag and the millionaire's widow all over again. She told about the dissolute actor. How many conversations she must have ridden through like this—laughing, insisting, rambling, recollecting. I wondered if this evening was something she would describe as fun. She would describe it. The house, the rugs, the dishes, the signs of money. It might not matter to her that Richard snubbed her. Perhaps she would rather be snubbed by a rich relative than welcomed by a poor one. But had she always been like this, always brash and greedy and scared; decent, maybe even admirable, but still somebody you hope you will not have to sit too long beside, on a bus or at a party? I was dishonest when I said that I wished we had met elsewhere, that I wished I had appreciated her, when I implied that Richard's judgments were all that stood in the way. Perhaps I could have appreciated her more, but I couldn't have stayed with her long.

I had to wonder if this was all it amounted to, the gaiety I remembered; the gaiety and generosity, the worldliness. It would be better to think that time had soured and thinned and made commonplace a brew that used to sparkle, that difficulties had altered us both, and not for the better. Unsympathetic places and people might have made us harsh, in efforts and opinions. I used to love to look at magazine advertisements showing ladies in chiffon dresses with capes and floating panels, resting their elbows on a ship's rail, or drinking tea beside a potted palm. I used to apprehend a life of elegance and sensibility, through them. They were a window I had on the world, and the cousins were another. In fact the cousin's flowery dresses used to remind me of them, though the cousins were so much stouter, and not pretty. Well, now that I think of it, what were those ladies talking about, in the balloons over their heads? They were discussing underarm odor, or thanking their lucky stars they were no longer chafed, because they used Kotex.

Iris collected herself, finally, and asked when the last bus ran. Richard had disappeared again, but I said that I would take her back to her hotel in a cab. She said no, she would enjoy the bus ride, truly she would, she always got into a conversation with somebody. I got out my schedule and walked her to the bus stop. She said she hoped she hadn't talked Richard's and my ears off and asked if Richard was shy. She said I had a lovely home, a lovely family, it made her feel grand to see that I had done so well in my life. Tears filled her eyes when she hugged me good-bye.

"What a pathetic old tart," said Richard, coming into the living room as I was gathering up the coffee cups. He followed me into the kitchen, recalling things she had said, pretentious things, bits of bragging. He pointed out grammatical mistakes she had made, of the would-be genteel variety. He pretended incredulity. Maybe he really felt it. Or maybe he thought it would be a good idea to start the attack immediately, before I took him to task for leaving the room, being rude, not offering a ride to the hotel.

He was still talking as I threw the Pyrex plate at his head. There was a piece of lemon meringue pie in it. The plate missed, and hit the refrigerator, but the pie flew out and caught him on the side of the face just as in the old movies or an *I Love Lucy* show. There was the same moment of amazement as there is on the screen, the sudden innocence, for him; his speech stopped, his mouth open. For me, too, amazement, that something people invariably thought funny in those instances should be so shocking a verdict in real life.

Row, row, row your boat
Gently down the stream.
Merrily, merrily, merrily, merrily,
Life is but a dream.

I lie in bed beside my little sister, listening to the singing in the yard. Life is transformed, by these voices, by these presences, by their high spirits and grand esteem, for themselves and each other. My parents, all of us, are on holiday. The mixture of voices and words is so complicated and varied it seems that such confusion, such jolly rivalry, will go on forever, and then to my surprise—for I am surprised, even though I know the pattern of rounds—the song is thinning out, you can hear the two voices striving.

Merrily, merrily, merrily, merrily,
Life is but a dream.

Then the one voice alone, one of them singing on, gamely, to the finish. One voice in which there is an unexpected note of entreaty, of warning, as it hangs the five separate words on the air. *Life is.* Wait. *But a.* Now, wait. *Dream.*

Chaddeleys and Flemings

2. The Stone in the Field

My mother was not a person who spent all her time frosting the rims of glasses and fancying herself descended from the aristocracy. She was a businesswoman really, a trader and dealer. Our house was full of things that had not been paid for with money, but taken in some complicated trade, and that might not be ours to keep. For a while we could play a piano, consult an Encyclopaedia Britannica, eat off an oak table. But one day I would come home from school and find that each of these things had moved on. A mirror off the wall could go as easily, a cruel stand, a horsehair loveseat that had replaced a sofa that had replaced a daybed. We were living in a warehouse.

My mother worked for, or with, a man named Poppy Cullender. He was a dealer in antiques. He did not have a shop. He too had a house full of furniture. What we had was just his overflow. He had dressers back-to-back and bed-springs upended against the wall. He bought things—furniture, dishes, bedspreads, doorknobs, pump handles, churns, flatirons, anything—from people living on farms or in little villages in the country, then sold what he had bought to antique stores in Toronto. The heyday of antiques had not yet arrived. It was a time when people were covering old woodwork with white or pastel paint as fast as they were able, throwing out spool beds and putting in blond maple bedroom suites, covering patchwork quilts with chenille bedspreads. It was not hard to buy things, to pick them up for next to nothing, but it was a slow business selling them, which was why they might become part of our lives for a season. Just the same, Poppy and my mother were on the right track. If they had lasted, they might have become rich and justified. As it was, Poppy kept his head above water and my mother made next to nothing, and everybody thought them deluded.

They didn't last. My mother got sick, and Poppy went to jail, for making advances on a train.

There were farmhouses where Poppy was not a welcome sight. Children hooted and wives bolted the door, as he came toiling through the yard in his greasy black clothes, rolling his eyes in an uncontrollably lewd or silly way he had and calling in a soft, pleading voice, "Ith anybody h-home?" To add to his other problems he had both a lisp and a stammer. My father could imitate him very well. There were places where Poppy found doors barred and others, usually less respectable, where he was greeted and cheered and fed, just as if he had been a harmless weird bird dropped out of the sky, valued for its very oddity. When he had experienced no welcome he did not go back; instead, he sent my mother. He must have had in his head a map of the surrounding country with every house in it, and just as some maps have dots to show you where the mineral resources are, or the places of historical interest, Poppy's map would have marked the location of every known and suspected rocking chair, pine sideboard, piece of milk glass, moustache cup. "Why don't you run out and take a look at it?" I would hear him say to my mother when they were huddled in the dining room looking at something like the maker's mark on an old pickle crock. He didn't stammer when he talked to her, when he talked business; his voice though soft was not humble and indicated that he had his own satisfactions, maybe his own revenge. If I had a friend with me, coming in from school, she would say, "Is that Poppy *Cullender?*" She would be amazed to hear him talking like an ordinary person and amazed to find him inside somebody's house. I disliked his connection with us so much that I wanted to say no.

Not much was made, really, of Poppy's sexual tendencies. People may have thought he didn't have any. When they said he was queer, they just meant queer; odd, freakish, disturbing. His stammer and his rolling eyes and his fat bum and his house full of throwaways were all rolled up into that one word. I don't know if he was very courageous, trying to make a life for himself in a place like Dalgleish where random insults and misplaced pity would be what was always coming at him, or whether he was just not very realistic. Certainly it was not realistic to make such suggestions to a couple of baseball players on the Stratford train.

I never knew what my mother made of his final disastrous luck, or what she knew about him. Years later she read in the paper that a teacher at the college I was going to had been arrested for fighting in a bar over a male companion. She asked me did they mean he was defending a friend, and if so, why didn't they say so? *Male companion?*

Then she said, "Poor Poppy. There were always those that were out to get him. He was very smart, in his way. Some people can't survive in a place like this. It's not permitted. No."

My mother had the use of Poppy's car, for business forays, and sometimes for a weekend, when he went to Toronto. Unless he had a trailer-load of things to take down, he travelled—unfortunately, as I have said—by train. Our own car had gone so far beyond repair that we were not able to take it out of town; it was driven into Dalgleish and back, and that was all. My parents were like many other people who had entered the Depression with some large possession, such as a car or a furnace, which gradually wore out and couldn't be fixed or replaced. When we could take it on the roads we used to go to Goderich once or twice in a summer, to the lake. And occasionally we visited my father's sisters who lived out in the country.

My mother always said that my father had a very odd family. It was odd because there had been seven girls and then one boy; and it was odd because six of those eight children still lived together, in the house where they were born. One sister had died young, of typhoid fever, and my father had got away. And those six sisters were very odd in themselves, at least in the view of many people, in the time they lived in. They were leftovers, really; my mother said so; they belonged in another generation.

I don't remember that they ever came to visit us. They didn't like to come to a town as big as Dalgleish, or to venture so far from home. It would have been a drive of fourteen or fifteen miles, and they had no car. They drove a horse and buggy, a horse and cutter in the wintertime, long after everyone else had ceased to do so. There must have been occasions when they had to drive into town, because I saw one of them once, in the buggy, on a town street. The buggy had a great high top on it, like a black bonnet, and whichever aunt it was was sitting sideways on the seat, looking up as seldom as it is possible to do while driving a horse. Public scrutiny seemed to be causing her much pain, but she was stubborn; she held herself there on the seat, cringing and stubborn, and she was as strange a sight, in her way, as Poppy Cullender was in his. I couldn't really think of her as my aunt; the connection seemed impossible. Yet I could remember an earlier time, when I had been out to the farm—maybe more than one time, for I had been so young it was hard to remember—and I had not felt this impossibility and had not understood the oddity of these relatives. It was when my grandfather was sick in bed, dying I suppose, with a big brown paper fan hanging over him. It was worked by a system of ropes which I was allowed to pull. One of my aunts was showing me how to do this, when my mother called my name from downstairs. Then the aunt and I looked at each other exactly as two children look at each other when an adult is calling. I must have sensed something unusual about this, some lack of what was expected, even necessary, in the way of balance, or barriers; else I would not have remembered it.

One other time with an aunt. I think the same one, but maybe another, was sitting with me on the back steps of the farmhouse, with a six-quart basket of clothespegs on the step beside us. She was making dolls for me, mannikins, out of the round-headed pegs. She used a black crayon and a red, to make their mouths and eyes, and she brought bits of yarn out of her apron pocket, to twist around to make the hair and clothes. And she talked to me; I am certain she talked.

"Here's a lady. She went to church with her wig on, see? She was proud. What if a wind comes up? It would blow her wig right off. See? You blow."

"Here's a soldier. See he only has the one leg? His other leg was blown off by a cannonball at the battle of Waterloo. Do you know what a cannonball is, that shoots out of a big gun? When they have a battle? Boom!"

Now we were going out to the farm, in Poppy's car, to visit the aunts. My father said no, he wouldn't drive another man's car—meaning he wouldn't drive Poppy's, wouldn't sit where Poppy had sat—so my mother drove. That made the whole expedition feel uncertain, the weight wrongly distributed. It was a hot Sunday late in the summer.

My mother was not altogether sure of the way, and my father waited until the last moment to reassure her. This was understood to be teasing, and yet was not altogether free of reservations or reproof.

"Is it here we turn? Is it one further? I will know when I see the bridge."

The route was complicated. Around Dalgleish most roads were straight, but out here the roads twisted around hills or buried themselves in swamps. Some dwindled to a couple of ruts with a row of plantain and dandelions running between. In some places wild berrybushes sent creepers across the road. These high, thick bushes, dense and thorny, with leaves of a shiny green that seemed almost black, reminded me of the waves of the sea that were pushed back for Moses.

There was the bridge, like two railway cars joined together, stripped to their skeletons, one lane wide. A sign said it was unsafe for trucks.

"We'll never make it," my father said, as we bumped on to the bridge floor. "There he is. Old Father Maitland."

My sister said, "Where? Who? Where is he?"

"The Maitland *River*," my mother said.

We looked down, where the guard-rails had fallen out of the side of the bridge, and saw the clear brown water flowing over big dim stones, between cedar banks, breaking into sunny ripples further on. My skin was craving for it.

"Do they ever go swimming?" I said. I meant the aunts. I thought that if they did, they might take us.

"Swimming?" said my mother. "I can't picture it. Do they?" she asked my father.

"I can't picture it either."

The road was going uphill, out of the gloomy cedar bush on the river bank. I started saying the aunts' names.

"Susan. Clara. Lizzie. Maggie. Jennet was the one who died."

"Annie," said my father. "Don't forget Annie."

"Annie. Lizzie. I said her. Who else?"

"Dorothy," said my mother, shifting gears with an angry little spurt, and we cleared the top of the hill, leaving the dark bush hollow behind. Up here were pasture hills covered with purple-flowering milkweed, wild pea blossom, black-eyed Susans. Hardly any trees here, but lots of elderberry bushes, blooming all along the road. They looked as if they were sprinkled with snow. One bald hill reached up higher than any of the others.

"Mount Hebron," my father said. "That is the highest point of land in Huron County. Or so I always was told."

"Now I know where I am all right," my mother said. "We'll see it in a moment, won't we?"

And there it was, the big wooden house with no trees near it, the barn and the flowering brown hills behind. The drive shed was the original barn, built of logs. The paint on the house was not white as I had absolutely believed but yellow, and much of it had peeled away.

Out in front of the house, in a block of shade which was quite narrow at this time of day, several figures were sitting on straight-backed chairs. On the wall of the house, behind them, hung the scoured milk-pails and parts of the separator.

They were not expecting us. They had no telephone, so we hadn't been able to let them know we were coming. They were just sitting there in the shade, watching the road where scarcely another car went by all afternoon.

One figure got up, and ran around the side of the house.

"That'll be Susan," my father said. "She can't face company."

"She'll come back when she realizes it's us," my mother said. "She won't know the strange car."

"Maybe. I wouldn't count on it."

The others stood, and stiffly readied themselves, hands clasped in front of their aprons. When we got out of the car and were recognized, one or two of them took a few steps forward, then stopped, and waited for us to approach them.

"Come on," my father said, and led us to each in turn, saying only the name in recognition of the meeting. No embraces, no touch of hands or laying together of cheeks.

"Lizzie. Dorothy. Clara."

It was no use, I could never get them straight. They looked too much alike. There must have been a twelve- or fifteen-year age span, but to me they all looked about fifty, older than my parents but not really old. They were all lean and fine-boned, and might at one time have been fairly tall, but were stooped now, with hard work and deference. Some had their hair cut short in a plain, childish style; some had it braided and twisted on top of their heads. Nobody's hair was entirely black or entirely gray. Their faces were pale, eyebrows thick and furry, eyes deep-set and bright; blue-gray or green-gray or gray. They looked a good deal like my father though he did not stoop, and his face had opened up in a way that theirs had not, to make him a handsome man.

They looked a good deal like me. I didn't know it at the time and wouldn't have wanted to. But suppose I stopped doing anything to my hair, now, stopped wearing makeup and plucking my eyebrows, put on a shapeless print dress and apron and stood around hanging my head and hugging my elbows? Yes. So when my mother and her cousins looked me over, anxiously turned me to the light, saying, "Is she a Chaddeley? What do you think?" it was the Fleming face they were seeing, and to tell the truth it was a face that wore better than theirs. (Not that they were claiming to be pretty; to look like a Chaddeley was enough.)

One of the aunts had hands red as a skinned rabbit. Later in the kitchen this one sat in a chair pushed up against the woodbox, half hidden by the stove, and I saw how she kept stroking these hands and twisting them up in her apron. I remembered that I had seen such hands before, on one of the early visits, long ago, and my mother had told me that it was because this aunt—was it always the same one?—had been scrubbing the floor and the table and chairs with lye, to keep them white. That was what lye did to your hands. And after this visit, too, on the way home my mother was to say in a tone of general accusation, sorrow, and disgust, "Did you see those hands? They must have got a Presbyterian dispensation to let them scrub on Sundays."

The floor was pine and it was white, gleaming, but soft-looking, like velvet. So were the chairs and the table. We all sat around the kitchen, which was like a small house tacked on to the main house; back and front doors opposite each other, windows on three sides. The cold black stove shone, too, with polishing. Its trim was like mirrors. The room was cleaner and barer than any I have ever been in. There was no sign of frivolity, no indication that the people who lived here ever sought entertainment. No radio; no newspapers or magazines; certainly no books. There must have been a Bible in the house, and there must have been a calendar, but these were not to be seen. It was hard now even to believe in the clothespin dolls, the crayons and the yarn. I wanted to ask which of them had made the dolls; had there really been a wigged lady and a one-legged soldier? But though I was not usually shy, a peculiar paralysis overcame me in this room, as if I understood for the first time how presumptuous any question might be, how hazardous any opinion.

Work would be what filled their lives, not conversation; work would be what gave their days shape. I know that now. Drawing the milk down through the rough teats, slapping the flatiron back and forth on the scorched-smelling ironing board, swishing the scrub-water in whitening arcs across the pine floor, they would be mute, and maybe content. Work would not be done here as it was in our house, where the idea was to get it over with. It would be something that could, that must, go on forever.

What was to be said? The aunts, like those who engage in a chat with royalty, would venture no remarks of their own, but could answer questions. They offered no refreshments. It was clear that only a great effort of will kept them all from running away and hiding, like Aunt Susan, who never did reappear while we were there. What was felt in that room was the pain of human contact. I was hypnotized by it. The fascinating pain; the humiliating necessity.

My father did have some idea of how to proceed. He started out on the weather. The need for rain, the rain in July that spoiled the hay, last year's wet spring, floods long past, the prospects or non-prospects of a rainy fall. This talk steadied them, and he asked about the cows, the driving horse whose name was Nelly and the workhorses Prince and Queen, the garden; did the blight get on their tomatoes?

"No it didn't."

"How many quarts did you do down?"

"Twenty-seven."

"Did you make any chili sauce? Did you make some juice?"

"Juice and chili sauce. Yes."

"So you won't starve next winter. You'll be falling into flesh, next."

Giggles broke from a couple of them and my father took heart, continued teasing. He inquired whether they were doing much dancing these days. He shook his head as he pretended to recall their reputation for running around the country to dances, smoking, cutting up. He said they were a bad lot, they wouldn't get married because they'd rather flirt; why, he couldn't hold up his head for the shame of them.

My mother broke in then. She must have meant to rescue them, thinking it cruel to tease them in this way, dwelling on just what they had never had, or been.

"That is a lovely piece of furniture," she said. "That sideboard. I always have admired it."

Flappers, my father said, that's what they were, in their prime.

My mother went over to look at the kitchen dresser, which was pine, and very heavy and tall. The knobs on all the doors and drawers were not quite round but slightly irregular, either from the making, or from all the hands that had pulled on them.

"You could have an antique dealer come in here and offer you a hundred dollars for that," my mother said. "If that ever happens, don't take it. The table and chairs as well. Don't let anybody smooth-talk you into selling them before you find out what they're really worth. I know what I'm talking about." Without asking permission she examined the dresser, fingered the knobs, looked around at the back. "I can't tell you what it's worth myself but if you ever want to sell it I will get it appraised by the best person I can find. That's not all," she said, stroking the pine judiciously. "You have a fortune's worth of furniture in this house. You sit tight on it. You have the old furniture that was made around here, and there's hardly any of that left. People threw it out, around the turn of the century, they bought Victorian things when they started getting prosperous. The things that didn't get thrown out are worth money and they're going to be worth more. I'm telling you."

So she was. But they could not take such telling. They could no more understand her than if she had been spouting lunacy. Possibly the word antique was not known to them. She was talking about their kitchen dresser but she was talking about it in terms they had no understanding of. If a dealer came into the house and offered them money? Nobody came into their house. Selling the dresser was probably as hard for them to imagine as selling the kitchen wall. None of them would look at anything but their aproned laps.

"So I guess that's lucky, for the ones that never got prosperous," my father said, to ease things, but they could not answer him, either. They would know the meaning of prosperous but they would never have used such a word, would never have got their tongues around it, nor their minds around the idea of getting that way. They would have noticed that some people, their neighbors even, were spending money, on tractors and combines and milking machines as well as on cars and houses, and I think this must have seemed to them a sign of an alarming, not enviable, lack of propriety and self-control. They would pity people for it, in a way, the same way they might pity girls who did run around to dances, and smoke and flirt and get married. They might pity my mother, too. My mother looked at their lives and thought of how they could be brightened, opened up. Suppose they sold some furniture and got hydro in the house, bought a washing machine, put linoleum on the floor, bought a car and learned to drive it? Why not? my mother would ask, seeing life all in terms of change and possibility. She imagined they would yearn for things, not only material things but conditions, abilities, which they did not even bother to deplore, did not think to reject, being so perfectly encased in what they had and were, so far beyond imagining themselves otherwise.

When my father was in the hospital for the last time he became very good-humored and loquacious under the influence of the pills they were giving him, and he talked to me about his life and his family. He told me how he had left home. Actually there were two leave-takings. The first occurred the summer he was fourteen. His father had sent him out to split some chunks of wood. He broke the ax-handle, and his father cursed him out and went after him with a pitchfork. His father was known for temper, and hard work. The sisters screamed, and my father, the fourteen-year-old boy, took off down the lane running as hard as he could.

"Could they scream?"

"What? Oh yes. Then. Yes they could."

My father intended to run only as far as the road, hang around, come back when his sisters let him know the coast was clear. But he did not stop running until he was halfway to Goderich, and then he thought he might as well go the rest of the way. He got a job on a lake-boat. He spent the rest of the season working on the boat, and the month before Christmas after the shipping season ended, he worked in a flour mill. He could do the work there, but he was underage; they were afraid of the inspector, so they let him go. He wanted to go home anyway, for Christmas. He was homesick. He bought presents for his father and his sisters. A watch was what he got for the old man. That and his ticket took every cent he had.

A few days after Christmas he was out in the barn, putting down hay, and his father came looking for him.

"Have you got any money?" his father wanted to know.

My father said he hadn't.

"Well, do you think then me and your sisters are going to spend all summer and fall looking up the arseholes of cows, for you to come home and sponge off us in the winter?"

That was the second time my father left home.

He shook with laughter in the hospital bed, telling me.

"Looking up the arseholes of cows!"

Then he said the funny thing was the old man himself had left home when he was a kid, after a fight with his own father. The father lit into him for using the wheelbarrow.

"It was this way. They always carried the feed to the horses, pail by pail. In the winter, when the horses were in the stalls. So my father took the notion to carry it to them in the wheelbarrow. Naturally it was a lot quicker. But he got beat. For laziness. That was the way they were, you know. Any change of any kind was a bad thing. Efficiency was just laziness, to them. That's the peasant thinking for you."

"Maybe Tolstoy would agree with them," I said. "Gandhi too."

"Drat Tolstoy and Gandhi. They never worked when they were young."

"Maybe not."

"But it's a wonder how those people had the courage once, to get them over here. They left everything. Turned their backs on everything they knew and came out here. Bad enough to face the North Atlantic, then this country that was all wilderness. The work they did, the things they went through. When your great-grandfather came to the Huron Tract he had his brother with him, and his wife and her mother, and his two little kids. Straightaway his brother was killed by a falling tree. Then the second summer his wife and her mother and the two little boys got the cholera, and the grandmother and both the children died. So he and his wife were left alone, and they went on clearing their farm and started up another family. I think the courage got burnt out of them. Their religion did them in, and their upbringing. How they had to toe the line. Also their pride. Pride was what they had when they had no more gumption."

"Not you," I said. "You ran away."

"I didn't run far."

In their old age the aunts rented the farm, but continued to live on it. Some got cataracts in their eyes, some got arthritis, but they stayed on and looked after each other, and died there, all except the last one, Aunt Lizzie, who had to go to the County Home. They lived a long time. They were a hardier clan, after all, than the Chaddeleys, none of whom reached seventy. (Cousin Iris died within six months of seeing Alaska.) I used to send a card at Christmas, and I would write on it: *to all my aunts, love and a Merry Christmas.* I did that because I could not remember which of them were dead and which were alive. I had seen their gravestone when my mother was buried. It was a modest pillar with all their names and dates of birth on it, a couple of dates of death filled in (Jennet, of course, and probably Susan), the rest left blank. By now more dates would be finished.

They would send me a card too. A wreath or a candle on it, and a few sentences of information.

A good winter so far, not much snow. We are all well except Clara's eyes not getting any better. Best wishes of the Season.

I thought of them having to go out and buy the card, go to the Post Office, buy the stamp. It was an act of faith for them to write and send those sentences to any place as unimaginable as Vancouver, to someone of their own blood leading a life so strange to them, someone who would read the card with such a feeling of bewilderment and unexplainable guilt. It did make me guilty and bewildered to think that they were still there, still attached to me. But any message from home, in those days, could let me know I was a traitor.

In the hospital, I asked my father if any of his sisters had ever had a boyfriend.

"Not what you could call that. No. There used to be a joke about Mr. Black. They used to say he built his shack there because he was sweet on Susan. I don't think so. He was just a one-legged fellow that built a shack down in a corner of the field across the road, and he died there. All before my time. Susan was the oldest, you know, she was twenty or twenty-one years old when I was born."

"So, you don't think she had a romance?"

"I wouldn't think so. It was just a joke. He was an Austrian or some such thing. Black was just what he was called, or maybe he called himself. She wouldn't have been let near him. He was buried right there under a big boulder. My father tore the shack down and used the lumber to build our chickenhouse."

I remembered that, I remembered the boulder. I remembered sitting on the ground watching my father who was fixing fence-posts. I asked him if this could be a true memory.

"Yes it could. I used to go out and fix the fences when the old man was sick in bed. You wouldn't have been very big."

"I was sitting watching you, and you said to me, do you know what that big stone is? That's a gravestone. I don't remember asking you whose. I must have thought it was a joke."

"No joke. That would be it. Mr. Black was buried underneath there. That reminds me of another thing. You know I told you, how the grandmother and the little boys died? They had the three bodies in the house at the one time. And they had nothing to make the shrouds out of but the lace curtains they had brought from the old country. I guess it would be a hasty business when it was cholera and in the summer. So that was what they buried them in."

"Lace curtains."

My father looked shy, as if he had given me a present, and said brusquely, "Well, that's the kind of a detail I thought might be interesting to you."

Some time after my father died I was reading some old newspapers on a microfilm reader in the Toronto Library; this was in connection with a documentary script I was working on, for television. The name Dalgleish caught my eye and then the name Fleming, which I have gone so long without.

HERMIT DIES NEAR DALGLEISH

It is reported that Mr. Black, a man about forty-five years old, Christian name unknown, has died on the farm of Mr. Thomas Fleming, where he has been living for
the last three years in a shack which Mr. Fleming allowed him to construct in the
corner of a field. He cultivated a few potatoes, subsisting mainly on those and on
fish and small game. He was believed to come from some European country but
gave the name Black and did not reveal his history. At some point in his life he had
parted company with one of his legs, leading some to speculate that he might have
been a soldier. He was heard to mutter to himself in a foreign language.

About three weeks ago Mr. Fleming, not having seen any smoke from the
recluse's shack, investigated, and found the man very ill. He was suffering from a
cancer of the tongue. Mr. Fleming wished to remove him to his own house for
care but Mr. Black would not agree, though he finally allowed himself to be taken
to Mr. Fleming's barn, where he remained, the weather being mild, and nursing care
being provided by the young Misses Fleming, who reside at home. There he died,
and was buried at his own request next to his hermit's shack, taking the mystery
of his life with him.

I began to think that I would like to see the stone, I would like to see if it was
still there. No one related to me lived in that country any more. I drove up on
a Sunday in June and was able to bypass Dalgleish completely; the highway had
been changed. I expected to have some trouble finding the farm, but I was on
it before I could have believed it possible. It was no longer an out-of-the-way
place. The back roads had been straightened; there was a new, strong, two-
lane concrete bridge; half of Mount Hebron had been cut away for gravel; and
the wild-pasture fields had been planted in corn.

The log drive-shed was gone. The house had been covered in pale-green alu-
minum siding. There were several wide new windows. The cement slab in
front, where my aunts had sat on their straight-backed chairs to watch the road,
had been turned into a patio, with tubs of salvia and geraniums, a metal table
with an awning, and the usual folding furniture with bright plastic webbing.

All this made me doubtful, but I knocked on the door anyway. A young,
pregnant woman answered. She asked me into the kitchen, which was a cheerful room with linoleum that looked something like red and brown bricks, and
built-in cupboards that looked very much like maple. Two children were watching a television picture whose colors seemed drained by the brightness of the
day outside, and a businesslike young husband was working at an adding machine, seemingly unbothered by the noise of the television as his children were
unbothered by the sunlight. The young woman stepped over a large dog to
turn off a tap at the sink.

They were not impatient of my story, as I had thought they might be. In fact
they were interested and helpful, and not entirely in the dark about the stone
I was looking for. The husband said that the land across the road had not been
sold to his father, who had bought this farm from my aunts; it had been sold previously. He thought it was over there that the stone was. He said his father had
told him there was a man buried over there, under a big stone, and they had
even gone for a walk once, to look at it, but he hadn't thought of it in years. He
said he would go and look for it now.

I had thought we would walk, but we drove down the lane in his car. We got out, and carefully entered a cornfield. The corn was just about to my knees, so the stone should have been in plain sight. I asked if the man who owned this field would mind, and the farmer said no, the fellow never came near it, he hired somebody else to work it for him.

"He's a fellow that has a thousand acres in corn in Huron County alone."

I said that a farmer was just like a businessman nowadays, wasn't he? The farmer seemed pleased that I had said this and began to explain why it was so. Risks had to be undertaken. Expenses were sky-high. I asked him if he had one of those tractors with the air-conditioned cabs and he said yes, he had. If you did well, he said, the rewards, the financial rewards, could be considerable, but there were trials and tribulations most people didn't know a thing about. Next spring, if all went well, he and his wife were going on their first holiday. They were going to Spain. The children wanted them to forget their holiday and put in a swimming pool, but his idea was to travel. He owned two farms now and was thinking of buying a third. He was just sitting working out some figures when I knocked on the door. In a way, he couldn't afford to buy it. In another way, he couldn't afford not to.

While carrying on this conversation we were walking up and down the corn rows looking for the stone. We looked in the corners of the field and it was not there. He said that of course the corner of a field then was not necessarily the corner of a field now. But the truth probably was that when the field got put in corn the stone was in the way, so they would have hauled it out. He said we could go over to the rock-pile near the road and see if we recognized it.

I said we wouldn't bother, I wasn't so sure I would know it, on a rock-pile.

"Me either," he said. He sounded disappointed. I wondered what he had expected to see, or feel.

I wondered the same thing about myself.

If I had been younger, I would have figured out a story. I would have insisted on Mr. Black's being in love with one of my aunts, and on one of them—not necessarily the one he was in love with—being in love with him. I would have wished him to confide in them, in one of them, his secret, his reason for living in a shack in Huron County, far from home. Later, I might have believed that he wanted to, but hadn't confided this, or his love either. I would have made a horrible, plausible connection between that silence of his, and the manner of his death. Now I no longer believe that people's secrets are defined and communicable, or their feelings full-blown and easy to recognize. I don't believe so. Now, I can only say, my father's sisters scrubbed the floor with lye, they stooked the oats and milked the cows by hand. They must have taken a quilt to the barn for the hermit to die on, they must have let water dribble from a tin cup into his afflicted mouth. That was their life. My mother's cousins behaved in another way; they dressed up and took pictures of each other; they sallied forth. However they behaved they are all dead. I carry something of them around in me. But the boulder is gone, Mount Hebron is cut down for gravel, and the life buried here is one you have to think twice about regretting.

Ann Copeland

(b. 1932)

ANN COPELAND TEACHES AT MOUNT ALLISON UNIVERSITY IN SACKVILLE, N.B. In *Fiddlehead* magazine, in 1982, in an introduction to her story, "Fame," she is quoted as finding that her sense of not being rooted in place "runs counter to much of what I see around me here"; perhaps as a consequence, she adds, "I place a...premium on searching out the most valuable continuities in my life and sustaining them. I suspect that may be behind much of my fiction...." The various oppositions between tradition and discontinuity inform much of the conflict in "The Bear's Paw"; a kind of reverse-Sam Slick story, it tells of the foreignness of what seems like a familiar culture, and of the disappointment and irritation that result alike when an outsider fails to respond appropriately to an insider's codes.

Familiar with the life of a Catholic convent, Copeland examined the nature of separateness and confinement in the stories of her first collection *At Peace* (1978); her second book, *The Back Room* (1979)—from which "The Bear's Paw" is taken—is a more disparate collection, focussing primarily on the secular world. *Earthen Vessels* appeared in 1984. Connecticut-born, and educated at the Catholic University of America (M.A. 1959) and Cornell University (Ph.D. 1971), the author has lived in a number of U.S. states, from Vermont to Idaho and Oregon. She now lives with her husband (Allan Furtwangler) and family near the Tantramar Marsh. "Ann Copeland" is a nom-de-plume.

For Further Reading

ANDREAS SCHROEDER, "Highjinks & Power," *Canadian Literature* 85 (Summer 1980): 144–48.

KATHLEEN TUDOR, Review of *The Back Room*, *Fiddlehead* 122 (Summer 1979): 140–42.

The Bear's Paw

From the beginning I had the feeling Honey might blow it, with her nose for a bargain and her hunger to win. She *is* shrewd though, and I've often under-estimated her before. So, despite my doubts, I took her along to see Minnie. I'd already placed my bet on who would win.

The day was bleak in a way that spells Maritime non-spring to me. Slate sky, nipping marsh wind, a chill to eat the heart out of any foolhardy crocus. Of these there were none, though we'd left plenty behind in Connecticut. Just miles and miles of evergreens here saving the landscape from total desolateness; and just as many miles of stripped maples, dead grey, and grey dead snow chunking and rutting here and there. Too cold to melt. Spring thaw is a joke here: it comes in May. *Late* May.

The road was even nastier than its border. Sprinkled with pot-holes—not slight bumps but deep wide holes that throttled the car and us inside, shaking our guts.

"Good God, Marion! This isn't what those gorgeous brochures promised! All those sailboats skimming along on blue ocean! Fresh lobster cheap. Charming rural countryside. Who'd want to live here? Don't they know win-ter's over?"

"No such thing as spring here, Honey. I warned you. They move right into summer. A gorgeous summer, too. No humidity. While we're boiling in Westchester barely able to drag ourselves around, they're enjoying clear fresh sunny weather here."

"I'll believe that when I see it, if I ever do. But this whole scene strikes me as the last word in dismal. What do they *do* here? Broken-down houses, col-lapsing barns. My God, it looks poor!"

She stared at rows of small pastel-coloured houses as we pulled into the village. Then she ground out her cigarette and pulled tight the lapels of her London Fog.

"Should've told me I needed my fur coat!"

"Hold on, Honey. We'll be back in civilization tomorrow. Do you really want to see Minnie or not? I wrote we *might* come, but it's easy enough to write again from the other end in a few days and say I'm sorry we didn't make it. What do you say?"

"Oh sure, sure." She turned toward me with that swift shift of mood that can devastate her customers. "I'd kick myself if I had this chance for a bargain and passed it up. You know that!"

Her father was a pawnbroker. She specializes in tag sales. Doesn't sound

From *The Back Room* (Ottawa: Oberon Press, 1979). Reprinted by permission of Oberon Press.

like much but she's made a bundle and continues to. One man's trash is another man's treasure. In her case that's true. She can sniff out a bargain miles away. If you could watch her scan the local *Bargain News* you'd see what I mean. A real pro. All business. If you need space, she'll rent you a place for your sale. If you've leftovers that didn't go, she'll buy them. She spends her Saturdays travelling around from neighbourhood to neighbourhood in Westchester County dickering, snapping up bargains. Fascinating to watch. She'll approach a housewife who has cleaned out her attic and inquire innocently about an item. Then she'll explain she's really shopping for a friend and offer a sum substantially below the price. She'll hang around long enough to size up the competition, go around the corner and call on the phone to say she's just talked her friend into going a dollar or two higher. In the end she gets her item, usually without making an enemy. Later—resells it for twice the price. She knows her goods. It seemed pointless to remind her we were light-years away from New York, in every sense. After all, she's been driving through that landscape with me for two days. So—on to Minnie's.

Her house is unobtrusive; grey clapboard with a small evergreen on either side of the cement steps leading up to the enclosed front porch. As we turned down Everett Street I saw the light on the porch and knew she'd be sitting there, sewing. Planning. Dreaming up designs. I honoured a twinge at the sight of that light: two summers since I'd seen Minnie. The usual Christmas cards, the occasional note. When I'd written that we would be coming through off season and might stop, I was prodded into it by Honey.

"Where did you *ever* find it, Marion?" she raved at the sight of the quilt Minnie sent my daughter Cathy for her birthday. The scent of a bargain was in the air. She knew I'd never pay the Bergdoff price—up to $500 these days.

"An old friend of ours, Honey. An ancient lady who lives in Nova Scotia. She spends her time quilting...does all her own work. Cathy fell in love with Minnie's quilts years ago. And this arrived for her fifteenth birthday."

"Well, what're we waiting for? *Let's go to Nova Scotia!*" Said in jest then but remembered later when the chance came to do just that. So here we were.

I hadn't minded having her along. Honey's good company. But we both knew that underneath all her good humour there was the hope of a kill. If she could snare one of these patchwork wonders for, say $50, she'd carry it back to Westchester crowing. To say nothing of what she'd do if she could work out some steady arrangement. I could feel her wheels turning.

One ding-a-ling of the bell and the chair inside squeaked. She was there. Predictably.

"Damn weather!" groaned Honey as she stamped her feet on the porch to warm her toes. "Perfect weather for quilts!"

The plastic curtain behind the door-window moved slightly. Then the latch jiggled.

I always forget just how tiny Minnie is until I am confronted by that frail body and have to look down into those deep-set grey eyes and wispy hair.

"Marion! Come in, come in!"

The fingers that grasped my arm were strong and urgent, drawing me in from the cold. With a quick eye toward Honey she indicated the door was to be shut tight.

"How *are* you, Marion! I've been hoping you'd get here. Sit down, sit down." She glanced about apologetically. Her porch was, as always, a mess. No chairs cleared, the card-table beside her chair heaped with tiny squares of coloured cloth, papers, magazines, needles, thread, scissors. "You'll have to clear a spot, I'm afraid. But take off your coats, sit down, sit down."

Honey was pulling off her pigskins finger by finger, bargain antennae already quivering.

"I've brought a friend who came up with me for the company, Minnie. We've checked out the damage at the cottage and are on our way back home, but she didn't want to pass up the chance to meet you." Beware, Minnie. "This is Honey Sterling."

"How do you do, Minnie? I've heard *so much* abut you from Marion."

Her best meet-the-potential-client manner. Not purely insincere mind you, just shrewdly calculated beneath a layer of real charm.

Minnie was easing back into her chair now, counting on us to clear our spaces, hang coats on the corner coat-tree, find a spot to sit and talk. While she got on with her work.

I could remember that from before. From always. Sit and talk. In such a formula rested the most agreeable way of passing the time for Minnie. Sit and talk. That meant sitting there while she sorted her pieces, snipped expertly, stitched a bit—working steadily away on one of the quilt-tops she always had going. *You* sat and talked. She sat and talked and worked. As if needle and thread, colour and design could catch the passing moment and fix it in place forever. One felt the possibility of timelessness on Minnie's porch: the tiny bent figure shaping her design, intent, while you sat there and chatted companionably in the pool of sunny warmth and clutter, wondering, perhaps, what sleeping body that quilt would warm long after Minnie's thread had been snipped.

She worked with unflagging enthusiasm—not so much for what she had just produced (though she loved appreciation and wanted to show her work) as for the pattern she'd begun to dream about: Daisy, Tulip, Ship of Dreams, Grandmother's Garden. Some new design was always working inside her age-ing head, pushing toward life through fingers that had knotted and swollen but refused yet to stop. You sensed a controlled urgency behind Minnie's steady output: when the needle stopped, she would.

"How did you find the cottage, Marion? Was the damage really that bad?"

"Not as bad as Jack made out in his note, Minnie." Jack is the fisherman who lives there year round and watches out for the place till we get up there summers. Honey was eyeing the bright pieces of cotton. Revving up for the kill. "But there was no way to be sure except to drive up and see. Luckily Honey could come along. Bill couldn't manage any time off and we didn't want to let it go any longer."

"And you, Mrs. Sterling." Minnie had picked up her needle, was threading it as she spoke, then let her hand rest a moment on the blue-and-white print housedress that covered her shallow lap. I couldn't imagine thighs under there:

just bones. She seemed to have shrunk even since I'd last seen her. "How do you like our spring?"

I watched Honey mentally select the suitable response. Medium: not too harsh. Negative enough to honour the obvious; positive enough not to insult anyone locked into this world.

"Well, to tell the truth Minnie—do you mind if I call you Minnie, for I've always heard of you that way, you know—it's a bit cold for my tastes!" She glanced about. "You certainly seem to have a few projects going here!"

The offensive was on.

Minnie stalks her prey, too. But not in any way Honey would recognize.

"Well, now, Marion may have told you this is what keeps me going." Minnie reached a knotted hand toward a pile of white squares with designs appliquéed on each piece. She tucked her needle in a pincushion and started to go through the patterns. "I'll show you what I'm working on now, if I can find the sample...let's see...Double Irish Chain, Drunkard's Patch, Nine Patch...."

As she leafed through the old patterns murmuring the litany of titles, that other world we'd so recently left—the world of monogramed bath towels, designer clothes, decorator décor and manicured lawns—seemed to fade like a suggestion of spring on the April marsh. We were back in maritime Canada, all right, O Canada—land of summer vistas and winter withdrawal. The only maple leaves around in this season were red on white, flying over the post office and the elementary school.

What did Honey feel sitting there in her red wool slacks and calfskin boots soaking up the warmth before we headed out again? Her diamonds gleamed in the sun.

"Here it is! The Bear's Paw!" She pulled forth a yellowing square of cotton on which a design was appliquéed: four tiny triangles for a claw, one square for the centre. "This is old. My mother's work." She held the pattern over for each of us to examine: yellow centre, soft purple (*mauve* she called it) claws. "I'm working on one of these right now, in prints. Almost all the squares are done."

I knew what Honey would think of these colours. Dull. Too pale. Faded. *They just didn't go, Marion. Whoever heard of yellow and—what did she call it?—mauve.* No *life!* Honey has that way about her. Very dismissive.

"But do you have any that are *finished,* Minnie?" Then, an afterthought. "This *is* lovely, of course."

You goofed, Honey. Royally. Time, friend. It takes time.

Minnie's sharp eyes stared at her for the shade of an instant before she turned back to me.

"And will you be back up this summer, Marion?"

Honey seemed oblivious. No telling. She's good at disguises. She'd picked up a pile of finished squares and was flipping through them, examining colours.

"Late July, it looks like. Eddie is off to camp but Cathy still can't imagine doing anything else with her summers except coming up here. She was thrilled with the quilt you sent. Minnie. She'd always wanted to ask you for one but was too shy."

"Good, I'm glad she likes it. Thought she would."

Unemphatic, but pleased. She had heard from Cathy, I knew. Cathy had joined in the annual visit to Minnie Glover's house ever since our accidental meeting ten years ago at the United Church Summer Bazaar where she sat quietly by her display of quilts and quilt-tops. Something in the quality of her dedication to her craft arrested me. Her prices even then were ridiculously low—if you could ever get her to quote a price. But I felt it then, and on each return visit since then: this whole business was a matter of heart with her. Nothing could induce her to part with one of these treasures unless she saw it would be valued. And that had little to do with dollars and cents. On the other hand, it might have everything to do with it. You could insult her if you offered too little. She knew the amount of time and labour that went into every quilt. A tricky woman to do business with.

I once watched her parry an eager-beaver from Ontario.

TOURIST: "Your work is *love-ly!* And such *de-tail!* Such colour!"
MINNIE: "Thank you. I'm glad you like it." Continuing to stitch.
TOURIST: "I would just love to bring home one of these to show my friends. They'd all be so jealous! You say you've been doing this for years?" Trying not to sound patronizing.
MINNIE: "About 70. My mother—"
TOURIST: "And can you tell me any of the prices? I don't see any marked...."
MINNIE: "Well now, that depends...."

And so it went on and on. The tourist eventually left without her quilt, having offered too little in every sense. Later on Minnie donated it to the Dominion Day Raffle.

Far be it from me to catechize Honey on the perils of bargaining.

Minnie was watching Honey.

"Would you have any *completed* quilt-tops or quilts for sale, Minnie? I just *love* them!"

What made her voice sound a trifle too eager, her crimson nails a shade too bright?

"A few," said Minnie hesitantly, as if wondering whether to drag them out. This was, I knew, just so much manner. They were ready, all of them, stacked neatly in the corner. She was just waiting to be asked.

"Would you show them to us?' Honey leaned forward ingratiatingly.

One point for you, Honey.

"I'll help you, Minnie." I forestalled her, got to the corner first, lifted the plastic garbage-bag and the carton beneath and carried them into the small living-room. "We can spread them out in here." How many times had Cathy and I been through this ritual!

Minnie moved her fragile bones into the living-room and Honey followed, settling herself quickly in the vinyl chair beside the upright—taking in, no doubt, the dog-earned hymn-book propped on the piano.

Minnie lowered herself onto the chesterfield, a long low affair with prickly upholstery and a granny Afghan folded over the back.

I set the bag and carton near her.

"If you'd like to see this—it's my Lovers' Knot," she said, grasping the other two ends while I spread it out on the floor. "My mother's variation on the pattern." Assuming we'd know the original, "I still have all her patterns. They're old, very old. Mother quilted from the time she was a little girl, as I did, and I'm 84, so..." Unhurrying.

"Perfectly lovely," murmured Honey in a tone I knew so well. She looked back toward the stack expectantly. Then she picked up one corner of the quilt before her to examine the stitching closely. "A real find! I like the design ever so much... but I might rather have an original. And I'm not partial to pink, really."

Minnie seemed not to hear. She was already pulling out another to spread over the Lovers' Knot.

"Dresden Plate," she explained.

It lay softly resplendent before us: plates delicately patterned in green, yellow and maroon paisley and spread in seven even rows, each plate a swirl of colour outlined in black feather-stitching.

"Gorgeous colours in this one," said Honey approvingly. "The turquoise is a bit sharp in the centre, but still it is lovely. Is the feather-stitching your own?"

Minnie caught her breath. No reply.

Strike two.

"This one, you see," she stared down at the quilt—"is for my grandchild." She has no grandchild. Her only child died at two. Her husband passed out of the picture long before we ever met her. "She's little now and this doesn't mean too much. But later...it may."

She started to refold it with me.

"And what will you do with it in the meantime?" asked Honey curiously.

"Hide it for the day," replied Minnie evenly. "And do you have any children?"

"None of my own, Minnie. But a dear little niece who right now has a Bloomingdale's quilt on her bed. I'd like to bring her a real handmade one."

One after another the wonders were displayed: two patchworks, one Aunt Lizzie's Star, one Drunkard's Path, one Maltese Cross. She explained the patterns to us in a way that assumed we already knew them and wanted only to hear it all again. I'd noticed that before about Minnie, about other Maritimers of her vintage: the assumption that things had always been like this, would always be like this. They had a way of making the world beyond the limits of their established habits a mirage, a fantasy. The Christmas ornaments were still around Minnie's small living-room. She was like the village itself: Christmas decorations up until late May, when summer at last became a sure bet.

"Do you know the work of the Mountain Artisans, Minnie?" asked Honey as we folded the Drunkard's Path away.

Minnie looked up inquiringly.

"Very beautiful," said Honey. "Their colours tend to be a bit brighter, but that" she conceded thoughtfully, "is a matter of taste, of course. My little niece Deirdre's quilt is a copy of their work."

No mention of the price they command on Madison Avenue.

"Would you care to see the one I'm working on now?"

Honey was beginning to simmer. How she loathes delay, being put off! There comes a moment when you can almost see her gathering her energies for the kill.

"Are you working on it right now, you mean?"

Stalling. Translate: what use is it to me? You're winding up for a strike, Honey.

"We'd love to, Minnie." This much I could do for Honey's cause....

"The Bear's Paw," said Minnie as she slowly pulled herself to the sun-porch and came back carrying a small pile of squares. Honey and I hastily folded away the riot of colour that had piled up on the floor. "I showed you the original pattern before.... My but cotton's gone sky-high here." She settled back down on the chesterfield. "Is it that way in the States? It's over a dollar a yard here now. Almost up to two. I can remember when we used to pay 38¢ a yard, years ago. And it gets harder and harder to find it with no stuffing. It's a good thing I've lots of leftovers, enough to keep me going a good long time." She waved toward the sun-porch with its clutter.

Honey's foot was tapping lightly. I could feel her longing for a cigarette.

"Now, Minnie, I really would like to buy one of your *completed* quilts. Can you tell me what you charge?"

Strike-out?

Minnie was bent over laying four squares on the floor.

"I've never done one in prints before," she said as she set down the finished paws, one by one. "When they're arranged like this we call it a block. I've completed enough for all but three blocks. Can't decide on the colour of the sashing. Guess I'll be able to tell when I spread them all out complete."

Honey was stifling a yawn.

"Here, I'll show you another block."

Was Minnie beginning to enjoy herself? What possessed her, I wondered frantically, as we bent down to spread out more blocks and stare at the possibilities of the Bear's Paw. I could feel Honey's eyes wandering back to the pile of folded quilts, trying still, no doubt, to size up her options. Plotting her next move.

"It'll be lovely," she breathed, leaning forward to do her duty by the design spread out on the floor, trying to suppress her irritation. "You never seem to run out of ideas, Minnie. Now could you give us a price on one of your quilts? Or even a quilt-top? I do have a superb seamstress back in Rowayton and I'm sure she could quilt it for me, if need be."

I've never been able to figure out exactly why the efficient approach doesn't work here. It's as if the more oil you apply to the machinery of getting business done, the more you gum up the works. It can be maddening in the extreme. My sympathies had begun to shift a bit. I could feel sorry for Honey now. *Don't say another word,* I thought. *You'll be sorry. You can't hurry them.*

"It would depend," said Minnie inscrutably, deliberately. "The bats are up to $5 now. It seems incredible to me. We used to get them for under a dollar." She smiled pleasantly.

"Yes, yes," said Honey half-attentively. I could almost feel the dryness in

her mouth. "Well, Minnie, what would the whole thing, one whole quilt put together say, be worth?"

Minnie looked at her steadily, holding between her swollen thumbs the
pieces of the Bear's Paw.

"Then too," she continued imperturbably and politely, "I try to get my quilting thread on sale but don't always succeed. Generally when she sees it on
sale at the 1¢ store my neighbour will bring some in."

3.45 PM. I'd promised Honey we'd be over the border before nightfall.
Unlikely. Things always took longer around here than you expected. A world
out of time.

"Was there one you were particularly interested in?" She looked directly at
Honey.

"I'd really settle for any one," Honey answered—lamely, I thought. Perhaps
she was beginning to suspect. "I suppose if I had my pick it would be the
Dresden Plate even though that's not exactly my shade of blue. But I know
that one's out. The Maltese Cross is interesting, too...but how about the
Drunkard's Path?"

The quilts were all folded up now and stacked back in the carton and
garbage-bag. In my own mind they had blurred into a composite thing of
beauty—soft, faded, sadly beautiful somehow. How could Honey possibly remember one from the other?

She was standing up, gripping her tooled-leather shoulder bag purpose-
fully, shifting her weight.

"The Drunkard's Path," repeated Minnie thoughtfully, looking up at her. "I
like that one, too. Would you want to see it again?"

"No, no!" almost groaned Honey, straining to sound polite. She lit a cigarette.

"It's an interesting quilt. I'm glad you like it. The local Kinsmen's Club
wants it for their Dominion Day Raffle. I still don't know if I'll part with it." She
looked faintly embarrassed.

"Well then," said Honey as she looked about hopelessly for an ashtray, then
tried to look casual as Minnie handed one up to her, "I can't take the Lover's
Knot. It wouldn't go in her bedroom. Patchworks can be found at home in
good imitation. Your Aunt Lizzie's Star I like a lot but you say it's for a niece."

Quickly she crushed out the cigarette and began pulling on her gloves.

Inscrutable Minnie. Was she hurt? Triumphant? Disappointed? That she
could use the money I was certain.

We managed to get ourselves quickly out to the sun-porch. I kissed her
good-bye.

"It's too bad, really. I've done less this winter than I'd planned," said she
apologetically as she opened the front door to a blast of cold. "But I'm always
planning ahead."

We'll stop for a drink, I thought. O Lord, where?

"Perhaps you could come back at the end of the summer," she went on,
seemingly unaware of the draught. "Or Marion could come back for you."

We knew it was courtesy. Old-world courtesy. With an edge. In the depths
of the old lady's eyes I seemed to catch a gleam that said she knew she'd won.

"If you come back in late summer," she said, "the Bear's Paw should be finished.... And good luck on your way home now. The prediction's pretty good for tonight, I believe." She surveyed the sky with knowing eyes. Honey was shivering. "But there are storm-warnings out for tomorrow. So be careful."

Tomorrow.

Already the forsythia was gleaming golden on the Henry Hudson Parkway. Back to that. Dogwood soon. The sky might be grey but there would be some sure sign of spring down there. None, absolutely none here.

The small figure stood watching from behind her storm-door until our car finally gasped to a start and jerked away.

"Good God!" snapped Honey. "Why didn't you warn me? It was like trying to do business with a sphinx. Let's get out of here! All that endless stuff about the price of cotton, bats, quilting thread! Who cares? How can you do business that way? It was hopeless. If the money meant so damn much to her why didn't she set me a good stiff price? Instead, we were to sit around watching every goddamn bear's paw being pieced, assembled and blended! I could feel it about to happen! Doesn't she have any sense of the value of time?"

A tiny yellow flame licked up from her lighter to meet the impatient cigarette. I turned on the heater.

Ahead of us the horizon was purple-blue shading into turquoise. Beyond that, a faint bank of pink faded off into grey, dead blank grey, the grey of winter enduring, distant summer buried far beneath the other side of that pale border.

Not even a mirage as yet.

Only a dream.

Rudy Wiebe

(b. 1934)

RUDY WIEBE WAS BORN ON THE FAMILY FARM—to parents who had emigrated from the Soviet Union in 1930—in a Mennonite community near Fairholme, Saskatchewan. Educated at the University of Alberta and at Tübingen, Germany, he has taught at the Mennonite Brethren Bible College and at Goshen College, and until he retired he taught creative writing at the University of Alberta. In their compulsion to explore the sources of moral behaviour, his stories (*Where Is the Voice Coming From?*, 1974; *The Angel of the Tar Sands and Other Stories*, 1982) and several novels all draw on his Mennonite commitment to both independence and community. *Peace Shall Destroy Many* (1962) most directly portrays Mennonite life; with more structural and linguistic complexity, *The Blue Mountains of China* (1970) traces the history of Mennonite wanderings during the 20th century and the recurrent tensions between visionary quest and social integration. Wiebe's fascination with the power of belief and the dimensions of private choice have also taken him into oral history and into an attempt to adapt the art of oral narrative to the telling of a novel, as in *The Temptations of Big Bear* (1973). In his more recent writing—e.g., *A Discovery of Strangers* (1994, a novel) and *Playing Dead: A Contemplation Concerning the Arctic* (1989)—he has further enquired into the mysteries of "knowledge," focussing in particular on the Arctic voyages of Sir John Franklin, and drawing on his own personal experience of the North.

This version of "Where Is the Voice Coming From?" is taken from *The Angel of the Tar Sands* (it first appeared, in slightly different form, in a 1971 anthology, *Fourteen Stories High*, eds. David Helwig and Tom Marshall). The story also draws on this distinction between the life of speech and art and the sterility of fact and record. Technically, it contrasts passive voice with active voice, as a way of contrasting historical artifact and documentary with art, belief, and vision. Given facts, we discover logical contradictions, Wiebe writes; if art and belief have the power to transcend them, how does this happen, and why? His story at once enacts the distinction and steps back from it, in order to invite the reader to reflect on the limits of fact and illusion, and on the fundamental difficulties of cross-cultural comprehension.

For Further Reading

DONALD CAMERON, *Conversations with Canadian Novelists*, vol. 2 (Toronto: Macmillan, 1973) 146–60.

W.J. KEITH, *Epic Fiction: The Art of Rudy Wiebe* (Edmonton: U Alberta P, 1981).

————, ed., *A Voice in the Land* (Edmonton: NeWest, 1981).

PENNY VAN TOORN, *Rudy Wiebe and the Historicity of the Word* (Edmonton: U Alberta P, 1995).

RUDY WIEBE, "Introduction" to *The Story-Makers* (Toronto: Macmillan, 1970) ix-xxx.

Where Is the Voice Coming From?

The problem is to make the story.

One difficulty of this making may have been excellently stated by Teilhard de Chardin: "We are continually inclined to isolate ourselves from the things and events which surround us...as though we were spectators, not elements, in what goes on." Arnold Toynbee does venture, "For all that we know, Reality is the undifferentiated unity of the mystical experience," but that need not here be considered. This story ended long ago; it is one of finite acts, of orders, or elemental feelings and reactions, of obvious legal restrictions and requirements.

Presumably all the parts of the story are themselves available. A difficulty is that they are, as always, available only in bits and pieces. Though the acts themselves seem quite clear, some written reports of the acts contradict each other. As if these acts were, at one time, too well-known; as if the original nodule of each particular fact had from somewhere received non-factual accretions; or even more, as if, since the basic facts were so clear perhaps there were a larger number of facts than any one reporter, or several, or even any reporter had ever attempted to record. About facts that are simply told by this mouth to that ear, of course, even less can be expected.

An affair seventy-five years old should acquire some of the shiny transparency of an old man's skin. It should.

Sometimes it would seem that it would be enough—perhaps more than enough—to hear the names only. The grandfather One Arrow; the mother Spotted Calf; the father Sounding Sky; the wife (wives rather, but only one of them seems to have a name, though their fathers are Napaise, Kapahoo, Old Dust, The Rump)—the one wife named, of all things, Pale Face; the cousin Going-Up-To-Sky; the brother-in-law (again, of all things) Dublin. The names of the police sound very much alike; they all begin with Constable or Corporal or Sergeant, but here and there an Inspector, then a Superintendent and eventually all the resonance of an Assistant Commissioner echoes down. More, Herself: Victoria, by the Grace of God etc., etc., QUEEN, defender of the Faith, etc., etc.; and witness "Our Right Trusty and Right Well-Beloved Cousin and Councillor the Right Honorable Sir John Campbell Hamilton-Gordon, Earl of Aberdeen; Viscount Formartine, Baron Haddo, Methlic, Tarves and Kellie in the Peerage of Scotland; Viscount Gordon of Aberdeen, County of Aberdeen in the Peerage of the United Kingdom; Baronet of Nova Scotia, Knight Grand Cross of Our Most Distinguished Order of Saint Michael and Saint George, etc., Governor General of Canada." And of course himself: in the award proclamation named "Jean-Baptiste" but otherwise known only as Almighty Voice.

From *The Angel of the Tar Sands and Other Stories* (Toronto: McClelland and Stewart, 1982). Reprinted by permission of the author.

But hearing cannot be enough; not even hearing all the thunder of A Proclamation: "Now Hear Ye that a reward of FIVE HUNDRED DOLLARS will be paid to any person or persons who will give such information as will lead... (etc. etc.) this Twentieth day of April, in the year of Our Lord one thousand eight hundred and ninety-six, and the Fifty-ninth year of Our Reign..." etc. and etc.

Such hearing cannot be enough. The first item to be seen is the piece of white bone. It is almost triangular, slightly convex—concave actually as it is positioned at this moment with its corners slightly raised—graduating from perhaps a strong eighth to a weak quarter of an inch in thickness, its scattered pore structure varying between larger and smaller on its perhaps polished, certainly shiny surface. Precision is difficult since the glass showcase is at least thirteen inches deep and therefore an eye cannot be brought as close as the minute inspection of such a small, though certainly quite adequate, sample of skull would normally require. Also, because of the position it cannot be determined whether the several hairs, well over a foot long, are still in some manner attached to it or not.

The seven-pounder cannon can be seen standing almost shyly between the showcase and the interior wall. Officially it is known as a gun, not a cannon, and clearly its bore is not large enough to admit a large man's fist. Even if it can be believed that this gun was used in the 1885 Rebellion and that on the evening of Saturday, May 29, 1897 (while the nine-pounder, now unidentified, was in the process of arriving with the police on the special train from Regina), seven shells (all that were available in Prince Albert at that time) from it were sent shrieking into the poplar bluffs as night fell, clearly such shelling could not and would not disembowel the whole earth. Its carriage is now nicely lacquered, the perhaps oak spokes of its petite wheels (little higher than a knee) have been recently scraped, puttied and varnished; the brilliant burnish of its brass breeching testifies with what meticulous care charmen and women have used nationally advertised cleaners and restorers.

Though it can also be seen, even a careless glance reveals that the same concern has not been expended on the one (of two) .44 calibre 1866 model Winchesters apparently found at the last in the pit with Almighty Voice. It is also preserved in a glass case; the number 1536735 is still, though barely, distinguishable on the brass cartridge section just below the brass saddle ring. However, perhaps because the case was imperfectly sealed at one time (though sealed enough not to warrant disturbance now), or because of simple neglect, the rifle is obviously spotted here and there with blotches of rust and the brass itself reveals discolorations almost like mildew. The rifle bore, the three long strands of hair themselves, actually bristle with clots of dust. It may be that this museum cannot afford to be as concerned as the other; conversely, the disfiguration may be something inherent in the items themselves.

The small building which was the police guardroom at Duck Lake, Saskatchewan Territory, in 1895 may also be seen. It had subsequently been moved from its original place and used to house small animals, chickens perhaps, or pigs—such as a woman might be expected to have under her responsibility. It is, of course, now perfectly empty, and clean so that the public may enter with no more discomfort than a bend under the doorway and a heavy encounter with disinfectant. The door-jamb has obviously been replaced; the bar network at one window is, however, said to be original; smooth still, very smooth. The logs inside have been smeared again and again with whitewash, perhaps paint, to an insistent point of identity-defying characterlessness. Within the small rectangular box of these logs not a sound can be heard from the streets of the, probably dead, town.

> *Hey Injun you'll get hung*
> *for stealing that steer*
> *Hey Injun for killing that government cow you'll get three weeks on the woodpile*
> *Hey Injun*

The place named Kinistino seems to have disappeared from the map but the Minnechinass Hills have not. Whether they have ever been on a map is doubtful but they will, of course, not disappear from the landscape as long as the grass grows and the rivers run. Contrary to general report and belief, the Canadian prairies are rarely, if ever, flat and the Minnechinass (spelled five different ways and translated sometimes as "The Outside Hill," sometimes as "Beautiful Bare Hills") are dissimilar from any other of the numberless hills that everywhere block out the prairie horizon. They are bare; poplars lie tattered along their tops, almost black against the straw-pale grass and sharp green against the grey soil of the plowing laid in half-mile rectangular blocks upon their western slopes. Poles holding various wires stick out of the fields, back down the bend of the valley; what was once a farmhouse is weathering into the cultivated earth. The poplar bluff where Almighty Voice made his stand has, of course, disappeared.

The policemen he shot and killed (not the ones he wounded, of course) are easily located. Six miles east, thirty-nine miles north in Prince Albert, the English Cemetery. Sergeant Colin Campbell Colebrook, North West Mounted Police Registration Number 605, lies presumably under a gravestone there. His name is seventeenth in a very long "list of non-commissioned officers and men who have died in the service since the inception of the force." The date is October 29, 1895, and the cause of death is anonymous: "Shot by escaping Indian prisoner near Prince Albert." At the foot of this grave are two others: Constable John R. Kerr, No. 3040, and Corporal C. H. S. Hockin, No. 3106. Their cause of death on May 28, 1897 is even more anonymous, but the place is relatively precise: "Shot by Indians at Min-etch-inass Hills, Prince Albert District."

The gravestone, if he has one, of the fourth man Almighty Voice killed is more difficult to locate. Mr. Ernest Grundy, postmaster at Duck Lake in 1897, apparently shut his window the afternoon of Friday, May 28, armed himself, rode east twenty miles, participated in the second charge into the bluff at about 6:30 p.m., and on the third sweep of that charge was shot dead at the edge of the pit. It would seem that he thereby contributed substantially not only to the Indians' bullet supply, but his clothing warmed them as well.

The burial place of Dublin and Going-Up-To-Sky is unknown, as is the grave of Almighty Voice. It is said that a Métis named Henry Smith lifted the latter's body from the pit in the bluff and gave it to Spotted Calf. The place of burial is not, of course, of ultimate significance. A gravestone is always less evidence than a triangular piece of skull, provided it is large enough.

Whatever further evidence there is to be gathered may rest on pictures. There are, presumably, almost numberless pictures of the policemen in the case, but the only one with direct bearing is one of Sergeant Colebrook who apparently insisted on advancing to complete an arrest after being warned three times that if he took another step he would be shot. The picture must have been taken before he joined the force; it reveals him a large-eared young man, hair brush-cut and ascot tie, his eyelids slightly drooping, almost hooded under thick brows. Unfortunately a picture of Constable R. C. Dickson, into whose charge Almighty Voice was apparently committed in that guardroom and who after Colebrook's death was convicted of negligence, sentenced to two months hard labour and discharged, does not seem to be available.

There are no pictures to be found of either Dublin (killed early by rifle fire) or Going-Up-To-Sky (killed in the pit), the two teen-age boys who gave their ultimate fealty to Almighty Voice. There is, however, one said to be of Almighty Voice, Junior. He may have been born to Pale Face during the year, two hundred and twenty-one days that his father was a fugitive. In the picture he is kneeling before what could be a tent, he wears striped denim overalls and displays twin babies whose sex cannot be determined from the double-laced dark bonnets they wear. In the supposed picture of Spotted Calf and Sounding Sky, Sounding Sky stands slightly before his wife; he wears a white shirt and a striped blanket folded over his left shoulder in such a manner that the arm in which he cradles a long rifle cannot be seen. His head is thrown back; the rim of his hat appears as a black half-moon above eyes that are pressed shut in, as it were, profound concentration; above a mouth clenched thin in a downward curve. Spotted Calf wears a long dress, a sweater which could also be a man's dress coat, and a large fringed and embroidered shawl which would appear distinctly Dukhobor in origin if the scroll patterns on it were more irregular. Her head is small and turned slightly towards her husband so as to reveal her right ear. There is what can only be called a quizzical expression on her crumpled face; it may be she does not understand what is happening and that she would have asked a question, perhaps of her husband, perhaps of the photographers, perhaps even of anyone, anywhere in the world if such questioning were possible for an Indian woman.

There is one final picture. That is one of Almighty Voice himself. At least it is purported to be of Almighty Voice himself. In the Royal Canadian Mounted Police Museum on the Barracks Grounds just off Dewdney Avenue in Regina, Saskatchewan, it lies in the same showcase, as a matter of fact immediately beside that triangular piece of skull. Both are unequivocally labelled, and it must be assumed that a police force with a world-wide reputation would not label *such* evidence incorrectly. But here emerges an ultimate problem in making the story.

There are two official descriptions of Almighty Voice. The first reads: "Height about five feet, ten inches, slight build, rather good looking, a sharp hooked nose with a remarkably flat point. Has a bullet scar on the left side of his face about $1^1/2$ inches long running from near corner of mouth towards ear. The scar cannot be noticed when his face is painted but otherwise is plain. Skin fair for an Indian." The second description is on the Award Proclamation: "About twenty-two years old, five feet ten inches in height, weight about eleven stone, slightly erect, neat small feet and hands; complexion inclined to be fair, wavey dark hair to shoulders, large dark eyes, broad forehead, sharp features and parrot nose with flat tip, scar on left cheek running from mouth towards ear, feminine appearance."

So run the descriptions that were, presumably, to identify a well-known fugitive in so precise a manner that an informant could collect five hundred dollars—a considerable sum when a police constable earned between one and two dollars a day. The nexus of the problems appears when these supposed official descriptions are compared to the supposed official picture. The man in the picture is standing on a small rug. The fingers on his left hand touch a curved Victorian settee, behind him a photographer's backdrop of scrolled patterns merges to vaguely paradisiacal trees and perhaps a sky. The moccasins he wears make it impossible to deduce whether his feet are "neat small." He may be five feet, ten inches tall, may weigh eleven stone, he certainly is "rather good looking" and, though it is a frontal view, it may be that the point of his long and flaring nose could be "remarkably flat." The photograph is slightly over-illuminated and so the unpainted complexion could be "inclined to be fair"; however, nothing can be seen of a scar, the hair is not wavy and shoulder-length but hangs almost to the waist in two thick straight braids worked through with beads, fur, ribbons and cords. The right hand that holds the corner of the blanket-like coat in position is large and, even in the high illumination, heavily veined. The neck is concealed under coiled beads and the forehead seems more low than "broad."

Perhaps, somehow, these picture details could be reconciled with the official description if the face as a whole were not so devastating.

On a cloth-backed sheet two feet by two and one-half feet in size, under the Great Seal of the Lion and the Unicorn, dignified by the names of the Deputy of the Minister of Justice, the Secretary of State, the Queen herself and all the heaped detail of her "Right Trusty and Right Well-beloved Cousin," this description concludes: "feminine appearance." But the pictures: any face of history, any believed face that the world acknowledges as *man*—Socrates, Jesus, Attila, Genghis Khan, Mahatma Gandhi, Joseph Stalin—no believed face is more *man* than this face. The mouth, the nose, the clenched brows, the eyes—the eyes are large, yes, and dark, but even in this watered-down reproduction of un-ending reproductions of that original, a steady look into those eyes cannot be endured. It is a face like an axe.

It is now evident that the de Chardin statement quoted at the beginning has relevance only as it proves itself inadequate to explain what has happened. At the same time, the inadequacy of Aristotle's much more famous statement becomes evident: "The true difference [between the historian and the poet] is that one relates what *has* happened, the other what *may* happen." These statements cannot explain the storymaker's activity since, despite the most rigid application of impersonal investigation, the elements of the story have now run me aground. If ever I could, I can no longer pretend to objective, omnipotent disinterestedness. I am no longer *spectator* of what *has* happened or what *may* happen: I am become *element* in what is happening at this very moment.

For it is, of course, I myself who cannot endure the shadows on that paper which are those eyes. It is I who stand beside this broken veranda post where two corner shingles have been torn away, where barbed wire tangles the dead weeds on the edge of this field. The bluff that sheltered Almighty Voice and his two friends has not disappeared from the slope of the Minnechinass, no more than the sound of Constable Dickson's voice in that guardhouse is silent. The sound of his speaking is there even if it has never been recorded in an official report:

hey injun you'll get
hung
for stealing that steer
hey injun for killing that government
cow you'll get three
weeks on the woodpile hey injun

The unknown contradictory words about an unprovable act that move a boy to defiance, an implacable Cree warrior long after the three-hundred-and-fifty-year war is ended, a war already lost the day the Cree watch Cartier hoist his guns ashore at Hochelaga and they begin the long retreat west; these words of incomprehension, of threatened incomprehensible law are there to be heard just as the unmoving tableau of the three-day siege is there to be seen on the slopes of the Minnechinass. Sounding Sky is somewhere not there, under arrest, but Spotted Calf stands on a shoulder of the Hills a little to the left, her arms upraised to the setting sun. Her mouth is open. A horse rears, riderless, above the scrub willow at the edge of the bluff, smoke puffs, screams tangle in rifle barrage, there are wounds, somewhere. The bluff is so green this spring, it will not burn and the ragged line of seven police and two civilians is staggering through, faces twisted in rage, terror, and rifles sputter. Nothing moves. There is no sound of frogs in the night; twenty-seven policemen and five civilians stand in cordon at thirty-yard intervals and a body also lies in the shelter of a gully. Only a voice rises from the bluff:

We have fought well
You have died like braves
I have worked hard and am hungry
Give me food

but nothing moves. The bluff lies, a bright green island on the grassy slope surrounded by men hunched forward rigid over their long rifles, men clumped out of rifle-range, thirty-five men dressed as for fall hunting on a sharp spring day, a small gun positioned on a ridge above. A crow is falling out of the sky into the bluff, its feathers sprayed as by an explosion. The first gun and the second gun are in position, the beginning and end of the bristling surround of thirty-five Prince Albert Volunteers, thirteen civilians and fifty-six policemen in position relative to the bluff and relative to the unnumbered whites astride their horses, standing up in their carts, staring and pointing across the valley, in position relative to the bluff and the unnumbered Indians squatting silent along the higher ridges of the Hills, motionless mounds, faceless against the Sunday morning sunlight edging between and over them down along the tree tips, down into the shadows of the bluff. Nothing moves. Beside the second gun the red-coated officer has flung a handful of grass into the motionless air, almost to the rim of the red sun.

And there is a voice. It is an incredible voice that rises from among the young poplars ripped of their spring bark, from among the dead somewhere lying there, out of the arm-deep pit shorter than a man a voice rises over the exploding smoke and thunder of guns that reel back in their positions, worked over, serviced by the grimed motionless men in bright coats and glinting buttons, a voice so high and clear, so unbelievably high and strong in its unending wordless cry.

The voice of "Gitchie-Manitou Wayo"—interpreted as "voice of the Great Spirit"—that is, The Almighty Voice. His death chant no less incredible in its beauty than in its incomprehensible happiness.

I say "wordless cry" because that is the way it sounds to me. I could be more accurate if I had a reliable interpreter who would make a reliable interpretation. For I do not, of course, understand the Cree myself.

Carol Shields

(b. 1935)

CAROL SHIELDS WAS BORN CAROL WARNER IN OAK PARK, Illinois, near Chicago; she married in 1957, the year of her graduation from Hanover College with a B.A. in English; and she and her husband then moved to Canada. She earned her M.A. at the University of Ottawa, with a study of the works of Susanna Moodie. Since that time she has been a lecturer and writer-in-residence at several colleges, and she now teaches English at the University of Manitoba in Winnipeg. A prolific writer, she has published over twenty books in a wide range of genres, from critical essays (*Susanna Moodie: Voice and Vision*, 1975) and poems (e.g., *Coming to Canada*, 1992) to stories (*Various Miracles*, 1985), a play (*Thirteen Hands*, 1993), and numerous novels (among them, *Small Ceremonies*, 1976; *The Box Garden*, 1977; *A Fairly Conventional Woman*, 1982; *Swann: A Mystery*, 1987; *The Republic of Love*, 1992; and *The Stone Diaries*, which won the 1993 Governor General's Award, a Booker Prize nomination, and—two years later, after its U.S. publication—the Pulitzer Prize). "Good Manners" appeared first in *West Coast Review* in 1987, and was collected in 1989 in a volume of stories called *The Orange Fish*.

Like much of her work, "Good Manners" looks at the language of polite—or "ordinary"—exchange, and then glimpses (or perhaps openly stares at) the kinds of violence that lie just below this veneer. *Swann: A Mystery*, for example, tells of a seemingly polite but actually quite fierce competition among a group of ostensibly civilized middle class academics and librarians. Comically, the novel traces their quest for the papers—the "life," the authority over—a recently dead and seemingly brilliant poet. All of the pursuers seem to believe that this authority will make them somehow unique, and as famous—or as important—as their writer-subject. "Authority" and "identity" are not easily bought here, however, nor (as "Good Manners" makes clear) are they equivalent to each other. But if the equation between identity and authority is assumed, what then? Perhaps it reveals something about motivation and desire?

For Further Reading

NEIL BESNER, ed., Carol Shields issue, *Prairie Fire* 16.1 (Spring 1995).

HARVEY DE ROO, "A little like flying: an interview with Carol Shields," *West Coast Review* 23.3 (Winter 1989): 38–56.

ELEANOR WACHTEL, ed., Carol Shields issue, *Room of One's Own* 13.1–2 (1989).

Good Manners

The stern, peremptory social arbiter, Georgia Willow, has been overseeing Canadian manners for thirty-five years. She did it in Montreal during the tricky fifties and she did it in Toronto in the unsettled sixties. In the seventies she operated underground, so to speak, from a converted Rosedale garage, tutoring the shy wives of Japanese executives and diplomats. In the eighties she came into her own; manners were rediscovered, particularly in the West where Mrs. Willow has relocated.

Promptly at three-thirty each Tuesday and Thursday, neatly dressed in a well-pressed navy Evan-Picone slub silk suit, cream blouse, and muted scarf, Georgia Willow meets her small class in the reception area of the MacDonald Hotel and ushers them into the long, airy tearoom—called, for some reason, Gophers—where a ceremonial spread has been ordered.

Food and drink almost always accompany Mrs. Willow's lectures. It is purely a matter of simulation since, wherever half a dozen people gather, there is sure to be a tray of sandwiches to trip them up. According to Mrs. Willow, food and food implements are responsible for fifty per cent of social unease. The classic olive pit question. The persisting problem of forks, cocktail picks, and coffee spoons. The more recent cherry-tomato dilemma. Potato skins, eat them or leave them? Saucers, the lack of. The challenge of the lobster. The table napkin quandary. Removing parsley from between the teeth. On and on.

There are also sessions devoted to hand-shaking, door-opening and rules regarding the wearing and nonwearing of gloves. And a concluding series of seminars on the all-important *langue de la politesse,* starting with the discourse of gesture, and moving on quickly to the correct phrase for the right moment, delivered with spiritual amplitude or imprecation or possibly something in between. Appropriateness is all, says Georgia Willow.

Our *doyenne* of good manners takes these problems one by one. She demonstrates and describes and explains the acceptable alternatives. She's excellent on fine points, she respects fine points. But always it's the philosophy *behind* good manners that she emphasizes.

Never forget, she tells her audience, what manners are *for.* Manners are the lubricant that eases our passage through life. Manners are the means by which we deflect evil. Manners are the first-aid kit we carry out on to the battlefield. Manners are the ceremonial silver tongs with which we help ourselves to life's most alluring moments.

She says these things to a circle of puzzled faces. Some of those present take notes, others yawn; all find it difficult to deal with Mrs. Willow's more exuberant abstractions. As a sensitive person, she understands this perfectly well; she sympathizes and, if she were less well-mannered, would illustrate her philosophy with personal anecdotes culled from her own experience. Like everyone else's, her life has been filled with success and failure, with ardor and the lack of ardor, but she is not one of those who spends her time unpicking the past, blaming and projecting and drawing ill-bred conclusions or dragging out pieces of bloodied vision or shame. She keeps her lips sealed about personal matters and advises her clients to do the same. Nevertheless, certain of her experiences refuse to dissolve. They're still on center stage, so to speak, frozen tableaux waiting behind a thickish curtain.

Only very occasionally do they press their way forward and demand to be heard. She is ten years old. It is an hour before dusk on a summer evening. The motionless violet air has the same density and permanence as a word she keeps tripping over in story books, usually on the last page, the word *forever*. She intuitively, happily, believes at this moment that she will be locked forever into the simplicity of the blurred summer night, forever throwing a rubber ball against the forever side of her house and disturbing her mother with the sound of childish chanting. It is impossible for her to know that the adult world will someday, and soon, carry her away, reject her thesis on the *Chanson de Roland* and the particular kind of dated beauty her features possess; that she will be the protagonist of an extremely unpleasant divorce case and, in the end, be forced to abandon a studio apartment on the twenty-fourth floor of an apartment building in a city two thousand miles from the site of this small wooden house; that she will feel in her sixtieth year as tired and worn down as the sagging board fence surrounding the house where she lives as a child, a fence that simultaneously protects and taunts her ten-year-old self.

On the other side of the fence is old Mr. Manfred, sharpening his lawnmower. She puts down her ball and watches him cautiously, his round back, his chin full of gray teeth, the cloud of white hair resting so lazily on top of his head, and the wayward, unquenchable dullness of his eyes. Twice in the past he has offered her peppermints, and twice, mindful of her mother's warnings, she has refused. "No, thank you," she said each time. But it had been painful for her, saying no. She had felt no answering sense of virtue, only the hope that he might offer again.

Tonight Mr. Manfred walks over to the fence and tells her he has a secret. He whispers it into her ear. This secret has a devious shape: grotesque flapping ears and a loose drooling mouth. Mr. Manfred's words seem ghosted by the scent of the oil can he holds in his right hand. In his left hand, in the folds of his cotton work pants, he grasps a tube of pink snouty dampish flesh. What he whispers is formlessly narrative and involves the familiar daylight objects of underwear and fingers and the reward of peppermint candy.

But then he draws back suddenly as though stung by a wasp. The oil can rolls and rolls and rolls on the ground. He knows, and Georgia, aged ten, knows that something inadmissible has been said, something that cannot be withdrawn. Or can it? A dangerous proposition has been placed in her hand. It burns and shines. She wants to hand it back quickly, get rid of it somehow, but etiquette demands that she first translate it into something bearable.

The only other language she knows is incomprehension, and luckily she's been taught the apt phrase. "I beg your pardon?" she says to Mr. Manfred. Her face does a courteous twist, enterprising, meek, placatory, and masked with power, allowing Mr. Manfred time to sink back into the lavender twilight of the uncut grass. "I'm afraid I didn't quite hear...."

Later, twenty-three years old, she is on a train, the Super Continental, traveling eastward. She has a window seat, and sunlight gathers around the crown of her hair. She knows how she must look, with her thin clever mouth and F. Scott Fitzgerald eyes.

"I can't resist introducing myself," a man says.

"Pardon?" She is clearly flustered. He has a beautiful face, carved cheeks, crisp gray hair curling at the forehead.

"The book," he points. "The book you're reading. It looks very interesting."

"Ah," she says.

Two days later they are in bed together, a hotel room, and she reflects on the fact that she has not finished the book, that she doesn't care if she ever does, for how can a book about love compare with what she now knows.

"I'm sorry," he says then. "I hadn't realized I was the first."

"Oh, but you're not," she cries.

This curious lie can only be accounted for by a wish to keep his love. But it turns out she has never had it, not for one minute, not love as she imagines it.

"I should have made things clear to you at once," he says. How was he to know she would mistake a random disruption for lasting attachment? He is decent enough to feel ashamed. He only wanted. He never intended. He has no business. If only she.

She seems to hear cloth ripping behind her eyes. The syntax of culpability—he's drowning in it, and trying to drown her too. She watches him closely, and the sight of his touching, disloyal mouth restores her composure. Courtesy demands that she rescue him and save herself at the same time. This isn't shrewdness talking, this is good manners, and there is nothing more economical, she believes, than the language of good manners. It costs nothing, it's portable, easy to handle, malleable, yet pre-formed. Two words are all that are required, and she pronounces them slippingly, like musical notes. "Forgive me," she says.

There. It's said. Was that so hard?

There is a certain thing we must all have, as Georgia Willow has learned in the course of her long life. We may be bankrupt, enfeebled, ill or depraved, but we must have our good stories, our moments of vividness. We keep our door closed, yes, and move among our scratched furniture, old photographs, calendars and keys, ticket stubs, pencil ends and lacquered trays, but in the end we'll wither away unless we have a little human attention.

But no one seems to want to give it away these days, not to Georgia Willow. It seems she is obliged to ask even for the unpunctual treats of human warmth. A certain amount of joyless groping is required and even then it's hard to get enough. It is especially painful for someone who, after all, is a personage in her country. She has her pride, her reputation—and a scattering of small bruise-colored spots on the back of her long thin hands. It makes you shudder to think what she must have to do, what she has to say, how she is obliged to open her mouth and say *please*.

Please is a mean word. A word in leg irons. She doesn't say it often. Her pleases and thank-yous are performed in soft-focus, as they like to say in the cinema world. It has nothing to do with love, but you can imagine how it is for her, having to ask and then having to be grateful. It's too bad. Good manners had such a happy childhood, but then things got complicated. The weave of complication has brought Georgia Willow up against those she would not care to meet again, not in broad daylight anyway, and others who have extracted far more than poor Mr. Manfred at the garden fence ever dreamed of. Good manners are not always nice, not nice at all, although Mrs. Willow has a way of banishing the hard outlines of time and place, and of course she would never think of naming names. Discretion is one of her tenets. She does a special Monday afternoon series on discretion in which she enjoins others to avoid personal inquiries and pointed judgments.

"Courtesy," concludes Georgia Willow, "is like the golden coin in the princess's silk purse. Every time it's spent worthily, another appears in its place."

Almost everyone agrees with her. However much they look into her eyes and think she is uttering mere niceties, they are sworn to that ultimate courtesy which is to believe what people want us to believe. And thus, when Mrs. Willow bids them good afternoon, they courteously rise to their feet. "Good afternoon," they smile back, shaking hands carefully, and postponing their slow, rhythmic applause and the smashing of the teacups.

Audrey Thomas

(b. 1935)

BORN AUDREY GRACE CALLAHAN, Audrey Thomas grew up in Binghamton, New York; the region is one she draws on as a setting for some of her stories and her first novel (and fourth book to be published) *Songs My Mother Taught Me,* 1973, and (in part) her subsequent *Graven Images* (1993). Educated at Smith College, the University of St. Andrews in Scotland, and the University of British Columbia, she emigrated to Canada in 1959; except for two years spent in Kumasi, Ghana (1964–66), and occasional sojourns abroad, she has since made her home on Galiano Island and in Vancouver. Repeatedly her novels and stories draw on her places of residence: Africa (the setting of her novels *Mrs. Blood* (1970) and *Coming Down from Wa* (1995) and several of the stories in *Ten Green Bottles,* 1967, and *Ladies and Escorts,* 1977), Greece (the setting of a novel called *Latakia,* 1979), Mexico ("The More Little Mummy in the World"), and the Gulf Islands (a novella called *Prospero on the Island,* 1971; some of the stories of *Real Mothers,* 1981; and her meticulously wrought novel of separation and survival, *Intertidal Life,* 1984). But always the landscape is part of the web of images and observations that texture her work. Islands, tides, inland cities: these are verbal landscapes as well as physical ones. Africa is a place of Otherness, the tangible expression of the difference that her (primarily female) characters do not know about themselves. And words, for the author, are a constant source of associational discovery and bilingual pun, producing *pain* and sustenance, disintegration and integration, playfulness and dislocation. *Alice in Wonderland* and Skeat's historical dictionary of English are valuable guidebooks to Thomas's prose. In her anecdotes are to be found small histories of humankind, and in her puns she records the doubleness she observes in experience, the uneasy truce between joy and desperation.

"The More Little Mummy in the World," collected in 1977, was first published in the Fall-Spring 1975–76 issue of *Capilano Review.* Fragmented and elliptical, it is a journal of emotional division, wavering between bitterness and wit, between the has-been and the might-have-been, resolving itself in caustic irony. Yet irony can be both a defensive weapon and a source of consolation. Some of Thomas's other stories, especially those that are steeped in cyclical imagery, occasionally permit her narrators to return to a quiet equilibrium. And perhaps that is also true even here.

For Further Reading

FRANK DAVEY, "Alternate Stories: the short fiction of Audrey Thomas and Margaret Atwood," *Canadian Literature* 109 (Summer 1986): 5–14.

Interview with Audrey Thomas, *Capilano Review* 7 (Spring 1975): 87–109.

Audrey Thomas issue, *Room of One's Own* 10.3–4 (1986).

AUDREY THOMAS, "Basmati Rice: An Essay About Words," *Canadian Literature* 100 (Spring 1984): 312–17.

———, "A Fine Romance, My Dear, This Is," *Canadian Literature* 108 (Spring 1986): 5–12.

The More Little Mummy
in the World

Oscar A. Lempe
Denver, Color U.S.   14-V-1876
*   23-XI-1958*

Guanauato, Gto.
  Recuerdo de Su Esposa
  Chijas
  Perpetuidad

Louis Montgomery Allen Sr.
New York City   Dec. 6-1887
*   Feb. 12-1957*

Guanauato, Gto.
  Perpetuidad   *in perpetuity*

Handprints on this one—of whom? *Su esposa? Su hermosa?* A passing, naughty, unrelated child?

  Elisabeth Carnes Allen, D.A.R.

She wandered through the cemetery looking at every stone, imagining the people, what had brought them there, what the town had been like nearly a hundred years before. The lure of what riches? The silver mines perhaps.

Everywhere there were flowers stuck in tins—Mobil Oil tins, paint tins, tomatoes, green chillies:

  Chiles Jalapenos, En Escapbeche

She took out her pocket dictionary.
  The wind blowing through the cypress trees rattled the tins like bones.

  To My Beloved Wife
  Maria Concepcion Buchnan

Although there had been a long line-up to see the mummies there were very few people in the Pantheon itself. A young couple with their arms around one another, laughing, exchanging kisses, some old women in black, a gardener. And the dead of course, the multitude of dead stacked six or seven high. The soft brown hills beyond and El Pipla, the boy hero, alone on a hill above the Jardin de la Union, his arm upraised.

From *Ladies & Escorts* (Ottawa: Oberon Press, 1977). Reprinted by permission of the author.

Ayer (yesterday), *Hoy* (today).
Mañana

Mother
Lily Mast McBride
Born Sept. 19-1882
Died July 22-1926

A pretty blue-grey stone, this one, beautifully incised.

It was very peaceful here with the wreaths, the plastic flowers and the real—gladioli, lilies—the white ones she saw everywhere here, Easter lilies back home—geraniums, carnations. The flowers dead too of course, or dying, sucking up the last dregs of rusty water from the tins. Still, she liked this place better than the churches with their bleeding Christs, their oppressive smell of hot wax, their plaster damned pleading to her for one last chance at salvation.

Some stones were casually propped against still-occupied cabinets. (They couldn't be called tombs and she couldn't think of a better word than "cabinet"—cabin, verb, to confine in a small space, cramp). She turned one over.

Naci Inocente!...
Muerto Ignorante
Freyre Jose E.
V-7-1925
Perpetuidad

So much for *perpetuidad!*
She had been thinking of failures and of suicides and had gone to mass on Palm Sunday in the hopes of finding something positive—if only for a second, if only for an instant, if only, even, an aura or a whiff of hope for her salvation.
Buenos dias. Adios.
She straightened a tin of gladioli which had fallen over in the wind.

Outside the Parroquia women and men were braiding palms into elaborate patterns. She bought a small crucifix and went in, covering her head, but the Mass was a disappointment. She stood up. She sat down. She prayed. The priest was way way way up in the chancel. Little bells rang. There was no pageantry, no music, nothing to draw her spirit up and away from the deep well of despair into which it seemed to have fallen. Over the words of the priest a poem of Yeats' kept running through her mind:

That is no country for old men
The young in one another's arms
Fish/Flesh/and fowl commend
all summer long
Whatever is begotten, born or dies

They had been going to come down here together. Had maps, dreams, destinations. Even a tape:

Siento molestarle!
No es ninguna molestia!
Salud!

How much too much please thank you don't mention it.

Instead he took her out (at her request) the night before she left. To a Greek restaurant (again at her request). She drank a lot of wine, and crumbling a bit of bread between her fingers, told him it was she all along whom he really loved.

"Do you think so?" he said and smiled at her over his wine glass. Then in an offhand manner he asked her if she'd ever been in any of the other Greek restaurants along the street, places where you just walked in and took whatever was going, places where the Greeks themselves went, cheaper places than this. (And he, who never went into a restaurant alone, whom had he lingered with in a small café full of the smell of lamb and garlic and the whine of recorded music. Who? Don't ask, or, as he would have put it, "why humiliate yourself?") He had always been Machiavellian; had always known how to put her in her place.

Once they had been at the house of his best friend and contemporary, Peter:

"I was coming in on the bus from the island," her lover said, "toward sunset—a beautiful evening. Suddenly I looked up and there was this incredible cloud formation—incredible! I said to the fellow next to me, without really thinking about it, you know, 'My God, that looks just like the Mushroom Cloud!' I saw the guy look at me and give a little frown and then I realized with a start that he was younger, younger than the Bomb—that he didn't even know what I was talking about. The only mushroom cloud he knew was psilocybin!"

Peter had laughed appreciatively. He was 35.

"It's true. People talk about the generation gap—as a metaphor I mean—but it seems to me there's a real gap—I almost see it as a physical space—between those born before or during the War and those born after it."

"Yes. There's a point at which Rachel and I just can't communicate; we were born into two different worlds." He had turned to her. "When I talk about Marlene Dietrich I don't know if you even know who I mean."

She was immediately defensive. He had wanted her to be, had set her up.

"Of course I know who Marlene Dietrich is."

"Ah yes—you know her name. But is your Marlene Dietrich the same as mine—I doubt it." Peter nodded and began singing "Lili Marlene." Her lover sat back and lit his pipe.

That night at the Greek restaurant he had given her a handsome present—a shoulderbag with three sections, or pouches, like a saddlebag.

"Now you will have three places to put all your clutter," he said, "instead of just one." ("It's not that she doesn't have a place for everything," he said once, at a party, "it's that she has several places." He was very tidy and they fought about the missing cap to the toothpaste.)

Buenos dias. Adios. No comprendo.

In one place there were freshly-dug graves, four in a row, an accident perhaps. This in a courtyard which led to a view of the city. Bougainvillaea had been splashed against the walls, the original purple and the scarlet, blood-coloured. In the distance she could hear the sound of children's voices.

Estoy esperando en paquete.
Lo tiene usted aqui?

When he came to get her at the hospital he was very brusque and efficient, annoyed that she was still in bed and crying. His sons were in the car—they were going camping. Yet still she wanted to buy him gifts—an onyx chess set, a heavy silver ring, a blanket for his bed. Things of beauty and whimsy, things that would make him think of her, remember her and want her.

Donde este? Where is?

He had told her there was nothing wrong, that maybe she should see a shrink. The gifts would only embarrass him. When she began to cry at the bus station, he kissed her quickly on the forehead and then walked away. She hated him; no, she loved him.

She had read in the guidebook that if the rent was not kept up on the crypts (yes, that was the word she had been searching for), the bodies were removed after five years and the bones thrown into a common bone-house to make room for new arrivals. But the region was very dry and some of the bodies would be mummified. When they were, they were put into the museum. Directly outside the cemetery were souvenir stands—skeletons, on horseback or playing fiddles or dancing, with springy arms and legs. Postcards of the mummies, earthenware, bone letter-openers and crochet hooks (human bone?). There were mummies of pale beige toffee with raisin eyes. These were wrapped in red or yellow cellophane. As she approached a man had offered her two large ones in one packet, *"Momias Matrimonias,"* and laughed at her discomfort. Now she was trying to get up enough courage to go into the mummy museum itself.

Death and disease were accepted here. Death was even made fun of, made into toffee to chew or chocolate to lick or tiny plaster figures to decorate, along with gilded pictures of miraculous virgins, the windows and mirrors of buses and cars. She knew now that almost certainly, whenever she saw a street musician, either he was blind or lame or leprous or there was a terribly deformed creature, just out of sight, on behalf of whom he was playing his music.

Her operation had been therapeutic and therefore covered by her insurance. No back streets or borrowed money—things were easier now.

Ayer (yesterday). *Hoy* (today).
Mañana

This was a very strange town to walk around in and easy to get lost. The main road ran underneath the town in places, reappearing above ground several hundred yards beyond. It was really a stone-arched tunnel and rather frightening. And there were six or seven main squares, not just one. She had already, in spite of her map, been lost several times. The night before, wandering steep alleys full of wrought-iron balconies, she had stumbled upon a strange religious ceremony in one of the smaller lamplit squares. There were bleachers set out and many of the people were already seated, men, women and children, facing an old church. The church bell began to ring and then a priest appeared high up on the church steps, intoning Hail Marys and Our Fathers. And she understood a bit of it, the history of the week leading up to the arrest of Jesus. Below the steps stood men in purple sackcloth and black hoods, very medieval and frightening. A lifesized statue of Christ (looking not unlike the "Jesu Christo Superstare" she had seen in Mexico City) was brought out of the church by more hooded men, carried down the steep steps and put on a flower-decked platform. There was a rope around his neck and it hung down his back, binding his hands behind him. A child-angel and one of the masked men climbed up and sat on either side of him. Torches were lit and as the rest of the masked men shouldered their burden the crowd gave a deep moan of pity and anticipation. The statue had real hair and jointed, movable arms. He terrified her, for he hovered somewhere in a strange space between icon and the living god. The wind blew his hair across his gentle, accepting face. His gown was purple like the garments of the men but his was of velvet, not hemp. A workman beat a drum and the entire affair—Christ, angel, masked men, flowers, scaffolding, torches, priest—began to move. A young boy followed behind, playing a simple pipe and the procession slowly moved out from the small square into the larger one beyond. Behind came small children, some on tricycles, the women in black, the men, balloon sellers, a thin brown pariah dog. The bowed, bound figure of Christ rode above them all. It was amateurish in a way but very powerful; she hid herself in the crowd.

Por que? Why? *No se.* I don't know.
Perdone.

It was as though once she had decided she didn't want it he had washed his hands of the whole affair.

"Ruth Barnes"
Just a small stone marker with a dried-up geranium obscuring the date. Presumably to be buried in this small courtyard was more expensive than to be deposited on the shelves. The wind blowing rattled the tins like bones.

If he were here he would have struck up a friendship with the gardener, would try out the little Spanish he knew and supplement it with laughter and broad gestures. His energy was one of the first things that had excited her. And his keen intelligence, his learning, the whole sum of his life experience. He had been married (twice), had children (one as old as her youngest sister), had suffered and taken chances.

"I find it impossible to live alone," he had said to her the first night, "and yet somehow I always seem to fuck it up—my relationships with women." He showed her pictures of his sons and took her home to bed.

Dispenseme. Excuse me.
Muchas gracias.

Everywhere down here men followed her and tried to feel her up—a woman alone deserved to be treated that way. Then they gave their paycheques to their mothers and went to mass on Sunday.

Hail Mary Full of Grace Blessed is
The Fruit of Thy Womb Jesus

On the train from Nuevo Laredo she had met a middle-aged man who lived in San Miguel. He said the happiest day of his life was the day when they nailed his wife's coffin shut. Federales came on the train looking for contraband. They wore their revolvers tucked in the back of their pants, Pancho Villa style.

"Watch for the Mordida," the American said.

She shook her head.

"'The Bite.' To force someone to give you a bribe. It's a game between the Federales and the people coming back."

Was that what she had done by getting pregnant? Put the bite on him?

The boy-hero stood unconcerned on the distant hill, his arm upraised forever. Her first day in the town she had followed the crude signs and climbed steep stairs and back alleys until she reached the top of that hill. She had taken some bread and fruit with her and sat in a little summer house just below the enormous figure, eating slices of pineapple and writing in her journal. The boy had set fire to the granary in which the Royalists had barricaded themselves. At his feet it said, in Spanish,

"There are still other castles to burn."

She felt quite happy there, after her climb, the whole town at her feet. But in the evening, at a band concert in the Jardin de la Union, she sat on a wrought-iron bench and longed to have him with her, next to her, observing, commenting, loving. Canaries mocked her from the laurel trees around the square.

Where is? *No comprendo.*

She retraced her steps, back through the main courtyard with all its stacked and silent dead, back through the black iron gate with its simple cross on top. There were very few people in line now so there was no reason not to wait.

He had been quite calm when she told him. Just said, "Well, what do you want to do about it?" He left it entirely up to her. Had she wanted him to be otherwise? Had she wanted to bear his child? She wanted to be a writer, a poet—had he not encouraged her, sung her praises? In Chapultapec Park in Mexico City she sat on the grass one Sunday and watched the fathers spoil their children. They were immaculate—it was the mothers, of course, who saw to that. There were funny animal heads on the trash cans in the children's playground. The children laughed and squealed when they stuck their little hands in.

She paid her five pesos and went into the mummy museum.

In Chapultapec Park she had sat on the grass and wept. She wanted to be six years old in a white dress and riding on her father's shoulders, her small hands tugging at his curly hair. She wanted to be held and to be forgiven. She wanted a red balloon.

Her mother was at home making a delicious Sunday dinner.

Ayer. (yesterday). *Hoy* (today).
Mañana.

The mummy museum was really a long artificially-lit corridor with the mummies displayed in glass cases along one side. The corridor was hot and very crowded, so that for a moment she experienced a wave of claustrophobia and almost turned around and ran.

Some of the names and dates on the stones had simply been scrawled in the wet plaster.

Aristo Perez
Manuel Torres M.
Maria de los Angeles Rodriguez

So there were the mummies, in glass cases like curios—which of course they were. Most were without clothes, jaundice-coloured and hideously wrinkled. A few had on mouldy shoes and there was one man who had on a complete suit of tattered black clothes. Very few had hair and this surprised her. Was it just an old wives' tale that the hair would keep on growing?

He read her, one night, from John Donne's "Funerale"

Whoever comes to shroud me,
  do not harme
Nor question much
That subtile wreathe of hair,
  which crowns my arme:

and from "A Feaver"

Oh doe not die, for I shall hate
  All women so, when thou art gone,
That thee I shall not celebrate,
  When I remember, thou wast one.

She got up and cut off a lock of her hair and gave it to him; he kissed her neck and put the lock in the back of his grandfather's gold watch.

Donde este? Where is?

The mummies' faces were full of anger and terror. Shrinkage had pulled their mouths open and their hands were clutched across their empty bellies. Her Spanish was not quick enough to understand everything the guides were saying, but there were abnormalities and tumours and other curious things being pointed out as they moved along. The mummies were tall or short, male and female, the men's papery genitals still visible, the women's wrinkled breasts.

She wrote him letter after letter and tore them all up.

Quiero comprar una postal. I wish to buy a postcard.

As she crossed the street to his car and his waiting sons, she stumbled, still drugged and swollen-eyed, against the curb, and turned her ankle. Suddenly she had to sit down on the grass and put her head between her knees. She knew the boys, his sons, were watching her. What had he said to them? Why had he brought them to the hospital? What was he trying to say?

People with limps, people with no legs, blind people, lepers, pariah dogs. The country swarmed with outcasts and with cripples. The tourists bought silver rings and onyx chess sets and turned their heads away. After all, it was not their problem. Charity begins....

"They hate us," the American man had said. "They want our money but they hate us. They would prefer if we just mailed it down."

Almost at the end of the corridor was a display case full of child mummies— some in christening gowns and bonnets, some naked or wrapped in tiny shrouds. In front of the smallest of these a cardboard sign was propped. She pushed closer, in order to read it, then tugged at the guide's elbow.

"Please. *Por favor.* What does the sign say? *Que quiere decir?*"

"*La Momia Mas Pequena del mundo.*" He smiled at her, showing perfect teeth.

"*Si, Si.* In English. *Habla Usted Inglis?*"

"*Ah, Inglis.*"

He smiled again.

"The more little mummy in the world."

It sat there, no bigger than the rubber babies she had played with as a child.

Where were the parents? Why had these children been removed to this terrible glass limbo? She looked at la momia mas Pequena but it refused to answer.

The American had asked her to come and spend a few days with him in San Miguel.

She pushed her way through the tourists and out the exit door. The sun struck her like a slap. She half-ran, half-walked toward the souvenir stands, rummaged quickly through the cards until she found the one she was looking for, the one she knew was certain to be there.

Back at the apartment he had said, "D'you think you could rustle us up some dinner—we'd like to get away before dark." The boys were looking at her curiously. She went into the bedroom and began to pack, tears running down her face, the little plastic hospital bracelet still locked around her wrist.

Go. Come. Are you ready?
Don't forget.

She fumbled in her bag for the change purse, then headed back down the hill. Tonight, drinking her cho-ko-la-tay in that little restaurant near the Plazuela where she had seen the Christ, she would get out the card and address it.

"Having a wonderful time," she would write.

"Wish you were here."

Alistair MacLeod

(b. 1936)

BORN IN NORTH BATTLEFORD, Saskatchewan, Alistair MacLeod went to high school in Cape Breton, then attended St. Francis Xavier University in Antigonish, Nova Scotia, the University of New Brunswick, and Notre Dame. Deeply attached to the Maritimes—and particularly to the rigorous world of the Cape Breton miners and fishermen—he has nevertheless lived away from the area since his university years, having taught at the University of Indiana and then at the University of Windsor, where he is now fiction editor for the *University of Windsor Review.* He had published in various journals since the mid-1950s—among them *Fiddlehead* and *Canadian Fiction Magazine.* Of these stories, two—including "The Boat," which first appeared in *The Southern Review* in 1974—were earlier selected for inclusion in the annual volume of *Best American Short Stories.* His two collections are called *The Lost Salt Gift of Blood* (1976), in which "The Boat" appeared, and *As Birds Bring Forth the Sun* (1986).

"The Boat" is a characteristic initiation or coming-of-age story, realistic in its detail, straightforward in form, and elegiac in tone. Like other stories in the collection, it speaks of the many shapes of loss, discovering the quality of possession in the moment of losing it, the nature of home in the realization of exile, or the power of memory to sustain one through problematic times. The memory that "The Boat" tells of is in the present, in the moment of tale-telling: a fact of central importance to the narrator. The event of choice, however—so important to all of MacLeod's characters, and never easy—lies in the past from which the present stems and to which it is somehow still connected. The past choice, in other words, continues to remind the narrator of change; hence the author's choice of narrative strategy itself serves to emphasize the interconnection between past and present and the ongoing effect of a moment of decision.

For Further Reading

LAURIE KRUK, "Alistair MacLeod: The World is Full of Exile" [interview], *Studies in Canadian Literature* 20.1 (1995): 150–60.

COLIN NICHOLSON, "The Region of Memory: The Fiction of Alistair MacLeod," *British Journal of Canadian Studies* 7.1 (1992): 128–37.

———, "Signatures of Time: Alistair MacLeod & His Short Stories," *Canadian Literature* 107 (Winter 1985): 90–101.

JOYCE CAROL OATES, "Afterword" to Alistair MacLeod, *The Lost Salt Gift of Blood* (rpt. Toronto: McClelland & Stewart, 1989) 157–60.

HOLLY RUBINSKY, "An Interview with Alistair MacLeod," *Brick* 36 (Summer 1989): 19–28.

SIMONE VAUTHIER, "Notes sur l'emploi du présent dans 'The Road to Rankin's Point' d'Alistair MacLeod," *Ranam*, 16 (1983): 143–58.

The Boat

There are times even now, when I awake at four o'clock in the morning with the terrible fear that I have overslept; when I imagine that my father is waiting for me in the room below the darkened stairs or that the shorebound men are tossing pebbles against my window while blowing their hands and stomping their feet impatiently on the frozen steadfast earth. There are times when I am half out of bed and fumbling for socks and mumbling for words before I realize that I am foolishly alone, that no one waits at the base of the stairs and no boat rides restlessly in the waters by the pier.

At such times only the grey corpses on the overflowing ashtray beside my bed bear witness to the extinction of the latest spark and silently await the crushing out of the most recent of their fellows. And then because I am afraid to be alone with death, I dress rapidly, make a great to-do about clearing my throat, turn on both faucets in the sink and proceed to make loud splashing ineffectual noises. Later I go out and walk the mile to the all-night restaurant.

In the winter it is a very cold walk and there are often tears in my eyes when I arrive. The waitress usually gives a sympathetic little shiver and says, "Boy, it must be really cold out there; you got tears in your eyes."

"Yes," I say, "it sure is; it really is."

And then the three or four of us who are always in such places at such times make uninteresting little protective chit-chat until the dawn reluctantly arrives. Then I swallow the coffee which is always bitter and leave with a great busy rush because by that time I have to worry about being late and whether I have a clean shirt and whether my car will start and about all the other countless things one must worry about when he teaches at a great Midwestern university. And I know then that that day will go by as have all the days of the past ten years, for the call and the voices and the shapes and the boat were not really there in the early morning's darkness and I have all kinds of comforting reality to prove it. They are only shadows and echoes, the animals a child's hands make on the wall by lamplight, and the voices from the rain barrel; the cuttings from an old movie made in the black and white of long ago.

I first became conscious of the boat in the same way and at almost the same time that I became aware of the people it supported. My earliest recollection of my father is a view from the floor of gigantic rubber boots and then of being suddenly elevated and having my face pressed against the stubble of his cheek, and of how it tasted of salt and of how he smelled of salt from his red-soled rubber boots to the shaggy whiteness of his hair.

When I was very small, he took me for my first ride in the boat. I rode the half-mile from our house to the wharf on his shoulders and I remember the

From *The Lost Salt Gift of Blood* (Toronto: McClelland and Stewart, 1976). Reprinted by permission of The Canadian Publishers McClelland and Stewart Ltd.

sound of his rubber boots galumphing along the gravel beach, the tune of the indecent little song he used to sing, and the odour of the salt.

The floor of the boat was permeated with the same odour and in its constancy I was not aware of change. In the harbour we made our little circle and returned. He tied the boat by its painter, fastened the stern to its permanent anchor and lifted me high over his head to the solidity of the wharf. Then he climbed up the little iron ladder that led to the wharf's cap, placed me once more upon his shoulders and galumphed off again.

When we returned to the house everyone made a great fuss over my precocious excursion and asked, "How did you like the boat?" "Were you afraid in the boat?" "Did you cry in the boat?" They repeated "the boat" at the end of all their questions and I knew it must be very important to everyone.

My earliest recollection of my mother is of being alone with her in the mornings while my father was away in the boat. She seemed to be always repairing clothes that were "torn in the boat," preparing food "to be eaten in the boat" or looking for "the boat" through our kitchen window which faced upon the sea. When my father returned about noon, she would ask, "Well, how did things go in the boat today?" It was the first question I remember asking: "Well, how did things go in the boat today?" "Well, how did things go in the boat today?"

The boat in our lives was registered at Port Hawkesbury. She was what Nova Scotians called a Cape Island boat and was designed for the small inshore fishermen who sought the lobsters of the spring and the mackerel of summer and later the cod and haddock and hake. She was thirty-two feet long and nine wide, and was powered by an engine from a Chevrolet truck. She had a marine clutch and a high speed reverse gear and was painted light green with the name *Jenny Lynn* stencilled in black letters on her bow and painted on an oblong plate across her stern. Jenny Lynn had been my mother's maiden name and the boat was called after her as another link in the chain of tradition. Most of the boats that berthed at the wharf bore the names of some female member of their owner's household.

I say this now as if I knew it all then. All at once, all about boat dimensions and engines, and as if on the day of my first childish voyage I noticed the difference between a stencilled name and a painted name. But of course it was not that way at all, for I learned it all very slowly and there was not time enough.

I learned first about our house which was one of about fifty which marched around the horseshoe of our harbour and the wharf which was its heart. Some of them were so close to the water that during a storm the sea spray splashed against their windows while others were built farther along the beach as was the case with ours. The houses and their people, like those of the neighbouring towns and villages, were the result of Ireland's discontent and Scotland's Highland Clearances and America's War of Independence. Impulsive emotional Catholic Celts who could not bear to live with England and shrewd determined Protestant Puritans who, in the years after 1776, could not bear to live without.

The most important room in our house was one of those oblong old-fashioned kitchens heated by a wood- and coal-burning stove. Behind the stove was a box of kindlings and beside it a coal scuttle. A heavy wooden table with leaves that expanded or reduced its dimensions stood in the middle of the floor. There were five wooden home-made chairs which had been chipped and hacked by a variety of knives. Against the east wall, opposite the stove, there was a couch which sagged in the middle and had a cushion for a pillow, and above it a shelf which contained matches, tobacco, pencils, odd fish-hooks, bits of twine, and a tin can filled with bills and receipts. The south wall was dominated by a window which faced the sea and on the north there was a five-foot board which bore a variety of clothes hooks and the burdens of each. Beneath the board there was a jumble of odd footwear, mostly of rubber. There were also, on this wall, a barometer, a map of the marine area and a shelf which held a tiny radio. The kitchen was shared by all of us and was a buffer zone between the immaculate order of ten other rooms and the disruptive chaos of the single room that was my father's.

My mother ran her house as her brothers ran their boats. Everything was clean and spotless and in order. She was tall and dark and powerfully energetic. In later years she reminded me of the women of Thomas Hardy, particularly Eustacia Vye, in a physical way. She fed and clothed a family of seven children, making all of the meals and most of the clothes. She grew miraculous gardens and magnificent flowers and raised broods of hens and ducks. She would walk miles on berry-picking expeditions and hoist her skirts to dig for clams when the tide was low. She was fourteen years younger than my father, whom she had married when she was twenty-six and had been a local beauty for a period of ten years. My mother was of the sea as were all of her people, and her horizons were the very literal ones she scanned with her dark and fearless eyes.

Between the kitchen clothes rack and barometer, a door opened into my father's bedroom. It was a room of disorder and disarray. It was as if the wind which so often clamoured about the house succeeded in entering this single room and after whipping it into turmoil stole quietly away to renew its knowing laughter from without.

My father's bed was against the south wall. It always looked rumpled and unmade because he lay on top of it more than he slept within any folds it might have had. Beside it, there was a little brown table. An archaic goose-necked reading light, a battered table radio, a mound of wooden matches, one or two packages of tobacco, a deck of cigarette papers and an overflowing ashtray cluttered its surface. The brown larvae of tobacco shreds and the grey flecks of ash covered both the table and the floor beneath it. The once-varnished surface of the table was disfigured by numerous black scars and gashes inflicted by the neglected burning cigarettes of many years. They had tumbled from the ashtray unnoticed and branded their statements permanently and quietly into the wood until the odour of their burning caused the snuffing out of their lives. At the bed's foot there was a single window which looked upon the sea.

Against the adjacent wall there was a battered bureau and beside it there was a closet which held his single ill-fitting serge suit, the two or three white shirts that strangled him and the square black shoes that pinched. When he took off his more friendly clothes, the heavy woollen sweaters, mitts and socks which my mother knitted for him and the woollen and doeskin shirts, he dumped them unceremoniously on a single chair. If a visitor entered the room while he was lying on the bed, he would be told to throw the clothes on the floor and take their place upon the chair.

Magazines and books covered the bureau and competed with the clothes for domination of the chair. They further overburdened the heroic little table and lay on top of the radio. They filled a baffling and unknowable cave beneath the bed, and in the corner by the bureau they spilled from the walls and grew up from the floor.

The magazines were the most conventional: *Time, Newsweek, Life, Maclean's, Family Herald, Reader's Digest.* They were the result of various cut-rate subscriptions or of the gift subscriptions associated with Christmas, "the two whole years for only $3.50."

The books were more varied. There were a few hard-cover magnificents and bygone Book-of-the-Month wonders and some were Christmas or birthday gifts. The majority of them, however, were used paperbacks which came from those second-hand bookstores which advertise in the backs of magazines: "Miscellaneous Used Paperbacks 10¢ Each." At first he sent for them himself, although my mother resented the expense, but in later years they came more and more often from my sisters who had moved to the cities. Especially at first they were very weird and varied. Mickey Spillane and Ernest Haycox vied with Dostoyevsky and Faulkner, and the Penguin Poets edition of Gerard Manley Hopkins arrived in the same box as a little book on sex technique called *Getting the Most Out of Love.* The former had been assiduously annotated by a very fine hand using a very blue-inked fountain pen while the latter had been studied by someone with very large thumbs, the prints of which were still visible in the margins. At the slightest provocation it would open almost automatically to particularly graphic and well-smudged pages.

When he was not in the boat, my father spent most of his time lying on the bed in his socks, the top two buttons of his trousers undone, his discarded shirt on the ever-ready chair and the sleeves of the woollen Stanfield underwear, which he wore both summer and winter, drawn half way up to his elbows. The pillows propped up the whiteness of his head and the goose-necked lamp illuminated the pages in his hands. The cigarettes smoked and smouldered on the ashtray and on the table and the radio played constantly, sometimes low and sometimes loud. At midnight and at one, two, three and four, one could sometimes hear the radio, his occasional cough, the rustling thud of a completed book being tossed to the corner heap, or the movement necessitated by his sitting on the edge of the bed to roll the thousandth cigarette. He seemed never to sleep, only to doze, and the light shone constantly from his window to the sea.

My mother despised the room and all it stood for and she had stopped sleeping in it after I was born. She despised disorder in rooms and in houses and in hours and in lives, and she had not read a book since high school. There she had read *Ivanhoe* and considered it a colossal waste of time. Still the room remained, like a solid rock of opposition in the sparkling waters of a clear deep harbour, opening off the kitchen where we really lived our lives, with its door always open and its contents visible to all.

The daughters of the room and of the house were very beautiful. They were tall and willowy like my mother and had her fine facial features set off by the reddish copper-coloured hair that had apparently once been my father's before it turned to white. All of them were very clever in school and helped my mother a great deal about the house. When they were young they sang and were very happy and very nice to me because I was the youngest and the family's only boy.

My father never approved of their playing about the wharf like the other children, and they went there only when my mother sent them on an errand. At such times they almost always overstayed, playing screaming games of tag or hide-and-seek in and about the fishing shanties, the piled traps and tubs of trawl, shouting down to the perch that swam languidly about the wharf's algae-covered piles, or jumping in and out of the boats that tugged gently at their lines. My mother was never uneasy about them at such times, and when her husband criticized her she would say, "Nothing will happen to them there," or "They could be doing worse things in worse places."

By about the ninth or tenth grade my sisters one by one discovered my father's bedroom and then the change would begin. Each would go into the room one morning when he was out. She would go with the ideal hope of imposing order or with the more practical objective of emptying the ashtray, and later she would be found spellbound by the volume in her hand. My mother's reaction was always abrupt, bordering on the angry. "Take your nose out of that trash and come and do your work," she would say, and once I saw her slap my youngest sister so hard that the print of her hand was scarletly emblazoned upon her daughter's cheek while the broken-spined paperback fluttered uselessly to the floor.

Thereafter my mother would launch a campaign against what she had discovered but could not understand. At times although she was not overly religious she would bring in God to bolster her arguments, saying "In the next world God will see to those who waste their lives reading useless books when they should be about their work." Or without theological aid, "I would like to know how books help anyone to live a life." If my father were in, she would repeat the remarks louder than necessary, and her voice would carry into his room where he lay upon his bed. His usual reaction was to turn up the volume of the radio, although that action in itself betrayed the success of the initial thrust.

Shortly after my sisters began to read the books, they grew restless and lost interest in darning socks and baking bread, and all of them eventually went to work as summer waitresses in the Sea Food Restaurant. The restaurant was run by a big American concern from Boston and catered to the tourists that flooded the area during July and August. My mother despised the whole operation. She said the restaurant was not run by "our people," and "our people" did not eat there, and that it was run by outsiders for outsiders.

"Who are these people anyway?" she would ask, tossing back her dark hair, "and what do they, though they go about with their cameras for a hundred years, know about the way it is here, and what do they care about me and mine, and why should I care about them?"

She was angry that my sisters should even conceive of working in such a place and more angry when my father made no move to prevent it, and she was worried about herself and about her family and about her life. Sometimes she would say softly to her sisters, "I don't know what's the matter with my girls. It seems none of them are interested in any of the right things." And sometimes there would be bitter savage arguments. One afternoon I was coming in with three mackerel I'd been given at the wharf when I heard her say, "Well I hope you'll be satisfied when they come home knocked up and you'll have had your way."

It was the most savage thing I'd ever heard my mother say. Not just the words but the way she said them, and I stood there in the porch afraid to breathe for what seemed like the years from ten to fifteen, feeling the damp moist mackerel with their silver glassy eyes growing clammy against my leg.

Through the angle in the screen door I saw my father who had been walking into his room wheel around on one of his rubber-booted heels and look at her with his blue eyes flashing like clearest ice beneath the snow that was his hair. His usually ruddy face was drawn and grey, reflecting the exhaustion of a man of sixty-five who had been working in those rubber boots for eleven hours on an August day, and for a fleeting moment I wondered what I would do if he killed my mother while I stood there in the porch with those three foolish mackerel in my hand. Then he turned and went into his room and the radio blared forth the next day's weather forecast and I retreated under the noise and returned again, stamping my feet and slamming the door too loudly to signal my approach. My mother was busy at the stove when I came in, and did not raise her head when I threw the mackerel in a pan. As I looked into my father's room, I said, "Well how did things go in the boat today?" and he replied, "Oh not too badly, all things considered." He was lying on his back and lighting the first cigarette and the radio was talking about the Virginia coast.

All of my sisters made good money on tips. They bought my father an electric razor which he tried to use for a while and they took out even more magazine subscriptions. They bought my mother a great many clothes of the type she was very fond of, the wide-brimmed hats and the brocaded dresses, but she locked them all in trunks and refused to wear any of them.

On one August day my sisters prevailed upon my father to take some of their restaurant customers for an afternoon ride in the boat. The tourists with their expensive clothes and cameras and sun glasses awkwardly backed down the iron ladder at the wharf's side to where my father waited below, holding the rocking *Jenny Lynn* in snug against the wharf with one hand on the iron ladder and steadying his descending passengers with the other. They tried to look both prim and wind-blown like the girls in the Pepsi-Cola ads and did the best they could, sitting on the thwarts where the newspapers were spread to cover the splattered blood and fish entrails, crowding to one side so that they were in danger of capsizing the boat, taking the inevitable pictures or merely trailing their fingers through the water of their dreams.

All of them liked my father very much and, after he'd brought them back from their circles in the harbour, they invited him to their rented cabins which were located high on a hill overlooking the village to which they were so alien. He proceeded to get very drunk up there with the beautiful view and the strange company and the abundant liquor, and late in the afternoon he began to sing.

I was just approaching the wharf to deliver my mother's summons when he began, and the familiar yet unfamiliar voice that rolled down from the cabins made me feel as I had never felt before in my young life or perhaps as I had always felt without really knowing it, and I was ashamed yet proud, young yet old and saved yet forever lost, and there was nothing I could do to control my legs which trembled nor my eyes which wept for what they could not tell.

The tourists were equipped with tape recorders and my father sang for more than three hours. His voice boomed down the hill and bounced off the surface of the harbour, which was an unearthly blue on that hot August day, and was then reflected to the wharf and the fishing shanties where it was absorbed amidst the men who were baiting their lines for the next day's haul.

He sang all the old sea chanties which had come across from the old world and by which men like him had pulled ropes for generations, and he sang the East Coast sea songs which celebrated the sealing vessels of Northumberland Strait and the long liners of the Grand Banks, and of Anticosti, Sable Island, Grand Manan, Boston Harbor, Nantucket and Block Island. Gradually he shifted to the seemingly unending Gaelic drinking songs with their twenty or more verses and inevitable refrains, and the men in the shanties smiled at the coarseness of some of the verses and at the thought that the singer's immediate audience did not know what they were applauding nor recording to take back to staid old Boston. Later as the sun was setting he switched to the laments and the wild and haunting Gaelic war songs of those spattered Highland ancestors he had never seen, and when his voice ceased, the savage melancholy of three hundred years seemed to hang over the peaceful harbour and the quiet boats and the men leaning in the doorways of their shanties with their cigarettes glowing in the dusk and the women looking to the sea from their open windows with their children in their arms.

When he came home he threw the money he had earned on the kitchen table as he did with all his earnings but my mother refused to touch it and the next day he went with the rest of the men to bait his trawl in the shanties. The tourists came to the door that evening and my mother met them there and told them that her husband was not in although he was lying on the bed only a few feet away with the radio playing and the cigarette upon his lips. She stood in the doorway until they reluctantly went away.

In the winter they sent him a picture which had been taken on the day of the singing. On the back it said, "To Our Ernest Hemingway" and the "Our" was underlined. There was also an accompanying letter telling how much they had enjoyed themselves, how popular the tape was proving and explaining who Ernest Hemingway was. In a way it almost did look like one of those unshaven, taken-in-Cuba pictures of Hemingway. He looked both massive and incongruous in the setting. His bulky fisherman's clothes were too big for the green and white lawn chair in which he sat, and his rubber boots seemed to take up all of the well-clipped grass square. The beach umbrella jarred with his sunburned face and because he had already been singing for some time, his lips which chapped in the winds of spring and burned in the water glare of summer had already cracked in several places, producing tiny flecks of blood at their corners and on the whiteness of his teeth. The bracelets of brass chain which he wore to protect his wrists from chafing seemed abnormally large and his broad leather belt had been slackened and his heavy shirt and underwear were open at the throat revealing an uncultivated wilderness of white chest hair bordering on the semi-controlled stubble of his neck and chin. His blue eyes had looked directly into the camera and his hair was whiter than the two tiny clouds which hung over his left shoulder. The sea was behind him and its immense blue flatness stretched out to touch the arching blueness of the sky. It seemed very far away from him or else he was so much in the foreground that he seemed too big for it.

Each year another of my sisters would read the books and work in the restaurant. Sometimes they would stay out quite late on the hot summer nights and when they came up the stairs my mother would ask them many long and involved questions which they resented and tried to avoid. Before ascending the stairs they would go into my father's room and those of us who waited above could hear them throwing his clothes off the chair before sitting on it or the squeak of the bed as they sat on its edge. Sometimes they would talk to him a long time, the murmur of their voices blending with the music of the radio into a mysterious vapour-like sound which floated softly up the stairs.

I say this again as if it all happened at once and as if all of my sisters were of identical ages and like so many lemmings going into another sea and, again, it was of course not that way at all. Yet go they did, to Boston, to Montreal, to New York with the young men they met during the summers and later married in those far-away cities. The young men were very articulate and handsome and wore fine clothes and drove expensive cars and my sisters, as I said, were very tall and beautiful with their copper-coloured hair and were tired of darning socks and baking bread.

One by one they went. My mother had each of her daughters for fifteen years, then lost them for two and finally forever. None married a fisherman. My mother never accepted any of the young men, for in her eyes they seemed always a combination of the lazy, the effeminate, the dishonest and the unknown. They never seemed to do any physical work and she could not comprehend their luxurious vacations and she did not know whence they came nor who they were. And in the end she did not really care, for they were not of her people and they were not of her sea.

I say this now with a sense of wonder at my own stupidity in thinking I was somehow free and would go on doing well in school and playing and helping in the boat and passing into my early teens while streaks of grey began to appear in my mother's dark hair and my father's rubber boots dragged sometimes on the pebbles of the beach as he trudged home from the wharf. And there were but three of us in the house that had at one time been so loud.

Then during the winter that I was fifteen he seemed to grow old and ill at once. Most of January he lay upon the bed, smoking and reading and listening to the radio while the wind howled about the house and the needle-like snow blistered off the ice-covered harbour and the doors flew out of people's hands if they did not cling to them like death.

In February when the men began overhauling their lobster traps he still did not move, and my mother and I began to knit lobster trap headings in the evenings. The twine was as always very sharp and harsh, and blisters formed upon our thumbs and little paths of blood snaked quietly down between our fingers while the seals that had drifted down from distant Labrador wept and moaned like human children on the ice-floes of the Gulf.

In the daytime my mother's brother who had been my father's partner as long as I could remember also came to work upon the gear. He was a year older than my mother and was tall and dark and the father of twelve children.

By March we were very far behind and although I began to work very hard in the evenings I knew it was not hard enough and that there were but eight weeks left before the opening of the season on May first. And I knew that my mother worried and my uncle was uneasy and that all of our very lives depended on the boat being ready with her gear and two men, by the date of May the first. And I knew then that *David Copperfield* and *The Tempest* and all of those friends I had dearly come to love must really go forever. So I bade them all good-bye.

The night after my first full day at home and after my mother had gone upstairs he called me into his room where I sat upon the chair beside his bed. "You will go back tomorrow," he said simply.

I refused then, saying I had made my decision and was satisfied.

"That is no way to make a decision," he said, "and if you are satisfied I am not. It is best that you go back." I was almost angry then and told him as all children do that I wished he would leave me alone and stop telling me what to do.

He looked at me a long time then, lying there on the same bed on which he had fathered me those sixteen years before, fathered me his only son, out of who knew what emotions when he was already fifty-six and his hair had turned to snow. Then he swung his legs over the edge of the squeaking bed and sat facing me and looked into my own dark eyes with his of crystal blue and placed his hand upon my knee. "I am not telling you to do anything," he said softly, "only asking you."

The next morning I returned to school. As I left, my mother followed me to the porch and said, "I never thought a son of mine would choose useless books over the parents that gave him life."

In the weeks that followed he got up rather miraculously and the gear was ready and the *Jenny Lynn* was freshly painted by the last two weeks of April when the ice began to break up and the lonely screaming gulls returned to haunt the silver herring as they flashed within the sea.

On the first day of May the boats raced out as they had always done, laden down almost to the gunwales with their heavy cargoes of traps. They were almost like living things as they plunged through the waters of the spring and manoeuvred between the still floating icebergs of crystal-white and emerald green on their way to the traditional grounds that they sought out every May. And those of us who sat that day in the high school on the hill, discussing the water imagery of Tennyson, watched them as they passed back and forth beneath us until by afternoon the piles of traps which had been stacked upon the wharf were no longer visible but were spread about the bottoms of the sea. And the *Jenny Lynn* went too, all day, with my uncle tall and dark, like a latter-day Tashtego standing at the tiller with his legs wide apart and guiding her deftly between the floating pans of ice and my father in the stern standing in the same way with his hands upon the ropes that lashed the cargo to the deck. And at night my mother asked, "Well, how did things go in the boat today?"

And the spring wore on and the summer came and school ended in the third week of June and the lobster season on July first and I wished that the two things I loved so dearly did not exclude each other in a manner that was so blunt and too clear.

At the conclusion of the lobster season my uncle said he had been offered a berth on a deep sea dragger and had decided to accept. We all knew that he was leaving the *Jenny Lynn* forever and that before the next lobster season he would buy a boat of his own. He was expecting another child and would be supporting fifteen people by the next spring and could not chance my father against the family that he loved.

I joined my father then for the trawling season, and he made no protest and my mother was quite happy. Through the summer we baited the tubs of trawl in the afternoon and set them at sunset and revisited them in the darkness of the early morning. The men would come tramping by our house at four A.M. and we would join them and walk with them to the wharf and be on our way before the sun rose out of the ocean where it seemed to spend the night. If I was not up they would toss pebbles to my window and I would be very embarrassed and tumble downstairs to where my father lay fully clothed atop his bed, reading his book and listening to his radio and smoking his cigarette. When I appeared he would swing off his bed and put on his boots and be instantly ready and then we would take the lunches my mother had prepared the night before and walk off toward the sea. He would make no attempt to wake me himself.

It was in many ways a good summer. There were few storms and we were out almost every day and we lost a minimum of gear and seemed to land a maximum of fish and I tanned dark and brown after the manner of my uncles.

My father did not tan—he never tanned—because of his reddish complexion, and the salt water irritated his skin as it had for sixty years. He burned and reburned over and over again and his lips still cracked so that they bled when he smiled, and his arms, especially the left, still broke out into the oozing salt-water boils as they had ever since as a child I had first watched him soaking and bathing them in a variety of ineffectual solutions. The chafe-preventing bracelets of brass linked chain that all the men wore about their wrists in early spring were his the full season and he shaved but painfully and only once a week.

And I saw then, that summer, many things that I had seen all my life as if for the first time and I thought that perhaps my father had never been intended for a fisherman either physically or mentally. At least not in the manner of my uncles; he had never really loved it. And I remembered that, one evening in his room when we were talking about *David Copperfield*, he had said that he had always wanted to go to the university and I had dismissed it then in the way one dismisses his father's saying he would like to be a tight-rope walker, and we had gone on to talk about the Peggottys and how they loved the sea.

And I thought then to myself that there were many things wrong with all of us and all our lives and I wondered why my father, who was himself an only son, had not married before he was forty and then I wondered why he had. I even thought that perhaps he had had to marry my mother and checked the dates on the flyleaf of the Bible where I learned that my oldest sister had been born a prosaic eleven months after the marriage, and I felt myself then very dirty and debased for my lack of faith and for what I had thought and done.

And then there came into my heart a very great love for my father and I thought it was very much braver to spend a life doing what you really do not want rather than selfishly following forever your own dreams and inclinations. And I knew then that I could never leave him alone to suffer the iron-tipped harpoons which my mother would forever hurl into his soul because he was a failure as a husband and a father who had retained none of his own. And I felt that I had been very small in a little secret place within me and that even the completion of high school was for me a silly shallow selfish dream.

So I told him one night very resolutely and very powerfully that I would remain with him as long as he lived and we would fish the sea together. And he made no protest but only smiled through the cigarette smoke that wreathed his bed and replied, "I hope you will remember what you've said."

The room was now so filled with books as to be almost Dickensian, but he would not allow my mother to move or change them and he continued to read them, sometimes two or three a night. They came with great regularity now, and there were more hard covers, sent by my sisters who had gone so long ago and now seemed so distant and so prosperous, and sent also pictures of small red-haired grandchildren with baseball bats and dolls which he placed upon his bureau and which my mother gazed at wistfully when she thought no one would see. Red-haired grandchildren with baseball bats and dolls who would never know the sea in hatred or in love.

And so we fished through the heat of August and into the cooler days of September when the water was so clear we could almost see the bottom and the white mists rose like delicate ghosts in the early morning dawn. And one day my mother said to me, "You have given added years to his life."

And we fished on into October when it began to roughen and we could no longer risk night sets but took our gear out each morning and returned at the first sign of the squalls; and on into November when we lost three tubs of trawl and the clear blue water turned to a sullen grey and the trochoidal waves rolled rough and high and washed across our bows and decks as we ran within their troughs. We wore heavy sweaters now and the awkward rubber slickers and the heavy woollen mitts which soaked and froze into masses of ice that hung from our wrists like the limbs of gigantic monsters until we thawed them against the exhaust pipe's heat. And almost every day we would leave for home, before noon, driven by the blasts of the northwest wind, coating our eyebrows with ice and freezing our eyelids closed as we leaned into a visibility that was hardly there, charting our course from the compass and the sea, running with the waves and between them but never confronting their towering might.

And I stood at the tiller now, on these homeward lunges, stood in the place and in the manner of my uncle, turning to look at my father and to shout over the roar of the engine and the slop of the sea to where he stood in the stern, drenched and dripping with the snow and the salt and the spray and his bushy eyebrows caked in ice. But on November twenty-first, when it seemed we might be making the final run of the season, I turned and he was not there and I knew even in that instant that he would never be again.

On November twenty-first the waves of the grey Atlantic are very very high and the waters are very cold and there are no signposts on the surface of the sea. You cannot tell where you have been five minutes before and in the squalls of snow you cannot see. And it takes longer than you would believe to check a boat that has been running before a gale and turn her ever so carefully in a wide and stupid circle, with timbers creaking and straining, back into the face of storm. And you know that it is useless and that your voice does not carry the length of the boat and that even if you knew the original spot, the relentless waves would carry such a burden perhaps a mile or so by the time you could return. And you know also, the final irony, that your father like your uncles and all the men that form your past, cannot swim a stroke.

The lobster beds off the Cape Breton coast are still very rich and now, from May to July, their offerings are packed in crates of ice, and thundered by the gigantic transport trucks, day and night, through New Glasgow, Amherst, Saint John and Bangor and Portland and into Boston where they are tossed still living into boiling pots of water, their final home.

And though the prices are higher and the competition tighter, the grounds to which the *Jenny Lynn* once went remain untouched and unfished as they have for the last ten years. For if there are no signposts on the sea in storm there are certain ones in calm and the lobster bottoms were distributed in calm before any of us can remember and the grounds my father fished were those his father fished before him and there were others before and before and before. Twice the big boats have come from forty and fifty miles, lured by the promise of the grounds, and strewn the bottom with their traps and twice they have returned to find their buoys cut adrift and their gear lost and destroyed. Twice the Fisheries Officer and the Mounted Police have come and asked many long and involved questions and twice they have received no answers from the men leaning in the doors of their shanties and the women standing at their windows with their children in their arms. Twice they have gone away saying: "There are no legal boundaries in the Marine area"; "No one can own the sea"; "Those grounds don't wait for anyone."

But the men and the women, with my mother dark among them, do not care for what they say, for to them the grounds are sacred and they think they wait for me.

It is not an easy thing to know that your mother lives alone on an inadequate insurance policy and that she is too proud to accept any other aid. And that she looks through her lonely window onto the ice of winter and the hot flat calm of summer and the rolling waves of fall. And that she lies awake in the early morning's darkness when the rubber boots of the men scrunch upon the gravel as they pass beside her house on their way down to the wharf. And she knows that the footsteps never stop, because no man goes from her house, and she alone of all the Lynns has neither son nor son-in-law that walks toward the boat that will take him to the sea. And it is not an easy thing to know that your mother looks upon the sea with love and on you with bitterness because the one has been so constant and the other so untrue.

But neither is it easy to know that your father was found on November twenty-eighth, ten miles to the north and wedged between two boulders at the base of the rock-strewn cliffs where he had been hurled and slammed so many many times. His hands were shredded ribbons as were his feet which had lost their boots to the suction of the sea, and his shoulders came apart in our hands when we tried to move him from the rocks. And the fish had eaten his testicles and the gulls had pecked out his eyes and the white-green stubble of his whiskers had continued to grow in death, like the grass on graves, upon the purple, bloated mass that was his face. There was not much left of my father, physically, as he lay there with the brass chains on his wrists and the seaweed in his hair.

Roch Carrier

(b. 1937)

A NATIVE OF THE BEAUCE REGION IN QUEBEC, Roch Carrier was born in Sainte-Justine-de-Dorchester, attended the University of Montreal and the Sorbonne, taught at the Collège Militaire de St. Jean, and in 1994 was named Director of the Canada Council. One of the most widely read Quebec novelists in English translation, he is noted for his trilogy about village and city confrontation during World War II and after. Marked by its black humour and fabular quality, the trilogy includes *La guerre, yes sir!* (1968, tr. 1970), *Floralie, where are you?* (1969, tr. 1971), and *Is it the sun, Philibert?* (1970, tr. 1972). Several more novels have appeared since then, together with many stories—some of them in journals for children, such as *Vidéo-presse*. His collection *Jolis deuils* appeared in 1964, and *Les enfants du bonhomme dans la lune* (from which "What Language Do Bears Speak?" comes) in 1979, translated as *The Hockey Sweater and Other Stories* that same year, by Sheila Fischman. The title story of this latter work has become a classic comic story of childhood trauma, especially for a generation that grew up with the T. Eaton Company catalogue and the perennial rivalry between the Montreal Canadiens and the Toronto Maple Leafs; it has also appeared in an illustrated children's version, and as a National Film Board animated short subject.

Like most of Carrier's work, "What Language Do Bears Speak?" draws on folktale idiom and folktale pattern: the iterative references to incomprehensible language cumulatively build to the characteristic climax of the tall tale, and the ironic exaggerations are held in check by the apparently direct, honest, naive point of view. The characters matter-of-factly accept the violence they witness because they take it to be a natural feature of the world that is alien to them. But several times in the story the tables turn; the humour derives from the reader's awareness of an indirect tale as well, about the consequences of mistaken identity, or of presuming too much—about language, politics, or the travelling circus.

For Further Reading

ROCH CARRIER, "Ceci n'est pas un conte," *Etudes françaises* 12 (avril 1976): 85–89.

MICHAEL DARLING, "Reading Carrier's 'The Nun Who Returned to Ireland,'" *Canadian Literature* 104 (Spring 1985): 24–33.

SHERRILL E. GRACE, "Duality and Series: Forms of the Canadian Imagination," *Canadian Review of Comparative Literature* 7 (Fall 1980): 438–51.

What Language
Do Bears Speak?
Translated by Sheila Fischman

Following our own morning ritual, to which we submitted with more conviction than to the one of saying our prayers when we jumped out of bed, we ran
to the windows and lingered there, silent and contemplative, for long moments. Meanwhile, in the kitchen, our mother was becoming impatient, for
we were late. She was always afraid we'd be late... Life was there all around
us and above us, vibrant and luminous, filled with trees; it offered us fields
of daisies and it led to hills that concealed great mysteries.

The story of that morning begins with some posters. During the night, posters
had been put up on the wooden poles that supported the hydro wires.

'Posters! They've put up posters!'

Did they announce that hairy wrestlers were coming? Far West singers?
Strong men who could carry horses on their shoulders? Comic artists who had
'made all America collapse with laughter'? An international tap-dance champion? A sword swallower? Posters! Perhaps we'd be allowed to go and see a
play on the stage of the parish hall—if the curé declared from the pulpit that the
play wasn't immoral and if we were resourceful enough to earn the money for
a ticket. Posters! The artists in the photographs would gradually come down
from the posters until they inhabited our dreams, haunted our games and accompanied us, invisible, on our expeditions.

'There's posters up!'

We weren't allowed to run to the posters and, trembling, read their marvellous messages; it was contrary to maternal law to set foot outside before we
had washed and combed our hair. After submitting to this painful obligation we
were able to learn that we would see, in flesh and blood, the unsurpassable Dr.
Schultz, former hunter in Africa, former director of zoos in the countries of
Europe, former lion-tamer, former elephant-hunter and former free-style
wrestling champion in Germany, Austria and the United Kingdom, in an unbelievable, unsurpassable show—'almost unimaginable.' Dr. Schultz would
present dogs that could balance on balls, rabbit-clowns, educated monkeys,
hens that could add and subtract; in addition, Dr. Schultz would brave a savage bear in an uneven wrestling match 'between the fierce forces of nature and
the cunning of human intelligence, of which the outcome might be fatal for
one of the protagonists.'

"What Language do Bears Speak?" by Roch Carrier, from *The Hockey Sweater and Other Stories*,
translated by Sheila Fischman (Toronto: House of Anansi Press, 1979). Reprinted by permission of the publisher.

We had seen bears before, but dead ones, with mouths bleeding, teeth gleaming. Hunters liked to tell how their victims had appeared to them: '...standing up, practically walking like a man, but a big man, hairy like a bear; and then it came at me roaring like thunder when it's far away behind the sky, with claws like knives at the end of his paws, and then when I fired it didn't move any more than if a mosquito'd got into its fur. Wasn't till the tenth bullet that I saw him fall down...' Loggers, too, had spotted bears and some, so they said, had been so frightened their hair had turned white.

Dr. Schultz was going to risk his life before our eyes by pitting himself against this merciless beast. We would see with our own eyes, alive before us, not only a bear but a man fighting a bear. We'd see all of that!

A voice that reached the entire village, a voice that was magnified by loudspeakers, announced that the great day had arrived: 'At last you can see, in person, the unsurpassable Dr. Schultz, the man with the most scars in the world, and his bear—a bear that gets fiercer and fiercer as the season for love comes closer!'

We saw an old yellow bus drive up, covered with stars painted in red, pulling a trailer on whose sides we could read: DR. SCHULTZ AND ASSOCIATES UNIVERSAL WONDER CIRCUS LTD. The whole thing was covered with iron bars that were tangled and crossed and knotted and padlocked. A net of clinking chains added to the security. Between messages, crackling music made curtains open at the windows and drew the children outdoors. Then the magical procession entered the lot where we played ball in the summer. The motor growled, the bus moved forward, back, hesitated. At last it found its place and the motor was silent. A man got out of the bus. He stood on the running-board; twenty or thirty children had followed the circus. He considered us with a smile.

'Hi, kids,' he said.

He added something else, words in the same language, which we'd never heard before.

'Either he's talking bear,' said my friend Lapin, 'or he's talking English.'

'If we can't understand him,' I concluded, 'it must be English.'

The man on the running-board was still talking; in his strange language he seemed to be asking questions. Not understanding, we listened, stupefied to see Dr. Schultz in person, alive, come down from the posters.

'We talk French here,' one of us shouted.

Smiling again, Dr. Schultz said something else we didn't understand.

'We should go get Monsieur Rancourt,' I suggested.

Monsieur Rancourt had gone to Europe to fight in the First World War and he'd had to learn English so he could follow the soldiers in his army. I ran to get Monsieur Rancourt. Panting behind his big belly, he hurried as fast as he could. He was looking forward to speaking this language. He hadn't spoken it for so many years he wasn't sure, he told me, that he could remember it. As soon as he saw the man from the circus he told me: "I'm gonna try to tell him hello in English.'

'Good day sir! How you like it here today?' ('I remember!' Monsieur Rancourt rejoiced, shouting with delight. 'I didn't forget!')

Dr. Schultz moved towards Monsieur Rancourt, holding out his hand. A hand wearing a leather glove, in the middle of summer.

'It's because of the bear bites,' my friend Lapin explained to me.

'Apparently the *Anglais* can't take the cold,' said one of our friends whose mother's sister had a cousin who worked in an *Anglais* house in Ontario.

The man from the circus and Monsieur Rancourt were talking like two old friends meeting after a number of years. They even laughed. In English, Monsieur Rancourt laughed in a special way, 'a real English laugh,' we judged, whispering. In French, Monsieur Rancourt never laughed; he was surly. We listened to them, mouths agape. This English language which we'd heard on the radio, in the spaces between the French stations when we turned the tuning knob, we were hearing now for real, in life, in our village, spoken by two men standing in the sun. I made an observation: instead of speaking normally, as in French, instead of spitting the words outside their lips, the two men were swallowing them. My friend Lapin had noticed the same thing, for he said:

'Sounds like they're choking.'

Suddenly something was overturned in the trailer; we could hear chains clinking, a bump swelled out the canvas covering and we saw a black ball burst out—the head of a bear.

Dr. Schultz and Monsieur Rancourt had rolled up their shirtsleeves and they were comparing tattoos.

'The bear's loose!'

The animal ran out on the canvas, came down from the roof of the bus and jumped to the ground. How could we tell that to Dr. Schultz who didn't understand our language, whose back was turned to the trailer and who was completely absorbed in his conversation?

'Monsieur Rancourt!' I shouted. 'The bear's running away!'

There was no need to translate. The man from the circus had understood. Waving a revolver, he sped towards the bear, which was fleeing into a neighbouring field. He shouted, pleaded, threatened.

'What's he saying?' we asked Monsieur Rancourt.

'Words that English children don't learn till they're men.'

'He must be saying the same words my father says when a cow jumps over the fence. They aren't nice.'

Dr. Schultz, whom we had seen disappear into the oats, came back after a long moment and spoke to Monsieur Rancourt, who ran to the village. The men who were gathered at the general store rushed off to find other men; they took out traps, rifles, ropes. While the mothers gathered up their children who were scattered over the village, the men set out, directed by fat Monsieur Rancourt. Because of his experience in the war, he took charge of the round-up. Dr. Schultz had confided to him, we learned later:

'That bear's more important than my own wife.'

They mustn't kill it, then, but bring it back alive.

The show was to begin in the early afternoon. Dr. Schultz, who had gone with the men into the forest, came back muttering; we guessed that he was unhappy. At his trailer he opened the padlock, unfastened the crossed iron bars, pulled out the pegs and undid the chains. We saw him transform his trailer into a stage, with the help of a system of pulleys, ropes and tripods. Suddenly we were working with the circus man: we carried boxes, held out ropes, unrolled canvas, stuck pickets in the ground, lined up chairs. Dr. Schultz directed our labours. Small, over-excited men that we were, we had forgotten he was speaking a language we didn't understand.

A piece of unrolled canvas suspended from a rope, which was held in place by stakes, formed a circular enclosure. It resembled a tent without a roof; we had built it. We were proud; would we, as long as we lived, ever have another day as beautiful as this one? From now on we were part of the circus.

At last it was time for the show. The music cried out as far as the horizon. In the stands there were mostly women: the men were still pursuing the lost bear.

In gleaming leather boots, in a costume sparkling with gilt braid, Dr. Schultz walked out on the stage. He said a few words and the crowd applauded fervently; the spectators no doubt considered it a mark of prowess to speak with such ease a language of which they couldn't utter a single word.

He opened a cage and a dozen rabbits came out. On the back of each he hung a number. At the other end of the platform was a board with holes cut out of it. Above each hole, a number. The man from the circus gave an order and the rabbits ran to the holes that bore their numbers. Unbelievable, wasn't it? We all raised rabbits, but our animals had never learned anything more intelligent than how to chew clover. Our hands were burning, so much had we applauded our friend Dr. Schultz. Next came the trained dogs' act: one danced a waltz; another rode around a track on a bicycle while his twin played a drum. We applauded our great friend hard enough to break our metacarpals.

The acrobatic chimpanzee's act had scarcely begun when a great uproar drowned the music from the loudspeakers. The canvas wall shook, it opened, and we saw the captured bear come in. The men from the village were returning it to its master, roaring, furious, screaming, clawing, kicking, gasping, famished. The men from the village, accustomed to recalcitrant bulls and horses, were leading it with strong authority; they had passed ropes around its neck and paws so the furious animal had to obey. Monsieur Rancourt was speaking French and English all at once.

When he saw his bear, Dr. Schultz let out a cry that Monsieur Rancourt didn't translate. The men's hands dropped the ropes: the bear was free. He didn't notice immediately. We heard his harsh breathing, and his master's too. The hour had come: we were going to see the greatest circus attraction in the Americas, we were going to see with our own eyes the famous Dr. Schultz, our friend, wrestle a giant black bear.

No longer feeling the ropes burning its neck, no longer submitting to the strength of the men who were tearing it apart, the bear stood up, spread its arms and shot forward with a roar. The bear struck Dr. Schultz like a mountain that might have rolled onto him. The bear and our friend tumbled off the stage. There was a ripple of applause; all the men together would never have succeeded in mustering half the daring of Dr. Schultz. The bear got up again, trampled on the great tamer of wild beasts and dived into the canvas enclosure, tearing it with one swipe of its claws before disappearing.

Dr. Schultz had lost his jacket and trousers. His body was streaked with red scratches. He was weeping.

'If I understand right,' said Monsieur Rancourt, 'he's telling us that the bear wasn't *his* bear...'

'It isn't *his* bear...'

The men shook and spluttered with laughter as they did at the general store when one of them told a funny story.

The men laughed so hard that Monsieur Rancourt could no longer hear Dr. Schultz's moans as he lay bleeding on the platform. The undertaker apologized for the misunderstanding.

'That bear was a bear that talked English, though, because I didn't understand a single word he said.'

Claire Harris

(b. 1937)

IN CLAIRE HARRIS'S OWN WORDS, she is "an African in the diaspora." She was born in Port of Spain, Trinidad, where she grew up and attended convent school. Subsequently she earned an Honours B.A. in English and Spanish at University College, Dublin (1961), a Diploma in Education at the University of the West Indies (1963), and a Diploma in Media Studies at the University of Lagos, Nigeria (1975). She immigrated to Canada in 1966 to teach in Calgary's Catholic school system. After retiring from teaching, she worked editorially for the literary magazines *Dandelion* (1981–89) and *blue buffalo* (1984–87). With her first book, she won a Commonwealth Prize for poetry, and several other honours have followed. She is the author of *Fables from the Women's Quarters* (1984), *The Conception of Winter* (1989), *Drawing Down a Daughter* (1992), and other books, and she acknowledges the influence on her work of Frantz Fanon and Aimé Césaire, bell hooks and Doris Lessing, Baudelaire, Lorca, and Kenneth Rexroth's Chinese translations. Her work is linguistically compact, politically charged, and highly critical of the racism and sexism which continue in Canada to marginalize those with black and Asian ancestry. Yet—as in "A Matter of Fact," where she draws on "La Diablesse" and other folk tales and traditions of Trinidad and Tobago—she also writes that cultural synthesis is possible. "A Matter of Fact" appeared first in *Imagining Women,* edited by the "Second, Second Story Collective" in 1988; it reappeared, revised and without a title, in *Drawing Down a Daughter.* The text printed here follows the revised version.

In "Why I Write" (see Morrell, 26–33), she declares that she found her subject when she committed herself to examine the nature of humanity in a fractured world, to take up the cause of women who suffer both racial and gender subjugation, and to address the need to reinscribe "Africa" on the consciousness of Westerners. The "I" in her work, she says, is neither disembodied nor universal nor naively autobiographical; it is the specific voice, crafted in narrative, of a modern African female, one who rejects the fragmentation of "minority" status and claims (perhaps in utopian fashion) the centre. Harris adds that "subject" alone is merely content; because of her interest in the overlap between "the metaphysics of the pre-Western world" and contemporary physics (chaos theory, for example, and space-time dimensions), she seeks to write these subjects into poetry.

For Further Reading

CLAIRE HARRIS, *"I dream of a new naming"* [interview] in Janice Williamson, *Sounding Difference: Conversations with Seventeen Canadian Women Writers* (Toronto: U Toronto P, 1993) 115–30.

————, "Ole Talk" in *Language in Her Eye: Writing and Gender,* ed. Libby Scheier, Sarah Sheard, and Eleanor Wachtel (Toronto: Coach House, 1990) 131–41.

LYNETTE HUNTER, "After Modernism: Alternative Voices in the Writings of Dionne Brand, Claire Harris, and Marlene Philip," *University of Toronto Quarterly* 62.2 (Winter 1992–93): 256–81.

CAROL MORRELL, ed., *Grammar of Dissent: poetry and prose by Claire Harris, M. Nourbese Philip, Dionne Brand* (Fredericton: Goose Lane, 1994) "Introduction," 9–24.

MONTY REID, "Choosing Control: An Interview with Claire Harris," *Waves* 13.1 (Fall 1984): 36–41.

ANDREW SALKEY, review of *Drawing Down a Daughter. World Literature Today* 67.2 (Spring 1993): 435–36.

A Matter of Fact

It is a matter of fact that the girl waits till the man from the capital begins to dress before she asks diffidently, "Where you leave your car?"

Burri buttons his shirt carefully before he replies, "It on the other side, near the big house. It park round the bend near the temple. Why you ask?"

"We could go for a drive."

"We could go for a drive!" He smiles. "Jocelyn, you ain't see how late it is? What your mother go say, girl?" His smile broadens, he strikes a pose and asks again, "You want she coming after me with a cutlass?"

"Well we have to talk."

"Eh, eh! I thought we was talking. What you have to say you can't say here?" He is laughing as he says this.

"It too late to stay here...I can't afford to catch cold!"

With a flourish, "Here, put on my jacket." Then seeing her seriousness, "You see how warm you get." His arm goes around her. He nibbles on her ear and chuckles.

"Look, I want to talk!"

"SO, talk!" He still nibbles, moving down the column of her neck, his fingers turn her face away from the river to face him.

"I ain't get my menses this month, again."

"What you saying..." he begins casually, then suddenly alert he sits up. "You ain't get... Look girl, what you trying on me?" His voice is rough. His movements abrupt.

"Nothing! Is true. I pregnant."

"Well, that's great!... So, you see a doctor? When?"

"I get the results Monday."

He stares at her, frowning.

"I want you to come and see my mother."

He has decided to be cool, "Me! What I want with your mother!" His eyes are wide. He is smiling. He puts his arm around her. "Is you I want." He pats her stomach. "I'll bet is a boy!"

"How we go marry if you ain't talk?"

"Marry!" He is amazed. "Look girl, I ask you to marry me? Is the man does ask!" He scowls, "I ain't ready to marry nobody."

"But ain't you say you love me? What you think my mother go say? Where I go go?"

He is contemptuous. "Is town you go to school? You never hear about tablet? If is mine, ask your grandmother to give you a tea to drink, because I ain't marrying nobody." He begins to gather his things together. He checks his car keys, his wallet. Draws his Seiko on over his wrist.

"But I can't...I ain't never...nobody..."

Now he is gentle again. He takes her hand and seems to think. "Girl, I sorry. Don't do anything yet. I go think of a way. Don't say nothing if you frighten."

"What you mean?"

"A way to fix everything. What? You think I just go leave you?" He smiles, bends to kiss her, straightens, looks around. "But look how late you keep me here! Is a good thing it have moon. How else to see to go through all that bush?"

"When you coming back?"

"Thursday."

The lie trips from his tongue as smooth as butter, and the girl hears it though she is desperate to believe. She stands on the ledge by the falls watching him bound down the hill towards the river. His jacket slung over one shoulder flaps in his lean surefooted grace. He does not look back until he comes to the clump of bamboo before the bend in the river and sets foot on the path. She knows he has turned, because she can see the trim white shirt tucked neatly back into his pants, and the gleaming silver buckle in his belt. He has come to her straight from his clean civil service job in the intimidating red pile of the Legislature. She does not return his wave. But waits to stop the tears that come of their own volition. When she is no longer shuddering, she wipes her face and begins to plan how to get to her room at the back of the house without coming face to face with her mother. Later she will claim a headache. This at least is true. She begins to climb up to the road to the village. Her fingers stray to the medallion dangling against her sore breasts.

Of all this: the river valley, the girl Jocelyn, the pregnancy, Burri as snake, the old storyteller will say nothing. She has no truck with this simple form, with its order and its inherent possibility of justice. Though she speaks the language, she knows the real world where men wander is full of unseen presences, of interruptions, of rupture. In such a world, men have only tricks and magic. When she makes her old voice growl, or rise and fall on the gutter and flare of candlelight, her tale is not only a small meeting: chance and the implacable at the crossroads, i.e. in the individual. Her tale is a celebration, and a binding of community. Her theme is survival in the current of riverlife. Her eyes scan the gathered children fiercely, "You can learn how to deal with life; you cannot avoid what nests in you." There is something of the ancestral, of Africa in this. The children hear. They are polite. They nod solemnly. But their eyes lust after the story.

She laughs in the disconcerting way of old women, lights the candles, orders the electric lights switched off. Now she is ready.

"*See-ah,*" she growls.

"*See-ah,*" the children growl back.

"*See-ah Burri See-ah.*"

"*See-ah Burri See-ah,*" the children sing hugging their knees and moving closer, almost huddling.

It have a man, Burri, he go see he girl by the river and he stay too late. They must have had talk or something because usually he leave while it light because he know about forest, riverbank, and La Diablesse. Well, this Burri, he hurry long through the tunnel form by the arching bamboo. All time he watching the forest, looking round and thing. He ain't really 'fraid, but he know in a few minutes darkness be King. Only moon for light. He ain't running, but he walking real fast. He feel he got to get to the car quick. It seem to him he walking and walking but he ain't getting nowhere. He think perhaps he miss the crossing stones. But he can't see how he do that because it ain't got no turn off. Well, this Burri, he decide to stop for a minute and light a cigarette. Well is who tell Burri do that?

"See-ah Burri See-ah
See-ah Burri Mammy oh.
See-ah Burri Mammy oh," respond the children.

"Crick-crack," says a small boy who wants to get on with the story.

First thing he know he can't find his lighter anywhere. He check breast pocket, breast pocket say, 'check shirt pocket.' He check shirt pocket, shirt pocket say, 'check pant pocket.' He check pant pocket, pant pocket say, 'check jacket pocket.' He check jacket pocket, and jacket pocket say, 'ain't my business if you drop it.'

Is now he in big trouble. Pitch black and no way to make a light. He begin to really hurry, and see heself looking straight into old eye of mappipi zanana. Snake straight and flat on the branch. Now he really begin to run. He run like he mad. Like snake chasing him. Branch catch at him, grass like it want to hold him back. A bird fly straight up out of the ground in front of him flapping and screaming. He running so hard that Burri half-way cross the clearing before he realize it.

He slow heself down. He bend over holding his knee like Olympic runner. When he heart return to he chest, he look back to the mouth of the bamboo grove. He ain't see nothing. He walk on now. He thinking how big and bright the moon. And is so it hanging low over the river. Well, is finally he come to the steppin stones and them. The water low in the river and he ain't think it go be slippery. And he standing there, shivering a little, because like is something cold trying to bind him, when he see a flash of something white. Like it moving in the trees on the other side of the river. Even before she come out in the moonlight he know is a woman. Is so some of those men does be. Anyhow she standing in the open looking frighten, and he see one time she pretty for so. Real pretty-pretty. And she got that high-boned face and full lips like the girl he just leave. Not that he thinking about she. What he thinking is how the moonlight so bright-bright, and how he clothes so mess up with all that running and thing. Instant he begin to fix up he shirt, and he jacket, he even take he tie out he pocket and put it back on.

And all the time he whistling. Like somebody give he something, and he real, real please...

"See-ah Burri See-ah
Burri cross de river oh
Burri itch he scratch-oh.

Burri itch he scratch-oh," sang the children happily.

"Crick-crack," says the small boy who knows his role.

The old woman turns to the small boy, "You is man, all you don't have no real sense. Is not only what you see that there." She pauses a moment, "And not all what smell sweet does taste sweet." Then she begins again.

Well, now that he tidy, Burri feel that he is who he is. He walk to the stones and all the whole time he smiling at the girl. He measure the first jump and he start crossing, jumping from stone to stone, and like he showing off a little for the girl. So he look up to see how she taking it, and he see her eyes. They like a lasso. They like a fishline, and Burri hook. He fall. He slip and he fall and feel heself struggling, the water close over he head, he thrash out and kick up, and he know the water ain't deep. But he head butt against sand, he eye open to the green wall of a pool. Current catch him, he toss like twig. His chest heavy and hurting, he see stars, and white light exploding, and red. Sudden he is boy again. This girl, Anita, skin like clay pot, that colour, her hair trailing in the water, her breast buds glistening, she floating on the surface of the river. Fragile and open as if she alone, as if none of the rest of them there. He swim over to her quiet, quiet, then he grab a bud in his mouth. How after the shock she scream and scream, and she grab his head and hold it down in the river bottom. How the thin wiry legs scissor and ride him. How the blood roar in he ears, and the darkness catch him. And then the weight lift and the light break through. How he jump and jerk and fight the line, the hooked finger. And how in the end he flop on the bank. How he lungs burn in the moonlight and water pour from eyes, nose, mouth. Meanwhile the woman just standing there under the cocoa. She ain't say nothing. He land on the riverbank at she feet where the skirt circle her in a frothing green frill.

Well, Burri fright leave as he see the woman kind of smiling, like she just too polite to laugh out loud. So now he start to feel stupid for so! But the girl bend down and give he a hand, and he stand up, and she say real nice, "You ain't careful, you catch cold!"

He just nod he head. Burri no fool, he figure he go let she do the talking and just nod and thing. He know if she start feeling sorry for him, he set. And right away he want to know she real, real well.

"You have far to go?" she voice have this sweet lilt.

Burri say, "It quite town I have to go!" He shiver a little bit then he say, "Is only my chest I 'fraid."

"You could come by me and dry out. Is only my grandmother there." And she smiling real sweet, and her voice like she promising something.

Burri ain't stop to ask heself how come a girl standing out there in the moonlight by sheself. He ain't ask heself how come he feeling so happy all of a sudden. He feeling happy, he just feel happy. And the woman herself, she just looking prettier and prettier. The woman self, she too happy because normally she does have to beg, but this one he just coming with her easy-easy.

"See-ah Burri See-ah." The old woman is drumming on her knees.

"See-ah Burri See-ah." The boy has got a bottle an' spoon.

"See-ah Burri See-ah

Burri lock in a box oh
What lock he in, can't open, oh."
Knees bent, turning slightly sideways, the old lady does a calypso shuffle,
"What lock he in, can't open oh."
Arms waving, pelvis shifting, the children dance around the room.
"What lock he in, can't open oh
See-ah Burri See-ah."
The boy gets tired of the bottle an' spoon. He decides to assert control.
"Crick-crack," he says. And again, "Crick-crack!" The old lady sighs, sits.
The children collapse at her feet. The old lady eyes the boy. "Your pee ain't
froth, you can't be man," she says. The boy's eyes go round with surprise. The
girls giggle. The old lady is talking rudeness! For a moment her voice crackles
as she picks up the tale.

Well now, Burri, he going up the hill with the lady. And he noticing how
sweet she smelling, like is flowers. And how she turn she head, and walk a little sideways. He thinking how lucky he is. And how he never realize Lopinot
have so many pretty girls. His head so full a plans for the girl, he never notice
she limping until they get to the car. Is when playing real gentleman he open
the car door for she that he see the funny foot. Still his mind ain't tell him
nothing. Is so when you talking love you don't see what you don't want to
see. Burri get in the car, take out he car keys, and say to the girl, real formal, "So
where do you live Miss...?" and he kind of pause like he waiting for she to
give he a name, but she ain't say no name. She just give him directions for a road
near the ravine. The ravine about a mile and a half up the road. Burri thinking
is so she want to play it? If she ain't give me a name, I ain't giving she one
neither. He look at she sitting there beside him, and he thinking how smooth
she skin, and he wondering what she grandmother going to say, and he hoping she real old. Perhaps is thinking of old that make he think of death. Anyway
it suddenly hit him what the scent in the car remind him of. Is how the house
smell when they bring all the wreaths for his mother funeral. Burri really love
he mother now she dead. Just thinking about her could bring tears to his eye.
The girl ain't saying nothing. She just sitting there smiling to sheself private like.
Burri car have signal in the engine. But he begin to do show-off drive. He open
the car window and begin to make pretty-pretty signal with his whole arm.
Then he reach for he cigarettes. As soon as she see the cigarette, she begin to
frown. She say "That does make me sick, yes?"

Burri forget all about he wet clothes, which practically dry by now. He thinking this woman bold, yes! She ask me for a lift. Now she telling me I can't
smoke in my own car! Is right now to see who is boss.

He say, "The window open, you don't see?" But she smart too. Quick as
crazy ants her hand move to the dashboard, and she grab the extra lighter he
does keep there. All the time she laughing like is joke. Burri ain't think is joke,
but he laugh like he think is joke.

He smiling and he smiling, but he mind working overtime. "God!" he say,
"but you stubborn yes! And in my own car too?" Is because he was looking
at her that he see she face slip a little when he say "God!" He think, "I ketch!

Now is Lawd help me!" And he see she face. He see it slip. And she put she hand up to hide it, and he grab the lighter from she. The whole car filling up with the scent of dead flowers. And he light the cigarette.

"Ah, Burri!" the children exclaim.

"So what you think happen next?" the old lady asks. She is relaxed, at ease. *"You lucky, eh Burri, You lucky."*

The children vie with each other in their banshee wailing,

"I woulda break you neck fuh you
de devil eat you, Burri."

They try to fill the room with wild laughter.

"Well, then she disappear," the old lady says, *"Is so Burri tell me and now I come here to tell you."*

A small girl fingers her face. "Ah, Burri," she sighs, eyes busy with the horror of a face slipping. Is it possible to be a La Diablesse and not know it, she wonders, where would you go when they found you out?

"But how she sitting here in the dark like that?"

"Girl, turn on the electricity and throw some light on things."

I'll try. But this isn't easy. For one thing, I doubt the ability of anyone to relate a series of facts accurately. For another, I doubt that it is possible to consider any event a fact except in the simplest use of that word. Take, for instance, the laughable, the incontrovertible idea that I am writing this. True, these are my hands that strike the keys. But I have so little control over what is being written that I know the story is writing me. I have been brooding over these events since I rediscovered them in 1983. Once I was determined to write a straightforward narrative. A soupçon of horror. A fiction. Yet this has become an autobiography. Of sorts. And this short paragraph a kick against that fate. For we do not know if any of this really happened. Yet I remember the story being told. I remember the old woman. And I am sure the story was told as I have written it because that is how the books say Afro-Caribbean tales are told. Your books, I mean. But this is not really about style. This is about plot. For, a few years later, seven years after the telling, to be precise, I met John Burian Armstrong.

He was dressed all in white except for a navy shirt. Close-cropped greying hair topped what I was later on to learn was called an ageless face. At the time I thought that in spite of the deep crevasses that ran down to the corner of his mouth, he was young. There I was curled up in my father's chair on the verandah, reading, I am sure, though I am not sure what I was reading. He stood there smiling at me, sucking at his lower lip as if I reminded him of food, and in spite of his cane, or perhaps because of it, managing to look Mr. Cool.

"You must be Mr. Williams's daughter!"

It crossed my mind suddenly to say coldly, "Not really, I'm a La Diablesse in waiting."

Well... Not really.

I'm trying for fact. A little artistic licence here, a little there, and the next thing you know I'm writing history.

A few minutes later I heard him say to my father, "I'm John Burian Armstrong. People around here say I should talk to you."

I was not very surprised by this opening. "Talking to my father" was something the villagers did regularly. He was the recipient of their dreams and their fears. As the only educated black man who came to the village regularly, he was frequently asked to help when anything 'official' or unusual came into their lives. Sometimes, perhaps often, the villagers simply needed someone to know what life, or 'they who does run everything' had done to them, again. So when Armstrong introduced himself, my father sat back in his dark mahogany easy chair with the cushioned slats and prepared to listen.

"Oh! So what is it you have to tell me, Mr. Armstrong?"

"Everyone calls me 'Burri'."

"Burri, then."

"Sir what I have to say is God's truth! People say I was drunk. But that time I didn't drink. A drink now and then, yes. But drink to get drunk, no! Not even till today."

It was the name, Burri, that did it. *"See-ah Burri See-ah."* I moved a Morris chair as close to the windows looking on the verandah as possible. Very quietly indeed I prepared to eavesdrop.

"Let me start from the beginning. Is true I get a girl pregnant. Is true I had no mind for marriage. We argue a bit and it get late. I leave her there and I start to walk along the river to get to the path what you cut there from the pool. Nothing so strange happen until I reach the steppin stones. Just before I cross to come to this side I see a girl standing on the bank, she just standing there on this side near the big cocoa tree where the steps begin."

"What time would that have been?"

"About what o'clock? About seven for the latest. I kind of wave to her and I start crossing. Half way I slip on the stones, fall into the water, and the current sweep me in to the little cave it have under the bank near the bend. I really thought I was gone. Every which way I turn I coming up water. Anyway the girl bend over and give me a hand."

"Did you see her do that yourself?"

"Well, Mr. Williams, there wasn't anybody else there! I figure it have to be her."

"Reasonable. But it's always better if you tell me exactly what you know for a fact. Not what you think it must have been."

"Well, when I get back my strength, I start talking and she offer to take me home with her to dry off my clothes. She tell me her mother gone to visit her sister in San Fernando, but the rest of the family, home. I ask her her name and she tell me 'Mera,' is short for 'Ramera.' I tell my name, Burri. Is true I never hear that name before, but they have lots of 'pagnol people living up here, so I ain't surprise."

"And she didn't look like anyone you know? Not even a little? You know how moonlight is tricky."

"To tell you the truth she look a lot like the girl I was seeing. I thought they might have been some relation. But she herself I never see before."

"Go on."

"We come to the top of the road, and as I crossing over to the car. I see she limping. I figure is a stone or something and I walk over to the other side. I open the car door and I get in. She tell me where she live and I start driving. The car smelling musty so I roll down the car window. I don't want the girl thinking my car nasty. Mosquitos start coming in the car so I reach for a cigarette. She say smoke does bother her. I reach for my lighter and my hand touch the bible with the Christopher medal my mother put there when I first buy the car. As God is my witness, Mr. Williams, I light the cigarette. The next thing I know the car rushing into the bank and I can't do anything. Sametime I look over, put out my hand, and the woman ain't there. Before the car hit the bank I see the whole thing. The car door stay close but the woman gone!

"The car crumple like somebody fold it up. I wait there half an hour before anybody come. Then they couldn't get me out."

"You never saw her again?"

"I'll tell you. While I was waiting for the ambulance and the police, I tell the people there was a woman in the car. I describe her. They say perhaps she fall out. They look all night. Nobody see anything. Two days later the police come, question me. They say nobody reported missing. Nobody dead."

"You sure you didn't lose consciousness? Sometimes it's hard to tell."

"Well, I'll admit. My doctor tell me so too. So I come up here and I question everybody. Nobody ever hear of the family. Is that what convince me."

"You know you ought to write that down. One hears of these things, but no one ever has first-hand experience."

"But if a thing like that could happen what kind of world is this?" What kind of world indeed! For Mr. Armstrong claimed to have had his amazing experience three years earlier. Four years after the night we had danced wildly around the back verandah chanting:

"De devil eat you, Burri"

First you point out to your sceptical parents that you have never before or since heard the name Burri. Have they? No they haven't. Infected by Newton and the church, they insist on coincidence. You are invited to clean up your imagination, to attend daily Mass. But something lovely has been given to you. A world in which each fact like the legs of runners photographed at slow speeds is an amalgam of variations of itself. Myriad versions of event reaching out of time, out of space, individual to each observer.

It is March, 1954. Though he has friends among the villagers, we never see Mr. Armstrong again. My father, however, has discovered that his cane is merely a matter of fashion. "Just practising," he says, looking at me quizzically, "just practising."

The fiction persists that autobiography is non-fiction. A matter of fact. The question, of course, is what is fact: what is reality. Though the myth of La Diablesse sticks to convention, the stories themselves are specific to a particular event. Is it possible that that old lady bodying forth a world in that long ago August night gave it flesh?

Or was it Burri himself? The power of his experience/delusion stretching both backwards and forwards into time.

Or did the face of reality slip?

Here are the notes I made over thirty years ago for the last half of the story.
   (i) In the darkness he slips and breaks his legs.
  (ii) The villagers hear him calling in delirium but are convinced that a spirit calls them to doom.
 (iii) He calls the girl by name: there is a dream sequence.
 (iv) He is found four days later by a hunting pack. Barely alive.
  (v) His leg never mends properly. (Serve him right!)

SEQUEL

He changes. Nice girl meets him and falls in love. He refuses to marry her and blight her life because of his leg. Somebody dies and leaves him a million dollars (US). The girl, who is poor, agrees to marry him because her little sister has nearly died from polio. The money helps them to buy better doctors. End on a kiss.

I could have been a romance novelist.

These I know to be facts: the 'Burri' tale; John Burian Armstrong; the Lopinot river; Jocelyn. By stopping here, I am being a purist. It is possible that the writing of this, this telling, began in 1983, when, on one of my rare trips to the island, I set out to visit the old lady, the storyteller of my childhood. I would have gone to see her anyway, but I also wanted to know if there had been an accident; more than that, I wanted to know where her story had come from. She was then 103 years old, this Great Aunt of mine, and she had the telegrams to prove it.

She looked at me cynically and observed, "All you so, ain't know what true from what ain't true!"

"You know. You tell me."

"You don't tell thing so to strangers."

"Come on! I am not a stranger!"

"Overseas water you blood! Don't know if you going or coming! Youself!"

She wouldn't sell me a plot of land either. She owned thirty acres, "All you had and you throw it away!"

But there had really been an accident. That much I had got from her. I discovered that a friend, Dr. Harry Wilson-Janes of UWI, could get me into the *Guardian* morgue. I wanted to find out if Mr. Armstrong's accident had been reported. It had been. Strong black lines to give it prominence. But I found it only by the merest fluke and in a paper dated *five* years after Mr. Armstrong's visit to my father:

> AROUCA—The police are interested in interviewing the woman who was riding with Mr. John B. Armstrong when his car crashed near the half mile post on the Lopinot Road at approximately 7:40 p.m. on Thursday, February 18, 1959. A witness saw a young woman get into the car about 7:36 p.m. You are asked to contact Inspector Jarvis at the Arouca police station. (J. Badsee)

After a few days of dithering, I called the Arouca police station. Inspector Jarvis had retired. But the desk sergeant cheerfully gave me his number at home.

Because I didn't have the nerve to ask a retired Superintendent of Police whether he remembered a traffic accident which had taken place twenty-four years earlier, face to face, I decided to phone him. It took me several tries to contact him, but when I did, his voice was strong and clear.

Mine was hesitant. Did he remember the Armstrong accident? He did. He certainly did. Why was I asking? Armstrong had been a friend of mine...I had been away...some very funny stories going around. When had the accident taken place? February 1959. He was certain. Had there been another accident in 1954? 1955? No. He was sure of it. Armstrong had had only one accident. God knows he had made it his business to find out everything there was to know about that man. And he went to his funeral in 1980, yes, and made sure to check out the coffin. Did he ever find the woman? That was a funny, funny thing happened there. He remembered it still. Couldn't get it out of his head.

(Here he paused for several minutes to check out my genealogy: Which Williams? Oh, so soandso is your cousin! Which brother was grandfather? Oh, so you relate to soandso!

In some quarters it takes three generations to establish trust. Both sides of the family.)

His next question was direct and much to the point. Did I believe in the old-time things? Convince me. I don't know what I believe. Like everybody else. Silence. W...ell, it was a long story, he would cut it short for me. When they got to the crash, Armstrong was conscious. Trapped. His legs twisted up. But his mind was clear. He said he picked up this woman and was taking her home when the car crashed. Asked him where the woman was. Funny look come over his face. Said he didn't know. To tell the truth, Jarvis thought it was going to be one of those gruesome cases. He and Sergeant Dick organized village search parties. Lanterns. Torchlight. Flambeaux. Ten groups of three spread out. Nothing. No woman. Next day, dogs and the police teams. Nothing. House to house; signals to every police station in the island. Signals to Tobago, Grenada. Nothing. He and Dick by themselves talked to every woman in the place. All the little tracks and hillhouses. Nothing.

By then the whole place started to panic. Country people. Taxi-drivers refused to drive after dark. Buses breaking down in the garage, come five-thirty. Visiting nurses sicken-off. Pressure! Pressure! He went to see Armstrong in the hospital, and Armstrong told him a strange, strange story. Went back to the accident reports. First thing, no skid marks. Yet that car, folded up like an accordion. De Silva, what own the plantation, he had called the station. Went back to see him. He wasn't there, he talked to his wife. The lady, English. At that time she was only here eight months. The lady didn't know anything about Trinidad. She swear she was sitting on her verandah having a drink after dinner. She, De Silva, and his brother. The car was parked under the hill, round the bend, after that is straight road. They saw the man come out the trees on the river track. They was watching for him. She know the girl young because she very slim, and though she had a limp she walk real queenly. Also she had on a very long skirt with a frill, like she was going to a ball. She thought it was funny to see that in the country, coming out of the bush. You know how those colonist type does think! She said it was bright moonlight.

Then the husband come in. He had hear all the rumours and he was kind of looking at Jarvis funny. Stressing that his wife English. He said they watch the couple get in the car. He stressed how modern they looked together. His wife laughed and said, "Like an advertisement." But then they get serious, and he said they watch the car drive real slow and kind of erratic as if the driver had only one hand on the wheel. Then the car head for the bank. De Silva gave him a queer look and said (he remembers his exact words), "The car head for the bank like it was going home. Quiet and peaceful. It hardly make any noise. The horn blare once and shut off." They stand on the verandah arguing about going down. His brother didn't believe the car crashed. They sent one of their men down to check and he came running back up the hill, shout up is a bad crash. De Silva said he didn't know why he asked him, but he ask his foreman, "How many people in the car?" The man said, "One."

There was a long silence. After a while I said, "Thank you. It's hard to get the truth of such a thing. The facts, I mean." Superintendent Jarvis wished me well. Then he said, "Nobody knows exactly what happen there that night. But is the kind of thing you think is story... You have to think is story."

Jack Hodgins

(b. 1938)

A NATIVE OF NORTHERN VANCOUVER ISLAND, Jack Hodgins was born to a logging family in Merville, near Courtenay, a landscape that figures largely in his prose fiction. He draws repeatedly on the anecdotal traditions and the vernacular exaggerations of local myth, and makes of the island a small universe, one which separates from the rest of the world at precisely those points where it joins it. Such paradoxes form part of the reality that fascinates him: the apparently nonchalant moments when fact wanders into fiction, and to which some critics have given the name "magic realism." "The Concert Stages of Europe," a story from *The Barclay Family Theatre* (1981)—which appeared in its original form in *Saturday Night* in 1978—is less typical of the fantastic side of Hodgins' creativity than of the purely anecdotal. Cast as a memoir, the story is a gentle comic account of childhood tribulations. It is shaped by Al Capp's Dogpatch as much as by Steinbeck's Salinas Valley and Gabriel Garcia Márquez's Macondo, and it is a gentle reminder of the painful comedy of growing up.

The Barclay Family Theatre tells a series of stories about Barclay Desmond, and about his fantastic family of excessive aunts. An earlier story collection, *Spit Delaney's Island* (1976), ranged among a different variety of characters, whose efforts to assert themselves often denied them the very kind of recognition they genuinely craved. Hodgins has also written numerous novels—*The Invention of the World* (1977) and *The Resurrection of Joseph Bourne* (1979) were followed by others, including *Innocent Cities* (1990) and *The Macken Charm* (1995)—and he has written for children and prepared three anthologies. The characters he writes about repeatedly draw attention to their own fictionality—"This is a story," they say: "believe it or not"—but repeatedly Hodgins asks the reader to look for the ways that myth permeates life. His is a world of simile: we are asked to see likenesses everywhere, but to keep an eye out for individuality at the same time. The author of *A Passion for Narrative* (1993), a widely-praised guide to writing fiction, he currently teaches creative writing at the University of Victoria.

For Further Reading

GEOFF HANCOCK, "An Interview with Jack Hodgins," *Canadian Fiction Magazine* 32–33 (1979–80): 33–63.

DAVID L. JEFFREY, "Jack Hodgins and the Island Mind," *Book Forum* 4 (1980): 70–78.

W.J. KEITH, "Jack Hodgins' Island World," *Canadian Forum* 61 (September-October 1981): 30–31.

J.R. (TIM) STRUTHERS, ed., *On Coasts of Eternity: Jack Hodgins' Fictional Universe* (Lantzville: Oolichan, 1996).

The Concert Stages
of Europe

Now I know Cornelia Horncastle would say I'm blaming the wrong person. I know that. I know too that she would say thirty years is a long time to hold a grudge, and that if I needed someone to blame for the fact that I made a fool of myself in front of the whole district and ruined my life in the process, then I ought to look around for the person who gave me my high-flown ideas in the first place. But she would be wrong; because there is no doubt I'd have led a different sort of life if it weren't for her, if it weren't for that piano keyboard her parents presented her with on her eleventh birthday. And everything—everything would have been different if that piano keyboard hadn't been the kind made out of stiff paper that you unfolded and laid out across the kitchen table in order to do your practising.

I don't suppose there would have been all that much harm in her having the silly thing, if only my mother hadn't got wind of it. What a fantastic idea, she said. You could learn to play without even making a sound! You could practise your scales without having to hear that awful racket when you hit a wrong note! A genius must have thought of it, she said. Certainly someone who'd read his Keats: *Heard melodies are sweet, but those unheard are sweeter.* "And don't laugh," she said, "because Cornelia Horncastle is learning to play the piano and her mother doesn't even have to miss an episode of *Ma Perkins* while she does it."

That girl, people had told her, would be giving concerts in Europe some day, command performances before royalty, and her parents hadn't even had to fork out the price of a piano. It was obvious proof, if you needed it, that a person didn't have to be rich to get somewhere in this world.

In fact, Cornelia's parents hadn't needed to put out even the small amount that paper keyboard would have cost. A piano teacher named Mrs. Humphries had moved onto the old Dendoff place and, discovering that almost no one in the district owned a piano, gave the keyboard to the Horncastles along with a year's free lessons. It was her idea, apparently, that when everyone heard how quickly Cornelia was learning they'd be lining up to send her their children for lessons. She wanted to make the point that having no piano needn't stop anyone from becoming a pianist. No doubt she had a vision of paper keyboards in every house in Waterville, of children everywhere thumping their scales out on the kitchen table without offending anyone's ears, of a whole generation turning silently into Paderewskis without ever having played a note.

They would, I suppose, have to play a real piano when they went to her house for lessons once a week, but I was never able to find out for myself, be-

From *The Barclay Family Theatre* (Toronto: Macmillan, 1981). Reprinted by permission of Macmillan Canada.

cause all that talk of Cornelia's marvellous career on the concert stages of Europe did not prompt my parents to buy one of those fake keyboards or sign me up for lessons with Mrs. Humphries. My mother was born a Barclay, which meant she had a few ideas of her own, and Cornelia's glorious future prompted her to go one better. We would buy a *real* piano, she announced. And I would be sent to a teacher we could trust, not to that newcomer. If those concert stages of Europe were ever going to hear the talent of someone from the stump ranches of Waterville, it wouldn't be Cornelia Horncastle, it would be Barclay Desmond. Me.

My father nearly choked on his coffee. "But Clay's a boy!"

"So what?" my mother said. *All* those famous players used to be boys. What did he think Chopin was? Or Tchaikovsky?

My father was so embarrassed that his throat began to turn a dark pink. Some things were too unnatural even to think about.

But eventually she won him over. "Think how terrible you'd feel," she said, "if he ended up in the bush, like you. If Mozart's father had worked for the Comox Logging Company and thought piano-playing was for sissies, where would the world be today?"

My father had no answer to that. He'd known since before his marriage that though my mother would put up with being married to a logger, expecting every day to be made a widow, she wouldn't tolerate for one minute the notion that a child of hers would follow him up into those hills. The children of Lenora Barclay would enter the professions.

She was right, he had to agree; working in the woods was the last thing in the world he wanted for his sons. He'd rather they take up ditch-digging or begging than have to work for that miserable logging company, or take their orders from a son-of-a-bitch like Tiny Beechman, or get their skulls cracked open like Stanley Kirck. It was a rotten way to make a living, and if he'd only had a decent education he could have made something of himself.

Of course, I knew he was saying all this just for my mother's benefit. He didn't really believe it for a minute. My father loved his work. I could tell by the way he was always talking about Ab Jennings and Shorty Cresswell, the men he worked with. I could tell by the excitement that mounted in him every year as the time grew near for the annual festival of loggers' sports where he usually won the bucking contest. It was obvious, I thought, that the man really wanted nothing more in this world than that one of his sons should follow in his footsteps. And much as I disliked the idea, I was sure that I was the one he'd set his hopes on. Kenny was good in school. Laurel was a girl. I was the obvious choice. I even decided that what he'd pegged me for was high-rigger. I was going to be one of those men who risked their necks climbing hundreds of feet up the bare lonely spar tree to hang the rigging from the top. Of course I would fall and kill myself the first time I tried it, I knew that, but there was no way I could convey my hesitation to my father since he would never openly admit that this was really his goal for me.

And playing the piano on the concert stages of Europe was every bit as unattractive. "Why not Kenny?" I said, when the piano had arrived, by barge, from Vancouver.

"He's too busy already with his school work," my mother said. Kenny was hoping for a scholarship, which meant he got out of just about everything unpleasant.

"What about Laurel?"

"With her short fat fingers?"

In the meantime, she said, though she was no piano-player herself (a great sigh here for what might have been), she had no trouble at all identifying which of those ivory keys was the all-important Middle C and would show it to me, to memorize, so that I wouldn't look like a total know-nothing when I showed up tomorrow for my first lesson. She'd had one piano lesson herself as a girl, she told me, and had learned all about Mister Middle C, but she'd never had a second lesson because her time was needed by her father, outside, helping with the chores. Seven daughters altogether, no sons, and she was the one who was the most often expected to fill the role of a boy. The rest of them had found the time to learn chords and chromatic scales and all those magic things she'd heard them practising while she was scrubbing out the dairy and cutting the runners off strawberry plants. They'd all become regular show-offs in one way or another, learning other instruments as well, putting on their own concerts and playing in dance bands and earning a reputation all over the district as entertaining livewires—The Barclay Sisters. And no one ever guessed that all the while she was dreaming about herself at that keyboard, tinkling away, playing beautiful music before huge audiences in elegant theatres.

"Then it isn't me that should be taking lessons," I said. "It's you."

"Don't be silly." But she walked to the new piano and pressed down one key, a black one, and looked as if I'd tempted her there for a minute. "It's too late now," she said. And then she sealed my fate: "But I just know that you're going to be a great pianist."

When my mother "just knew" something, that was as good as guaranteeing it already completed. It was her way of controlling the future and, incidentally, the rest of us. By "just knowing" things, she went through life commanding the future to fit into certain patterns she desired while we scurried around making sure that it worked out that way so she'd never have to be disappointed. She'd had one great disappointment as a girl—we were never quite sure what it was, since it was only alluded to in whispers with far-off looks—and it was important that it never happen again. I was trapped.

People were always asking what you were going to be when you grew up. As if your wishes counted. In the first six years of my life the country had convinced me it wanted me to grow up and get killed fighting Germans and Japanese. I'd seen the coils of barbed wire along the beach and knew they were there just to slow down the enemy while I went looking for my gun. The teachers at school obviously wanted me to grow up and become a teacher just like them, because as far as I could see nothing they ever taught me could be of any use or interest to a single adult in the world except someone getting paid to teach it to someone else. My mother was counting on my becoming a pianist with a swallow-tail coat and standing ovations. And my father, despite all his noises to the contrary, badly wanted me to climb into the crummy every morning with him and ride out those gravelly roads into mountains and risk my life destroying forests.

I did not want to be a logger. I did not want to be a teacher. I did not want to be a soldier. And I certainly did not want to be a pianist. If anyone had ever asked me what I did want to be when I grew up, in a way that meant they expected the truth, I'd have said quite simply that what I wanted was to be a Finn.

Our new neighbours, the Korhonens, were Finns. And being a Finn, I'd been told, meant something very specific. A Finn would give you the shirt off his back, a Finn was as honest as the day is long, a Finn could drink anybody under the table and beat up half a dozen Germans and Irishmen without trying, a Finn was not afraid of work, a Finn kept a house so clean you could eat off the floors. I knew all these things before ever meeting our neighbours, but as soon as I had met them I was able to add a couple more generalizations of my own to the catalogue: Finnish girls were blonde and beautiful and flirtatious, and Finnish boys were strong, brave, and incredibly intelligent. These conclusions were reached immediately after meeting Lilja Korhonen, whose turned-up nose and blue eyes fascinated me from the beginning, and Larry Korhonen, who was already a teenager and told me for starters that he was actually Superman, having learned to fly after long hours of practice off their barn roof. Mr. and Mrs. Korhonen, of course, fitted exactly all the things my parents had told me about Finns in general. And so I decided my ambition in life was to be just like them.

I walked over to their house every Saturday afternoon and pretended to read their coloured funnies. I got in on the weekly steam-bath with Larry and his father in the sauna down by the barn. Mr. Korhonen, a patient man whose eyes sparkled at my eager attempts, taught me to count to ten—*yksi, kaksi, kolme, nelja, viisi, kuusi, seitseman, kahdeksan, yhdeksan, kymmenen.* I helped Mrs. Korhonen scrub her linoleum floors and put down newspapers so no one could walk on them, then I gorged myself on cinnamon cookies and *kala loota* and coffee sucked through a sugar cube. If there was something to be caught from just being around them, I wanted to catch it. And since being a Finn seemed to be a full-time occupation, I didn't have much patience with my parents, who behaved as if there were other things you had to prepare yourself for.

The first piano teacher they sent me to was Aunt Jessie, who lived in a narrow, cramped house up a gravel road that led to the mountains. She'd learned to play as a girl in Toronto, but she had no pretensions about being a real teacher, she was only doing this as a favour to my parents so they wouldn't have to send me to that Mrs. Humphries, an outsider. But one of the problems was that Aunt Jessie—who was no aunt of mine at all, simply one of those family friends who somehow get saddled with an honorary family title—was exceptionally beautiful. She was so attractive, in fact, that even at the age of ten I had difficulty keeping my eyes or my mind on the lessons. She exuded a dreamy sort of delicate femininity; her soft, intimate voice made the hair on the back of my neck stand on end. Besides that, her own playing was so much more pleasant to listen to than my own stumbling clangs and clunks that she would often begin to show me how to do something and become so carried away with the sound of her own music that she just kept right on playing through the rest of my half-hour. It was a simple matter to persuade her to dismiss me early every week so that I'd have a little time to play in the creek that ran past the back of her house, poling a homemade raft up and down the length of her property while her daughters paid me nickels and candies for a ride. At the end of a year my parents suspected I wasn't progressing as fast as I should. They found out why on the day I fell in the creek and nearly drowned, had to be revived by a distraught Aunt Jessie, and was driven home soaked and shivering in the back seat of her old Hudson.

Mr. Korhonen and my father were huddled over the taken-apart cream separator on the verandah when Aunt Jessie brought me up to the door. My father, when he saw me, had that peculiar look on his face that was halfway between amusement and concern, but Mr. Korhonen laughed openly. "That boy lookit like a drowny rat."

I felt like a drowned rat too, but I joined his laughter. I was sure this would be the end of my piano career, and could hardly wait to see my mother roll her eyes to the ceiling, throw out her arms, and say, "I give up."

She did nothing of the sort. She tightened her lips and told Aunt Jessie how disappointed she was. "No wonder the boy still stumbles around on that keyboard like a blindfolded rabbit; he's not going to learn the piano while he's out risking his life on the *river!*"

When I came downstairs in dry clothes Aunt Jessie had gone, no doubt wishing she'd left me to drown in the creek, and my parents and the Korhonens were all in the kitchen drinking coffee. The Korhonens sat at either side of the table, smoking hand-rolled cigarettes and squinting at me through the smoke. Mrs. Korhonen could blow beautiful white streams down her nostrils. They'd left their gumboots on the piece of newspaper just inside the door, of course, and wore the same kind of grey work-socks on their feet that my father always wore on his. My father was leaning against the wall with both arms folded across his chest inside his wide elastic braces, as he sometimes did, swishing his mug gently as if he were trying to bring something up from the bottom. My mother, however, was unable to alight anywhere. She slammed wood down into the firebox of the stove, she rattled dishes in the sink water, she slammed cupboard doors, she went around the room with the coffee pot, refilling mugs, and all the while she sang the song of her betrayal, cursing her own stupidity for sending me to a friend instead of to a professional teacher, and suddenly in a flash of inspiration dumping all the blame on my father: "If you hadn't made me feel it was somehow pointless I wouldn't have felt guilty about spending more money!"

From behind the drifting shreds of smoke Mr. Korhonen grinned at me. Sucked laughter between his teeth. "Yust *teenk,* boy, looks like-it you're saved!"

Mrs. Korhonen stabbed out her cigarette in an ashtray, picked a piece of tobacco off her tongue, and composed her face into the most serious and ladylike expression she could muster. "Yeh! Better he learn to drive the tractor." And swung me a conspirator's grin.

"Not on your life," my mother said. Driving a machine may have been a good enough ambition for some people, she believed, but the Barclays had been in this country for four generations and she knew there were a few things higher. "What we'll do is send him to a real teacher. Mrs. Greensborough."

Mrs. Greensborough was well known for putting on a public recital in town once a year, climaxing the program with her own rendition of Grieg's Piano Concerto—so beautiful that all went home, it was said, with tears in their eyes. The problem with Mrs. Greensborough had nothing to do with her teaching. She was, as far as I could see, an excellent piano teacher. And besides, there was something rather exciting about playing on her piano, which was surrounded and nearly buried by a thousand tropical plants and dozens of cages full of squawking birds. Every week's lesson was rather like putting on a concert in the midst of the Amazon jungle. There was even a monkey that swung through the branches and sat on the top of the piano with the metronome between its paws. And Mrs. Greensborough was at the same time warm and demanding, complimentary and hard to please—though given a little, like Aunt Jessie, to taking off on long passages of her own playing, as if she'd forgotten I was there.

It took a good hour's hard bicycling on uphill gravel roads before I could present myself for the lesson—past a dairy farm, a pig farm, a turkey farm, a dump, and a good long stretch of bush—then more washboard road through heavy timber where driveways disappeared into the trees and one dog after another lay in wait for its weekly battle with my right foot. Two spaniels, one Irish setter, and a bulldog. But it wasn't a spaniel or a setter or even a bulldog that met me on the driveway of the Greensborough's chicken farm, it was a huge German shepherd that came barking down the slope the second I had got the gate shut, and stuck its nose into my crotch. And kept it there, growling menacingly, the whole time it took me to back him up to the door of the house. There was no doubt in my mind that I would come home from piano lesson one Saturday minus a few parts. Once I had got to the house, I tried to get inside quickly and shut the door in his face, leaving him out there in the din of cackling hens; but he always got his nose between the door and the jamb, growled horribly and pushed himself inside so that he could lie on the floor at my feet and watch me hungrily the whole time I sat at the kitchen table waiting for Ginny Stamp to finish off her lesson and get out of there. By the time my turn came around my nerves were too frayed for me to get much benefit out of the lesson.

Still, somehow I learned. That Mrs. Greensborough was a marvellous teacher, my mother said. The woman really knew her stuff. And I was such a fast-learning student that it took less than two years for my mother to begin thinking it was time the world heard from me.

"Richy Ryder," she said, "is coming to town."

"What?"

"Richy Ryder, CJMT. *The Talent Show.*"

I'd heard the program. Every Saturday night Richy Ryder was in a different town somewhere in the province, hosting his one-hour talent contest from the stage of a local theatre and giving away free trips to Hawaii.

Something rolled over in my stomach.

"And here's the application form right here," she said, whipping two sheets of paper out of her purse to slap down on the table.

"No thank you," I said. If she thought I was going in it, she was crazy.

"Don't be silly. What harm is there in trying?" My mother always answered objections with great cheerfulness, as if they were hardly worth considering.

"I'll make a fool of myself."

"You play beautifully," she said. "It's amazing how far you've come in only two years. And besides, even if you don't win, the experience would be good for you."

"You have to go door-to-door ahead of time, begging for pledges, for money."

"Not begging," she said. She plunged her hands into the sink, peeling carrots so fast I couldn't see the blade of the vegetable peeler. "Just giving people a chance to vote for you. A dollar a vote." The carrot dropped, skinned naked, another one was picked up. She looked out the window now toward the barn and, still smiling, delivered the argument that never failed. "I just know you'd win it if you went in, I can feel it in my bones."

"Not this time!" I shouted, nearly turning myself inside out with the terror. "Not this time. I just can't do it."

Yet somehow I found myself riding my bicycle up and down all the roads around Waterville, knocking at people's doors, explaining the contest, and asking for their money and their votes. I don't know why I did it. Perhaps I was doing it for the same reason I was tripping over everything, knocking things off tables, slamming my shoulder into doorjambs; I just couldn't help it, everything had gone out of control. I'd wakened one morning that year and found myself six feet two inches tall and as narrow as a fence stake. My feet were so far away they seemed to have nothing to do with me. My hands flopped around on the ends of those lanky arms like fish, something alive. My legs had grown so fast the bones in my knees parted and I had to wear elastic bandages to keep from falling apart. When I turned a corner on my bicycle, one knee would bump the handlebar, throwing me into the ditch. I was the same person as before, apparently, saddled with this new body I didn't know what to do with. Everything had gone out of control. I seemed to have nothing to do with the direction of my own life. It was perfectly logical that I should end up playing the piano on the radio, selling myself to the countryside for a chance to fly off to Hawaii and lie on the sand under the whispering palms.

There were actually two prizes offered. The all-expense, ten-day trip to Hawaii would go to the person who brought in the most votes for himself, a dollar a vote. But lest someone accuse the radio station of getting its values confused, there was also a prize for the person judged by a panel of experts to have the most talent. This prize, which was donated by Nelson's Hardware, was a leatherette footstool.

"It's not the prize that's important," people told me. "It's the chance to be heard by all those people."

I preferred not to think of all those people. It seemed to me that if I were cut out to be a concert pianist it would be my teacher and not my parents encouraging me in this thing. Mrs. Greensborough, once she'd forked over her two dollars for two votes, said nothing at all. No doubt she was hoping I'd keep her name out of it.

But it had taken no imagination on my part to figure out that if I were to win the only prize worth trying for, the important thing was not to spend long hours at the keyboard, practising, but to get out on the road hammering at doors, on the telephone calling relatives, down at the General Store approaching strangers who stopped for gas. Daily piano practice shrank to one or two quick run-throughs of "The Robin's Return", school homework shrank to nothing at all, and home chores just got ignored. My brother and sister filled in for me, once in a while, so the chickens wouldn't starve to death and the woodbox would never be entirely empty, but they did it gracelessly. It was amazing, they said, how much time a great pianist had to spend out on the road, meeting his public. Becoming famous, they said, was more work than it was worth.

And becoming famous, I discovered, was what people assumed I was after. "You'll go places," they told me. "You'll put this place on the old map." I was a perfect combination of my father's down-to-earth get-up-and-go and my mother's finer sensitivity, they said. How wonderful to see a young person with such high ambition!

"I always knew this old place wouldn't be good enough to hold you," my grandmother said as she fished out a five-dollar bill from her purse. But my mother's sisters, who appeared from all parts of the old farmhouse in order to contribute a single collective vote, had some reservations to express. Eleanor, the youngest, said she doubted I'd be able to carry it off, I'd probably freeze when I was faced with a microphone, I'd forget what a piano was for. Christina announced she was betting I'd faint, or have to run out to the bathroom right in the middle of my piece. And Mabel, red-headed Mabel who'd played accordion once in an amateur show, said she remembered a boy who made such a fool of himself in one of these things that he went home and blew off his head. "Don't be so morbid," my grandmother said. "The boy probably had no talent. Clay here is destined for higher things."

From behind her my grandfather winked. He seldom had a chance to contribute more than that to a conversation. He waited until we were alone to stuff a five-dollar bill in my pocket and squeeze my arm.

I preferred my grandmother's opinion of me to the aunts'. I began to feed people lies so they'd think that about me—that I was destined for dizzying heights. I wanted to be a great pianist, I said, and if I won that trip to Hawaii I'd trade it in for the money so that I could go off and study at the Toronto Conservatory. I'd heard of the Toronto Conservatory only because it was printed in big black letters on the front cover of all those yellow books of finger exercises I was expected to practise.

I don't know why people gave me their money. Pity, perhaps. Maybe it was impossible to say no to a six-foot-two-inch thirteen-year-old who trips over his own bike in front of your house, falls up your bottom step, blushes red with embarrassment when you open the door, and tells you he wants your money for a talent contest so he can become a Great Artist. At any rate, by the day of the contest I'd collected enough money to put me in the third spot. I would have to rely on pledges from the studio audience and phone-in pledges from the radio audience to rocket me up to first place. The person in second place when I walked into that theatre to take my seat down front with the rest of the contestants was Cornelia Horncastle.

I don't know how she managed it so secretly. I don't know where she found the people to give her money, living in the same community as I did, unless all those people who gave me their dollar bills when I knocked on their doors had just given her two the day before. Maybe she'd gone into town, canvassing street after street, something my parents wouldn't let me do on the grounds that town people already had enough strangers banging on their doors every day. Once I'd got outside the vague boundaries of Waterville I was to approach only friends or relatives or people who worked in the woods with my dad, or stores that had—as my mother put it—done a good business out of us over the years. Cornelia Horncastle, in order to get herself secretly into that second place, must have gone wild in town. Either that or discovered a rich relative.

She sat at the other end of the front row of contestants, frowning over the sheets of music in her hands. A short nod and a quick smile were all she gave me. Like the other contestants, I was kept busy licking my dry lips, rubbing my sweaty palms together, wondering if I should whip out to the bathroom one last time, and rubbernecking to get a look at people as they filled up the theatre behind us. Mrs. Greensborough, wearing dark glasses and a big floppy hat, was jammed into the far corner at the rear, studying her program. Mr. and Mrs. Korhonen and Lilja came partway down the aisle and found seats near the middle. Mr. Korhonen winked at me. Larry, who was not quite the hero he had once been, despite the fact that he'd recently beat up one of the teachers and set fire to the bus shelter, came in with my brother Kenny—both of them looking uncomfortable—and slid into a back seat. My parents came all the way down front, so they could look back up the slope and pick out the seats they wanted. My mother smiled as she always did in public, as if she expected the most delightful surprise at any moment. They took seats near the front. Laurel was with them, reading a book.

My mother's sisters—with husbands, boyfriends, a few of my cousins— filled up the entire middle section of the back row. Eleanor, who was just a few years older than myself, crossed her eyes and stuck out her tongue when she saw that I'd turned to look. Mabel pulled in her chin and held up her hands, which she caused to tremble and shake. Time to be nervous, she was suggesting, in case I forgot. Bella, Christina, Gladdy, Frieda—all sat puffed up like members of a royal family, or the owners of this theatre, looking down over the crowd as if they believed every one of these people had come here expressly to watch their nephew and for no other reason. "Look, it's the Barclay girls," I heard someone behind me say. And someone else: "Oh, *them*." The owner of the first voice giggled. "It's a wonder they aren't all entered in this thing, you know how they like to perform." A snort. "They *are* performing, just watch them." I could tell by the muffled "Shhh" and the rustling of clothing that one of them was nudging the other and pointing at me, at the back of my neck. "One of them's son." When I turned again, Eleanor stood up in the aisle by her seat, did a few steps of a tap dance, and quickly sat down. In case I was tempted to take myself seriously.

When my mother caught my eye, she mouthed a silent message: stop gawking at the audience, I was letting people see how unusual all this was to me, instead of taking it in my stride like a born performer. She indicated with her head that I should notice the stage.

As if I hadn't already absorbed every detail. It was exactly as she must have hoped. A great black concert grand with the lid lifted sat out near the front of the stage, against a painted backdrop of palm trees along a sandy beach, and—

in great scrawled letters—the words "Richy Ryder's cjmt Talent Festival". A long blackboard leaned against one end of the proscenium arch, with all the contestants' names on it and the rank order of each. Someone named Brenda Roper was in first place. On the opposite side of the stage, a microphone seemed to have grown up out of a heap of pineapples. I felt sick.

Eventually Richy Ryder came out of whatever backstage room he'd been hiding in and passed down the row of contestants, identifying us and telling us to get up onto the stage when our turns came without breaking our necks on those steps. "You won't be nervous, when you get up there," he said. "I'll make you feel at ease." He was looking off somewhere else as he said it, and I could see his jaw muscles straining to hold back a yawn. And he wasn't fooling me with his "you won't be nervous" either, because I knew without a doubt that the minute I got up on that stage I would throw up all over the piano.

Under the spotlight, Richy Ryder acted like a different person. He did not look the least bit like yawning while he told the audience the best way of holding their hands to get the most out of applause, cautioned them against whistling or yelling obscenities, painted a glorious picture of the life ahead for the talented winner of this contest, complimented the audience on the number of happy, shiny faces he could see out there in the seats, and told them how lucky they were to have this opportunity of showing off the fine young talent of the valley to all the rest of the province. I slid down in my seat, sure that I would rather die than go through with this thing.

The first contestant was a fourteen-year-old girl dressed up like a gypsy, singing something in a foreign language. According to the blackboard she was way down in ninth place, so I didn't pay much attention until her voice cracked open in the middle of a high note and she clutched at her throat with both hands, a look of incredulous surprise on her face. She stopped right there, face a brilliant red, and after giving the audience a quick curtsey hurried off the stage. A great beginning, I thought. If people were going to fall to pieces like that through the whole show no one would even notice my upchucking on the Heintzman. I had a vision of myself dry-heaving the whole way through "The Robin's Return".

Number two stepped up to the microphone and answered all of Richy Ryder's questions as if they were some kind of test he had to pass in order to be allowed to perform. Yes sir, his name was Roger Casey, he said with a face drawn long and narrow with seriousness, and in case that wasn't enough he added that his father was born in Digby, Nova Scotia, and his mother was born Esther Romaine in a little house just a couple of blocks up the street from the theatre, close to the Native Sons' Hall, and had gone to school with the mayor though she'd dropped out of Grade Eight to get a job at the Safeway cutting meat. And yes sir, he was going to play the saxophone because he'd taken lessons for four years from Mr. D. P. Rowbottom on Seventh Street though he'd actually started out on the trumpet until he decided he didn't like it all that much. He came right out to the edge of the stage, toes sticking over, leaned back like a rooster about to crow, and blasted out "Softly As in a Morning Sunrise" so loud and hard that I thought his bulging eyes would pop right out of his head and his straining lungs would blast holes through that red-and-white shirt. Everyone moved forward, tense and straining, waiting for something terrible to happen—for him to fall off the stage or explode or go sailing off into the air from the force of his own fantastic intensity—but he stopped suddenly and everyone fell back exhausted and sweaty to clap for him.

The third contestant was less reassuring. A kid with talent. A smart-aleck ten-year-old with red hair, who told the audience he was going into show business when he grew up, started out playing "Swanee River" on his banjo, switched in the middle of a bar to a mouth organ, tap-danced across the stage to play a few bars on the piano, and finished off on a trombone he'd had stashed away behind the palm tree. He bowed, grinned, flung himself around the stage as if he'd spent his whole life on it, and looked as if he'd do his whole act again quite happily if the audience wanted him to. By the time the tremendous applause had died down my jaw was aching from the way I'd been grinding my teeth the whole time he was up there. The audience would not have gone quite so wild over him, I thought, if he hadn't been wearing a hearing aid and a leg brace.

Then it was my turn. A strange calm fell over me when my name was called, the kind of calm that I imagine comes over a person about to be executed when his mind finally buckles under the horror it has been faced with, something too terrible to believe in. I wondered for a moment if I had died. But no, my body at least hadn't died, for it transported me unbidden across the front of the audience, up the staircase (with only a slight stumble on the second step, hardly noticeable), and across the great wide stage of the theatre to stand facing Richy Ryder's enormous expanse of white smiling teeth, beside the microphone.

"And you are Barclay Philip Desmond," he said.

"Yes," I said.

And again "yes", because I realized that not only had my voice come out as thin and high as the squeal of a dry buzz-saw, but the microphone was at least a foot too low. I had to bend my knees to speak into it.

"You don't live in town, do you?" he said. He had no intention of adjusting that microphone. "You come from a place called...Waterville. A logging and farming settlement?"

"Yes," I said.

And again "yes" because while he was speaking my legs had straightened up, I'd returned to my full height and had to duck again for the microphone.

He was speaking to me but his eyes, I could see, were busy keeping all that audience gathered together, while his voice and his mind were obviously concentrated on the thousands of invisible people who were crouched inside that microphone, listening, the thousands of people who—I imagined now—were pulled up close to their sets all over the province, wondering if I was actually a pair of twins or if my high voice had some peculiar way of echoing itself, a few tones lower.

"Does living in the country like that mean you have to milk the cows every morning before you go to school?"

"Yes."

And again "yes".

I could see Mrs. Greensborough cowering in the back corner. I promise not to mention you, I thought. And the Korhonens, grinning. I had clearly passed over into another world they couldn't believe in.

"If you've got a lot of farm chores to do, when do you find the time to practise the piano?"

He had me this time. A "yes" wouldn't be good enough. "Right after school," I said, and ducked to repeat. "Right after school. As soon as I get home. For an hour."

"And I just bet," he said, throwing the audience an enormous wink, "that like every other red-blooded country kid you hate every minute of it. You'd rather be outside playing baseball."

The audience laughed. I could see my mother straining forward; she still had the all-purpose waiting-for-the-surprise smile on her lips but her eyes were frowning at the master of ceremonies. She did not approve of the comment. And behind that face she was no doubt thinking to herself "I just know he's going to win" over and over so hard that she was getting pains in the back of her neck. Beside her, my father had a tight grin on his face. He was chuckling to himself, and sliding a look around the room to see how the others were taking this.

Up at the back, most of my aunts—and their husbands, their boyfriends—had tilted their chins down to their chests, offering me only the tops of their heads. Eleanor, however, had both hands behind her neck. She was laughing harder than anyone else.

Apparently I was not expected to respond to the last comment, for he had another question as soon as the laughter had died. "How old are you, son?"

"Thirteen."

For once I remembered to duck the first time.

"Thirteen. Does your wife like the idea of your going on the radio like this?"

Again the audience laughed. My face burned. I felt tears in my eyes. I had no control over my face. I tried to laugh like everyone else but realized I probably looked like an idiot. Instead, I frowned and looked embarrassed and kicked at one shoe with the toe of the other.

"Just a joke," he said, "just a joke." The jerk knew he'd gone too far. "And now seriously, one last question before I turn you loose on those ivories over there."

My heart had started to thump so noisily I could hardly hear him. My hands, I realized, had gone numb. There was no feeling at all in my fingers. How was I ever going to play the piano?

"What are you going to be when you grow up?"

The thumping stopped. My heart stopped. A strange, cold silence settled over the world. I was going to die right in front of all those people. What I was going to be was a corpse, dead of humiliation, killed in a trap I hadn't seen being set. What must have been only a few seconds crawled by while something crashed around in my head, trying to get out. I sensed the audience, hoping for some help from them. My mother had settled back in her seat and for the first time that surprise-me smile had gone. Rather, she looked confident, sure of what I was about to say.

And suddenly, I was aware of familiar faces all over that theatre. Neighbours.

Friends of the family. My aunts. People who had heard me answer that question at their doors, people who thought they knew what I wanted.

There was nothing left of Mrs. Greensborough but the top of her big hat. My father, too, was looking down at the floor between his feet. I saw myself falling from that spar tree, high in the mountains.

"Going to be?" I said, turning so fast that I bumped the microphone with my hand, which turned out after all not to be numb.

I ducked.

"Nothing," I said. "I don't know. Maybe...maybe nothing at all."

I don't know who it was that snorted when I screwed up the stool, sat down, and stood up to screw it down again. I don't know how well I played, I wasn't listening. I don't know how loud the audience clapped, I was in a hurry to get back to my seat. I don't know what the other contestants did, I wasn't paying any attention, except when Cornelia Horncastle got up on the stage, told the whole world she was going to be a professional pianist, and sat down to rattle off Rachmaninoff's Rhapsody on a Theme of Paganini as if she'd been playing for fifty years. As far as I know it may have been the first time she'd ever heard herself play it. She had a faint look of surprise on her face the whole time, as if she couldn't quite get over the way the keys went down when you touched them.

As soon as Cornelia came down off the stage, smiling modestly, and got back into her seat, Richy Ryder announced a fifteen-minute intermission while the talent judges made their decision and the studio audience went out into the lobby to pledge their money and their votes. Now that the talent had been displayed, people could spend their money according to what they'd heard rather than according to who happened to come knocking on their door. Most of the contestants got up to stretch their legs but I figured I'd stood up once too often that night and stayed in my seat. The lower exit was not far away; I contemplated using it; I could hitch-hike home and be in bed before any of the others got out of there.

I was stopped, though, by my father, who sat down in the seat next to mine and put a greasy carton of popcorn in my lap.

"Well," he said, "that's that."

His neck was flushed. This must have been a terrible evening for him. He had a carton of popcorn himself and tipped it up to gather a huge mouthful. I had never before in my life, I realized, seen my father eat popcorn. It must have been worse for him than I thought.

Not one of the aunts was anywhere in sight! I could see my mother standing in the far aisle, talking to Mrs. Korhonen. Still smiling. She would never let herself fall apart in public, no matter what happened. My insides ached with the knowledge of what it must have been like right then to be her. I felt as if I had just betrayed her in front of the whole world. Betrayed everyone.

"Let's go home," I said.

"Not yet. Wait a while. Might as well see this thing to the end."

True, I thought. Wring every last drop of torture out of it.

He looked hard at me a moment, as if he were trying to guess what was going on in my head. And he did, he did, he always knew. "My old man wanted me to be a doctor," he said. "My mother wanted me to be a florist. She liked flowers. She thought if I was a florist I'd be able to send her a bouquet every week. But what does any of that matter now?"

Being part of a family was too complicated. And right then I decided I'd be a loner. No family for me. Nobody whose hearts could be broken every time I opened my mouth. Nobody expecting anything of me. Nobody to get me all tangled up in knots trying to guess who means what and what is it that's really going on inside anyone else. No temptations to presume I knew what someone else was thinking or feeling or hoping for.

When the lights had flickered and dimmed, and people had gone back to their seats, a young man with a beard came out onto the stage and changed the numbers behind the contestants' names. I'd dropped to fifth place, and Cornelia Horncastle had moved up to first. She had also, Richy Ryder announced, been awarded the judges' footstool for talent. The winner of the holiday in sunny Hawaii would not be announced until the next week, he said, when the radio audience had enough time to mail in their votes.

"And that," my mother said when she came down the aisle with her coat on, "is the end of a long and tiring day." I could find no disappointment showing in her eyes, or in the set of her mouth. Just relief. The same kind of relief that I felt myself. "You did a good job," she said, "and thank goodness it's over."

As soon as we got in the house I shut myself in the bedroom and announced I was never coming out. Lying on my bed, I tried to read my comic books but my mind passed from face to face all through the community, imagining everyone having a good laugh at the way my puffed-up ambition had got its reward. My face burned. Relatives, the aunts, would be ashamed of me. Eleanor would never let me forget. Mabel would remind me of the boy who'd done the only honourable thing, blown off his head. Why wasn't I doing the same? I lay awake the whole night, torturing myself with these thoughts. But when morning came and the hunger pains tempted me out of the bedroom as far as the breakfast table, I decided the whole wretched experience had brought one benefit with it: freedom from ambition. I wouldn't worry any more about becoming a pianist for my mother. Nor would I worry any more about becoming a high-rigger for my father. I was free at last to concentrate on pursing the only goal that ever really mattered to me: becoming a Finn.

Of course I failed at that too. But then neither did Cornelia Horncastle become a great pianist on the concert stages of Europe. In fact, I understand that once she got back from her holiday on the beaches of Hawaii she announced to her parents that she was never going to touch a piano again as long as she lived, ivory, or cardboard, or any other kind. She had already, she said, accomplished all she'd ever wanted from it. And as far as I know, she's kept her word to this day.

Eric McCormack

(b. 1938)

BORN IN SCOTLAND, Eric McCormack immigrated to Canada in 1966, after having graduated with an M.A. at the University of Glasgow four years earlier. He attended the University of Manitoba, earning a Ph.D. in 1973, and has taught English at St. Jerome's College in Waterloo, Ontario, since 1970, specializing in contemporary and 17th-century literature. In addition to *Inspecting the Vaults* (1987), which won a Commonwealth Writers' Prize, McCormack has written other works of speculative fiction, including two novels: *The Paradise Motel* (1989) and *The Mysterium* (1992). His stories have appeared in such journals as *Prism International, West Coast Review,* and *Malahat Review.* "Inspecting the Vaults" appeared first in *New Quarterly* (Waterloo) in 1985.

"Inspecting the Vaults," using the deceptively "flat" *report* as a technical device, probes in part the relation between the politics of behaviour and the politics of language. A phrase such as "my function is clearly defined" leads to speculations about ritual and regulation (are they necessary or merely habitual?). It also exposes the false neutrality of categories (the terminology of "founders" and "housekeepers" is similar to the restrictive vocabulary that classifies persons and possibilities in Margaret Atwood's 1985 novel *The Handmaid's Tale*). And it also reveals the subtle force of the passive voice (who, after all, is the agent of control?). What the story makes clear is that techniques of expression can apparently construct and consolidate techniques of victimization—and then it (obliquely, perhaps) probes the consequences of such a connection. The world of speculative fiction, finally, asks not so much about division as about overlap. It draws attention to reality not by trying to define it but by asking questions about its generally accepted limits. *What if* something were true? it asks—and *if* something *were* true, what then?

For Further Reading

STANLEY FOGEL, "'McBorges,'" *Essays on Canadian Writing* 37 (Spring 1989): 137–45.

CHRISTOPHER GITTINGS,"Eric McCormack's 'Institute for the Lost': The Scottish Expatriate Writer's Reconstruction of Self and Place in English Canadian Literature," *British Journal of Canadian Studies* 7.1 (1992): 138–47.

Inspecting the Vaults

I

The founders of this settlement have built it near the fjord, on the edge of a ravine whose sides are crumbling like stale cake. But the buildings are solid. They squat upon spacious "vaults," as they like to call them here, not "basements," and especially not "dungeons"—a most unsuitable word. The housekeepers, in particular, who live in the upper, visible parts of the buildings, stress their pride in conditions below ground. I would not deny that these vaults are "well-appointed," fitted with "most mod cons." I have inspected them all and can testify that certain comforts—a wooden frame, say, with a straw mattress; a cold water spigot, low in the cement wall; even the occasional roughly made book-case or table—are ungrudgingly supplied. Yet there are times when, no matter how generous the efforts made at muffling sound— twelve-inch-thick layers of insulation, for example, or cheerful military marches played non-stop over the PA system—the anguish of one of the vault-dwellers, as they like to call them here, penetrates all barriers, the howling insinuates itself into the ears of the passer-by. It should be physically impossible for the other vault-dwellers, underground, to hear the cry, yet invariably they all take it up. Yes, they all take up the cry, so that it mingles with the wind's constant whine down the ravine, along the great slit of the fjord, and it exposes, beyond all dispute, the fact of their unhappiness.

This, then, is the settlement, a place of many zones, built all along the ravine on land that once was forest. Each zone consists of six buildings, each with a vault, and one other house where the inspector lives. For each zone has its official inspector who lives in a seventh building that looks similar to the others but lacks a vault. The name-plate "INSPECTOR" is nailed to its front door.

The buildings of my zone (I am the inspector) rim the jagged edge of the ravine like sutures on a wound. My task is suitable for a man of retiring disposition. I inspect the vaults of the six houses once a month, then write a report which is picked up by the official courier at the end of each month, assuring the administration that the housekeepers are efficient, the vault-dwellers well looked after. The rest of the time I spend in my own house, reading, or writing my journal, for the administration discourages all outdoor activities, all movement between zones. No social gatherings of the housekeepers take place— none, at least, to which I have ever been invited.

Inspections are necessary. Experience has shown that we cannot always trust the housekeepers. They never fail to smile, to reassure me when I inquire about the vault-dwellers. They shake their heads disarmingly at my concern, they are quick with appropriate phrases: "...quite happy...," "...turn for the better...," even "...soon be on the mend...." If I stare long enough into their friendly eyes, however, I begin to feel uncomfortable.

The houses are a uniform brown in accordance with administration guidelines—last year the prescribed colour was dark blue. These houses have no windows, no eavestroughing. Gardens are forbidden. As a result, the untrained eye would have difficulty distinguishing one house from the other. The housekeepers, therefore, take pride in the *names* they have given their houses. They have named each house individually, burning the letters into wooden shingles they hang above their front doors. In this way, each house achieves some uniqueness in a landscape whose identifying features have been minimized. The great forest and the earth around the houses have been levelled. High brown canvas backdrops curtain the zones from the ravine and from each other. No effort has been made to tamper with the distant roar of the sea battering the cliffs of the fjord, for though that sound is irregular, it embraces all of the buildings without distinction.

On inspection days, I always begin my round of visitations during a period when no wailing has erupted for some time—"a quiet spell," they like to call it. On some days, if the wailing is incessant, I cancel the inspection. "Timing is all," was the final advice my predecessor, a man with a sure touch in such matters, passed on. "No inspector can survive if his visits coincide with the wailing. No matter how strong-willed he may be, the wailing will undermine him."

I knock, as always, first on the brown painted door of *Trade Winds*—a peculiar name for a house that sits within a hundred miles of the tundra.

The door swings open. A rather heavy, round-faced, middle-aged woman welcomes me. She tries to look surprised, although I am expected—mine are the only visits she will receive in the year. Always, I encounter the same ritual: a plain woman or a fresh-faced, wiry man, both honest-looking, both accustomed to looking honest. Always they beckon me into the dim interior with its dark mahogany furniture, its absence of mirrors. Always they press me to sit in the overstuffed armchair. Always they insist I share the pot of tea they have just, by coincidence, brewed. Always I refuse.

I remember how, on my first inspection of the zone, I expressed to the housekeepers of *Trade Winds* my surprise at the name of their house. I asked them how they came to choose such a name in such a place. The plain woman, or the wiry man, I cannot now remember which, laughed heartily, and assured me the name was the most natural thing in the world, absolutely the most natural thing in all the world. I have not asked about house names since.

The formalities, at this point, always begin to flounder, and I am aware of the anxiety in their smiles, their chatter. I tell them I must now see the vault-dweller. As expected, they demur feebly for a while, mumbling about his condition without much conviction: "...getting over it...," "...quiet today...," "...such a pleasant chap...." All too clearly, their eyes show how, at this moment, they loathe me.

Yet I must insist. I unhook the heavy red-enamel storm lantern which, by regulation, must hang near the entrance to the vault—the stairs have no electric light. I place the lantern on the dark mahogany table and light it, holding the match steady, for they are alert to any weakness on my part. The man then peels back the worn carpet in the corner of the living room to reveal the trap door. He swings the door over heavily against the wall. Without hesitation, I step down into the darkness.

The light gradually spills over the stairs, and I follow it down till I stand in a pool of brightness on a flagstone floor. The leaden door of the vault in front of me glistens with damp. I put the lantern on the floor beside me and slide back the viewing-grille.

The stink immediately seeps out, offending my nose, the smell of dampness and decay. The man himself lies there, on his bunk, withdrawn as ever. His arm across his face wards off the glare from the caged bulb in the ceiling. He is blubbering softly, rhythmically. There is an indefinable, shapeless quality about him. His protecting arm looks like a fallen log in an undergrowth of wild grey hair and matted beard.

I do not speak to him. I never speak to these vault-dwellers even when they wish to speak to me. For my function is clearly defined: I am to inspect, to have visual association only with them. Nor am I at all sure I could survive any other way.

This vault-dweller, like all the others, is not identified by name even in our files. But though their names have been taken away, an inspector is required to be familiar with their case histories so that he may record any behaviour that might be of interest to the administration. I am not certain yet what kind of behaviour this might be, and so, acting on the advice of my predecessor, I report everything.

This man I observe through the grille is the last survivor of a great family from the North. Over a period of several hundred years his ancestors erected a man-made forest around their manor house. From the mid-sixteenth century, the family devoted itself to removing carefully each natural tree, each shrub surrounding the house, and to shaping instead copies of them—the details were not precise, but the general outlines were persuasive—made from a kind of papier mâché strengthened in the early days with wire, and, as time passed, with plastic and synthetic supports. They made hop hornbeams and dwarf chinquapins; they made bebb willows and panicled dogwoods; they made balms of Gilead and tacamahacs; they made shagbarks and bracted balsams; they made trees-of-heaven and madronas; they made arbor vitaes and witherods; they made Judas-trees. They copied even the root systems, and by ingenious engineering techniques, inserted them into the holes left by their natural predecessors.

The results were quite remarkable—a private facsimile forest of a thousand acres, utterly convincing at a distance. No seasons violated its constancy. In the fall, there were no deaths.

When our administration came to power, it denounced all such aberrations. A regiment of the élite Blue Guards, like beetles in their sleek blue fatigues and flame-throwing antennae, was sent in with orders to scorch the forest to ashes.

The incineration began, great clouds of black smoke and sparks erupting into the air, visible as far away as the capital. The forest was doomed.

What no one was prepared for was the animals. As the fire rolled towards the outer edges of the forest, like water tilted on a table, the forest animals in their thousands ran blundering right into our men. It was not the eyes of these animals, shining with unnatural understanding, that frightened the Blue Guards, soldiers chosen for their fearlessness; it was not their *polyphonic howling* (I use the report's exact phrase). No, observers say it was the shapes of the animals themselves—no one had ever seen such creatures before. They *resembled*, in a general way, all the animals one would expect to find in a forest—rabbits, squirrels, bears, deer—but they ran in a stiff, disjointed manner, and their shapes were not clearly defined. Their strangely wise and multicoloured eyes of different sizes were irregularly placed around the amorphous lumps that suggested heads. Mouths were gaping caverns situated anywhere on the body, rimmed with jagged bone that served as teeth. Legs were awkwardly located, some dangling uselessly from the backs or bellies of the animals. When these animals stumbled too near the flames, they would suddenly melt into pools of liquid, or explode like living shrapnel with a bang. The Blue Guards were ordered to remain calm and to kill every one of them.

This man lying here, when he saw what our soldiers were doing, came rushing towards them, screaming at them, "Murderers! Murderers!" They pushed him to one side, and he wept, begging them to spare at least some of the animals. The men ignored him, and after a few minutes he was at them again, this time slashing with a machete, so that they were obliged to defend themselves and club him to the ground.

The morning after the incineration, when that forest had become a vast cemetery of smouldering stalagmites, they transported him here. And here he lies, in his odd, shapeless way. He is one of those who, over the years, has never made any effort to speak, as though he thinks that by saying nothing he will disappear. Our administration hopes that one day he will speak, say something about the birds that lived in the forest—the birds that vanished during the fire, but are still seen from time to time throughout the country, startling our children as they hurtle clumsily overhead more like flying clumps of earth than birds.

The man never speaks, however, though he often weeps soundlessly, as now, and can be relied upon to join in the general wailing.

I close the grille and climb the steep stairs. I thank the housekeepers (their relief is patent, mine hidden), and step out into the chilly air before the stifling fumes of the doused lantern upset my stomach. The first of my visits is over.

The rituals will be repeated with minor variations at the remaining houses: the same rehearsed surprise of the good-hearted, untrustworthy housekeepers, the same damp descents into the damp vaults, the same heartfelt relief on all sides at the end of the visit. We all share one great hope: that the wailing will not begin. We cannot be sure what starts it, for whilst we, the inspector and the housekeepers, understand each other, we do not, as yet, understand the vault-dwellers. Perhaps it is the secret of the wailing the administration hopes to uncover.

Six vault-dwellers live in this zone. I know them all yet I do not know them. They will always be familiar strangers.

II

The second vault-dweller lives under the brown house called *Chez Nous*. He, according to his file, is an inventor, a natural genius without formal education. He can see right into the heart of machines, this small, bent man with the wheezing in his chest, looking up now from where he lies on his bunk towards the grille. Looking up, but not moving.

He is the inventor of a compact throwing machine that keeps throwing a ball for a dog to chase *interminably*. The dog fetches the ball, returns it to an open container on the machine, which instantly throws it away for the dog to fetch again. And so on, *interminably*. No, not *interminably*, only for a limited period of time, a modification brought about after one of his prototypes ran his wife's pet Irish wolfhound to death by exhaustion.

He is the inventor of a machine that feeds horses measured quantities of oats whilst the owners are away from home on weekends. One of his prototypes kept feeding the horses till they overate. The shocked owners, friends of his wife, returned to find the horses swollen and feverish. They tried to make the horses walk off the fermenting oats, but it was too late: the animals ballooned into elephants and burst. The inventor learnt from this disaster, made some adjustments and perfected the machine.

He is the inventor of a machine that rolls through meadows in the dawn light and collects exotic mushrooms. An earlier model, made for a friend of his wife, gathered, by accident, a lethal variety of toadstools. The consequences were too unpleasant to consider.

In the capital, he was renowned as a machine doctor, a man able to heal the indispositions of machines of any sort. Members of our own administration relied on him to repair their presentation antique watches.

His wife turned him in. She began to notice an excess of bloodstains on his white working overalls whose pockets bulged with wrenches and screwdrivers. One day she saw, horrified, a thick trickle of blood seeping under the door of the backyard shed where he developed his inventions in seclusion. Our agents answered her plea, coming to the house whilst he was away on business. They smashed open his shed door and fell over the raggedly decapitated bodies of a dozen German shepherd dogs and an assortment of alley-cats piled on the floor beside his latest invention, a device that looked like a guillotine, three feet tall.

His guillotine operated in a unique way: after the button was pressed, a set of double blades with saw teeth began to sink very slowly to the wooden chopping-block below. The teeth moved back and forth, back and forth, in a sawing motion. Our agents realized that when the blades—which were still congested with fur and flesh—came into contact with a victim's neck, they would very deliberately sever the head from the body, like a slice from a roast of beef.

Our agents never did find the two human heads: only the headless bodies of two of his wife's friends lay under the heap of animal corpses.

The inventor was arrested in the city and brought to the settlement—our administration feels his skills may yet be valuable to us. He lies on his back on the bunk, wheezing heavily, and smiles as the sliding grille rasps into its slot.

The third vault-dweller lives under the brown house called *Hill Top* (there is no hill). She is still young, astonishingly beautiful, with brown hair to the waist.

I slide back the grating and she looks up towards me from where she sits on her bunk. She is unsmiling as she rises, as she loosens the buttons of her dress, exposing her full breasts and her dark sex to me. She whispers words I cannot quite make out, as though she is speaking to me from under several inches of water, and fixes me with her eyes, knowing I am watching her, though she cannot see me in the darkness outside the door.

The administration ordered her to this place after one of our most respected magistrates visited, on his annual circuit, the country village where she lived. The villagers dragged her before him—according to our files—accusing her of being a mouth-sorceress, a manipulator of spells. Two village policemen held her at a safe distance by ropes, avoiding looking directly into her eyes, avoiding contact with her body for fear that their clothing would burst into flames.

The magistrate began to question her but she screamed and cursed so much she started to vomit. According to our files she vomited up: four Moray eels, each one a foot-and-a-half long; seven hanks of wool, all the colours of the rainbow, braided together like intertwined snakes; a bone-handled carving knife; a loaded .44 automatic pistol; a dozen compacted balls of cat and dog hair, mainly ginger and black; three engraved granite rocks, each six inches in diameter (she heaved them up, they say, like a snake regurgitating eggs); an unknown quantity of dung of such animals as cows, horses, and rabbits; countless pints of blood, not her own type, according to our pathologists; a book written in a language experts have not yet been able to identify; and a parchment that contained a detailed description of this very encounter with the elderly magistrate—had he chosen to pick it up and read it as soon as she vomited it up, tragedy might have been averted. He chose not to, which the parchment had foretold.

This fit of vomiting lasted for four hours. The old magistrate himself, shocked, begged her to stop, but did not know how to help her. The spectators were too terrified to touch her.

Eventually, she could vomit no more, and knelt moaning hollowly, like an animal that has given birth to a steaming litter, her eyes empty, her face lined with exhaustion.

There is no confusion over what happened next. Eyewitnesses record that, after a while, she raised her head and said in a soft voice to the elderly magistrate, "You have sucked me dry." Then she picked up the pistol from the glistening heap in front of her, and fired the full barrel point-blank at the man's stomach before anyone had the power to stop her. And she fell into a coma. All of this happened exactly as the parchment predicted.

She has lived under *Hill Top* for seven years, and the administration has made it clear she will never go free. Now she is sitting quite still on the bunk. Now she shakes her long brown hair back over her shoulder and catches it in her hand, and looks up towards me. Her eyes are smiling. She is usually the one who starts the howling. Her voice seems able to penetrate any barrier. Always when I visit her, I hold my breath, hoping she will not begin. All that I have ever heard from her during the inspections are her seductive whispers. If I ever understood the words, would I have the power to walk away?

The fourth vault-dweller lives under the brown house called *Home Sweet Home*. Through the grille, I see him as usual, this bald-headed, benevolent-looking man in wire glasses, studying, as always, one of his frayed charts, spread out on the table under the dim bulb, his big, farmer's hands fingering lightly the fragile parallel rulers as though they were the first leaves of some spring plant.

For twenty-eight years, according to his file, in a clearing in a pine forest known for its strange sighing and groaning sounds, not far from his fieldstone house, this farmer, this kind father and husband, devoted all his spare hours to a secret task. Using only children's construction sets consisting of small pieces of plastic less than one inch in size, he built a replica, exact in all its measurements (150ft L.O.A., 40ft beam), of the *Santa Cruz*, the galleon of an admiral of the fleet in the Spanish Armada. He fitted together, without any kind of glue, according to our records, sixty billion pieces. The masts and the booms were built in this way, only the ropes and the rigging, the Manilla sheets and the chains were made from any other material.

Our soldiers discovered the galleon by accident in the dark wood during the early days of our administration when all woods, even this one fifty miles from any body of water, were being searched for precisely such objects. They spread out and hid themselves in the undergrowth in the hope of capturing the unknown shipwright.

Just before dusk, they heard someone stumbling along the path (he was a clumsy walker) without any attempt to be silent. He hummed to himself as he climbed aboard the galleon by its dangling rope-ladder. He mounted the quarter deck and entered the Admiral's state-room at the stern. Our men slinked aboard after him. They could not help marvelling at the strength and the precision of the structure. The rigging creaked soothingly in the night breeze and the smell of salt air hung about the ship as though it had just put into port after a long voyage.

They thought they heard voices from the direction of the stateroom, laughing and debating good-humouredly in what sounded like Spanish. They crept up to the door, and with their guns at the ready, burst into the cabin. They found the farmer seated at a wide chart-table, poring over ancient charts, plotting out courses with parallel rulers and hand compass. He looked up at them without any show of surprise. He was completely alone.

They carefully searched the rest of the ship but found no one, not in the cramped crew's quarters before the mast, nor in the cargo hold, even though provisions of dried beef and biscuits enough to last fifty men for six months were stored there. They did disturb several large ships' rats, which scuttled overboard and disappeared into the forest. The farmer was placed under close arrest.

Our administration was uncertain about this man, feeling that perhaps he was not irretrievably lost. They did something rare, they gave him a second chance, appointing him under-watchman at the northern, sunless gate of the capital. He would be both watcher and watched.

Unfortunately, he began acting in a disturbing manner almost immediately. Each morning, as the sun laid a withered arm on the eastern horizon, he would climb the watch turret of the great wall that surrounds the city, a wall built in some forgotten fashion without mortar or machinery—we are gradually replacing it—by our forgotten ancestors. Once up there, he would screech, at the top of his lungs, "Light! Light!". The other guards would seize him and drag him away, watched fearfully by all the people who lived near the gate.

After a while, there was no option but to bring him here. The housekeepers have claimed from time to time that they hear other voices in his cell speaking to him in strange languages, but that when they open the grille, he is, of course, alone. Our administration has warned the housekeepers that there can be no other voices.

I myself will not admit to having heard anything. I know this: on some occasions at the end of a visitation, I have watched him working anxiously over his charts at some projected odyssey he alone knows about. Sometimes, after I have slid the grille shut and started up the stairs, I hear a babble of what seem to be voices coming from his vault. I never go back to check, I avoid the knowing looks of the housekeepers at the top of the stairs, and I move on to my next visit without delay.

The fifth vault-dweller lives under the brown house called *The Nest*. Through the grille I see him dangling by the finger tips of his right hand from a tiny crack in the brickwork near the angle of the wall and ceiling of the vault, whilst with his left hand he hammers a piton into the concrete. He has climbed over every inch of the vault, marking the route over particularly dangerous pitches, fixing ropes to impossible overhangs. The vault looks like the home of a giant spider.

He pays no attention to me.

He is thin like an ascetic bird, he is an albino with a red beak. His hair is long, straight and fair. His mother, according to our file, was a West African princess, his father a Scottish ship's engineer who brought her back with him to the North-western Islands. Too alien to survive on the bleak islands, she died of pneumonia after giving birth to a boy. The father died in a storm on his next voyage, and a maiden aunt was left with the responsibility of the child.

A useless task. After a few years, the pimpled and surly boy wanted only to be alone, to clamber over the sea cliffs pounded by that northern ocean, clinging to treacherous rock-faces with the limpets and the cold barnacles.

In time, he made his name as a climber. By the age of twenty-one, he had climbed all the fearsome rock faces of the world. There are photographs of him in our files, standing high against killing blue skies.

He became a philosopher of mountains. He began to talk of "climbing beyond the peak." He came to feel that no earthly mountain could challenge him. Yet he still had ambitions. "I must make my own mountain," he told his small circle of mountain-climbing friends. He found a collaborator, an engineer who loved ingenious projects, and together they planned to build, on an island by the northern ocean, a man-made mountain that would dwarf any natural mountain. They were beginning to move in the first shiploads of granite when the plan fell into the hands of our administration. They sensed the danger and immediately transported the climber here.

Yet though he has scaled heights inaccessible to all other men, he shows no dismay at being locked in this vault. He never stops climbing. Even when he sleeps, he lies face down, his arms and legs moving incessantly, like a man groping for holds on some steep rock face. When I slide back the grille, I never know where to look for him. Yes, I see him now, hanging upside down in the corner, calculating all possible angles before he makes his next move. I am happy to leave him dangling there.

The sixth vault-dweller lives under the brown house called *Cozy Corner*. She is the dignified one, the little mayoress, sitting upright on her bunk as though ready to preside over a council meeting, her mayor's chain still around her neck, her mayor's robes a little shabby after so many years. The sound of the grille opening elicits a trained smile in my direction, but the eyes are lifeless. For many years, she was mayoress of a small town in the western wilderness. She it was who introduced monthly festivals in which she encouraged all her townspeople to exchange their clothing with their neighbours and adopt each other's lives for twenty-four hours (black face-masks, she suggested, would give the necessary anonymity).

The festivals flourished, according to our files. For one day a month, the lives of her people were transformed. The newly created day-long marriages were filled with love and excitement. Men who had been lifelong enemies often became firm friends for a day, not recognizing each other. Parents for a day, children for a day, found fresh delight in each other. The townspeople even adopted the occupations of their neighbours for a day: no job that lasted only one day seemed to them intolerable.

After a year of this, the mayoress and her council, delighted by the results, decreed that the practice should become permanent: the townspeople need never return to their original selves, but might forever disguise themselves as someone else, changing roles whenever they became bored.

Time passed. The townspeople began to forget who they once had been, often inadvertently returning to their original roles. In the end, all problems seemed minor, even when the bread from the baker's would occasionally be burnt to a cinder, or the plumber would be unable to fix a leak. The doctor's surgery was always deserted.

When our administration came to power, it moved rapidly to remedy the situation. The mayoress was arrested by a squadron of our soldiers, and an interim military tribunal ordered the townspeople to resume their former selves— so far as they could be established (our files hint that a significant number of sex changes had occurred).

The little mayoress was sent here, and so she sits, looking sad, though as dignified as ever. She sits here, without question, but is she the mayoress? Because of the confusion brought about by the festival, our administration can never be sure we have arrested the right person. Our policy is, therefore, to replace her periodically with another of the townspeople, just in case. In this way we are certain we will eventually have her.

III

Six vault-dwellers live in this zone, twelve housekeepers, and one inspector. It is not always easy for a man like myself to understand how our administration decides who should be the vault-dwellers, who the inspectors.

When I first came to the capital, with its strange walls and its watch-towers, I registered with the police, as was required. I gave them the name of the place I had lived all my life, a remote fishing village by the northern sea. They looked at me suspiciously as they copied down the information from my creased papers.

Late that night, two of their black-coated agents quietly forced the room door of the seedy hotel I had booked into, and placed me, quite discreetly, under arrest. On the way back to the city jail in their limousine, with its black windows, they accused me of falsifying my papers, and said that there was no such place as the village named there. I laughed: although the village might be too small to appear on their maps, it had existed for centuries, and had a population of three hundred people of whom every single one knew me.

They did not argue. They locked me up for the night in the city jail, in a small, brick-walled private cell—quite unlike these vaults. I lay there soothed by the chirruping of the cicadas. In the middle of the night their singing suddenly stopped, and I was afraid.

Next morning the guards brought me, worn out with anxiety, to the hearing room where the jail commandant, a spruce, fat man, a retired officer of the Blue Guard, presided. His face showed no sympathy for me. I was made to stand to attention behind a worn wooden railing whilst he addressed me briefly: "We have checked your story with all of our agencies in the northern area. They have assured us there is no such village as you claim. Your name does not occur in any of our files. You will remain in custody and will appear in court again within a few days." He rose abruptly and left the room.

I was returned to my cell where a lawyer appointed to help me was waiting, a small man with a brown mole on his left cheek and a tired voice. I repeated everything I had already said about my village, remembering clearly how it had looked on the morning I left, somehow aware, even then, that it would be my last look. I told him about the little granite buildings running down either side of the cobbled street with its post office, its commercial hotel, its general store, its steepled church, towards the harbour gleaming in the sun at low tide, the pilings erect and dry as matchsticks, the scissor-tailed birds crashing into the calm water, the work-boats (one of them skippered by my own father) nosing towards their tasks like anxious dogs swimming out of their depth, the debris of old ships exposed on the oily sand like fossils from some distant era.

I gave him names, unhesitating, the names of a hundred villagers to testify on my behalf. The lawyer, the mole on his left cheek twitching as though independent of him, seemed persuaded and said he would try to do something.

Two days later, they awoke me early, ordered me to wash and shave myself, and brought me before the commandant again. He was more spruce, more grim than ever. Administration agents had, he said, at the insistence of my lawyer (I could see him standing in the corner of the hearing room avoiding my eyes, I could see his mole pulsing rapidly), gone to the area where I had indicated my village was located. They had not found any village, but they had found, there by the edge of the ocean, the ruins of what might not long ago have been a village—the outline of a street, charred pieces of wood, fragments of brick and mortar.

More alarmingly, they had found in a nearby meadow a massive mound of freshly bulldozed earth which they feared might cover something unthinkable.

The commandant now spoke, in a controlled voice, about the house, the only intact house the agents had found, down among the jack pines by the shore.

The house was empty, the agents had reported; but in the backyard, with its trim privet hedge and its blossoming flowers, they again found the signs of a burial on the otherwise smooth lawn. Carefully, with the long-handled shovel lying nearby, they dug till they struck what was buried. At first it seemed like a large brown leather bag, but as they uncovered more of it and tried to pull it out of the hole, they saw to their horror that it was in fact the tanned hide, completely empty of bones and organs, of a young woman. It was completely intact, in texture like the deflated rubber inner tube of a car. The insides had been removed without any sign of a scar.

As they wiped some of the mud from the area of the face, they saw that it was covered with tiny tattoo marks. One of the agents cleaned the mud from other parts of the body and they realized it was completely tattooed from head to toe with columns of words, so that it looked like the remnants of an old newspaper left in a damp cellar.

The agents rolled up the body and carried it with them in a suitcase to the capital where experts could examine it.

The commandant's distaste for me shone plainly in his eyes:

"Until our inquiries have been completed, therefore, you will be held here in the capital indefinitely. Dismissed."

A year ago, on a sparkling summer day, I was brought to this settlement in a military jeep escorted by a motor-cycle platoon of armed Blue Guards. When I arrived here, I was informed I had been appointed inspector of this zone, and that I was to take up my duties immediately. I was installed in the inspector's house, handed the final report of my predecessor, and the files of the vault dwellers.

These are dark times. I do not sleep well. I think constantly about that buried girl, I wonder why the administration has told me nothing more about its findings. I try to keep up appearances, for fear of being reported by the housekeepers because of some imagined grievance. I avoid (an easy matter here) any form of intimacy. At all costs, I suppress the temptation to join in the wailing. Do you hear it? Listen carefully. There it is now—difficult for the untrained ear to pick out at first. Yes, that's it, that high-pitched lament rising above the distant base of the sea's percussion, drifting steadily down the fjord, converging, at last, with the endless moaning of the northern winds.

John Metcalf

(b. 1938)

A NATIVE OF CARLISLE, in the north of England, John Metcalf was educated at the University of Bristol, and emigrated to Canada in 1962, to teach in high schools in Montreal and Cold Lake, Alberta. In 1969 he took a position at Loyola College in Montreal, where he was also active in establishing the Montreal Story-Tellers; and since 1971 he has spent his time as a writer, editor, part-time teacher, devotee of contemporary art, and caustic satirist of Canadian inertia, whether he finds it in literary pretension or in academic staleness, in social blindness or in bureaucracy and behaviour. The satiric thrust of much of his writing is most evident in two of his novels, *Going Down Slow* (1972) and *General Ludd* (1980)—both of them anatomies of pedagogical practice, of an academic taste for power and system, and of the current educational susceptibility to technocrats and fads—and in his personal account of literary reception and reputation, *Kicking Against the Pricks* (1982). Coupled with the reformative impulse of such works is his clear empathy for people who are made victims of system. The satire works partly to expose the arbitrariness of the victimizers' presumptions—most insidious, perhaps (as in "Robert, standing"), when the victimizers are unaware that they are even being presumptuous—and partly to buttress the self-respect of the victims. Reinforced by such admirable qualities as love, kindness, a recognition of the need for privacy, and an ability to see past stereotypes, self-respect is, in Metcalf's work, nonetheless also elusive. Many of his stories pause over moments when it threatens to disappear for the characters altogether; but repeatedly the irony of the author's method draws the reader back from despair and disintegration, and insists upon the enduring values of humanity and civilization, even in the face of ignorance and gaucherie.

Among Metcalf's volumes of novellas and short stories are *The Lady Who Sold Furniture* (1970) and *The Teeth of My Father* (1975); "Robert, standing" appeared in his 1982 volume, *Selected Stories*. He has also edited several more volumes, and his anthologies include some of the most influential guides to modern English-Canadian prose style: *The Narrative Voice* (1972), for example, and *Making It New* (1982), both of which collect important statements on the craft of fiction by writers themselves. Like the writers he admires (Blaise, Hood, Munro, Rooke, Levine)—and like the writers who have influenced him (the English satirist Anthony Powell, most directly)—Metcalf attaches great importance to the choice and arrangement of words. "Robert, standing" is remarkable for its accuracy of dialogue, and for the effect of its shifting cadences. The rhythms of the prose convey a contrast (and a tension) between resentment and equanimity, between silence and speech, between the awkward reach for self-respect and the easy clichés of mechanical articulateness. "Intrusion" comes in many forms, and resistance to it may often prove ineffectual. The story recognizes at the level of *theme* that people do not easily shed their preconceptions, recognizes that they are "shocked" and "surprised" more than "educated" when an intense reaction to their behavior seems to them out of all proportion to the occasion. But at the level of *form* the story argues that such resistance takes place constantly in ordinary human behaviour; it is recognizable in the tones of speech and the character of action. And only the insensitive fail to understand.

For Further Reading

BARRY CAMERON, "An Approximation of Poetry: the Short Stories of John Metcalf," *Studies in Canadian Literature* 2.1 (Winter 1977): 17–33.

————, "Practice of the Craft: A Conversation with John Metcalf," *Queen's Quarterly* 82 (Autumn 1975): 402–24.

GEOFF HANCOCK, "An Interview with John Metcalf," *Canadian Fiction Magazine*, 39 (1981): 97–123.

Robert, standing

The hot-water bottle bulgy in his lap, Robert pushed himself down the passage and into the bathroom. The wheels of his chair rippled over the uneven wood-block floor and squawked as he made the turn. A strong push with his right hand brought the chair round to face the washbasin. Gripping the edge of the basin with his right hand, he pulled the chair closer.

Tipping the chair forward, he reached up and over the basin to open the bathroom cabinet. He took down the bottle of Dettol and stood it between the taps. Holding the hot-water bottle pressed against his chest with his left arm he unscrewed the stopper and then poured the urine down the sink.

He ran the water for a few moments and then flopped the mouth of the hot-water bottle under the tap. When it was half full he held it pressed against the edge of the basin with his left hand while he poured in some Dettol so that it wouldn't smell.

He pushed against the basin and moved himself over to the bath. Leaning out from the chair, he turned on both taps. The bath was an old fashioned one his brother had bought from a demolition company, legs and claw feet, its enamel chipped away in spots leaving blue-black roughnesses. The original bath had been too low for him to get into without help.

He took off his pyjama jacket and draped it over the back of his chair. He lifted himself with his good arm and worked the pyjama bottoms from under him, pushing them down his legs to wrinkle round his ankles. He sat naked in the canvas chair as the bathroom filled with steam.

From his broad shoulders hung the single, paunchy mound of his chest and stomach. His left arm was stick thin, the wrist and hand twisted, fingers splayed. Below, both legs were thin and useless, the kneecaps rising like huge swellings. At the end of the wasted legs his feet sat like big boots on a rag puppet.

He freed his feet from the folds of the pyjamas and then, jamming the wheel-chair against the tub, worked himself forward to the edge of the blue canvas seat. Holding the pressure against the bath to try and stop the chair from being pushed away, he heaved up his bulk on the strength of his right arm. The chair tipping, sliding, he lurched sideways, straining upwards to lodge one buttock on the white enamel. The breath soughing in and out of him, he rested there for a moment, and then worked himself higher until he was sitting on the edge of the tub.

Using both arms, he lifted up his right leg, hoisted it over the rim, and dumped it into the water. Then the left leg. He sat resting again, facing the wall.

The skin of his back and buttocks was pitted with the scars of boils and

---

From *Selected Stories* (Toronto: McClelland and Stewart, 1982). Reprinted by permission of The Canadian Publishers McClelland and Stewart Ltd.

sores, wounds which erupted again and again from the same chafed sites leaving scar tissue like soft scale.

He shuffled himself along the edge of the bath to the curved end. His legs dragged out behind him. Then, getting a good grip with his hand, he allowed his buttocks to slide down. His quivering arm held for a moment and then his bulk fell, water slopping out onto the floor. The shock of the hot water stopped his breath. He lay motionless as the water surged up and down. When his breathing returned, he levered himself into a sitting position and hauled at his legs to straighten them out.

Sweat was standing out on his forehead. A vein, a muscle, something in his neck was jerking. He lay back in the rising steam, his eyes closed, waiting for the pounding of his heart to slow. He could feel the water still lapping at the island of his stomach. He opened his eyes and stared up at the tiled wall. It was furred with gathering beads of moisture.

Grey cement lines between the white spaces climbing, zigzags, verticals, building block lines, near the top edge a band of blue tiles, a single drop hung. Already impossibly heavy. Still on his desk. The weekly folder of playscripts from the CBC still lay on his desk. They'd have to be mailed off today or he'd have to pay for special delivery. But if he could finish reading the last play and write the four reports by eleven and then get the last three chapters of the novel read for the *Gazette* review—say twelve, twelve-thirty—he could get the carriage out and go to the drive-in on Decarie for lunch. The drop of water pulled others tributary and hung swelling. It broke suddenly into a meandering run. It was three days now since he'd been out. But if he went a bit later she wouldn't be so busy. One-thirty. One-thirty might be better, when the cars had thinned out.

As it checked, and paused, and changed direction to run again, it was leaving a clear trail shining down the tiles. One-thirty might be better. The soap slipped from his hand and he groped for it under his wasted thighs.

Bringing his tray, the edge of the peasant blouse decorated with blue and pink stitched flowers. Leaning into the carriage, the blouse falling away, a tiny gold crucifix on a gold chain deep between her breasts. The drop of water gathered again and then streaked down below the edge of the tub and out of sight.

"Are you going to be long, Bob?" yelled his brother.

"Nearly finished," he called back.

He could hear Jim in the kitchen now; the tap running, a pan on the gas-stove. He pushed himself higher and twisted round to reach the two towels on the chair behind him. He spread the first on the seat of his wheelchair so that he wouldn't have to sit on wet canvas for hours. He draped the other down the inside curve of the bath and splashed water on it. He heaved himself up again on his right arm and grunted his way up the towel's roughness until he was lodged on the rim of the bath.

Jim rapped on the bathroom door and rushed in. He was wearing a dark suit and carrying a briefcase. "Sorry, Bob," he said. "It's half-past eight." He wrenched on the cold tap and splashed water on his face.

"Didn't you sleep again?" he said.

"Fair. I just woke up early."

Jim squeezed toothpaste onto his brush and leaned over the basin. When he had wiped his mouth, Robert said, "You've still got toothpaste on your moustache."

"Okay. See you tonight then. There's some coffee for you in the kitchen." He peered into the mirror again. "Nothing you want?"

"No, I don't think so, thanks." Then he called after him, "Jim! Are you going to be late tonight?"

"No. Usual."

"Shall I make supper?"

"Okay. Bye."

The front door slammed shut. Robert sat on the edge of the bath.

He struggled back into his chair and started to dry himself. When he touched his legs the flesh dented into white fingerprints which slowly faded up again to red.

He wheeled himself over to the basin and waited for the water to run hot. He propped the small hand-mirror between the taps and reached down his razor and the can of foam. As he peered into the mirror his fingertips explored a nest of spots under the angle of his jaw.

He put his hand into the water to test the heat and sat staring down into the basin. No scrubbing ever cleaned his calloused palm and fingers which were grimy with an ingrained dirt from the rubber wheels. He sat in the silence, staring. His hand looked disembodied, yellowish, like some strange creature in an aquarium.

Before going back to his room, he dusted his buttocks and groin with Johnson's Baby Powder.

Sitting tailor fashion on his bed, he worked the socks onto his feet. Then pulling his legs apart, he stuffed his feet into his underpants. He got the pants up round his knees and then rolled onto his back to pull them up. He repeated the manoeuvre to get his trousers on. As he had decided on going out, he put on his new turtle-neck sweater. Then he rolled back into his chair again and wheeled himself over to face his desk.

The empty apartment was shifting, settling into silence. He moved the folder of plays to one side and taking a large manila envelope from the middle drawer wrote:

The Script Department,
CBC,
P.O. Box 500,
Toronto.

He found his mind drifting into the clock's rhythm, speeding up and slowing down, emphasizing now this beat, now that. He could hear the faint twinge of cooling metal from the gas-stove in the kitchen. Outside on the street he could hear the rattle of tricycles, the faint shouts of children. If he looked up he would see the side wall of the next duplex and in the top left corner of the window part of a branch. The desk top was a sheen of light.

The room behind him was familiar country, his own unchanging landscape. On top of the chest of drawers stood the photographs of his mother and father, ebony and silver frames. Beside them stood the small silver cup won long ago in his school days. On the end wall were the two rows of Hogarth prints—a complete set of *The Rake's Progress* and three odd prints from *Marriage à la Mode.* By the fake fireplace and the green armchair were his record player, tape-recorder, and the FM radio. And the rank and order of his books memorized, the colours of their bindings.

Facing him on the desk were three shoeboxes. They were packed with file cards—the bones of his abandoned thesis for the University of Montreal. He was always intending to move the boxes and put them away but he never seemed to get round to it.

The wild yapping of the upstairs dog aroused him. His eyes focused and he found that his pen had covered the envelope with doodling lines and squiggles. He quickly wheeled himself out to the front door. The mailman was just walking up the concrete ramp.

"Hello!" said Robert. "How are you?"

"Oh, fine. Just fine."

He handed Robert two letters.

"Did you go away anywhere?" Robert asked.

"No, I took it easy, you know. Did a few jobs round the house."

He smiled and started to walk away down the slope.

"The man replacing you got everybody's mail mixed up all the time," called Robert.

"Oh, these temporaries, *they* don't care," he said.

"It must be hard getting back to it after a holiday," Robert called. The mailman paused on the pavement and shrugged. "Oh, it gets kind of boring round the house," he said. He hitched up his bag and walked on up the road. Robert sat in the open doorway and looked at the letters. One was a bill from Hydro-Quebec and the other contained a three cent voucher for New Luxol detergent.

He backed his chair and closed the door. He knew it must be at least nine-thirty. Perhaps more coffee would help. He was just about to wheel himself into the kitchen when the dog started its frantic barking again. He sat in the hall waiting. It had to be somebody for upstairs. But then the bell rang. He waited for a few moments and then moved up to open the door. Two young women stood looking at him.

"Good morning," said one.

"We're messengers of the Lord," said the other.

"Well, you'd better come in, then," said Robert.

He ushered them into his room. "Do sit down," he said, pointing to the armchair by the record-player. "I'll just...." He started to drag over a wooden kitchen chair.

"Can I help you with that?" asked the younger one.

"No, no. I can manage, thank you."

He placed the chair and the two of them sat down. The older one smoothed her skirt carefully, pulling it down taut over her knees. Robert guessed she was in her late twenties. She had straight hair, cut short, and a pale, almost pasty face. She bent to take something from her briefcase.

The younger one was prettier except that her hair was rigidly permed. She was wearing white ankle socks, a tartan skirt, and a blue blazer with brass buttons.

"Well," said the older one, "we'd like to talk with you for a few minutes if you can spare us the time?"

"Sure," said Robert. "Certainly."

"We'd like to talk about the Lord Jesus?"

"Can I get you anything?" asked Robert. "Tea, coffee?"

"No, thank you."

He moved his wheelchair so that he could look at both of them at once.

"We're members of the Church of Jesus Christ of Latterday Saints," said the younger one.

"Commonly called 'Mormons,'" said the other, pointing to a blue, paperback book she had taken from her briefcase. On the bookcover, a man in gold robes was blowing a trumpet. "After this book, *The Book of Mormon.*"

"Yes," said Robert. "Would you like some lemonade, perhaps?"

"We should have introduced ourselves," said the older one. "This is Miss Adetti and I'm Miss Stevens."

"Hardwick," said Robert. "Robert Hardwick."

"Tell me, Mr. Hardwick, are you a member of a church?"

"No, I don't go to church," said Robert.

"Do you believe in the Lord Jesus Christ?" asked Miss Stevens.

"Not in any active way," said Robert.

"We'd like to present the Lord Jesus to you this morning, if you'll let us?" said Miss Stevens.

"By all means...." said Robert.

She fixed him with her eyes. "Mr. Hardwick. Why did the Lord Jesus come into the world?"

"Allegedly to save it," said Robert.

"'And he cometh into the world that he may save all men if they harken unto his voice; for behold, he suffereth the pains of all men, yea, the pains of every living creature....'" said Miss Stevens.

"Second Book of Nephi. Chapter Nine. Verse twenty-one," said Miss Adetti.

"There are many misconceptions about the Mormon faith, Mr. Hardwick," said Miss Stevens.

"You mean wives and so on?" said Robert.

"Some people say we aren't even Christians and that *The Book of Mormon* is our Bible," said Miss Stevens.

"Which just isn't true," said Miss Adetti.

"*The Book of Mormon,*" said Miss Stevens, "*reinforces* the Bible. It *doesn't* replace it. It adds its witness to Christ's word."

"'Wherefore murmur ye,'" said Miss Adetti, "'because that ye shall receive more of my word?'"

"And again from Second Nephi," said Miss Stevens. "'And because my words shall hiss forth—many of the Gentiles shall say: A Bible! A Bible! We have got a Bible and there cannot be any more Bible!'"

She paused and then said, "And what was the Lord God's answer, Mr. Hardwick?"

"'O fools!'" said Miss Adetti.

"Well, that certainly seems a reasonable point," said Robert.

Miss Stevens bent into her briefcase again and came out with a long cylinder. She took the cap off and pulled out an assortment of metal rods. Robert hauled his feet further in on the footplate and shifted his buttocks on the hard canvas. Miss Stevens did not shave her legs and he stared at the matted hair under her nylons.

The Book of Mormon," she said—her fingers were building the rods into a sort of frame or easel—"was first given to the world in 1830. We'd like to tell you a little of the miraculous history of that book. I have here a visual aid...." She stretched over and stood the easel thing on top of the record-player. Robert saw with sudden interest that her baggy blouse concealed absolutely enormous breasts.

"But you see," said Robert, "it's not history that concerns me. Before we bother about history we ought to answer other questions. How do we know that the Lord God even exists?"

"'And by the power of the Holy Ghost ye may know the truth of all things,'" said Miss Adetti. "Moroni 10:4–5," she added.

"But I don't know that the Holy Ghost exists," said Robert.

"I have known the Lord Jesus in my life, Mr. Hardwick," said Miss Stevens.

"But I haven't," said Robert.

"You must have faith," said Miss Adetti. "'For the natural man is an enemy to God and has been from the fall of Adam, and will be, forever and ever, unless he yields to the enticings of the Holy Spirit.' Mosiah 3:19–20."

"'He who wishes to become a saint must become as a child,'" said Miss Stevens. "'Submissive, meek, humble, patient, full of love, willing to submit to all things which the Lord seeth fit to inflict upon him, even....'"

"But how," interrupted Robert, "can you have faith in something you don't believe in?"

"There's such a beautiful story in The Book of Alma," said Miss Adetti, "that answers that very question. May I tell it to you?" Miss Stevens nodded.

"'Korihor said to Alma: If thou wilt show me a sign that I may be convinced that there is a God'—you see—the very question you asked us. 'But Alma said unto him: Thou hast had signs enough; will ye tempt your God? Will ye say, Show unto me a sign, when ye have the testimony of all these thy brethren, and also all the holy prophets? The scriptures are laid before thee, yea, and all things denote there is a God; yea, even the earth, and all things that are upon the face of it, yea, and its motion, yea, and also all the planets which move in their regular form do witness that there is a Supreme Creator.'"

She finished and there was a silence. Her face was flushed. The silence deepened. Robert nodded slowly. He bent and pushed his left foot forward on the footplate. He straightened up and looked at them.

"Oh, Mr. Hardwick!" burst out Miss Stevens. "Let the Lord Jesus enter into your life!"

"Let us say a prayer!" said Miss Adetti.

He leaned back in his chair and watched them. They screwed up their eyes tight like children and lifted up their faces. They intoned their words antiphonally and his eyes followed from face to face.

"And let us," said Miss Stevens, "remind ourselves of that promise thou hast made to us in The Book of Moroni: 'If ye by the grace of God are perfect in Christ, and deny not his power, then are ye sanctified in Christ by the grace of God...'"

Miss Adetti's voice took up, "'...through the shedding of the blood of Christ, which is in the covenant of the Father...'"

Both voices rose in unison, "'...unto the remission of your sins, that ye become holy, without spot.'"

They lowered their heads and sat for a few moments in silence.

"Thank you," said Robert quietly.

Miss Stevens glanced at Miss Adetti and then said, "Mr. Hardwick, we'd like to leave this book with you for a few days. We'd like to have you read it?" She stood up and picked up her briefcase. Miss Adetti got up and took the wooden chair back to the other side of the room. "And perhaps we could call back on you in a few days' time?"

"I shall look forward to it," said Robert. He wheeled himself ahead of them and opened the door. As they stood by the front door, Miss Adetti said, "Well, it's been just fine meeting you, Mr. Hardwick." She smiled warmly at him.

He backed his chair away and started to close the door. They were just turning out onto the pavement. Miss Stevens hitched her briefcase higher under her arm. Suddenly he pulled the door open again and rammed his chair forward, bucking the wheels over the fibre mat.

"Hey! You!"

Two startled faces turned to stare at him. His body bent forward from the chair.

"If I was standing up," he bellowed, "I'd be six foot three."

Margaret Atwood

(b. 1939)

AN OTTAWA NATIVE, Margaret Atwood grew up in Sault St. Marie and Toronto, and graduated from Victoria College (Toronto) and Radcliffe College (Harvard) as a specialist in English literature; she has taught at various universities, chaired the Writers' Union of Canada, been a cartoonist for *This Magazine,* an editor for House of Anansi, a writer-in-residence in the U.S.A. and Canada; and she currently lives near Toronto, with her husband, the novelist Graeme Gibson. A provocative lecturer, she is much in demand as a speaker on topics that range from literature to women's rights to Amnesty International, and she has written and edited over thirty books. Among these are the volumes of poetry (her first, *Double Persephone,* appeared in 1961) and novels (among them *The Edible Woman,* 1969; *The Handmaid's Tale,* 1985; and *The Robber Bride,* 1993) on which her substantial international reputation primarily rests. Her books of short fiction (which include *Dancing Girls,* 1977; *Wilderness Tips,* 1991; and *Good Bones,* 1992) have extended her readership even further. She has also published two books of criticism (including the influential *Survival,* 1972) and has edited the *New Oxford Book of Canadian Verse in English* (1982) and the *Oxford Book of Short Stories* (1995).

"Bluebeard's Egg," which appeared first in *Chatelaine,* was the title story of a 1983 collection. Like much of her other work, it displays Atwood's talent for witty political analysis, her intellectual substance, and her articulate fascination with folk culture and fairy tale. Traditional tellers of fairy tale and folk myth found ways to make narratives out of the games of power that people play—each stated story telling an unstated one as well. As inheritors of "popular culture," people in the present live with a variety of gothic fairytale relationships. They tend, however, to dramatize these relationships as romance and soap opera, sometimes without even recognizing the connection between folk and fairy tale and real life. Atwood's "Bluebeard"—a contemporary folk tale—specifies that the traditional Bluebeard story has taken many literary forms (the French version, as told by Charles Perrault, is perhaps the most familiar). The unstated story in Atwood's version uncovers the folk tale's covert presumptions and uses them to expose the fears and to challenge the power ploys of contemporary society.

For Further Reading

MARGARET ATWOOD, *Second Words* (Toronto: House of Anansi, 1982).

FRANK DAVEY, *Margaret Atwood: A Feminist Poetics* (Vancouver: Talonbooks, 1984).

BARBARA GODARD, "Tales within Tales: Margaret Atwood's folk narratives," *Canadian Literature* 109 (Summer 1986): 5–14.

EARL G. INGERSOLL, ed., *Margaret Atwood in Conversation* (Princeton, N.J.: Ontario Review P, 1990).

JUDITH McCOMBS, ed. *Critical Essays on Margaret Atwood* (Boston: G.K. Hall, 1988).

JEROME H. ROSENBERG, *Margaret Atwood* (Boston: Twayne, 1984).

GEORGE STEINER, *In Bluebeard's Castle* (New Haven: Yale UP, 1971).

KATHRYN VANSPANCKEREN and JAN GARDEN CASTRO, *Margaret Atwood: Vision and Forms* (Carbondale: Southern Illinois UP, 1988).

JENNIFER WAELTI-WALTERS, *Fairytales and the Female Imagination* (Montreal: Eden Press, 1982).

Bluebeard's Egg

Sally stands at the kitchen window, waiting for the sauce she's reducing to come to a simmer, looking out. Past the garage the lot sweeps downwards, into the ravine; it's a wilderness there, of bushes and branches and what Sally thinks of as vines. It was her idea to have a kind of terrace, built of old railroad ties, with wild flowers growing between them, but Edward says he likes it the way it is. There's a playhouse down at the bottom, near the fence; from here she can just see the roof. It has nothing to do with Edward's kids, in their earlier incarnations, before Sally's time; it's more ancient than that, and falling apart. Sally would like it cleared away. She thinks drunks sleep in it, the men who live under the bridges down there, who occasionally wander over the fence (which is broken down, from where they step on it) and up the hill, to emerge squinting like moles into the light of Sally's well-kept back lawn.

Off to the left is Ed, in his windbreaker; it's officially spring, Sally's blue scylla is in flower, but it's chilly for this time of year. Ed's windbreaker is an old one he won't throw out; it still says WILDCATS, relic of some team he was on in high school, an era so prehistoric Sally can barely imagine it; though picturing Ed at high school is not all that difficult. Girls would have had crushes on him, he would have been unconscious of it; things like that don't change. He's put-tering around the rock garden now; some of the rocks stick out too far and are in danger of grazing the side of Sally's Peugeot, on its way to the garage, and he's moving them around. He likes doing things like that, puttering, humming to himself. He won't wear work gloves, though she keeps telling him he could squash his fingers.

Watching his bent back with its frayed, poignant lettering, Sally dissolves; which is not infrequent with her. *My darling Edward,* she thinks. *Edward Bear, of little brain. How I love you.* At times like this she feels very protective of him.

Sally knows for a fact that dumb blondes were loved, not because they were blondes, but because they were dumb. It was their helplessness and confu-sion that were so sexually attractive, once; not their hair. It wasn't false, the rush of tenderness men must have felt for such women. Sally understands it.

For it must be admitted: Sally is in love with Ed because of his stupidity, his monumental and almost energetic stupidity: energetic, because Ed's stupidity is not passive. He's no mere blockhead; you'd have to be working at it to be that stupid. Does it make Sally feel smug, or smarter than he is, or even smarter than she really is herself? No; on the contrary, it makes her humble. It fills her with wonder that the world can contain such marvels as Ed's colossal and en-dearing thickness. He is just so *stupid.* Every time he gives her another piece of evidence, another tile that she can glue into place in the vast mosaic of his stu-

From *Bluebeard's Egg* (Toronto: McClelland and Stewart, 1983). Reprinted by permission of The Canadian Publishers McClelland and Stewart Ltd.

pidity she's continually piecing together, she wants to hug him, and often does; and he is so stupid he can never figure out what for.

Because Ed is so stupid he doesn't even know he's stupid. He's a child of luck, a third son who, armed with nothing but a certain feeble-minded amiability, manages to make it through the forest with all its witches and traps and pitfalls and end up with the princess, who is Sally, of course. It helps that he's handsome.

On good days she sees his stupidity as innocence, lamb-like, shining with the light of (for instance) green daisied meadows in the sun. (When Sally starts thinking this way about Ed, in terms of the calendar art from the service-station washrooms of her childhood, dredging up images of a boy with curly golden hair, his arm thrown around the neck of an Irish setter—a notorious brainless beast, she reminds herself—she knows she is sliding over the edge, into a ghastly kind of sentimentality, and that she must stop at once, or Ed will vanish, to be replaced by a stuffed facsimile, useful for little else but an umbrella stand. Ed is a real person, with a lot more to him than these simplistic renditions allow for; which sometimes worries her.) On bad days though, she sees his stupidity as wilfulness, a stubborn determination to shut things out. His obtuseness is a wall, within which he can go about his business, humming to himself, while Sally, locked outside, must hack her way through the brambles with hardly so much as a transparent raincoat between them and her skin.

Why did she choose him (or, to be precise, as she tries to be with herself and sometimes is even out loud, *hunt him down*), when it's clear to everyone she had other options? To Marylynn, who is her best though most recent friend, she's explained it by saying she was spoiled when young by reading too many Agatha Christie murder mysteries, of the kind in which the clever and witty heroine passes over the equally clever and witty first-lead male, who's helped solve the crime, in order to marry the second-lead male, the stupid one, the one who would have been arrested and condemned and executed if it hadn't been for her cleverness. Maybe this is how she sees Ed; if it weren't for her, his blundering too-many-thumbs kindness would get him into all sorts of quagmires, all sorts of sink-holes he'd never be able to get himself out of, and then he'd be done for.

"Sink-hole" and "quagmire" are not flattering ways of speaking about other women, but this is what is at the back of Sally's mind; specifically, Ed's two previous wives. Sally didn't exactly extricate him from their clutches. She's never even met the first one, who moved to the west coast fourteen years ago and sends Christmas cards, and the second one was middle-aged and already in the act of severing herself from Ed before Sally came along. (For Sally, "middle-aged" means anyone five years older than she is. It has always meant this. She applies it only to women, however. She doesn't think of Ed as middle-aged, although the gap between them is considerably more than five years.)

Ed doesn't know what happened with these marriages, what went wrong. His protestations of ignorance, his refusal to discuss the finer points, is frustrating to Sally, because she would like to hear the whole story. But it's also cause for anxiety: if he doesn't know what happened with the other two, maybe the same thing could be happening with her and he doesn't know about that, either. Stupidity like Ed's can be a health hazard, for other people. What if he wakes up one day and decides that she isn't the true bride after all, but the false one? Then she will be put into a barrel stuck full of nails and rolled down-hill, endlessly, while he is sitting in yet another bridal bed, drinking cham-pagne. She remembers the brand name, because she bought it herself. Champagne isn't the sort of finishing touch that would occur to Ed, though he enjoyed it enough at the time.

But outwardly Sally makes a joke of all this. "He doesn't *know,*" she says to Marylynn, laughing a little, and they shake their heads. If it were them, they'd know, all right. Marylynn is in fact divorced, and she can list every single thing that went wrong by item. After doing this, she adds that her divorce was one of the best things that ever happened to her. "I was just a nothing before," she says. "It made me pull myself together."

Sally, looking across the kitchen table at Marylynn, has to agree that she is far from being a nothing now. She started out re-doing people's closets, and has worked that up into her own interior-design firm. She does the houses of the newly rich, those who lack ancestral furniture and the confidence to be shabby, and who wish their interiors to reflect a personal taste they do not in reality process.

"What they want are mausoleums," Marylynn says, "or hotels," and she cheerfully supplies them. "Right down to the ash-trays. Imagine having some-one else pick out your ash-trays for you."

By saying this, Marylynn lets Sally know that she's not including her in that category, though Sally did in fact hire her, at the very first, to help with a few details around the house. It was Marylynn who redesigned the wall of closets in the master bedroom and who found Sally's massive Chinese ma-hogany table, which cost her another seven hundred dollars to have stripped. But it turned out to be perfect, as Marylynn said it would. Now she's dug up a nineteenth-century keyhole desk, which both she and Sally know will be ex-actly right for the bay-windowed alcove off the living room. "Why do you need it?" Ed said in his puzzled way. "I thought you worked in your study." Sally ad-mitted this, but said they could keep the telephone bills in it, which appeared to satisfy him. She knows exactly what she needs it for: she needs it to sit at, in something flowing, backlit by the morning sunlight, gracefully dashing off notes. She saw a 1940s advertisement for coffee like this once; and the hus-band was standing behind the chair, leaning over, with a worshipful expression on his face.

Marylynn is the kind of friend Sally does not have to explain any of this to, because it's assumed between them. Her intelligence is the kind Sally respects.

Marylynn is tall and elegant, and makes anything she is wearing seem fash-ionable. Her hair is prematurely grey and she leaves it that way. She goes in for loose blouses in cream-coloured silk, and eccentric scarves gathered from interesting shops and odd corners of the world, thrown carelessly around her neck and over one shoulder. (Sally has tried this toss in the mirror, but it doesn't work.) Marylynn has a large collection of unusual shoes; she says they're unusual because her feet are so big, but Sally knows better. Sally, who used to think of herself as pretty enough and now thinks of herself as doing quite well for her age, envies Marylynn her bone structure, which will serve her well when the inevitable happens.

Whenever Marylynn is coming to dinner, as she is today—she's bringing the desk, too—Sally takes especial care with her clothes and make-up. Marylynn, she knows, is her real audience for such things, since no changes she effects in herself seem to affect Ed one way or the other, or even to register with him. "You look fine to me," is all he says, no matter how she really looks. (But does she want him to see her more clearly, or not? Most likely not. If he did he would notice the incipient wrinkles, the small pouches of flesh that are not quite there yet, the network forming beneath her eyes. It's better as it is.)

Sally has repeated this remark of Ed's to Marylynn, adding that he said it the day the Jacuzzi overflowed because the smoke alarm went off, because an English muffin she was heating to eat in the bathtub got stuck in the toaster, and she had to spend an hour putting down newspaper and mopping up, and only had half an hour to dress for a dinner they were going to. "Really I looked like the wrath of God," said Sally. These days she finds herself repeating to Marylynn many of the things Ed says: the stupid things. Marylynn is the only one of Sally's friends she has confided in to this extent.

"Ed is cute as a button," Marylynn said. "In fact, he's just like a button: he's so bright and shiny. If he were mine, I'd get him bronzed and keep him on the mantel-piece."

Marylynn is even better than Sally at concocting formulations for Ed's particular brand of stupidity, which can irritate Sally: coming from herself, this sort of comment appears to her indulgent and loving, but from Marylynn it borders on the patronizing. So then she sticks up for Ed, who is by no means stupid about everything. When you narrow it down, there's only one area of life he's hopeless about. The rest of the time he's intelligent enough, some even say brilliant: otherwise, how could he be so successful?

Ed is a heart man, one of the best, and the irony of this is not lost on Sally: who could possibly know less about the workings of hearts, real hearts, the kind symbolized by red satin surrounded by lace and topped by pink bows, than Ed? Hearts with arrows in them. At the same time, the fact that he's a heart man is a large part of his allure. Women corner him on sofas, trap him in bay-windows at cocktail parties, mutter to him in confidential voices at dinner parties. They behave this way right in front of Sally, under her very nose, as if she's invisible, and Ed lets them do it. This would never happen if he were in banking or construction.

As it is, everywhere he goes he is beset by sirens. They want him to fix their hearts. Each of them seems to have a little something wrong—a murmur, a whisper. Or they faint a lot and want him to tell them why. This is always what the conversations are about, according to Ed, and Sally believes it. Once she'd wanted it herself, that mirage. What had she invented for him, in the beginning? A heavy heart, that beat too hard after meals. And he'd been so sweet, looking at her with those stunned brown eyes of his, as if her heart were the genuine topic, listening to her gravely as if he'd never heard any of this twaddle before, advising her to drink less coffee. And she'd felt such triumph, to have carried off her imposture, pried out of him that minuscule token of concern.

Thinking back on this incident makes her uneasy, now that she's seen her own performance repeated so many times, including the hand placed lightly on the heart, to call attention of course to the breasts. Some of these women have been within inches of getting Ed to put his head down on their chests, right there in Sally's living room. Watching all this out of the corners of her eyes while serving the liqueurs, Sally feels the Aztec rise within her. *Trouble with your heart? Get it removed,* she thinks. *Then you'll have no more problems.*

Sometimes Sally worries that she's a nothing, the way Marylynn was before she got a divorce and a job. But Sally isn't a nothing; therefore, she doesn't need a divorce to stop being one. And she's always had a job of some sort; in fact she has one now. Luckily Ed has no objection; he doesn't have much of an objection to anything she does.

Her job is supposed to be full-time, but in effect it's part-time, because Sally can take a lot of the work away and do it at home, and, as she says, with one arm tied behind her back. When Sally is being ornery, when she's playing the dull wife of a fascinating heart man—she does this with people she can't be bothered with—she says she works in a bank, nothing important. Then she watches their eyes dismiss her. When, on the other hand, she's trying to impress, she says she's in P.R. In reality she runs the in-house organ for a trust company, a medium-sized one. This is a thin magazine, nicely printed, which is supposed to make the employees feel that some of the boys are doing worthwhile things out there and are human beings as well. It's still the boys, though the few women in anything resembling key positions are wheeled out regularly, bloused and suited and smiling brightly, with what they hope will come across as confidence rather than aggression.

This is the latest in a string of such jobs Sally has held over the years: comfortable enough jobs that engage only half of her cogs and wheels, and that end up leading nowhere. Technically she's second-in-command: over her is a man who wasn't working out in management, but who couldn't be fired because his wife was related to the chairman of the board. He goes out for long alcoholic lunches and plays a lot of golf, and Sally runs the show. This man gets the official credit for everything Sally does right, but the senior executives in the company take Sally aside when no one is looking and tell her what a great gal she is and what a whiz she is at holding up her end.

The real pay-off for Sally, though, is that her boss provides her with an endless supply of anecdotes. She dines out on stories about his dim-wittedness and pomposity, his lobotomized suggestions about what the two of them should cook up for the magazine; *the organ,* as she says he always calls it. "He says we need some fresh blood to perk up the organ," Sally says, and the heart men grin at her. "He actually said that?" Talking like this about her boss would be reckless—you never know what might get back to him, with the world as small as it is—if Sally were afraid of losing her job, but she isn't. There's an unspoken agreement between her and this man: they both know that if she goes, he goes, because who else would put up with him? Sally might angle for his job, if she were stupid enough to disregard his family connections, if she coveted the trappings of power. But she's just fine where she is. Jokingly, she says she's reached her level of incompetence. She says she suffers from fear of success.

Her boss is white-haired, slender, and tanned, and looks like an English gin ad. Despite his vapidity he's outwardly distinguished, she allows him that. In truth she pampers him outrageously, indulges him, covers up for him at every turn, though she stops short of behaving like a secretary: she doesn't bring him coffee. They both have a secretary who does that anyway. The one time he made a pass at her, when he came in from lunch visibly reeling, Sally was kind about it.

Occasionally, though not often, Sally has to travel in connection with her job. She's sent off to places like Edmonton, where they have a branch. She interviews the boys at the middle and senior levels; they have lunch, and the boys talk about ups and downs in oil or the slump in the real-estate market. Then she gets taken on tours of shopping plazas under construction. It's always windy, and grit blows into her face. She comes back to home base and writes a piece on the youthfulness and vitality of the West.

She teases Ed, while she packs, saying she's going off for a rendezvous with a dashing financier or two. Ed isn't threatened; he tells her to enjoy herself, and she hugs him and tells him how much she will miss him. He's so dumb it doesn't occur to him she might not be joking. In point of fact, it would have been quite possible for Sally to have had an affair, or at least a one- or two-night stand, on several of these occasions: she knows when those chalk lines are being drawn, when she's being dared to step over them. But she isn't interested in having an affair with anyone but Ed.

She doesn't eat much on the planes; she doesn't like the food. But on the return trip, she invariably saves the pre-packaged parts of the meal, the cheese in its plastic wrap, the miniature chocolate bar, the bag of pretzels. She ferrets them away in her purse. She thinks of them as supplies, that she may need if she gets stuck in a strange airport, if they have to change course because of snow or fog, for instance. All kinds of things could happen, although they never have. When she gets home she takes the things from her purse and throws them out.

Outside the window Ed straightens up and wipes his earth-smeared hands down the sides of his pants. He begins to turn, and Sally moves back from the window so he won't see that she's watching. She doesn't like it to be too obvious. She shifts her attention to the sauce: it's in the second stage of a *sauce suprême*, which will make all the difference to the chicken. When Sally was learning this sauce, her cooking instructor quoted one of the great chefs, to the effect that the chicken was merely a canvas. He meant as in painting, but Sally, in an undertone to the woman next to her, turned it around. "Mine's canvas anyway, sauce or no sauce," or words to that effect.

Gourmet cooking was the third night course Sally has taken. At the moment she's on her fifth, which is called *Forms of Narrative Fiction*. It's half reading and half writing assignments—the instructor doesn't believe you can understand an art form without at least trying it yourself—and Sally purports to be enjoying it. She tells her friends she takes night courses to keep her brain from atrophying, and her friends find this amusing: whatever else may become of Sally's brain, they say, they don't see atrophying as an option. Sally knows better, but in any case there's always room for improvement. She may have begun taking the courses in the belief that this would make her more interesting to Ed, but she soon gave up on that idea: she appears to be neither more nor less interesting to Ed now than she was before.

Most of the food for tonight is already made. Sally tries to be well organized: the overflowing Jacuzzi was an aberration. The cold watercress soup with walnuts is chilling in the refrigerator, the chocolate mousse ditto. Ed, being Ed, prefers meatloaf to sweetbreads with pine nuts, butterscotch pudding made from a package to chestnut purée topped with whipped cream. (Sally burnt her fingers peeling the chestnuts. She couldn't do it the easy way and buy it tinned.) Sally says Ed's preference for this type of food comes from being pre-programmed by hospital cafeterias when he was younger: show him a burned sausage and a scoop of instant mashed potatoes and he salivates. So it's only for company that she can unfurl her *boeuf en daube* and her salmon *en papillote,* spread them forth to be savoured and praised.

What she likes best about these dinners though is setting the table, deciding who will sit where and, when she's feeling mischievous, even what they are likely to say. Then she can sit and listen to them say it. Occasionally she prompts a little.

Tonight will not be very challenging, since it's only the heart men and their wives, and Marylynn, whom Sally hopes will dilute them. The heart men are forbidden to talk shop at Sally's dinner table, but they do it anyway. "Not what you really want to listen to while you're eating," says Sally. "All those tubes and valves." Privately she thinks they're a conceited lot, all except Ed. She can't resist needling them from time to time.

"I mean," she said to one of the leading surgeons, "basically it's just an exalted form of dress-making, don't you think?"

"Come again?" said the surgeon, smiling. The heart men think Sally is one hell of a tease.

"It's really just cutting and sewing, isn't it?" Sally murmured. The surgeon laughed.

"There's more to it than that." Ed said, unexpectedly, solemnly.

"What more, Ed?" said the surgeon. "You could say there's a lot of embroidery, but that's in the billing." He chuckled at himself.

Sally held her breath. She could hear Ed's verbal thought processes lurching into gear. He was delectable.

"Good judgment," Ed said. His earnestness hit the table like a wet fish. The surgeon hastily downed his wine.

Sally smiled. This was supposed to be a reprimand to her, she knew, for not taking things seriously enough. *Oh, come on, Ed,* she could say. But she knows also, most of the time, when to keep her trap shut. She should have a light-up JOKE sign on her forehead, so Ed would be able to tell the difference.

The heart men do well. Most of them appear to be doing better than Ed, but that's only because they have, on the whole, more expensive tastes and fewer wives. Sally can calculate these things and she figures Ed is about par.

These days there's much talk about advanced technologies, which Sally tries to keep up on, since they interest Ed. A few years ago the heart men got themselves a new facility. Ed was so revved up that he told Sally about it, which was unusual for him. A week later Sally said she would drop by the hospital at the end of the day and pick Ed up and take him out for dinner; she didn't feel like cooking, she said. Really she wanted to check out the facility; she likes to check out anything that causes the line on Ed's excitement chart to move above level.

At first Ed said he was tired, that when the day came to an end he didn't want to prolong it. But Sally wheedled and was respectful, and finally Ed took her to see his new gizmo. It was in a cramped, darkened room with an examining table in it. The thing itself looked like a television screen hooked up to some complicated hardware. Ed said that they could wire a patient up and bounce sound waves off the heart and pick up the echoes, and they would get a picture on the screen, an actual picture, of the heart in motion. It was a thousand times better than an electrocardiogram, he said: they could see the faults, the thickenings and cloggings, much more clearly.

"Colour?" said Sally.

"Black and white," said Ed.

Then Sally was possessed by a desire to see her own heart, in motion, in black and white, on the screen. At the dentist's she always wants to see the X-rays of her teeth, too, solid and glittering in her cloudy head. "Do it," she said, "I want to see how it works," and though this was the kind of thing Ed would ordinarily evade or tell her she was being silly about, he didn't need much persuading. He was fascinated by the thing himself, and he wanted to show it off.

He checked to make sure there was nobody real booked for the room. Then he told Sally to slip out of her clothes, the top half, brassière and all. He gave her a paper gown and turned his back modestly while she slipped it on, as if he didn't see her body every night of the week. He attached electrodes to her, the ankles and one wrist, and turned a switch and fiddled with the dials. Really a technician was supposed to do this, he told her, but he knew how to run the machine himself. He was good with small appliances.

Sally lay prone on the table, feeling strangely naked. "What do I do?" she said.

"Just lie there," said Ed. He came over to her and tore a hole in the paper gown, above her left breast. Then he started running a probe over her skin. It was wet and slippery and cold, and felt like the roller on a roll-on deodorant.

"There," he said, and Sally turned her head. On the screen was a large grey object, like a giant fig, paler in the middle, a dark line running down the centre. The sides moved in and out, two wings fluttered in it, like an uncertain moth's.

"That's it?" said Sally dubiously. Her heart looked so insubstantial, like a bag of gelatin, something that would melt, fade, disintegrate, if you squeezed it even a little.

Ed moved the probe, and they looked at the heart from the bottom, then the top. Then he stopped the frame, then changed it from a positive to a negative image. Sally began to shiver.

"That's wonderful," she said. He seemed so distant, absorbed in his machine, taking the measure of her heart, which was beating over there all by itself, detached from her, exposed and under his control.

Ed unwired her and she put on her clothes again, neutrally, as if he were actually a doctor. Nevertheless this transaction, this whole room, was sexual in a way she didn't quite understand; it was clearly a dangerous place. It was like a massage parlour, only for women. Put a batch of women in there with Ed and they would never want to come out. They'd want to stay in there while he ran his probe over their wet skins and pointed out to them the defects of their beating hearts.

"Thank you," said Sally.

Sally hears the back door open and close. She feels Ed approaching, coming through the passages of the house towards her, like a small wind or a ball of static electricity. The hair stands up on her arms. Sometimes he makes her so happy she thinks she's about to burst; other times she thinks she's about to burst anyway.

He comes into the kitchen, and she pretends not to notice. He puts his arms around her from behind, kisses her on the neck. She leans back, pressing herself into him. What they should do now is go into the bedroom (or even the living room, even the den) and make love, but it wouldn't occur to Ed to make love in the middle of the day. Sally often comes across articles in magazines about how to improve your sex life, which leave her feeling disappointed, or reminiscent: Ed is not Sally's first and only man. But she knows she shouldn't expect too much of Ed. If Ed were more experimental, more interested in variety, he would be a different kind of man altogether: slyer, more devious, more observant, harder to deal with.

As it is, Ed makes love in the same way, time after time, each movement following the others in an exact order. But it seems to satisfy him. Of course it satisfies him: you can always tell when men are satisfied. It's Sally who lies awake, afterwards, watching the pictures unroll across her closed eyes.

Sally steps away from Ed, smiles at him. "How did you make out with the women today?" she says.

"What women?" says Ed absently, going towards the sink. He knows what women.

"The ones out there, hiding in the forsythia," says Sally. "I counted at least ten. They were just waiting for a chance."

She teases him frequently about these troops of women, which follow him around everywhere, which are invisible to Ed but which she can see as plain as day.

"I bet they hang around outside the front door of the hospital," she will say, "just waiting till you come out. I bet they hide in the linen closets and jump out at you from behind, and then pretend to be lost so you'll take them by the short cut. It's the white coat that does it. None of those women can resist the white coats. They've been conditioned by Young Doctor Kildare."

"Don't be silly," says Ed today, with equanimity. Is he blushing, is he embarrassed? Sally examines his face closely, like a geologist with an aerial photograph, looking for telltale signs of mineral treasure: markings, bumps, hollows. Everything about Ed means something, though it's difficult at times to say what.

Now he's washing his hands at the sink, to get the earth off. In a minute he'll wipe them on the dish towel instead of using the hand towel the way he's supposed to. Is that complacency, in the back turned to her? Maybe there really are these hordes of women, even though she's made them up. Maybe they really do behave that way. His shoulders are slightly drawn up: is he shutting her out?

"I know what they want," she goes on. "They want to get into that little dark room of yours and climb up onto your table. They think you're delicious. They'll gobble you up. They'll chew you into tiny pieces. There won't be anything left of you at all, only a stethoscope and a couple of shoelaces."

Once Ed would have laughed at this, but today he doesn't. Maybe she's said it, or something like it, a few times too often. He smiles though, wipes his hands on the dish towel, peers into the fridge. He likes to snack.

"There's some cold roast beef," Sally says, baffled.

Sally takes the sauce off the stove and sets it aside for later: she'll do the last steps just before serving. It's only two-thirty. Ed has disappeared into the cellar, where Sally knows he will be safe for a while. She goes into her study, which used to be one of the kids' bedrooms, and sits down at her desk. The room has never been completely redecorated: there's still a bed in it, and a dressing table with a blue flowered flounce Sally helped pick out, long before the kids went off to university: "flew the coop," as Ed puts it.

Sally doesn't comment on the expression, though she would like to say that it wasn't the first coop they flew. Her house isn't even the real coop, since neither of the kids is hers. She'd hoped for a baby of her own when she married Ed, but she didn't want to force the issue. Ed didn't object to the idea, exactly, but he was neutral about it, and Sally got the feeling he'd had enough babies already. Anyway, the other two wives had babies, and look what happened to them. Since their actual fates have always been vague to Sally, she's free to imagine all kinds of things, from drug addiction to madness. Whatever it was resulted in Sally having to bring up their kids, at least from puberty onwards. The way it was presented by the first wife was that it was Ed's turn now. The second wife was more oblique: she said that the child wanted to spend some time with her father. Sally was left out of both these equations, as if the house wasn't a place she lived in, not really, so she couldn't be expected to have any opinion.

Considering everything, she hasn't done badly. She likes the kids and tries to be a friend to them, since she can hardly pretend to be a mother. She describes the three of them as having an easy relationship. Ed wasn't around much for the kids, but it's him they want approval from, not Sally; it's him they respect. Sally is more like a confederate, helping them get what they want from Ed.

When the kids were younger, Sally used to play Monopoly with them, up at the summer place in Muskoka Ed owned then but has since sold. Ed would play too, on his vacations and on the weekends when he could make it up. These games would all proceed along the same lines. Sally would have an initial run of luck and would buy up everything she had a chance at. She didn't care whether it was classy real estate, like Boardwalk or Park Place, or those dingy little houses on the other side of the tracks; she would even buy train stations, which the kids would pass over, preferring to save their cash reserves for better investments. Ed, on the other hand, would plod along, getting a little here, a little there. Then, when Sally was feeling flush, she would blow her money on next-to-useless luxuries such as the electric light company; and when the kids started to lose, as they invariably did, Sally would lend them money at cheap rates or trade them things of her own, at a loss. Why not? She could afford it.

Ed meanwhile would be hedging his bets, building up blocks of property, sticking houses and hotels on them. He preferred the middle range, respectable streets but not flashy. Sally would land on his spaces and have to shell out hard cash. Ed never offered deals, and never accepted them. He played a lone game, and won more often than not. Then Sally would feel thwarted. She would say she guessed she lacked the killer instinct; or she would say that for herself she didn't care, because after all it was only a game, but he ought to allow the kids to win, once in a while. Ed couldn't grasp the concept of allowing other people to win. He said it would be condescending towards the children, and anyway you couldn't arrange to have a dice game turn out the way you wanted it to, since it was partly a matter of chance. If it was chance, Sally would think, why were the games so similar to one another? At the end, there would be Ed, counting up his paper cash, sorting it out into piles of bills of varying denominations, and Sally, her vast holdings dwindled to a few shoddy blocks on Baltic Avenue, doomed to foreclosure: extravagant, generous, bankrupt.

On these nights, after the kids were asleep, Sally would have two or three more rye-and-gingers than were good for her. Ed would go to bed early—winning made him satisfied and drowsy—and Sally would ramble about the house or read the endings of murder mysteries she had already read once before, and finally she would slip into bed and wake Ed up and stroke him into arousal, seeking comfort.

Sally has almost forgotten these games. Right now the kids are receding, fading like old ink; Ed on the contrary looms larger and larger, the outlines around him darkening. He's constantly developing, like a Polaroid print, new colours emerging, but the result remains the same: Ed is a surface, one she has trouble getting beneath.

"Explore your inner world," said Sally's instructor in *Forms of Narrative Fiction,* a middle-aged woman of scant fame who goes in for astrology and the Tarot pack and writes short stories, which are not published in any of the magazines Sally reads. "Then there's your outer one," Sally said afterwards, to her friends. "For instance, she should really get something done about her hair." She made this trivial and mean remark because she's fed up with her inner world; she doesn't need to explore it. In her inner world is Ed, like a doll within a Russian wooden doll, and in Ed is Ed's inner world, which she can't get at.

She takes a crack at it anyway: Ed's inner world is a forest, which looks something like the bottom part of their ravine lot, but without the fence. He wanders around in there, among the trees, not heading in any special direction. Every once in a while he comes upon a strange-looking plant, a sickly plant choked with weeds and briars. Ed kneels, clears a space around it, does some pruning, a little skilful snipping and cutting, props it up. The plant revives, flushes with health, sends out a grateful red blossom. Ed continues on his way. Or it may be a conked-out squirrel, which he restores with a drop from his flask of magic elixir. At set intervals an angel appears, bringing him food. It's always meatloaf. That's fine with Ed, who hardly notices what he eats, but the angel is getting tired of being an angel. Now Sally begins thinking about the angel: why are its wings frayed and dingy grey around the edges, why is it looking so withered and frantic? This is where all Sally's attempts to explore Ed's inner world end up.

She knows she thinks about Ed too much. She knows she should stop. She knows she shouldn't ask, "Do you still love me?" in the plaintive tone that sets even her own teeth on edge. All it achieves is that Ed shakes his head, as if not understanding why she would ask this, and pats her hand. "Sally, Sally," he says, and everything proceeds as usual; except for the dread that seeps into things, the most ordinary things, such as rearranging the chairs and changing the burnt-out lightbulbs. But what is it she's afraid of? She has what they call everything: Ed, their wonderful house on a ravine lot, something she's always wanted. (But the hill is jungly, and the house is made of ice. It's held together only by Sally, who sits in the middle of it, working on a puzzle. The puzzle is Ed. If she should ever solve it, if she should ever fit the last cold splinter into place, the house will melt and flow away down the hill, and then....) It's a bad habit, fooling around with her head this way. It does no good. She knows that if she could quit she'd be happier. She ought to be able to: she's given up smoking.

She needs to concentrate her attention on other things. This is the real reason for the night courses, which she picks almost at random, to coincide with the evenings Ed isn't in. He has meetings, he's on the boards of charities, he has trouble saying no. She runs the courses past herself, mediaeval history, cooking, anthropology, hoping her mind will snag on something; she's even taken a course in geology, which was fascinating, she told her friends, all that magma. That's just it: everything is fascinating, but nothing enters her. She's always a star pupil, she does well on the exams and impresses the teachers, for which she despises them. She is familiar with her brightness, her techniques; she's surprised other people are still taken in by them.

Forms of Narrative Fiction started out the same way. Sally was full of good ideas, brimming with helpful suggestions. The workshop part of it was anyway just like a committee meeting, and Sally knew how to run those, from behind, without seeming to run them: she'd done it lots of times at work. Bertha, the instructor, told Sally she had a vivid imagination and a lot of untapped creative energy. "No wonder she never gets anywhere, with a name like Bertha," Sally said, while having coffee afterwards with two of the other night-coursers. "It goes with her outfits, though." (Bertha sports the macramé look, with health-food sandals and bulky-knit sweaters and hand-weave skirts that don't do a thing for her square figure, and too many Mexican rings on her hands, which she doesn't wash often enough.) Bertha goes in for assignments, which she calls learning by doing. Sally likes assignments: she likes things that can be completed and then discarded, and for which she gets marks.

The first thing Bertha assigned was The Epic. They read *The Odyssey* (selected passages, in translation, with a plot summary of the rest); then they poked around in James Joyce's *Ulysses,* to see how Joyce had adapted the epic form to the modern-day novel. Bertha had them keep a Toronto notebook, in which they had to pick out various spots around town as the ports of call in *The Odyssey,* and say why they had chosen them. The notebooks were read out loud in class, and it was a scream to see who had chosen what for Hades. (The Mount Pleasant Cemetery, McDonald's, where, if you eat the forbidden food, you never get back to the land of the living, the University Club with its dead ancestral souls, and so forth.) Sally's was the hospital, of course; she had no difficulty with the trench filled with blood, and she put the ghosts in wheelchairs.

After that they did The Ballad, and read gruesome accounts of murders and betrayed love. Bertha played them tapes of wheezy old men singing traditionally, in the Doric mode, and assigned a newspaper scrapbook, in which you had to clip and paste up-to-the-minute equivalents. The *Sun* was the best newspaper for these. The fiction that turned out to go with this kind of plot was the kind Sally liked anyway, and she had no difficulty concocting a five-page murder mystery, complete with revenge.

But now they are on Folk Tales and the Oral Tradition, and Sally is having trouble. This time, Bertha wouldn't let them read anything. Instead she read to them, in a voice, Sally said, that was like a gravel truck and was not conducive to reverie. Since it was the Oral Tradition, they weren't even allowed to take notes; Bertha said the original hearers of these stories couldn't read, so the stories were memorized. "To recreate the atmosphere," said Bertha, "I should turn out the lights. These stories were always told at night." "To make them creepier?" someone offered. "No," said Bertha. "In the days, they worked." She didn't do that, though she did make them sit in a circle.

"You should have seen us," Sally said afterwards to Ed, "sitting in a circle, listening to fairy stories. It was just like kindergarten. Some of them even had their mouths open. I kept expecting her to say, 'If you need to go, put up your hand.'" She was meaning to be funny, to amuse Ed with this account of Bertha's eccentricity and the foolish appearance of the students, most of them middle-aged, sitting in a circle as if they had never grown up at all. She was also intending to belittle the course, just slightly. She always did this with her night courses, so Ed wouldn't get the idea there was anything in her life that was even remotely as important as he was. But Ed didn't seem to need this amusement or this belittlement. He took her information earnestly, gravely, as if Bertha's behaviour was, after all, only the procedure of a specialist. No one knew better than he did that the procedures of specialists often looked bizarre or incomprehensible to onlookers. "She probably has her reasons," was all he would say.

The first stories Bertha read them, for warm-ups ("No memorizing for *her,*" said Sally), were about princes who got amnesia and forgot about their true loves and married girls their mothers had picked out for them. Then they had to be rescued, with the aid of magic. The stories didn't say what happened to the women the princes had already married, though Sally wondered about it. Then Bertha read them another story, and this time they were supposed to remember the features that stood out for them and write a five-page transposition, set in the present and cast in the realistic mode. ("In other words," said Bertha, "no real magic.") They couldn't use the Universal Narrator, however: they had done that in their Ballad assignment. This time they had to choose a point of view. It could be the point of view of anyone or anything in the story, but they were limited to one only. The story she was about to read, she said, was a variant of the Bluebeard motif, much earlier than Perrault's sentimental rewriting of it. In Perrault, said Bertha, the girl has to be rescued by her brothers; but in the earlier version things were quite otherwise.

This is what Bertha read, as far as Sally can remember:

There were once three young sisters. One day a beggar with a large basket on his back came to the door and asked for some bread. The eldest sister brought him some, but no sooner had she touched him than she was compelled to jump into his basket, for the beggar was really a wizard in disguise. ("So much for United Appeal," Sally murmured. "She should have said, 'I gave at the office.'") The wizard carried her away to his house in the forest, which was large and richly furnished. "Here you will be happy with me, my darling," said the wizard, "for you will have everything, your heart could desire."

This lasted for a few days. Then the wizard gave the girl an egg and a bunch of keys. "I must go away on a journey," he said, "and I am leaving the house in your charge. Preserve this egg for me, and carry it about with you everywhere; for a great misfortune will follow from its loss. The keys open every room in the house. You may go into each of them and enjoy what you find there, but do not go into the small room at the top of the house, on pain of death." The girl promised, and the wizard disappeared.

At first the girl contented herself with exploring the rooms, which contained many treasures. But finally her curiosity would not let her alone. She sought out the smallest key, and, with beating heart, opened the little door at the top of the house. Inside it was a large basin full of blood, within which were the bodies of many women, which had been cut to pieces; nearby were a chopping block and an axe. In her horror, she let go of the egg, which fell into the basin of blood. In vain did she try to wipe away the stain: every time she succeeded in removing it, back it would come.

The wizard returned, and in a stern voice asked for the egg and the keys. When he saw the egg, he knew at once she had disobeyed him and gone into the forbidden room. "Since you have gone into the room against my will," he said, "you shall go back into it against your own." Despite her pleas he threw her down, dragged her by the hair into the little room, hacked her into pieces and threw her body into the basin with the others.

Then he went for the second girl, who fared no better than her sister. But the third was clever and wily. As soon as the wizard had gone, she set the egg on a shelf, out of harm's way, and then went immediately and opened the forbidden door. Imagine her distress when she saw the cut-up bodies of her two beloved sisters; but she set the parts in order, and they joined together and her sisters stood up and moved, and were living and well. They embraced each other, and the third sister hid the other two in a cupboard.

When the wizard returned he at once asked for the egg. This time it was spotless. "You have passed the test," he said to the third sister. "You shall be my bride." ("And second prize," said Sally, to herself this time, "is *two* weeks in Niagara Falls.") The wizard no longer had any power over her, and had to do whatever she asked. There was more, about how the wizard met his come-uppance and was burned to death, but Sally already knew which features stood out for her.

At first she thought the most important thing in the story was the forbidden room. What would she put in the forbidden room, in her present-day realistic version? Certainly not chopped-up women. It wasn't that they were too unrealistic, but they were certainly too sick, as well as being too obvious. She wanted to do something more clever. She thought it might be a good idea to have the curious woman open the door and find nothing there at all, but after mulling it over she set this notion aside. It would leave her with the problem of why the wizard would have a forbidden room in which he kept nothing.

That was the way she was thinking right after she got the assignment, which was a full two weeks ago. So far she's written nothing. The great temptation is to cast herself in the role of the cunning heroine, but again it's too predictable. And Ed certainly isn't the wizard; he's nowhere near sinister enough. If Ed were the wizard, the room would contain a forest, some ailing plants and feeble squirrels, and Ed himself, fixing them up, but then, if it were Ed the room wouldn't even be locked, and there would be no story.

Now, as she sits at her desk, fiddling with her felt-tip pen, it comes to Sally that the intriguing thing about the story, the thing she should fasten on, is the egg. Why an egg? From the night course in Comparative Folklore she took four years ago, she remembers that the egg can be a fertility symbol, or a necessary object in African spells, or something the world hatched out of. Maybe in this story it's a symbol of virginity, and that is why the wizard requires it unbloodied. Women with dirty eggs get murdered, those with clean ones get married.

But this isn't useful either. The concept is so outmoded. Sally doesn't see how she can transpose it into real life without making it ridiculous, unless she sets the story in, for instance, an immigrant Portuguese family, and what would she know about that?

Sally opens the drawer of her desk and hunts around in it for her nail file. As she's doing this, she gets the brilliant idea of writing the story from the point of view of the egg. Other people will do the other things: the clever girl, the wizard, the two blundering sisters, who weren't smart enough to lie, and who will have problems afterwards, because of the thin red lines running all over their bodies, from where their parts joined together. But no one will think of the egg. How does it feel, to be the innocent and passive cause of so much misfortune?

(Ed isn't the Bluebeard: Ed is the egg. Ed Egg, blank and pristine and lovely. Stupid, too. Boiled, probably. Sally smiles fondly.)

But how can there be a story from the egg's point of view, if the egg is so closed and unaware? Sally ponders this, doodling on her pad of lined paper. Then she resumes the search for her nail file. Already it's time to begin getting ready for her dinner party. She can sleep on the problem of the egg and finish the assignment tomorrow, which is Sunday. It's due on Monday, but Sally's mother used to say she was a whiz at getting things done at the last minute.

After painting her nails with *Nuit Magique,* Sally takes a bath, eating her habitual toasted English muffin while she lies in the tub. She begins to dress, dawdling; she has plenty of time. She hears Ed coming up out of the cellar, then she hears him in the bathroom, which he has entered from the hall door. Sally goes in through the other door, still in her slip. Ed is standing at the sink with his shirt off, shaving. On the weekends he leaves it until necessary, or until Sally tells him he's too scratchy.

Sally slides her hands around his waist, nuzzling against his naked back. He has very smooth skin, for a man. Sally smiles to herself: she can't stop thinking of him as an egg.

"Mmm," says Ed. It could be appreciation, or the answer to a question Sally hasn't asked and he hasn't heard, or just an acknowledgement that she's there.

"Don't you ever wonder what I think about?" Sally says. She's said this more than once, in bed or at the dinner table, after dessert. She stands behind him, watching the swaths the razor cuts in the white of his face, looking at her own face reflected in the mirror, just the eyes visible above his naked shoulder. Ed, lathered, is Assyrian, sterner than usual; or a frost-covered Arctic explorer; or demi-human, a white-bearded forest mutant. He scrapes away at himself, methodically destroying the illusion.

"But I already know what you think about," says Ed.

"How?" Sally says, taken aback.

"You're always telling me," Ed says, with what might be resignation or sadness; or maybe this is only a simple statement of fact.

Sally is relieved. If that's all he's going on, she's safe.

Marylynn arrives half an hour early, her pearl-coloured Porsche leading two men in a delivery truck up the driveway. The men install the keyhole desk, while Marylynn supervises: it looks, in the alcove, exactly as Marylynn has said it would, and Sally is delighted. She sits at it to write the cheque. Then she and Marylynn go into the kitchen, where Sally is finishing up her sauce, and Sally pours them each a Kir. She's glad Marylynn is here: it will keep her from dithering, as she tends to do just before people arrive. Though it's only the heart men, she's still a bit nervous. Ed is more likely to notice when things are wrong than when they're exactly right.

Marylynn sits at the kitchen table, one arm draped over the chairback, her chin on the other hand; she's in soft grey, which makes her hair look silver, and Sally feels once again how banal it is to have ordinary dark hair like her own, however well-cut, however shiny. It's the confidence she envies, the negligence. Marylynn doesn't seem to be trying at all, ever.

"Guess what Ed said today?" Sally says.

Marylynn leans further forward. "What?" she says, with the eagerness of one joining in a familiar game.

"He said, 'Some of these femininists go too far,'" Sally reports. "'*Femininists.*' Isn't that sweet?"

Marylynn holds the pause too long, and Sally has a sudden awful thought: maybe Marylynn thinks she's showing off, about Ed. Marylynn has always said she's not ready for another marriage yet; still, Sally should watch herself, not rub her nose in it. But then Marylynn laughs indulgently, and Sally, relieved, joins in.

"Ed is unbelievable," says Marylynn. "You should pin his mittens to his sleeves when he goes out in the morning."

"He shouldn't be let out alone," says Sally.

"You should get him a seeing-eye dog," says Marylynn, "to bark at women."

"Why?" says Sally, still laughing but alert now, the cold beginning at the ends of her fingers. Maybe Marylynn knows something she doesn't; maybe the house is beginning to crumble, after all.

"Because he can't see them coming," says Marylynn. "That's what you're always telling me."

She sips her Kir; Sally stirs the sauce. "I bet he thinks I'm a femininist," says Marylynn.

"You?" says Sally. "Never." She would like to add that Ed has given no indication of thinking anything at all about Marylynn, but she doesn't. She doesn't want to take the risk of hurting her feelings.

The wives of the heart men admire Sally's sauce; the heart men talk shop, all except Walter Morly, who is good at by-passes. He's sitting beside Marylynn, and paying far too much attention to her for Sally's comfort. Mrs. Morly is at the other end of the table, not saying much of anything, which Marylynn appears not to notice. She keeps on talking to Walter about St. Lucia, where they've both been.

So after dinner, when Sally has herded them all into the living room for coffee and liqueurs, she takes Marylynn by the elbow. "Ed hasn't seen our desk yet," she says, "not up close. Take him away and give him your lecture on nineteenth-century antiques. Show him all the pigeon-holes. Ed loves pigeon-holes." Ed appears not to get this.

Marylynn knows exactly what Sally is up to. "Don't worry," she says, "I won't rape Dr. Morly; the poor creature would never survive the shock," but she allows herself to be shunted off to the side with Ed.

Sally moves from guest to guest, smiling, making sure everything is in order. Although she never looks directly, she's always conscious of Ed's presence in the room, any room; she perceives him as a shadow, a shape seen dimly at the edge of her field of vision, recognizable by the outline. She likes to know where he is, that's all. Some people are on their second cup of coffee. She walks towards the alcove; they must have finished with the desk by now.

But they haven't, they're still in there. Marylynn is bending forward, one hand on the veneer. Ed is standing too close to her, and as Sally comes up behind them she sees his left arm, held close to his side, the back of it pressed against Marylynn, her shimmering upper thigh, her ass to be exact. Marylynn does not move away.

It's a split second, and then Ed sees Sally and the hand is gone; there it is, on top of the desk, reaching for a liqueur glass.

"Marylynn needs more Tia Maria," he says. "I just told her that people who drink a little now and again live longer." His voice is even, his face is as level as ever, a flat plain with no signposts.

Marylynn laughs. "I once had a dentist who I swear drilled tiny holes in my teeth, so he could fix them later," she says.

Sally sees Ed's hand outstretched towards her, holding the empty glass. She takes it, smiling, and turns away. There's a roaring sound at the back of her head, blackness appears around the edges of the picture she is seeing, like a television screen going dead. She walks into the kitchen and puts her cheek against the refrigerator and her arms around it, as far as they will go. She remains that way, hugging it; it hums steadily, with a sound like comfort. After a while she lets go of it and touches her hair, and walks back into the living room with the filled glass.

Marylynn is over by the french doors, talking with Walter Morly. Ed is standing by himself in front of the fireplace, one arm on the mantelpiece, his left hand out of sight in his pocket.

Sally goes to Marylynn, hands her the glass. "Is that enough?" she says.

Marylynn is unchanged. "Thanks, Sally," she says, and goes on listening to Walter, who has dragged out his usual piece of mischief: some day, when they've perfected it, he says, all hearts will be plastic, and this will be a vast improvement on the current model. It's an obscure form of flirtation. Marylynn winks at Sally, to show that she knows he's tedious. Sally, after a pause, winks back.

She looks over at Ed, who is staring off into space, like a robot which has been parked and switched off. Now she isn't sure whether she really saw what she thought she saw. Even if she did, what does it mean? Maybe it's just that Ed, in a wayward intoxicated moment, put his hand on the nearest buttock, and Marylynn refrained from a shriek or a flinch out of good breeding or the desire not to offend him. Things like this have happened to Sally.

Or it could mean something more sinister: a familiarity between them, an understanding. If this is it, Sally has been wrong about Ed, for years, forever. Her version of Ed is not something she's perceived but something that's been perpetrated on her, by Ed himself, for reasons of his own. Possibly Ed is not stupid. Possibly he's enormously clever. She thinks of moment after moment when this cleverness, this cunning, would have shown itself if it were there, but didn't. She has watched him so carefully. She remembers playing Pick Up Sticks, with the kids, Ed's kids, years ago: how if you moved one stick in the tangle, even slightly, everything else moved also.

She won't say anything to him. She can't say anything: she can't afford to be wrong, or to be right either. She goes back into the kitchen and begins to scrape the plates. This is unlike her—usually she sticks right with the party until it's over—and after a while Ed wanders out. He stands silently, watching her. Sally concentrates on the scraping: dollops of *sauce suprême* slide into the plastic bag, shreds of lettuce, rice, congealed and lumpy. What is left of her afternoon.

"What are you doing out here?" Ed asks at last.

"Scraping the plates," Sally says, cheerful, neutral. "I just thought I'd get a head start on tidying up."

"Leave it," says Ed. "The woman can do that in the morning." That's how he refers to Mrs. Rudge, although she's been with them for three years now: *the woman.* And Mrs. Bird before her, as though they are interchangeable. This has never bothered Sally before. "Go on out there and have a good time."

Sally puts down the spatula, wipes her hands on the hand towel, puts her arms around him, holds on tighter than she should. Ed pats her shoulder. "What's up?" he says; then, "Sally, Sally." If she looks up, she will see him shaking his head a little, as if he doesn't know what to do about her. She doesn't look up.

Ed has gone to bed. Sally roams the house, fidgeting with the debris left by the party. She collects empty glasses, picks up peanuts from the rug. After a while she realizes that she's down on her knees, looking under a chair, and she's forgotten what for. She goes upstairs, creams off her make-up, does her teeth, undresses in the darkened bedroom and slides into bed beside Ed, who is breathing deeply as if asleep. *As if.*

Sally lies in bed with her eyes closed. What she sees is her own heart, in black and white, beating with that insubstantial moth-like flutter, a ghostly heart, torn out of her and floating in space, an animated valentine with no colour. It will go on and on forever; she has no control over it. But now she's seeing the egg, which is not small and cold and white and inert but larger than a real egg and golden pink, resting in a nest of brambles, glowing softly as though there's something red and hot inside it. It's almost pulsing; Sally is afraid of it. As she looks it darkens: rose-red, crimson. This is something the story left out, Sally thinks: the egg is alive, and one day it will hatch. But what will come out of it?

Clark Blaise

(b. 1940)

CLARK CLAISE HAS REPEATEDLY CROSSED BORDERS, and his fiction pursues the cultural implications not of rootlessness so much as the problem (and advantage) of having roots in a variety of places. Born to Canadian parents in Fargo, North Dakota, Blaise grew up there, and in the American South, the urban North, and Manitoba. Much of his work is semi-autobiographical, but displaced into story, taking confessional or satiric form. His story "How I Became a Jew" tells of a Southern boy's initiation into the language and persecution of a Northern playground; another story, "A Class of New Canadians," exposes the egocentric disillusionment of a second-language teacher in Montreal. Chapters in autobiography—under the title *Resident Alien*—appeared in 1986. With his wife Bharati Mukherjee—herself the author of a striking 1985 story collection about majority cultures and immigrant surrender, called *Darkness*—he wrote an openly autobiographical journal of a year spent in India, *Days and Nights in Calcutta* (1977), the title an allusion to a film by Satyajit Ray. The cinematic sensibility is strong in Blaise's writing. He sees scenes and hears speech with remarkable fidelity; but as with film, his narrative scenes and dialogues function metaphorically as well as reportorially. In form is meaning. Many of Blaise's stories have been collected in *A North American Education* (1973) and *Tribal Justice* (1974), and he has written several essays on his experiences learning the craft of fiction, and on the art of short story form. A graduate of Denison University and the University of Iowa, and a student of Bernard Malamud, Blaise has taught at Concordia, York, Skidmore, Iowa, Saratoga Springs, and David Thompson University Centre; he is the author of such novels as *Lunar Attractions* (1979) and *Lusts* (1983), and is currently director of the International Writers programme at the University of Iowa.

"Eyes," from *A North American Education* (the story was first published in *Fiddlehead* in 1971), is remarkable not only for its graphic account of terror but also for its controlled handling of what might be called "second-person" point of view. The emphasis on "you" at once generalizes the experience (from fear on the part of one person to the neuroses of contemporary society) and involves the reader as an agent in the problem and the narrative. The story is "about" itself, and its own method, as well as "about" alien life in Montreal. It is about seeing and being seen. The art of fiction, it transpires, is in some ways itself to be seen as an act of voyeurism, as discomforting as it is revelatory.

For Further Reading

CLARK BLAISE, "The Border As Fiction," *American Review of Canadian Studies* 23.2 (Summer 1993): 308–11.

——, "On Ending Stories," *Canadian Forum,* 62 (September 1982): 7, 37.

——, "To Begin To Begin" in *A 20th Century Anthology,* ed. W.E. Messenger and W.H. New (Toronto: Prentice-Hall, 1984) 415–18.

ROBERT LECKER, *On the Line* (Toronto: ECW, 1982).

——, *An Other I: The Fictions of Clark Blaise* (Toronto: ECW, 1988).

J.R. (TIM) STRUTHERS, ed., *The Montreal Story Tellers: Memoirs, Photographs, Critical Essays* (Montreal: Véhicule, 1985).

Eyes

You jump into this business of a new country cautiously. First you choose a place where English is spoken, with doctors and bus lines at hand, and a supermarket in a *centre d'achats* not too far away. You ease yourself into the city, approaching by car or bus down a single artery, aiming yourself along the boulevard that begins small and tree-lined in your suburb but broadens into the canyoned aorta of the city five miles beyond. And by that first winter when you know the routes and bridges, the standard congestions reported from the helicopter on your favorite radio station, you start to think of moving. What's the good of a place like this when two of your neighbors have come from Texas and the French paper you've dutifully subscribed to arrives by mail two days late? These French are all around you, behind the counters at the shopping center, in a house or two on your block; why isn't your little boy learning French at least? Where's the nearest *maternelle?* Four miles away.

In the spring you move. You find an apartment on a small side street where dogs outnumber children and the row houses resemble London's, divided equally between the rundown and remodeled. Your neighbors are the young personalities of French television who live on delivered chicken, or the old pensioners who shuffle down the summer sidewalks in pajamas and slippers in a state of endless recuperation. Your neighbors pay sixty a month for rent, or three hundred; you pay two-fifty for a two-bedroom flat where the walls have been replastered and new fixtures hung. The bugs *d'antan* remain, as well as the hulks of cars abandoned in the fire alley behind, where downtown drunks sleep in the summer night.

Then comes the night in early October when your child is coughing badly, and you sit with him in the darkened nursery, calm in the bubbling of a cold-steam vaporizer while your wife mends a dress in the room next door. And from the dark, silently, as you peer into the ill-lit fire alley, he comes. You cannot believe it at first, that a rheumy, pasty-faced Irishman in slate-gray jacket and rubber-soled shoes has come purposely to your small parking space, that he has been here before and he is not drunk (not now, at least, but you know him as a panhandler on the main boulevard a block away), that he brings with him a crate that he sets on end under your bedroom window and raises himself to your window ledge and hangs there nose-high at a pencil of light from the ill-fitting blinds. And there you are, straining with him from the uncurtained nursery, watching the man watching your wife, praying silently that she is sleeping under the blanket. The man is almost smiling, a leprechaun's face that sees what you cannot. You are about to lift the window and shout, but your wheezing child lies just under you; and what of your wife in the room next door? You could, perhaps, throw open the window and leap to the ground, tackle the man before he runs and smash his face into the bricks, beat him senseless then call the cops... Or better, find the camera, afix the flash, rap once at the window and shoot when he turns. Do nothing and let him suffer. *He is at your mercy,* no one will ever again be so helpless—but what can you do? You know, somehow, he'll escape. If you hurt him, he can hurt you worse, later, viciously. He's been a regular at your window, he's watched the two of you when you prided yourself on being young and alone and masters of the city. He knows your child and the park he plays in, your wife and where she shops. He's a native of the place, a man who knows the city and maybe a dozen such windows, who knows the fire escapes and alleys and roofs, knows the habits of the city's heedless young.

And briefly you remember yourself, an adolescent in another country slithering through the mosquito-ridden grassy fields behind a housing development, peering into those houses where newlyweds had not yet put up drapes, how you could spend five hours in a motionless crouch for a myopic glimpse of a slender arm reaching from the dark to douse a light. Then you hear what the man cannot; the creaking of your bed in the far bedroom, the steps of your wife on her way to the bathroom, and you see her as you never have before: blond and tall and rangily built, a north-Europe princess from a constitutional monarchy, sensuous mouth and prominent teeth, pale, tennis-ball breasts cupped in her hands as she stands in the bathroom's light.

"How's Kit?" she asks. "I'd give him a kiss except that there's no blind in there," and she dashes back to bed, nude, and the man bounces twice on the window ledge.

"You coming?"

You find yourself creeping from the nursery, turning left at the hall and then running to the kitchen telephone; you dial the police, then hang up. How will you prepare your wife, not for what is happening, but for what has already taken place?

"It's stuffy in here," you shout back, "I think I'll open the window a bit," You take your time, you stand before the blind blocking his view if he's still looking, then bravely you part the curtains. He is gone, the crate remains upright. "Do we have any masking tape?" you ask, lifting the window a crack.

And now you know the city a little better. A place where millions come each summer to take pictures and walk around must have its voyeurs too. And that place in all great cities where rich and poor co-exist is especially hard on the people in-between. It's health you've been seeking, not just beauty; a tough urban health that will save you money in the bargain, and when you hear of a place twice as large at half the rent, in a part of town free of Texans, English, and French, free of young actors and stewardesses who deposit their garbage in pizza boxes, you move again.

It is, for you, a city of Greeks. In the summer you move you attend a movie at the corner cinema. The posters advertise a war movie, in Greek, but the uniforms are unfamiliar. Both sides wear mustaches, both sides handle machine guns, both leave older women behind dressed in black. From the posters out-side there is a promise of sex; blond women in slips, dark-eyed peasant girls. There will be rubble, executions against a wall. You can follow the story from the stills alone: mustached boy goes to war, embraces dark-eyed village girl. Black-draped mother and admiring young brother stand behind. Young sol-dier, mustache fuller, embraces blond prostitute on a tangled bed. Enter soldiers, boy hides under sheets. Final shot, back in village. Mother in black; dark-eyed village girl in black. Young brother marching to the front.

You go in, pay your ninety cents, pay a nickel in the lobby for a wedge of *halvah*-like sweets. You understand nothing, you resent their laughter and you even resent the picture they're running. Now you know the Greek for "Coming Attractions," for this is a gangster movie at least thirty years old. The eternal Mediterranean gangster movie set in Athens instead of Naples or Marseilles, with smaller cars and narrower roads, uglier women and more sinister killers. After an hour the movie flatters you. No one knows you're not a Greek, that you don't belong in this theater, or even this city. That, like the Greeks, you're hanging on.

Outside the theater the evening is warm and the wide sidewalks are clogged with Greeks who nod as you come out. Like the Ramblas in Barcelona, with children out past midnight and families walking back and forth for a long city block, the men filling the coffeehouses, the women left outside, chatting. Not a blond head on the sidewalk, not a blond head for miles. Greek music pours from the coffeehouses, flies stumble on the pastry, whole families munch their *torsades molles* as they walk. Dry goods are sold at midnight from the sidewalk, like New York fifty years ago. You're wandering happily, glad that you moved, you've rediscovered the innocence of starting over.

Then you come upon a scene directly from Spain. A slim blond girl in a flo-ral top and white pleated skirt, tinted glasses, smoking, with bad skin, ignores a persistent young Greek in a shiny Salonika suit. "Whatsamatta?" he de-mands, slapping a ten-dollar bill on his open palm. And without looking back at him she drifts closer to the curb and a car makes a sudden squealing turn and lurches to a stop on the cross street. Three men are inside, the back door opens and not a word is exchanged as she steps inside. How? What re-finement of gesture did we immigrants miss? You turn to the Greek boy in sympathy, you know just how he feels, but he's already heading across the street, shouting something to his friends outside a barbecue stand. You have a pocketful of bills and a Mediterranean soul, and money this evening means a woman, and blond means whore and you would spend it all on another blond with open pores; all this a block from your wife and tenement. And you hurry home.

Months later you know the place. You trust the Greeks in their stores, you fear their tempers at home. Eight bathrooms adjoin a central shaft, you hear the beatings of your son's friends, the thud of fist on bone after the slaps. Your child knows no French, but he plays cricket with Greeks and Jamaicans out in the alley behind Pascal's hardware. He brings home the oily tires from the Esso station, plays in the boxes behind the appliance store. You watch from a greasy back window, at last satisfied. None of his friends is like him, like you. He is becoming Greek, becoming Jamaican, becoming a part of this strange new land. His hair is nearly white; you can spot him a block away.

On Wednesdays the butcher quarters his meat. Calves arrive by refrigerator truck, still intact but for their split-open bellies and sawed-off hooves. The older of the three brothers skins the carcass with a small thin knife that seems all blade. A knife he could shave with. The hide rolls back in a continuous flap, the knife never pops the membrane over the fat.

Another brother serves. Like yours, his French is adequate. *"Twa lif d'hamburger,"* you request, still watching the operation on the rickety sawhorse. Who could resist? It's a Levantine treat, the calf's stumpy legs high in the air, the hide draped over the edge and now in the sawdust, growing longer by the second.

The store is filling. The ladies shop on Wednesday, especially the old widows in black overcoats and scarves, shoes and stockings. Yellow, mangled fingernails. Wednesday attract them with boxes in the window, and they call to the butcher as they enter, the brother answers, and the women dip their fingers in the boxes. The radio is loud overhead, music from the Greek station.

"Une et soixante, m'sieur. Du bacon, jambon?"

And you think, taking a few lamb chops but not their saltless bacon, how pleased you are to manage so well. It is a Byzantine moment with blood and widows and sides of dripping beef, contentment in a snowy slum at five below.

The older brother, having finished the skinning, straightens, curses, and puts away the tiny knife. A brother comes forward to pull the hide away, a perfect beginning for a gameroom rug. Then, bending low at the rear of the glistening carcass, the legs spread high and stubby, the butcher digs in his hands, ripping hard where the scrotum is, and pulls on what seems to be a strand of rubber, until it snaps. He puts a single glistening prize in his mouth, pulls again and offers the other to his brother, and they suck.

The butcher is singing now, drying his lips and wiping his chin, and still he's chewing. The old black-draped widows with the parchment faces are also chewing. On leaving, you check the boxes in the window. Staring out are the heads of pigs and lambs, some with the eyes lifted out and a red socket exposed. A few are loose and the box is slowly dissolving from the blood, and the ice beneath.

The women have gathered around the body; little pieces are offered to them from the head and entrails. The pigs' heads are pink, perhaps they've been boiled, and hairless. The eyes are strangely blue. You remove your gloves and touch the skin, you brush against the grainy ear. How the eye attracts you! How you would like to lift one out, press its smoothness against your tongue, then crush it in your mouth. And you cannot. Already your finger is numb and the head, it seems, has shifted under you. And the eye, in panic, grows white as your finger approaches. You would take that last half inch but for the certainty, in this world you have made for yourself, that the eye would blink and your neighbors would turn upon you.

Ken Mitchell
(b. 1940)

A NATIVE OF MOOSE JAW, Ken Mitchell attended the University of Saskatchewan, and since 1967 he has taught creative writing at the University of Regina. The author of three comic novels—*Wandering Rafferty* (1972), *The Meadowlark Connection* (1975), and *The Con Man* (1979)—and the book of short stories from which "The Great Electrical Revolution" is taken (*Everybody Gets Something Here*, 1977), Mitchell is also a critic and a regional anthologist (*Horizon*, 1977). He is most noted, however, as a playwright. He is the author of *Cruel Tears* (1976), *The Great Cultural Revolution* (1979), and several other plays and screenplays, and he has been associated with the performance group Humphrey and the Dumptrucks. A self-proclaimed "popularist," Mitchell addresses the political experience of people by exploring the surface elements of the daily culture that frequently declares their immediate needs. His characters are nonconformists, always resisting conventions and authorities. They are ordinary individuals. But there is another set of conventions that gives them their vigorous power of speech, and gives their speech its own confident authority. Ordinary people, in Mitchell's tales, become extraordinary (possibly even heroic) by the simple, difficult feat of being true to themselves.

The playwright's ear for speech helps shape the dialogue of "The Great Electrical Revolution." First published in *Prism International* in 1970, the story is a highly conventional tall tale, dependent on its ironic cadences, almost ritually exaggerating events and character types until it reaches its inevitable, melodramatic point of climax, and snappily closes off. Mitchell uses the tall tale technique as it is typically used in Western Canada: as a spoof of those centralized systems of power that are so large they are inadequately aware of their fringes, and as a declaration of the residual power of local individualism.

For Further Reading

GEOFF HANCOCK, Interview with Ken Mitchell, *Books in Canada* 14.4 (May 1985): 37, 39.

DICK HARRISON, *Unnamed Country: The Struggle for a Canadian Prairie Fiction* (Edmonton: U Alberta P, 1977).

The Great Electrical Revolution

I was only a little guy in 1937, but I can remember Grandad being out of work. Nobody had any money to pay him, and as he said, there wasn't much future in brick-laying as a charity. So mostly he just sat around in his suite above the hardware store, listening to his radio. We *all* listened to it when there was nothing else to do, which was most of the time, unless you happened to be going to school like me. Grandad stuck right there through it all—soap operas, weather reports, and quiz shows—unless he got a bit of cash from somewhere. Then he and Uncle Fred would go downtown to the beer parlour at the King William Hotel.

Grandad and Grandma came from the old country long before I was born. When they arrived in Moose Jaw, all they had was three children—Uncle Fred, Aunt Thecla, and my Dad; a trunk full of working clothes; and a twenty-six-pound post maul for putting up fences to keep "rogues" off Grandad's land. Rogues meant Orangemen, cattle rustlers, capitalists, and Indians. All the way on the train from Montreal, he glared out the Pullman window at the endless flat, saying to his family:

"I came here for land, b'Christ, and none of 'em's goin' to sly it on me."

He had sworn to carve a mighty estate from the raw Saskatchewan prairie, although he had never so much as picked up a garden hoe in his life before leaving Dublin.

When he stepped off the train at the C.P.R. station in Moose Jaw, it looked like he was thinking of tearing it down and seeding the site to oats. It was two o'clock in the morning but he kept striding up and down the lobby of the station, dressed in his good wool suit with the vest, puffing his chest like a bantam rooster in a chicken run. My dad and Uncle Fred and Aunt Thecla sat on the trunk, while Grandma pleaded with him to go and find them a place to stay. (It was only later they realized he was afraid to step outside the station.) He finally quit strutting long enough to get a porter to carry their trunk to a hotel across the street.

The next morning they went to the government land office to secure their homestead. Then Grandad rented a democrat and took my Dad and Uncle Fred out to inspect the land they had come halfway around the world to find. Grandma and Aunt Thecla were told to stay in the hotel room and thank the Blessed Virgin for deliverance. They were still offering their prayers three hours later, when Grandad burst back into the room, his eyes wild and his face pale and quivering.

"Sweet Jesus Christ!" he shouted at them. "There's too much of it! There's just too damn much of it out there." He ran around the room several times, knock-

From *Everybody Gets Something Here* (Toronto: Macmillan, 1977). Reprinted by permission of Bella Pomer Agency Inc.

ing against the walls and moaning, "Miles and miles of nothing but miles and miles!" He collapsed onto one of the beds, and lay staring at the ceiling.

"It'ud drive us witless in a week!"

The two boys came in and told the story of the expedition. Grandad had started out fine, perhaps just a bit nervous. But the further they went from the town, the more agitated and wild-eyed he became. Soon he stopped urging the horse along and asked it to stop. They were barely five miles from town when they turned around and came back, with Uncle Fred driving. Grandad could only crouch on the floor of the democrat, trying to hide from the enormous sky, and whispering at Fred to go faster. He'd come four thousand miles to the wide open spaces—only to discover he suffered from agoraphobia.

That was his last excursion onto the open prairie. (He did make one special trip to Bulkhead in 1928 to fix Aunt Thecla's chimney, but that was a family favour. Even then Uncle Fred had to drive him there in an enclosed Ford sedan in the middle of the night, with newspapers taped to the windows so he couldn't see out.) He abandoned the dream of a country manor. There was nothing he could do but take up brick-laying again in Moose Jaw, where there were trees and tall buildings to protect him from the vastness. Maybe it was a fortunate turn of fate; certainly he prospered from then until the Depression hit, about the time I was born.

Yet—Grandad always felt guilty about not settling on the land. It was his conscience that prompted him to send my Dad to work at a cattle ranch in the hills, the day after he turned sixteen. He married Aunt Thecla off to a Lutheran farmer at Bulkhead who threshed about five hundred acres of wheat every fall. Uncle Fred was the eldest and an apprentice brick-layer, so he stayed in town and lived with Grandad and Grandma in the suite above the hardware store.

I don't remember much about the cattle ranch my father eventually took over, except whirls of dust and skinny animals dragging themselves from one side of the range to the other. Finally there were no more cattle, and no money to buy more, and nothing to feed them if we *did* buy them, except wild foxtail and Russian thistle. So we moved into Moose Jaw with Grandad and Grandma, and went on relief. It was better than the ranch, where there was nothing to do but watch tumbleweeds roll through the yard. We would have had to travel into town to collect our salted fish and government pork anyway. Grandad was happy to have us, because when my Dad went down to the railway yard to get our ration, he collected Grandad's too. My Dad never complained about waiting in line for a handout, but Grandad would have starved to death first. "Damned government drives us all to the edge," he'd say. "Then they want us to queue up for the God-damned swill they're poisoning us with."

That was when we spent so much time listening to Grandad's radio, a great slab of black walnut cabinet he had swindled, so he thought, from a secondhand dealer on River Street. An incandescent green bulb glowed in the centre of it when the tubes were warming up. There was a row of knobs with elaborate-looking initials and a dial with the names of cities like Tokyo, Madrid, and Chicago. Try as we might on long winter evenings to tune the needle in and hear a play in Japanese or Russian, all we ever got was CHMJ Moose Jaw, The Buckle of the Wheat Belt. Even so, I spent hours lying on the floor, tracing the floral patterns on the front of the speaker while I listened to another world of mystery and fascination.

When the time came that Grandad could find no more work, he set a kitchen chair in front of the radio and stayed there, not moving except to go to the King William with Uncle Fred. My Dad managed to get a job with the city, gravelling streets for forty cents a day. But things grew worse. The Moose Jaw Light and Power Company came around one day in the fall of 1937 and cut off our electricity for non-payment. It was hard on Grandad not to have his radio. Not only did he have nothing to do, but he had to spend all his time thinking about it. So he stared out the parlour window, which looked over the alley behind the hardware store. There was a view of the rear of the Rainbow Laundry, probably the dreariest vista in town.

That was what he was doing the day of his discovery, just before Christmas. Uncle Fred and my Dad were arguing about who had caused the Depression— R.B. Bennett or the C.P.R. Suddenly Grandad turned from the window. There was a new and strange look on his face. "Where does that wire go?" he said.

"Wire?" said Uncle Fred, looking absent-mindedly around the room. He patted his pockets looking for a wire.

"What wire?" my Dad said.

Grandad nodded toward the window. "This wire running right past the window." He pointed to a double strand of power line that ran from a pole in the back alley to the side of our building. It was a lead-in for the hardware store below.

"Holy Moses Cousin Harry. Isn't that a sight now!" Grandad said, grinning crazily.

"You're nuts!" Uncle Fred told him. "You'll never get a tap off that line there. They'd find you out in nothing flat."

Grandma, who always heard everything that was said, called from the kitchen: "Father, don't you go and do some foolishness will have us all electrinated."

"By Jayzuz," he muttered. He never paid attention to anything she said. "Cut off *my* power, will they?"

That night, after I went to bed, I listened to him and Uncle Fred banging and scraping as they bored a hole through the parlour wall. My Dad wouldn't have anything to do with it and took my mother to the free movie at the co-op. He said Grandad was descending to the level of the Moose Jaw Light and Power Company.

As it happened, Grandad was an experienced electrician. He had known for a long time how to jump a wire from one side of the meter to the other, to cheat the power company. I had often watched him under the meter, stretched out on tip-toe at the top of a broken stepladder, yelling at Grandma to lift the God-damned Holy Candle *higher* so he could see what the Christ he was doing.

The next day, Grandad and Uncle Fred were acting like a couple of kids, snorting and giggling and jabbing each other in the ribs. They were eager for the King William beer parlour to open so they could go and tell their friends about Grandad's revenge on the power company. There they spent the day like heroes, telling over and over how Grandad had spied the lead-in, and how they had bored the hole through the wall, and how justice had finally descended on the capitalist leeches. They came home for supper, but as soon as they ate they headed back to the King William. Everybody was buying them free beer.

Grandma didn't think much of their efforts, though she claimed to enjoy the benefits of electrical power. The line came through the hole in the wall, across the parlour floor to the kitchen and the hall. Other cords were attached which led to the two bedrooms. Grandma muttered in irritation when she had to sweep around the black tangle of wires and sockets. She had that quaint old-country belief that electricity leaked from every connection and with six of us living in the tiny suite, somebody was forever tripping on one of the cords and knocking things over.

But we lived with all that because Grandad was happy again. We might *all* have lived happily if Grandad and Uncle Fred could have kept silent about their revenge on the power company.

One night about a week later we were in the parlour listening to Fibber McGee and Molly when somebody knocked at the door. It was Mrs. Pizak, who lived next door in a tiny room.

"Goot evening," she said, looking all around. "I see your power has turnt beck on."

"Ha," Grandad said. "We turned it on *for* 'em. Damned rogues."

"Come in and listen to the show with us," Grandma said. Mrs. Pizak kept looking at the black wires running back and forth across the parlour, and at Grandad's radio. You could tell she wasn't listening to the show.

"Dey shut off my power, too," she said. "I alvays like listen de Shut-In program. Now my radio isn't vork."

"Hmmm," Grandad said, trying to hear Fibber and the Old-Timer. Grandma and my Dad watched him, not listening to the radio any more either. Finally he couldn't stand it.

"All right, Fred," he said. "Go and get the brace and bit."

They bored a hole through one of the bedroom walls into Mrs. Pizak's cubicle, and she was on Grandad's power grid, too. It didn't take long for everybody else in the block to find out about the free power. They all wanted to hook up. There were two floors of apartments above the hardware store, and soon the walls and ceiling of Grandad's suite were as full of holes as a colander, with wires running in all directions. For the price of a bottle of whiskey, people could run their lights twenty-four hours a day if they wanted. By Christmas Day, even those neighbours who *paid* their bills had given notice to the power company. It was a tolerable Christmas in a bad year—and Grandad and Uncle Fred liked to take credit for it. Which everyone gave them. There was a lot of celebration up and down the halls, where they always showed up as guests of honour. A funny feeling ran through the block, like being in a state of siege, or a revolution, with Grandad and Uncle Fred leading it.

One late afternoon just before New Year's, I was lying on the parlour floor, reading a second-hand Book of Knowledge I had gotten for Christmas. Grandma and my mother were knitting socks, and all three of us were half-listening to Major Bowes' amateur show. From the corner of my eye, I thought I saw Grandad's radio move. I blinked and stared at it, but the big console just sat there quoting the Major's tactful enthusiasm. I turned a page. Again, it seemed to move in a jerk.

"Grandma," I said. "The radio—"

She looked up from her knitting, already not believing a word I might have to say. I gave up and glared at the offending machine. While I watched, it slid at least six inches across the parlour floor.

"Grandma!" I screamed. "The radio's moving! All by itself!"

She looked calmly at the radio, then the tangle of wires spread across the floor, and then out the parlour window.

"Larry-boy, you'd best run and fetch your grandfather. He's over at McBrides'."

McBrides' suite was along the gloomy hall a few doors. I sprinted the whole distance and pounded frantically at the door. Someone opened it the width of a crack. "Is my Grandad in there?" I squeaked.

Grandad stepped out into the hall with a glass in his hand, closing the door behind him. "What is it, Larry?"

"Grandma says for you to come quick. There's something wrong with the radio!"

"My radio!" Like most small men, he had the energy of a race-horse. He started walking back up the hall, broke into a trot, then a steady gallop, holding his glass of whiskey out in front at arm's length so it wouldn't spill. He burst through the door and skidded to a stop in front of the radio, which sat there, perfectly normal except that it stood maybe a foot to the left of his chair.

"By the Holy Toenails of Moses—what is it?"

Grandma looked up and jerked her chin ominously toward the window. Her quiet firmness usually managed to calm him, but now, in two fantastic bounds, Grandad stood glaring out the window.

"Larry," he said, turning to me with a pale face, "fetch your Uncle Fred." I tore off down the hall again to number eight and fetched Uncle Fred. When we entered the suite, the two women were still knitting. Grandma was doing her stiches calmly enough, but my mother's needles clattered like telegraph keys, and she was throwing terrified glances around the room.

Grandad had not moved. "Have a gawk at *this*, will you, Fred."

Uncle Fred and I crowded around him to see out. There, on a pole only twenty feet from our parlour window, practically facing us eye-to-eye, was a lineman from the power company. He was replacing broken glass insulators; God knows why he was doing it in the dead of winter. He could not have noticed our home-made lead-in, or he would have been knocking at the door. We could only pray he wouldn't look at the wire too closely. Once, he lifted his eyes toward the lighted window where we stood gaping out at him in the growing darkness. He grinned at us, and raised his hand in a salute. He must have thought we were admiring his work.

"Wave back!" Grandad ordered. The three of us waved frantically at the lineman, to make him think we appreciated his efforts, although Grandad was muttering some very ugly things about the man's ancestry.

Finally, to our relief, the lineman finished his work and got ready to come down the pole. He reached out his hand for support—and my heart stopped beating as his weight hung on the contraband wire. Behind me, I could hear the radio slide another foot across the parlour floor. The lineman stared at the wire he held. He tugged experimentally, his eyes following it up to the hole through our wall. He looked at Grandad and Uncle Fred and me standing there in the lit-up window, with our crazy horror-struck grins and our arms frozen above our heads in grotesque waves. Understanding spread slowly across his face.

He scrambled around to the opposite side of the pole and braced himself to give a mighty pull on our line. Simultaneously, Grandad leaped into action, grabbing the wire on our side of the wall. He wrapped it around his hands, and braced his feet against the baseboard. The lineman gave his first vicious yank, and it almost jerked Grandad smack against the wall. I remember thinking what a powerful man the lineman must be to do that to my Grandad.

"Fred, you feather-brained idiot!" he shouted. "Get over here and *haul* before the black-hearted son of a bitch pulls me through the wall."

Uncle Fred ran to the wire just in time, as the man on the pole gave another, mightier heave. From the window, I could see him stiffen with rage and determination. The slender wire sawed back and forth through the hole in the wall for at least ten minutes, first one side, then the other, getting advantage. The curses on our side got very loud and bitter. I couldn't hear the lineman, but I could see him—with his mouth twisted in an awful snarl, throwing absolutely terrible looks at me in the window, and heaving on the line. He was not praying to St. Jude.

Grandad's cursing would subside periodically when Grandma warned: "Now, now, father, not in front of the boy." Then she would go back to her knitting and pretend the whole affair wasn't happening, and Grandad's blasphemies would soar to monumental heights.

The lineman must have been in extra-good condition, because our side quickly began to play out. Grandad yelled at Grandma and my mother, even at me, to throw ourselves on the line and help. But the women refused to leave their knitting, and they would not allow me to be corrupted. I didn't want to leave my viewpoint at the window, anyway.

Grandad and Uncle Fred kept losing footage until the huge radio had scraped all the way across the floor and stood at their backs, hampering their efforts.

"Larry!" Grandad shouted. "Is he weakenin' any?"

He wanted desperately for me to say yes, but it was useless. "It doesn't look like it," I said. Grandad burst out in a froth of curses I'd never heard before. A fresh attack on the line pulled his knuckles to the wall and barked them badly. He looked tired and beaten. All the slack in the line was taken up. He was against the wall, his head twisted, looking at me. A light flared in his eyes.

"All right, Fred," he said. "If he wants the God-damned thing so bad—let him have it!" They both jumped back—and nothing happened.

I could see the lineman, completely unaware of his impending disaster, literally winding himself up for an all-out assault on our wire. I wanted, out of human kindness, to shout a warning at him. But it was too late. With an incredible backward lunge, he disappeared from sight behind the power pole.

A shattering explosion of wild noises blasted around us, like a bomb had fallen in Grandad's suite. Every electric appliance and light that Grandma owned flew into the parlour, bounding off the walls and smashing against each other. A table lamp from the bedroom caromed off Uncle Fred's knee. The radio collided against the wall and was ripped off its wire. Sparking and flashing like lightning, all of Grandma's things hurled themselves against the parlour walls, popping like a string of firecrackers as the cords went zipping through the hole. A silence fell—like a breath of air to a drowning man. The late afternoon darkness settled through the room.

"Sweet Jesus Christ!" Grandad said. Then there came a second uproar: a blood-curdling series of roars and shouting, as all our neighbours recovered from seeing their lamps, radios, irons, and toasters leap from their tables and collect in ruined piles of junk around the "free power" holes in their walls. Uncle Fred turned white as a sheet.

I looked out the window. The lineman sat at the foot of his pole, dazed. He looked up at me with one more hate-filled glare, then deliberately snipped our wire with a pair of cutters, taped the end and marched away into the night.

Grandad stood in the midst of the total darkness and the ruins of his home, trying to examine his beloved radio for damage. Grandma sat in her rocking chair, knitting socks and refusing to acknowledge the adventure.

It was Grandad who finally broke the silence. "Well! They're lucky," he said. "It's just damned lucky for them they didn't scratch my radio!"

Michel Tremblay

(b. 1942)

MICHEL TREMBLAY WAS BORN ON THE RUE FABRE IN MONTREAL, the urban setting of most of his plays and novels. Following the family business as a linotype operator at first, he soon turned to the theatre. Though his first play was written in 1959, he attracted major attention with *Les Belles-Soeurs* (1965, published 1968), a play disclosing the basic cultural presumptions and ambitions of a group of working-class women who gather to celebrate (and excoriate) the chance good fortune of one of them. The play also set in motion a cycle of ten plays on the related theme of the cultural family, written over the next twelve years. The alienation of individuals in Tremblay's dramatized family has its parallel (according to Jean-Cléo Godin) in the cultural alienation felt by modern Quebec. The divided family angrily resists its destiny for a long time; then abruptly admits to transvestitism and prostitution and incestuous longings (declarations of narrative fact and social metaphor); and finally, in the play *Hosanna* (1973), strips itself of its artificial trappings and declares its true identity.

A translator and a fiction writer as well, Tremblay has embarked on a sequence of novels which traces the continuing lives of characters whose world is shaped by East End Montreal. He has also written a number of stories, of which *Contes pour buveurs attardés* (1966) was translated by Michael Bullock in 1978 as *Stories for Late Night Drinkers*. This 1974 translation of "The Thimble" (1966)—a seriocomic nightmare about the end of the world—is by Jay Bochner.

For Further Reading

PIERRE LAVOIE, "Bibliographie commentée," *Voix et images,* 7.2 (hiver 1982): 225–306.

ROCH TURBIDE, "Michel Tremblay: Du texte à la représentation," *Voix et images* 7.2 (hiver 1982): 213–24.

RENATE USMIANI, *Michel Tremblay* (Vancouver: Douglas & McIntyre, 1982).

The Thimble

Translated by Jay Bochner

If Bobby Stone had known what was to happen that day, he probably would never have got out of bed. And...well, the catastrophe might have been avoided.

Bobby Stone wasn't bad fellow. He worked in an office, drank in moderation, went to mass every Sunday, and had a weakness for plump women. He was neither old nor young, though he wore a hat to cover an expanding bald spot.

Bobby Stone had not the slightest inkling that he was going to be the cause of the catastrophe.

"Now, now, my dear lady, please stop this silly game. People are looking at us!" He was right. A throng of loafers had gathered around them and some were beginning to eye Bobby Stone reproachfully, because this woman was weeping and wailing. "Sir, I beg of you," she cried, "take it! Take it! I give it to you. It's yours!" But Bobby Stone didn't want it; he didn't want to have anything to do with it. "What do you expect me to do with it?" he said. "And besides, it's a...thing that belongs to women." More and more people gathered on the sidewalk and Bobby Stone began to sweat. He took out his handkerchief to wipe his forehead, but he didn't remove his hat. *She's crazy. That's it, she's crazy. And all those people looking at us. But I don't want to have her thimble!*

A man emerged from the crowd and grabbed Bobby Stone by the collar. "So," he said, breathing a rotten smell into his face, "we make women cry in the middle of the street?" Bobby Stone was trembling. "But Mister, I don't know this woman! She wants to give me her thimble, and I don't want her thimble, I don't...." Really, Bobby Stone had had enough. In an abrupt surge of courage— or was it cowardice?—he slammed his fist into the face of the man who was threatening him and took off, knocking over two or three people who tried to stop him.

As you might have expected, he worked very poorly that day. The columns of figures swayed on the page, and when he closed his eyes Bobby Stone saw the strange woman offering him the thimble. "It is yours."

The five o'clock bell rang. Bobby Stone slumped in his desk chair, his tie undone and one hand on his chest. *I never would have believed such a stupid incident....*

Michel Tremblay, "The Thimble," in Philip Stratford, ed., *Stories from Québec* (Toronto: Van Nostrand Reinhold Canada, 1974). Translated by Jay Bochner. Originally published in *Contes pour buveurs attardés* (Montréal: Les Editions du Jour, 1966).

Oh, no that's too much, following me to my office! But it was no vision this time; his eyes were wide open. She was sitting in the chair directly in front of him on the other side of his desk. "If you do not take it immediately," said the woman. "I will have to forbid you from taking it, and then you'll run after me to steal it from me. I'm telling you, you'll steal it from me." Bobby Stone, mad with fear, jumped up and ran towards the door. "Very well then," the woman cried out, "I forbid you to take my thimble!" Bobby Stone stopped short. Oh, what a fine thimble, such a fine beautiful thimble! Made out of plastic with tiny dimples in it. A fine thimble! He must have this thimble. Nothing else in the world existed outside of this pink and yellow thimble. He ran after the woman, who pretended to flee but was careful to lose ground all the while....

Smack! And another! You bitch! So, you wanted to keep it all to yourself, did you? The thimble for you and nothing for me! This is for you. Some good kicks, you see, and the back of my hand, and a few with the knee....

When he left the building his clothes were all mussed and there was some blood on his fingernails, but he had the thimble. It was his and no one—but no one, do you hear?—would ever be able to take it from him. He knew the secret of the thimble now. Before she died the woman had whispered, "In the thimble...in the thimble...I have locked the universe."

When he awoke the next morning Bobby Stone remembered nothing. He found a pink and yellow thimble on his night-table. What an ugly thimble! He threw it in the garbage. But before he left for the office Bobby Stone tore a loose button from his overcoat. He found some thread and a needle and thought of the thimble at the bottom of the garbage pail. He went and got it. And so as not to prick himself while he sewed on his coat button, Bobby Stone pushed his little finger into the little thimble. He squashed the entire universe.

Thomas King

(b. 1943)

OF CHEROKEE AND GREEK-GERMAN DESCENT, Thomas King was born in Sacramento, California, and grew up in Roseville. Leaving California for the first time in 1964, he travelled to New Zealand and Australia on a tramp steamer, and lived there for the next three years, learning photography and journalism. Subsequently he returned to the United States and pursued a number of other careers—including working as a draftsman for Boeing in Seattle—before attending the University of Utah, earning a Ph.D. in history and literature. At the invitation of Leroy Littlebear, he emigrated to Canada in 1980, to teach Native Studies at the University of Lethbridge. Since then he has chaired the American Indian Studies Department at the University of Minnesota, and worked for CBC-TV in Toronto. He currently teaches at the University of Guelph.

A prolific writer and editor, King brought First Nations writing to widespread public attention with such books as *The Native in Literature* (1984; edited with Cheryl Carver and Helen Hoy) and *All My Relations: An Anthology of Contemporary Canadian Native Prose* (1990). These works made clear the moral role of the trickster figure in First Nations tale-telling, and also the importance of interconnectedness, or community. King's own fictions—the novels *Medicine River* (1990; which he subsequently adapted as a CBC-TV movie) and *Green Grass, Running Water* (1993), for example—provide further evidence of these motifs. They temper social critique with a comic vision of human behaviour.

"A Seat in the Garden," which first appeared in *Books in Canada* in 1990 and then was collected in *One Good Story, That One* in 1993, uses the "trickster" technique inventively (juxtaposing "elevated" and vernacular conventions) and in literary and social context. Written at a time when W.P. Kinsella's "Silas Ermineskin" stories were being critiqued for "appropriating" another culture, King's story *parodically* "appropriates" in order to talk about appropriation—adapting to comic ends the most famous phrase in Kinsella's *Shoeless Joe* (1982; turned into the film *Field of Dreams* in 1989): "if you build it, they will come." George Bowering's use of "first and second Indians" in his novel *Caprice* (1987) perhaps also comes in for parodic recognition here, and added to this mix is a series of references to American actors who "played" Indians in Hollywood films—Jeff Chandler ("Cochise" in *Broken Arrow*, 1950), for example, or Victor Mature (the title character in *Chief Crazy Horse*, 1955). By allowing parody and self-mockery to work small miracles, King reclaims social reality from movie (and other) conventions. For while pompousness and presumption do not last long in King's fictional universe, love does, and so does community—in large part because of laughter.

For Further Reading

JEANNETTE ARMSTRONG, ed. *Looking at the Words of our People: First Nations Analysis of Literature* (Penticton, B.C.: Theytus, 1993).

MARGARET ATWOOD, "A Double-Bladed Knife: Subversive Laughter in Two Stories by Thomas King," *Canadian Literature* 124–125 (Spring-Summer 1990): 243–50.

GRETCHEN M. BATAILLE and CHARLES P. SILET, *The Pretend Indians: Images of Native Americans in the Movies* (Ames, Iowa: Iowa State UP, 1980).

JEFFREY CANTON, "An Interview with Thomas King," *Paragraph* (Stratford) 16.1 (Summer 1994): 2–6.

THOMAS KING, "Godzilla vs. Post-Colonial," *WLWE* 30.2 (1990): 10–16.

DAVID LATHAM, "From Richardson to Robinson to King: Colonial Assimilation and Communal Origination," *British Journal of Canadian Studies* 8.2 (1993): 180–90.

CONSTANCE ROOKE, "Interview with Tom King," *WLWE* 30.2 (1990): 62–76.

A Seat in the Garden

Joe Hovaugh settled into the garden on his knees and began pulling at the wet, slippery weeds that had sprung up between the neat rows of beets. He trowelled his way around the zucchini and up and down the lines of carrots, and he did not notice the big Indian at all until he stopped at the tomatoes, sat back, and tried to remember where he had set the ball of twine and the wooden stakes.

The big Indian was naked to the waist. His hair was braided and wrapped with white ermine and strips of red cloth. He wore a single feather held in place by a leather band stretched around his head, and, even though his arms were folded tightly across his chest, Joe could see the glitter and flash of silver and turquoise on each finger.

"If you build it, they will come," said the big Indian.

Joe rolled forward and shielded his eyes from the morning sun.

"If you build it, they will come," said the big Indian again.

"Christ sakes," Joe shouted. "Get the hell out of the corn, will ya!"

"If you build it..."

"Yeah, yeah. Hey! This is private property. You people ever hear of private property?"

"...they will come."

Joe struggled to his feet and got his shovel from the shed. But when he got back to the garden, the big Indian was gone.

"Alright!" Joe shouted and drove the nose of the shovel into the ground. "Come out of that corn!"

The corn stalks were only about a foot tall. Nevertheless, Joe walked each row, the shovel held at the ready just in case the big Indian tried to take him by surprise.

When Red Mathews came by in the afternoon, Joe poured him a cup of coffee and told him about the big Indian and what he had said, and Red told Joe that he had seen the movie.

"Wasn't a movie, Red, damn it. It was a real Indian. He was just standing there in the corn."

"You probably scared him away."

"You can't let them go standing in your garden whenever they feel like it."

"That's the truth."

The next day, when Joe came out to the garden to finish staking the tomatoes, the big Indian was waiting for him. The man looked as though he was asleep, but, as soon as he saw Joe, he straightened up and crossed his arms on his chest.

"You again!"

"If you build it..."

"I'm going to call the police. You hear me. The police are going to come and haul you away."

"...they will come."

Joe turned around and marched back into the house and phoned the RCMP, who said they would send someone over that very afternoon.

"Afternoon? What am I supposed to do with him until then. Feed him lunch?"

The RCMP officer told Joe that it might be best if he stayed in his house. There was the chance, the officer said, that the big Indian might be drunk or on drugs and, if that were the case, it was better if Joe didn't antagonize him.

"He's walking on my corn. Does that mean anything to you?"

The RCMP officer assured Joe that it meant a great deal to him, that his wife was a gardener, and he knew how she would feel if someone walked on her corn.

"Still," said the officer, "it's best if you don't do anything."

What Joe did do was to call Red, and, when Red arrived, the big Indian was still in the garden waiting.

"Wow, he's a big sucker, alright," said Red. "You know, he looks a little like Jeff Chandler."

"I called the police, and they said not to antagonize him."

"Hey, there are two of us, right?"

"That's right," said Joe.

"You bet it's right."

Joe got the shovel and a hoe from the shed, and he and Red wandered out into the garden as if nothing was wrong.

"He's watching us," said Red.

"Don't step on the tomatoes," said Joe.

Joe walked around the zucchini, casually dragging the shovel behind him. Red ambled through the beets, the hoe slung over his shoulder.

"If you build it, they will come."

"Get him!" shouted Joe. And before Red could do anything, Joe was charging through the carrots, the shovel held out in front like a lance.

"Wait a minute, Joe," yelled Red, the hoe still on his shoulder. But Joe was already into the tomatoes. He was closing on the big Indian, who hadn't moved, when he stepped on the bundle of wooden stakes and went down in a heap.

"Hey," said Red. "You okay?"

Red helped Joe to his feet, and, when the two men looked around, the big Indian was gone.

"Where'd he go?" said Joe.

"Beats me," said Red. "What'd you do to get him so angry?"

Red helped Joe to the house, wrapped an ice pack on his ankle, and told him to put his leg on the chair.

"I saw a movie a couple of years back about a housing development that was built on top of an ancient Indian burial mound."

"I would have got him, if I hadn't tripped."

"They finally had to get an authentic medicine man to come in and appease the spirits."

"Did you see the look on his face when he saw me coming?"

"And you should have seen some of those spirits."

When the RCMP arrived, Joe showed the officer where the Indian had stood, how he had run at him with the shovel, and how he had stumbled over the bundle of stakes.

After Joe got up and brushed himself off, the RCMP officer asked him if he recognized the big Indian.

"Not likely," said Joe. "There aren't any Indians around here."

"Yes, there are," said Red. "Remember those three guys who come around on weekends every so often."

"The old winos?" said Joe.

"They have that grocery cart, and they pick up cans."

"They don't count."

"They sit down there by the hydrangea and crush the cans and eat their lunch. Sometimes they get to singing."

"You mean drink their lunch."

"Well, they could have anything in that bottle."

"Most likely Lysol."

The RCMP officer walked through the garden with Joe and Red and made a great many notes. He shook hands with both men and told Joe to call him if there was any more trouble.

"Did you ever wonder," said Red, after the officer left, "just what he wants you to build or who 'they' are?"

"I suppose you saw a movie."

"Maybe we should ask the Indians."

"The drunks?"

"Maybe they could translate for us."

"The guy speaks English."

"That's right, Joe. God, this gets stranger all the time. Ed Ames, that's who he reminds me of."

On Saturday morning, when Joe and Red walked out on the porch, the big Indian was waiting patiently for them in the corn. They were too far away to hear him, but they could see his mouth moving.

"Okay," said Red. "All we got to do is wait for the Indians to show up."

The Indians showed up around noon. One man had a green knapsack. The other two pushed a grocery cart in front of them. It was full of cans and bottles. They were old, Joe noticed, and even from the porch, he imagined he could smell them. They walked to a corner of the garden behind the hydrangea where the sprinklers didn't reach. It was a dry, scraggly wedge that Joe had never bothered to cultivate. As soon as the men stopped the cart and sat down on the ground, Red got to his feet and stretched.

"Come on. Can't hurt to talk with them. Grab a couple of beers, so they know we're friendly."

"A good whack with the shovel would be easier."

"Hey, this is kind of exciting. Don't you think this is kind of exciting?"

"I wouldn't trip this time."

When Joe and Red got to the corner, the three men were busy crushing the cans. One man would put a can on a flat stone and the second man would step on it. The third man picked up the crushed can and put it in a brown grocery bag. They were older than Joe had thought, and they didn't smell as bad as he had expected.

"Hi," said Red. "That's a nice collection of cans."

"Good morning," said the first Indian.

"Getting pretty hot," said the second Indian.

"You fellows like a drink?" said the third Indian, and he took a large glass bottle out of the knapsack.

"No thanks," said Red. "You fellows like a beer?"

"Lemon water," said the third Indian. "My wife makes it without any sugar so it's not as sweet as most people like."

"How can you guys drink that stuff?" said Joe.

"You get used to it," said the second Indian. "And it's better for you than pop."

As the first Indian twisted the lid off the bottle and took a long drink, Joe looked around to make sure none of his neighbors were watching him.

"I'll bet you guys know just about everything there is to know about Indians," said Red.

"Well," said the first Indian, "Jimmy and Frank are Nootka and I'm Cree. You guys reporters or something?"

"Reporters? No."

"You never know," said the second Indian. "Last month, a couple of reporters did a story on us. Took pictures and everything."

"It's good that these kinds of problems are brought to the public's attention," said Red.

"You bet," said the third Indian. "Everyone's got to help. Otherwise there's going to be more garbage than people."

Joe was already bored with the conversation. He looked back to see if the big Indian was still there.

"This is all nice and friendly," said Joe. "But we've got a problem that we were hoping you might be able to help us with."

"Sure," said the first Indian. "What's the problem?"

Joe snapped the tab on one of the beers, took a long swig, and jerked his thumb in the direction of the garden. "I've got this big Indian who likes to stand in my garden."

"Where?" asked the second Indian.

"Right there," said Joe.

"Right where?" asked the third Indian.

"If you build it, they will come," shouted the big Indian.

"There, there," said Joe. "Did you hear that?"

"Hear what?" said the first Indian.

"They're embarrassed," said Red under his breath. "Let me handle this."

"This is beginning to piss me off," said Joe, and he took another pull on the beer.

"We were just wondering," Red began. "If you woke up one day and found a big Indian standing in your cornfield and all he would say was, 'If you build it, they will come,' what would you do?"

"I'd stop drinking," said the second Indian, and the other two Indians covered their faces with their hands.

"No, no," said Red. "That's not what I mean. Well...you see that big Indian over there in the cornfield, don't you?"

The Indians looked at each other, and then they looked at Joe and Red.

"Okay," said the first Indian. "Sure, I see him."

"Oh, yeah," said the second Indian. "He's right there, all right. In the...beets?"

"Corn," said Joe.

"Right," said the third Indian. "In the corn. I can see him, too. Clear as day."

"That's our problem," said Red. "We think maybe he's a spirit or something."

"No, we don't," said Joe.

"Yes, we do," said Red, who was just getting going. "We figure he wants us to build something to appease him so he'll go away."

"Sort of like...a spirit?" said the first Indian.

"Hey," said the second Indian, "remember that movie we saw about that community that was built..."

"That's the one," said Red. "What we have to figure out is what he wants us to build. You guys got any ideas?"

The three Indians looked at each other. The first Indian looked at the cornfield. Then he looked at Joe and Red.

"Tell you what," he said. "We'll go over there and talk to him and see what he wants. He looks...Cree. You guys stay here, okay."

Joe and Red watched as the three Indians walked into the garden. They stood together facing the beets.

"Hey," shouted Joe. "You guys blind? He's behind you."

The first Indian waved his hand and smiled, and the three men turned around. Red could see them talking, and he tried to watch their lips, but he couldn't figure out what they were saying. After a while, the Indians waved at the rows of carrots and came back over to where Joe and Red were waiting.

"Well," said Red. "Did you talk to him?"

"Yes," said the first Indian. "You were right. He is a spirit."

"I knew it!" shouted Red. "What does he want?"

The first Indian looked back to the cornfield. "He's tired of standing, he says. He wants a place to sit down. But he doesn't want to mess up the garden. He says he would like it if you would build him a...a...bench right about...here."

"A bench?" said Joe.

"That's what he said."

"So he can sit down?"

"He gets tired standing."

"The hell you say."

"Do you still see him?" asked the second Indian.

"You blind? Of course I still see him."

"Then I'd get started on the bench right away," said the third Indian.

"Come on, Red," said Joe, and he threw the empty beer can into the hydrangea and opened the other one. "We got to talk."

Joe put the pad of paper on the kitchen table and drew a square. "This is the garden," he said. "These are the carrots. These are the beets. These are the beans. And this is the corn. The big Indian is right about here."

"That's right," said Red. "But what does it mean?"

"Here's where those winos crush their cans and drink their Lysol," Joe continued, marking a spot on the pad and drawing a line to it.

"Lemon water."

"You listening?"

"Sure."

"If you draw lines from the house to where the big Indian stands and from there to where the winos crush their cans and back to the house...Now do you see it?"

"Hey, that's pretty good, Joe."

"What does it remind you of?"

"A bench?"

"No," said Joe. "A triangle."

"Okay, I can see that."

"And if you look at it like this, you can see clearly that the winos and the big Indian are there, and the house where you and I are is here."

"What if you looked at it this way, Joe," said Red and he turned the paper a half turn to the right. "Now the house is there and the old guys and the big Indian are here."

"That's not the way you look at it. That's not the way it works."

"Does that mean we're not going to build the bench?"

"It's our battle plan."

"A bench might be simpler," said Red.

"I'll attack him from the house along this line. You take him from the street along that line. We'll catch him between us."

"I don't know that this is going to work."

"Just don't step on the tomatoes."

The next morning, Red waited behind the hydrangea. He was carrying the hoe and a camera. Joe crouched by the corner of the house with the shovel.

"Charge!" yelled Joe, and he broke from his hiding place and lumbered across the yard and into the garden. Red leaped through the hydrangea and struggled up the slight incline to the cornfield.

"If you build it, they will come," shouted the Indian.

"Build it yourself," shouted Joe, and he swung the shovel at the big Indian's legs. Red, who was slower, stopped at the edge of the cornfield to watch Joe whack the Indian with his shovel and to take a picture, so he saw Joe and his shovel run right through the Indian and crash into the compost mound.

"Joe, Joe...you alright? God, you should have seen it. You ran right through that guy. Just like he wasn't there. I got a great picture. Wait till you see the picture. Just around the eyes, he looks a little like Sal Mineo."

Red helped Joe back to the house and cleaned the cuts on Joe's face. He wrapped another ice pack on Joe's ankle and then drove down to the one-hour photo store and turned the film in. By the time he got back to the house, Joe was standing on the porch, leaning on the railing.

"You won't believe it, Joe," said Red. "Look at this."

Red fished a photograph out of the pack. It showed Joe and the shovel in mid-swing, plunging through the corn. The colors were brilliant.

Joe looked at the photograph for a minute and then he looked at the cornfield. "Where's the big Indian?"

"That's just it. He's not there."

"Christ!"

"Does that mean we're going to build the bench?"

The bench was a handsome affair with a concrete base and a wooden seat. The Indians came by the very next Saturday with their knapsack and grocery cart, and Red could tell that they were impressed.

"Boy," said the first Indian, "that's a good-looking bench."

"You think this will take care of the problem?" asked Red.

"That Indian still in the cornfield?" said the second Indian.

"Of course he's still there," said Joe. "Can't you hear him?"

"I don't know," said the third Indian, and he twisted the lid off the bottle and took a drink. "I don't think he's one of ours."

"What should we do?"

"Don't throw your cans in the hydrangea," said the first Indian. "It's hard to get them out. We're not as young as we used to be."

Joe and Red spent the rest of the day sitting on the porch, drinking beer, and watching the big Indian in the garden. He looked a little like Victor Mature, Red thought, now that he had time to think about it, or maybe Anthony Quinn, only he was taller. And there was an air about the man that made Red believe—believe with all his heart—that he had met this Indian before.

Andreas Schroeder

(b. 1946)

BORN IN HOHENEGGELSEN, GERMANY, Andreas Schroeder immigrated to Canada with his parents in 1951. He studied creative writing at the University of British Columbia, founded the *Journal of Contemporary Literature in Translation* (which ran from 1968 to 1980), and has been a newspaper columnist, a creative writing instructor, an anthologist of short fiction, chairman of the Writers' Union of Canada, and director of the Public Lending Right programme. His volumes of poetry include *The Ozone Minotaur* (1969), *File of Uncertainties* (1971) and u*niVERSE* (1971), the last a collection of concrete poems. His book-length sequence of surreal stories, *The Late Man*, appeared in 1972, and *Shaking It Rough*, a revealing 8-month prison journal, was published in 1976. Since then he has written on Mennonite culture and published a nonfiction novel, *Dustship Glory* (1987).

"The Cage" is the closing story of *The Late Man*, a collection in which seemingly bizarre and ritual events enclose the actions of individual characters. A quiet, plain, even matter-of-fact prose shifts seamlessly into the fantastic, deliberately blurring easy distinctions between the two. Schroeder's eye falls on the art and the artist, and on the separate, enclosed, even isolating process the artist goes through, struggling to shape art into existence. Fabular in effect, if not strictly so in form, "The Cage" is in many ways a modern creation story, a story about the birth of consciousness and the nature of metaphor. Metaphoric in its own technique, it probes the power of word, colour, image, and sound to isolate experience exactly, or sometimes—however miraculously and rarely—to effect connection.

For Further Reading

GEORGE BOWERING, ed., *Fictions of Contemporary Canada* (Toronto: Coach House, 1980), "Introductory Notes" 7–21.

GEOFF HANCOCK, ed., *Magic Realism* (Toronto: Aya, 1980), "Magic Realism" 7–15.

The Cage

There was nothing at first. No colors for anyone to see; no shape.

Later, the flat, thin layers of day and night fell across each other like cast-off leaves; wind scuffed along the sand and bushes with the absent-minded sound of listless feet.

In this desert not even the knowledge of being desert was certain. The fixtures of desert were only concessions arranged to ward off the threat of total vacuum. Silence buckled and twisted in the air like invisible mountain ranges on the move. There was a possibility of animals, of cautious paws and hoofs on dry ground, but nothing was ever certain. The alternating currents of heat and cold loped across the land until it cowered like a charged beast, bristling at the touch, and narrow-eyed.

I was, as my father had been, a rock, a bush, a leaf or a vacuum: there was nothing at first: no color for anyone to see, no shape.

•••

Someone, something, must have spent a lot of time stringing this bone frame with carefully stretched and heated nerves. At first consciousness I felt as if I had been suddenly dropped from some unexpected height. All around me the dust seemed to be constantly in the process of settling, and the shape of everything I did not know stretched and compressed like gaunt lizards trapped by fire. The desert wind gabbled and fluttered like a flock of new-born geese.

I came to enjoy the thin, lean thoughts I found scattered among the debris my brain continually drifted into me; long flexible strands, useful for repairing or re-weaving ornate, synthetic memories, hanging oneself, or simply collecting. I learned to propel myself through the present by simply fabricating and spinning out an ever-lengthening past, at the end of which I floated, pawing lazily through the air toward the future.

I received much, returned little. Occasionally an argument with myself, as the cave of me grew too crowded for my unruly demands. I used everything I could think up uses for and discarded the rest. I was offended at my birth and delighted with its irreversibility, but I was never certain of either.

•••

Now and then, in this desert, there are people. I know little about them. Some time ago I kicked over a rock and several of them scuttled away. That was the first I'd ever seen of them. In the mornings, occasionally, I catch glimpses of them scrabbling about in the half-light, arguing and gesticulating, but few of them ever risk the brute illusion of the mid-day sun. I suspect many of them are blind.

From *The Late Man* (Port Clements, B.C.: Sono Nis Press, 1972). Reprinted by permission of the publisher.

I am almost deaf. Half my life ago I remember noticing the sound of the earth slowly fading, until eventually I could no longer hear it turning at all. There was visible movement, but no discernible sound. In its place I gradually became aware of color, bouncing with an increasing violence off the rocks and bushes; edges hardened, sharpened to a painful intensity, and I began to discern shapes that cut their outlines into the air so quietly, I could almost feel the fabric of the atmosphere separating with the unprotesting, mute subjugation of a lump of meat under a well-honed butcher knife. I kept my eyes heavily shaded in those days, until they were accustomed to the moods of a rippling desert under glass.

As I gained increasing use of my vision I seemed to lose the power of speech. I spoke less and less, hardly moved at all, only slid my eyes over smooth, grinning surfaces, groping, probing the tight mesh of molecules, the epidermal layers which from a distance blurred together to form the apparent shapes of things.

I stared for an interminable time, eventually concentrating my entire gaze on a single rock, until the only movement was the slowly sliding focusing of my irises trying to adjust to my determination to penetrate the rock's exterior. When it finally fell away, I saw exposed the proof I had suspected since first consciousness, the proof I had always felt I would find if I could just force my vision into the unsuspecting rock's interior before it could prepare itself to appear to me simply as a known quantity, a thing with a name, a category.

Inside this rock, I discovered, was only rock.

Then it dawned on me, what an outrageous fraud had been perpetrated on us all by a two-faced universe; all around me I discovered only reality masquerading as reality; nothing was what it was but was only itself in disguise. The rocks, in short, were not rocks at all, but rocks masquerading as rocks.

I remember this incident well, for it occurred again and then again, many times later, though the circumstances differed slightly in each case. Each time I made this discovery, I rushed back to apply it to all that I had left behind, but when I arrived I found nothing left; I had been away too long; I had forgotten that one cannot safely afford to leave one's beliefs on their own even for an instant. There was, consequently, nothing to do but to retrace the entire travelled distance, it being, after all, not uncommon for a man to lose his place in his own line and be forced to begin again.

•••

Eventually, there was the problem of fear. The fear of an empty man constantly beginning again to defend nothing at all with nothing less than his life. The fear of a man not yet accustomed to coming upon himself, without warning, in unexpected places. The fear of a man who suspects he is to himself as unpredictable as he is to the world around him. The fear of a man who knows no other method but reason.

I sat, somewhere on the outskirts of myself, afraid to disclose myself to me, afraid of the vacuum I might not find, worried that I might succeed in deluding myself and hoping that I would. I couldn't understand the purpose of the purposelessness of all my acts, and I remained confused by the lack of confusion on the part of everything I perceived around me. And yet, though I had no doubt that my own purposelessness was important, I was unable to determine the point, or for that matter the intention, of the existence of anything else in the world.

It remained for me to discover that at the base of every animal's movements, every plant's existence, every man's handshake, lay the search for water. The unexpectedly orange flower among rocks was merely camouflage, an attempt to divert my attention from the search for the water it naturally required for its own survival. The tenuously non-violent co-existence between all animate and inanimate things rested stealthily on the suspicion that each was subsisting on a source of water the other might eventually be able to usurp. All around me the sidelong glances, the squinted, furtive optics of a landscape using its light mainly for reconnaissance succeeded only in creating a mirage of water, on the strength of which countless numbers migrated to the desert and died. Many of me, also, collapsed of thirst during the long, hot run toward an ever-receding ocean.

It was when I learned to live without the water everything else required, however, that my survival stood in greatest jeopardy, for a man who needs no water can provoke an entire landscape into revolt. A strange fear, an instinctive panic hovered over all that existed around me; a hatred which desired to kill by surprise and run for cover. I was forced to make a great show of clanging pails and digging shallow wells whenever I was exposed to general view outside my dwelling, and even then the rumours continued to grow that I was not consuming enough water to warrant being considered harmless, and therefore safe.

My safety, finally, came in the ever-increasing numbers of me which became evident to those who attempted to hunt me down. As the food and water shortage became more intense and the inhabitants of the desert correspondingly decreased, I began to constitute a larger and larger percentage of its population. Eventually, when I was in the uncontested majority, I began to examine the possibilities of becoming the desert, and its mirage, as well.

•••

How many of me there now are, I have no idea—the numbers vary considerably, depending on how many can be supported or provoked at any given time. Those who become extraneous or for some reason unneeded fade without incident and reappear only where a future situation warrants their return. In difficult times it is not unusual for the numbers to become reduced to only one. In the severest of times, I have often discovered myself with my body between my own teeth.

As more and more things in this desert die, more and more becomes possible. I have developed the habit of killing something every day. Each evening I retrace my tracks, carrying some dead thought, strangled emotion or shot belief slung onto my gamebelt. Soon there will be no more interference. I have written a time into my life when I shall discover my own footsteps leading continually away from me. Where those footsteps end (abruptly, for no reason, in mid-step) I begin, constantly. There is, in fact, no end to my beginning....

Douglas Glover

(b. 1948)

DOUGLAS GLOVER WAS BORN IN SIMCOE, Ontario, and raised on an Ontario tobacco farm. A widely-published journalist and a prize-winning writer of fiction, he was educated at York University, the University of Edinburgh, and the University of Iowa, where in addition to graduating with an M.F.A. he edited the *Iowa Review*. He has been a lecturer and writer-in-residence at numerous colleges in Canada and the United States, including U.N.B., Lethbridge, SUNY (Albany), and Skidmore, and his writing has appeared in periodicals as diverse as *Canadian Fiction Magazine, Saturday Night,* and *Playgirl*. He now lives part of the time in Waterford, Ontario, and part in Gansevoort, in upstate New York.

As well as working on his own writing, he has actively encouraged other writers, both by drawing attention to the talents of emerging storytellers and by highlighting excellence in a range of genres. He has edited, for example, *The Journey Prize Anthology 6* (1995) and, with Maggie Helwig, *Coming Attractions 93,* one of the annual Oberon Press series devoted to the work of new writers.

Glover's fictions include *A Guide to Animal Behaviour* (1991), *The Life and Times of Captain N.* (1993), and several other novels and volumes of short stories. "Dog Attempts to Drown Man in Saskatoon" is the title story of a 1985 collection; it first appeared in *Canadian Fiction Magazine* in 1983. It is a "postmodern" story, about language and fragmentation as much as empirical realities. Concerned with "separation," it is consequently concerned also with "connection"—with "bridges" and with the difficulty of "reading the bridge," the signs of division and/or understanding. Hence Glover's work also probes the unstable dividing line between the real and the invented, between the empirical details that provide the illusion of actuality and the arbitrariness of apparent "plotted" narrative. But where and how, then, does a story "actually" happen? In the sequence of events? In the conflict among characters? In the techniques of organization and design? Or ("only") in the mind of the teller?

For Further Reading

LINDA HUTCHEON, *The Canadian Postmodern: a study of contemporary English-Canadian fiction* (Toronto: Oxford, 1988).

PATRICIA WAUGH, *Metafiction: The Theory and Practice of Self-Conscious Fiction* (London & New York: Methuen, 1984).

Dog Attempts to Drown Man
in Saskatoon

My wife and I decide to separate, and then suddenly we are almost happy together. The pathos of our situation, our private and unique tragedy, lends romance to each small act. We see everything in the round, the facets as opposed to the flat banality that was wedging us apart. When she asks me to go to the Mendel Art Gallery Sunday afternoon, I do not say no with the usual mounting irritation that drives me into myself. I say yes and some hardness within me seems to melt into a pleasant sadness. We look into each other's eyes and realize with a start that we are looking for the first time because it is the last. We are both thinking, "Who is this person to whom I have been married? What has been the meaning of our relationship?" These are questions we have never asked ourselves; we have been a blind couple groping with each other in the dark. Instead of saying to myself, "Not the art gallery again! What does she care about art? She has no education. She's merely bored and on Sunday afternoon in Saskatoon the only place you can go is the old sausage-maker's mausoleum of art!" instead of putting up arguments, I think, "Poor Lucy, pursued by the assassins of her past, unable to be still. Perhaps if I had her memories I also would be unable to stay in on a Sunday afternoon." Somewhere that cretin Pascal says that all our problems stem from not being able to sit quietly in a room alone. If Pascal had had Lucy's mother, he would never have written anything so foolish. Also, at the age of nine, she saw her younger brother run over and killed by a highway roller. Faced with that, would Pascal have written anything? (Now I am defending my wife against Pascal! A month ago I would have used the same passage to bludgeon her.)

•

Note. Already this is not the story I wanted to tell. That is buried, gone, lost—its action fragmented and distorted by inexact recollection. Directly it was completed, it had disappeared, gone with the past into that strange realm of suspended animation, that coatrack of despair, wherein all our completed acts await, gathering dust, until we come for them again. I am trying to give you the truth, though I could try harder, and only refrain because I know that that way leads to madness. So I offer an approximation, a shadow play, such as would excite children, full of blind spots and irrelevant adumbrations, too little in parts; elsewhere too much. Alternately I will frustrate you and lead you astray. I can only say that at the outset, my intention was otherwise; I sought only clarity and simple conclusions. Now I know the worst—that reasons are out of joint with actions, that my best explanation will be obscure, subtle and unsatisfying, and that the human mind is a tangle of unexplored pathways.

•

"My wife and I decide to separate, and then suddenly we are almost happy together." This is a sentence full of ironies and lies. For example, I call her my wife. Technically this is true. But now that I am leaving, the thought is in both our hearts: "Can a marriage of eleven months really be called a marriage?" Moreover, it was only a civil ceremony, a ten-minute formality performed at the City Hall by a man who, one could tell, had been drinking heavily over lunch. Perhaps if we had done it in a cathedral surrounded by robed priests intoning Latin benedictions we would not now be falling apart. As we put on our coats to go to the art gallery, I mention this idea to Lucy. "A year," she says. "With Latin we might have lasted a year." We laugh. This is the most courageous statement she has made since we became aware of our defeat, better than all her sour tears. Usually she is too self-conscious to make jokes. Seeing me smile, she blushes and becomes confused, happy to have pleased me, happy to be happy, in the final analysis, happy to be sad because the sadness frees her to be what she could never be before. Like many people, we are both masters of beginnings and endings, but founder in the middle of things. It takes a wise and mature individual to manage that which intervenes, the duration which is a necessary part of life and marriage. So there is a sense in which we are not married, though something *is* ending. And therein lies the greater irony. For in ending, in separating, we are finally and ineluctably together, locked as it were in a ritual recantation. We are going to the art gallery (I am guilty of over-determining the symbol) together.

•

It is winter in Saskatoon, to my mind the best of seasons because it is the most inimical to human existence. The weather forecaster gives the temperature, the wind chill factor and the number of seconds it takes to freeze exposed skin. Driving between towns one remembers to pack a winter survival kit (matches, candle, chocolate, flares, down sleeping bag) in case of a breakdown. Earlier in the week just outside the city limits a man disappeared after setting out to walk a quarter of a mile from one farmhouse to another, swallowed up by the cold prairie night. (This is, I believe, a not unpleasant way to die once the initial period of discomfort has been passed.) Summer in Saskatoon is a collection of minor irritants: heat and dust, blackflies and tent caterpillars, the night-time electrical storms that leave the unpaved concession roads impassable troughs of gumbo mud. But winter has the beauty of a plausible finality. I drive out to the airport early in the morning to watch jets land in a pink haze of ice crystals. During the long nights the *aurora borealis* seems to touch the rooftops. But best of all is the city itself which takes on a kind of ghostliness, a dreamlike quality that combines emptiness (there seem to be so few people) and the mists rising from the heated buildings to produce a mystery. Daily I tramp the paths along the riverbank, crossing and re-crossing the bridges, watching the way the city changes in the pale winter light. Beneath me the unfrozen parts of the river smoke and boil, raging to become still. Winter in Saskatoon is a time of anxious waiting and endurance; all that beauty is alien, a constant threat. Many things do not endure. Our marriage, for example, was vernal, a product of the brief, sweet, prairie spring.

•

Neither Lucy nor I was born here; Mendel came from Russia. In fact there is a feeling of the camp about Saskatoon, the temporary abode. At the university there are photographs of the town—in 1905 there were three frame buildings and a tent. In a bar I nearly came to blows with a man campaigning to preserve a movie theatre built in 1934. In Saskatoon that is ancient history, that is the cave painting at Lascaux. Lucy hails from an even newer settlement in the wild Peace River country where her father went to raise cattle and ended up a truck mechanic. Seven years ago she came to Saskatoon to work in a garment factory (her left hand bears a burn scar from a clothes press). Next fall she begins law school. Despite this evidence of intelligence, determination and ability, Lucy has no confidence in herself. In her mother's eyes she will never measure up, and that is all that is important. I myself am a proud man and a gutter snob. I wear a ring in my left ear and my hair long. My parents migrated from a farm in Wisconsin to a farm in Saskatchewan in 1952 and still drive back every year to see the trees. I am two courses short of a degree in philosophy which I will never receive. I make my living at what comes to hand, house painting when I am wandering; since I settled with Lucy, I've worked as the lone overnight editor at the local newspaper. Against the bosses, I am a union man: against the union, I am an independent. When the publisher asked me to work days I quit. That was a month ago. That was when Lucy knew I was leaving. Deep down she understands my nature. Mendel is another case: he was a butcher and a man who left traces. Now on the north bank of the river there are giant meat-packing plants spilling forth the odours of death, guts and excrement. Across the street are the holding pens for the cattle and the rail lines that bring them to slaughter. Before building his art gallery Mendel actually kept his paintings in this sprawling complex of buildings, inside the slaughterhouse. If you went to his office, you would sit in a waiting room with a Picasso or a Rouallt on the wall. Perhaps even a van Gogh. The gallery is down-river at the opposite end of the city, very clean and modern. But whenever I go there I hear the panicky bellowing of the death-driven steers and see the streams of blood and the carcasses and smell the stench and imagine the poor beasts rolling their eyes at Gauguin's green and luscious leaves as the bolt enters their brains.

•

We have decided to separate. It is a wintry Sunday afternoon. We are going to the Mendel Art Gallery. Watching Lucy shake her hair out and tuck it into her knitted hat, I suddenly feel close to tears. Behind her are the framed photographs of weathered prairie farmhouses, the vigorous spider plants, the scarred child's school desk where she does her studying, the brick-and-board bookshelf with her meagre library. (After eleven months there is still nothing of me that will remain.) This is an old song; there is no gesture of Lucy's that does not fill me instantly with pity, the child's hand held up to deflect the blow, her desperate attempts to conceal unworthiness. For her part she naturally sees me as the father who, in that earlier existence, proved so practised in evasion and flight. The fact that I am now leaving her only reinforces her intuition—it is as if she has expected it all along, almost as if she has been working toward it. This goes to show the force of initial impressions. For example I will never forget the first time I saw Lucy. She was limping across Broadway, her feet swathed in bandages and jammed into her pumps, her face alternately distorted with agony and composed in dignity. I followed her for blocks—she was beautiful and wounded, the kind of woman I am always looking for to redeem me. Similarly, what she will always remember is that first night we spent together when all I did was hold her while she slept because, taking the bus home, she had seen a naked man masturbating in a window. Thus she had arrived at my door, laughing hysterically, afraid to stay at her own place alone, completely undone. At first she had played the temptress because she thought that was what I wanted. She kissed me hungrily and unfastened my shirt buttons. Then she ran into the bathroom and came out crying because she had dropped and broken the soap dish. That was when I put my arms around her and comforted her which was what she had wanted from the beginning.

•

An apology for my style: I am not so much apologizing as invoking a tradition. Heraclitus whose philosophy may not have been written in fragments but certainly comes to us in that form. Kierkegaard who mocked Hegel's system-building by writing everything as if it were an afterthought, *The Unscientific Postscript.* Nietzsche who wrote in aphorisms or what he called "attempts," dry runs at the subject matter, even arguing contradictory points of view in order to see all sides. Wittgenstein's *Investigations,* his fragmentary response to the architectonic of the earlier *Tractatus.* Traditional story writers compose a beginning, a middle and an end, stringing these together in continuity as if there were some whole which they represented. Whereas I am writing fragments and discursive circumlocutions about an object that may not be complete or may be infinite. "Dog Attempts to Drown Man in Saskatoon" is my title cribbed from a facetious newspaper headline. Lucy and I were married because of her feet and because she glimpsed a man masturbating in a window as her bus took her home from work. I feel that in discussing these occurrences, these facts (our separation, the dog, the city, the weather, a trip to the art gallery) as constitutive of a non-system, I am peeling away some of the mystery of human life. I am also of the opinion that Mendel should have left the paintings in the slaughterhouse.

•

The discerning reader will by now have trapped me in a number of inconsistencies and doubtful statements. For example, we are not separating—I am leaving my wife and she has accepted that fact because it reaffirms her sense of herself as a person worthy of being left. Moreover it was wrong of me to pity her. Lucy is a quietly capable woman about to embark on what will inevitably be a successful career. She is not a waif nor could she ever redeem me with her suffering. Likewise she was wrong to view me as forever gentle and forbearing in the sexual department. And finally I suspect that there was more than coincidence in the fact that she spotted the man in his window on my night off from the newspaper. I do not doubt that she saw the man; he is a recurring nightmare of Lucy's. But whether she saw him that particular night, or some night in the past, or whether she made him up out of whole cloth and came to believe in him, I cannot say. About her feet, however, I have been truthful. That day she had just come from her doctor after having the stitches removed.

•

her toes   <u>Lucy's clumsiness.</u> Her clumsiness stems from the fact that she was born with six toes on each foot. This defect, I'm sure, had something to do with the way her mother mistreated her. Among uneducated folk there is often a feeling that physical anomalies reflect mental flaws. And as a kind of punishment for being born (and afterwards because her brother had died), Lucy's feet were never looked at by a competent doctor. It wasn't until she was twenty-six and beginning to enjoy a new life that she underwent a painful operation to have the vestigial digits excised. This surgery left her big toes all but powerless; now they flop like stubby white worms at the ends of her feet. Where she had been a schoolgirl athlete with six toes, she became awkward and ungainly with five.

•

Her mother Celeste, is one of those women who make feminism a *cause célèbre*—no, that is being glib. Truthfully, she was never any man's slave. I have the impression that after the first realization, the first inkling that she had married the wrong man, she entered into the role of submissive female with a strange, destructive gusto. She seems to have had an immoderate amount of hate in her, enough to spread its poison among the many people who touched her in a kind of negative of the parable of loaves and fishes. And the man, the father, was not so far as I can tell cruel, merely ineffectual, just the wrong man. Once, years later, Lucy and Celeste were riding on a bus together when Celeste pointed to a man sitting a few seats ahead and said, "That is the one I loved." That was all she ever said on the topic and the man himself was a balding, petty functionary type, completely uninteresting except in terms of the exaggerated passion Celeste had invested in him over the years. Soon after Lucy's father married Celeste he realized he would never be able to live with her—he absconded for the army, abandoning her with the first child in a drover's shack on a cattle baron's estate. (From time to time Lucy attempts to write about her childhood—her stories always seem unbelievable—a world of infanticide, blood feuds and brutality. I can barely credit these tales, seeing her so prim and composed, not prim but you know how she sits very straight in her chair and her hair is always in place and her clothes are expensive if not quite stylish and her manners are correct without being at all natural; Lucy is composed in the sense of being made up or put together out of pieces, not in the sense of being tranquil. But nevertheless she carries these *cauchemars* in her head: the dead babies found beneath the fencerow, blood on sheets, shotgun blasts in the night, her brother going under the highway roller, her mother's cruel silence.) The father fled as I say. He sent them money orders, three-quarters of his pay, to that point he was responsible. Celeste never spoke of him and his infrequent visits home were always a surprise to the children; his visits and the locked bedroom door and the hot, breathy silence of what went on behind the door; Celeste's rising vexation and hysteria; the new pregnancy; the postmarks on the money orders. Then the boy died. Perhaps he was Celeste's favourite, a perfect one to hold over the tall, already beautiful, monster with six toes and (I conjecture again) her father's look. The boy died and the house went silent— Celeste had forbidden a word to be spoken—and this was the worst for Lucy, the cold parlour circumspection of Protestant mourning. They did not utter a redeeming sound, only replayed the image of the boy running, laughing, racing the machine, then tripping and going under, being sucked under—Lucy did not even see the body, and in an access of delayed grief almost two decades later she would tell me she had always assumed he just flattened out like a cartoon character. Celeste refused to weep; only her hatred grew like a heavy weight against her children. And in that vacuum, that terrible silence accorded all feeling and especially the mysteries of sex and death, the locked door of the bedroom and the shut coffin lid, the absent father and the absent brother, somehow became inextricably entwined in Lucy's mind; she was only nine, a most beautiful monster, surrounded by absent gods and a bitter worship. So that when she saw the naked man calmly masturbating in the upper storey window from her bus, framed as it were under the cornice of a Saskatoon rooming house, it was for her like a vision of the centre of the mystery, the scene behind the locked door, the corpse in its coffin. God, and she immediately imagined her mother waiting irritably in the shadow just out of sight with a towel to wipe the sperm from the windowpane, aroused, yet almost fainting at the grotesque denial of her female passion.

●

Do not, if you wish, believe any of the above. It is psychological jazz written *en marge;* I am a poet of marginalia. Some of what I write is utter crap and wishful thinking. Lucy is not "happy to be sad"; she is seething inside because I am betraying her. Her anger gives her the courage to make jokes; she blushes when I laugh because she still hopes that I will stay. Of course my willingness to accompany her to the art gallery is inspired by guilt. She is completely aware of this fact. Her invitation is premeditated, manipulative. No gesture is lost; all our acts are linked and repeated. She is, after all, Celeste's daughter. Also do not believe for a moment that I hate that woman for what she was. That instant on the bus in a distant town when she pointed out the man she truly loved, she somehow redeemed herself for Lucy and for me, showing herself receptive of forgiveness and pity. Nor do I hate Lucy though I am leaving her.

●

My wife and I decide to separate, and then suddenly we are almost happy together. I repeat this crucial opening sentence for the purpose of reminding myself of my general intention. In a separate notebook next to me (vodka on ice sweating onto and blurring the ruled pages) I have a list of subjects to cover: 1) blindness (the man the dog led into the river was blind); 2) a man I know who was gored by a bison (real name to be withheld); 3) Susan the weaver and her little girl and the plan for us to live in Pelican Narrows; 4) the wolves at the city zoo; 5) the battlefields of Batoche and Duck Lake; 6) bridge symbolism; 7) a fuller description of the death of Lucy's brother; 8) three photographs of Lucy in my possession; 9) my wish to have met Mendel (he is dead) and be his friend; 10) the story of the story or how the dog tried to drown the man in Saskatoon.

•

Call this a play. Call me Orestes. Call her mother Clytemnestra. Her father, the wandering warrior king. (When he died accidentally a year ago, they sent Lucy his diary. Every day of his life he had recorded the weather; that was all.) Like everyone else, we married because we thought we could change one another. I was the brother-friend come to slay the tyrant Celeste; Lucy was to teach me the meaning of suffering. But there is no meaning and in the labyrinth of Lucy's mind the spirit of her past eluded me. Take sex for instance. She is taller than I am; people sometimes think she must be a model. She is without a doubt the most beautiful woman I have been to bed with. Yet there is no passion, no arousal. Between the legs she is as dry as a prairie summer. I am tender, but tenderness is no substitute for biology. Penetration is always painful. She gasps, winces. She will not perform oral sex though sometimes she likes having it done to her, providing she can overcome her embarrassment. What she does love is for me to wrestle her to the living-room carpet and strip her clothes off in a mock rape. She squeals and protests and then scampers naked to the bedroom where she waits impatiently while I get undressed. Only once have I detected her orgasm—this while she sat on my lap fully clothed and I manipulated her with my fingers. It goes without saying she will not talk about these things. She protects herself from herself and there is never any feeling that we are together. When Lucy's periods began, Celeste told her she had cancer. More than once she was forced to eat garbage from a dog's dish. Sometimes her mother would simply lock her out of the house for the night. These stories are shocking; Celeste was undoubtedly mad. By hatred, mother and daughter are manacled together for eternity. "You can change," I say with all my heart. "A woman who only sees herself as a victim never gets wise to herself." "No," she says, touching my hand sadly. "Ah! Ah!" I think, between weeping and words. Nostalgia is form; hope is content. Lucy is an empty building, a frenzy of restlessness, a soul without a future. And I fling out in desperation, Orestes-like, seeking my own Athens and release.

•

More bunk! I'll let you know now that we are not going to the art gallery as I write this. Everything happened some time ago and I am living far away in another country. (Structuralists would characterize my style as "robbing the signifier of the signified." My opening sentence, my premise, is now practically destitute of meaning, or it means everything. Really, this is what happens when you try to tell the truth about something; you end up like the snake biting its own tail. There are a hundred reasons why I left Lucy. I don't want to seem shallow. I don't want to say, well, I was a meat-and-potatoes person and she was a vegetarian, or that I sometimes believe she simply orchestrated the whole fiasco, seduced me, married me, and then refused to be a wife—yes, I would prefer to think that I was guiltless, that I didn't just wander off fecklessly like her father. To explain this, or for that matter to explain why the dog led the man into the river, you have to explain the world, even God—if we accept Gödel's theorem regarding the unjustifiability of systems from within. Everything is a symbol of everything else. Or everything is a symbol of death as Levi-Strauss says. In other words, there is no signified and life is nothing but a long haunting. Perhaps that is all that I am trying to say...) However, we *did* visit the art gallery one winter Sunday near the end of our eleven-month marriage. There were two temporary exhibitions and all of Mendel's slaughterhouse pictures had been stored in the basement. One wing was devoted to photographs of grain elevators, very phallic with their little overhanging roofs. We laughed about this together; Lucy was kittenish, pretending to be shocked. Then she walked across the hall alone to contemplate the acrylic prairie-scapes by local artists. I descended the stairs to drink coffee and watch the frozen river. This was downstream from the Idylwyld Bridge where the fellow went in (there is an open stretch of two or three hundred yards where a hot water outlet prevents the river from freezing over completely) and it occurred to me that if he had actually drowned, if the current had dragged him under the ice, they wouldn't have found his body until the spring breakup. And probably they would have discovered it hung up on the weir which I could see from the gallery window.

•

Forget it. A bad picture: Lucy upstairs "appreciating" art, me downstairs thinking of bodies under the ice. Any moment now she will come skipping toward me flushed with excitement after a successful cultural adventure. That is not what I meant to show you. That Lucy is not a person, she is a caricature. When legends are born, people die. Rather let us look at the place where all reasons converge. No. Let me tell you how Lucy is redeemed: preamble and anecdote. Her greatest fear is that she will turn into Celeste. Naturally, without noticing it, she is becoming more and more like her mother every day. She has the financial independence Celeste no doubt craved, and she has been disappointed in love. Three times. The first man made himself into a wandering rage with drugs. The second was an adulterer. Now me. Already she is acquiring an edge of bitterness, of why-me-ness. But, and this is an Everest of a but, the woman can dance! I don't mean at the disco or in the ballroom; I don't mean she studied ballet. We were strolling in Diefenbaker Park one summer day shortly after our wedding (this is on the bluffs overlooking Mendel's meatpacking plant) when we came upon a puppet show. It was some sort of children's fair: there were petting zoos, pony rides, candy stands, bicycles being given away as prizes, all that kind of thing in addition to the puppets. It was a famous troupe which had started in the sixties as part of the counter-culture movement—I need not mention the name. The climax of the performance was a stately dance by two giant puppets perhaps thirty feet tall, a man and a woman, backwoods types. We arrived just in time to see the woman rise from the ground, supported by three puppeteers. She rises from the grass stiffly then spreads her massive arms toward the man and an orchestra begins a reel. It is an astounding sight. I notice that the children in the audience are rapt. And suddenly I am aware of Lucy, her face aflame, this crazy grin and her eyes dazzled. She is looking straight up at the giant woman. The music, as I say, begins and the puppet sways and opens her arms towards her partner (they are both very stern, very grave) and Lucy begins to sway and spread her arms. She lifts her feet gently, one after the other, begins to turn, then swings back. She doesn't know what she is doing; this is completely unselfconscious. There is only Lucy and the puppets and the dance. She is a child again and I am in awe of her innocence. It is a scene that brings a lump to my throat: the high, hot, summer sun, the children's faces like flowers in a sea of grass, the towering, swaying puppets, and Lucy lost in herself. Lucy, dancing. Probably she no longer remembers this incident. At the time, or shortly after, she said, "Oh no! Did I really? Tell me I didn't do that!" She was laughing, not really embarrassed. "Did anyone see me?" And when the puppeteers passed the hat at the end of the show, I turned out my pockets, I gave them everything I had.

•

I smoke Gitanes. I like to drink in an Indian bar on 20th Street near Eaton's. My nose was broken in a car accident when I was eighteen; it grew back crooked. I speak softly; sometimes I stutter. I don't like crowds. In my spare time, I paint large pictures of the city. Photographic realism is my style. I work on a pencil grid using egg tempera because it's better for detail. I do shopping centres, old movie theatres that are about to be torn down, slaughterhouses. While everyone else is looking out at the prairie, I peer inward and record what is merely transitory, what is human. Artifice. Nature defeats me. I cannot paint ripples on a lake, or the movement of leaves, or a woman's face. Like most people, I suppose, my heart is broken because I cannot be what I wish to be. On the day in question, one of the coldest of the year, I hike down from the university along Saskatchewan Drive overlooking the old railway hotel, the modest office blocks, and the ice-shrouded gardens of the city. I carry a camera, snapping end-of-the-world photos for a future canvas. At the Third Avenue Bridge I pause to admire the lattice of I-beams, black against the frozen mist swirling up from the river and the translucent exhaust plumes of the ghostly cars shuttling to and fro. Crossing the street, I descend the wooden steps into Rotary Park, taking two more shots of the bridge at a close angle before the film breaks from the cold. I swing round, focussing on the squat ugliness of the Idylwyld Bridge with its fat concrete piers obscuring the view upriver, and then suddenly an icy finger seems to touch my heart: out on the river, on the very edge of the snowy crust where the turbid waters from the outlet pipe churn and steam, a black dog is playing. I refocus. The dog scampers in a tight circle, races toward the brink, skids to a stop, barks furiously at something in the grey water. I stumble forward a step or two. Then I see the man, swept downstream, bobbing in the current, his arms flailing stiffly. In another instant, the dog leaps after him, disappears, almost as if I had dreamed it. I don't quite know what I am doing, you understand. The river is no man's land. First I am plunging through the knee-deep snow of the park. Then I lose my footing on the bank and find myself sliding on my seat onto the river ice. Before I have time to think, "There is a man in the river," I am sprinting to intercept him, struggling to untangle the camera from around my neck, stripping off my coat. I have forgotten momentarily how long it takes exposed skin to freeze and am lost in a frenzy of speculation upon the impossibility of existence in the river, the horror of the current dragging you under the ice at the end of the open water, the creeping numbness, again the impossibility, the alienness of the idea itself, the dog and the man immersed. I feel the ice rolling under me, throw myself flat, wrapped in a gentle terror, then inch forward again, spread-eagled, throwing my coat by a sleeve, screaming, "Catch it! Catch it!" to the man whirling toward me, scrabbling with bloody hands at the crumbling ledge. All this occupies less time than it takes to tell. He is a strange bearlike creature, huge in an old duffel coat with its hood up, steam rising around him, his face bloated and purple, his red hands clawing at the ice shelf, an inhuman "awing" sound emanating from his throat, his eyes rolling upwards. He makes no effort to reach the coat sleeve trailed before him as the current carries him by. Then the dog appears, paddling toward the man, straining to keep its head above the choppy surface. The dog barks, rests a paw on the man's shoulder, seems to drag him under a little, and then the man is striking out wildly, fighting the dog off, being twisted out into the open water by the eddies. I see the leather hand harness flapping from the dog's neck and suddenly the full horror of the situation assails me: the man is blind. Perhaps he understands nothing of what is happening to him, the world gone mad, this freezing hell. At the same moment, I feel strong hands grip my ankles and hear another's laboured breathing. I look over my shoulder. There is a pink-cheeked policeman with a thin yellow moustache stretched on the ice behind me. Behind him, two teenage boys are in the act of dropping to all fours, making a chain of bodies. A fifth person, a young woman, is running toward us. "He's blind," I shout. The policeman nods: he seems to comprehend everything in an instant. The man in the water has come to rest against a jutting point of ice a few yards away. The dog is much nearer, but I make for the man, crawling on my hands and knees, forgetting my coat. There seems nothing to fear now. Our little chain of life reaching toward the blind drowning man seems sufficient against the infinity of forces which have culminated in this moment. The crust is rolling and bucking beneath us as I take his wrists. His fingers, hard as talons, lock into mine. Immediately he ceases to utter that terrible, unearthly bawling sound. Inching backward, I somehow contrive to lever the dead weight of his body over the ice lip, then drag him on his belly like a sack away from the water. The cop turns him gently on his back; he is breathing in gasps, his eyes rolling frantically. "Tank you. Tank you," he whispers, his strength gone. The others quickly remove their coats and tuck them around the man who now looks like some strange beached fish, puffing and muttering in the snow. Then in the eerie silence that follows, broken only by the shushing sound of traffic on the bridges, the distant whine of a siren coming nearer, the hissing river and my heart beating, I look into the smoky water once more and see that the dog is gone. I am dazed; I watch a drop of sweat freezing on the policeman's moustache. I stare into the grey flux where it slips quietly under the ice and disappears. One of the boys offers me a cigarette. The blind man moans; he says, "I go home now. Dog good, I all right. I walk home." The boys glance at each other. The woman is shivering. Everything seems empty and anticlimactic. We are shrouded in enigma. The policeman takes out a notebook, a tiny symbol of rationality, scribbled words against the void. As an ambulance crew skates a stretcher down the river bank, he begins to ask the usual questions, the usual, unanswerable questions.

•

This is not the story I wanted to tell. I repeat this *caveat* as a reminder that I am willful and wayward as a storyteller, not a good storyteller at all. The right story, the true story, had I been able to tell it, would have changed your life— but it is buried, gone, lost. The next day Lucy and I drive to the spot where I first saw the dog. The river is once more sanely empty and the water boils quietly where it has not yet frozen. Once more I tell her how it happened, but she prefers the public version, what she hears on the radio or reads in the newspaper, to my disjointed impressions. It is also true that she knows she is losing me and she is at the stage where it is necessary to deny strenuously all my values and perceptions. She wants to think that I am just like her father or that I always intended to humiliate her. The facts of the case are that the man and dog apparently set out to cross the Idylwyld Bridge but turned off along the approach and walked into the water, the man a little ahead of the dog. In the news account, the dog is accused of insanity, dereliction of duty and a strangely uncanine malevolence. "Dog Attempts to Drown Man," the headline reads. Libel law prevents speculation on the human victim's mental state, his intentions. The dog is dead, but the tone is jocular. *Dog Attempts to Drown Man*. All of which means that no one knows what happened from the time the man stumbled off the sidewalk on Idylwyld to the time he fell into the river and we are free to invent structures and symbols as we see fit. The man survives, it seems, his strange baptism, his trial by cold and water. I know in my own mind that he appeared exhausted, not merely from the experience of near-drowning, but from before, in spirit, while the dog seemed eager and alert. We know, or at least we can all agree to theorize, that a bridge is a symbol of change (one side to the other, hence death), of connection (the marriage of opposites), but also of separation from the river of life, a bridge is an object of culture. Perhaps man and dog chose together to walk through the pathless snows to the water's edge and throw themselves into uncertainty. The man was blind as are we all; perhaps he sought illumination in the frothing waste. Perhaps they went as old friends. Or perhaps the dog accompanied the man only reluctantly, the man forcing the dog to lead him across the ice. I saw the dog swim to him, saw the man fending the dog off. Perhaps the dog was trying to save its master, or perhaps it was only playing, not understanding in the least what was happening. Whatever is the case my allegiance is with the dog; the man is too human, too predictable. But man and dog together are emblematic—that is my impression at any rate— they are the mind and spirit, the one blind, the other dumb; one defeated, the other naive and hopeful, both forever going out. And I submit that after all the simplified explanations and crude jokes about the blind man and his dog, the act is full of a strange and terrible mystery, of beauty.

•

9th repetition

My wife and I decide to separate, and then suddenly we are almost happy together. But this was long ago, as was the visit to the Mendel Art Gallery and my time in Saskatoon. And though the moment when Lucy is shaking down her hair and tucking it into her knitted cap goes on endlessly in my head as does the reverberation of that other moment when the dog disappears under the ice, there is much that I have already forgotten. I left Lucy because she was too real, too hungry for love, while I am a dreamer. There are two kinds of courage: the courage that holds things together and the courage that throws them away. The first is more common; it is the cement of civilization; it is Lucy's. The second is the courage of drunks and suicides and mystics. My sign is impurity.

By leaving, you understand, I proved that I was unworthy. I have tried to write Lucy since that winter—her only response has been to return my letters unopened. This is appropriate. She means for me to read them myself, those tired, clotted apologies. I am the writer of the words; she knows well enough they are not meant for her. But my words are sad companions and sometimes I remember...well...the icy water is up to my neck and I hear the ghost dog barking, she tried to warn me; yes, yes, I say, but I was blind.

Lee Maracle

(b. 1950)

LEE MARACLE GREW UP IN NORTH VANCOUVER, and attended Simon Fraser University in nearby Burnaby, B.C. She has worked as a writer-in-residence at the En'owkin Centre for Native Artists in Penticton, B.C. A poet, novelist, essayist, and effective *speaker,* Maracle draws variously on her heritage—Métis, Cree, and Coast Salish—to examine the kinds of conflict that affect contemporary First Nations people in Canada, especially women.

In *I Am Woman* (1988), *Sun Dogs: a novel* (1992), and *Ravensong* (1993), she reveals how the values encouraged by a Native upbringing often collide with the values of the social majority; she also celebrates her characters'—and her culture's—capacity to survive, and to move forward. *Bobbi Lee, Indian rebel* (1990) is an autobiographical work, following her travels in quest of reclaiming home; it protests against the treatment of Indians in Canada, particularly the prejudice and the social conditions that perpetuate colonial disparities. "Yin Chin," which first appeared in *Canadian Literature* in 1990 and was collected the same year in *Sojourner's Truth and Other Stories,* honours Maracle's friendship with the novelist Sky Lee and the poet Jim Wong-Chu. While openly acknowledging that prejudice can take root in any culture, it also insists that individual people can resist—even overcome—prejudice, and so change the society in which they live. The act of resistance, that is, does not stop at being oppositional; it seeks, finally, the means to cross and erode the boundary lines of discrimination.

For Further Reading

BARBARA GODARD, "The Politics of Representation," *Canadian Literature* 124–125 (Spring-Summer 1990): 183–225.

AGNES GRANT, "Contemporary Native Women's Voices in Literature," *Canadian Literature* 124–125 (Spring-Summer 1990): 124–32.

LEE MARACLE, "an infinite number of pathways to the centre of the circle" [interview] in Janice Williamson, *Sounding Difference: Conversations with Seventeen Canadian Women Writers* (Toronto: U Toronto P, 1993) 166–78.

———, "Oratory: Coming to Theory," *Essays on Canadian Writing,* 54 (Winter 1994): 7–11.

Yin Chin

for Sharon Lee, whose real name is Sky, and for Jim Wong-Chu

she is tough,
she is verbose,
she has lived a thousand lives

she is sweet,
she is not,
she is blossoming
and dying every moment

a flower
unsweetened by rain
untarnished by simpering
uncuckolded by men
not coquettish enough
for say the gals
who make a career of shopping
at the Pacific Centre Mall

PACIFIC CENTRE, my gawd
do North Americans never tire
of claiming the centre
of the universe, the Pacific and
everywhere else...

I am weary
of North Americans
so I listen to SKY

Standing in the crowded college dining hall, coffee in hand, my face is drawn to a noisy group of Chinese youth; I mentally cancel them out. No place to sit—no place meaning there aren't any Indians in the room. It is a reflexive action on my part to assume that any company that isn't Indian company is generally unacceptable, but there it was: the absence of Indians, not chairs, determined the absence of a space for me. Soft of heart, guilt-ridden liberals might argue defensively that such sweeping judgement is not different from any of the generalizations made about us. So be it; after all, it is not their humanity I am calling into question. It is mine. Along with that thought dances another. I have lived in this city in the same neighbourhood as Chinese people for twenty-two years now and don't know a single Chinese person.

It scares me just a little. It wasn't always that way. The memory of a skinny little waif drops into the frame of moving pictures rolling across my mind. Unabashed, she stands next to the door of Mad Sam's market across from the Powell Street grounds, surveying "Chinamen" with accusatory eyes. Once a month on a Saturday the process repeats itself: the little girl of noble heart studies the old men. Not once in all her childhood years did she ever see an old man steal a little kid. She gave up, not because she became convinced that the accusation was unfounded, but because she got too big to worry about it.

"Cun-a-muck-ah-you-da-puppy-shaw, that's Chinee for how are you," and the old Pa'pa-y-ah* would laugh. "Don't wander around town or the old Chinamen will get you, steal you,… Chinkee, chinkee Chinamen went down town, turned around the corner and his pants fell down," and other such truck is buried somewhere in the useless information file tucked in the basement of my mind, but the shape of my social life is frighteningly influenced by those absurd sounds. The movie is just starting to lag and the literary theme of the pictures is coming into focus when a small breath of air, a gentle touch of a small woman's hand invites me to sit. How embarrassing. I'd been gaping and gawking at a table-load of Hans long enough for my coffee to cool.

It doesn't take long. Invariably, when people of colour get together they discuss white people. They are the butt of our jokes, the fountain of our bitterness and pain and the infinite well-spring of every dilemma life ever presented to us. The humour eases the pain, but always whites figure front and centre of our joint communication. If I had a dollar for every word ever said about them, instead of to them, I'd be the richest welfare bum in the country. No wonder they suffer from inflated egoism.

I sit at the table-load of Chinese people and towards the end of the hour I want to tell them about Mad Sam's, Powell Street and old men. Wisely, I think now, I didn't. Our sense of humour was different then. In the face of a crass white world we had erased so much of ourselves, and sketched so many cartoon characters of white people over top of the emptiness inside, that it would have been too much for us to face the fact that we really did feel just like them. I sat at that table more than a dozen times but not once did it occur to any of us that we were friends. Eventually, the march of a relentless clock, my hasty departure from college the following semester and my failure to return for fifteen years took its toll—now even their names escape me.

Last Saturday—seems like a hundred years later—was different. This time the table-load of people was Asian and Native. We laughed at ourselves and spoke very seriously about our writing. "We really believe we are writers," someone said, and the room shook with the hysteria of it all. We ran on and on about our growth and development, and not once did the white man enter the room. It just seemed too incredible that a dozen Hans and Natives could sit and discuss all things under heaven, including racism, and not talk about white people. It had only taken a half-dozen revolutions in the third world, seventeen riots in America, one hundred demonstrations against racism in Canada

---

*grandfather

and thirty-seven dead Native youth in my life to become. I could have told them about the waif, but it didn't seem relevant. We had crossed a millennium of bridges over rivers swollen with the floodwaters of dark humanity's tenacious struggle to extricate ourselves from oppression, and we knew it. We had been born during the first sword wound that the third world swung at imperialism. We were children of that wound, invincible, conscious and movin' on up. We could laugh because we were no longer a joke. But somewhere along the line we forgot to tell the others, the thousands of our folks who still tell their kids about old Chinamen.

•••

It's Tuesday and I'm circling the block at Gore and Powell trying to find a parking space, windows open, driving like I belong here. A sharp, "Don't come near me, why you bother me?" jars me loose. An old Chinese woman swings a ratty old umbrella at a Native man who is pushing her, cursing her and otherwise giving her a hard time. I lean towards the passenger side and shout at him from the safety of my car: "Leave her alone, asshole."

"Shuddup you f.ck.ng rag-head." I jump out of the car without bothering to park it. No one honks; they just stare at me. The man sees my face and my cowichan, bends deeply and says sarcastically that he didn't know I was a squaw. Well, I am no pacifist, I admit: I belt him, give him what for, and the coward leaves. I help the old woman across the street, then return to park my car. She stays there, where I left her, still shaking, so I stop to try and quell her fear.

She isn't afraid. She is ashamed of her own people—men who passed her by, walking around her or crossing the street to avoid trying to rescue her from the taunts of one of my people. The world rages around inside me while she copiously describes every Chinese man who saw her and kept walking. I listen to her in silence and think of me and old Sam again.

Mad Sam was a pioneer of discount foods. Slightly overripe bananas (great for peanut-butter-and-banana bannock sandwiches), bruised apples and day-old bread were always available at half the price of Safeway's, and we shopped there regularly for years. I am not sure if he sold meat. In any case, we never bought meat; we were fish-eaters then. I doubt very much that Sam knew we called him "Mad" but I know now that "mad" was intended for the low prices and the crowds in his little store, not for him. In the fifties, there were still storeowners who concerned themselves with their customers, established relationships with them, exchanged gossip and shared a few laughs. Sam was good to us.

If you press your nose up against the window to the left of the door you can still see me standing there, ghost-like, skinny brown body with huge eyes riveted on the street and the Powell Street grounds. Sometimes my eyes take a slow shift from left to right, then right to left. I'm watchin' ol' Chinamen, makin' sure they don't grab little kids. Once a month for several years I assume my post and keep my private vigil. No one on the street seems to know what I'm doing or why, but it doesn't matter. The object of my vigil is not appreciation but catchin' the old Chinamen in the act.

My nose is pressed up against the window pane; the cold circles the end of my flattened nose; it feels good. Outside, the window pane is freckled with crystal water drops; inside, it is smooth and dry, but for a little wisp of fog from my breath. Round *o*'s of water splotch onto the clear glass. Not perfectly round, but just the right amount of roundness that allows you to call them *o*'s. Each *o* is kind of wobbly and different, like on the page at school when you first print *o*'s for teacher.

I can see the rain-distorted street scene at the park through the round *o*'s of water. There are no flowers or grass in this park, no elaborate floral themes or landscape designs, just a dozen or so benches around a wasteland of gravel, sand and comfrey root (weeds), and a softball backstop at one end. (What a bloody long time ago that was, mama.)

Blat. A raindrop hits the window, scrunching up the park bench I am looking at. The round *o* of rain makes the park bench wiggle towards my corner of the store. I giggle.

"Mad Sam's... Mad Sam's... Mad Sam's?" What begins as a senseless repetition of a household phrase ends as a question. I know that Mad Sam is a Chinaman... Chinee, the old people call them—but then, the old people can't speak goot Inklish. But what in the world makes him mad? I breathe at the window. It fogs up. The only kind of mad I know is when everyone runs aroun' hollering and kicking up dust.

I rock back and forth while my finger traces out a large circle which my hand had cleared. Two old men on the bench across the street break my thoughts of Sam's madness. One of them rises. He is wearing one of those grey tweed wool hats that people think of as English and associate with sports cars. He has a cane, a light beige cane. He half bends at the waist before he leaves the bench, turns, and with his arms stretched out from his shoulders flails them back and forth a few times, accentuating his words to the other old man seated there.

It would have looked funny if Pa'pa-y-ah had done it, or ol' Mike, but I am acutely aware that this is a Chinaman. Ol' Chinamen are not funny. They are serious, and the words of the world echo violently in my ears: "Don't wander off or the ol' Chinamen will get you and eat you." I wonder about the fact that mama has never warned me about them.

A woman with a black car coat and a white pill box hat disturbs the scene. Screech, the door of her old Buick opens. Squeak, slam, it bangs shut. There she be, blonde as all get out, slightly hippy, heaving her bare leg, partially constrained by her skirt, onto the bumper of her car and cranking at whatever has to be cranked to make the damn thing go. There is something humorously inelegant about a white lady with spiked heels, tight skirt and a pill box hat cranking up a '39 Buick. (Thanks, mama, for having me soon enough to have seen it.) All of this wonderfulness comes squiggling to me through a little puddle of clear rain on the window. The Buick finally takes off and from the tail end of its departure I can see the little old man still shuffling his way across the street. Funny, all the cars stop for him. Odd, the little Chinee boy talks to him, unafraid.

Shuffle, shuffle, plunk of his cane, shuffle, shuffle, plunk; on he trudges.

The breath from the corner near my window comes out in shorter and louder gasps. It punctuates the window with an on-again, off-again choo-choo rhythm of clarity. Breath and fog, shuffle, shuffle, plunk, breath and fog. BOOM! And the old man's face is right on mine. My scream is indelicate. Mad Sam and mama come running.

"Whatsa matter?"... "Wah iss it?" from Sam and mama respectively.

Half hesitating, I point out the window. "The Chinaman was looking at me." I can see that that is not the right answer. Mama's eyes yell *for pete's sake* and her cheeks shine red with shame—not embarrassment, shame. Sam's face is clearly, definably hurt. Not the kind of hurt that shows when adults burn themselves or something, but the kind of hurt you can sometimes see in the eyes of people who have been cheated. The total picture spells something I cannot define.

Grandmothers, you said if I was ever caught doing nothing you would take me away for all eternity. The silence is thick, cloying and paralyzing. It stops my brain and stills my emotions. It deafens my ears to the rain. I cannot look out to see if the old man is still there. No grannies come to spare me.

My eyes fall unseeing on a parsnip just exactly in front of my face. They rest there until everyone stops looking at my treacherous little body and resumes talking about whatever they were talking about before I brought the world to a momentary halt with my astounding stupidity. What surprises me now, years later, is that they did eventually carry on as though nothing were wrong.

The floor sways beneath me, while I try hard to make it swallow me. A hand holding a pear in front of my face jars my eyes loose from the parsnip.

"Here," the small, pained smile on Sam's face stills the floor, but the memory remains a moving moment in my life.

•••

The old woman is holding my hands, saying she feels better now. All that time I wasn't thinking about what she said, or speaking. I just nodded my head back forth and relived my memory of Mad Sam's.

"How unkind of the world to school us in ignorance" is all I say, and I make my way back to the car.

David Adams Richards

(b. 1950)

A NATIVE OF NEWCASTLE, New Brunswick, where he now lives, David Adams Richards briefly attended St. Thomas University in Fredericton but left to continue writing. The sombre mood of his poems *Small Heroics* (1972) characterizes the entire body of his work. A trilogy of novels—*The Coming of Winter,* 1974; *Blood Ties,* 1976; and *Lives of Brief Duration,* 1981—was followed by another prizewinning sequence, including *Nights Below Station Street* (1988) and *Evening Snow Will Bring Such Peace* (1990). These works find little joy in the constrained lives they portray, nor do the stories of *Dancers at Night* (1978) promise much in the way of escape from violence, truculence, despair, and decay. The Miramichi Valley turns here into a kind of pressured cauldron of constraints, one which psychology and sociology alike can explain but which neither can tame or change. Deprivation shapes character—deprivation at once cultural and economic and emotional.

Typically, Richards' characters—cut off from the options that might develop them—slide from failure to failure, unable to make human relationships work any better than they can make their farms produce or their machinery operate smoothly. Even their language is constrained. Cut off from any range of expression, they are reduced to their lowest common oaths, which substitute inadequately for personal communication. Violence, comparably, must be seen less as a measure of quality of character than as a desperate gesture of inarticulate hope. The phlegmatic and the laconic disguise but scarcely cover the intensity of ambition and desire that lies at the heart of Richards' characters. His talent is to evoke the prevailing moods of such an environment, and to give voice to a people whose very lack of language mutely declares their predicament. "Dane" first appeared in *Fiddlehead* magazine in April 1982 under the title "La Roche."

For Further Reading

"A novel celebration of the Miramichi," *Globe & Mail* (Toronto) 30 July 1983: E1.

DAVID ADAMS RICHARDS, *A Lad from Brantford & other essays* (Fredericton: Broken Jaw P, 1994).

SUSAN LEVER, "Against the Stream: The Fiction of David Adams Richards," *Canadian-Australian Studies* 12.1 (1994): 81–89.

———, "An Interview with David Adams Richards," *Canadian-Australian Studies* 12.1 (1994): 91–97.

Dane

All the wino huts have been washed away with the years, and new houses have arisen in their stead, and apartment buildings also. There is an apartment building where his house once stood—in that dirty yard in the midst of a gully, where a perpetual sad smell of smoke came from the broken doorway.

A man, who may be a Chartered Accountant, comes out of that apartment building on this winter morning to start his car, wraps the heavy fur-lined coat about him, and wipes his mouth with a handkerchief.

The winos used to sit out here on moonlit nights in summer and sometimes in winter. Just beyond this embankment overlooking the river the real town began, but the winos weren't concerned with the real town but rarely, or what went on in it. And the town, of course, had nothing to do with them.

The first time I met him we got into a fight, and then we were friends. At five years old he was disappearing for whole afternoons into those small back streets of town, that I as yet had no idea existed—finding the haunts and the alleyways of those people of the moonlit nights. And when he found those people he'd sit with them, run small errands for them and collect their bottles— the ones that could be brought back to the liquor store for 2 or 3 cents. What dark things he managed to witness on those days, when the liquor store was down on Castle Street, I have no idea, but he was as quick as a monkey and funny and alive and none bothered him.

He wore thick soled shoes until they were worn to nothing and you could hear them scraping along as he walked. He wore shirts with a button or two missing and pants that often came above his ankle bones, and thin red socks that often slid beneath his shoes. When other children in the neighbourhood were going to bed, he was heading down along the worn pathway crowded by over-hanging gully alders, toward the mysterious lights of town, the sheds and haunts that are so distant now, so much like a part of that dead age.

He had to earn his own money to buy baseball bats or hockey sticks, and he was a fine and agile sports enthusiast at a young age, and a leader in most things he did. We'd follow him back home, to the house with the broken door-way, where he'd talk about his plans to form baseball or hockey teams, or legions of soldiers that would attack and destroy our enemies on the other side of the gully.

He was the best at rock fights, and he'd give no quarter to any rock fight coward or rock fight loser. He was a fine shot with a sling shot—but he never hunted birds or squirrels like many of us did. He hunted the neighbour's windows, porch flower pots, and the lights that shone near his street. Consequently he became known to police as a vandal while those who slaughtered squir-

From *Fiddlehead,* No. 132 (April 1982). First published as "La Roche." Reprinted by permission of the author.

rels and birds were considered good mannered. I feel he would have been known by the police no matter how he behaved himself—his soiled clothes spoke of a dark knowledge behind the eyes.

One day I invited him to see a movie in the theatre my father managed, and we were almost there when he fell in with a group of other youngsters and waved me away. I went on to the movie alone. I was resentful that he'd waved me away, but within two minutes after the lights were lowered he was sitting beside me.

"Ho-lo," he said.

"You came did you"

"Ya—I snuck past yer old ticket taker—there"

"You didn't pay"

"No"

I was angry, not so much because he did this, but that he told me, as if he was testing my loyalty. I said nothing.

"Yes—I snuck right in" he said.

"Why" I asked.

"Wanted to"

"Then don't tell me about it" I said, "Do it—but don't tell me about it"

"But weren't you going to invite me here—for nothing?"

"Sure I was"

"Well then"

"Well then what"

"Well then you didn't want me to pay did you?"

"No—I didn't"

"Well I didn't"

And I couldn't answer or argue that. Then he asked me if I had ever snuck into any place and I had to admit that yes I had—I had snuck into the skating rink. He seemed much happier after that, because he helped clean the ice at the skating rink, and could feel that I'd done him an injustice. So we were even.

He began to work the boats when he was 12, as waterboy. Day after day, all day long he'd carry buckets of water from the spring to the men in the holds, while the great loads of pulp wood teetered overhead. The long gangplanking and the shadows of men. And later he would stand on the bow of the lumber ship and dive into the water, a distance of over 40 feet. His head would bob in the black waves at sunset, the charred scent of a shore fire.

One night he cut his head open and we had to carry him home. There must have been ten of us with him, and we carried him into the house, that smelled slightly of spoiled fish. The heat caught the greasy flycatchers at twilight, and blood soaked my white T-shirt that we'd wrapped his head in. There was no one home, and he refused to go to the doctor. He held his head with my T-shirt, and now and then dabbed a wet face cloth to the cut. He didn't know where any of his family was or when they'd be back, but he wasn't going to go to any hospital without letting them know, and none of us could change his mind.

The last 2 years I knew him well he excelled in everything he wished to. He was on the all star hockey team, and he was the first of us ever to swim the river. He'd formed his own baseball team and cricket squad and he arranged tournaments with other parts of town. About this time he won 2 hundred dollars playing bingo. There was a strange freedom about him that frightened mothers and fathers, that allowed him to spend his nights playing bingo, because no one minded if he had school in the morning or lessons to do. He bought a coat for his mother and a coat for his brother, a pair of boots for himself—and he gave the rest to his father.

He went on a trip with the all star hockey squad that winter and was billeted in one of the houses in the town the tournament was being played. However he liked that I didn't know—I heard later from a member of the Recreation Council, that it was intentional that he was put into 'one of the better families' so he could see how they lived, and could be given, for those 3 or 4 days, anything he wanted.

I didn't see him much after that. He'd stopped working as a rinkrat, and he'd stopped taking any interest in school—he was one of the top students at one time, but now he was repeating a year. I don't remember the first time I saw him drunk, but it was the summer after he'd quit the all star hockey squad. He might have been fifteen. With drink came his vicious fistfights against the world, and a parade of sad young girls. And jail.

My later memories of him see a brooding, heavyset young man staggering along the street with his shirt tail out, and saying "Ho-lo" in a gruff suspicious voice.

The jail was not only for drink, but also for criminal activity. As youngsters we all used to break into places—with a great mischievous sense of adventure. But now he was stealing almost anything he could get his hands on, and trying to sell it to the second hand shops. And he was continually getting caught. It just reinforced the policemen's opinion that they were right all along.

He was away periodically. You'd forget about him, and then one day you'd see him sitting in the back room of a corner store drinking rum. He'd nod and laugh, and wink as if he was sharing a secret with you.

When he was in jail in town they'd be hard pressed to keep him in it, because he'd sawed through the bar and had replaced it with a broom handle—a scene which might be played by Abbot and Costello. But each night after playing checkers with the jailer, he'd lift away the broom handle and make his way into the haunts of the town again, into the back rooms of bootleggers that he knew. Or he'd take a jaunty walk to the circus to see the strippers. There was an hilariousness in all of this that he couldn't help—as if he sought after and needed, however briefly, the great universal laugh.

One night my father received a phone call that he had broken into the theatre. "How can that be—isn't he in jail"

"That's where we thought he was" the policeman told my father, "But his fingerprints are all over your safe—all over your cigarette machine—all over—"

Going into his cell they found stuffed into his mattress, cartons of cigarettes and boxes of chocolates and other things that look absolutely absurd to be caught with.

Many times that last winter he would have frozen in the snow on his way home if certain of the neighbourhood teenagers hadn't looked out for him. His face was filled with a bloated but comical remorse. He'd still wink; 'Ho-lo' he'd say. He was the first man I'd ever met that would sometimes lose his voice to drink. He was 19 years old. He sat out on the bank with the winos and the older women who wet their pants from drinking, when the moon was out.

The last time I saw him, he grabbed my shirt as if he wanted to hit me. I called his name, and he recognized who I was and gave a half smile—somewhere between a savage and a saint. "Ho-lo—Jess I didn't recognize you—Ho-lo" he said.

Two days later he was in a car accident and killed instantly. And people said that was for the best, because he'd made quite a mess of his life.

Rohinton Mistry

(b. 1952)

BORN IN BOMBAY, INDIA, Rohinton Mistry grew up in a Parsi family, absorbing the rites of his religion and closely observing the intricacies of Indian social structure. He attended the University of Bombay, earning a B.Sc. in mathematics and economics. In 1975, he emigrated to Canada, and some time after his arrival, he secured work in a Toronto bank. But after earning a second university degree—a B.A. in English and Philosophy at the University of Toronto—he resigned from the bank and began in 1985 to write full time.

Mistry's first book was the 1987 collection of stories from which "Exercisers" (first published in *Canadian Fiction Magazine* in 1986) is taken. Called *Tales from Firozsha Baag*, the collection brings together a set of stories about the interconnected lives of the families who live in "Firozsha Baag," a Bombay apartment complex. One of the book's main narratives concerns a young man who leaves his Parsi home, and its linked symbols of water and fire, and who ends up in a Toronto apartment house, "learning to swim" in the language and culture of a new world. Intertwined with this narrative are tales of the not-quite-parallel lives of other young men in the Bombay community, each seeking himself and some sort of fulfillment, in a world where death is certain but unexpected, where sexuality is insistent but somehow dislocating, and where custom and power do not always coincide with opportunity and desire.

Two novels have followed this collection: *Such a Long Journey* (1991) and *A Fine Balance* (1995). Both examine the complicated lives of ordinary individuals, whose aspirations and hopes seem always also to lead them further into desperation. "Exercisers" echoes this motif. Asking if the ties of attachment, authority, and custom are stronger than those of desire—or are fundamentally the same—the story focuses on characters who do not necessarily recognize the connections that bind them. Those who exercise their bodies are not always the same as those who exercise their rights; and exercising judgment might sometimes elude them all.

For Further Reading

AJAY HEBLE, "A Foreign Presence in the Stall: towards a poetics of cultural hybridity," *Canadian Literature* 137 (Summer 1993): 51–61.

GEOFF HANCOCK, "An Interview with Rohinton Mistry," *Canadian Fiction Magazine* 65 (1989): 143–50.

W.H. NEW, "A Shaping of Connections" in *A Shaping of Connections*, ed. Hena Maes-Jelinek, K.H. Petersen, and Anna Rutherford (Aarhus: Dangaroo, 1989) 154–63.

DAGMAR NOVAK, Interview with Rohinton Mistry, in *Other Solitudes: Canadian Multicultural Fictions*, ed. Linda Hutcheon and Marion Richmond (Toronto: Oxford, 1990) 256–62.

Exercisers

"If you don't want to take our word for it," said Jehangir Bulsara's parents to him, "that's fine. Ask Bhagwan Baba. Let *him* decide, with his holy wisdom, that the girl is unsuitable for you."

That was last week. Now the day of the journey was here; Mr and Mrs Bulsara, with Jehangir, were bound for Bhagwan Baba's dwelling place in the suburbs. From outside the gates of Firozsha Baag they took the bus to Bombay Central Station, and boarded the Sunday morning local.

Such guidance-seeking train journeys were customary for the parents, but this one was solely for Jehangir's benefit. "Your entire life's happiness is at stake," they had insisted. "When Bhagwan Baba speaks your eyes will open, all will become clear."

At first, Jehangir had refused to go. But: "You had double pneumonia when you were eight," Father had reminded him, "and even the doctor was despairing. I came to Bhagwan Baba and your health returned."

And Mother added, "After Father lost his job, who do you think helped, his friends, our relatives, who? Bhagwan Baba, and we have enough to eat and wear, thanks to him."

Thus it went, although the examples were dredged with difficulty out of the past. Due to the passage of time they had relinquished the greater part of their preternatural lustre, and appeared in a disappointingly mundane light. But when Jehangir was younger, he used to think it wonderful that there was a Baba who aided his mother and father with blessings and advice and kind words. Life was hard, always full of want and worry, and assistance from any quarter was welcome. The little boy who used to sit on the steps of C Block to watch the others at play, and who used to spend Sunday mornings with Dr Mody and his stamps, would ask God every night to help his father and mother.

The boy was now nineteen and in his third year at university, but he still carried the distinct memories of poverty and anxiety, memories of envelopes labelled Rent, School Fees, Ration, Kerosene, Light, and Water, envelopes which were forever examined and shuffled and re-examined because there was never enough money in them (and never would be), and were worn ragged and tattered along the edges due to such constant handling and scrutinizing, as if the shuffling and sorting and re-examining would lead to some discovery that would make the money last longer.

So in the end Jehangir agreed to consult the holy man of the suburbs and let him exercise his tenuous infallibility. He looked out of the train window. What he had not realized, till the moment of boarding, was the full baseness of it all. It struck suddenly, in the pit of his stomach, like nausea. Cringing inwardly, he wondered what *she* would say if she knew about the act of betrayal

From *Tales from Firozsha Baag* by Rohinton Mistry. Used by permission of the Canadian Publishers, McClelland & Stewart, Toronto.

he was shortly to perpetrate. Probably despise him forever, and he would deserve it.

The suburban local was at the outskirts of Bombay; they would arrive at their destination in forty-five minutes. The "17 Standees Allowed" by the scratched and peeling sign had already been exceeded by the crush of Sunday morning commuters, but not to the extent of a weekday train: as yet, there were no roof-riders or window-clingers. In the sky the sun was higher than when the train left Bombay Central. The heat began to strengthen rapidly now, seeming to feed on itself, growing more oppressive with every breath. From metal straps hung the standees, listless, upraised arms revealing identical damp patches under sleeves of shirts and blouses. Overhead, the fans turned ineffectively, whirring and rattling, their blades labouring with feeble rotations, trying to chop the air thick with heat and odour, scattering it around uselessly in the compartment.

In fitful sleep his parents leaned against each other. They swayed as one with the train's motion, on the wooden bench that constituted third-class seats. The bench, and the compartment in general, was randomly adorned with red stains of *paan:* the oral effluences of past passengers, relics of journeys done and gone. Time and dust had done their work, too, aging and dulling the tobacco-betel-nut juices to varying degrees of redness.

Mother held a brown paper bag in her lap. It contained three oranges and three bananas for Bhagwan Baba. Offerings were not compulsory but people brought gifts out of gratitude, she had explained to Jehangir: "And Bhagwan Baba usually gives back half after blessing it. Very rich people bring expensive gifts, boxes of almonds and pistachios, large cartons of *mithai,* whole baskets of prime *alphonso* mango, sometimes even jewellery. But the beautiful thing is, he does no more for them than he does for the poorest. It is one of the signs of his saintliness."

All in the compartment were now asleep or trying to attain that envious state. Even the ones hanging from the straps like drowsy trapeze artists, lost in a swaying, somnolent exercise. Occasionally a new set of people entered when the train stopped. They were noisy and fidgety at first. But the contagion of lethargy quickly subdued them. They fell silent under the spell of the whirring fans which swivelled jerkily from side to side. With a nervous tic, twitching like victims of a heat-induced malady.

Sleep was one way to escape the discomfort; Jehangir shut his eyes to see if he could. He ceased bracing himself against the movement of the train, allowed the head and shoulders to droop forward to sway, and let his whole body sway with the train, unresisting. Like his parents' opposite him, his movement became one with the movement of the compartment. Rolling to and fro, swaying side to side, as the train decreed. Surrendering to the torridity of the air and the hypnotic drone of the fans, the close click-click of the standees' metal straps and the seemingly remote clackety-clack of the rails, he was ready to cross over from the edge of torpor into slumber, succumbing slowly to the swaying, swaying slowly.

The train stopped, and Jehangir straightened with a start. Did I really fall asleep? He anxiously scanned the platform for the station's name. No, this was not the one. The compartment lurched into motion. The train resumed its journey, and the possibility of sleep was now crowded out by thoughts of Bhagwan Baba, his parents, and her; but mainly of her.

She was the first girl he had ever gone out with.

Jehangir's school years had been devoid of girls. His parents could not afford the exorbitant fees which, for some peculiar reason, were common to all co-educational high schools, and from whence issued rumours, periodically, about students being "dismissed for attempting sexual intercourse on school property." The rumours, vicariously relished and savoured when they reached the boys' schools, fuelled and stoked high the envy and frustration rife within those walls. Their occupants had a heavy study load. Besides the regular subjects, they learned to forgo things taken for granted by their wealthy counterparts in coeducational schools—things such as music lessons, camping trips, and guided tours to Jammu and Kashmir. But they discovered ways to make up for it. They learned how to use their eyes to undress their female teacher and gaze longingly at the outline of her bra, drop erasers or pencils and linger at floor level to retrieve them while she sat at her desk on an elevated platform (the days when she wore a sari were barren, black days), and carry home unforgettable images of flowery panties.

These pursuits went a long way in honing imaginations and developing agility and suppleness in tight places. Unfortunately, the supply of female teachers dwindled drastically in the higher grades, when their need was greatest. But the students believed that within the egalitarianism of university life all wrongs would be righted, and continued to believe until they arrived, bright-eyed and optimistic despite their awkwardness, to discover their faith had been groundless.

Jehangir had been trapped in St Xavier's Boys School; its effects lingered, and even in college his first two years had been fallow. He lacked the sophistication of the chaps from coeducational schools, in their Levis and other imported clothes, who took pleasure in flaunting the ease with which they mingled and joked in the college canteen before the gawky ones from boys' schools or the "vernacs" from non-English medium schools (at the bottom of the sophistication hierarchy) who continued shamefacedly to clothe themselves in old school uniforms at their parents' insistence to get the full wear out of them.

Jehangir suffered the superciliousness of the boys from coeducational schools with a silent rage. Sometimes he was consumed by bouts of inferiority which he palliated by trying to accept with calm resignation that the gulf between them and him was no wider than the one between him and the dolts in Firozsha Baag. But such fatalism did not make things less embittering. He despised their sardonic comments to the innocent ones who kept using 'periods' instead of 'lectures': "Periods, my friend, occur for menstruating females and schoolboys. In college we attend lectures." He envied their long and loud laughter laden with confidence, their clearly forceful and distinct speech during class discussions, which he could not help but compare to the diffident mumbles of the others.

He observed them, tried to learn from them and be like them, but remained inevitably mired in his reticence when it came to girls.

She started talking to him one day while they waited for choir practice to begin. It had taken a lot of courage, two years' worth of it, to join the college choir. As he correctly guessed, it was comprised mainly of members of that hateful species from coeducational schools who, in addition to their sartorial advantage, came equipped with prior experience from school choirs and corresponding portions of arrogance. All he had was a love of music and a good but untrained ear. After the first meeting he decided never to go again. He had felt like a gatecrasher at an exclusive party.

But a week went by during which he re-collected his courage, and the day for choir practice arrived. She was a soprano, he sang bass. She started the conversation, and Jehangir was relieved to find he had no trouble keeping it going. She had a lot to say, especially about Claude, the conductor: "The pompous jackass thinks all the girls in the choir are his personal property. The next time he puts his arm around me, I'm going to take his baton and poke it in his froggy eyes." Jehangir laughed, surprised at how naturally it came.

They had talked often after that. His fear of blushing when spoken to, or stumbling over his words if he thought they were being overheard gradually diminished. They discovered a common interest in reading, and she invited him to her house. He borrowed books, met her parents, and went back often for more. She sometimes mentioned movies she had seen or wanted to see, and how it would be fun to go together, but they always stopped short of making definite plans.

Jehangir had never been much of a cinema-goer. Amidst the bunch of envelopes marked Rent, Water, Light, and others, the last was labelled Pocket Money. But this one always stayed empty. And if sometimes he had enough money for a cinema ticket, there was no one at school or in Firozsha Baag he really cared to go with. The low opinion he had of the boys in the Baag, formed during the days of Pesi *paadmaroo* and the misery his life had been then, persisted. He preferred to sit on the steps of C Block and read, or watch the activity in the compound. Sometimes, he heard them heroically recounting their feats in the cinema: chucking paper balls of empty potato-chip bags at strangers, or hooting and whistling in the dark to provoke shushing sounds from the audience. He felt nothing but contempt for their puerile antics. A delight in Nariman Hansotia's yarns on the steps of A Block was the only thing he shared with them.

When Mrs Bulsara decided he was old enough to go out alone provided he always returned by eight o'clock, Jehangir varied the routine of his evenings. He began going for walks to the Hanging Gardens. His favourite place there was the children's playground after the children left at dusk. Then, it was occupied by men who transformed it into a gym every night. They came regularly, and improvised by using the various combinations of bars and railings of the slide or swing for pull-ups and push-ups, and the plank of the see-saw for sit-ups. They must have had an arrangement with the night-watchman, because the playground was strictly for children. Jehangir, hidden behind a bush or tree, watched the exercisers. They fascinated him. Their rippling, sweating muscles were magnified versions of the bodies of the boys in the school gym. Watching their powerful torsos and limbs had a strange effect on his own skinny body, it sometimes triggered a longing for brawn and sinew in his slender arms and legs.

Later, in college, Jehangir stopped going to the Hanging Gardens. He was suddenly very conscious of his aloneness, and felt silly wandering around amidst ayahs with children or couples looking for solitude. Hiding and watching the exercisers did not seem right, either.

The cinema became his new haunt. In the dark movie theatres it did not matter that he was alone. If he sat next to a girl, he would fantasize that she had come with him and was throbbing just like him. He let his elbow touch her arm as if by accident on the arm-rest they shared. When she edged past him during intermission or after the movie, he gently grazed the back of her thighs with his knees, almost like a light caress. He would maneouvre to make a show of allowing her maximum room, but made sure to get the most feel. Those were moments of pure ecstasy, moments which he re-lived in bed at night. Sometimes, if there was a particularly active couple next to him, he spent more time watching them than the screen, employing the contortions of a head trained in school under desks and benches. But a stiff neck and an ache at his centre were his only companions when he emerged from the theatre.

Several choir practices later, she went with him to the cinema, and Jehangir found it hard to believe that he had not come alone again to the darkened hall of possibilities. After the intermission she was gently massaging her right wrist, having sprained it the day before. He asked if it was hurting terribly, and later remembered the moment with pride, that he had had the courage and presence of mind to stroke the wrist without a word when she held it out for him over his lap. The stirring which began at his centre swelled with each stroke; after a while their fingers entwined, clumsily, until the index, middle, and ring found their proper places, and interlocked in a tight clasp. He was tremendously aroused but did not dare do anything else. Much too soon the flag appeared on the screen and the audience rose for *Jana Gana Mana*. His tremendous arousal was quickly doused. All that remained was a nasty ache, the unpleasant residue of lust unreleased, as though he had been kneed in the groin.

It was a while since the train had stopped at a station. Jehangir crossed his legs. He was disgusted with himself. Getting excited again at the mere memory of holding hands. He had read in various magazines and books that boys of fifteen in America enjoyed regular sex, and had the privacy to do it, while he at nineteen was still a virgin, worked up just at the thought of holding her hand, and it was all very unfair and frustrating.

The train was passing by farmland. The fields were sere, brown and bare, and the little vegetation persisting tenaciously was parched yellow. The monsoons were late again, and here, outside the city, the delay was writ harsh across the landscape.

In the city, too, there were hardships. The quota of tap water had been curtailed, and Jehangir had been waking up at five A.M. for the past month to help Mother fill up storage drums for bathing and cleaning and cooking, before the supply was cut off at six A.M.

Scrawny cattle foraged amidst the stubble in the fields. Telegraph poles whizzed by, menacingly close. Poles which periodically cracked open the skulls of commuters who travelled hanging from doors and windows, and provided fodder for the death toll faithfully recorded by city newspapers. A death toll sharing the inconspicuity of inside pages. Side by side with assaults on scheduled castes in one village and murders of *harijans* by brahmins in another.

When he had brought her home the first time, it had been for a very short visit. He had warned his parents beforehand, praying that Mother would take the hint and remove the *mathoobanoo* from her head; the white mulmul square made her look like a backward village Parsi from Navsari, he had recently decided. But he was not spared what he thought was a moment of shame and embarrassment. There were quick introductions and several awkward silences, then they left for choir practice.

Later, when Jehangir returned, Mother said during dinner that he should not be seeing so much of the girl. "This is not the time for going out with girls anyway. The proper time will come after finishing college, when you are earning your own living and can afford it." In the meantime, if he did go out occasionally after asking for permission, he would have to continue to be home by eight o'clock. It would not do to stay out later than that and let things get too serious.

Jehangir said that he would be home by eight if she did not wear that *mathoobanoo*.

"I am not going to tolerate your ifs-bifs," said Mrs Bulsara, covering her hurt with brusqueness, "what I am saying is for your own good." It was obvious, she said, that the girl came from a family better off than they were, her life-style would make him uncomfortable. "Trust a mother's instinct. It is only your happiness I think of. Besides, she is the first girl you have gone out with, you might meet someone you like more. Then what?"

"Then I'll stop going out with her."

"But what of her feelings? You might be giving her serious hopes."

"No one has any serious hopes. It's so silly, all these objections."

"It is always a serious matter where a girl is involved. You will not understand that at your age."

Dinner finished without any real unpleasantry. But not for many nights after that. The dinner-table talk grew sharper as days passed. At first, words were chosen carefully in an effort to preserve a semblance of democratic discussion. Soon, however, the tensions outgrew all such efforts, and a nightly routine of debilitating sarcasm established itself. Every dinner saw the same denunciations brought forth, sometimes with a new barb twisted through them.

"There's something about the way she talks. Without proper respect."

"Saw what she was wearing? Such a short skirt. And too much makeup."

"Because you are going out with her you think electricity is free of charge? Ironing shirt and pant from morning till evening." The ancient dented servingspoon, descended through hands of foremothers, struck the pot of brinjal with a plangency denoting more to come.

"Why must a girl wear so much makeup unless she is hiding something underneath."

"Shines his shoes till I can see my unhappy face. More shoe polish has been used after meeting her than in all the years before."

"If she does not respect your parents, how will she respect you? Your whole life will be unhappy."

Father said only one thing: "Trust your mother's instincts. I always do, they are never wrong."

Things rapidly became worse. Not a day passed without quarrelling. They said things to each other which they would not have dreamt of saying at one time; bitter, vindictive things. Every few days there was a reconciliation at Father's insistence, with sincere hugs and tears of remorse which sprang from the depths of their beings, so fervent was the desire to let peace and understanding reign again. But this would last for a short time only. The strange new emotions and forces which had taken hold, indecipherable and inscrutable, would soon be manifest again; then the quarrels and hurtful words would resume.

After the first few visits Jehangir did not bring her home any more. Besides, she always refused to come under some pretext—she had felt the antagonism that silently burgeoned on her arrival. There was no outward sign of it, on the surface all was decorum and grace, welcome and kindness. But to sense what lay underneath did not take much. She also picked up the unintentional hints he dropped during those evenings when they met after an excessively trying time at home. Then she would try to help him, and before they parted he would agree to stand up to his parents, become independent, and many more promises.

But the promises were always smothered by a fresh wave of reproaches awaiting him at home. If he managed to speak in the spirit of autonomy that she had inspired in him earlier in the evening, it still turned out unfavourably.

"See?" Mother would say with mournful satisfaction, "see how it proves my point that she is a bad influence? He goes to her and returns with such cruel words in his mouth. And who put them there, that is all I am asking. Because such words were not there before. Now I must start all over again to remove her effect on him. Then he will be more like the son I once knew. But how long can I go on like this, how long?" she would conclude dolefully, whereupon Jehangir abandoned the balance of his painstakingly prepared words.

He looked at his parents now, supporting each other as they slept through heat and dust. The photograph was in his wallet. They had told him to bring it along. He had taken it with her camera during the college picnic at Elephanta Caves. She later gave him a copy. It was a black-and-white, and as he gazed at it he could feel the soft brown of her eyes drawing him in, ready to do her will. The will of my enchantress, he liked to imagine.

Mother had taken to going through his trousers and wallet. He was aware of these secret searches but had said nothing, not wanting to add to her sorrow and to the bitterness that filled the house.

The day after he received the photograph, she triumphantly found it: "What is this, why must you carry her photo with you?"

"What right did you have to look in my wallet?"

"What right? What right, he says! To his own mother he says what right! A mother does not need any rights. A mother exercises her judgement out of love. A mother does whatever she knows is right for her son."

The photograph was brought up constantly for days after, and with each passing day the rhetoric grew increasingly forceful and wildly inventive.

"It is not enough to see her makeup-covered face in the evening. He must also keep her photograph."

"People have been made to go crazy by a photo with a magic spell on it. Maybe her parents are involved in this, trying to snare my son for their daughter."

"She knows you will go to study in America one day and settle there. By thrusting her photo on you she is making sure you will sponsor her. Oh yes, it begins with a photograph."

"Be careful you don't forget your own mother's face, you don't have much time to see it these days."

And always, the eight o'clock ultimatum: "Remember, the door will never open for you after eight o'clock."

In the end Mother was glad to have the photograph. "One good thing she did by giving it to you. Now we have something to show Bhagwan Baba."

The train braked in preparation for the approaching station. A *kayrawalli* climbed aboard to flop upon the floor with her basket of plantains. She mopped her brow with one corner of her sari, rubbed her eyes, and sat with drawn-up knees after administering a good scratching in some region under the sari-folds. Any minute now she'll start badgering the passengers to buy her plantains, thought Jehangir. But she sat where she was, enervated, with no inclination to acquire business. Perhaps she did not dare to wake the slumbering people. In school they used to say that for a quarter rupee a *kayrawalli* would lift her sari and flash for you. For a rupee she would even perform with a plantain. He wondered if it was true.

The glass bangles on her wrists tinkled as the train swayed along, and she fell asleep. The plantains in her basket looked bruised and battered, beginning to show black patches because of the heat. They would have to be thrown away if they remained unsold. Granny had a saying about eating them: a plantain in the morning turns to gold in the stomach and a plantain at noon is silver; a plantain in the evening turns to brass in the belly, but a plantain at night is iron in the gut.

He wondered why the *kayrawalli* was travelling away from the city and towards the suburbs. People like her brought fruit to the city. Maybe she was on the wrong train.

Just like Father and Mother and me. To think that I put the thought in their heads.

Once, in the midst of a bitter outburst, he had said, "Why don't you ask your famous Bhagwan Baba if he also handles matchmaking? Maybe he'll be in my favour." He spoke with what he thought was biting sarcasm. Everything now had a habit of degenerating into a sarcasm contest.

But they liked the idea very much. "It was only a joke," Jehangir pleaded, sarcasm retreating in alarm.

Mother and Father thought it was the best way to decide his future. They tried to convince him to make the visit. Mother was harshly dictatorial at first, then lachrymose and pleading. "What we want," she tearfully entreated, "is for you to come and talk to Bhagwan Baba about the girl, to find out if she is right for you. Agree that Bhagwan Baba is never wrong, believe again as you believed once when you were younger."

And Jehangir stopped objecting when reminded of the many miracles wrought within the world of his childhood. Miracles were no doubt easier to believe in that long ago world. But the memories began to prey on his notions of loyalty to the past, his nostalgia for a home happy and loving despite its material meagreness, and guilt for considering (however briefly) repudiation of Bhagwan Baba. Besides, he reasoned, he had nothing to lose, it could not get worse. If he was lucky, a favourable pronouncement would make things much easier.

And with the agreement to take Bhagwan Baba's advice, a measure of calm returned to their lives. Hostilities were suspended and the harsh words temporarily silenced.

The *kayrawalli* awoke and balanced the basket of plantains on her head. She got off at the next station, which was also the one Jehangir and his parents were waiting for.

The medium-sized house had a spacious veranda at the front. A wooden bench sat on the veranda, and around the house a lush vegetable garden with several pumpkin vines and tomato plants. Tucked away in one corner was a large bench-swing, hanging still. Still, too, was the greenery in the garden. Not a breath of breeze.

A large crowd was waiting for Bhagwan Baba, People stood in a line leading up to the veranda, in silence or soft conversation, reverent hands clutching packets with offerings for Bhagwan Baba. There was none of the hysterical activity usually associated with holy men, no burning of incense, no chanting, no peddling of holy pictures or religious artifacts.

Jehangir's parents explained that when Bhagwan Baba was ready he came out to the wooden bench. The visitors then went up to the veranda and sat with him, one by one or in a group if it was a group consultation.

A man just ahead of them in line overheard, and spoke up as though waiting for the cue: "There is *no*thing to worry about. Bhagwan Baba is *won*derful. What*ever* he will say or do, it is only for your own benefit." Bhagwan Baba started granting audiences at eleven A.M. It was now eleven-thirty. With the air of one privy to special information the man said, "Bhagwan Baba knows best. If he is late it is for a good reason." His hands performed practised gestures to embellish the earnestly devout speech: fingers bunched together to describe a vertical line in the air; right index finger wisely held aloft and lowered through an arc into the left hand; palms together in a clasp; and so on. "We are only simple human beings, so *how* to understand *eve*rything Bhagwan Baba will say or do, how to know *why* his spirituality is manifesting in one way and not in another?" He paused, then added unctuously, "For us, it is only to stand and wait till Baba is ready to mingle with poor souls like you and me."

Jehangir found the man's effusive devotional talk embarrassing. He wished his parents would stop encouraging him by nodding pious looks of agreement. Bhagwan Baba appeared now, supported by two men. Something like a collective suspiration was audible in the garden. Then the scattered whispering fell silent. He was dressed in a white *kurta-pyjama,* and looked quite frail, with bare feet. His head was bald but he had a white beard. A short stubbly beard. And he wore dark glasses.

"Sometimes he takes off the glasses," the man whispered, "then at once puts them back on. *Everyone* waits for that, to see his eyes. *Exactly* what it means I don't understand. But it is absolutely significant, *most* definitely."

Two little boys and their older sister climbed onto the bench-swing in the corner of the vegetable garden. Their clambering set it into a gentle, squeaky oscillation. The sister sustained the motion of the swing with a pushing-kicking movement of her legs. During the forward swing her skirt billowed, then fell with the retreat; forward and back, billowed and fell.

Out of a long-formed habit Jehangir, craning, positioned himself to obtain the best view. When he had newly started going to college he discovered a pastime to which the Law of Diminishing Returns did not apply. The excitement of descending the stairs sometimes kept him from paying proper attention during class. There were two flights to each floor, and as he rounded the splendidly carved newel at the end of the first flight, his eyes lifted upwards. Above him flowed a stream of panties, a cascade of crotches out of the heavens, while he descended slowly, hand upon the balustrade to keep his balance, for it was heady stuff.

The thrills of this sport suffered greatly after that day at choir practice when she spoke to him. He realized that she could be amidst the descending crowd while his head was thrown back at a right angle to his trunk. It would be mortifying if she spotted him in this stance, she who believed him shy and, doubtless, pure of mind. Like Mother who, until recently, would say with pride, "My Jehangir, such a quiet good boy, *aitlō dahyō,* won't make *chooñ* or *chaañ.* Does everything I tell him." What a revelation if she could enter his prurient mind. Ironic that two women so different could share the same misconception, both beguiled in identical ways.

The bench-swing reminded him of the exercisers in the children's playground. He now gave that place a wide berth when he visited the Hanging Gardens, preferring to think that the playground and the exercisers belonged to a part of his life which had concluded for good. He wondered if the exercisers still went there every night, if their muscles had developed further since he last saw them more than two years ago.

The children lost interest in the swing. It slowed down, steadying into its former stillness, with the squeaks coming further and further apart, then dying away completely. Jehangir turned away from it, feeling victorious after his sighting. Not only had he succeeded, he had done so in Bhagwan Baba's garden amidst devotees thinking pious thoughts, and the touch of blasphemy was particularly satisfying. The sanctimonious fellow in front had been quiet for a while, not sharing any more of his insider's information. His turn was next. He smiled at Jehangir and his parents, and stepped up to the veranda. The sun had progressed in its descent, and the pumpkin vines and tomatoes would soon need watering. A slight breeze was evident in the faint rustle of leaves.

Now they were first in line. Jehangir's apprehension and uncertainty returned. He began digging frantically in his trousers for the photograph before remembering that on the train, while his parents slept, he had transferred it from his wallet to his shirt pocket. "How do we start this?" he asked. "Do I show the photo first?"

Mother said she would take care of that. All he should do was listen carefully when Bhagwan Baba spoke.

From Bhagwan Baba's house to the railway station was a short walk along a dirt road. Jehangir and his parents hurried along silently in the face of a rising wind. A somber, rainless cloud cover dominated the sky.

The dirt road was deserted. The sun's midday sharpness had been replaced by a heavy, stifling air mass moving over the land. Clouds of dust rose at the least provocation and Mother held a handkerchief over her nose and mouth. A few simple shacks and shanties on either side of the road were the only structures on the barren plain. Their sunken-cheeked occupants watched with empty eyes as the three figures made their way to the station.

The shelter of the waiting-room was a relief. It was deserted except for the man attending to the cold-drink stand. They purchased three bottles of Limca and settled on a bench to await their train. The bottles were closer to tepid than the ice-cold promised by the sign, but the drink was refreshing.

Bathrooms were located next to the cold-drink stand. From behind one of the doors emerged the song of a broken tap, the copious drip splashing in complex, agitated rhythms upon the stone floor.

"Shortage of water everywhere. But listen, listen to the shameful waste," said Father. He sipped Limca through the straw, anticipating the final empty gurgle to signal the end. "It was a little disappointing. He removed his dark glasses to see the photo, but did not say much. And three hours in line."

Mother said, "That is normal. Bhagwan Baba never speaks unless you ask him specific things. Jehangir did not open his mouth *sidhō-padhrō,* to speak clearly. Not one word. What do you expect Bhagwan Baba to do?"

"But you said you would explain..."

"I said I would begin for you. That does not mean you show no interest in what is your problem."

"I don't have a problem. You do because you don't like her." The entire day had passed without argument. Now it seemed the heat and dust would take their toll.

"I never said I do not like *her.* But no sense talking to you, you don't want to understand. We decided to come, you should have shown more concern. Now we still don't know what is the best thing for you."

Jehangir returned the empty Limca bottles to the cold-drink counter. A ceiling fan hung motionless in the waiting-room, and he pointed to it when the cold-drink man caught his eye. "Power shortage," the cold-drink man replied. "No lights even. At night I sell by lantern light. And kerosene is not cheap. So price of cold-drinks had to go up."

Jehangir nodded indifferently and returned to the bench. Father said, "Bhagwan Baba did not say much. But it seems to me he did give an answer. He said life is a trap, full of webs. Ask yourself, what does the sensible person do if a trap is facing him? Avoid, get away from it. So I think Bhagwan Baba was saying that Jehangir should stay away from that girl." He was pleased with his interpretation.

"But if that was what Bhagwan Baba meant, why not say it plainly?" said

Mother. "Every other time he has given us plain answers, simple language."

"I don't know. There is always a reason for what Bhagwan Baba does. That much I know. To me his words sounded like a warning for Jehangir."

"But Jehangir is not saying anything. Again you are staying quiet, like you did with Bhagwan Baba. Tell us whatever is on your mind."

And he was tempted to tell: of the sight which had shocked and embarrassed him one night when he had come home, changed his clothes, and left them on the pile for the *gunga* to wash next morning. A few minutes later he had returned, having forgotten his pen in one of the pockets. But Mother was there, sniffing, scrutinizing the gusset under the light. To find smells of illicit sex? Stains to corroborate her suspicions of the girl's sluttishness? Evidence that her boy had been ravished by a flesh-and-blood succubus? She had started counting garments for next day's washing quota when she saw him.

Trying to conceal the rough edge of resentment that crept into his voice now, he was only partly successful. "You keep saying the girl, the girl, the girl. You know her name is Behroze, why don't you use it? Do you think if you pronounce her name she will become more real than she is?"

His parents shifted uncomfortably. "You never talk to us these days," said Mother. "You were not like that in school. How you used to come home and tell me everything. The little butter we could afford I would always save for you, make your tea, help with homework. And how you used to go running to Dr Mody every Sunday at ten o'clock, do you remember, with your stamps." Those happy years brought a wistful smile to her face. She reached out as if to stroke his cheek. But the memories also exacerbated the imperfection of the present, and she left the gesture unfinished.

"We never treated you like other parents when you misbehaved. That old Karani woman in B Block, she used to make her boy stand naked out on the steps for punishment, to shame him. A brilliant CA he is now, but to this day the poor man has not completely recovered from that cruelty. And Dr Mody, rest his soul, would slap his son Pesi left-right on the face. Outside in the compound for all Firozsha Baag to see." Mother paused, remembered the point she was trying to make, and continued.

"Maybe it is because you have changed so much that we fret. You used to care about our problems, worry just like Daddy and me. More and more selfish you seem to be now, so what am I to think? That your new life in college, and your new friends, and that girl—Behroze—have changed you."

"Again we are starting to argue. No use talking of it now," said Father, "when we are all so tired."

"But I want to tell you what I think," said Jehangir. "Bhagwan Baba talked about a trap. He also said no one can do anything about it. No one means not you or I or Bhagwan Baba himself. So what is the point of a warning no one can act upon?"

"You see what I mean?" asked Mother, turning in despair to Father. "What I mean when I say he has changed? He takes all these logic and philosophy courses in college and gives us smart answers. We begged and borrowed to pay his college fees, and this is the result. Not afraid even to twist the words of Bhagwan Baba. Don't forget, all your smartness and your ambition to go to

America will come to nothing. This girl will change you and keep you here. Then you will finish your days like your father and me, in poverty and filth."

The suburban local to Bombay Central was announced over the loudspeaker. As the train swept in, Mother realized that the brown paper bag of oranges blessed by Bhagwan Baba was missing. Jehangir raced into the waiting-room and back to the compartment where they had found seats.

"You can eat one every day for the next three days," Mother said. "It will help you think clearly about your problem."

Jehangir did not tell Behroze about Bhagwan Baba. She would dismiss him as a fake, lumping him in the same category as the quacks and charlatans of whom there was no dearth in Bombay, who sold their charms and potions and had a thriving trade among the educated and the uneducated alike. It would lead to an argument, and he did not want to have to defend Bhagwan Baba.

That week, he missed choir practice and went to the Hanging Gardens. He walked, taking the short cut up the hill as he had done so many times with her. He mulled over the words of Bhagwan Baba. Not that it matters one way or the other what he meant, he kept assuring himself. A trap, he had said. Did he mean Behroze trapped me? That was absurd. Why would she want to? If anything, he had trapped Behroze, luring her with his melancholy looks and the sad and gentle air which so became him and his shyness. Or had Bhagwan Baba meant trap in a larger—sort of cosmic—sense, so that he and his parents and Behroze were all trapped, and must work out their lives within its confines? This interpretation at least had some metaphysical appeal to it.

The sun was on the verge of setting when he arrived at the Gardens. There was yet another possibility: that he could not break with Behroze even if he wanted because these things were out of man's control. Ludicrous, the thought that he was seeing her impelled by some higher force.

On weekdays the Gardens were empty except for ayahs with their charges and the elderly out for a constitutional. They left when it got dark. Then couples arrived to seek privacy behind bushes and trees. But shortly after dusk a gang of men roamed through the Gardens, flushing out twosomes in their sanctuaries. They would stand around and snicker, or yell out obscene encouragement punctuated by lewd flourishes of hands and fingers, till the couples took flight in frustration and embarrassment.

Jehangir walked till the sun went down. The ayahs and the little children departed with their prams and toys, and across the greying skies a flock of sparrows ushered them to the exits, chirping urgently. He could go on seeing Behroze as if nothing had changed. But then the squabbles, the scenes verging on hysteria, the bitter taunting would continue to fester. In one way Bhagwan Baba's words made sense; life is a trap—I cannot solve both problems. How long could such terrible discord persist without rupturing something vital? He never understood that so much unhappiness could come upon the happy, loving family they used to be. A horrible end would come of it, some awful mess, if things continued in their clamorous, disturbed manner.

He emerged from the Gardens through the gate opposite the one he had entered by. Where the *shik-kababwalla* sat. Fanning his coals, and the skewers ready in his basket, loaded with bits of beef and liver. Nodding at Jehangir in recognition. Then across the road and into Kamala Nehru Park, with its hedges sculpted into the shapes of animals and birds. In bright sunlight, when freshly trimmed, the figures were delightful to look at. But now the hour was passing through the final moments of dusk, and the shapes were indefinable. Looming in a strange, unearthly manner. Possessing neither the randomness of nature nor the manicured discipline imposed by man.

He left quickly. Something eerie about the place. Back into the Hanging Gardens, to retrace his steps homeward, down the hill.

And then a slight detour occurred to him, through the children's playground. His heart raced a little as he approached, wondering if the exercisers would be there.

He heard their panting before he saw them, and hurried to turn the bend in the hedge and position himself at his old place. Unnoticed, he watched their sweating bodies perform. The old fascination returned at the sight of their rippling, bulging muscles. In their rhythm and symmetry, in the sureness of their pulse, in the obedient responses of their limbs he rediscovered what he had always found strangely enticing, and remembered the days in the gym at St Xavier's: the smell of sweat, the camaraderie that flowed, the slapping of flesh, the search for the hairiest chest, bushiest armpit, longest pubic hair, the grabbing and jostling, all the fun which he was never a part of, always ignored by the boys, always isolated.

And now, regarding these fellows building bodies by night, a wild urge came over him. To step out of his concealed spot and touch their muscles, feel the hardness, make his body join theirs in the exercises. To engage in good-hearted physical competition, to see who could do the most push-ups, to arm-wrestle, to grunt and heave together.

But it was only momentary. I was never good at such things, I'll look foolish. He laughed at himself and left, feeling better now. As if the straining, exerting muscles of these men at exercise had kneaded away the disquietude and anxiety he had been feeling about Behroze, about Bhagwan Baba, about his parents. Nothing is a trap, I exercise control over my own destiny.

To discover where he had been, Mother began some skilful questioning. She stalked around, observing his face for suspicious-looking marks or blemishes, his shirt and collar for questionable discolouration. Instead of ignoring this customary examination he said, "You won't see anything. Behroze never puts on makeup when we go out for *kissie-koatie.*"

She clutched at her throat with both hands. "When a son speaks so shamelessly to his mother it is the end." And Father scolded in his mild way: "It is a disgrace when you talk like that."

Next evening he was drawn again to the Hanging Gardens. Lack of rain was obvious in the fading lushness of the lawns, but what green remained was still soothing. All the foundations were dry, their coloured lights switched off, and the little waterfall was a slope of grey sun-dried rock. After a few minutes of aimless strolling he went down to the overhang. It was the most secluded spot in the Gardens, at the edge overlooking the sea. Thick with bushes and trees on all three sides, and two wooden benches affording a spectacular view of Chaupatty Beach, from the Queen's Necklace along Marine Drive to the modern skyscrapers mushrooming at Nariman Point.

Behroze and he had come here once when both benches were unoccupied, on a slightly cool December evening. There was a gentle breeze. They sat down, his arm around her, watching the sky till the first star appeared. The gang of voyeurs was nowhere in sight, and Jehangir had a plan: to turn her head and kiss her when it was darker. A few moments later she reached her hands up to his face—she must have had a plan, too. But there were footsteps. He froze, then tore away from her hands.

The newcomers, a man and woman, occupied the other bench and began kissing desperately. The man's hands seemed to be everywhere, down her blouse, up her skirt. Jehangir and Behroze did not need to look; they could feel the heat of the feverish activity.

When Jehangir finally snatched a glance, the man was supine on the bench, his fly undone. The woman's face buried in his lap. Moans of pleasure. And a vague memory was transported from a great distance, pitting his intense desire to watch against an urgent need to leave, to cover up his eyes, to blot it all out: it was an evening on the veranda of their flat; the little boy stood with Mother at the window, taking the evening air and looking out beyond the compound wall. A boisterous group of men approached from the direction of Tar Gully, and down the main road three young women. As they closed the distance between them, one of the men suddenly cupped his hands around his crotch and said something the little boy could not hear, something about suck and mouth and money. There was giggling among the girls. The little boy tried hard to see what happened next. But Mother dragged him away, saying he shouldn't be looking at the filthy behaviour of wicked *mawaalis* and evil women; he should forget what he saw and heard or God would punish him and their whole house.

The evening had been spoilt. As they got up to leave, the night-watchman who patrolled the Gardens appeared. The fellating couple remained oblivious to the banging of his nightstick and other diversionary tactics. Finally, without going closer, in stentorian *Pathani* tones he called out, "*Arré bhaisahib,* lying on the benches is prohibited, please sit up straight," and the couple broke apart.

The night-watchman left; Jehangir and Behroze followed. Jehangir cast one backward glance: the couple was down again upon the bench, her mouth upon his lap. And fleeing the overhang, he recalled the panicked tearing of his own face from Behroze's hands. "I'm sorry," he said, "I just couldn't help it." He bundled up his frustrated desires into a tight, aching package and descended the hill in silence. Images of the couple on the bench abandoning themselves to their wild and desperate lust had danced unendingly before his eyes.

Jehangir sat on the grass now, under a lamp just outside the overhang. The overhang and its benches. Benches everywhere. *Paan*-stained ones in the train were third-class seats. Bhagwan Baba's veranda bench—sit on it and he told you a riddle. The one in the waiting-room was for drinking lukewarm Limca. And the overhang bench—reserved for sucking lessons, and wet dreams that trickled down your thighs to make embarrassing starched pyjama legs, which the *gunga* probably examined with interest when she washed the clothes.

A shower of gravel descended upon him, striking his head and neck and back. He jumped up. Saw three boys sprinting away. Started to give chase, then stopped. What will I do even if I manage to catch the urchins?

He was trembling and could not sit down again. Breathing hard. Quick short breaths. Hands shaking. Armpits damp. He decided to walk. To the children's playground. The gym-by-night. Where children's game equipment became the parallel bars of the poor: where the stone-broke used the see-saw to bench-press, with flagstones for weights. Yes, they would build their muscles, one way or another.

As the twilight faded the exercisers arrived, and stripped down to *lungoatee* and vest. A little adjustment of the pouch with a swift downward movement. Tucking in and fine-tuning of the formation within. Then tightening expertly the knots of the waistband.

Their bodies moved through the various exercises, and once again Jehangir felt the urge to join them, join them in their sweating, rippling activity. He imagined meeting them every evening, taking off his clothes with them, down to his shorts and *sudra*; they would sweat and pant together, a community of men, and when the exercises were done they would all go arm in arm, laughing and joking, for a hot and spicy *shik-kabab* and sugar cane juice. He could even learn to smoke a *bidi* with them.

He seriously considered taking up exercising. He was tired of being a skinny-armed, stoop-shouldered weakling. He would start in private, at home, and after his body strengthened he could join them in the open air. Surely they would welcome him. It would be a fraternity sufficient and complete.

He would go to Behroze's house on Saturday and say he had to speak to her about a serious matter. Make a clean break.

He prepared a mental list. He decided to conclude by saying that their relationship was making everyone unhappy: first, his parents were; she was, too, because they did not like her; besides, she could not tolerate their influence on him. Now she could resume her life as it was before he trespassed into it. Yes, trespassed, that was a good word, he'd use it.

The Kamala Nehru Park beckoned from across the road, through the dusk. The *maali* must have been at work, cuttings and twigs and leaves lay in heaps around the hedges. The sculptures looked magnificent, the birds on the verge of flight, the camel and elephant and giraffe about to lumber off into the darkness. But all of them ultimately frozen. Trapped, like Bhagwan Baba said. The words of Bhagwan Baba. Should be labelled A Philosophy For The Faint Of Heart And Weak Of Spirit. Or better still, The Way Of The Sculpted Hedges.

Behroze was alone when Jehangir arrived on Saturday evening. Her parents were out, so was the servant.

"You missed choir practice on Thursday," she said accusingly, crossing her legs. Her skirt slipped above the knee, exposing part of her thigh, and she did not pull it down.

Jehangir sensed nervously that somewhere in this was a challenge to him. The trace of hostility in the air narrowed the distance between them and made the room more intimate. Outside in the compound a game of volleyball was in progress, and the dull thuds as the ball met flesh and bone could be heard inside the flat.

"I'm sorry. I had something very important to do. It concerns us. I would like to talk to you about it." The note of formality in his short, complete sentences sounded reassuringly in his ears. "This is the first time you've been alone at home," he ventured with an echo of her accusing tone.

"You didn't come since last weekend. Maybe my parents think we've broken up, and they didn't need to stick around to guard my virginity."

Jehangir turned away to look outside the window. He felt very uncomfortable when she talked like this. The flat was on the ground floor at an elevation that raised it above the compound, and he could see the volleyball in its flight over the net but not the boys who smacked it. A few minutes of daylight remained. When the room began edging towards darkness she reached out to switch on the table-lamp. Her movement caused the skirt to rise a little more.

"They've gone to a wedding at Albless Baag. Won't be back till eleven o'clock," she said.

"And Shanti?"

"Gone to visit her family. Has the weekend off."

"I could not come last Sunday, I went with my parents to Bhagwan Baba—"

"Your string is showing again," she interrupted. He reached behind, thinking his *kusti* had slipped out over the waistband of his trousers.

She laughed scornfully. "Not your *kusti,* I meant your mother's extra-long apron string. Anyway, tell me about your Baba. This should be good."

"If you're going to mock me even before I..."

"I'm sorry, go on."

Jehangir described the visit to Bhagwan Baba and the pronouncement. He paused before announcing his own decision about them. She adjusted her skirt properly over the knee and said, "But does that make any difference? Surely you don't believe all that mumbo-jumbo."

"But that's not the reason—"

"Your parents will try anything, you know they hate me."

"They don't hate you," he started, and stopped. His well-tempered sentences wrought for the occasion now seemed silly—he realized he had known it all along, even as he rehearsed the words in the Hanging Gardens. He looked outside. The volleyball no longer flew over the net, and the boys had either gone home or down to the *bhelpuriwalla* for a snack. The sudden gloom was due to the sky's fierce clouding, which had overtaken the gradual change from dusk to night. In the window the curtains flapped, violently at times.

The decision made in the Hanging Gardens was no comfort. No comfort at all. Refused to buoy him up. Instead, it suddenly started to dissolve. Where was the peace and serenity he experienced that night in the Hanging Gardens? How could it come and go so quickly? To recapture his elusive confidence he imagined himself in the Gardens amidst the community of exercising men, sculpted hedges, chirping sparrows. But they swam pointlessly through his mind now. It was all meaningless.

Drawn by his anguished face, she came and sat beside him on the sofa. She slipped her hand in his; the scorn had gone out of her eyes, leaving them soft and brown. She moved closer, and he put his arm around her. His confusion and anxiety started to evaporate. He remembered the other time on the overhang bench: what would have been their first kiss had been interrupted by the unrestrained, coarse, unabashed passion of the other couple. Today there would be no interruptions. She switched off the lamp. Outside, there was the first rumbling of thunder, very distant, and the first drops of rain. The fresh, wholesome smell of earth was soon in the air.

It was still raining when Jehangir was racing homeward. People waited, huddled under awnings of shops or overhangs of buildings, under whatever shelter was afforded till the shower passed. There was gladness on all faces at the rain which had at long last arrived.

Outside a *jhopadpatti,* where even at the best of times a hundred and twenty residents depended on one water tap or the fortuity of a malfunctioning fire-hydrant, the joy of celebration was the most intense. Children and grownups soaped their bodies, tattered clothes and all, and stood gratefully under the cleansing waters from heaven. Mothers washed naked babies to the accompaniment of gleeful squeals. Some women were scouring their grimy, greasy pots and pans. Little rivulets of soapy water were soon running down the pavements leading from the *jhopadpatti* into the main street.

Jehangir was soaked to the skin. But he did not notice it, as he noticed nothing else around him. He was oblivious to the celebration of rain, to its freshness and abundance, to the delicious coolness and comfort that graced the air which barely an hour ago had been vile and full of threat.

With long desperate strides he splashed through the puddles. Some of them were ankle-deep, and his shoes were soon water-logged, but he hurried along. The rubbled pavement abandoned in mid-construction was impossible, so he took to the road.

A car fixed his soaking figure in its headlights, honking in annoyance. Sweat mingled with the rain-water coursing down his face. Waiting for a bus back to Firozsha Baag in this weather was pointless, it would take too long. He was panting hard, gasping for breath, but did not slow down. And his wretched, anguished mind would not be rid of her seated figure on the sofa, her hair over her soft brown eyes in which there were traces of moisture.

And to think that just a few minutes before he'd been sitting beside her on the same sofa, they were holding each other so close. Things could not be more perfect, it had seemed to him at that moment.

"Isn't this like a Hindi movie?" she had said smiling, adding wickedly to make him blush, "only thing is, I should be wearing a sari made transparent by rain. Even the thunder and lightning sound-track is perfect for lovers." Lovers? Was that a hint? She had stroked his hair. "Tell your parents and your Baba they did not succeed."

Jehangir had rested his cheek against hers, at peace with life and all its tangled complexities. His eyes wandered around in the dark, passed over the clock (a flash of lightning showed eight-fifteen), the outline of the bookcase, the piano and the frowning bust of Beethoven.

Eight-fifteen. Was that the right time? He had to find out. The radium-painted numbers of his watch dial would glow in the dark and show the correct time. He shifted, uneasy, and tried to move his hand. But she'd noticed immediately.

"If you want to look at your watch don't be so sneaky about it." She shook off his hand.

"I'm supposed to be home by eight." He looked at his watch.

"I know. You remind me every time you see me."

"In my watch it's almost eight. It's set with the clock at home. We eat dinner by it," he added apologetically, as if that would set things right. Short, complete sentences again, for reassurance. He got up.

"Going home on time for your mother is more important than—?" and she broke off. Her eyes rested for a moment on the cushions which lay about the sofa, comfortably rumpled, still holding the heat of their bodies, then returned to his face. He did not reply, just glanced at his watch again. Tidying up in great haste, he tucked in his shirt, put the crease back in pants, smoothed down the tousled hair: raced with the clock of Mother.

Behroze watched in stark disbelief at this exhibition of terror, the transformation from man to cowering child. "Calm down, will you? Your mother's world won't end if you are late. Haven't you learned yet? All these are just her tactics to—"

"I've told you before I know they are tactics," he snapped back, "and I'm doing it all because I want to, because her life has been troubled enough, because I don't want to add more misery to it. Because, because, because! Do you want me to repeat everything again?"

Then he had stooped to pull up his socks. As he was leaving he turned around, and that was when he saw what he'd least expected—two tiny tears moistening her lower lashes.

And side by side with this image that refused to go away was the sickening thought which had struck in the pit of his stomach, like nausea—the one interpretation of Bhagwan Baba's words which he had never considered during all his rumination in the Hanging Gardens: that the trap was the one laid by Bhagwan Baba himself. To trick him into ending it this way.

He rushed through the streets like a madman, shivering, tormented and confused, glancing at his watch again and again. His breath was coming hard, he thought he would collapse. Finally, he turned into the compound and stumbled up the three steps of the C Block entrance and into the lift.

He rang the doorbell. Just one short burst. His finger slid off, the arm fell limply to his side. There was no energy to complete the prearranged signal of rings that the family members used: two short and one long.

Mother opened the door narrowly, leaving on the chain. "Trying to fool me or what, with just one ring?"

Jehangir shook his head. He clung feebly to the door, wanting to speak, but the words could not form through the panting.

"You know what time it is?"

He nodded, holding up his watch. Eight-thirty.

"This time you crossed the limit. Your father says be patient, he is just a boy. Just a boy, yes, but the boy has climbed to the roof." She shook off his hand and slammed the door shut.

Still leaning against the door, he reached for the bell and rang it. Desperately, again and again, two short bursts and one long burst, two short and one long, over and over, as if that familiar signal would magically open the door. It remained shut. From inside the flat, silence. His arm fell. He slid to the floor and settled down to wait.

His breathing returned to normal but the wet clothes clung to him, he was very cold. During his school years, Mother used to accompany him on rainy mornings with a towel, a change of socks and shoes; at school she would dry his feet, help him into fresh socks, exchange his gumboots for the dry shoes.

He pulled his handkerchief and wiped his face, then pushed back the wet hair. The door was exposed to a gusting wind from the balcony. It made him shiver, and he shuffled into the narrow corridor sheltered by the staircase. He looked at his watch. Still eight-thirty. Must have stopped, clogged with rain water. It was a gift from Mother and Father for getting first class with distinction in his SSC exams. He hoped the neighbours would not open their doors: the news would spread through all three blocks of Firozsha Baag. Then the boys would find new names for him. He fell into a light sleep, leaning against the wall, till the soft clanking of the chain being removed from the door woke him up.

Neil Bissoondath

(b. 1955)

BORN IN TRINIDAD, Neil Bissoondath emigrated in 1973 to Canada, where he majored in French at York University. A teacher of English and French, he now lives in Toronto and devotes as much time as possible to writing. His stories have been broadcast on CBC *Anthology* and printed in *Saturday Night*. The collection *Digging Up the Mountains*, from which "Insecurity" is taken, appeared in 1985.

Like the other stories in this volume, "Insecurity" compassionately probes the sore points of Third World experience: the facts of violence (even brutality at times), of corruption (or of specialized techniques for manipulating the system), and of poverty (or of acute disparities between economic groups), against which the North American version of a tropical tourist paradise abruptly pales. This is a story in which shifts in dialect tell of political and generational difference, but it is not a portrait of a dualistic world. "Virtue" is not found all on one side, or in one place. In this story such terms as "success" and "accommodation" are defined in various ways, as—implicitly—is "failure." The story tells of social changes over time as well as of social differences from place to place; it is a story about possession and exile, of consequence and discovery, of power and the transfer of power: even of a kind of transfer that the characters only appreciate after the fact, when the insecurity that they have not even thought to prepare for replaces the insecurity they once held at bay.

Bissoondath's subsequent work includes such novels as *A Casual Brutality* (1988) and a controversial critique of Canadian "multiculturalism" in practice, *Selling Illusions: the cult of multiculturalism in Canada* (1994).

For Further Reading

"Caribbean Connections," special Caribbean-Canadian literature issue of *Canadian Literature* 95 (Winter 1982).

HELEN TIFFIN, "'Continental Drift' and the Fourth Naipaul," *CRNLE Reviews Journal* 1 (1987): 7–10.

Insecurity

"We're very insecure in this place, you know." Alistair Ramgoolam crossed his fat legs and smiled beatifically, his plump cheeks, gouged by bad childhood acne, quivering at the effect his words had had. "You fly down here, you look around, you see a beautiful island, sun, coconut trees, beaches. But I live here and I see a different reality, I see the university students parading Marx and Castro on the campus, I see more policemen with guns, I see people rioting downtown, I see my friends running away to Vancouver and Miami. So you can see, we are very insecure down here. That is why I want you to put the money your company owes me into my Toronto bank account. It is my own private insurance. The bank will notify me the money has been deposited and the government here won't notice a thing."

Their business concluded, the visitor pocketed Mr. Ramgoolam's account number and stood ready to leave. He asked to use the phone. "I'd like to call a taxi. My flight leaves early in the morning."

"No, no." Mr. Ramgoolam gestured impatiently with his plump arm. "Vijay will drive you into town. You're staying at the Hilton, not so?"

The visitor nodded.

"Vijay! Vijay!" Mr. Ramgoolam's silver hair—stirred, the visitor noticed, by the slightest movement—jumped as if alive.

Vijay's voice rattled like a falling can as it came in irritated response from the bowels of the house. "Coming, Pa, coming."

The tick-tock of Vijay's table-tennis game continued and Mr. Ramgoolam, chest heaving, bellowed. "Vijay!"

Still smiling beatifically, Mr. Ramgoolam turned to his visitor and said, "So when you'll be coming back to the islands again?"

The visitor shrugged and smiled. "That depends on the company. Not for a long time probably."

"You like Yonge Street too much to leave it again soon, eh?" Mr. Ramgoolam chuckled. The visitor smiled politely.

Vijay, rake thin and wild-eyed, shuffled into the living room.

Mr. Ramgoolam saw the visitor to Vijay's sports car, the latest model on the road. "You won't forget to get the letter to my son, eh? Remember, it's Markham Street, the house number and phone number on the envelope. You won't forget, eh?"

"I won't forget," the visitor said. They shook hands.

Mr. Ramgoolam was back in his house before the gravel spat up by the tires of the car had settled. He followed the tail-lights through a heavily burglar-proofed window—Vijay was speeding again, probably showing off; he'd need

From *Digging Up the Mountains* (Toronto: Macmillan, 1985). Reprinted by permission of Macmillan Canada.

another talking to. Nodding ponderously, he muttered, "We're very insecure in this place, yes, very insecure."

Alistair Ramgoolam was a self-made man who thought back with pride to his poor childhood. He credited this poverty with preventing in him the aloofness he often detected in his friends: a detachment from the island, a sneering view of its history. He had, he felt, a fine grasp on the island, on its history and its politics, its people and its culture. He had developed a set of "views" and anecdotes which he used to liven up parties. It distressed him that his views and anecdotes rarely had the desired effect, arousing instead only a deadpan sarcasm. He had written them down and had them privately published in a thin volume. Except for those he'd given away as gifts, all five hundred copies were collecting dust in cardboard boxes under the table-tennis board.

Mr. Ramgoolam had seen the British when they were the colonial masters and he had attended the farewell ball for the last British governor. He had seen the Americans arrive with the Second World War, setting up their bases on large tracts of the best agricultural land; and he had seen the last of them leave, the Stars and Stripes tucked securely under the commander's arm, more than twenty years after the end of the war. He had seen the British, no longer masters and barely respected, leave the island in a state of independence. And he had seen that euphoric state quickly degenerate into a carnival of radicals and madmen.

His life at the fringe of events, he felt, had given him a certain authority over and comprehension of the past. But the present, with its confusion and corruption, eluded him. The sense of drift nurtured unease in Mr. Ramgoolam.

He would always remember one particular day in late August, 1969. He had popped out of his air-conditioned downtown office to visit the chief customs officer at the docks. As an importer of foreign foods and wines, Mr. Ramgoolam made it his business to keep the various officials who controlled the various entry stamps happy and content. On that day, he was walking hurriedly past the downtown square when a black youth, hair twisted into worm-like pigtails, thrust a pink leaflet into his unwilling hands. It was a socialist tract, full of new words and bombast. Mr. Ramgoolam had glanced irritatedly at it, noticed several spelling mistakes, crumpled it up, and thrown it on the sidewalk. Then he remembered he was a member of the Chamber of Commerce Keep-Our-City-Clean committee and he picked it up. Later that evening he found it in his pants pocket. He smoothed it out, read it, and decided it was nothing less than subversion and treason. At the next party he attended, he expounded his views on socialism. He was told to stop boring everyone.

Not long after the party, riots and demonstrations—dubbed "Black Power" by the television and the newspaper—occurred in the streets. Mr. Ramgoolam's store lost a window pane and the walls were scribbled with "Socialism" and "Black Communism". The words bedevilled the last of Mr. Ramgoolam's black hairs into the mass of silver.

As he watched the last black stripe blend in, Mr. Ramgoolam realized that, with an ineffectual government and a growing military, one night could bring the country a change so cataclysmic that the only issue would be rapid flight. And failing that, poverty, at best.

He had no desire to return to the moneyless nobility of his childhood; pride was one thing, stupidity quite another, and Alistair Ramgoolam was acutely aware of the difference.

He began looking for ways of smuggling money out of the island to an illegal foreign bank account. A resourceful man, he soon found several undetectable methods: buying travellers' cheques and bank drafts off friends, having money owed him by foreign companies paid into the illegal account, buying foreign currency from travellers at generous rates of exchange. His eldest son was attending university in Toronto, so it was through him that Mr. Ramgoolam established his account.

The sum grew quickly, Mr. Ramgoolam became an exporter of island foods and crafts, deflating the prices he reported to the island's government and inflating those he charged the foreign companies. The difference was put into the Toronto account. Every cent not spent on his somewhat lavish lifestyle was poured into his purchases of bank drafts and travellers' cheques.

The official mail service, untrustworthy and growing more expensive by the day, was not entrusted with Mr. Ramgoolam's correspondence with his son. Visitors to or from Toronto, friend or stranger, were asked to perform favors.

Over the years, with a steadily developing business and ever-increasing foreign dealings, Mr. Ramgoolam's account grew larger and larger, to more than forty thousand dollars.

He contemplated his bankbooks with great satisfaction. Should flight be necessary—and the more time passed, the more Mr. Ramgoolam became convinced it would—there would be something to run to beyond bare refuge.

The more insecure he saw his island becoming, the more secure he himself felt. From this secure insecurity a new attitude, one of which he had never before been aware, arose in him. The island of his birth, on which he had grown up and where he had made his fortune, was transformed by a process of mind into a kind of temporary home. Its history ceased to be important, its present turned into a fluid holding pattern which would eventually give way. The confusion had been prepared for, and all that was left was the enjoyment that could be squeezed out of the island between now and then. He could hope for death here but his grandchildren, maybe even his children, would continue the emigration which his grandfather had started in India, and during which the island had proved, in the end, to be nothing more than a stopover.

When the Toronto account reached fifty thousand dollars, Mr. Ramgoolam received a letter from his eldest son. He reminded his father that Vijay would be coming to Toronto to study and that the fifty thousand dollars was lying fallow in the account, collecting interest, yes, but slowly. Wouldn't it be better to invest in a house? This would mean that Vijay—Mr. Ramgoolam noticed his eldest son had discreetly left himself out—would not have to pay rent and, with the rapidly escalating property prices in Toronto, a modest fifty-thousand-dollar house could be resold later at a great profit.

His first reading of the letter brought a chuckle to Mr. Ramgoolam's throat. His independent-minded son, it seemed, was looking for a way of not paying rent. But then he felt a ripple of quiet rage run through him: his son had always made an issue of being independent, of making it on his own. Paying for the privilege, Mr. Ramgoolam thought, was the first requisite of independence. He put the suggestion out of his mind.

Later that night, just before bed, he read the letter aloud to his wife. This had long been their custom. She complained continually of "weakness" in the eyes. As he lay in bed afterwards, the words "great profit" stayed with him.

His wife said, "You going to buy it?"

He said, "Is not such a bad idea. I have to think."

When he awoke at four the next morning for his usual Hindu devotions, Mr. Ramgoolam's mind was made up. He walked around the garden picking the dew-smothered flowers with which he would garland the deities in his private prayer room and, breathing in the cool, fresh air of the young dawn's semi-light, he became convinced that the decision was already blessed by the beauty of the morning.

After a cold shower, Mr. Ramgoolam draped his fine cotton dhoti around his waist and prayed before his gods, calling their blessings onto himself, his wife, his sons, and the new house soon to be bought, cash, in Toronto. It was his contention that blessed business dealings were safer than unblessed ones.

He spent the rest of the morning writing a letter to his son, giving instructions that before any deals were made he was to be consulted. He didn't want any crooked real estate agent fooling his son, Toronto sophisticate or not. He also warned that the place should be close enough to Vijay's school that he wouldn't have to travel too far: a short ride on public transportation was acceptable but his son should always remember that it was below the station of a Ramgoolam to depend on buses and trains.

That was an important point, Mr. Ramgoolam thought. It might force his independent son to raise his sights a little. He probably used public transportation quite regularly in Toronto, whereas here on the island he would not have heard of sitting in a bus next to some sweaty farmer. The letter, Mr. Ramgoolam hoped, would remind his eldest son of the standards expected of a member of his family.

The letter was dispatched that evening with the friend of a friend of a friend who just happened to be leaving for Toronto.

A week passed and Mr. Ramgoolam heard nothing from his son. He began to worry: if *he* were buying a house, you could be sure *he'd* have found a place and signed the deal by now. That son of his just had no business sense: didn't he know that time was money? A week could mean the difference of a thousand dollars! Mr. Ramgoolam said to his wife, "I just wish he'd learn to be independent on somebody else's money."

He was walking in the garden worrying about his money and kicking at the grass when Vijay shouted from the house, "Pa, Pa! Toronto calling."

Mr. Ramgoolam hurried in, his cheeks jiggling. "Hello." It was the real estate agent calling.

The operator said, "Will you accept the charges?"

Accept the charges? Mr. Ramgoolam was momentarily unsettled. "No." He slammed the phone down. He glared at Vijay sitting at the dining table. "What kind of businessman he is anyway? Calling collect. He's getting my money and he expects me to pay for his business call? He crazy or what, eh?" Incensed, he ran out into the garden. Every few minutes, Vijay could hear him muttering about "cheapness".

The telephone rang again half an hour later.

This call was from his son and, luckily, not collect. The first thing Mr. Ramgoolam said was, "Get rid of that cheap agent. I don't trust him. Get somebody else."

The son agreed. Then he asked whether his father would be willing to go above fifty thousand, to, say, sixty or sixty-five. Only such a sum would assure a good house in a proper location. Less would mean a good house, yes, but a long way on public transportation for Vijay.

Mr. Ramgoolam pictured Vijay riding on some rickety bus with a smelly fish vendor for company. He broke out in a cold sweat. "Now wait up a minute...awright, awright, sixty or sixty-five. But not a cent more. And close the deal quickly. Time is money, you know."

Time dragged by. Nothing was heard from Toronto for a week. Mr. Ramgoolam began to worry. What was that no-good son of his up to now? Wasting time as usual, probably running off somewhere being independent.

Another week went by and Mr. Ramgoolam began brooding over the house in Toronto. He couldn't get his mind off it. He stopped going to the office. Not even prayer seemed to ease his growing doubts. Wasn't it better to have the cash safely in the bank, slowly but surely collecting its interest? And what about Vijay? The money for his schooling was to have come from that account: now he'd have to take money with him, and Mr. Ramgoolam hadn't counted on that. Above all, the house was going to cost ten to fifteen thousand more than the Toronto account contained: that was a lot of money to smuggle out. Would it mean a mortgage? He hated mortgages and credit. He hated owing. Buy only when you could pay: it was another of his convictions.

After three more days and a sleepless night, Mr. Ramgoolam eased himself out of bed at 3.30 a.m. He might as well pray. It always helped, eased the mind however little.

There was very little light that morning and the flowers he collected were wilted and soggy. He stubbed his toe on a stone and cursed, softly, in Hindi. The cold shower felt not so much refreshing as merely cold.

He prayed, his dhoti falling in careless folds, his gods sad with their colorless flowers.

When he finished he wrote a quick letter to his son, ordering him to leave all the money in the bank and to forget about buying a house. He couldn't afford it at the present time, he said.

He signed it and sealed it. He wondered briefly whether he should telephone or telegram but decided they were both too expensive. The next problem was to find someone who was going to Toronto. That was easy: the representative of his biggest Toronto client, the one staying at the Hilton, would be coming to the house this evening to finalize a deal and to get the Toronto account number. He could take the letter.

Five days passed and Mr. Ramgoolam heard nothing from his eldest son. Once more he began to worry. Couldn't the fool call to say he'd got the letter and the money was safe? He spent the morning in bed nursing his burning ulcer.

On the morning of the sixth day the call came.

"Hello, Pa?" His son's voice was sharp and clear, as if he were calling from across the street. "You're now the proud owner of a house in Toronto. The deal went through yesterday. It's all finalized."

Mr. Ramgoolam's jaw fell open. His cheeks quivered. "What? You didn't get my letter?"

"You mean the one the company rep brought up? Not yet. He just called me last night. I'm going to collect the letter this evening, before the ballet."

"Be-be-be-fore the ballet?" Mr. Ramgoolam ran his pudgy fingers down the length of his perspiring face. He could feel his heart thumping heavily against the fat in his chest.

"Yes, I'm going to the ballet tonight. Good news about the house, eh? I did exactly as you told me, Pa. I did it as quickly as possible. Time is money, as you always say."

"Yes-yes," said Mr. Ramgoolam. " Time is money, son, time is money. We're very insecure in this place, you know."

His son said, "What?"

"Nothing." Mr. Ramgoolam ran his hand, trembling, through his hair. "Goodbye." He replaced the receiver. The wooden floor seemed to dance beneath him and, for a moment, he had a sense of slippage, of life turned to running liquid. He saw his son sitting in the living room of the Toronto house—sitting, smiling, in a room Mr. Ramgoolam knew to be there, but the hardened outlines of which he could not distinguish—and he suddenly understood how far his son had gone. Just as his father had grown distant from India; just as he himself had grown even further from the life that, in memory, his father had represented and then, later in life, from that which he himself had known on the island, so too had his eldest son gone beyond. Mr. Ramgoolam had been able to picture the money sitting in the bank, piles of bills; but this house, and his son sitting there with ballet tickets in his hand: this was something softer, hazier, less graspable. He now saw himself as being left behind, caught between the shades of his father and, unexpectedly, of his son. And he knew that his insecurity, until then always in the land around him, in the details of life daily lived, was now within him. It was as if his legs had suddenly gone hollow, two shells of utter fragility.

There was only one thing left, one thing to hold on to. He hurried to his room and, brushing his wife aside, dressed quickly. Then he swallowed two hefty gulps of his stomach medicine and called out to Vijay to drive him to the office.

Steven Heighton

(b. 1961)

BORN IN TORONTO, Steven Heighton was raised there and in Red Lake, Alberta. After graduating from Queen's University in Kingston (with an M.A. in English, 1986), he travelled to Japan to teach English as a Second Language. His first volume of stories, *Flight Paths of the Emperor* (1992), in which "Five Paintings of the New Japan" appeared, grew out of his Asian experiences and observations.

Subsequently, Heighton returned to Canada—and to Kingston, where he now lives. Editor for six years (1988–1994) of the Kingston-based literary magazine *Quarry*, he has himself written poetry and prose and won prizes for both, including the 1989 Air Canada Award for short fiction and the 1990 Gerald Lampert Award for poetry. His volumes of poetry include *Stalin's Carnival* and *Foreign Ghosts* (both 1989); the latter also includes some travel commentary. A second volume of stories, *On Earth As It Is*, appeared in 1995.

"Five Paintings of the New Japan" looks at a world in which the idea of "translation" is more than verbal. For a culture undergoing radical transition, the signs of "success" become abruptly less universal and more difficult to agree upon, especially as the border between "local" and "foreign" itself becomes more diffuse. But the new signs of success (like the old ones) are easy enough to identify. *Bushido*—the old warrior culture—had its rules; so does the contemporary culture of possession and profit. The story also asks, however, if closed societies (whether Eastern or Western) can ever truly open. Who is the foreigner in this culture? Who sees whom? And what does the collection of artifacts—the Van Goghs and Picassos that sign the story's subtitles, for example—imply? Heighton's control over tone here permits a story that begins in parody to end in a different tonal register, revealing both the humour and the pathos to which cross-cultural encounters sometimes give rise.

For Further Reading

ARNOLD E. DAVIDSON, "Intersections of East and West," *Essays on Canadian Writing* 55 (Spring 1995): 220–29.

Five Paintings of the New Japan
A National Gallery

I. SUNFLOWERS:

I was the first foreigner to wait tables in the Yume No Ato. Summer enrolment was down at the English school where I taught so I needed to earn extra money, and since I'd been eating at the restaurant on and off for months it was the first place I thought of applying. It was a small establishment built just after the war in a bombed-out section of the city, but when I saw it the area was studded with bank towers, slick boutiques, coffee shops and flourishing bars and the Yume No Ato was one of the oldest and most venerable places around. I was there most of the summer and I wish I could go back. I heard the other day from Nori, the dishwasher, who works part-time now in a camera store, that our ex-boss Mr Onishi has just fought and lost a battle with cancer.

'We have problems here every summer,' Mr Onishi sighed during my interview, 'with a foreign tourist people.' He peered up at me from behind his desk, two shadowy half-moons drooping under his eyes. 'Especially the Americans. If I hire you, you can deal to them.'

'With them,' I said automatically.

'You have experienced waitering?'

'A little,' I lied.

'You understand Japanese?'

'I took a course.'

'Say something to me in Japanese.'

I froze for a moment, then was ambushed by a phrase from my primer.

'*Niwa ni wa furu-ike ga arimasu.*'

'In the garden,' translated Mr Onishi, 'there is an old pond.'

I stared abjectly at his bald patch.

'You cannot say a sentence more difficult than that?'

I told Mr Onishi it was a beginners' course. He glanced up at me and ran his fingers through a greying Vandyke beard.

'How well do you know the Japanese cuisine?'

'Not so well,' I answered in a light bantering tone that I hoped would disarm him, 'but I know what I like.'

He frowned and checked his watch, then darted a glance at the bank calendar on the wall.

'Morinaga speaks a little English,' he said. 'He will be your trainer. Tomorrow at 1600 hours you start.'

Reprinted with permission of Steven Heighton and the Porcupine's Quill, Inc.

'You won't be sorry, sir,' I told him.

'I shall exploit you,' he said, 'until someone more qualitied applies.'

*

Nori Morinaga leaned against the steam table and picked his nose with the languid, luxurious gestures of an epicure enjoying an after-dinner cigar. He was the biggest Japanese I'd ever seen and the Coke-bottle glasses perched above his huge nose seemed comically small.

'Ah, *gaijin-san!*' he exclaimed as he saw me, collecting himself and inflating to his full height. 'Welcome in! Hail fellow well-hung!'

I wondered if I'd heard him correctly.

'It gives me great pressure!'

I had. I had.

Nori Morinaga offered me his hand at the same moment I tried to bow. Nervously we grinned at each other, then began to laugh. He was a full head taller than I was, burly as a linebacker but prematurely hunched as if stooping in doorways and under low ceilings had already affected his spine. He couldn't have been over twenty-five. His hair was brush-cut like a Marine's and when he spoke English his voice and manner seemed earnest and irreverent at the same time.

'Onishi-san tells me I will help *throw you the ropes,*' he chuckled. 'Ah, I like that expression. Do you know it? I study English at the University but the *gaijin-sensei* always says Japanese students must be more idiomatic so I picked up this book'—his giant hand brandished a thick paperback—'and I study it *like a rat out of hell.*'

He grinned enigmatically, then giggled. I couldn't tell if he was serious or making fun of me.

Nori pronounced his idiomatic gleanings with savage enthusiasm, his magnified eyes widening and big shoulders bunching for emphasis as if to ensure his scholarship did not pass unseen. I took the book and examined it: a dog-eared, discount edition of UP-TO-DATE ENGLISH PHRASES FOR JAPANESE STUDENTS— in the 1955 edition.

'We open in an hour,' he said. 'We are *oppressed for time.* Come on, *I'm going to show you what's what.*'

Situated in a basement, under a popular *karaoke* bar, the Yume No Ato's two small rooms were dimly lit and the atmosphere under the low ceiling was damp and cool, as in an air-raid shelter or submarine. I wondered if this cramped, covert aura hadn't disturbed some of the earliest patrons, whose memories of the air raids would still have been fresh—but I didn't ask Nori about that. The place had always been popular, he said, especially in summer, when it was one of the coolest spots in Ōsaka.

A stairway descended from street level directly into the dining room so on summer days, after the heat and bright sunshine of the city, guests would sink into a cool aquatic atmosphere of dim light and swaying shadows. The stairway was flanked on one side by a small bar and on the other by the sushi counter where I'd eaten before. An adjoining room contained a larger, more formal dining space which gave onto the kitchen through a swinging door at the back. Despite the rather Western-style seating arrangements (tables and chairs instead of the traditional *zabuton* and *tatami*) the dining area was decorated in authentic Japanese fashion with hanging lanterns, calligraphic scrolls, a *tokonoma* containing an empty *maki-e* vase, *bonsai* and *noren* and several framed, original *sumi-e* prints. The only unindigenous ornament was a large reproduction of Van Gogh's *Sunflowers* hung conspicuously on the wall behind the sushi bar.

'Onishi-san says it's for the behoof of the American tourists,' Nori explained, 'but I'd *bet my bottom* he put it there for the bankers who come *in the wee-wee hours*. It's the bankers who are really interested in that stuff.' He sniffed and gestured contemptuously toward *Sunflowers* and toward the *sumi-e* prints as well, as if wanting me to see he considered all art frivolous and dispensable, no matter where it came from.

I didn't realize till much later the gesture meant something else.

Nori showed me around the kitchen and introduced me to the cooks, who were just arriving. Kenji Komatsu was head chef. Before returning to Japan and starting a family he'd worked for a few years in Vancouver and Montréal and his memories of that time were good, so he was delighted to hear I was Canadian. He insisted I call him Mat. 'And don't listen to anything this big whale tells you,' he warned me affably, poking Nori in the stomach. 'So much sugar and McDonald's the young ones are eating these days.... This one should be in the *sumo* ring, not my kitchen.'

'*Sumo* is for old folk,' Nori said, tightening his gut and ironically saluting a small, aproned man who had just emerged from the walk-in fridge.

'*Time is on the march*,' Nori intoned. '*Nothing can stop it now!*'

Second chef Yukio Miyoshi glared at Nori then at me with frank disgust and muttered to himself in Japanese. He marched toward the back of the kitchen and began gutting a large fish. 'Doesn't like the foreigners,' Nori grinned indifferently. 'So it is. You can't pleasure everybody.'

The swinging door burst open and a small dark form hurtled into the kitchen and disappeared behind the steam table. Nori grabbed me by the arm.

'It's Oh-san, the sushi chef—come, we must hurry.'

Mr Oh was a jittery middle-aged man who scurried through the restaurant, both hands frantically embracing a mug of fresh coffee. Like all the elder folks, Nori explained, Mr Oh worked too hard....

We finally cornered him by the walk-in fridge and Nori introduced us. Clearly he had not heard of Mr Onishi's latest hiring decision—he flung down his mug and gawked as if I were a health inspector who'd just told him twenty of last night's customers were in the hospital with food poisoning.

The *yukata* which Mr Oh insisted I try on looked all right, and in the change room I finally gave in and let him Brylcreem and comb back my curly hair into the slick, shining facsimile of a typical Japanese cut. As he worked with the comb, his face close to mine, I could see the tic in his left eye and smell his breath, pungent with coffee.

'You look *marvellous*,' Nori laughed on my return, 'and you know who you are!' He winked and blew me a kiss.

Mr Onishi entered and snapped some brusque truculent command. When the others had fled to their stations he addressed me in English.

'I hope you are ready for your first shift. We will have many guests tonight.

Come—you will have to serve the aliens.'

From the corner of my eye I could see Nori clowning behind the grille, two chopsticks pressed to his forehead like antennae.

As I trailed Mr Onishi into the dining room two men and a woman, all young, tall, clad smartly in *yukata,* issued from behind the bar and lined up for inspection. One of the men wore a pearl earring and his hair was unusually long for a Japanese, while the woman had a rich brown, luminous skin and plump attractive features. Mr Onishi introduced the other man as Akiburo. He was a college student and looked the part with his regulation haircut and sly, wisecracking expression.

With patent distaste Mr Onishi billed the long-haired man as 'your bartender, who likes to be known as Johnnie Walker'. The man fingered his earring and smiled out of the side of his mouth. 'And this is Suzuki Michiko, a waitress.' She bowed awkwardly and studied her plump brown hands, the pale skin on the underside of her wrists.

My comrades, as Mr Onishi called them, had been expecting me, and now they would show me to my sector of the restaurant—three small tables in the corner of the second room. In this occidental ghetto, it seemed, Mr Onishi thought I would do the least possible damage to the restaurant's ambience and reputation. Michiko explained in simple Japanese that since my tables were right by the kitchen door I could ask Nori for help as soon as I got in trouble.

The *tokonoma,* I now saw, had been decorated with a spray of poppies.

'We open shortly,' Mr Onishi declared, striding toward us. His manner was vigorous and forceful but his eyes seemed tired, their light extinguished. 'We probably will have some American guests tonight. Your job will be to service them.'

'I'll do my best, sir.'

'And coffee—you will now take over from Michiko and bring Mr Oh his coffee. He will want a fresh supply every half-hour. Do not forget!'

For the first hour the second room remained empty, as did the tables of the front room, but the sushi bar was overrun within minutes by an army of ravenous, demanding guests. 'Coffee,' cried Mr Oh, and I brought him cup after cup while the customers gaped at me and hurled at Mr Oh questions I could not understand. The coffee yellowed his tongue and reddened his eyes, which took on a weird, narcotic glaze, while steam mixed with sweat and stood out in bold clear beads on his cheeks and upper lip. Orders were called out as more guests arrived. Mr Oh's small red hands scuttled like sand crabs over the counter, making predatory forays into the display case to seize hapless chunks of smelt or salmon or eel and then wielding above them a fish-silver knife, replacing the knife deftly, swooping down on speckled quail eggs and snapping shells between thumb and forefinger and squeezing the yolk onto bricks of rice the other hand had just formed. Then with fingers dangling the hands would hover above an almost completed dish, and they would waver slightly like squid or octopi in currents over the ocean floor, then pounce, abrupt and accurate, on an errant grain of rice or any garnish or strip of ginger imperfectly arranged, and an instant later the finished work, irreproachable and beyond time like a still life or a great sculpture, would appear on the glass above the display case from which it was snatched within seconds by the grateful customers or attentive staff.

The process was dizzying. I was keenly aware of my ignorance and when I was not airlifting coffee to the sushi bar I was busy in my own sector studying the menu and straightening tables.

Around eight o'clock Mr Onishi entered the second room, carrying menus, followed by a man and woman who were both heavyset, tall and fair-haired. The man wore a tailored navy suit and carried a brief-case. The woman's hair was piled high in a steep bun that resembled the nose-cone of a rocket, and her lipstick, like her dress, was a pushy, persistent shade of red.

'Take good care with Mr and Mrs Cruikshank,' Onishi-san murmured as he passed me and showed them to their seats. 'Mr Cruikshank is a very important man—a diplomat, from America. Bring two dry Martinis to begin.'

Mr Cruikshank's voice was genteel and collected, his manner smooth as good brandy. 'How long have you been working in this place?' he inquired.

'Two hours,' I told him, serving the Martinis.

'Surprised they'd have an American working here.' With one hand he yanked a small plastic sabre from his olive, then pinched the olive and held it aloft like a tiny globe.

'I'm not American,' I said.

There was a pause while Mr and Mrs Cruikshank processed this unlooked for information.

'Well surely you're not Japanese?' Mrs Cruikshank asked, slurring her words a little. 'Maybe half?'

Mr Cruikshank swallowed his olive then impaled his wife's with the plastic sword. He turned back to me, inadvertently aiming the harmless tip at my throat.

'*Nihongo wakaru?*' he asked in plain, masculine speech. *You understand Japanese?* I recognized his accent as outstanding.

'Only a little,' I said.

'I'll bet he's Dutch,' Mrs Cruikshank wagered. 'The Dutch speak such beautiful English—hardly any accent at all.'

'You'll find it hard here without any Japanese,' Mr Cruikshank advised me, ignoring his wife, drawing the sword from his teeth so the gleaming olive stayed clenched between them.

'*Coffee,*' Mr Oh called from the sushi bar.

'I'll only be serving the foreign customers, sir.'

Mr Cruikshank bit into his olive. 'Some of the foreign customers,' he said, 'prefer being served in Japanese.'

'Or maybe German,' said Mrs Cruikshank.

'I can speak some German,' I said. 'Would you like it if—'

'*Coffee,*' cried Mr Oh from the sushi bar.

Mrs Cruikshank was beaming. 'I was right,' she said, lifting her Martini glass in a kind of toast. '*Wie geht's?*'

'We'd like some sushi,' Mr Cruikshank interrupted his wife, who was now grimacing at her drink as if trying to recall another German phrase.

I fumbled with my pad.

'An order each of *maguro, saba, hamachi,* and—why not?—some sea urchin.

Hear it's full of mercury these days, but hell, we've got to eat something.'
'Yes, sir.'
'And two more Martinis.' He pointed at his glass with the plastic sword.
'Got it.'
'Danke schön,' roared Mrs Cruikshank as I hurried from the room.

While waiting for Johnnie Walker to finish the Martinis I noticed an older guest rise from the sushi bar and stumble toward the washrooms. As he saw me, his red eyes widened and he lost his footing and crashed into the bar, slamming a frail elbow against the cash register. He righted himself with quick slapstick dignity and stood blushing. When I moved to help him he waved me off.

Johnnie Walker smirked and muttered as he shook the Martinis and for a moment the words and the rattling ice took on a primitive, mocking rhythm, like a chant. The older man began to swear at him and reached out as if to grab his earring, his long hair. *Shin jin rui,* the old man muttered—*Strange inscrutable creature!* I'd heard it was a new phrase coined by the old to describe the young.

'Wake up old man,' Johnnie snapped in plain Japanese as he poured the Martinis. 'Watch out where you're going.'

The man lurched off.

'Always drunk, or fast asleep in their chairs.'

'Coffee,' cried Mr Oh from the sushi bar.

II. THE DREAM:

'Tell me something about the restaurant.' I said to Nori, sweeping my hand in a half circle and nodding at the closed bar. 'How old is the place?'

Nori finished his Budweiser and balanced the empty tin on a growing tower of empties. 'It was built after the war ends,' he belched—and I couldn't help noticing how casually he used the word *war.* His expression was unchanged, his voice was still firm, his eyes had not recoiled as if shamed by some unspeakable profanity. That was how my older students reacted when The War came up in a lesson. No doubt Mr Onishi would react the same way. But not Nori. For him the war was history, fiction—as unreal and insubstantial as a dimly remembered dream, a dream of jungles, the faded memory of a picture in a storybook. He wasn't much younger than me.

'What about the name,' I said, 'Yume No Ato? I mean, I can figure out the individual words, but I can't make sense of the whole thing.' *Yume,* I knew, meant 'dream', *no* signified possession, like an apostrophe and an 's', and *ato,* I thought, meant 'after'.

Nori lit a cigarette and trained a mischievous gaze on my hairline. His capacity for drink was larger than average for a Japanese but now after four tins of beer he was flushed, theatrical and giddy. He wrinkled his broad nose, as if at a whiff of something rotten, and spat out, 'It's a line from a poem we had to study in the high school. Ah, Steve-san, university is so much better, we have fun in the sun, we make whoopee, we live for the present tense and forget all our yesterdays and tomorrows.... I hated high school, so much work. We had to study this famous poem.'

He stood and recited the lines with mock gravity:

'*Natsu kusa ya!*
  Tsuamono domo ga
    Yume no ato.'

'It's *a haiku*,' I said.

'Aye, aye, captain.' He slumped down and the tower of beer cans wobbled. 'Do you watch "Star Trek"?'

'I'm not sure,' I said, 'that I understand it.'

'Oh, well, it's just a TV show—about the future and the stars.'

'I mean the poem, Nori, the *haiku*.'

'Ah, the poem—naturally you don't understand. It's old Japanese—old Japanese language, old Japanese mind—not so easy for us to understand either. It's Matsuo Bashō, dead like Shakespeare over three hundred years. Tomorrow and tomorrow and tomorrow. We had to study them both in school. Full fathom five and all that.'

'But about that last line....'

'*Yume no ato?*'

I nodded.

'That's the name of the restaurant. You see, when Mr Onishi's uncle built the place after the war he gave it that name. It's a very strange name for a restaurant! Mr Onishi was just a boy then.'

'What does it mean?'

'I don't think Mr Onishi would have called it that, but when his uncle went over the bucket he didn't want to change the name. Out of respect.'

I finished my own beer and contributed to the tower of cans. The other staff had gone upstairs to the *karaoke* place but they'd drunk a lot of Bud and Kirin beforehand and the tower was growing high.

'I wonder,' I said, 'if the words mean "when the dream is over?"'

Nori took a long drag on his cigarette. 'I don't think they do,' he finally said. 'And besides, the dream had only just begun.... The uncle was smart and he built Yume No Ato to attract foreigners as well as Japanese and it's done really well, as you can see.' His eyes brightened. '*We're going great guns.*'

Mr Onishi's telephone began to ring from the back of the restaurant, where he was still working. We heard him answer.

'The first line,' I said, 'is "Ah! Summer grasses", right?'

Nori seemed to be weighing this, then blurted out, '*Yume no ato* means...it means what's left over after a dream.'

Mr Onishi's voice could be heard faintly. I surveyed the shaky tower, the ashtrays, the skeletons of fish beached on the sides of our empty plates.

'Leftovers,' I said, ironically.

'There's another word.'

'What about vestige? No? Remnant?'

Nori stubbed out his cigarette like a game-show panelist pressing a buzzer. '*Remnant!*' he cried, '*your choice is absolutely correct, for five thousand dollars and a dream home!*' Suddenly he grew calm, thoughtful. 'So many foreign words sound alike,' he mused. 'There's a famous Dutch painter with that name.'

'You mean Rembrandt?'

'That's him. A bank here in Umeda just bought a Remnant for nine hundred million yen.'

'*Yume no ato,*' I said, 'must mean "the remnant of dreams".'

Nori furrowed his brow, then nodded.

'Funny name for a restaurant,' I said. 'You like game shows?'

As if in a fresh wind the paper *noren* in the doorway behind the sushi bar blew open and a haggard phantom came in. Mr Onishi. He seemed to look right through us. Nori suggested we clean up and leave. We began to pile the chopsticks and empty plates onto a tray; I glanced up and saw Mr Onishi beckoning Nori.

'Please go examine the guest toilet,' Nori told me.

The guest washroom was immaculate—I'd cleaned it myself two hours before—but I spent a few minutes checking it again so Nori and Mr Onishi would know I was thorough. For the second time that night I was intrigued by a notice in the stall, pencilled on the back of an old menu and taped to the door—

TO ALL FOREIGNERS:
OUR TUBES ARE IN ILL REPAIR, PLEASE
DO NOT THROW YOUR PEEPERS
IN THE TOILET.

When I came out of the washroom Mr Onishi was gone. 'The boss looks awful,' I whispered to Nori, my smile forced. 'When he was on the phone before—maybe a guest was calling to complain about the new waiter, eh?'

'Possibly,' Nori said, 'but more likely it was a banker.'

'What, at this time of night?'

Nori shrugged. 'The elder folks, I told you, they're working late. And early, too—there was a banker here first thing this morning to talk at Mr Onishi.'

'Bankers,' I scoffed, shaking my head. 'Not trouble, I hope....'

Nori laughed abruptly. Arm tensed karate-style he approached the tower of cans.

III. THE KERMESS:
KAMPAI!

A month has gone past and the whole staff, *gaijin-san* included, are relaxing after a manic Saturday night in the Yume No Ato. August in Ōsaka: with other waiters and students and salarymen we sit in a beer garden under the full moon above twenty-two storeys of department store merchandise, imported clothing and cologne and books and records, Japanese-made electronics, wedding supplies, Persian carpets and French cigarettes and aquariums full of swordfish and coral and casino-pink sand from the Arabian Sea, appliances and appliqué, blue-china chopstick-holders computers patio-furniture coffee-shops chefs and friendly clerks and full-colour reproductions of well-known Western portraits, etchings, sketches, sculptures, landscapes that Japanese banks are buying like real estate and bringing back to Ōsaka, anything, anything at all, SPEND AND IT SHALL BE GIVEN, endless armies of customers and ah, summer tourists billowing like grain through the grounds of Ōsaka's most famous department store. SURELY, quoth the televangelist from the multitudinous screens, SURELY THE PEOPLE IS GRASS.

(For a moment the tables shudder as a tremor ripples through toxic earth under the Bargain Basement, and passes.)

KAMPAI! Western rock and roll music blasts from hidden speakers. In a few minutes the *O-bon* fireworks are due to start and we've got the best seats in the house. The plastic table sags and may soon buckle as another round of draft materializes and is swiftly distributed. A toast to this, a toast to that, *kampai,* KAMPAI, every time we lift our steins to take a drink, someone is proposing another toast: in a rare gesture Komatsu toasts the wait-staff (Akiburo and Johnnie and Michiko and me) because (this in English) we were really on the balls tonight and made no errors at all. *Kampai!* Akiburo toasts Komatsu and Mr Oh and second chef Miyoshi in return, presumably for turning out so much food on such a busy night and making it all look easy. *Kampai!* Mr Oh raises his glass of ice-coffee in thanks while second chef Miyoshi, drunk and expansive, in a rare good mood, toasts Nori for not smacking his head in the storeroom when he went back for extra soy sauce, KAMPAI, (this translated by the delighted Nori, who immediately hefts his stein and decrees a toast to Michiko, the waitress, simply because he's mad about her and isn't it lucky she doesn't speak English?)

The blushing Michiko lifts her heavy stein with soft plump hands and meekly suggests, in Japanese, that it might be possible, perhaps, to maybe if it isn't too much trouble drink a toast to our skillful bartender, Johnnie Walker, without whom we would hardly have survived the night, it seems to me, after all, or maybe we might have? *Kampai! Kampai!* The flesh of Johnnie's ear lobe reddens around his pearl stud. He smirks and belts back another slug of whisky.

'To Onishi-san,' he says in English. 'To Yume No Ato.' And he quickly adds some other remark in harsh, staccato Japanese.

'KAMPAI!' I holler, hoisting my stein triumphantly so that beer froths up and sloshes over the lip of the glass. But no one else has followed suit. They are all gazing without expression at the table or into their drinks. Johnnie Walker's head hangs lowest, his features hidden.

Komatsu glances at his watch and predicts that the fireworks will start in thirty seconds.

I turn to Nori. 'Did I do something wrong?'

Miyoshi and Mr. Oh both snap something at him. I can't make out a word.

'Well, not at all,' says Nori, softly, 'I guess people just don't feel like talking about work after a busy night.'

I purse my lips. 'I have the feeling you're not being completely honest with me.'

'Of course I'm not!' Nori protests—and I wonder if we've understood each other.

At that moment the fireworks start. Everyone at our table looks up, relieved. '*O-bon,*' Nori says to me, relaxed again. 'Tonight the ancestors return.' Flippantly he rolls his eyes, or only seems to—I can't be sure because his Coke-bottle lenses reflect the moonlight and the fierce red glare of the first rockets. One after another they are up out of the dark expanse of Nagai Park, miles to the north, then slow down and pause at their zenith and explode in corollas of violet, emerald, coral, cream, apricot and indigo. *Hanabi,* they call them in Japanese: fire-flowers. The steins are raised again, glasses rammed together, toasts made and spirits drawn skyward by the aerial barrage.

My flat is somewhere down there on the far side of Nagai Park and now I picture a defective missile veering off course and buzzing my neighborhood, terrifying the old folks, plunging with a shriek like an air-raid siren through the roof of my flat....

Nori grabs my arm with steely fingers. 'Steve-san, listen—do you hear what I hear?' I'm still concentrating on the look and sound of the exploding flowers, but suddenly I pick it out: the bouncy unmistakable opening bars of 'Like a Virgin'.

'It's the Madonna!'

'I hear it, Nori.'

He lumbers to his feet. 'You want to dance? Hey, get up! Come off it!'

Michiko and Johnnie Walker are already up beside the table, strobelit by the fireworks, shaking themselves to the beat, Michiko with a timid, tentative look and Johnnie with self-conscious abandon. The older staff sit motionless and watch the exploding rockets. Nori glances at them, at Michiko, at me, and I can tell he doesn't want to lose her. As she dances her small hands seem to catch and juggle the light.

'Life is so curt,' he pleads. 'You only lived once!' He gives me a half-smile, a sly wink, and I'm no longer sure he doesn't know exactly what he's saying.

KAMPAI! Nori hauls me to my feet and heaves me from the table in a blind teetering polka, out toward Johnnie and Michiko, his big boorish feet beating a mad tattoo on my toes. Komatsu and Mr Oh, the elders in the crowd, link arms and start keening some old Japanese song. Steins raised they sway together to a stately rhythm much slower than Madonna's, their voices rolling mournfully over the antique minors and archaic words. The rockets keep exploding. Their sound takes on a rhythm which seems to fall between the beats of the opposing songs—then as I watch, one of the rockets fails to burst. Like a falling star it streaks earthward in silence and disappears over the city.

IV. GUERNICA

I woke early the next morning with a headache and a burning stomach. I'd been dreaming. I dreamed Michiko had come home with me to my flat and we stood together hand in hand on the threshold, staring in at a gutted interior. The guilty rocket, however, had not actually exploded—it was resting in perfect condition, very comfortably, on an unburnt, freshly-made futon in the centre of the room.

Michiko took me by the hand and led me into the ruin. When the smoke began to drown me she covered my mouth with her own. Her breath was clean and renewing as wind off an early-morning sea and when she pulled away the smell of burning was gone. She removed her flowered kimono and stood naked before me. The nipples of her firm small breasts were now the accusing eyes of a seduced and betrayed woman—then I was naked too, and utterly absolved, and we were lying side by side amid the acrid wreckage by the futon. She climbed atop me and took me inside her, slowly, making small articulate sighs and rolling her head back and forth so her dark bangs rippled like a mid-night waterfall across my nipples, and the blue-black hair was curved as space-time and full of sparks like the Milky Way, which in the Japanese tongue is called *ama no gawa*, the river of heaven.

I wanted to come, to fill the gathering space inside her, and I wanted to run my tongue down the soft pale line of hair from her breasts to her belly and on up the wooded mound of Venus and lick the nectar from her tender orchid, as the Japanese poets say, but then it came to me that Nori had meant to tell me something important—about Michiko? About a poem? Or was there some-thing I'd asked him that he hadn't answered?

Summer grasses.... Something left over after dreams....

What a stupid time to be thinking about poetry.

I woke embarrassed but with a feeling of desperate tenderness for Michiko, to whom I'd hardly ever spoken and who had inspired, I thought, no more than a passing interest on my part. It was like missing a lover who'd slept be-side me all night and had just left and gone home before I woke....

Well, I reflected, a dream like that was better than the waitering nightmares I'd had all the time till recently, and still woke from now and then. Usually I'd enter the restaurant and be told I was two hours late and none of the other wait-staff had shown up and the restaurant was full and we were booked solid till midnight. Other times I would realize I'd forgotten a couple or threesome who'd been seated two hours ago in the back corner of the second room and would they believe now it was just an honest mistake and I'd really been busy and meaning to get to them all along? Sometimes they were the Cruikshanks, and sometimes Mr. Sato, who (Nori had told me) was a professor at the uni-versity in Kyōto but had been demoted and now taught primary kids in Nagai, and that was why he drank so much and was so cold and pedantic when he spoke to you. In fact the unrequited dream-diners could be just about anyone, because the summer had been busy and now I was serving both foreigners and Japanese alike.

It had been the busiest summer in years, Komatsu said, and we were at-tracting more tourists than ever before—so why the visible anxiety whenever talk after hours came round to the restaurant? Mr Onishi did not look like a man with a flourishing business. Perhaps he was ill and everyone was worried? I'd been reading articles lately about the soaring incidence of cancer in Japan, the spread of big business and factories into the countryside, toxins in the soil, polluted water, poisonous seafood....

'I think you'd better level with me,' I told Nori the night of my dream.

Miyoshi was standing by the walk-in fridge, reading the *Sangyo Keizai,* and Komatsu was behind the steam table chopping onion. But I had the feeling they were listening to us, and so did Nori.

'*Not here,*' he whispered.

'Ah, such good news,' growled Miyoshi, lowering his paper with an un-pleasant smile. Since he hardly ever spoke English I knew the remark was aimed at me. 'Such good news about the yen!'

Nori shook his head. 'For some the war has never ended.'

'*Nihon ichiban!*' Miyoshi cried. 'Japan is number one!'

'And he wasn't even born till after,' Nori grumbled. 'I don't understand.'

'Maybe we should talk somewhere else,' I said.

Nori nodded but Komatsu set down his knife and said quickly 'No. It's all right. Steve-san is part of the restaurant now—we should tell him the truth.' Eyes pink and glistening, he walked out from behind the steam table and pulled the newspaper from Miyoshi's hands.

Miyoshi scowled, did an about-face and marched into the fridge.

'Look at this,' Komatsu sniffled, handing me the paper.

'You know I can't read Japanese.'

'Of course. Don't read, just look—the pictures.'

In the lower right-hand corner of the front page several well-known pieces of European art were reproduced in hazy black and white. One was a Rousseau, the second a Gauguin, the third a Brueghel, I couldn't read the caption beneath but I could make out the name of a prominent Ōsaka bank, written in *romaji*.

'And Van Gogh,' Komatsu said, frowning. 'I hear they have just bought another costly painting by Van Gogh—so many paintings they are buying and bringing to Japan.'

We could hear Miyoshi in the fridge, muttering to himself, furiously shifting things around.

'They're buying everything in their sights,' Nori said, his usual gusto tangibly absent.

I told them I knew a bit about these purchases, but didn't see what they had to do with us.

'Well,' Komatsu started, 'they need some place to put these paintings....' His voice tapered off on the last words. I sensed I was being counted on, in customary Japanese fashion, to finish the sentence mentally so that everyone would be spared embarrassment.

'Chagall, too,' Komatsu resumed, 'and Rembrandt and Picasso.' *Bigasshole*, it sounded like, but I knew who he meant. 'Costly things...they need to find a place to put them all....'

'Like an art gallery,' I said.

Komatsu rubbed his eyes with a corner of his apron. 'I'm afraid so.'

It had been just like *Dallas*, Nori groaned, describing how the bank had first made polite offers to the dozen businesses operating in the block where they meant to build, and most were politely accepted. But several proprietors (including Mr Onishi and the owner of the Idaho Caffeine Palace, a large coffee shop dating from the late forties) had refused to consider them. Secretly the bank had made more attractive offers, then a final offer which the firm's representative begged Mr Onishi to accept, because if a negotiated settlement proved necessary then payment would revert to the level of the initial sum—or, conceivably, somewhat less.

Mr Onishi had ignored the bank's covert threats and a negotiated settlement proved necessary. Unfortunately it did not involve negotiation. The bank produced lawyers who showed that actual title to the land had belonged to the bank till the end of the war and they argued that the transfer of deeds had been improperly handled by the overworked civil authorities of the time.

The young lawyers (I could just hear them) moved further that since the art gallery would be a public facility of great benefit to all citizens of the prefecture and would attract hundreds of thousands of foreigners to Ōsaka, it was in effect a civic institution, albeit privately owned, and the city should urge Mr Onishi to come to terms.

'The court is asking Mr Onishi to accept,' Nori said, 'but he just says no.'

Nihon ichiban, we heard faintly from the fridge.

Komatsu took the newspaper from me and walked back around the steam table. He began to giggle, like a bad comedian setting up a punchline. 'They're going to tear us down,' he said, laughing openly. 'Soon!'

Nori was chuckling, too, as the Japanese often will when speaking of their own misfortunes. Komatsu was laughing harder than I'd ever seen him, so I knew he really must be upset.

I paused respectfully. 'Listen, I'm really sorry to hear this.'

Komatsu roared with laughter. Nori continued to cackle. I asked them if they knew when these things were going to happen.

'There's no time like presently,' Nori said, slapping me on the shoulder a bit harder than he needed to. 'Come on, it's a busy night tonight, we'd better get happening.'

'Please take coffee now to Mr Oh-san,' Komatsu giggled.

Miyoshi was still marching around in the fridge.

V. THE STARRY NIGHT:

September in Ōsaka is just as hot as July or August and this year it was worse. Though many of the tourists were gone, the Yume No Ato was busier than ever: Mr Onishi's struggle with the bank was now common knowledge, so old customers came often to show their support and the sushi bar was crowded with curious locals. Meanwhile enrolment was picking up at the school and I had to cut back on my hours as a waiter.

Mr Onishi was upset when I told him, but since I knew now of the epic struggle he was waging each day in the courts (Nori got the details from Komatsu and passed them on to me) I found it hard to feel angry in return. The boss, after all, was showing tremendous pluck. Sure, he was of another generation, a hardy breed of industrious survivors, and as a child he would have absorbed with his mother's milk the bracing formula of *bushido*, but this was valour way beyond the call of duty. He was giving Japan's second biggest bank the fight of its life. Already the original date for demolition was three weeks in arrears....

I heard that after receiving the court's final decision, Mr Onishi sighed and said, '*Yappari, nah*. It is as I expected. They will build a museum and a new country and fill both with foreign things.'

The demolition was set for the end of September and the Yume No Ato was to close a week before.

On the last night, a Saturday, the dining room was booked solid from five till closing with regular customers, both Japanese and foreign. We assembled by the bar a few minutes before five to wait for Mr Onishi, and at five sharp he emerged from his office. He marched up to us, a menu tucked under one arm like a swagger stick, then briefed us in a formal and highly nuanced Japanese that I could not follow—though the general tenor of his speech was easy enough to guess. Or was it? Sometimes I wondered if I'd ever done more than misimagine what these people felt and believed.

A current of laughter rippled through the staff and Nori nudged me appreciately, forgetting for a moment that I did not understand.

Mr Onishi dismissed us and we hurried off to complete our preparations as he climbed the stairs and opened the door. A long shaft of dirty sunlight pierced the cool gloom, and a few seconds later our guests began to descend, bringing with them the hot muggy air of the street.

'Meet me in the back,' I told Nori.

We stood in the kitchen on either side of the open rice machine, slowly filling it with the contents of two clay cooking pots. Thick billows of steam rose between us and Nori's face was intermittently clouded, his eyes nacreous, indistinct, like a man under a foot of water.

'So what did Onishi-san just say,' I asked, scooping the soft, sweet-smelling grains into the machine.

'He was apologizing.'

'Apologizing,' I said.

'Sure. He was apologizing for letting the bank close the Yume No Ato. He says it's all on his shoulders. He feels responsible for the jobs we will lose. He says he is sorry because he has felled us.'

The steam was thinning and I could see Nori clearly. His big face was pink and sweating.

'He says his uncle was a soldier in the old navy and after the war he built this restaurant with his own two hands. So he says that by losing the restaurant he has felled his uncle, too.'

'But isn't his uncle dead?'

Nori put down his pot and gave me a faintly disappointed look. 'For many years. But so the old people believe—they can fell the dead as well as the breathing. Like being caught *between the devil and the deep blue sea, neh?*'

I nodded and stared into the rice cooker, its churning steam spectral and hypnotic.

'I feel sorry for him.' I said.

'So it is, all the while. The big fish eat the little.'

There was a harsh grating sound as he scraped rice from the bottom of his pot.

It was the busiest night of the summer but the customers were gentle and undemanding and the atmosphere, as at a funeral reception, was chastened and sadly festive and thick with solidarity. The foreigners left huge tips and Mr Oh grunted graciously whenever I freshened his coffee. It fell to Michiko to serve the disagreeable Mr Sato for the last time and though he usually deplored the grammar and fashions of her generation, he was tolerant tonight and even remarked at one point on her resemblance to his own daughter. The Cruikshanks were among the last to arrive. When they left, just before closing, Mrs Cruikshank said she trusted I wouldn't have to go home to Germany just yet and surely with my good English I could land another job....

The last guests, our oldest customers, intoxicated and teary-eyed, staggered up the stairs around midnight and we dragged together a few tables and sank

down for a last meal. Mat and Nori and second chef Miyoshi filed from the
kitchen bearing platters of steaming rice and salmon terriyaki; at Mr Onishi's be-
hest Johnnie Walker opened the bar to all staff. And now, though I'd felt more
and more a part of things over the last months, I sensed my saddened colleagues
closing ranks, retreating into dialect, resorting to nuance, idiom and silence, a
semaphore of glances and tics and nods. Nori loomed on the far side of the table
with Michiko beside him. They were talking quietly. In the shadows by their
chair-legs I could see two hands linked, like sinuous seacreatures, twined and
mating in the deep.

Johnnie had finished the last of the Johnnie Walker Red and was now working on a bottle of Old Granddad. Mr Oh was not drinking. He sat mutely, his
agile hands wrapped around one beer tin after another, crushing them and laying them to rest among the plates and ashtrays. Komatsu and second chef
Miyoshi were smoking side by side, eyes half-closed, meditating on the fumes
that rose and spread outward over their heads.

Mr Onishi, I suppose, was in his office. At one-thirty he came out and told
everyone it was time to leave. There were some last half-hearted toasts and
deep bowing and then we all stumbled upstairs and outside. The night air was
cool and fresh. We looked, I thought, like a beaten rabble. As if wounded, Nori
tottered over and proffered a scrap of paper the size of a cheque or phone bill.
'Here,' he said, his speech slurred, 'I almost forgot. That poem they called the
restaurant for.... Remember?'

He and Michiko swayed before me, their features painted a smooth flaw-
less amber by the gentle light of the doorway. Behind them the brooding profiles of bank and office towers and beyond those in long swirling ranks the
constellations of early autumn.

I took the slip of paper and held it to the light:

> *Ah! summer grass/this group of warriors'/remnant of dream*
> *(this poem by Matsuo Bashō, lived same time as Shakespeare)*

> *So long and take care of yourself. Nori.*

He shrugged when I thanked him. 'We had to study it back then. A real pin
in the ass.'

'Drop by the school sometime,' I said. 'Please, both of you....'

I knew they wouldn't come.

Gradually the rest straggled off alone or in pairs and I headed for the station.
Waves of heat rising from sewers, smokestacks and vacant pavement set the
stars quivering, like the scales of small fish in dark water. In the late-summer
heat of 1945, after the surrender, Japanese armies trudged back through the
remains of Ōsaka and there was little where these buildings now stood but
rubble, refuse, dust and blowing ash. A stubble of fireweed and wildflowers
bloomed on the ruins, rippled in the hot wind. There was nothing for the children to eat. I heard these things from a neighbour, a toothless old man who
had been a soldier at that time, and I heard other things as well: how faceless

Japan had been, how for a while it had been a different place—beaten, lev-elled and overrun, unable to rise—waiting for the first touch of a foreign hand. For a sea change, into something rich, and strange.

On the train to Nagai I had a half-hour to experiment with the words on Nori's farewell card. By the time I got home I had the translation done, though the line '*Yume no ato*' was still troublesome and I found it hard to focus on the page.

Ah, summer grass!
   All that survives
      Of the warrior's dream....

I keep thinking I should send a copy to Nori.

Caroline Adderson
(b. 1963)

CAROLINE ADDERSON LIVES ON THE WEST COAST and teaches English as a Second Language at Vancouver Community College. Actively involved in questions of public education, she is the author of *Humans and the Environment* (1987), a set of pedagogical ideas for lessons on ecological issues; but she came to national attention when her first collection of stories, *Bad Imaginings* (1993)—in which "Gold Mountain" appeared—was named a finalist for the Governor-General's Award for English-language fiction. She also won the CBC Literary Competition in 1988 and 1991, and the B.C. Book Prize for her 1993 collection.

"Gold Mountain" displays one facet of the author's remarkable technical range. Most obviously, the narrative form emulates that of John Bunyan's 17th-century allegory *Pilgrim's Progress,* which charts the journey of a man named Christian on his eventful quest to find the Celestial City. Stylistically, however, Adderson's story "re-creates" the world of expansionist European imperial history only to subvert its claim on truth. European wealth, law, custom, and expectations run up against alternative realities here—star maps instead of conventional exploration cartography, cross-dressing instead of fixed identities, *"Gumshan"* (i.e., "Gold Mountain": the Cantonese name for North America) instead of *"British Columbia."* The narrative quest thus at once re-enacts and exposes the illusions of history; the realities of dream and fact intrude upon one another, till the destination changes. Over the course of time, the "yellow gold" that was one object of the narrator's quest proves misleading and unreliable, and then—perhaps (like the narrator himself)—it undergoes a strange kind of alchemical transformation.

For Further Reading

ANTHONY B. CHAN, *Gold Mountain: The Chinese in the New World* (Vancouver: New Star, 1983).

GRAHAM HUGGAN, *Territorial Disputes: Maps and Mapping Strategies in Contemporary Canadian and Australian Fiction* (Toronto: U Toronto P, 1994).

LINDA HUTCHEON, *A Theory of Parody: the teaching of twentieth-century art forms* (New York: Routledge, Chapman & Hall, 1985).

Gold Mountain
(A Tale of Fortune-Seeking in British North America)

Showing in brief my present Straits and their pitiful Origin

Now I am a remittance man of the worst kind, the unwitting kind who leaves home expressly to support his needy, but ends up gnawing on their empty outstretched hands. Example: in England my poor mother, before opening my letters, will shake them, listening vainly for a coin-like jangle. Finding instead more beggarly words, she rebukes me by return post. Financial insecurity distresses her digestion. When my father was alive and providing amply, she never so much as broke wind.

My father owned a shoe shop in Salisbury where he dressed men's feet as a priest might souls. His passion for the vamp, the heel and upper I inherited, though not his knack at turning pennies. For sums I have no nerve. Thus my widowed mother's suggestion that I come to the colonies where I might practise a simpler commerce, man-to-man from the back of a horse, my breast pocket for a bank.

Landing in Montreal, I was brash and optimistic. My mercantile scheme I had bolstered with a loftier ideal: the civilizing influence of fine footwear. I heard a wretched plea from deep in the wilderness and so, as the missionary goes bearing The Word to the isolated and deprived, I went to the barefoot and clod-hoppered with Bluchers and Balmorals. A season later, having crossed the maddening plains, I had become a ragged peripatetic, my neck scabbed with horsefly bites, a fungal garden growing on my tongue. How in good conscience could I continue thrusting the corns and calluses of peasants into the shoe of lords? I flung my peddler's case into the river and, though never wont to indulge in spirits, vowed to finish my days in the Dominion of Failure on a saloon stool, marinating myself in brandy, then, like a Christmas pudding, setting myself aflame.

That saloon was here in Everlasting, this frontier town, these hundred meanly-shod inhabitants. Everlasting. Try to find it on your map.

In which, cajoled by Drink, I seal my Fate as a Gold-Seeker

I am a slight man, two inches and five feet in stacked heels—a near match for the slumbering dog I met in the saloon doorway. Recalling a certain wise old adage, I hastened to retreat. Just then a voice from inside the saloon hailed me.

'Step on over 'im! He's more an angel than a hound!'

The cur's owner proved to be Mr Bernard Coop. (The day before, ignoring that he wore no collar, that his flies were spotty and partially unbuttoned, I had

---

tried to sell him a truly resplendent pair of Balmorals, the self-same pair now on its way to sea.) He bade me take a seat, then bought a quantum of brandy that plied my shameless tongue. Before long I had disclosed the trouble with my mother's digestion. 'Selling dancing slippers never made a body rich,' snorted Coop. 'All the smart ones are going to Cariboo for staking claims.'

Coop had a scheme which he outlined thus: assemble a party of rude young men and lead them into Cariboo. Give them tents and meals and wages for their placer mining. The gold itself, keep yourself—at a handsome profit. Coop was to be the overseer. He was looking for someone to recruit the men and keep the camp tidy. I being, in Coop's words, 'runty and very spruce' was just the man. Did I agree?

'Where is Cariboo?' I enquired.

'I've no hell idea.'

He refilled my glass, then held his own out to make a toast. There I sat, penniless, my livelihood bobbing down a river—a beggar, not a chooser. Reluctantly I too raised my glass. We drank and afterward, to doubly seal our fate, shook hands. I recoiled. Where on his right hand his middle fingers should have been, were two unsightly stumps. 'At least the good one's left, Mr Merritt,' he said, wagging the finger at me, then, with it, reaming out his ear.

How, in a clean and starched Shirt Front, I am truly smitten

A decent change of boots (capped toes, four gay buttons) was still in my possession, but for clothes I had only those clinging to my back. Needs were, I hired myself a laundress, a sympathetic lady who let me wait undraped in her parlour while the wash water evaporated from my shirt tails. 'Funny. I'm not a bit ashamed,' she confessed. 'You seem more a lady than a fellow. What's your trade?'

'I ease and beautify mankind's weary tread.'

'A cobbler?'

'A peddler, alas. But I hope now to try my luck at gold.' Then I told her of Coop's and my plan for Cariboo, could we ever find the place.

'My cousin Evaline is a cartographer.'

'A lady cartographer?'

'Of sorts.'

'Of sorts a lady or of sorts a cartographer?' I jested.

'Both.' She hesitated a moment, then divulged to me the rare nature of her cousin's craft. With her head on her pillow here in Everlasting, Miss Evaline could find me Cariboo. She could find it in her dreams.

When my garments were dried and pressed, my laundress buttoned me. 'Go and see her,' she said.

I had thought a cartographer who dreamed her maps and mapped her dreams would be as airily constructed as an angel. Miss Evaline was a giantess. (Anvil-footed in derby boots, a torso like a stove.) I found her in her barn, arm to her elbow in the backside of a horse. Her mare was late to foal, she bashfully explained, wiping on her skirt the equine slime. 'She'll drop before the stars come out. Upon my word.'

Then she invited me to tea and in our brief amble to the house I recognized her considerable manly talents. Already demonstrated were her gifts in husbandry. Now I learned that both her barn and house were built by her person alone. Further, she was sole master of this range, a full one hundred and sixty acres.

In her parlour she poured me a cup of mire, then proffered on a washboard her stony biscuits. I cast a glance around—at hides and burlap sacks, sundry implements, unpapered walls. Espying a rack of scrolls, I asked, 'Are those your maps?'

She rose to fetch one and together we unfurled it.

'It's just a pastime.'

'On the contrary,' I declared. 'It's a gift!' Here was a sheet of snow-white parchment. Only close inspection revealed minutiae rendered, not in line, but subtle iridescent shading. Any skills she lacked in pure cartography were made up for in artistry. I saw rills and drifts and locked-in floes. It was indeed snow white; it was snow.

'The North Pole,' she said.

'But it's undiscovered!'

'If it were discovered, I would have drawn a flag.'

Then she showed me the Hawaiian Islands—volcanoes and pineapple plantations—and in New England the terrible charred place where a witch had been burned.

My astonished accolades I could not restrain. Abashed, Miss Evaline set aside the maps and asked if I cared to promenade. At first I mistook her, thinking she meant a dance. 'Walk my range,' she tittered, all afluster, her big hand covering her face. I helped tie her bonnet strings, for she was trembling with shyness, though once we got out walking she grew braver. She took my arm. I took two steps to her every one. 'I have a goodly herd,' she said, so we clambered up a grassy butte and viewed them grazing in the distance. Below us was a sere creek bed, lacy as the bas-relief of a fossil fern. Small clouds cast clear shadows on the flatland. I wondered if in those shapes she read countries.

When we returned to the house, the foal, unborn that morning, was standing in the yard on wavering legs. I was struck then by the marvellous workings of a mere handful of hours. What had not previously existed came into being— ineffably, delightfully! Then, as if it heard and liked my thought, the foal twitched with joy.

Miss Evaline agreed to help me, though she said it was nothing she had ever done before. To absorb my dream of Cariboo, she brought me to her bed, and it was nothing I had ever done before. In one eager puff she extinguished both her shyness and the lamp, gathered me in hirsute arms, made fly the dust and straw while I, I lay passive—a virgin maid. Why are women named the weaker sex? In intellect they have always seemed to me superior. And now I knew by experience how a woman's fleshly potency can vanquish a man's heart. A long time I lay listening to her windy snore, for once I fell asleep she travelled on to Cariboo, left me behind—alone in love in Everlasting.

Containing the Account of our Travelling out, its Perils, and the droll Characters that We meet upon the Way

It took a week to ride into British Columbia, where other men with a different dog might have done it in four days. Coop called his creature Bruin, for that was the size and strength of him. At night Bruin molested me in my bedroll. By day he strayed off course to mangle squirrels. As for Coop, he imbibed continuously, dismounting on the hour and making water. All the while I pined for Evaline. At least I had her map which guided us as well as any star.

Note, too, how we were unaccompanied by rude young men. I had petitioned every lad in Everlasting, many of whom gave me an attentive ear, but upon hearing Coop's name, recoiled. Truly, I regretted Coop's and my handshake, but, severed fingers notwithstanding, it bound me to him.

Perilous alpine passes, frigid streams, the omnipresent fear of bears—all this so taxed me that when we finally reached Frazer's River, I was spent. I begged Coop to let me take some days recovering, but as we were then sharing the trail with a contingent of seasoned miners, he feared they would beat us to the best claims. We pressed on, tagging these rivals like, not one, but three smitten dogs. It was they, though, who finally relented, not granting us leave to pass, but inviting us to join them.

Sympathetic to my enfeebled condition, they offered me their freight wagon in which to convalesce. There I lay dreaming of my darling Evaline. I recalled, as a poem learnt in childhood, every detail of her person: her ropy hands and plenteous thighs, the whorl of whiskers round her paps. Delight a potent medicine, before long I had recovered, refreshed and idealistic, my fortune waiting to be panned. With the gold I found I vowed to fashion my love a ring, a seal ring with which to mark her maps. And the beauty of the land revived me further—fireweed blazing along our trail, new growth shivering on the pines, a pale green aura. The river itself, sunlight coloured gold.

Since neither Coop nor I had panned before, I was greedy for good counsel. For the next part of the journey I rode alongside the two hoariest of the fellows, life-long miners flattered to impart their combined wisdom.

On panning itself, one instructed, 'Dunk yer pan, but not too deep.'

The other resounded this advice. 'By God, not too deep!'

'Flush out the silt, but not too much.'

'By God, not too much!'

To discourage bears sing bawdy ditties, not for the lyrics but the din. Burn green wood to repel flies. They warned me, too, against the villains we might encounter: the travelling pastor, the savage Native and the Gold Commissioner. As for the moon-eyed Chinese, he is the lowest man in the golden economy.

'A scavenger,' they told me. 'Where you see a Celestial, there's only dregs.'

One night, as we sat around a leaping fire, someone took out a violin and began sawing a despondent tune. The clearing—towering columns of trees, vault of branches—might have been the great choirspace of Salisbury. My soul, an even smaller being hunkering down inside me, was greatly soothed. Then one of the men cried, 'How about a dance?' Immediately the dirge became a reel and a bale of calico was thrown down from the freight wagon.

When it hit the ground, the bale burst open to reveal a sampling of ladies' dresses. Some of the men stripped to the waist and began donning this unlikely garb with great anticipation. Indeed, the same hoary fellows whose counsel I had esteemed, were now quarrelling over female frippery. Even Bruin, yelping in indignation, was forced into a petticoat.

'Henry Merritt,' someone addressed me. 'Will you be a lady or a fellow?'
'I'll be neither.'
'You dance or you play the fiddle. Can you fiddle?'
'No, sir.'
'Then you dance.'
And into my arms lunged an obscene partner, Coop himself, straining his calico seams at the waist and oxters. When he took my hand, my fingers mingled
with his hideous stumps. Most of that macabre night we jigged and swigged and
reeled. One lady pirouetting near the fire was set aflame, but kept on twirling
till her very beard was singed. It was a nightmare. I mourned the laws of nature even as I danced.

*Relating how We are duped into Making Camp and the shocking Truth about our
Neighbours. Also, the low Particulars of a Panner's Life*

The map showed we had not reached Cariboo, but where our party halted,
men were panning in the river below. One eager miner cried, 'Boys, it must
be loaded here!' and a hot discussion followed. Some wanted to make camp and
reap this certain bounty, while others held steadfast to the promise of Cariboo.
'Henry Merritt, we are bailing out!' Coop suddenly announced. Astonished, I
recalled to him our proper destination only to have torn from my hands the
precious map. The other fellows then reached immediate accord—they would
remain a band and proceed on to Cariboo. This parting advice they offered:
exchange with them our horses for staples of victuals and drink. Then Coop
and I, against my timid judgement, descended the wooded slope alone.
Of a sudden the mountains reared around us. Their heads, crowned in red,
reminded me of a view at ruddy sunset—the line of stony kings on the face of
Salisbury Cathedral. And the river, hailing us with its stately roar, magnified
my awe. Kneeling at its edge, I saw the mighty workings of that current, how
it had ground down the mountains to liberate the gold. For those clear waters
were scintillant with gold, with jade too, green nuggets blinking up at me,
wildcats' eyes. I pictured the seal on Evaline's ring carved from that verdant
stone, the ring upon her sturdy hand, that hand in mine. Then Coop, having
gone to investigate the encampment we had seen from the trail, came racing
back, hollering and breaking off my vision.
'Celestials! They are Celestials!'
I gaped at him, for this was the import of his discovery: our journey, having
worn down equally my boot soles and my nerves, had now ended in an abandoned claim. With neither transport nor lucre, we were stranded, just as sure as
Mr Crusoe.
'This, Mr Coop, is what comes of going off the map!'
Though I knew it would but augment my despair, I went to see for myself
our Chinese neighbours. Approaching through the trees, I spotted them—five
in number, toiling by the river. Down each bent back hung a plait like the long
tail of a bell. My mother dressed her hair thus when convalescing, and Evaline,
too, abed. They were ladies then! Five Celestial ladies! But an incongruity left
me blinking: each was clad in *trousers*. Baffled, I drew within an earshot so as
to determine their sex from their voices, yet such clangorous speech told me

only that they might have had, too, the tongues of bells. At last one chanced to turn and I saw a bony face of unmistakable masculinity. Shuddering then at the queerness of these people, I hastened back to Coop.

I found him huddled close to Bruin, dog from master indistinguishable in their despondency. I made a fire and prepared our customary meal: salt pork fried in suet, beans and gruel. We ate in silence, then Coop, with a percolating sniff, laid his dish down for Bruin to clean. Hitherto in our journey I had not perceived in him an emotion that might signify the presence of a soul. Now, tears glistened on his stubbly countenance. It occurred to me also that our weeks together had made him my familiar, that this mutual predicament at least united us, as did, of course, our race. Reaching out, I patted his mutilated hand.

'We'll make the best of this,' I said.

'They'll cut our throats as we sleep!'

'Bruin will be our guard.'

That night a perturbing contradiction set me tossing in my bedroll: abandoned claims the Celestials were said to work, yet I had seen the river sparkle, an aquatic coffer. The next morn this same enigma spurred me headlong to the water. Seeing the Celestials already labouring in the stream, I stopped short, pressed my pan to my breast and in this solemn pose vowed to do the work of five. Then I squatted and commenced to earn my fortune as per the instructions of my erstwhile mentors—filling the pan and swirling it, using the current to flush out the silt. Accordingly, the pan should then have brimmed with nuggets; it brimmed instead with gravel, the gold having washed away. The whole course I then repeated to the same worthless result. Only after many dogged efforts did I learn the trouble: the gold was not formed in nuggets, but flakes like the scales of an auriferous fish. Soon Coop came down to pan as well. 'It's arse gold,' he said, disgusted. 'We're the arses, Henry Merritt.'

If panning was no good to us, we would try another method. First we endeavoured to cull the flecks directly, but our fingers stiffened hopelessly in that frigid water. More successful was extraction by toothpick, after two days, we were a full teaspoon richer.

In the end, I returned to the old method. Toiling thus, I was one day arrested by a dazzling sight: a gold leviathan gliding through our river shedding as it went the glinting scales of its splendour. Rapt, I dropped my pan and hastened after it. Ahead on the bank I met a Celestial, not panning, but crouching in perfect immobility. Loath to pass him, I stopped and waited for him to move. When he did, it was a most peculiar motion; he cast into the air his own plait. To my further astonishment the plait continued soaring as an angling line uncoiling from a reel. On it stretched, and on, in a wondrous elongation, finally landing with a splash in the river. At the same moment, a monstrous gold tail burst from the water and the Celestial lurched forward violently. Scrambling for purchase among the rocks, he began his tug o' war—a Chinese Jonah against a gilded whale. When I finally awoke, the Celestial reigned triumphant, hauling upon the rocks that priceless catch.

Thus our neighbours' tenacity and good fortune mocked our failure, even in our dreams. We coveted their laughter as they came up from the river, balancing on a pole their teeming baskets. 'Children of the Mother Lode', they had no need for teaspoons; she fed them directly from her paps. Coop called them 'heathen alchemists'. To ascertain their golden secret, he concealed himself near to where they worked, but their method was simple panning, he confoundedly reported, differing from ours in only speed and mirth.

To numb disconsolation and the bombarding effect of Coop's snores, I began to indulge, too, in a nightly tipple. (The sweetness of the whisky I tasted not upon my tongue, but in my thirsting heart. From the first draught I had discovered a thrifty mode of transport; though my love lay a vast distance from me, if I had sufficiently imbibed, when I closed my eyes, I felt her near.) One night as we shuttled the bottle to and fro, an idea, sure as a river stone, struck me on the head. Salvation would come not by angel or Messiah, but in another party of our race. With this end in mind, we agreed that while I panned Coop would keep watch upon the trail. The prospect of delivery cheering us greatly, I allowed myself a double measure of drink.

That night Evaline's tangibility so aroused me, I found myself rolling upon her bosom. Her formidable scent I truly breathed. If these were the delightful workings of an extra dram, I wished I had indulged more frequently! Of a sudden, though, the fancy vanished and I sensed a most unimaginary squeeze. With ardour unmistakable, Coop was gripping me, wheezing hotly on my neck. The last time we had thus entwined had been by the miner's fire a-jigging. The queer semblance (how it had unnerved me then!) now admitted no denial: Coop's embrace and Evaline's were twins. Thus I came to know by experience how loneliness is a dread affliction, worse even than self-disgust.

Gold Mountain, in which I am enlightened to the good Humanity of our Neighbours

'I am ill,' I told Coop. 'I am dying.'

'You don't know their parleyvoo!'

This did not deter me. I set off to the Chinese camp with a need more pressing than even that of gold.

The Celestials had a flock of scabious hens and a garden made from terracing the bank. Approaching, I found a fellow stooping between the rows of greens. 'My bowels have not moved in weeks,' I abashedly confessed. 'Could I beg from you a—?' I gestured to the unfamiliar cousin of our cabbage at his feet.

When he straightened, I saw before me my equal in physical insignificance. He squinted, perplexed, so I pantomimed my complaint. Then he bade me wait as he repaired to their tent. (When he drew aside the flap I saw it stacked inside with blankets.) A moment later he returned with a different cure: a handful of foul-smelling sticks and leaves.

'Tea,' he said in a toothy exhibition.

Within two days this potion had done the trick. In truth, I might have set a watch by my visits to the earth closet. 'Those Celestials are good fellows,' I told Coop.

He spat his whisky on the ground. 'They're little dandies in their pigtails, just like you! That's why you love them!' Then he crawled into the tent and, till morn, blat not a further word.

I was roused as usual by the insistent buzz of flies and the clack of Bruin's jaws as he caught them. Then Coop issued forth his cheery reveille.

'Shite! Shite! Shite!'

He had taken to wearing a lady's bonnet stolen from the dancers. 'It comes to this!' he griped. 'Sluicing dregs with Celestials!'

We were not even sluicing. That required an apparatus we did not possess. I hastened to remind him of this and how we had come unfortunately to land there. Pronouncing me a cretin, he stalked off toward the trail, stopping first to make poor Bruin yelp for mercy.

Since first we fell stranded in the wilderness I had maintained that pleasant manners would keep us civilized and therefore sane. That evening I entered the Celestial camp again. I found them by the fire, watching the progress of a kettle, their voices tolling merrily. Perceiving me, though, they at once ceased conversing. I had come to thank the good apothecary, but unable to tell one from the other, was struck as mum. In the eerie silence, the firelight warped and made sinister their features. Somewhere an owl shrieked. Then one leapt up, jabbed his finger at me and made the cruel pronouncement all men loathe to hear.

'Die... Die.'

I swooned. Luckily one nimble fellow arrested my fall. A second applied himself to my revival by a vigorous fanning of his hat. Then, as a flock of birds will wake in one clamorous burst, they resumed their chatter and in a throng helped me to a seat. Finally I recognized the apothecary as the one whose dire utterance had instilled in me such terror. Now he explained himself, mostly by dumb-show. It was my pallor that had startled them; as I had taken them for my murderers, they had supposed I was a ghost.

Ready in the kettle was a manner of dumpling which they served in bowls with cabbage. Though they kindly pressed this meal upon me, I repeatedly declined, for instead of spoons, they ate with sticks. (These implements, I perceived, required no small dexterity. Had poultry been on the menu, however, or even a fresh egg, I might have happily employed my fingers!) When I accepted tea, served likewise in a bowl, they were satisfied and settled down to eat. I soon surmised that the apothecary alone knew a little English. Lee Hon was his name. The others, though, were eager students. Throughout the meal they used their sticks as pointers, asking how I called things.

'Fire,' I told them. 'Mountain. River. Gold.'

I was not the only tutor. Lee Hon opened wide his arms to embrace the lonely place we inhabited, then taught me its Chinese name. Later I informed Coop, 'We are at Gold Mountain.'

'Ask them then,' he retorted, 'how they are making their mountain of gold!'

I wondered if something in the Chinese camp recalled to me my darling Evaline, or if disillusionment with my own lot endeared them to me. Once I had felt a kinship with Coop, but could no longer abide his crude manners and philosophies. Though we spoke the same language, and glared at one another through same-shaped eyes, I surely did not love him.

In which a good Fellow joins our jolly Company

'Where have all the men gone?' I asked Coop.

I meant the scores of eager miners rushing off to Cariboo. Coop's post on the trail served the hope that we might accost a passing party, yet not a soul had he encountered, not even Natives who I had understood were numerous in these parts. This had begun to irk me as much as the flies and the stones that made their unaccountable entry into my boots. One unprofitable afternoon I therefore put away my pan and clambered up the slope to spy on Coop. I found him nowhere on the trail, but in the wood slumbering behind a tree. Shaking him to consciousness by his slobbery bonnet strings, I roared an ultimatum. Until he came with news of fellow panners, he was banished from the camp; I would henceforth bring his supper to the trail. When he failed to appear that night, I was truly astonished, marvelling that he had actually paid me heed. Then I settled happily into a solitude infinitely less lonely than keeping vexatious company.

Two nights hence I woke to Bruin baying in mortal terror and a frightful crashing in the trees. Both I and the Celestial party dashed from our tents with lanterns lit hastily. Upright and staggering toward us was a maddened and vociferous bear. I held the musket but, ignorant of its workings, stood with clacking knees. With great relief I espied a familiar gleam: the bear was wearing shoes.

He was drunk beyond language (which accounted for his animal roars) and miserably tattered. Coop by then had caught up and together we cajoled him to our tent.

'There he is,' said Coop when we had tucked him in. 'Yer good fellow.'

The following day, when our visitor had regained his wits, Coop recounted to him his words. 'Samuel Goodfellow,' the stranger rejoined, his grin so blackened he might lately have supped on charcoal. 'That's sure enough my name.'

I did not believe him. To pry from him a little of his history, I enquired after his excellent and grossly incongruous shoes.

'I kilt a man for 'em in Californee, but it was hardly worth it. They pinch me in the heels.'

Describing the rising Hostilities in and among the Camps. Revealing also a Scheme of mine and how It is thrown over for One better. Further, the Account of the Death of a certain Character for which the Reader will require a Handkerchief

The presence of the Celestial fowl grieved us all, having known for too long only salt pork for meat. Bruin especially coveted them. (Once daring to enter the Celestial camp, he had been soundly thrashed by Coop.) When Goodfellow joined our company, Bruin's ration became his and Bruin was forced to seek sustenance for himself. Mainly he gnawed our boots, his bulk daily diminishing until love of life surpassed his love of Coop and he went and got himself a hen. Goodfellow, witness to the deed, pursued Bruin and wrested away his banquet. After the manner of the best French chefs, he and Coop impaled it on a stick and roasted it in its feathery jacket. For Bruin's trouble, they tossed him the well-sucked bones.

That night one of the Chinese burst into our camp accompanied by all his fury. Brandishing a knife and with choppy gesticulation, he informed us he was full prepared to quarter Bruin. Goodfellow, by way of rebuttal, issued forth a sonorous belch.

Soon afterward, I found a sign fixed to a tree outside our camp.

Nottiss! To Seleteels!
You are Hearbi noteefed that iff
yo gow intu this camp
you will ketch hell!

That my own name was not recorded there surprised me. Despite a certain handshake, Coop and Goodfellow were now rightful partners—in sloth instead of gold—and I, I was their object of derision. They retorted upon me noisome slander: if I polished my boots or performed ablutions in the river, I was a 'dandy' or a 'maid'. For my acquaintance with Lee Hon, they called me 'Hen Ree'.

I loved that sobriquet. My few visits to the Chinese camp had been my only peace. Once, wretched with a longing for Evaline, I had crossed over and like the peddler that I had been, put on display the woeful contents of my heart. I had not expected comprehension, just a sympathetic ear, yet Lee Hon rose and went into the tent. He fetched a tin box and from it took a daguerreotype of his wife. Her hair was pulled tight in the Celestial plait and she wore a striking costume: flowered slippers fitting to tread the ground of the Flowery Kingdom (Lee Hon's name for China), a short jacket that fastened at the side, and, I am decidedly not mistaken—trousers.

Since Goodfellow's arrival and the incident with the hen, my relations with the Celestials had ailed. Lee Hon no longer saluted me if we happened to meet at the river and I dared not pay a visit to their camp. Something cheered me though. With Evaline's map as my true guide I intended to try again for Cariboo. My breast pocket a bank, I had a modest account, enough to quit Gold Mountain. The gold was rightly mine—flake by flake I had extracted it—though Coop and Goodfellow were sure to call it common wealth. My departure would therefore be stealthy; I had already begun to squirrel provisions in the woods.

From my bed by the fire (having been thus displaced), I watched a shadow-show on the tent wall: Coop and Goodfellow, card-sharpers, cheating one another. With no gold to wager, they played for punitive stakes—the winner bashing the loser on the pate. One evening, in the course of this jollification, Coop and Goodfellow began a suspiciously subdued colloquy.

'We'll kill the lot of 'em,' was what reached my ears. I sat up alarmed. From the Celestial camp, I could see a fire still burning.

It being so far into night, I had expected to find them reposing, but they were busily at work. Onto several blankets, spread out on the ground, they were pouring silt from sacks.

'They plan to take your hens!' I cried, translating with gesticulation.

They stopped short and gaped at me. Then Lee Hon came forward with an exaggerated grin and took me by the arm. 'Thank you, Hen Ree,' he told me and began to steer me off. Glancing over my shoulder, I saw the others hastening to conceal their occupation. I realized then that Coop had been correct; steady toil alone did not enrich them. I had chanced upon their secret art.

I clutched Lee Hon's hand. 'Show me. I beg you, show me.'

Why he conceded, I do not know. Perhaps it was to return the favour I had done them in my warning, or that I had already seen the greater part of it. It occurred to me also that there might be a fondness between us, despite his being a Celestial and I a Ghost.

The more they stoked the fire, the hungrier it grew, many-tongued, lapping at the night. A glittering silt, a fortnight's panning, they spread across the blankets. When folded, these blankets and their contents became their noble offering and by way of rite were fed into the flames. I was awe-struck. In this simple method I fancied a golden enchantment, heard in their unfathomable parlance incantation. Now I know no manner of utterance can speed or slow this truth: anything fire loves will burn. For fire has a mouth and a thousand teeth and its bite is all-transforming. In the slow-burning the tiny flakes amalgamated to nuggets. At dawn we sifted through the cool ash, retrieving in handfuls the metamorphosed gold.

My second plan for Cariboo I then abandoned and applied myself to panning with reborn hope. Compared to my previous exacting labour—gleaning pure flake—collecting the silt required little wit. In truth, as I panned a pleasant drowsiness ofttimes suffused me, almost as if I dreamt awake. Then, gazing at the swirling contents of my pan, I would behold an image. Formed not of gold or gravel, they were visions, as in the tales of prophets and saints. I saw, for example, my mother back in England mixing soda tonic for her wind. Also revealed: the ideal shoe. Evaline I saw dreaming, and then I saw her dream. In my half-dream she was smiling at her own dream—at ladies dressed in breeches and fellows wearing plaits.

One morning a raucous commotion from the Celestial camp broke off my reverie. Leaving my pan, I raced to learn the trouble, stood watching from a safe vantage behind a tree. The Celestials were shouting and waving cudgel-like their fists. Lee Hon, in the centre of the camp, was clutching fast to Bruin's tail while Bruin, fuelled by famine and oblivious to his passenger, was pursuing in crazed circles a shrieking hen. This carousel of starvation continued its merry rotations until the fowl finally collapsed. Immediately, Bruin seized hold of his feast. But a second Celestial pounced likewise upon Bruin and with no ado whatsoever plunged into his wasted scruff a knife.

Coop and Goodfellow, also witnesses to this carnage, were strangely gleeful. Coop refused to bury Bruin. He left the corpse to rot under his warning sign, saying the Gold Commissioner would soon pass by and bring justice to the river. Hitherto I would not have believed the flies could plague us worse. Bluebottles swirled over the swelling carcass, an opaque confusion. In the autumn heat, Bruin's bursting open was the crack of doom.

An Account of the scandalous Trial and its Fatal Repercussions. Also, my Experience with the Celestial Method of Gold Retrieval and What was caught in Justice's Pan

'This was damshur more an angel than a dog!' Coop told the Gold Commissioner who had appeared while on his route downstream. 'In cold blood they kilt 'im!' By then Bruin's bones were protruding whitely from his putrid flesh. Bending over to examine them, the Commissioner gagged behind his handkerchief.

'And Yer Highness, look what they done to Coop!' Goodfellow cried. Coop drew from his pocket a bandaged hand; Goodfellow proceeded to unswaddle it. Then Coop, bawling, a debauched baby in his bonnet, thrust in the Commissioner's face his freshly scored and bleeding stumps.

The Gold Commissioner is the lawful adjudicator of all disputes under fifty English pounds. He seemed a just enough fellow, albeit haggard and with one eye listing sightless in its socket. Declaring Bruin worth two pounds and Coop's severed fingers ten pounds apiece, he drew his pistol and rounded up the terrified Celestials. Having assembled on the river bank both disputing parties, he produced a Bible and set to swearing in the Christians. Coop repeated his libellous testimony with Goodfellow's perfidious corroboration, but since the Celestials could neither utter a language intelligible to the Commissioner, nor be sworn to oath, their defence was disqualified.

I then proceeded to describe in exacting detail how Bruin came to lose his life, for just reason and with due warning. The Commissioner turned his blind eye to me.

'Surely, sir,' I protested, 'you won't take the word of these vulgarians over that of honest gentlemen!'

'Having no words from them, how can I presume honesty? Furthermore, your title 'gentlemen' is the grossest of misnomers. Do you know who these pathetic fellows are?'

I looked to the Celestials, tattered and made even more diminutive by incomprehension and fear. It occurred to me then that I more truly belonged in their party than my own. In truth, welling up inside me was a new allegiance which I now felt called upon to defend. I turned to the Commissioner.

'They are my friends, sir.'

'They are slaves,' he retorted, 'indentured to a coolie broker to repay their passage to this hell! Imagine the hell they come from, if they would go to such expense! And now I shall fine them, Mr Merritt, for their injury to this man, thus happily prolonging their misery!' He broke off coughing.

'They are innocent of your charge, sir, and my testimony will prove it!' I paused to let him finish retching. His handkerchief, I noted, was stained with bloody sputum. 'I had several occasions to remark Mr Coop's stumps before we ever came in contact with Celestials.'

'When, Mr Merritt?'

'We shook to seal our bargain before we set out for Cariboo. Once, too, I comforted him as he wept.'

'Lies!' screamed Coop.

'We danced together! He was a lady and I a fellow!'

Now Goodfellow, too, set to railing, but the Commissioner objected. 'Mr Coop and Mr Goodfellow! I shall question this witness without interruption or molestation! Do you mark my words?'

Coop shrunk down in obeisance; Goodfellow expectorated on the ground.

'At any other time,' the Commissioner continued, 'did you note Mr Coop's disfigurement?'

This question caused me to blush deeply, but having laid my hand upon the Bible, I was fettered to the truth. The matter of Coop's and my nocturnal tussling, of which we ourselves had never spoken, I now shame-facedly confessed.

'You say he squeezed you?' queried the flabbergasted Commissioner.

'Aye, sir, he did.'

'How often?'

'While we shared a tent, sir, almost every night.'

(Here Coop and Goodfellow, with violent expletives, renewed their denials, but were silenced once again by threat of contempt of court.)

'And, Mr Merritt, did you enjoy this treatment?' asked the Commissioner.

'It gave a bit of comfort, sir. I miss so much my lady.'

'A moment ago you called Mr Coop a lady.' Then the Commissioner, disgust marring his countenance, dismissed my evidence on the grounds that I was unsound of mind. His judgement: the Celestials were without a doubt guilty of the aforementioned crimes. The confiscation of their gold and its disbursement among the Commissioner and the aggrieved plaintiffs was the swiftest retribution.

Coop and Goodfellow were equally swift in leading the Commissioner to the Celestials' tent and their unsecret cache. Then erupted a most hellish skirmish as the Chinese tried to defend their store. Clearly Lee Hon did not understand my part in these outrageous proceedings; when I approached him, he drew a knife.

I fast retreated to the safety of the nearby trees, but my nostrils were immediately assailed by a potent stench—Bruin's corrupting carcass billowing gas. Although all the men found sufficient air with which to fuel their fight, it nearly stifled me. I fled the tainted atmosphere, stumbling up the wooded slope.

Waiting on the trail was the Commissioner's horse. I grabbed its halter and was about to take up the unlikely trade of pony stealing, when I heard shots fired at the river. I could not go without learning my friends' fate, though nearly an hour passed before the Commissioner reached the trail.

'Who is shot?' I asked.

'Celestials. The whole party.'

'Take me with you!' I implored him, feeling my breast pocket for a bribe. To my immense shock I found it empty, all my earnings scattered on the slope. 'Sir, I beg you! Take me!'

'Where I am going, Mr Merritt,' the Commissioner replied, 'I will no other man to go.'

I watched him ride away. I could not run myself, for night was settling like a million flies. Nor did the prospect of the morning's light offer any hope; I was penniless and without a morsel. Coop and Goodfellow, in possession at last of real stakes, would shuffle and deal through the night. Already I could hear their roisterous carousing far below. I felt certain they would not welcome a third player.

In the end I huddled upon the trail, insensible with shock and grief. Above me the constellations were like minuscule flecks of gold set in everlasting patterns in the firmament. As I crouched, I fell to wondering why the Chinese were called Celestials, whether it was their shaved forelocks that earned them the appellation—their naked brows round and smooth like planets—or that, when smiling, their eyes folded into pleasing crescents that brought to mind the waning moon. They had, too, tails like black comets and voices that mimicked the tonal music of the spheres. Then the stars themselves, indeed the whole bespangled sky, seemed to unswirl in an astronomical tribute to my friends. Lying back to watch this wonder, I drifted off to sleep.

In my dream, Smoke Personified was leaning over me in an oppressive cloak of black, forcing up my nose its ghastly fingers. I woke gasping. Below in the darkness, gold sparks were shooting. I saw them glinting, as in my pan, but would not touch them, lest I burn: *something in our camp had caught on fire.* The tent. Blazing up of a sudden, it made a mighty pyre, Coop and Goodfellow trapped within.

If the compound of feelings churning in me could have been distilled, it would have made an insanity potion. At once I battered my skull against a tree and hummed a ditty I had learned upon the trail. ('We are dancing girls in Cariboo, and we're liked by all the men...') Then, thinking of Coop's corpse braising in the embers, I set to wailing, only to find myself a moment later jigging. Thus I passed the remainder of that hellish night.

At daybreak, exhausted and in awful trepidation, I ventured back down the slope. About their camp the Chinese lay in various wracked postures, all bearing monstrous wounds. Lee Hon's very arm was severed from his person as he stared heavenward from a pool of gore. I turned away in horror. They were the sole men with whom I had felt affinity, perhaps in all my sorry life. Now they had travelled on to a place not even Evaline could map.

As for Coop and Goodfellow—drunk, they must have knocked the lamp down in the tent while gambling their booty. I knelt beside the fire's remains. The Celestials' gold, twice-consumed by flame, had fused to weighty nuggets. I might have been a rich man. I might have made my love a ring. But gold washed in blood loses all its lustre, makes an ugly trinket and a foul currency. To fund my escape, I was obliged to take a handful. A more grisly chore I cannot imagine, combing through those ashes, sorting gold from charred stubs of bone.

Wherein I arrive back in Everlasting, greatly down at the Heel

By the time I found my Evaline snow lay upon the ground and I was a tatterdemalion, as much a pauper as when I left her. In my absence she seemed to have accumulated flesh, that or trial and hunger had shrivelled me. And though she greeted me with the same bashful manner I adored, I saw at once I had not been missed. Knowing well she would refuse me, nonetheless I begged her hand, then with my tears I washed her boots.

'It would be too comic, Mr Merritt,' she told me. 'As if I were the man and you the lady.'

At least she consented to make for me a map. She shooed me to her bed and while I tumbled headlong in its frowzy comfort, she made a coy show of removing her hair pins and letting her plait fall down her back.

'What if I can no longer dream?' I asked her.

'How do you know you are not dreaming now?' Turning, she smiled at me in the lamp-light and for a moment I thought she was Coop.

How true her words! What had happened to me awake was infinitely more terrible and strange than anything I had encountered in a nightmare. As a lad I was wont to contemplate the simple workings of a boot-lace, how eye-to-eye it made its criss-cross pattern—certain, predetermined and everlasting. So too, I had thought, would be my life. Now even elemental truths—justice, for example, or what defines a race of people, or even, for that matter, a man or woman—all this seemed to me reversed. I was lost and knew not where to go.

We slept like babes and, in dreaming, awoke together to find ourselves upon a forest trail. This sylvan path we trod but a short distance before it opened in a field. In truth, we had reached a vista glittering and vast—a plain of golden stars. Evaline turned to me in amazement. 'This is the Celestial Route!' And so I learned my proper destination. I took her hand, she took mine, and as one we ventured forth. In the morn she sat up in the bed, her visage radiant with our shared dream. 'Such a lovely place!' she exclaimed. 'Are you certain it exists?'

Now I am waiting out the winter in a room above the saloon, replying to my mother's bombastic correspondence, taking her pennies to pay my keep. Sometimes I wax despondent, lamenting what has happened to me and my boots. Mostly, though, I pass the hours studying Evaline's map of China, its mighty wall, the two great rivers wending to the sea. Somehow it stirs me. It seems as much a work of art as of cartography. When first I saw it, I proposed she travel with me to be sure that this time I would not stray off course. She only laughed and told me she could sojourn far more economically.

My boots! Of the original laces, only one remains, the left I now fasten with a bit of string. Part of the stacking on that heel is also gone, giving me a most ungainly limp. As for the right, being so punctured by Bruin's gnawing it would make a perfect sieve. Yet these mean scraps of leather have brought me so great a distance I am loath now to part with them. If they endure this one last journey, then I shall retire them—for a pair of flowered slippers.

Lisa Moore

(b. 1964)

LISA MOORE WAS BORN AND RAISED IN ST. JOHN'S, Newfoundland, where (after completing a B.F.A. at the Nova Scotia College of Art and Design) she returned to live. The author of art criticism as well as fiction, she has attended the Banff Workshop, read her work at centres across the country, had radio plays produced on the CBC network, and been one of the writers featured in *Coming Attractions* (1994). She has won prizes in the Newfoundland and Labrador Arts and Letters Competition and in the *Prism International* short fiction contest. Her stories have appeared in *Event, New Quarterly, Tickleace,* and other journals. "Meet Me in Sidi Ifni" appeared in *Canadian Fiction Magazine* in 1990 and was collected in her first book-length publication, *Degrees of Nakedness,* in 1995.

"Sidi Ifni"—the coastal capital of Ifni, now part of the province of Agadir in Morocco—serves here, like "Timbuktu" in popular idiom, as an archetypal "alternative," a place so distant as to be romantic, so remote as to be unreal. But the conventions of romance ("Meet Me in St. Louis"?) are always as open to distortion as are the "actual" terms of a relationship that has itself gone conventional. The fiction here is founded on contrast: between reality and desire, between the demands of habit and the unreachability of dream. The narrator recognizes that the life she leads is limited, a kind of desert, and she wants it to be something other—or at least *like* something else. Yet when the world of simile takes over from the world of recognition, it is not clear that the alternative is any more fulfilling than the life she resents. The problem for the imagination is that mundane detail always intrudes upon it; the problem with mundane detail is that it so often leaves no room for romance.

For Further Reading

LAWRENCE MATHEWS, "New Writing on the Rock," *Canadian Fiction Magazine* 72 (1990): 4–9.

Meet Me in Sidi Ifni

Look for me in Sidi Ifni. I'm leaving the back yard. Those weeds you spent half the summer thrashing have returned unscarred, thicker, greener, and the perfume from them makes the air moist. They grew back when you stopped to have a bottle of pop. We can't just stop like that.

These are the things I'm leaving. I'm leaving the toys all over the stairs. That magic wand with the glow-in-the-dark star sitting on the coffee table, so that if you walk into the living room at night it seems to float. The paperweight with the unicorn and the snowstorm you shake. It's May and we haven't taken down the Christmas wreath from the back door, but the stuffed dove is under the kitchen table on its back, beak open, claws stretched forward. I'm leaving my water colours in the cookie tin.

Once we made love in a blackout. There were brass candle holders in sluffing drifts of wax. At the bottom of Cathedral street cars swished their tails like lethargic crocodiles. Engines straining.

You said, I'll blow out the candles.

The wicks curled to protect themselves, flared orange against your breath, then out.

You said, Over here on the chair.

A passing headlight gleamed on the worn rose brocade of the armchair, and where the covering is torn, the stuffing and a coiled spring, just by the inside of your wrist. The shadows of the rubber plants climbed across the ceiling like blind crustaceans, and crawled back into themselves when the car passed.

People will see, I said.

But the whole island is dark.

Saliva soaked, water colours bled from your fingers. Burnt sienna spine, cherries on my nipples, ink black strokes. My knees dug into the back corners of the chair around your waist. I rose and dropped over the wavelets of frost on the window like a mermaid. A horn honked. And honked and honked.

Never mind, you whispered, never mind.

I'm leaving the cockroaches in the shower on the dirty tiles and all the foreign coins we saved for parking meters.

Your daughter, who doesn't know how to swim, almost choking me, terror-locks her arms around my neck. Her naked body shivers, lips bluish, she squeals in a shrill pitch. Then we look into each other's eyes, our noses almost touching. I'm trying to make her remember me always. She opens her mouth suddenly and shrieks and bashes her fist in the water. Her magnetic letters on the fridge arrange themselves, HA HA HA.

I'm leaving on the train. The first train we rode together. Holding each other on the narrow cot, people on both the cots beneath us. The darkness squeezing down on the train so it vibrated, the vibration passing through us into our toes. The conductor shook his black ringlets when he ripped the morning sunshine through the curtain.

Sunlight falling through the slatted roof over the souks, striping the brass pots, diagonals over your face, your freckled arms. The snake charmer tipping the lid off the woven basket with his big toe. Earthy coloured pyramids of spice, a boy with a bright green lizard on his outstretched palm. Don't forget the German toy maker who could find his way by facing the sun. His spectacles pressed into his flushed cheeks like teeth biting apples. The sturdy way he set down his feet, two puffs of dust. Dripping loops of dyed fabric, fuchsia, turquoise, the odour of urine, light piercing the loose weave.

I'm going to Sidi Ifni. I'm leaving the shadows from the venetian blinds on the kitchen table and the fridge that makes so much noise it sounds like a spaceship. I can't wait all night for you to move. You survey the board with your eyes squinted up, your beer bottle cuddled near your crotch, and then with a gesture of triumph you shoot a bishop across the board and put your own king in check.

Look for me in Sidi Ifni. The Spanish conquered it. An old man pushes a wheelbarrow filled with sizzling donuts glazed and hissing like wasps. Remember him? The ocean barely lifts its lip. It behaves like a pond. I'll hire the blue Mercedes with the miniature weather vane on the hood. The windshield is cracked, and inside the car smells like American cigarettes.

I'll leave from Tiznit, silver capital of the country. There's a salesman there who claims he is the grandson of the chief of the caravan. He wears an Adidas jacket under his djellaba and accepts credit cards. I'll leave in the middle of a festival, when the streets are squeezed full of people, shoulder to shoulder. Boys in tree branches, boiled eggs, mandarins in dusty plastic bags. Women with tambourines, singing from their throats, heads thrown back. They hold in the air gowns on crucifixes with bushes of mint stuffed in the necks. The dignitaries drive their cars over Persian carpets and are showered with rose petals.

What was that woman's name? The Swedish woman in the tight floral print. She was a chaise longue, soft as a swimming pool. You think I didn't smell her kitchen, all crushed camomile and coconut suntan oil? Oh, you could sleep in with her, the phone company would come and disconnect the alarm clock by mistake. Her seeds sprout as she flings them. She made me mince my garlic. I said she was dewy-eyed, bucolic. But you would remind me, her caesar salad's creamy and her pubic hair is magenta. I'll be in Sidi Ifni.

The taxi driver's horn will blast, nasal singing, fast impossible banjo. We'll drive as fast as that.

I'll be running a hotel of pink chalky colour. The paint is peeling in the shape of continents and oceans that I can read like tea leaves.

I'll have an affair with the projectionist from the movie theatre. The theatre has many smashed light bulbs in its sign. He speaks only Spanish and grunts "Me gusta" while he grinds. The film in the noisy projector. You on the screen. You on the highway where the car broke down, in your yellow rain coat. You, swallowed by the fog of Signal Hill. You, jerking your body to screaming Bob Dylan in the kitchen. Your voice through the wall, overanimated, reading your daughter bedtime stories. You, crouched with the hose waiting for your sister, spraying your mother by mistake, spraying all the years away from her, so when she scurried back inside, her face looked like she was fourteen.

I'll be dancing with my Spanish ghost in the dust. We'll dance the tango, very seriously. Sweat makes my make-up run, and our cheeks are pressed together. We'll smell of gin that has come through our skin in the thinnest film. His coarse moustache will tickle. He'll say, "Me amore, Me amore"—and then you— having ridden on Air Canada, a rickety bus and finally a blue Mercedes—you will burst through the doors, crushing the rusty locks in your fist. You will be wearing your jeans and suspenders, but instead of that pink t-shirt, you will for once have dressed for the occasion, a white cotton shirt with pirate sleeves. You will pull out a sword. One by one you will pop the buttons off the shirt of my Spanish troubadour. They will fall to the floor with a click click that resembles the grinding of your teeth.